NORTHERN WOLVES

BOOK 1-4

DEBRA DUNBAR

debra dunbar
FIENDISHLY FUN FICTION

JUNEAU TO KENAI

NORTHERN WOLVES BOOK 1

BRENT

"You're an idiot."

I was, but it wasn't my second's place to tell me so. Not that Sabrina had ever had any marked respect for authority. The woman was loyal, tough, and just as much of an alpha as I was. I'd encouraged her many times over the last five years to start her own pack—a spin-off from our main one, but she was content to remain second in charge and a pain in my butt.

"So what do you expect me to do, Sabrina?"

"Go after her. You haven't looked at a woman like that in…well, you've never looked at a woman like that. You're a wolf. You're an Alpha. Don't be an insecure wuss. Go win her love."

If only it were that easy. "She's a surgeon. She's got a career in Seattle that she spent fifteen years and a gazillion dollars in student loans studying for. She's forty-three. She's got a life she's happy with. She's got friends at home. She's probably got a boyfriend at home."

Sabrina snorted. "If she's got a boyfriend at home, he's on

the edge of being kicked to the curb. That woman wants you. And you want her."

True, but there was more to building a long-term relationship than lust. I'd found that out too many times in my life. "The attraction was one of those heat-of-battle things. I want more than sex; I want a partner. She won't want to abandon the life she's built to come up to Alaska and be my mate, and I have responsibilities that I can't—and won't—leave. There's no sense in pursing something that clearly wouldn't work, that would only end in heartbreak for us both."

Well, heartbreak for me. I was physically attracted to her. I was ridiculously physically attracted to her. And I admired her. She was smart, with a quick, dry wit. She was brave, kept calm in a crisis, had good judgement. I could depend on her. I respected her council. I saw her as more than an equal; in some regards I viewed her as having superior skills and knowledge—skills and knowledge that complimented mine. Together we'd make an amazing team.

And did I mention I wanted to bury myself into her softness, make her cry out my name in the heat of passion, wrap myself around her as we slept. I wanted to feed her, protect her, trust her with my soft underbelly, lean on her in dark hours. She was strong and steady. Seeing her walk away to her hotel and turning my back on her had been the hardest thing I'd ever done in my life.

"Idiot." Sabrina swatted me on the shoulder. My second and I had known each other since we were pups. She, Ahia, and Zeph were my closest friends, my confidents, the ones that saw the *me* behind the Alpha.

"She's gone off on some ten-day hiking/climbing thing up in Kenai," I told Sabrina. "Then she'll fly from Anchorage to Seattle, and go back to work at the hospital. What am I supposed to do, conduct a long-distance romance? Fly back and forth to Seattle every two weekends? Her schedule is all over the place crazy. She hardly ever gets days off. It's not going to work."

Sabrina gave me a knowing one-eyebrow-raised look. "Seems like you've thought an awful lot about why this isn't going to work. How about you just go with it? Hunt her down, see where the next ten days take you, then make your decision. I'll hold down the fort with the pack. Go get your woman."

Where the next ten days would take me? They'd take me into a broken heart, that's where they'd take me. I, the Alpha of the Juneau Pack, was scared of a diminutive, confident woman. No, I was scared of me. I was scared of losing my heart at the age of forty-five and feeling the ache for the rest of my life.

Those sleepy bedroom eyes. That slim, wiry, athletic body. The dark, fine hair, soft as strands of silk. Every cell in my body wanted her. And my heart wanted her too.

"What does your wolf feel?" Sabrina asked.

I grimaced. My wolf wholeheartedly approved. My wolf wanted me to take her to bed that first night we'd met, in the cave. My wolf wanted me to shift and haul ass across the state to find her.

"Fine. I'll go. But if she thinks I'm a complete weirdo-stalker for showing up uninvited on her hiking/climbing vacation, I'm going to be thoroughly humiliated."

Sabrina grinned. "Don't worry, Brent. I won't tell a soul."

She would though. I'd have the whole pack waiting for me to come out of the wilderness, Kennedy scooped up in my arms like a bride on her wedding day. They'd cheer. They'd toast our nuptials. They'd plan the details of our mating ceremony. Werewolves might have a fierce reputation, but we were suckers for weddings and babies. And when I came out of the wilderness alone, I'd have to endure years of sad, sympathetic looks. Half the pack would bring casseroles to my door. The other half would try to drag me out to titty bars to drown my sorrows. The reaction of my pack would be worse than the rejection itself. Well, not really, but close.

But Sabrina was right. I doubted Kennedy would ever want to give up her career, her life's purpose, to move here with me, but I needed to know that for sure. I needed to see if the slim chance we had a future together might be enough. And if I suffered the inevitable heartbreak, well, so be it.

I was an idiot. These things didn't last. I'd been in the Army. I'd seen my share of romances forged in the stress of battle. Heck, I'd *had* my share of adrenaline-sparked romances, where life-threatening circumstances gave rise to some of the most passionate sex I'd ever had. Those relationships never survived outside of the environment they'd been born in, and I was sure the same would be true of whatever that werewolf and I had been heading toward. It wouldn't have lasted. But it would have been nice to have actually had sex with him before we were rescued and went on about our normal lives.

No, it wouldn't have. Sex with him would have been a high-speed journey to heartbreak.

I'd watched him in the tourist store, because who could keep their eyes away from a powerful, sexy guy like that? He had a presence to go along with his good looks—the sort of presence that made everyone take notice, that made everyone jump to obey his orders, to long for his smile and nod of approval.

And I'd watched him close in conversation with a curvy,

pretty native girl at the counter. I'd seen him pinch her chin, give her a soft, affectionate kiss on the forehead, and look at her with love in his face as he turned to leave. But after what happened on the other side of that interdimensional rift, I was pretty sure what he felt for that angel was the same as I felt for my brother, or my best friend back in Seattle. She was in love with the other angel, and that left Brent available. But available didn't mean squat if he wasn't interested in anything beyond a heat-of-the-moment quickie.

He'd walked away. I'd given the police my very weird statement, then gotten in the squad car for them to take me back to my hotel. When I glanced back as the officer drove off, I'd seen him heading away with his friends. He hadn't watched me leave. He hadn't given me any indication that he ever wanted to see me again. Whatever might have been didn't happen, and I needed to stop obsessing over his broad shoulders, his deep voice, the feel of his fingers as he tucked my hair behind my ear, his calm, authoritative, commanding presence.

Gah, I had it bad. *Stop thinking about Brent and enjoy your vacation.* I had this ten-day hike and climb that included some rafting, then I'd return to Anchorage and board the plane back to Seattle and the hospital. Once there, I'd throw myself into my job, and forget about everything except the patients rushed through the emergency room door.

"You up for s'mores, Kennedy?"

I looked up at Leon. I'd felt a little uncomfortable at first that this hike/climb excursion consisted of only me and a guide. Seems I was the sole weirdo wanting to tromp through the snow and ice of late April in Alaska, which left me with a private tour.

I'd missed a day hike in Juneau because I'd been caught in the tourist-shop explosion that sucked me, six other humans, and a werewolf through an interdimensional rift. Not that I'd known Brent was a werewolf at the time. We'd been rescued and rather than just go back to Seattle, I'd decided to salvage what I could of my vacation and do this planned ten-day hike in Kenai.

Leon and I had loaded up a plane first thing this morning. Another outfitter employee had flown us to our entry zone, landing on a glacier lake so we could promptly start our hike. I liked to think of myself as fairly athletic but after spending the entire day tromping through boreal forests and ascending to the alpine tundra, I was tired. Not so tired that I didn't plan on doing our climbs tomorrow, though. And not so tired that I'd turn down an offer for s'mores.

"Sure. I'll grab some sticks for the marshmallows."

I walked away from the campsite and down a narrow trail that was barely the size of a deer path to search for sticks, careful of my surroundings. I had bear spray. I didn't have a rifle, although Leon had one. I guess if I ran out of bear spray I could always beat one over the head with a camp chair. Oddly, I wasn't all that concerned about encountering a bear out here. Fighting raggedy bug-guys with laser shooting sticks just a few days ago tended to make wildlife seem harmless in comparison.

S'mores weren't the only highlight of our meal. When I got back from my stick-gathering, I found Leon grilling up salmon and vegetables. My stomach knotted with hunger as I smelled the lemon and herb marinade. After tomorrow we'd be back to more traditional backpacking food—stuff that was lightweight enough to haul for the remaining eight days through the mountains, but for now I was going to savor every bite of that salmon.

Once we'd eaten and finished clean-up, I decided I was done for the evening. Pulling my collapsible crutches out of my pack, I sat down and unzipped the side of my hiking pants. With a push of a button I released the vacuum lock on the socket, and eased my leg off. Setting it aside, I took off the sealing sleeve and sock, then began to carefully remove the liner.

"You're an amputee?" Leon's voice conveyed his disbelief and shock. I was used to this. I'd rather people come right out and ask me about my accident and my prosthesis then stay silent and wonder.

"Yep. I lost my leg in a car accident sixteen years ago. I'm lucky to be alive. I'm even luckier to have only lost the one leg. I was told it was touch-and-go with the other one."

He shook his head. "I had no idea. I mean, you don't walk like you've got an artificial leg or anything. Are you going to be able to do this trip? We're going to be covering some challenging terrain. We'll be ascending over four thousand feet, then back down. We'll be crossing rivers and streams, walking on rocky trails. There will be some muddy spots that are really slippery."

I got it. This was a difficult excursion for a fit, two-legged person. Leon was afraid I'd gotten in over my head and that he'd somehow have to drag me out of here to a spot where he could call for an airlift rescue. He couldn't imagine doing all this as an above-the-knee amputee, so he assumed it was impossible. In sixteen years, I'd learned there was very little in life that was impossible—if you were creative, persistent, willing to fail over and over without giving up, and open to trying new things.

"I've climbed in Colorado. I've skied in Wyoming. I've kayaked in Oregon. I've hiked all over Washington State, Montana, and Utah. I think you'll find that I'm just as capable as any other experienced backpacker."

"But..." He looked skeptically at the leg I'd just removed. "You really can hike all day with that on? Did I mention crossing streams and muddy, slippery spots?"

"The days of the wooden pirate leg are far gone, my

friend." I held up the prosthesis. "This here sucker is one hundred thousand dollars of top-notch technology. Waterproof. Sand proof. Five-day battery life, which I brought a back-up for, thank you very much. I'm just as stable in slippery mud as you are. Even standing for an eighteen-hour surgery doesn't bother me. Trust me, I'll be fine. I'll probably be tired as all heck, but I'll be fine."

He eyed the leg with surprise. "A hundred grand? Sheesh, that's as much as some houses."

I nodded. "But what price do you put on your mobility? On being able to do all the things you love to do?"

I was lucky that I'd managed to scrape together the money and loans for such an expensive prosthesis. Yeah, I had a fortune in loans, both from this and from my schooling but as a trauma surgeon, I made good money. Eventually everything would be paid off, and I'd look for houses in some of Seattle's nicer areas. Unbidden, an image of a brawny dark-haired man surfaced in my mind. I would love to come home to him, to share my life with him, but he was the leader of his pack, and he clearly wasn't interested.

He grinned. "Yeah, I'd live in my car and eat Ramen noodles for that. Okay, bionic woman, let's drink our wine, get some sleep, and tomorrow we climb."

* * *

LEON WAS UP BEFORE ME, frying pancakes that were more blueberries than batter. It was colder here than in Juneau and I was grateful for my thick sleeping bag and puffy coat. After breakfast, we gathered our climbing gear, I put on the prototype climbing leg I was testing, and we set out.

I'd used the leg once when we'd been sucked through that interdimensional rift, and felt confident enough in it that I left the prosthesis with the microprocessor knee back at the camp. We were going to climb all day, then return to the camp at night. Tomorrow we'd head out for a long hike, then hopefully the weather would cooperate and we'd be able to get on the river and do some paddling.

The climb Leon had chosen to start was a mixed pitch with a snowy approach, a forty-five degree snow and ice covered slope leading to a rock headwall. The second pitch had an ice overhang that looked fun and some rather menacing jagged daggers of ice over a rock roof.

Down in Juneau there had been patches of snow here and there, but only in the higher elevations and shaded areas. Here, in spite of it being nearly May, there was a good bit of white. Some spots in the lower alpine area would still have basins of foot-deep snow. I wanted to come back here, to hike and climb in Denali, to kayak the Lemon Creek Canyon, to explore the ice fields outside of Juneau.

That wasn't the only reason I kept thinking of Juneau. If I came back for another vacation, would I see him? Would I be able to make up some excuse to look him up? *Hey, I was just in the area cross-country skiing and thought we could catch up over a beer.*

Yeah. No. I'd be better off avoiding Juneau. I'd be better off avoiding this state. Otherwise I'd be thinking up ways to look like a pathetic, love-struck idiot.

I shook off thoughts of the sexy werewolf and started climbing. My experience was mostly in sport climbing and I'd done very little ice climbing in the lower forty-eight. By the time we were heading up the first pitch, I realized I needed to spend more time in the gym. I belayed while Leon climbed, then I did a top-rope climb on the first section. After that, Leon and I took turns belaying. It was a blast, thinking about the best route up, working out the handholds and footholds. Climbing required strength, but it also required balance and equilibrium, a calm, cool head and the patience to backtrack when the route you thought was ideal didn't quite work out the way you wanted.

At the top of the headwall, we chilled on a ledge for a bit, then set up a second belay point and continued up the third pitch. There I got to use my crampons and tools and really fall in love with ice climbing. It made me want to come back...but I probably shouldn't come back. Although Alaska was a huge state. There was no reason I couldn't vacation here without thinking about Brent.

No. Alaska to me would always be about Brent. Every bit of rock and ice, each spruce and hemlock, every breathtaking view reminded me of him—made me wish he was here to share the beauty with me.

We rested again at the top of the ice-ledge, looking down at the green treetops in the valleys, the deep blue-gray of the lakes and rivers. The ridgeline went on for miles, in the background cloud-covered mountains, monochromatic with their black rock and white snow.

It was breathtaking. The enormity of it all, the scale, the brutal beauty—it made me feel small and insignificant. In a world where it was easy to fall into a state of hubris, to think that we humans had conquered all, that we reigned supreme, a place like this was humbling. I was a nobody kneeling before such glory. When we finally rose to head back to the camp, I felt almost as though I'd had a religious awakening, that I'd seen the face of God.

But as awe-inspiring as the experience was, it was less than perfect because Brent wasn't there to share it with me.

I climbed down, while Leon cleaned the anchors and rappelled down each section. After chicken and fire-roasted potatoes, we packed all we could to head out early tomorrow, then I sat by the fire, while Leon went early to bed.

I'd never been one to be afraid of the dark. The fire crackled and spit, filling our camping area with a golden glow. I could hear insect song, the call of a hoot owl, the wind stirring the trees. I was safe. I had my bear spray. Leon had a rifle. But still something sent a prickly feeling up my spine and raised the hair on the back of my neck.

There was a faint rustling sound, like something in the bush. I saw a flash, as if the moonlight reflected off a metallic surface, or silvery eyes caught the firelight. It was gone in a blink, making me wonder if in my tired, half-dreamy state I'd imagined it.

I thought about getting up to check, but it wasn't like I could see much in the dark. Besides, what would I do, whack whatever it was with my s'more stick? I debated waking Leon, but didn't want to seem like some wimpy city girl afraid of a fox in the woods, or the wind whistling through the trees. I was too proud to wake Leon. I was too scared to go investigate. So instead I put out the fire and scurried off to the safety of my tent and sleeping bag.

CHAPTER 3

BRENT

The plane touched down in Kachemak Bay, water spraying as we pivoted and taxied across the water to the dock.

"Be careful out there," Dustin warned me.

I looked over to him in surprise. I'd been running in the lower part of Alaska since I was a cub and had been up this way for some joint hunts with the Swift River Pack. It had been a long time since I'd visited Kenai, but I wasn't likely to get lost, and there were few animals who'd attack me.

"I asked and received permission from Jake," I told Dustin. This wasn't my territory, and it would have been rude to trespass without first asking the Swift River Alpha's blessing to run on his land.

"It's not that." Dustin turned to look at me as he pulled alongside the dock. "The grizzlies are saying one of theirs went missing in Kenai. Just flat-out vanished."

Grizzly shifters were an independent bunch. They weren't pack-oriented like we were and didn't always let the others in their sloth know their whereabouts. This time of year they were out of their hibernation and eating everything in sight. And looking for a mate. We were friendly with a few of them in our territory and it wasn't uncommon to have them vanish for months, only to appear just in time for the August barbeque.

"He's probably in Fairbanks trying to get some sow into his bed. He'll turn up."

Dustin shrugged. "Maybe. His sloth doesn't usually get this worked up over a bear on the prowl. They were worried enough to contact Jake."

"What do they think happened?" Grizzly shifters were pretty top of the food chain. The only thing they had to fear beyond avalanche, falling off a cliff, or decapitation from being clotheslined while snowmobiling, was losing a fight with another grizzly shifter, or losing a fight with a whole pack of wolves.

Or a really pissed-off sow. Female grizzly shifters were downright scary during mating season. If I were a male grizzly, I'd seriously contemplate a life of celibacy.

"They think someone killed him."

What? "Did Swift River have any problems with him? Was he trying to grab another bear's woman?"

"Heck if I know. We were fine with the guy. Jake didn't have any beef with him, and nobody in our pack takes a piss without the Alpha's okay. Those grizzlies are all grumpy until late May. Maybe one of his sloth killed him and didn't want to admit it."

Well then, I wouldn't have anything to fear. I'd just give any grumpy bear a wide berth and we'd all be happy campers. "Thanks for the lift, Dustin. I owe you one."

The werewolf grinned. "Nah. I owed you for taking me out on that fishing trip last summer."

I grabbed my pack and hopped out of the plane onto the

dock. "Join us this year. And tell Jake he needs to get his furry butt down to the barbeque this August."

"Will do." Dustin waved, pivoted the plane and taxied into position for take-off. I heard the propeller engine rev, then watched the plane zip by and take flight before I headed into the woods. This wasn't exactly a high-traffic area, but tour groups did like to use the bay and this dock for pickups and drop-offs. I'd done some sleuthing and found out which tour group Kennedy was using. They put in at any one of the glacier lakes in the area, then customized the excursion depending on what the customer wanted to do. I was betting that Kachernak Bay was their end point. I'd just need to trace back the general area of the itinerary and catch up with her. Then I'd need to find a good excuse for me showing up nine hundred miles from my home in the middle of the wilderness.

I'd figure that out later, once I managed to find her in this enormous preserve. And I'd do that better on four legs than two. I set down my pack, which was a modified type of saddlebag, and began the arduous process of shifting to my wolf form. If I rushed it, I could change in five minutes or less, but there was no need to endure that sort of pain so I took my time and fifteen minutes later was picking up the pack with my teeth and wiggling into it. Once around my chest, I stepped into the leg holds, then grabbed the strap with my teeth and tightened it. It would chafe if I ran more than a few hours with it on, but I was a werewolf, I'd heal as soon as I took it off. And I could deal with a little discomfort. Hunting for food and drinking from a stream weren't a problem, nor was staying warm while sleeping. My main reason for the saddlebag was clothing. I couldn't talk to Kennedy in my wolf form, and standing in front of her naked wouldn't make conversation any easier. Find her. Shift back to my human form. Put on some pants at a minimum. Then see if the sparks we'd both felt a few days ago were still there —and if they'd burst into the sort of flame that could make a smart, bad-ass surgeon with bedroom eyes fall in love with a werewolf.

CHAPTER 4

KENNEDY

We were up at dawn, breaking down camp and hitting the trail. I'd had to pop a couple of aspirin to combat the headache from the altitude and ease sore muscles from yesterday's climbing. I'd assured Leon that I could keep up, and was determined to prove to him that I was up for a challenging excursion.

We weren't climbing today, but that didn't mean we weren't doing hours of scrambling as we climbed over rocks and up hills. Both of us used hiking poles for additional balance on the steep slopes. By lunch time we'd hopped across two creeks, and forded a good-sized stream. My waterproof hiking shoes were starting to be less waterproof, my pants were covered in mud from sliding down a slippery trail, and I'd hacked my way through more brush than I'd ever expected. I was never so glad for leather gloves or my hands would have been shredded from the prickly Devil's Club and stinging nettles. This last hour was less back-packing and more trailblazing, and I was thrilled to be able to sit on a somewhat dry rock and devour my sandwich.

I paused midbite when a gunshot echoed through the canyon. "There's hunting this time of year?" I asked Leon.

"It's mostly trapping in the spring, but yeah there's hunting. Brown bear and muskox primarily. Could be someone with a special permit, or a ranger taking down an injured animal, though."

There was a worried look on Leon's face. I thought of last night by the fire, the feeling that there was something out there, that eyes had blinked from out of the darkness. Maybe a ranger was taking down a dangerous animal, and I'd sleep better tonight.

"Is it close? Where did the shot come from?" Hopefully we wouldn't be shot by some idiot who mistook two hikers for moose or something.

"It's hard to tell with the sound bouncing off the mountains. It seemed pretty far away, maybe closer to the bay?"

Kachemak Bay was our finish point, where the plane would pick us up in another seven days. If the shot came from there, the hunter should be long gone by the time we arrived. Reassured that I wasn't going to be accidently shot, I finished my sandwich and we pressed onward.

By late afternoon, we'd started our descent to a gorgeous alpine lake that sat at the foot of a glacier, dark blue water sparkling in the sunlight. Patches of snow dotted the rocky beach and the glacier's bright blue ice made the whole scene look like something from a fairy tale. We pitched our tents and Leon started a fire while I gnawed on a granola bar and took in the scenery. Again the feeling of magic washed over me. I could be happy here. I could be more than happy here, but where would I work? I loved my job, and I'd invested fifteen years and huge money in my career. I couldn't toss it all away to wander around the wilderness for the rest of my life. Was there a trauma center I could apply to in Anchorage? In Fairbanks?

In Juneau?

Or maybe I should just stick to Seattle and schedule some two and three day trips up here. It wasn't that long of a plane flight. I could afford it if I put the house purchase on hold another five years or so.

"Here. We're going to forage for our meal."

I looked up to see Leon, his eyes twinkling as he held out a collapsible bowl.

"I'm not eating Devil's Club, if that's what you have in mind."

He grinned. "Nope, although the roots are edible and kinda like ginseng we're not going to eat Devil's Club. We're gathering salmon berries."

I took the bowl. He picked up another and I followed him out into the woods, undecided whether the appeal of fresh berries was greater than sitting down for the evening and not getting up until morning.

Berries won.

The salmon berries looked like yellow and dark orange raspberries but with a milder flavor. They were everywhere, bushes loaded with them. Before long my bowl was full and I was just eating them straight from the branch.

Leon looked over at me and laughed. "Your mouth is orange. You look like you took a marker to your lips and teeth.

I flashed my orange teeth at him, and stuck out my equally orange tongue. "These are good. I might just skip dinner and eat berries. No wonder bears like them so much."

"Normally these bushes would have been picked clean, but our pack has a deal with the grizzlies to leave a few for us." He shot me a quick, panicked look, realizing what he'd just said. "Ha ha, we guides like to ensure we're on the good side of the bears."

He was trying to play it off as a joke, and a week ago I

would have totally laughed along. But after what had happened on the other side of the rift, I knew. Well, I knew about the existence of werewolves and angels, but I hadn't known until this moment that Leon was a supernatural being.

"You're part of the Swift River Pack? They're the ones who have this territory, right?"

He eyed me warily. "No, Ice Mountain Adventures. And we're not the only outfit operating in this part of Alaska."

"It's okay, Leon. I know Brent Phillips of the Juneau Pack."

He blinked. "Oh. Sorry, tourists usually don't know about us. I didn't realize…he's the Alpha there. Are you and he…?"

"No! No, we're not." I wish we were. The thought of it had me all flustered. "We wound up on the other side of a rift together. That's how I know."

"I heard about that. Glad you all got back alive." Leon tilted his head, his smile reaching his eyes. "I didn't want to have Jake chew me out for offending Brent's mate. But since you're not—" Leon scooped up a handful of berries and smashed them against my mouth.

"Hey," I protested, laughing. He danced out of reach as I tried to do the same to him. "That's unfair. Give a poor one-legged girl a chance here."

"No way. I saw you climb that rock face yesterday. You're better on one leg then most guys are on two."

I feinted right then dove. Leon was quicker than I'd expected so the berries smeared across his cheek, leaving chunks of yellow and orange in his beard.

"Peace, peace!" He raised his hands.

"All right, but only because you're adorable with food in your beard." I reached into a nearby bush to grab another handful of berries, only to jerk my fingers back with a squeak. *Darn, those thorns are sharp.*

"Here." Leon plucked a berry and shoved it into my mouth. I was too slow opening, and it squished against my lips, smearing yellow on them and dripping juice down my chin.

"Think I've had enough berries." I wiped my mouth on my sleeve, amused to see a streak of berry juice. "What's on our itinerary for tomorrow?"

"Pack rafting at dawn if the weather is good. Otherwise we're in for another long day of hiking."

I looked over at the tangerine sky around the setting sun. Paddling. It would give my legs a break, but I'd heard Alaska rivers and lakes were rough and rowdy, and especially challenging. "Well then, either way, I think I need to get off my feet. Or foot."

"Wine by the lake while you watch the sunset?"

It was one of the things I was learning to like about Leon. He was a good guide. He was fun. He made a mean grilled salmon. And he knew when I wanted to be alone. He knew when to be quiet for hours at a time so I could lose myself in my thoughts, in the ache of my muscles, in the beauty of my surroundings.

"Wine by the lake sounds glorious."

CHAPTER 5

BRENT

I was surprised that I managed to catch up with them just after sunset. I'd run along the banks of Fox River, took miles of switchbacks up into the mountains and along the ridge—all with that brisk werewolf gallop that ate up distance while pausing every now and then so I could scent the air. Around noon I heard a gunshot echo across the valley. My ears perked, but I didn't hear anything further. It wasn't close. And in Alaska, guides and hunters all knew how to tell the difference between a shifter in animal form and prey.

About four hours later I finally found what I was looking for. A faint breeze brought me a hint of fruity-floral that was her body wash, and the warm aroma that was all Kennedy. Every nerve ending snapped to attention, every cell sparked. My body spun midstride, and I ran as fast as I could down slopes and through brush and briar. My heart thudded in my chest, but all I could do was run straight toward her, my nose lifted high to keep the scent.

Once I saw her I slowed and edged through the trees, trying to stay out of sight. I recognized the guide she was with as one of the Swift River Pack and felt like even more of an idiot. How embarrassing to come strolling out of the wilderness with no good excuse for my presence, and have the whole thing witnessed by another werewolf. What if she was weirded out, thought me some kind of stalker? What if the moment had passed and she'd turned her back on me, never caring if she ever saw me again? This was going to be the most humiliating moment of my life.

So instead of shifting, donning my pants, and screwing up my courage to go see her, I hid in the bush, watching as she picked berries. She'd been eating them and both her hands and mouth were stained with the juice. I wondered if her lips tasted like berries—tart and full of flavor? Was this the right time? Should I shift now? Then I heard her speak my name.

Leon asked her if we were an item. And she denied it vehemently. Well, there was my answer. She did think of me, but whatever attraction we'd had on the other side of the rift, it hadn't lasted. I watched as she and Leon got into a berry-fight, watched as he gently fed her one.

It was just as well I hadn't come out of the woods and laid my heart bare to be tromped on. She wasn't attracted to me any longer. And it seemed Leon might have the advantage right now. Far be it from me to get in the way of another wolf, especially when the woman had made it her feelings known. I adjusted the saddlebag with my teeth and left, slowly returning to the bay where I could call Dustin for a lift back to Juneau. This time I wasn't in any hurry, and as the sun went down, I decided I wasn't in any mental or emotional state to be wandering around mountaintops in the dark, so I found a sheltered place out of the wind, curled my tail around my nose, and went to sleep.

I stretched my four legs, yawning and shivering to get my circulation going in the cold morning air. Clouds had moved in overnight, obscuring the mountain peaks and drizzling a light rain in the lower elevations. It mirrored my mood. I wanted to just run through these woods for weeks, let my wolf take over and give me time to reset my course. Kennedy was a gorgeous, smart, capable woman. I'd met other women like that, but I'd been dating very casually the past few years. Maybe I needed to get serious and really look for a mate. Maybe if I put forth the effort, made it a priority, I'd find someone that lit me up inside like Kennedy did. Maybe even another werewolf.

But I was forty-five. It's not like I'd been a monk. I'd had plenty of relationships as well as short flings, and nobody stirred me like this gutsy doctor. It hurt, but some people went through their lives alone. The stars didn't align for them and they lived perfectly fulfilling lives on their own.

And yes, I was beginning to think that would be my future. Casual dating. Some booty calls. It wasn't what I wanted. I wanted someone to wake up next to, someone who knew my quirks, someone to laugh with, to share my day with just as I shared theirs. I wanted someone I couldn't wait to see each evening.

I descended down the mountainside into the mist, feeling the drops of rain bead on my fur. The brush snagged at me as I walked by, trees waving as the wind picked up and the rain increased. Even at this pace I'd be back home late tomorrow. There were still chimera to hunt down, the weekly meeting with the sheriff, and the pack mud-races to finalize. I needed to get Sabrina more involved in leadership—that had become clear. I was young, but if that rift had gone somewhere else, the pack would have needed her to step right into my shoes. And Zeph too. Anything could happen and I didn't want the pack to fall apart just because I'd met an untimely death.

I was so lost in thought that I almost missed hearing the noise from deep in the brush. It was a sort of whine-moan. It was the sound of an animal dying. I couldn't let an animal suffer, so I headed into the briars, following the sound. I was sure the animal could hear me coming, but anything in that much pain wouldn't take notice. The next cry I heard ended on a growl and the hair went up on my neck as I recognized the sound.

It was a bear—a grizzly. A shifter grizzly. Could this be the missing bear? If so, then where had he been for the last week? I doubted he'd been lying in the bush injured for that long. Anything that would take seven days to kill a shifter would be something we could heal on our own. If he'd fallen over a cliff, or gotten in a fight, he'd either die right away or he'd heal.

An injured grizzly shifter wasn't something I wanted to mess with, but I couldn't just walk away and leave someone to die alone, so I went forward, making as much noise as possible. Far enough away that he couldn't reach me, I shifted, rushing the process. Once I was human, I walked closer, separating the thorny briars to see a huge grizzly stretched full length on the ground. He'd trampled everything within a ten square foot area, and clearly had been thrashing around at one point. Right now he was rigid, his teeth bared and his eyes wide.

"I'm Brent Phillips, Alpha of the Juneau pack. I'm here to help you."

At my words the eyes shifted, an outstretched paw flexed showing eight-inch long claws.

"Where are you hurt? Can I touch you?"

The grizzly twitched a paw and whined, his tongue licking his nose. I wasn't sure if that was a yes or no since I'd had minimal contact with grizzly shifters in their animal form, but I figured any mauling he did at this point wouldn't kill me. I walked slowly over to him, making soothing noises as I ran my hands over his fur. He was a big guy, so it took me a while to find it, but I felt the blood on his leg and traced it up to the wound on his hip. He'd been shot, but obviously it hadn't been with a normal bullet.

Getting shot hurt like a mo-fo, but it wasn't a death sentence. Our bodies expelled the bullet then healed. Didn't matter whether we were shot in the heart or the hip, we healed. Head was dicey. Depending on what part of the brain was damaged a shot to the head could kill us, but it was a rare occurrence. And contrary to legend, we didn't have problems with silver. A silver bullet would do no more damage than any other metal.

But this smelled foul. It had a sickening sweet odor to it— a chemical odor. It reminded me of the odor tranquilizer darts gave off, but this wasn't the same, and animal tranquilizers didn't affect us. What in the world was on or in this bullet? And who had shot this man?

I felt a paw on my arm and looked over to see the grizzly watching me, his claws gently touching my skin.

"Do you want me to try to get it out?" I was guessing his body hadn't expelled the bullet if he was still not healing. When had this happened? How much of this chemical had been introduced into his system? And why hadn't he shifted?

The bear nodded. Digging in my saddlebags I pulled out a hunting knife and parted the hair around the wound, praying that this bear didn't lash out at me in pain for what I was about to do. With a deep breath, I cut into his flesh, digging with fingers and knife to find the bullet. It was in deep, and the slimy feel of it against my fingers made me want to wretch. I eased it out, then stood back to wait for the bear to heal.

Instead he shifted. It was horrible to watch his bones twisting and muscles contorting. This wasn't normal, and after fifteen minutes, a half-man/half-bear lay on the ground, the wound in his hip still not healing.

"He shot me," the shifter told me in between gasps. "Shot me. I ran. I got away before he could finish me off."

Had a hunter mistaken this guy for an actual grizzly? But if so, the shifter would be healing from a bullet wound and pissed as all get-out. Plus, I didn't know of any hunters who'd be hunting for bear with these weird bullets.

"They killed Charlie last week, I'm sure of it. I came here to look for him and I found them. And they shot me."

He was rambling, sweat coating the parts of him that were skin. I smelled the cloying sweet odor of decaying flesh and realized that even with the bullet removed, this shifter wasn't going to make it.

"What's your name? Do you know who shot you?"

"Ian." Every muscle in the bear's body tensed and he let out a growl before continuing. "Two men. Guns. Traps. They killed Charlie, I know it," he whispered.

I leaned closer to hear him. "Hunters? They were shooting bear and you were in your grizzly form?"

Ian shook his head. "I was in human form when they shot me. They're not shooting bears, they're shooting shifters."

I recoiled in shock. Tourists didn't know about us, and we lived in harmony with the humans here in Alaska. Who would be so depraved as to hunt us?

And who would be so stupid? My wolf snarled as blood lust swept through me. We were descended from angels but outside of a handful of special skills, we'd lost the majority of any angelic supernatural advantage. We'd become shifters, and as the generations passed, we found ourselves living a dual existence with an animalistic amorality barely kept at bay.

Although having met a few angels and a demon or two, I wondered if the amorality wasn't a trait that had held true through the millennia. We prided ourselves on holding it in check, on letting the human part of ourselves take precedence. But times like this, when I felt an injustice, when the need for revenge poured through me, I became more of an animal. I needed to protect my pack, as well as the other shifters in Alaska. I needed to avenge Ian and Charlie.

And I needed to protect Kennedy. She was with a shifter, and if whoever had shot Ian was still hunting in the preserve, he might set his sights on Leon. And he might not care if the human woman with the werewolf also died.

As panicked as I was about Kennedy, I couldn't leave Ian, so I used some sticks and a tarp from my saddlebag to make a shelter from the rain and sat beside him. Just around nightfall the clouds cleared, the setting sun lighting them salmon-pink. As the sky grew dark, the insects sang. Peepers from a nearby pond chirped. The breeze shifted, bringing the scent of bluebells and fireweed. Night was warm and damp, the air full of the sounds of spring. And right as the morning sun peeped over the top of the mountains, Ian drew his last breath.

CHAPTER 7

KENNEDY

I awoke to a foggy mist that hung over the lake and obscured the mountains. Breakfast was short and we quickly broke camp, unsure how much paddling we'd get done before needing to head back to land. In preparation, I put on my slicker and made sure my pack had the rain shield up. Good thing too, since two hours into the five hour water portion of our day the skies opened up and a deluge of rain poured on us. Even with a brimmed hat, it was hard to see. I just kept Leon in view and powered through it, thinking this was the most miserable thing I'd ever paid good money to do.

We lunched under a tree that did nothing to keep the rain off us. Even with the slicker I was wet, my fine hair plastered to my neck. Water dripped off the brim of my hat and rolled down my back. Calling it a day, we pulled in the rafts and made camp, forgoing any attempts at making a fire and getting our tents up as quickly as possible.

I stripped out of my wet clothing and dove naked into my thankfully dry sleeping bag, dozing to the sound of rain on my tent. When I woke, the sunset was lighting up my tent with a faint pink, and the rain had stopped. Digging some dry clothes out of my pack, I dressed and hauled the wet ones out of the tent to drape across tree limbs. With any luck they'd dry by morning. Or possibly be frozen stiff.

"Started a fire. Do you mind tending it while I take a little walk?"

Leon's hair was a tousled mess, his face creased from where he'd lain on his sleeping bag. My stomach growled and I eyed the fire. I'd taken my prosthetic off and was hobbling around on my collapsible crutches. Leon could take a stroll while I made sure the fire kept going. It would give me time to grab a quick snack and don my leg. When he got back, I'd go out for a bit and stretch my own muscles.

"Sure. Want me to start dinner?"

He nodded. "They're instant, so just heat water. And coffee would be a good idea. I filtered some water over by my tent for you to use."

I waved him off with one of my crutches and headed back to set another log on the fire and put a pot of water on to boil. By the time I had my leg on, the coffee was ready and we had hot water for breakfast. Leon was still not back. He'd been gone a long time for a number two. I debated going to find him and dealing with the embarrassment to interrupting a guy doing his morning business. I couldn't imagine him getting lost, even if he weren't a werewolf. How far *had* he gone? Maybe he just liked his privacy? Maybe he needed to walk a few miles to get the old digestion in gear?

I was just getting ready to sit down for a second cup of coffee when I heard the gunshot. It was closer than I wanted a gunshot to be. Immediately I looked over to Leon's tent. My first thought was that he'd needed to defend himself against a moose or bear while his pants were down, but I hadn't remembered him taking the rifle.

He hadn't. It was right there propped against his tent. My

stomach twisted with dread and I ran, snatching up the rifle on my way. It was loaded. I didn't have time to grab any additional bullets, so whatever was in the gun would have to do.

I ran through the brush, briars snagging at my pants as I wove in and out of trees and larger bushes, trying to figure out where the shot came from. It might be nothing, but my gut told me otherwise. A few minutes later I heard another shot and adjusted course, now sure I was heading in the right direction. About twenty yards out, I slowed, carefully watching my footfalls and listening. I heard the sound of heavy boots crashing through the brush, a growl, a triumphant "yeah." As I came into view I saw two guys in camo giving each other a high-five. On the ground was a man—Leon, and he was in the process of shifting.

I didn't hesitate to chamber a round, take aim, and shoot to kill. I know that sounds extreme, but every bit of my army background screamed that these two guys were hostiles, that they'd shot Leon in his human form on purpose, and that they wouldn't hesitate to take me down either. I'd been a medic, I couldn't administer medical care unless the scene, which included both me and Leon, was safe.

The guy dropped like a stone. I chambered another round, but the second guy was on the move, cursing as he hit the ground and frantically tried to aim his own rifle. He shot and it went wide of me by around twenty feet.

I seethed with anger. These guys probably picked up a gun once or twice a year, and for some psychotic reason felt tough and macho blindsiding someone just walking through the forest. Well one if not both of those guys weren't getting up again. If I finished stabilizing Leon and the dudes were still alive, I'd render minimal aid. Hippocratic oath and all that, but I wasn't going to go out of my way to help people who gunned down another in cold blood.

I shot again and missed, churning up a divot right where the guy's shoulder had just been. He looked over at his buddy and decided to bolt, cowardly abandoning his friend and fleeing through the forest. As much as I wanted to chase him down, I was a doctor and now that the area was safe, Leon came first.

I ran to him, chambering another round and keeping the rifle close. Feeling through his blood-soaked fur, I found two entry points—his torso and his neck. The neck wound was an in-and-out and beginning to clot. The torso wound was dire, bubbling blood from where I assumed a wolf's lung would be.

"Hang in there. I've got you," I told Leon, yanking my shirt over my head and slapping it over the wound. I applied pressure and mentally calculated the distance back to the camp and my surgical kit.

Yes, I had a surgical kit. After having to deal with injuries using a basic first-aid kit across the rift, I'd decided it would be wise to carry the tools of my trade with me. I'd bought supplies in Juneau and kept them in a nifty holder. But I couldn't apply pressure to Leon's wound and run for my surgical kit in the same time.

But improvise was my middle name, so I wadded up my shirt and with one hand took off my belt.

"Just hold still. I'm going to do a very light sort of tourniquet to keep you from bleeding too much. It won't be so tight that you can't breathe, okay? Then I'm going to run back to the camp and get my doctor's kit. Did I tell you I'm a doctor? It's your lucky day, Leon. If you were going to be shot, it's good to have a trauma surgeon nearby."

By the time I'd finished talking, I'd secured the belt, pulling a pitiful whine from Leon as I rolled him slightly to ease the leather strap around his torso. Tightening it as much as I dared, I gave him a reassuring smile, then ran.

I'd seen that look in his eyes so many times before that I'd lost count. Every single one of my patients had that same desperate, pleading, frightened expression. They didn't need to say a word. I knew they were terrified. I knew they didn't want to die. I knew they were putting every bit of faith in my ability to pull them through this. I was the one who stood between my patients and the grim reaper. I was the one who beat that scythe-bearing jerk back with my bare hands.

I lost more than I won. All my years as an army medic and as a trauma surgeon, I'd learned that the reaper was a powerful foe. But every life I saved was a victory. Every life I snatched away from the bony hands of death made all those years of school and training worth it. Every one that I saved made up for all those patients I'd lost throughout the years.

Tearing into the camp, I ransacked my tent and snatched both the surgical kit and a bottle of water. Leon hadn't moved from where he'd been, but he looked relieved to see me.

"You've got a wound in your neck, but I'm going to deal with the one in your chest first. I can't see an exit wound, so I need to open you up, get the bullet out of there, and, more importantly, stitch everything up. I don't usually operate without anesthesia, so I'm hoping that as a werewolf you can take this."

This was so unnerving. Throughout history surgeons had been operating with nothing more than a shot of whisky, and sometimes not even that, but I wasn't used to doing a delicate operation with the patient potentially screaming and thrashing about. I seem to remember that in the Civil War, doctors had assistants to hold the patient still. I didn't have that luxury, and I didn't have time on my side, so I quickly shaved the fur around the entry wound, and made a careful cut.

Nothing sanitized. Nothing to cauterize the wound. I'd

been an army medic, but my job back then had been to stabilize the patient for transport to the actual surgeons. My surgery experience hadn't been in the field, but I had the feeling Leon's life was on the line. We were in the middle of nowhere. It wasn't like a Black Hawk helicopter was going to come out of nowhere to lower a stretcher. It was me, a handful of surgical tools, and a whole lot of prayer.

Leon lost consciousness after the first cut, which made my job easier. I'd used all my clamps by the time I found the bullet lodged deep in his left lung, just missing his heart. After I removed it, I carefully stitched everything, wishing for a cauterizing tool, for more gauze, for an additional clamp or two. After I closed him up, I prayed that nothing broke open again and got to work on his neck.

Why wasn't any of this stuff healing? I'd seen Brent heal a torn ligament within hours. He'd told me that werewolves could generally repair even the most serious of injury within a day. I would have expected to see clotting, to see new tissue growth, but there was none of that.

The bad guy never came back. When I finished with Leon, I went to check on the hunter and wasn't surprised to find him dead. By this point it was late morning. In a matter of hours my whole vacation had been turned on its head. Déjà vu. I might not be doing any hiking for the next two days, but sometimes life took a left-hand turn.

Making sure that Leon's heart rate and breathing were stable, I headed back to the campsite and grabbed a tarp. I was pretty strong, but I was still a five-foot-one-inch tall woman who weight one hundred and eight pounds. It might take me the rest of the day to safely move Leon, but I needed to get him back to the camp where we had a fire and water, and he could rest on a sleeping bag.

I doubted the other killer would be back. His buddy was dead and I'd witnessed their murder. Plus, he knew I had a rifle and was a good shot. I couldn't see him coming back to hunt me down for revenge. Cowards like him would just have kept running.

Leon's breathing was ragged when I returned to him, and his heart rate was a bit fast. I took his temperature the only way I could—up his butt. It was high, but I wasn't sure what a normal werewolf temperature should be. Brent had always seemed warm to me, even when the outside air felt close to freezing, so maybe Leon's was normal. He didn't seem on the edge of death.

Carefully easing him onto the tarp, I slowly dragged Leon through the brush, grateful that we were on fairly flat land and the rocks weren't overly large. It took hours. Even with the cool temps, I was sweating like crazy by the time I made it back to camp, my altitude headache pounding its way through my skull. The fire was down to coals, so I stoked it and put on more wood, then checked Leon once more.

He hadn't regained consciousness. This whole thing wasn't good. Gunshot wound, backwoods surgery. We needed to get out of here, and Leon clearly wasn't in any condition to travel. I powered up my cell phone, and as expected couldn't get a signal. Then I ransacked Leon's tent, hoping that he'd brought a satellite phone. We'd always had them in the military, but lots of civilian outfitters didn't. They were pricey, and required a costly purchase of minutes that expired. The other hiking groups I'd been with hadn't bothered, but we'd never had any issue requiring an emergency medical evacuation.

There's always a first time, and here I was in the middle of nowhere Alaska with a werewolf who might die. I had two choices—hike to a higher elevation and hope I could pick up a cell signal to call for help, or try to get Leon well enough to get to our meeting point at the bay. If we didn't show up at the agreed upon time, I'm sure his company would send someone in to find us, but that would be another six days at the minimum. I wasn't sure Leon would live that long. And I was afraid to leave him right now to go hunt for a cell signal.

I eventually decided to stay through the night and see how Leon fared. Worse or better, I'd need to start hunting for a place to make a call tomorrow morning, but in the meantime my goal was to keep my guide alive.

When I checked on him again, his chest wound was seeping, which wasn't unusual. Normally I would have put a drain in there, but I didn't have anything suitable. If I saw too much fluid building up, I'd need to open him up again, but in the meantime I was hoping his supernatural healing would take over.

It didn't. I sat there, keeping the fire going, the rifle locked and loaded in my lap, praying for rescue as Leon's breathing grew choppy, and his heart rate stuttering. I'd had this helpless feeling before, but I never got used to it.

The sun dropped low on the horizon. I'd opened Leon's chest wound to allow it to drain and ate a granola bar to try to keep my strength up. Just as the sky was turning a beautiful lavender-gray, I heard a faint noise in the brush. I know I'd called for rescue, but I still brought the rifle up to my shoulder, seating my finger firmly on the trigger.

The bushes burst apart, but instead of men with a stretcher, or a bad guy with a gun, the being jumping into my campsite was a wolf—a huge wolf with dark gray fur and golden-yellow eyes.

I traced my way back to where I'd last seen Leon and Kennedy, then tracked them from that point, only to lose the scent at the lake. There were two ways they could have gone, but judging from the rough itinerary I'd gotten, only one made sense. I followed along the shore, knowing that I'd be traveling twice the distance as by raft.

Hours of running and I heard a gunshot. I put on a burst of speed, hearing a second gunshot. Would I be too late? Were these the same hunters who had killed Ian? Who had killed the other grizzly shifter?

Leon was a shifter, and as much as I didn't want him to die, I was more concerned that these hunters might not stop with shifters. They might decide that the human witness needed to die also. And my guts twisted into a knot at the thought that Kennedy might right now be bleeding out from a gunshot wound.

Another shot. And another. I was running as fast as I could, tracking the sound of the shots as well as any human scent I could find, Kennedy's or not. There was silence and for an hour I pounded through the forest and brush, afraid of what I'd find.

I caught a scent and followed it, alarmed when I smelled the odor of blood. When I burst into the clearing I saw trampled grasses, blood everywhere, a human body. Pausing to take in the scene, I smelled the human body first. It had been dead for at least three hours, a rifle shot to the head. It was a clean kill—better than most hunters I'd known in my life. Whoever shot this man knew how to kill a human as opposed to hunting animal prey. Military experience. And judging from the attire and the rifle nearby, I was assuming this was one of the shifter hunters. And I was also assuming the person who'd pulled the trigger had been Kennedy. My heart swelled at the thought that my woman would have taken down a killer. My woman. Because no matter whether she'd chosen to give her affections to another or not, she'd always be my woman.

I scented the pool of blood and smelled a werewolf. Leon. I immediately thought of Ian and worried Leon might be suffering the same fate. Carefully, I traced the trail of scent and blood, following it to a camp near the shore of the lake. There was a fire and two tents. The smell of blood mixed with the smell of necrotic flesh. And I also recognized the floral-fruity scent of Kennedy's body wash, faded and dominated by the warm scent of her own flesh. With a dizzying sensation of relief, I burst into the camp, not caring whether I was in wolf form or human form, and came face-to-face with Kennedy.

CHAPTER 9

KENNEDY

"**B**rent!" I flung myself at the werewolf, burying my face in his warm fur. Then I pulled back to look into his golden eyes as I told him all about what had happened. After I was done, Brent went over and sniffed Leon, then he shrugged a pair of saddlebags off and began to shift.

His body twisted, bone and muscle reshaping, hair fading from his back and neck. I'd seen this before, I knew what was happening. It seemed rude to watch Brent go through this agonizing process, so I turned to stand guard, waiting until he was fully in human form. Then I turned back around to watch him put his pants on because Brent naked was one of the great marvels of nature.

Wait. "Why are you here? I mean, I'm really glad to see you, but it's kind of weird that you appeared out of the blue like this." Even if he'd had some romantic ESP about me being in danger, he wouldn't have had time to fly here from Juneau and hike in.

Brent stood a moment, looking uncharacteristically embarrassed. "I…well, I…was in the neighborhood? No, I wasn't. I wanted to see you and…to just know whether or not. Because you're leaving, and I needed to know."

What in the world was he talking about? I shook my head, but before I could ask him he grabbed me by the shoulders and pulled me against him.

"This. I needed to do this." Then he kissed me. In spite of the firm arms he'd wrapped around me, his kiss was soft and gentle—tentative, almost as if he were afraid I was going to jump back and swat him on the nose. It made me want to laugh. A tall, muscle-bound, Alpha wolf, as if I'd *not* want him kissing me.

I waited a few seconds, then took charge, sliding my hands up under his shirt and stroking the hard planes of his back. Pressing myself against him, I made a little moan noise and parted my lips to lick the seam of his mouth.

It was like lighting a match to dry tinder. Brent scooped an arm under my hips and lifted me up against him, his other arm holding me steady. His tongue brushed into my mouth and with a growl he kissed me with an intensity I'd never known before. Then his mouth left mine to trail kisses across my jaw and down my neck, nipping the skin and tasting the hollow of my throat. I was wet, shaking with need, every nerve in my body coming to life.

And the best thing about it was that he was shaking too, an undeniable erection pressed against me.

He pulled back, easing me slowly down, his eyes never leaving mine. "We need to talk."

"Talk? Can we have sex first then talk? I'm assuming we need to address the fact that there's an attempted murderer at large, a seriously injured werewolf twenty feet away, and a dead guy that I shot growing cold about a quarter of a mile in the bush. I'm hoping we can get a quickie in before we have to address that situation"

"No, we need to talk about *us*. And we need to do it

before, because once I have sex with you, I'm not letting you go." He cupped my face with both hands and brushed his thumbs across my cheeks. "I'm not letting you go regardless, so we'll just have to figure something out."

It was so gloriously caveman-like that everything south of my navel quivered. Then he kissed me on the tip of my nose. "But you're right. We do need to address this situation. It's probably crude to be having sex with a seriously injured werewolf twenty feet away and a dead guy that you shot a quarter mile off in the bush. I'm a pretty crude kinda guy, but even I have my limits."

I laughed. In spite of the "situation" we were in, I laughed. He was gorgeous and funny and I was so relieved that he was here. I'd been feeling completely out of my league in the middle of nowhere with a murderer on the loose and no way out, but with Brent, I felt I could take on the world.

"So, first issue is we need to get out of here," he told me.

"Really? You think so? Because this is a beautiful spot for us to reenact the last stand at the Alamo," I teased.

He smiled, his hands still cupping my face. "No Alamo. Not if I can help it, anyway. I am worried that guy who ran off might be back with a friend or two. Leon isn't the only one who has been shot. There was a grizzly shifter that went missing last week, and I found another weregrizzly who'd been shot. He managed to get away from his attackers before he collapsed."

And now I had not the slightest urge to continue our lighthearted banter. These guys were murderers who targeted shifters, which didn't make me feel any better. They must have a method of telling the weres from humans, because dead tourists would have caused an uproar. Murderers. Hunters. And they wouldn't like the idea that I had been a witness to what they'd done any more than the fact that I'd killed one of them. I shivered and hugged myself.

"I couldn't get a cell signal and I couldn't find that Leon had a satellite phone. Maybe if one of us can climb up to a higher elevation we can call for a medivac."

Brent looked over at Leon. "I don't want you to climb up on your own," he told me. "And I'm not about to leave you to do so. We'll have to get closer to the bay so we can call in. I can carry Leon, but it will slow us down."

"Well we can't just leave him here." Leon wasn't looking good, but I couldn't abandon him.

"No, we can't." Brent ran a hand through his hair. "We're easy to find here. We're exposed. Maybe we should try to take him via one of the rafts or something." His expression turned grim. "If he lives, that is. The grizzly didn't make it. There has to be something in the bullets that keeps us from healing and keeps us in our animal form."

"But I removed the bullet and Leon still hasn't shifted back."

"He might have a chance then. The grizzly had that bullet in him for almost twenty-four hours. Maybe since Leon has limited exposure to whatever the toxin was, he'll eventually heal."

Brent didn't sound confident. I'll admit I didn't feel particularly confident either. If Leon had been a human, he most likely would have been dead by now. I didn't know much about werewolf healing, but I was hoping that I got that bullet out in time for him to pull through.

"Let's stay here for the night," Brent said. "I'll set up some traps around the area that might give us advance notice if the hunters come back. Hopefully they aren't savvy enough to be looking for them. In the meantime, let's go look at the one you killed. Maybe we can get an idea of who these guys are, how they're identifying us, and why they're trying to hunt us down."

I did a quick check on Leon then Brent and I went to

where I'd shot the one guy. He was still in the same position, lying in a pool of thick, cold blood. Brent turned him over to search his pockets and I saw the purplish tinge of lividity on the side of his face. While Brent pulled a cell phone and a wallet out of the guy's jacket pocket, I picked up the rifle.

"Can you get these bullets out of his pocket here?" Brent asked. "I'm not sure if touching them is going to do anything to me."

I was pretty sure whatever was on the bullets didn't harm humans or this hunter wouldn't have had a box of them in his pocket. Still, I slid on my gloves before I pulled out the box. When he was done with his search, Brent stood and we began to head back to the campsite.

"He only had a bottle of water and some snacks, so they must have had a camp less than a day's hike from here."

"Do you think it's the same guys who shot the grizzly shifter?"

"I hope so. I don't like the idea that there are multiple bands of hunters here."

"So, a day's hike? Do you think that guy is going to come back here tonight or tomorrow to attack us?"

"I don't know. He ran off, which makes me think he's a coward. You showed him you're no novice with a gun and that you're not afraid to pull the trigger, so I'm hoping he got the heck out of here."

"But the game's up if I live to tell what's going on. I can't believe those two guys were behind this. I get the feeling they're tourists like me, paying for a hunting excursion where they get to kill shifters."

"That's what I'm worried about." Brent paused at the edge of the camp to look around. "If he ran back to camp and got a call in to whoever is running these expeditions, we might have more experienced, and dangerous, people after us."

"At night? I know I wouldn't want to hike around here in the dark."

"If they know the area and are using night-vision goggles, it's a possibility." Brent scowled. "Or they could be shifters themselves."

"Killing their own kind?"

He nodded. "We tend to get along, but it wouldn't be inconceivable for someone to be carrying an old grudge, or maybe they hate any shifter except their own breed. Either way, I'd feel safer if we were on the move. As soon as Leon is stable, we need to go."

I walked over to the injured werewolf and put my hand on his forehead. We'd leave as soon as Leon was stable—or he was dead.

Kennedy took care of Leon and fired up the little camp stove to boil water. We'd agreed that a fire wasn't a good idea—either during the day or the night. If a shifter came looking for us, he'd be able to find us even faster with the smell and light of a campfire.

I grabbed the rope she and Leon had been using for climbing along with a bunch of carabiners and a multi-tool and headed into the brush and wooded area around the camp to set some traps. On the deer tracks I made some snares. They wouldn't hold a human for long, but at least they'd cause enough commotion that we'd be alerted that someone was coming. In a few other areas I put together a trip wire system that would snap a branch at anyone who sprang the trap. Again, it wouldn't do more than cause enough noise to let us know about an approach. Done, I headed back to the camp to check on Kennedy.

She was sponging Leon's face with water. When she saw me she smiled and my heart skittered.

"Hungry? I boiled water for dinner. You have a choice of pad Thai or chili mac."

"Ooo, fancy gourmet food. Shrimp pad Thai?" I was hungry. All I'd brought with me to eat was a packet of beef jerky.

"Vegetarian." I wrinkled my nose and she laughed. "Okay, beef chili mac it is."

She added boiling water to the packets and set them aside as she made instant coffee. I went over to help, enjoying this bit of domestic bliss. I loved that she was outdoorsy. If things worked out between us, we could do all sorts of camping, hiking, and paddling trips together. I added instant creamer to my coffee, envisioning Kennedy in a bikini on my boat as we went fishing. I wasn't much of a climber, but I'd happily join her exploring the Juneau ice fields and mountains.

When our dinner was done, she dumped the chili mac into tin bowls and handed me a fork. We spread a tarp on top of an old log and sat, chatting as we ate. After we cleaned our dishes, she again went to check on Leon.

"How is he?" I asked.

"I don't know. You tell me. He's hot, but you guys seem to run three to four degrees hotter than we do normally. His heart rate is a bit fast, but again that might be normal."

What wasn't normal was the smell of necrotic tissue I was getting from the wound. Leon was hanging in there, but his body wasn't healing like a normal werewolf's would. "I think it's up to him at this point. He'll either fight it off and heal, or whatever was on or in those bullets will win."

She made a helpless wave of her hand. "What do you guys do when this happens? Is there something I can give him? Anything I can do to help?"

"You've already helped." I walked over and put my arm around her. "You removed the bullet, stitched him up. When werewolves get hurt, they heal themselves. The only time I've seen one not heal is when they were instantly killed or something prevented them from healing, like drowning or a severe brain injury."

"I guess I'll just make him comfortable and pray for the best." She leaned into me. "Are you going to take first watch? I've got the two rifles, and I loaded that other one with the tainted bullets just in case the bad guys come back with a shifter. I'll take that one and you can take Leon's rifle."

I rubbed her shoulder. "Deal. I'm going to shift into my wolf and do some reconnaissance before nightfall. Since we haven't seen or heard anything yet, I think the remaining guy ran back to camp and called in reinforcements. If that's the case, we've got until tomorrow earliest for someone to hike in from the nearest landing zone."

She turned to smile up at me. "Go on with your furry self, then. And make sure you give me plenty of warning when you come back so I don't shoot you."

I put my clothes inside her tent then shifted, lifting my nose to scent the air once I was done. Then I ran, exploring a several mile circumference around the camp as I determined any likely approaches for attack. There was a steep section with snow to the east leading up to the mountains, and like-wise to the south. They'd most likely be coming from the north or west, and if I were a betting man I'd say west.

Eyeing the sky, I headed west a few extra miles, trying to pick up the scent of humans or campfire, or another shifter, and pausing frequently to listen.

Nothing. Even if the other hunter had back-up on the ground, I didn't think they'd attack tonight. They'd want to be cautious and plan. Plus, they thought they were dealing with one human with one rifle. Under other circumstances, Leon would be dead. Under other circumstances, Kennedy would have been alone out here, trying to get to the bay for a plane out. They'd know her route. Instead of risking themselves trying to sneak up on her in the dark and winding up like the dead guy in the brush, they'd plan a better attack. They'd find a good spot for ambush and they'd wait.

And we'd be ready for them.

I unzipped Leon's sleeping bag and wrapped him in it, thinking it would be best to not move him unless it was threatening rain. It was warmer tonight, and I'd noted that shifters didn't seem as affected by cold as we humans were.

That done I went to sit over by the unlit fire pit.

"Cold?"

I nodded. "A bit."

Brent disappeared into my tent and came out with my sleeping bag. He unzipped it turning it into a big blanket, but instead of wrapping me in it he sat down beside me, his back against a tree. Then he pulled me off the cold ground and onto his lap, wrapping the sleeping-bag blanket around the two of us. Our little cocoon. Warm with my face against his neck, he had one arm around my shoulder and had snuck one hand between my legs.

"Can we talk now? I think, I mean you know, that I want more than just a vacation fling here. But I understand that you wouldn't want to rush into something. I can't leave my pack, and you have your career. I can fly down to Seattle a couple of times per month, so we can see how things go with us, but I don't want that long term."

I didn't either. "That's a lot of money on airfare, Brent. And my schedules are all over the place. There needs to be at least one trauma surgeon on twenty-four seven, so there are times I sleep at the hospital and am on-call."

"I'm not worried about spending money on flights. And if you get called in while I'm there, that's fine. Believe me, I understand responsibility. Your dedication to your patients is one of the things I lo—like about you."

Did he almost say the "L" word? Holy cow.

"I'll fly up here too. If I pull long shifts, I usually get three days off in a row. I'll warn you, though, I might spend most of my time sleeping."

"Or not sleeping." He said the words with a growly undertone that made me weak.

Could this possibly work? As a surgeon, I was rarely home. Would he get frustrated with all the back and forth, with me getting called in occasionally and leaving him alone for days, with me being exhausted and not the most entertaining company after coming out of a long surgery? I'd need to make changes, because I didn't want to spend the rest of my life alone, I wanted to spend it with Brent.

"There's a level two trauma center in Anchorage," he said. "It's less than a two-hour flight from Juneau. You could commute, especially if you have long shifts where you can stay at the hospital for a few days, then fly back home."

Home. I thought of a life in Juneau with Brent. I thought of him waiting for me, curling up with him in front of a fireplace. A life together. And he'd cared enough not only to work out a whole lot of back-and-forth travel, but to research what hospitals would have trauma surgeons on staff. My eyes stung with tears at the thought.

"I looked into the hospital in Juneau, but it's just a regional hub. They stabilize then medivac patients up to Anchorage." He turned his head to kiss my forehead. "You'd be bored. And all your talent would be wasted there. I wish I could move to Anchorage, but this is Swift River Pack territory, not ours."

His voice had a nervous edge to it that made me smile. He was worried I'd say no, that I'd think this was all too much bother, or that I wouldn't want to leave Seattle. Silly wolf.

"There are actually two level two trauma centers in Anchorage," I told him. "I should apply to them now, since I don't know how long it will take for a position to open up. Not bragging, but I've got a bit of a reputation in professional circles, so I'm sure they'll figure out the budget to bring me on sooner rather than later."

He caught his breath. "It's not bragging if it's true. I'm sure they'll snap you up right away. I live in the Alpha's house. It's huge and I think you'd like it, but it's not always the most private place in the world. The pack tends to come and go. We host most of our get-togethers there as well as meetings. It's not uncommon for half a dozen wolves to spend the night in the guest rooms. Sometimes it's more like living in a resort hotel than a home. If that's not your thing, we can get something smaller, just for the two of us."

"No. This is *your* responsibility and the pack is your family. Your dedication to your pack is one of the things I love about you."

There. No more tip-toeing around.

His arm tightened around me. "I fell for you the moment I met you on the other side of the rift, when you elbowed me out of the way and called me 'Muscles.'"

"So you like a bossy woman, do you?" I teased.

"I love *you*. Bossy, take-charge, smart, kind, compassionate, sexy. Did I mention sexy?"

I scooted my butt a bit on his lap. "We're going to do the frequent-flyer thing until I get a job in Anchorage, then I'm moving all my crap up to your giant house/hotel, and we'll live happily ever after. Are we done talking? Can we get to the sex part of our itinerary now?"

He chuckled and I felt it rumble through his chest. "Absolutely."

His one hand slid farther up, stroking between my thighs. I shifted to give him better access and his fingers pressed harder, working their magic. I bunched up his shirt, exploring the ridges of his glorious abs up to firm pecs. He made a low noise, then took his hand away. Before I could protest he was unbuttoning my pants and easing his hand inside.

"Maybe I should take those off," I suggested.

"Maybe I should help you." He scooped me up as he stood then set me on my feet, our sleeping bag blanket still wrapped around us. Then he let the blanket slide to the ground and hooked his thumbs in my waistband, easing my cargo pants slowly down.

I shivered, the air cold on my thighs. Once my pants hit my knee he let them drop and skated his fingers up the back of my legs. I leaned against him, my hands on his shoulders for balance as I wiggled the pants free of my feet, which put my thighs right against his cheek. I felt the brush of his beard, heard him inhale sharply, then he kissed the inside of my thighs, sucking and licking as he worked his way upward. Hooking a finger at the base of my panties, he pulled them aside and explored me with his fingers and mouth. There was something so incredibly sexy having him on his knees before me, not even waiting to get my underwear off first.

"You're so wet," he murmured against me. "You taste amazing. I could do this forever."

"Oh, good," I gasped. Or maybe it was "Oh, God." I wasn't sure because at that point all I could do was try to keep my balance as I rocked my hips against him. He was slow and methodical, bringing me to the edge over and over, but keeping my orgasm teasingly out of reach. My legs shook, my fists bunching his shirt at the shoulders as he explored every crease and fold, tasting, sucking, gently nipping. Just when I thought I'd go insane he made a low growl that rumbled through me and speared me with his tongue, thumb working my nub. I fell apart, shaking and crying out as I came against him.

Then he gently eased off my underwear and stood to lift my shirt over my head. While he unsnapped my bra, I unbuttoned his pants, carefully easing the zipper down.

"I'll get that. You're cold," he said, stooping to grab the discarded sleeping bag and wrap me in it. I was cold, but my shivering had more to do with desire than the chill spring air. I pulled the blanket around me and watched as Brent wiggled out of his pants and yanked off his shirt.

He was so gorgeous, a wall of tanned muscle with dark curls scattered across his chest and down his abdomen to a darned impressive erection. I opened my arms to welcome him into the sleeping bag and we stood for a moment pressed against each other, his heat instantly warming me.

I held the blanket while he sat down on, me straddling his lap. He was sitting on a log, and my legs were spread on either side of his waist. The length of his cock rested against my stomach and I wasn't sure how he intended this to work.

"Hold my shoulders," he told me.

I looked up into his warm brown eyes and saw love, desire, and a naughty twinkle. I'd barely got my hands on his shoulders before he lifted me upward and maneuvered me into position, then he slowly lowered me down. I gasped with the glorious feel of myself stretching around him as he slid into place. He lowered me all the way until my pelvis rested against his, the whole time watching me, his eyes reflecting every sensation he felt. We sat for a few heartbeats, then I tightened myself around him and shifted my hips.

"Easy," he chuckled. "Give me a second or this going to be over way too fast."

I obliged, instead tracing the lines of his shoulders with my fingers, working them up the column of his neck to feel the angle of his jaw under the dark beard. He dropped his head and kissed me. He tasted warm and wild, with a hint of my own scent on his tongue. It reminded me of how incredible his mouth and fingers had felt, and I tightened against him once more.

"Screw it," he murmured against my mouth. "Slow next time. I can't wait any longer."

His fingers curled around my hips and he began to lift and lower me, thrusting his pelvis in rhythm. I threw my head back, losing myself in the feeling of him inside me, of his muscled arms against me, of his mouth kissing down the column of my neck. Faster. Harder. I felt every muscle in my body tighten, felt him swell inside me. He drove himself deep and held me there, and with a cry I came. His release was a split second after mine, his body shaking as he pulsed inside me.

Then his hands left my hips to wrap around my waist and pull me tightly against him. Our breaths mingled, our bodies still joined, our hearts beating in time as we rode the lessening tide of orgasm.

"Love you," I whispered as I brushed my lips against his.

"And I love you," he whispered back.

I felt him twitch inside me and smiled, giving him a quick soft kiss. "And in about ten to twenty minutes, I'm going to show you just how much I love you."

He twitched again. "Blow job? Anal? You on top? Doggie style?"

"All of the above. Although maybe not at the same time."

"Well then," he rocked his hips against me. "Let's get this party started."

CHAPTER 12

BRENT

I was up before Kennedy and left her snoozing in the sleeping bag to go put on water for coffee and breakfast. Neither of us had gotten much sleep, and the remembrance of how we'd passed the night had me pitching a tent in my pants. Later. We needed to get moving as soon as we ate and broke camp. Once we were safely out of here, I intended to spend whatever remained of Kennedy's vacation in bed with her, but right now, in the harsh dawn light, the danger of our situation was weighing heavily on me.

Digging out the breakfast food packets, I left the water to heat up and went to check on Leon. The werewolf opened his eyes when I approached and wiggled a paw.

"Hey, look who's back from the dead. We're going to nickname you Lazarus," I teased. As relieved as I was to see Leon conscious, he was still in his wolf form and still had that horrible smell of dead flesh about him.

He stuck out his tongue at me and carefully stretched.

"I'm going to get you some water. Can you shift back?" I asked.

The wolf whined, so I took that as a no and put the water

in one of the bowls, lifting his head to help him drink. "Can you eat anything? I've got some beef jerky, or you can wait for breakfast."

I was feeding Leon chunks of jerky when Kennedy woke. "Look who decided to join us for breakfast this morning," I told her.

She grabbed her crutches and came over. "Dude, we thought you were a goner." She smiled and knelt down beside him. "We're going to try to get you out of here. I think the plan is to make it to the river and paddle out. Can you shift back to a human form?"

Leon furrowed his brow and chewed thoughtfully on a piece of jerky.

"Let's give him some time," I told Kennedy. "You wash up and I'll get us coffee and breakfast. Hopefully by the time we're ready to break camp, he'll at least be able to stand."

As we were beginning to clean up from breakfast I noticed that Leon was trying to shift. It took him nearly half an hour, but by the time we'd gotten the tents put away and our packs together, he was in human form, although still curled up on the ground.

"Leon, what can we do for you?" Kennedy asked in a soft voice as she checked his heart rate and temperature, then examined the gunshot wounds, the whole time completely unfazed by the fact that the werewolf was buck naked.

"Shoot me." He grimaced. "This time in the head. I've never felt so horrible in my life. Why am I not healing?"

"You're lucky you're not dead," I told him. "Remember that grizzly shifter that went missing last week? Well, one of his sloth came out looking for him—Ian. I found him shot and dying. He said there are a group of hunters targeting weres, and they've got bullets coated with something that makes us shift and not heal."

"Why make us shift?" Leon winced and curled up tighter.

"I'd rather face a grizzly shifter in his human form than in his bear one."

"Yeah, well mounting a human head on a wall will get you a life sentence. Mounting a bear head on the wall will get you a thumbs-up from fellow hunters—especially ones who can tell the difference between a shifter and a really big animal."

Leon looked even more pale at the idea. "We need to get out of here. It's a thirteen-mile hike to Fox River, then a thirty-mile paddle to the bay."

"You're in no condition to do a thirteen-mile hike," Kennedy protested.

"I don't have a choice. Help me up."

Before I could give Leon a hand, Kennedy elbowed me out of the way. "No. You're not getting up until I check you out. Now hold still."

I watched with amusement as she pressed on his abdomen and had him take several breaths while she had her ear pressed to his back. The whole time Leon looked at me wide-eyed. I shrugged. Bossy doctor always won over even the most assertive werewolf. When she was done she stood and gave me a nod.

"We go slow. Brent, you carry his pack along with yours and we need to pause every hour so I can check on him. If I say we're done for the day, we're done. Got it?"

"Can I at least put on clothes?" Leon asked, his voice full of awed wonder.

"Most definitely. I don't want to have to yank stinging nettles and Devil's Club thorns out of your behind tonight."

She headed off to break down the tents, leaving the pair of us to stare after her.

"So she *is* your woman," Leon finally said. "Can't think of any other reason for you to be up here, out of your territory, tracking us through hundreds of miles of trails."

I smiled, watching Kennedy's ass as she tied her sleeping bag to the bottom of her backpack. "Yeah. She's my woman."

Leon nodded. "Just so you know, I've kept my hands to myself. Don't want you to think I crossed any lines or been anything but respectful."

I thought about the exchange I'd witnessed with the berries. I'd never fault a man for flirting or being playful, even if it was with a mated woman. Yeah, I got jealous, but I would have been a crappy Alpha to let it cloud my common sense. And I knew Leon. He had a reputation for being an honorable guy.

"I've got no problem with you Leon. It's all good."

He relaxed, and smiled at me. "She's a gutsy girl, Brent. She'd make a fine mate for an Alpha."

Yes. Yes, she would.

KENNEDY

About five miles along Leon was unable to continue. I wanted to camp, but Brent was determined to make it to the river. After a rather heated argument he grabbed my pack, picked Leon up in his arms and kept going—which meant he was carrying everything including my guide. I fumed, trailing after him. I'll admit that we were able to travel faster that way, although I'm sure Leon's pride was bruised.

Ten hours after we'd left camp we made it to the river. Brent deposited Leon and the packs, then scouted around for a defensible spot for us to settle in for the night. I yanked out the tiny camp stove and filtered water, figuring I might as well get us some dinner. Leon was looking pasty and weak, but I managed to get him to swallow a few aspirin with some water and eat a granola bar. Brent still wasn't back by the time the water was ready, so I got the pad Thai ready, made tea, and wrapped Leon in his sleeping bag as he rested.

I was done eating and keeping Brent's food warm by the time he returned, sweaty, muddy, and covered in briars.

"I found a spot a few miles downriver." He picked up the backpacks and I pulled them from his hands.

"Sit. Eat. Let Leon sleep a bit longer. We've got enough time to get two miles before it gets dark."

He shook his head. "No fire and no flashlights. Unless you can set up tents in the dark, we should leave now."

"Sit." I scowled and pointed to a boulder. "You overruled me once today, you won't get your way this time. Take ten darned minutes to eat, and we'll go."

His lips twitched, but he sat. I brought over his meal and handed it to him.

"Are you mad at me for earlier?" he asked. "And thank you, by the way, for getting dinner together."

I sat beside him. "You're welcome. And no, I'm not mad at you. I'm a doctor and you're...I don't know. I guess you're more like the sergeant. We both have the same goal; we just prioritize things differently because we are looking at a situation from a different angle."

He nodded between bites of the pad Thai. Which I noticed he was eating at super speed. "Good. Because we're both strong-willed. We're going to butt heads pretty often."

"I'm sure we will. When it comes to matters about your pack, I'll advise, but you're the boss. When it comes to health and safety, I'm hoping you'll allow my expertise to sway you, even when it comes to your pack."

Brent got up to take his bowl over to wash and I followed.

"Absolutely. And I did take your expertise into consideration earlier today, but as much as I'm worried about Leon, my priority is getting you out of here alive and unhurt." He set down the dish and took me in his arms. "You can argue with me all you want, but you, my dear, will always come first."

It was a weird feeling, knowing that someone was looking out for me. I hadn't had that since I'd left the army.

Every soldier's life was important, but they especially guarded their medics. Good thing too, since once I was concentrating on helping the wounded, I wasn't paying much attention to people trying to shoot me.

"I never would have made it this far in life if I couldn't have a civil disagreement with someone and get past it." I grinned. "Although a shouting match generally takes a bit longer to put behind me."

"Hey, we weren't shouting, just having a rather loud quarrel." He ran a finger across my bottom lip. "So how long do you hold a grudge? What do I need to do to get back in your good graces?"

"Naked groveling? Breakfast in bed? A massage?" I suggested.

"All three once we get back home." He leaned in and gave me a soft lingering kiss, pulling at my lower lip with gentle teeth. "In the meantime, I'll set up your tent. My night vision is better, and that way you can check on Leon before it gets too dark to see. Deal?"

I kissed him back, leaning into him. "Deal."

Brent carried Leon's pack and his, plus the werewolf bundled up in his sleeping bag. I followed behind with my pack. Two miles never seemed so far. We went off the trail and took a circuitous route to our camp spot, but once there I agreed wholeheartedly with Brent. It was a defensible spot with the river looping around two thirds, and a tall monolith of a rockface at our back. There were two narrow spots to get in and out—easy for us to shoot anyone who tried to come up on us. There was enough room to maneuver around too, in case one of the bad guys was a mountain goat shifter and decided to climb the monolith and shoot down at us.

And beyond that, it was beautiful. The river was swift, with white splashing around and against a scattered mess of rocks. The sound of the water mixed with the evening bird-

song and the hum of the insects were a perfect accompani-
ment to the late-day beams of sun filtering through the trees
to dance across the water.

Our camping spot was a beach full of round rocks. Not
the most comfortable spot for sleeping, but we'd make due.
Brent, good to his word, set up the tents while I took Leon's
vitals. He seemed to be improving, and I think his deep sleep
was more about healing then any setback caused by our
travel.

Brent had set Leon's tent in a sheltered area under an
overhang where he'd be protected if a firefight broke out.
Before it got too dark, we tucked him in for the night, then
sat together, listening to the river as the sky grew dark.

"Bed?" I reached out and ran a hand down his back,
feeling the muscles jump under my palm.

"You go to bed. I'll take first watch."

I slipped my fingers under his shirt and ran them along
the edge of his waistband. "Are you watching in your wolf or
human form?"

He hesitated a moment. "Wolf. It's a compromise. I'd like
to be able to shoot a rifle, but my sense of smell and hearing
is better as a wolf. Plus, big teeth, you know."

"The better to eat you with, my dear?"

He groaned. "Don't give me ideas. I'd much rather be
going down on you than waiting for an attack to come."

"A couple more days and you can put those fantasies to
good use. I'll even delay my flight if I have to. Or we can do it
in the airport. I've got business lounge privileges. That's got
to at least give me a booth in a dark corner where you can
sneak under the table and turn me into a quivering mess."

"Ideas. Stop. I won't be able to focus, and we'll all die.
Then you'll never get oral sex, so cut it out."

"Nope." I leaned over and kissed him, deep and long, my
hands lightly tracing a path along his waist. "I want to give

you a reason to focus. All this is yours baby. All yours once we get out of here. Now go guard the camp, and kick some murdering hunter ass."

He growled deep in his throat and grabbed the back of my head, twisting my hair in his fist. "I'd fight to the death to protect you."

I smiled and pulled away. Even with his hold on my hair, he loosened his grip the moment before it pulled. "Now that's a little extreme. How about you not die, and we both protect each other? I'm a pretty good shot, and in case one of them is a were-mountain-goat, I can use the special bullets. Deal?"

He tilted his head, a puzzled smile curling up his mouth. "Were-mountain-goat? If there is such a thing, then I know what we're having for dinner tomorrow night."

I laughed. "Eww. Isn't that cannibalism? Weirdo. I've fallen in love with a cannibal shifter. Great."

He got to his feet and pulled his shirt over his head. "Normally the thought would never cross my mind, but if there are such things as were-rabbits, were-chickens, and were-goats, all bets are off."

And with that, he shucked off his pants and walked into the woods to shift while I admired his incredibly tight backside. Yum.

But "yum" would have to wait for later, because while Brent was guarding, I didn't intend to sleep in my tent where I'd be in a world of trouble if we were attacked. No, better to sleep out here leaning against the rockface with the sleeping bag wrapped around me and a rifle in my hand. And the other rifle, loaded and ready, beside me.

CHAPTER 14

BRENT

I spent the night making loops around our camp, widening out my circle then coming back in to watch Kennedy sleep bundled up in her green sleeping bag, two rifles at the ready. She'd left her leg on, just in case there was trouble. I knew it had to be bothering her to have it on for such a long period of time. She'd told me once that it was so well fitted and crafted that she could spend eighteen hours standing in surgery without any more fatigue or pain than someone with two legs would feel. Even so, this had been a tough day of hiking, and she'd spent several days beforehand hiking and climbing. Beyond tight and sore muscles, I'm sure she was longing for a length of time without the prosthetic.

But she'd push through it, because that's what she did. That's what I did too. We were so alike. I know that opposites were supposed to attract, but decades of dating my opposite only led me to frustration and a migraine that wouldn't quit. The few times I'd felt that click had been with someone who walked on the same side of life as I did. And never had I felt that click like I had with Kennedy.

Night passed without incident, but I couldn't stop that

prickling up my spine that told me danger was just out of my line of sight, waiting and biding its time to make a move. When the sky was the light gray that heralds the coming dawn, I went back to camp and started water for coffee and breakfast, checking on Leon. He was sleeping peacefully, seeming better than he had been yesterday, even after our strenuous hike.

Kennedy slept like a baby, soft little snores from her slumped-over position. I made coffee as quietly as I could, then waved a cup in front of her nose to awaken her.

She blinked open those gorgeous, sleepy, bedroom eyes and gave me a smile that sent blood rushing right down to my cock. I wished I wasn't so uneasy about our situation, or I'd take the time to wake her up properly.

"Is it… It's morning. You were on watch all night? You didn't wake me?"

I kissed the top of her head. "I'm waking you now. Oatmeal or reconstituted scrambled eggs?"

She frowned at me but took the coffee. "Oatmeal sounds good. How's Leon?"

"Sleeping. He seems better."

"Good." She stood, rubbing her back. "Ugh. I don't recommend sleeping on a bed of rocks."

I turned and something caught my eye—a flash of light reflected on something on the other bank of the river. Instinctively I reached out for Kennedy, pushing her against the rock and covering her with my body as I heard the echo of a gunshot. Something hot grazed my side, spreading a burning sensation through every nerve.

Kennedy cursed and pushed at me, wiggling down to grab one of the rifles. Everything happened in slow motion—me learning against the rock feeling bones and muscles twist and reshape with a blinding pain, Kennedy sliding the bolt on the rifle and aiming through the scope, another gunshot, this one pinging off the rock beside me. Then Kennedy fired.

I dropped to all fours, shifting faster than I'd ever been able to do before, feeling as if the whole process was completely out of my control. More shots. A hand at my shoulder shoved me flat to the ground and I saw Kennedy dart behind a boulder.

Fur, paws, fangs. Everything sharpened, every scent and sound pouring into me like water. A feeling of power and strength surged through me and I pushed through the burning pain and snarled. They'd killed too many of us. It was my turn to kill some of them.

I'd never been so angry, so determined, in my life. They'd shot Brent, and even though the bullet just grazed him, I saw the spreading stain of blood and I saw him begin to shift. A memory of Leon sprawled across the ground, two hunters congratulating each other on their kill resurfaced in my mind. I wouldn't let that happen to Brent. Leon had survived whatever was in those bullets. Brent would too—as long as he didn't take any additional shots.

I shoved him flat to the ground, feeling his rough fur and the wet of blood against my hand. Then I found cover and took aim. I couldn't see the guy across the river, but a few well-placed shots would flush him out, and I'd be ready.

Another shot, this one from the narrow path leading into our camp. They were hemming us in, guarding the two easy exits out of here with another making sure we didn't take to the river. I was willing to bet there was another one climbing up the rockface to shoot down on us. Whether that one was a mountain-goat shifter or a human skilled in climbing it didn't matter. We'd be trapped and between the guy above and the guy across the river, they'd eventually kill us all.

So the key was to kill the guy across the river before mountain-climber got into position. He obviously wasn't there yet or there would be bullets raining down from above, which made me believe the guy across the water had jumped the mark. If I could kill him, I'd be able to concentrate on climbing guy who wouldn't be able to shoot down at us without exposing himself.

Take both of them down, and the other two would need to either make a move or change position, either of which was fine with me. I could gun down anyone coming into camp, and if they moved away from the entrance, it would put us at equal advantage.

I saw a movement in the brush through the scope and shot. Another movement, and I shot again. The briars undulated. The guy was on the move. Now that I'd flushed him out, made him reveal his position, I took aim and prayed.

The movement ceased. I wasn't sure if I'd hit him, killed him, or if he suddenly become smart and decided to hold still, so I let off another two shots just to make sure, then pivoted to look above.

The sound of a snarl raised the hair on the back of my neck and I looked over to see Brent. Blood dripped from his hip, but that was the only indication of his injury. I'd seen him several times in his wolf form, but never like this. He was normally huge—much larger than a normal wolf, but right now he seemed gigantic. Fur bristled in a line from his neck down his back. His yellow eyes glowed feverishly bright, and his bared teeth looked lethal.

He was pissed—really, really pissed. And I wasn't sure if he'd recognize me in this state. My adrenaline went into overdrive and I pressed my back against the rock, trying to look above me for an attack and keep an eye on him as well.

The next gunshot didn't come from above, but from the entrance to our camp. It hit my shoulder, and I gasped, nearly dropping the rifle. Brent roared, and I cringed, but instead of jumping on me, he spun about and ran straight for shooter. The man screamed, firing off two more rounds before Brent was on him.

I couldn't watch. Not because I was particularly squeamish about seeing a giant wolf rip someone to bits, but because I'd seen something above me. A gun muzzle. A rain of small rocks and dirt hitting my face. My shoulder was on fire, but Brent was right in this guy's line of sight, so I fired straight up, hoping to throw off the man's aim.

Bits of rock flew off the lip of the monolith. I shot again and again, determined to keep this guy's attention on me.

"Brent, get out of there," I shouted. "Get back against the rock."

I heard a shot, not from above as I'd feared, but from inside the camp. I spun around, my heart pounding. The fourth guy. I'd been so busy worrying about the dude overhead that I'd forgotten about him and let him have opportunity to come in and shoot Brent.

As I turned I saw a man in camouflage lying facedown on the ground, a bloody hole in the back of his head. I kept pivoting, and saw Brent still savaging the other man, then Leon. The werewolf was holding the second rifle in shaking hands. With a weak smile my direction, he dropped to his knees.

Once again I looked up, worried that what I hoped was the sole remaining bad guy might be aiming to kill either of the two werewolves. I heard falling rock, the scramble of feet and the crash of a heavy body landing on top of brush and dead wood.

Brent heard it too. Lifting his blood-soaked muzzle he cocked his head, ears twitching. Then with a growl he took off. I hesitated, not thrilled that he was running after a guy who most probably had bullets that could kill him, but I could never catch him judging from the speed at which he could run, so instead I went to Leon.

The werewolf was breathing heavy, holding his chest. I didn't see any signs of a massive hemorrhage, so I helped him back to a more sheltered area and propped him against a rock, watching him for indications of internal injury.

"You okay?" he asked, eyeing my shoulder.

"I'll live," I told him, checking his stitches. My shoulder was on fire, but it wasn't a serious wound, and unlike the werewolves, whatever was in the bullets didn't seem to do me any additional damage. I wasn't a stranger to pain, and there was plenty of time to cry and doctor myself up once all my soldiers were safe.

"Here." I handed Leon the rifle he'd used, just in case he needed it, then got the sleeping bag to support him and keep him upright. I'd just gotten him comfortable when I heard another shot.

This time it was me that took off, gun in hand. Brent was in wolf form, which meant he was most likely the one being shot at. I followed the trampled brush and spots of blood, terrified at what I might find. I hadn't brought my medical kit with me. If Brent was shot, I'd need to run back to get my supplies.

It was the longest ten minutes of my life, that panicked scramble through the woods. I was afraid to call out for him, and equally afraid that I'd find him dead. I nearly fainted when I saw him staggering toward me on the trail, and I'm not a fainting kind of woman.

Rushing toward him, I resisted the urge to throw myself at him and wrap my arms around his neck. Brent's yellow eyes were wide and he panted heavily as he came toward me. The wound on his hip where the bullet grazed him was still bleeding, and on his rump was another bloody wound.

I wasn't sure how much time I had to get the bullet out of

him. Leon had been shot twice and he'd barely pulled through even though I was able to perform my makeshift surgery right away. We were half a mile from the camp and my kit.

"Keep heading to the camp," I told Brent, hoping he wasn't in so much pain that he wandered off the path and blacked out where I couldn't find him. "I'm going to run back for my kit and return."

He nodded, his pace slow but determined. I sprinted, my lungs on fire by the time I tore into camp, grabbed my kit and ran back.

Brent wasn't much farther than he'd been when I left him, but he was still on his feet, taking one agonizing step at a time.

"Rest here. Lie down so I can get to where you're shot." I examined the wound, breathing easier once I discovered the bullet lodged in the muscle tissue of his rump.

He let out a sigh and closed his eyes. His breathing was labored, but his heart rate was steady, which was better than Leon's condition had been.

"This is terribly unsanitary and there's no anesthesia, so you're just going to have to clench your sharp teeth and get through it."

I trimmed the hair around the wound and rinsed it, using gauze to keep the blood from obscuring my view of the bullet.

"Okay. I'm going to do this. Just don't bite me. I've already lost one limb; I'd really like to keep the remaining three."

He made a huff noise that I took to be a laugh. The laugh turned to a pained growl as I carefully inserted my forceps into the wound, using my fingers around the area to keep the bullet from working in deeper or slipping sideways. Once I had a good grip on it, I extracted it then cleaned and stitched the wound. For good measure, I cleaned and stitched the minor graze on his hip that didn't seem to want to clot.

By the time I was done, he was out, breathing easier and the bleeding around the stitches slowing. I hated to leave Leon alone in the camp, especially since he was just recovering from his own injuries, but my priority would always be with Brent. He was far too big and heavy for me to drag back to camp as I'd done Leon, even if I didn't have an injury of my own hindering me. So instead, I sat down beside him, one hand resting on top of his head, the other hand holding the rifle. And there I stayed until the sun began its descent toward the horizon.

It was mid-afternoon when Brent opened his eyes and began to shift. Normally I didn't watch him go through the painful process, but this time I was worried and kept an eye on him. It was like something out of a horror movie, and he whined and yelped with each twist of bone and sinew. After what seemed like an eternity, he was human once more, with stitches intact both on his neck and on his ass.

And it was a very fine ass, even with a gunshot wound in it.

"Your shoulder. You got shot," he said, his voice rough and gravely.

"I did. And it hurts like a mo-fo too. When we get back to the camp, I'll have you or Leon clean it and put a bandage on it."

He growled. "Leon isn't touching you. I'll stitch you up."

I stroked his short, dark hair. "No offense hon, but I'd rather just bandage it up and wait until we get to a medical professional. I've got enough scars without adding to them."

"I love your scars." His voice slurred a bit. "The ones on

your legs, the one around your ribs, the one across your hip. Beautiful. Beautiful."

Oh Lord, he was feverish if he thought my scars were beautiful. My one leg was a mess of divots from where the surgeons had needed to place pins after the accident, then there was the scar on my residual limb, then the huge one where they'd needed to crack my ribs open and stop internal bleeding, then the one where they'd needed to put my pelvis back together. It was a miracle I'd survived that accident. It made me appreciate every day I had.

"You're beautiful," I told him, still stroking his hair. I let him rest, my hands roving over his head and back and keeping watch until he was ready to stand. Once he was upright, I put my arm around his waist and draped his arm across my neck, wincing as I transferred the rifle to my arm with the injured shoulder.

"I appreciate the snuggle, but there's no way you can support my weight." He chuckled, breathing in a sharp breath afterward. "Plus I'm a foot taller than you. Maybe if I hunched over?"

He must not be feeling too horrible if he was joking, although with Brent, I never knew. "Then consider it a snuggle. Come on, Muscles. Let's get a move on."

When we got back to camp, I was amazed to see that Leon had inflated the rafts, and gathered essentials into both our backpacks, leaving the tents behind.

"Good idea," Brent told him. "The one guy got away and I don't know how much time we have before more show up."

"That's what I was thinking." Leon eyed Brent's wounds. "You gonna be okay to travel?"

"I don't have any other choice."

I helped Brent over to one of the rafts, sucking in my breath as the cold water came over the tops of my boots and soaked through my hiking pants. Then I carried the packs to the rafts and helped Leon into his before climbing in with Brent. Leon still had the one rifle. I made sure to reload mine, then pushed us off with the paddle.

Brent kept insisting that he help paddle and we had yet another of what I assumed were going to become our famous arguments. I won this one, probably because he was hurt and exhausted, so he ended up dozing.

The river was quite a bit rougher than I would have liked, and it was difficult to paddle with the wound in my shoulder. I was beginning to feel as if I were on the edge of going into shock, but I managed to hold myself together. Leon had tethered the two rafts together and after a few hours I noticed I was doing the lion's share of the paddling. After five hours I pushed past my pain and tried to increase my speed. Leon got his second wind and helped, but I was pretty sure we wouldn't make it to the bay by nightfall. I was debating how far we could go before I found a place to put in, and hoping it wouldn't rain since we didn't have the tents when I heard the sound of a helicopter.

Friend or foe? I glanced back at Brent and Leon, worried that we were going to be shot out of the water, but the chopper that circled above us was a Bell Jet Ranger, and not equipped with guns. Unless they were going to hover over us and shoot with rifles, this wasn't the bad guys.

Leon obviously felt the same since he nearly capsized his raft by standing and waving. The helicopter circled around, then set down ahead and to the west of us. By the time we reached the shore, there were two men waiting for us, both cradling rifles in their arms.

"It's Dustin and Jake," Brent reassured me, his voice tired and husky. "The Swift River Alpha and one of his pack. Dustin flew me here in his bush plane, but Jake runs a helicopter tour company."

Leon and I picked up the pace, and the two other werewolves waded out into the river to help us pull the rafts in. Brent managed to make it to the helicopter by pride and sheer will alone, but I didn't truly feel safe until we were back in Anchorage—actually until our wounds had been treated and Dustin flew us back to Juneau.

Getting out of the plane in Gastineau Bay, I saw a group of people waiting for us. I recognized a few from when we'd come back from the rift. They were Brent's friends, members of his pack. Instead of waving or greeting them, he turned to me and yanked my pack out of my hand. Then with a wince of pain, he scooped me up into his arms and headed toward the group.

"You're not coming out of the woods, but close enough," one woman shouted.

"Is this a yes?" another asked.

Brent shifted my weight so he could rest his chin on the top of my head. "It's a yes."

They all cheered, and I felt myself blush, realizing that the entire pack knew about us. Oh well. If they hadn't before, they sure were going to when I moved all my hiking and climbing gear along with my collection of vintage board games into the Alpha house. I wondered if werewolves liked to play Parcheesi?

EPILOGUE

I rolled over, burying my face in Kennedy's silky-soft dark hair. Every time she had a day or two off I flew down to Seattle or she came up to Juneau. The grizzlies were mourning the loss of two of their sloth. Between them and Jake, I was sure the hunters targeting shifters in Kenai would soon be found and brought to our own sort of justice. I'd offered the assistance of the Juneau Pack, but so far they hadn't asked for our help. Just as well since I was busy with other matters. And I was busy spending as much time as I could with Kennedy.

"Morning." Her voice was soft and husky. Her hands stroked down my waist and curled around my hips.

"Don't you have to go to work?" I asked, mentally calculating how fast I'd need to make things happen before she had to head out.

"Yes." She sighed, warm palms sliding around to grip my ass. Her fingers traced the round scar from the gunshot wound that had finally, after six weeks, healed. It was an unbelievable amount of time for a shifter to heal from something so minor and to have a scar was unheard of. I wasn't complaining, given that two grizzly shifters had died and Leon had scars of his own.

"I'll pop by the hospital to see you before I leave," I told her. This was killing me, only seeing her for a few days at a time. Killing. Me. But she'd had an interview at both hospitals in Anchorage within weeks of submitting her resume, and she seemed optimistic that she'd be receiving an offer within the next month.

"I'll be in Juneau Tuesday," she reminded me, kissing my shoulder. "Can't miss the mud races, you know."

Warmth spread from my torso through every limb. The mud races were a pack event. Kennedy would be there as my mate, helping officiate and playing the role of hostess. I was thrilled she had eagerly embraced these duties. My pack already adored her, and everyone was counting the days until she moved to Juneau.

And until our wedding. My fingers traced the ring on her finger, the platinum, diamond-encrusted band and moonstone solitaire that I'd given her just two days ago.

"So...am I going to be late for work today, or what?"

"Absolutely." I gathered her close and kissed the warm skin of her shoulder. "If I have my way, you'll be very, very late."

She let out a soft sound of pleasure, draping her leg across mine. "Make me late, baby. Make me very, very late."

***

Don't miss Rogue, Book 2 in the Northern Wolves Series.

DEBRA DUNBAR
ROGUE
BOOK 2 OF THE NORTHERN WOLVES SERIES

ROGUE

NORTHERN WOLVES BOOK 2

PROLOGUE

"Who is *that?*" I transferred the bottle of beer that I'd been nursing for the last hour to my other hand so I could point rudely at the man emerging from the woods at the end of Brent's property.

"That's Karl." Ahia took a swig from her own bottle. The Nephilim had been drinking steadily since we were setting up this morning, but she never seemed to get drunk. Werewolves had a heck of a tolerance when it came to booze, but Ahia always could drink us under the table.

"The grizzly shifter?" I asked. Every year there was an open invitation to all shifters to attend the Juneau Pack barbeque, but no one except for wolves had ever come. This was a first.

"Yeah. Hot, isn't he? Damn, I've been trying to hit that for the last five years, but he always says no. And he says no in a way that makes me think he'll punch me in the face if I ask again." The Nephilim chuckled. "So, of course, I keep asking. Not that the answer is ever different."

I could see why Ahia was so persistent. Wow, the guy was smoking. He was tall and broad-shouldered, with wavy hair that brushed his shoulders and a scruffy look that said he didn't like to shave more than once a week. He walked with a graceful lope across the lawn, shaking hands with Brent, our Alpha, who'd walked over to meet him.

The grizzly shifter looked like a wild man come out of the woods after decades in seclusion. And that contributed just as much to his hotness factor in my eyes as his powerful form. It was funny, actually, that I'd be attracted to this kind of guy when I was the type of werewolf who owned a walk-in closet full of tailored clothing, loved scented bath gels, and never left the house without my make-up perfectly done. Yeah, I loved to shift and hunt down deer as much as the next wolf, but once I shifted back, I at least touched up the mascara and the lipstick and ensured my glossy red curls weren't a tangled mess.

I broke out of my thoughts, realizing that Brent was leading the grizzly shifter over to us.

"Karl, this is my second, Sabrina. And you know Ahia."

The grizzly grunted. I got the idea that was his go-to method of communication. Not that I could say anything polite or welcoming in response to Brent's introduction. I was too busy staring at his amazing eyes—hazel with flecks of gold that were far too bright to pass as human.

There was something dark behind those eyes, something dangerous and amoral, something predatory. Smoking hot. Radiating a power that nearly suffocated me. And scary. The last two turned me on as much, if not more, than the first.

"Karl! My man! Wanna fuck?"

Oh Lord. Times like this I just wanted to stab Ahia.

For some reason the grizzly's eyes jerked to meet mine at Ahia's proposal. I sucked in a breath. That brooding, smoldering expression seemed like it was designed to make me come at a glance. And it nearly did. Holy crap where had this guy been the last few years? I knew why Ahia was constantly trying to get him in the sack. He might not be my type at all, but I'd sell my soul for a night with this guy. I'd bet he was amazing in bed. Amazing.

His gaze left mine to glare at the Nephilim. "I've got no interest in beddin' you, Ahia. Go fuck a tree stump if you're that horny."

His voice was rough and gravelly, as if he seldom spoke or he was a chain-smoker. I didn't smell any tobacco on him and I had a werewolf's nose, so I could only assume he was a man of few words. A wild man. A grizzly shifter who'd come out of the woods to eat burgers and drink beer with a rowdy bunch of werewolves. This was going to be the most interesting party we'd ever had. And judging from that intense look in his eyes, I was full of hope that this party would end with the pair of us naked and sweaty in one of the upstairs bedrooms.

"I'M DONE. Done, I tell you," Zeph slurred, his forehead hitting the top of the table. We'd been at it all day—food, beer, horseshoes, volleyball, cannonball contests in the pool, more beer, bonfires. Eventually beer turned to shots which meant nearly half the pack was sprawled out in the grass, inebriated.

I wasn't. Second to the Alpha meant I needed to not be passed out in the dirt. I was tipsy, but I could function.

"Thought you wolves were tougher. Next time I'll bring some milk."

Zeph lifted his head and trained his bleary eyes on the man across from him. "Normally I'd pin you to the ground with my teeth at your throat for those words, but I'm drunk and I'm not stupid enough to mess with a bear. Here." He slid a bottle across the table. "You won. Take it and leave me to sleep it off here at the table.

The "bear" reached out and grabbed the bottle with far less deference one should have given Woodford Reserve bourbon. "That'll teach you to try to outdrink a grizzly," he said. Then he grinned and examined the label on the bottle of bourbon.

A grizzly shifter. At our barbeque. I still couldn't get over the novelty of it. Most of the black bear shifters were down in the lower forty-eight, but Alaska was home to the majority of the brown bear shifters. There were a few coastal brown bears in the south and up in Anchorage, one or two Kodiak shifters that roamed all over the north, and anywhere from fifty to seventy grizzlies at any given time. No one knew exactly how many. They were independent, solitary, and introverted. We all got along just fine, we just didn't run across bear shifters more than once a month. We'd nod, exchange a few words, then go on our way. It wasn't only that it was a novel occurrence for a grizzly shifter to join a party full of noisy, physically demonstrative, rowdy wolf shifters, it was that Karl truly appeared to be enjoying himself. He wasn't the most loquacious guy I'd ever met, but he'd joined in every game, chatted amicably with the members of my pack, took a turn flipping burgers on the grill.

And all night his eyes had followed me. If I went inside, he was watching for my reappearance. If I went to sit by the pool, he left whatever he was doing and moved nearby. He was never creepy or stalkery, just present. A werewolf would have made a move four hours ago. Heck, a werewolf would have propositioned me right after he'd grabbed that beer from the cooler. But this guy seemed content to just be near me.

Weird. And honestly the best sexual build-up I'd ever

experienced. If the guy didn't make a move soon, I would. And if he said no, I'd be spending a lot of quality time with my vibrator tonight.

I hesitated, watching the bear's hand on the bottle. Then my eyes traveled up his arm to his hazel eyes. He lifted the bottle.

"This any good?"

I swallowed. His voice was deep, gruff, husky—so very sexy.

"Yeah. It's really good."

He stood and I looked upward because the guy was well over six feet tall and proportioned accordingly. "Then let's share it."

Share it, or *share* it? I made a quick decision. "There's a stream that runs through the back of the property. There's a mossy bank where you can hear the gurgle of water over rocks, and see the fireflies against the dark woods on the other side."

"This a date?"

I hesitated, then chickened out. "No, just a quiet place to drink some whisky."

He grunted and waved the bottle. "Then lead the way."

We walked away from the light of the bonfire, my eyes adjusting to the darkness. The sounds of laughter died away, replaced by insect song and the brush of our feet through the tall grass. The bear shifter followed me down a steep embankment, through a wooded area and to a clearing where moonlight reflected off the surface of the stream, the golden blink of fireflies giving the whole scene a fairy-like atmosphere.

I heard the crack of the seal breaking on the bottle and the nudge of glass against my bare arm.

"Here. You first."

Crap. I'd forgotten glasses. I can't believe I was about to drink hundred-dollar booze out of the bottle.

I lifted it to my lips and took a sip. Warm and smooth with a honey and oak aroma and a sweet, slightly bitter finish. Just because it was so very nice, I took another sip before handing it back to the bear.

He took it and sat on the moss, his back against a tree. I dropped down beside him, chuckling as I watched him gulp the bourbon.

"Whoa there, wild man. We're not at a frat party here, that's sipping whisky."

He eyed the label then passed the bottle back to me. "I *was* sipping. Otherwise half the bottle would be gone."

Sheesh. How this guy was still standing after drinking two werewolves under the table was beyond me. "So…Karl the grizzly shifter at a werewolf party," I said, taking another sip. "What made you decide to come to the barbeque? Were you in the neighborhood and drawn in by the amazing aroma of hamburgers and ribs?"

"Get asked every year and figured I'd see if you wolves had any decent food and booze."

He was such a bear. "So…?"

He took the bottle from me. "Ribs were good. Burgers were better."

Yes, they were. Brent, our Alpha, had made a mix of beef, venison, and sausage. We'd been taste-tasting spice blends for a month, and Allison had ordered in some specialty goat cheese. Drew had even cooked a bunch of pork loin and shredded them to use as a topping.

"Next year I'll bring some smoked trout. You like fish?" He nudged my arm again with the bottle.

Surprisingly I liked the idea of a "next year" with Karl. Being second to the Alpha had kind of put a damper on my dating life. The dominant wolves chafed at my superior position in the hierarchy, and I wasn't attracted to the submissive wolves. I'd tried dating some of the guys from the other packs, hoping to find a dominant wolf that wouldn't want to constantly be in a battle for control, but the distance killed any idea of a relationship with them. When it's three hours by plane to see your main squeeze, romance snaps from the strain—at least for me.

So that left me with humans who, although they made for fine bedfellows, lacked the connection I needed, that something more. Yeah, I was picky—too picky according to my parents who were desperate to see me mated and bringing a guy home for the holidays. I'd kind of given up at this point, throwing myself into my careers—both in marketing and with the pack management. It's not like it was that weird to be unmated. Our Alpha was and he was in his midforties. It shouldn't be a big deal, but for me it was. But I'd never thought to try to date a bear. Shifters were shifters, but bear society was very different than ours.

Wait. What was I thinking? This wasn't a date. It wasn't anything long-term. This was a booty call, if it was even that. Afterward he'd go back to his den to prep for the winter, coming out in the spring to go hunt down and screw a sow in Fairbanks or Anchorage, and I'd work my butt off, spend Christmas with my folks, and hope he meant it about bringing smoked trout to the next year's barbeque.

Yum. Smoked trout.

"Absolutely. I love fish. If it's meat, then I'll eat," I joked. I took more than a sip this time. I'd been nursing my beers all night and this bourbon was really going to my head. I scooted closer, my thigh resting against Karl's, my shoulder brushing his. It was a toasty August night and the booze was warming my blood, but nothing compared to the heat I felt coming off this bear shifter. His hand touched my leg and worked its way up to the hem of my shorts. My breath hitched and I mentally willed his hand to go higher. I was sure the scent of my arousal was filling the air.

Which was totally okay, because his was too.

Karl took the bottle from my hand, carefully setting it aside. I watched him, watched his muscles flex under the snug shirt, watched the swing of his shoulder-length wavy hair. My thoughts swirled in a bourbon haze, my inhibitions nowhere to be found. When he turned and slid me onto his lap, I pivoted to straddle him, feeling myself perfectly positioned against what was clearly a raging hard-on.

"Prettiest wolf I've ever seen," he murmured, wrapping one of my red curls around his finger. Then his hand moved up to the back of my scalp and he pulled me to him.

His lips met mine. I'd expected something gentle, tentative and soft. This kiss wasn't. He was demanding and forceful. His hand twisted into my curls, pulling the hair so tight it stung. I was trapped, his one hand controlling my head, his mouth devouring mine, his other arm pinning me against him. I, second to the Alpha, was well aware that this guy could crush me, could do whatever he wanted to me and beyond inflicting some minor damage, I'd lose in a fight against him. It wasn't just that a grizzly would always beat a lone wolf, it was the force of his personality, the internal strength of the man. I'd met powerful Alphas before. Jake of the Swift River Pack was like a current of hot, dangerous electricity, unpredictable and deadly. Karl was...he was like the mountains that separated us from Canada—huge, quiet, unmovable, and even more deadly in his own way.

It made me feel unsettled and on edge to lose control to another like this. And it turned me on beyond belief.

I shuddered, my tongue playing with his as I slid my hands up his chest. Everything about this man filled and touched every sense. I tasted his mouth, felt the hard muscles of his chest and shoulders, smelled his wild woodsy scent mixing with my light perfume. He growled, a low rumble deep in his throat, then pulled his mouth from mine, releasing my hair to fumble with the buttons on my shirt.

"Don't want to tear your shirt," he said.

It was adorable, this rough sexy man trying to undo tiny pearl-shaped buttons and not rip them off in his hurry to get me naked.

"Here." I helped, popping them loose one at a time, then slid the fabric from my shoulders.

He drew in a ragged breath, his eyes devouring me. Then he took a finger and traced the lacy edge of my scarlet red bra. I felt my nipples harden as he brushed his palm over one. With a snap he'd unhooked the center closure and the bra hung loose on my breasts. I went to shrug the undergarment off, but he stopped me, slowly nudging the lace aside with his fingers until the small globes popped free.

He cupped one breast in his hand and bent his head to the other, licking and nibbling across the skin before pulling my taut nipple into his mouth.

I arched my back, losing myself in the feel of him. He pinched and rolled, nipped and sucked. I moaned, grinding against the bulge in his pants. He might have not wanted to rip my shirt, but I had no such restraint. Putting my werewolf strength to the test, I gripped the cotton neckline and tore downward, running my hands over the warm skin of his chest.

He made that low, deep growl again and the sound shot heat right between my legs.

"Pants." He muttered, shoving me backward onto the damp mossy ground. Before I could protest at the caveman tactics, he'd removed my shorts and undergarments. Then he stood, towering over me as he shucked off his jeans. My breath hitched as I watched. I was sprawled naked on the ground in front of him as he loomed over me, muscled and powerful, eyeing me like a cougar watches a snared rabbit. Me. A wolf. Wet and quivering, feeling helpless before an apex predator. I'd never been so turned on in my life. And judging from the incredible boner the grizzly shifter was sporting, he was equally aroused.

I took action, springing to my feet and slamming into him, driving him back against a tree as I pressed myself against his torso. He was so darned tall that I could do no more than kiss his chest, nipping and licking as he'd done to me. I reached a hand between us to grip him, giving his shaft a few quick, firm strokes.

He groaned and slid down the tree, pulling free from my hand, and yanking me down on top of him once more. I squealed, losing my balance and squashing my face against his shoulder where I felt the rumble of his laugh. His arm flexed, pulling me firmly against his broad chest, holding me steady as he trailed a line of hot kisses down my throat. I squirmed against him, trying to rise up so I could sheathe his cock between my legs, but he held me tight.

Then his fingers slid down the crack of my ass, skating between my folds and brushing against my nub. I arched back in his arms, my fingers digging into his shoulders. His breath caught, then his finger slid into me. I opened for him, eager for more, and he obliged.

"Damn. You're tight," he murmured against my neck. "This might not work."

"It will work," I gasped, riding his hand. "Trust me, it will work."

Pulling his fingers free, he glided the slick wetness along my folds. I rose on my knees as he positioned himself, then lowered slowly onto his cock—slowly because he was a lot to take in. I stretched around him, feeling the burn of being widened almost to the edge of pain. He gripped my hips, holding me still a moment to adjust before letting me slide down an inch at a time.

The whole time I couldn't stop watching his face. There was a muscle that tightened in his jaw, a hiss that escaped his full lips, an unfocused sheen in those eerie gold-flecked eyes.

"You're right. I think you *might* be too much for me." I was only half teasing, and I didn't just mean the size of his dick either. He *was* too much for me—too intense, too wild, too primal. He made me feel unbalanced, buffeted by a force greater than me. It was like a carnival ride gone crazy, with no safety harness whatsoever.

"I think you might need someone who's too much for you," he growled. "And next time I'm ripping that shirt right off you. Pretty bra too. With my teeth."

I drew in a ragged breath at the suggestion and lowered all the way, feeling the incredible fullness of him balls-deep inside me. Then slowly I moved. His muscles tensed, fighting to hold himself back as he let me set the pace, his hands on my hips for support. As I increased the speed, leaning forward so I could rise all the way up, then sink completely down onto him, his fingers tightened, digging into my flesh. They'd leave bruises. I didn't care. Actually, the pressure spurred me on and I rocked against him, tightening internal muscles.

He groaned, and took over, thrusting into me, harder longer faster, pushing his hips upward to meet mine on every stroke. Everything merged together—the intoxicating wild scent of him, his cock pounding into me, his low growl of pleasure, the golden glowing flecks in his hazel eyes. It all became one sensation, and my muscles tightened around him, everything tensing as I felt my orgasm crest and crash over me.

I cried out, and bit down on his shoulder hard enough to draw blood.

"Bad girl," he chuckled, then bucked into me harder, his rhythm going off the rails. I gasped and tightened around him once more, moaning something incoherent that sounded an awful lot like begging.

"Fuck," he shouted, closing his eyes and jerking his head back. I shook, muscles weak only to feel another wave of ecstasy, this one stronger than the last, rush through me. He thickened inside me, and I felt his release, felt it spill into me as I trembled with another wave.

He was going to kill me. And what a way to go. I slumped on top of him, smelling the metallic tang of blood from my bite, the scent of our sex, the aroma of his skin, warm and woodsy.

I was panting, like I'd just run a record-breaking sprint. I was sweaty. My hair was a tangled mess of red against his tanned chest. No doubt my mascara was smudged under my eyes and my lipstick smeared halfway across my cheek. I didn't care. All I could do was lay there on top of him.

He stirred inside me.

"Seriously?" I gasped, using his chest to push myself upright. "You're getting hard already? What are you, Superman?"

"Better. I'm a bear shifter." He grinned up at me. "Why? Got somewhere you need to be, wolf-girl?"

I tried to lift off of him, but he held me tight, skewered on his cock. "Not until morning. Why?"

That grin turned downright salacious. "'Cause I was hoping to make a night of this. You game?"

Was I ever. "All night? Like we just did?"

A concerned frown creased his brow. "That was gentle. Was hoping we could have some fun, maybe get a little rough." His hand reached up to touch the bite on his shoulder. "I promise I won't draw blood, but kinda like it when you do."

Yes, this man was going to be the death of me. I wiggled on his lap, thrilled to see that muscle twitch in his jaw again. "I'm totally game, wild man. And I've got all night."

* * *

THE SKY WAS peach and orange with the sunrise, birds chirping. I hadn't slept a wink and was sore in all the right places. I wanted to stay and see how long this crazy grizzly could keep it up, but I had responsibilities. Someone had to help Brent with clean-up from the party, and I needed to check on an ad campaign I was running so I could have a weekend effectiveness report ready first thing Monday morning. So instead of going in for round six, or seven, or whatever we were at, I kissed Karl on the nose and stood, gathering up my clothes.

"That was a whole lot of fun, wild man. Don't be a stranger."

His hazel eyes were intent as they watched me walk away. "I don't intend to."

CHAPTER 1

"Hey Sabrina."

I matched Kennedy's high-five, walking out the door of the Alpha house as I walked in. I liked Brent's new mate. And I liked him even better now that his woman was living here in Juneau instead of down in Seattle. Having her fly up to Anchorage for the trauma center every three days was better than having a grumpy Alpha who only saw his mate twice a month. They'd had a whirlwind romance this spring, and already she was an integral part of our pack. Kennedy was human, but a kick-ass human with a great sense of humor and a quick mind. She'd become one of my best friends, and I couldn't wait for her and Brent's mating ceremony this fall.

"Is Brent in the great room?" I asked.

Kennedy grabbed a roll-aboard suitcase and a slung a duffle over her shoulder. "Kitchen. We still on for a trail run next weekend?"

"Absolutely." I held the door for her, watching the woman jog down to her car before heading toward the kitchen. The Alpha House was enormous—eight bedrooms, a dining room that seated thirty, a great room that took up half of the first floor, and a commercial-sized kitchen. That's where I found my Alpha, scrubbing a fry pan.

"S'up, boss?" I plopped down at the long kitchen table, propping my feet up on the chair across from me and snagging an apple from a basket.

"We've got a rogue bear down Ketchikan way."

I put the apple back, suddenly not hungry. "Who'd he kill?"

Brent didn't mean a regular bear, he meant a bear shifter. We were all descended from Nephilim, our diluted angel powers giving us added strength, speed, healing, and the ability to shift form. Ninety-five percent of us were wolves, but that other five percent could be bears, cougars, falcons. Heck, I'd even heard there was some badass boar dude down in Nebraska. Since werewolves were the dominant shifter breed, we were the ones with the big target on our backs. The angels might no longer consider us one wrong move away from extinction, but they still were pretty heavy-handed when it came to us following their endless rules and restrictions. Killing humans was a big no-no. Bigger than big.

"A group of five human scientists studying fungal strains in glacier ice."

What the heck? Did they annoy the guy? Steal his smoked salmon? Play loud music in their tents at night? Bear shifters were weird. They were reclusive, introverted, quick to anger, insanely territorial, and notoriously grumpy. And I wasn't being sexist in thinking the rogue was a male. Females, sows, were only one in ten of the bear shifter population. They tended to be slightly more social, living in cities, and having sexual relations with humans except for a few months in the spring when the bear shifter males reluctantly put on clothes and ventured into town to get laid.

No wonder the males were grumpy. Their solitary existence, and the scarcity of females, meant they only got the chance to bury their sticks in some fur a few times per year. Of course it was their own fault that they didn't make more of an effort. And sexual frustration was no excuse for killing five scientists.

Even so, it wasn't our problem. Well, maybe tangentially it was our problem, but there were others better suited to deal with this guy.

"So let the bears deal with it. Did you call the sloth?"

Brent put the fry pan in a cabinet and turned to me with a pained expression on his face. "I did. I called four of them. I'm sure you can guess how they reacted."

Yeah. Although it was midsummer and the bears should be downright jovial. Well, jovial for a bear, anyway. "Isn't that Eric guy down near Ketchikan? Tell him he's got a rogue trying to poach his fish and see how fast he gets his furry butt in gear."

"Eric's phone is out of service, and from what I've heard he's roamed east, over the mountains into Canada."

That was the problem. Bear shifters were territorial, but many weren't opposed to pulling up stakes and moving their "territory" five hundred miles elsewhere. No forwarding address. No social media or friends to tell you where the heck they'd gone. We had a hierarchy, a pack. Wolves didn't just vanish without a thorough manhunt twenty-four hours later. Bears had their sloth, but it was more a loose affiliation of the shifter breed. Black bears were a little better since they tended to cluster in family groups, but the brown bears were as individualistic as they came. They had no Alpha, no directory, no regular meetings or check-ins. There were so few of them that the angels didn't bother to keep track of them. And even if they did attempt to do so, I doubted even those all-powerful winged-beings could manage to find a grumpy, reclusive bear who'd been mostly off-the-grid from the day he was born.

"Humans? Who's that sheriff down there we met with last October? He seems competent." I was grasping for straws. I really didn't want to spend this week tromping through wet forests, battling a gazillion stinging insects while I sniffed out a rogue bear. I had a job, and although I could move deadlines around and manage my marketing campaigns on the fly, it wasn't an easy thing to put aside my career for my pack responsibilities.

But pack came first. Pack always came first.

Brent folded his arms across his chest and raised one inky-dark eyebrow. "Rogue, Sabrina. Humans are working with us about the shifter-hunters up north, but it's our responsibility to police rogue shifters and bring them to justice."

I winced. Justice for a rogue wolf would be exclusion from hunts, banishment, or a transfer to another pack. Our society was our life. But bears… Justice for a bear shifter meant death.

"Fine. Who am I taking with me? I'm assuming at least six or seven other wolves?" I was Brent's second, next in line for Alpha, but I wasn't tough enough to bring down a bear shifter solo. No one was.

"Normally, but one of the bears agreed to go, so it's just you and him."

I felt my muscles lock up, my breath stuck in my lungs. No. Just, no. "Who?"

"Karl. You met him at the barbeque last August."

I'd more than met the grizzly shifter at the barbeque last August, I'd gotten naked and sweaty with him in a crazy drunken night that still haunted my dreams and had me reaching between my thighs at least once a week since then. My whole life I'd lived in Alaska and I'd never met him—

that's how much a loner this guy was. For some reason he'd tromped out of the forest to eat burgers and drink beers with us wolves last year. We'd wound up down by the creek with a bottle of whisky. Just the two of us. And thinking about that night was bringing back the sort of memories that had me squirming in my chair.

"You okay?" Brent shot me an odd look.

"Yeah." Crap. All I needed was my Alpha to scent the lust that was curling through me. There was nothing wrong with a hook-up between shifter breeds, but after that night Karl had walked back into the forest in typical bear fashion. No phone call. No flowers. Not even a thanks-for-the-sex text. Eleven months, one week, and two days. It was darned embarrassing. If I'd been like Zeph or Ella, known for keeping relationships strictly to one-night stands, it wouldn't have mattered. I wasn't. And I didn't need the whole pack fussing over me, bringing over sympathy casseroles and chick flicks because they thought I'd lost my heart to an anti-social grizzly who probably didn't even have running water in his den.

"Does he know he's working with me?" Okay, that was pathetic, but I had to know. Did Karl volunteer when Brent told him he was sending me in? My stupid heart thumped at the thought.

Brent's forehead creased into a puzzled frown. "I don't think so. I told him I'd send someone down to Ketchikan to meet him, but I don't remember specifying who. Why? Did you guys rub each other wrong at the barbeque?"

No, we rubbed each other right. And that was the problem. I leaned back in my chair, trying for a casual, indifferent posture. "Nah, we're good. When do I meet him?"

"This afternoon." Brent tossed me a set of keys. I caught them and blinked, wide-eyed. He was letting me take his boat?

"Dude, that's an eighteen-hour trip. Did you put magical motors in the boat?"

The Alpha rolled his eyes. "Dustin is flying you down. That's for a rental Jeep."

Oh. That made more sense, although I liked the idea of magical motors. Someone needed to get right on that. Still, a flight down and a rental Jeep came in a close second.

I stood and gave Brent a quick salute and spun about to leave. "I'm on it, boss."

"Sabrina?" I paused at the door and turned to face him. His normally cheerful face was full of worry. "Be careful. If things get out of hand, get out of the way and let Karl handle it. Understand? Leave him to kill the rogue while you get to safety."

Grizzly shifters were brutal in a fight, and rogues even worse. I was hard to kill, but if a fight went south I didn't have any problem with retreating. And normally I wouldn't have any problem letting Karl take the lead, but I wasn't about to turn tail and leave him to fight this rogue solo.

So I looked Brent straight in the eyes, and for the first time ever, I lied to my Alpha. "Will do, boss."

CHAPTER 2

The Jeep was right where Brent said it would be. I hopped in and headed out of town onto narrow roads that eventually became gravel as they slid into the lush green on both sides of me. After an hour of bumpy travel, I saw the signpost—a two-foot thick stump with a metal pole driven through the center. Bears. Go figure.

Parking the Jeep, I made my way down a well-traveled path marked on either side with clawed trees, their bark hanging in shreds. It made me shiver. Yeah, I'd had sex with this bear. Yeah, I was abnormally fascinated with him. Yeah, he scared the heck out of me—that was a good bit of the attraction.

There was a tiny clearing in the woods, barely big enough to accommodate the postage-stamp-sized frame house with plank siding. Outside was a man wearing faded jeans and nothing else. His light brown hair hung to his shoulders in loose waves. Dark blond scruff edged his jaw. Muscles flexed in his arms as he swung an axe. Wiping sweat from his forehead, he picked up the split log and stacked it neatly. Judging by the pile, he'd been doing this for a few hours.

Clearly he was busy, and clearly this wood chopping activity in late July was a critical activity because he didn't even acknowledge my presence. He was a shifter. As quiet as I moved, he'd heard me before I ever came into the clearing, and even without that he surely smelled me. He was downwind of me. He knew I was there. And after our intimacy last year, he knew exactly who I was.

My face burned with shame. A bear. Why couldn't I have become infatuated with a wolf shifter, or even a human. No, instead I was hot and bothered over this guy who felt splitting an additional five logs was more important than greeting the woman he'd had sex with, the wolf who was partnering with him on tracking down a rogue.

Karl stacked the last split log, and buried his axe in the stump. Then he turned to me, his jacked body glistening with sweat, those faded jeans tight. My eyes drifted lower, and I reluctantly forced them back up.

"Ready to track down a rogue, or do you need to split another cord? Winter is coming, you know."

He grunted.

"Was that a 'yes' grunt, or a 'no' grunt?"

His eyes met mine. They were green with brown and gold flecks that I couldn't see at this distance but remembered oh so well. "Want me to put a shirt on first?" he asked.

No. No, I didn't. "That's up to you, wild man. It's July. Bugs are gonna be nasty out there."

"Don't care." He walked past me and headed down the path. Sometimes sweat smells acrid and sour, but Karl smelled warm and wild with a hint of leather, clove, and pine. It was intoxicating and I turned and followed him like he was the pied piper. At my Jeep, Karl climbed into the passenger seat and sat silently, waiting for me to join him.

He didn't care about being eaten alive by mosquitoes. Because he was so badass that even the bugs stayed away. I fought to keep my libido in check as I climbed into the driver's seat and started the Jeep. Karl was freaking huge and my hand nudged against his thigh and knee each time I shifted. I couldn't help myself from spreading out my fingers and brushing along the top of his leg as I dropped the Jeep down into second.

A soft growl rumbled through his chest and I hid a smile. That wasn't a growl of warning, it was a growl of arousal. Karl wasn't as unaffected by me as I'd thought.

"So you live here? I thought you were closer in to Juneau?" I asked, breaking the silence.

He grunted. Clearly that was his go-to communication. "Sometimes. Sometimes I'm as far north as Skagway. Depends on how I'm feelin'"

"What kind of feeling do you have when you're in the Ketchikan area?"

"Summer's nice here. I like to chop my wood for winter. Smoke some fish."

"So what kind of rolling papers do you need to smoke a halibut? Extra wide, I assume?"

He shot me a puzzled glance, obviously not getting the pot reference. It didn't matter since it afforded me an opportunity to see his beautiful eyes.

"Are you coming up to the barbeque in a few weeks?" I couldn't help it. I'm sure I was pouring out all sorts of lusty pheromones right now. The guy might slap me down, but I needed to know.

"Depends."

"Depends on what?"

Those hazel eyes with the gold flecks pinned me to my seat. I was lucky I didn't wreck the Jeep because I just couldn't turn away.

"Depends on whether I'm gonna get laid or not."

Oh my. I swallowed hard and squirmed in my seat, every

bump in the road ratcheting up the lust pouring through me, hitting the excruciatingly sensitive nerve endings between my legs.

Here goes nothing. "Karl, you could have been getting laid hundreds of times in the last year. All you had to do was call."

His eyebrows furrowed and he tilted his head. "Don't like using a phone. Don't even have one. And sex is once a year."

No. Just no. Please don't have me lusting after a shifter with a sex drive that only kicked in once per year. But we'd done it in August, and bear shifters typically sought out a sow in March and April, so they had to at least get horny two or three times per year. None of that would be enough for me. I wondered if we could meet in the middle—as in every other day in the middle.

"You could have sent a letter, a courier, smoke signals. And Karl? Sex for me is ideally an everyday occurrence. Twice or three times a day if I'm on a roll."

Desire rolled off him and I nearly wrecked the car. Dang it all, I was wet, and struggling to keep my attention on the road.

He grunted. And didn't say one more word even after we arrived at the murder scene. The bodies were long gone, but nobody did a crime scene clean-up out in the middle of nowhere, especially when the local police knew we needed as much scent as possible.

The both of us hopped out of the Jeep. I did a slow half-circle of the area, careful not to cross any obvious scent trail —not that I couldn't tell my own smell from that of others. There was blood, lots of blood. It was sprayed on the trees, soaked into the ground, splattered onto the bushes. This rogue had been pissed, and he'd slashed these five humans to ribbons judging from all the stains of red.

Blood. Urine. And that horrible smell that comes when

large intestines get lacerated and all the half-digested food and bacteria hits the air.

"Someone shot him," Karl said. I walked over to where he was and knelt down, sniffing. The human blood was still strong in my nose—overpoweringly strong, but this here was shifter blood.

"It's not a lot," I commented. But it was more than there should have been. Shifters healed fast. It was a mixed blessing when it came to gunshot wounds. As nice as it was to have your wound clotting and scabbing immediately, and healed within an hour, it wasn't so nice when that happened with a bullet still lodged in your body. Getting shot worked better when there was someone nearby to quickly get the bullet out, otherwise, you had to go through it all over again once they cut it out of your healed flesh.

"Didn't clot," Karl grumbled, sticking his finger in the blood and eyeing it. "Smells weird too."

I immediately thought about the shifter hunters up in Kenai. They were to blame for one grizzly shifter death, possibly two, and had shot both Brent and Leon from the Swift River Pack. Those wounds didn't heal, and they festered, spreading a poison that would eventually kill a shifter. The only reason Brent and Leon had made it was because Kennedy had been there, and she was a quick-thinking trauma surgeon badass who was one of the best shots with a rifle I'd ever known.

Magically coated bullets were what we'd discovered when Kennedy dug the shrapnel out of Brent and Leon. But these five humans weren't hunters out on a private, illegal, expedition to kill shifters. These were scientists. What in the world would they have been doing with the tainted bullets? Honestly, I was surprised they even were carrying a gun.

We both stood and looked around, having gained as much

information as we could in this form. To better track the rogue, at least one of us would need to be on four feet.

"You or me, big guy?"

Karl grunted.

"That a 'me' grunt, or a 'you' grunt?"

"Your nose is better than mine," he grumbled reluctantly. "'Sides, wouldn't mind seeing you naked again."

Oh, Lord. I wasn't about to argue against that, so I walked back to the Jeep and peeled off my shirt. Karl leaned against the tailgate, his arms folded across his chest, his eyes glued to *my* chest.

"Want me to carry your clothes for when you shift back?" he asked.

The heat of his gaze was disconcerting, and I had to pause to gather my thoughts. "Yes, please. It gets cold at night and I might need to shift back before we return." I hoped to shift back before we returned, because a wolf screwing a grizzly was kind of weird and I had a feeling we'd be doing it in the next twenty-four hours. At least, that was what I hoped.

"You won't get cold at night."

I caught my breath, then exhaled as I unbuttoned my pants and shimmied them down my legs. Karl's eyes followed their motion.

"Take my clothes, just in case you change your mind."

He grunted. "I'll take your clothes, but I'm not changing my mind. You're a damned fine lay, wolf. Been thinking about you all year, waiting for the next barbeque."

Damn. *Damn.* I pulled off my underwear and my bra and began my shift, well aware of how horrible the whole long process appeared. Karl was a grizzly shifter. He wouldn't be turned off by twisting bones and contorting muscles. Normally I was insensible with pain during my fifteen-minute shift, but I noticed Karl gathering up my clothes, carefully folding each item and packing them in my duffle bag, except for the underwear. Those he brought to his face, inhaling deeply. His eyes flared gold, glowing with a supernatural light. I didn't even feel the pain of my shift, I was so turned on just from watching him take in my scent, watching the desire on his face and smelling the thick aroma of pheromones that filled the clean forest air.

But I was now a wolf, and as much as I wanted this bear, we needed to both be in human form to make that happen. I wasn't a prude by any definition, but *that* was where I drew the line. Maybe. I'd never had sex with another shifter breed before. Some werewolves enjoyed getting it on in their animal form. But wolf-wolf was different than wolf-bear, and far different than human-wolf or human-bear.

And why was I even thinking about this? Having sex once in a year was clearly eroding my sense of morality.

Karl grinned, brushing the silk of my underwear across his lips before folding them and putting them in the duffle bag. "First time I've seen your animal."

I'd never seen his. And I was suddenly very concerned what he thought of my wolf. Some shifters felt a strong division between themselves and their beast, almost as though they were suffering from Multiple Personality Disorder. Others were all one. My wolf and I were of the same mind. There was no division, and although I often referred to my wolf as a separate entity, she was merely a facet of my own personality—a more instinctual and physical facet. Although even in human form I tended to be more instinctual and physical than most humans.

"Silver with tawny streaks. Eyes like dark roast coffee. Muscular. Strong. I wouldn't want to face you in a fight."

I warmed at his praise, even though I knew he, as a grizzly shifter, could kick my ass in a fight. Then he walked over and stroked my head, scratching behind my ears. I closed my eyes and leaned against his hand, nearly toppling as he moved his fingers down along my spine to rub right at the joint of my tailbone. Oh, ecstasy. I danced my back legs, lifting my nose to the sky and arching my back as I pressed my rear against his hand.

He chuckled. "That's the spot, huh? You know, like beast, like human. I'm gonna hit that ass at the barbeque. Or before, if you're in rut. Although it sounds like you're always in rut."

This was so embarrassing. I sounded like a total slut by his description, and I could do nothing but groan and push against his palm.

"I like standing here and rubbing you, but guessing we best catch this rogue first."

Yeah. That. I sighed and pulled away from his magic fingers, dropping my nose to the grass. Starting from the outer edges of the crime scene, I worked my way in a spiral inward. Karl waited outside the area, watching me with a hooded gaze. Everything was so crisp and clear in this form, every scent like a distinct shade or color. The odor formed trails extending outward. I sorted and catalogued each one, the humans with their distinct aromas—and the killer. As Brent had said, the rogue was definitely a bear, and from what my nose told me a brown bear. I wasn't as savvy in determining the difference between Kodiak, grizzly, and the standard brown bear, but I could tell them apart from black bears and polar bears. This scent had a different tang than Karl, whose aroma I'd memorized with intimate detail, but I wasn't sure if that was just an individual or a race difference.

Looking over toward Karl and tilting my head, I headed into the brush. He followed. I rolled my eyes hearing the crash of his booted feet on the branches and ground. Grizzlies. When you were an apex predator, you didn't give a crap if anyone heard you.

Blocking out the background noise, I followed the scent, moving slowly to make sure I didn't miss anything. By nightfall I was hungry and tired and ready to call it quits until morning. We hadn't yet found the rogue, but as I'd tracked him I'd discovered a few things. And if I wanted to share those things with Karl, I'd need to change back into human form.

It was quite a dilemma. As a wolf I'd be toasty warm and comfortable sleeping on the hard ground tonight, plus I'd be in the form best equipped to defend myself if the rogue doubled back and attacked us in the night. Human form meant I could tell Karl what I'd discovered and have a better chance of getting some action, although it probably wasn't a good idea to be distracted with sexual activity when there was a killer on the loose.

Switching back and forth was an option, but a last-resort one. It took me fifteen minutes to change form, ten if I was rushing it. And shifting exhausted me. One or two changes I could deal with. Three and I'd be dipping into energy reserves I might need if we were attacked. So I needed to pick one or the other.

Karl had set my bag in a dry spot and stood beside it, his back against the trunk of a sturdy tree, his eyes glowing slightly as he watched me. "Come here."

I pawed at the ground to convey my indecision.

"I'll tell you what I know, then you can decide if you want to stay a wolf or not," he said. "The rogue is a male grizzly, about fifty years old and I'm guessing seven hundred to seven fifty pounds given the tracks and the broken brush and tree limbs. His winding path makes me think he's truly a rogue and not just a grumpy bear who had a bone to pick with a group of humans."

In other words, the bear was crazy. Which meant an already dangerous grizzly was even more unpredictable and lethal.

"He doesn't smell right. I can even tell that with this nose.

From the trail, he's probably a half-day out, but with a rogue there's no saying he won't come back around." Karl's expression was serious as he stared at me. "Wolf or human tonight, that's your choice. I won't run the risk that he'll come back around and I'm not ready."

And with a nod he turned and shucked his pants, giving me a breathtaking view of his tight ass as he strode off into the woods. I knew when he meant. He'd be in bear form tonight. And if he was going to prepare for an attack, I was too.

I was second to the Alpha, not some helpless damsel to stand by while Karl fought the rogue single-handedly. Brent had told me to hold back, to let the grizzly shifter deal with one of his own, but I knew that wasn't how this was going to go down. I'd fight beside Karl. I'd always fight beside him. My dominant wolf nature demanded it, and so did the human side of me.

My decision made dinner a little difficult. Using my teeth and a strategically placed paw I managed to get the outer pocket of my duffle bag open and tear through a packet of beef jerky, eating the whole thing. There were another three bags in there along with a summer sausage, but I got the feeling that Karl was out getting his own food.

Less than an hour later I heard the crash of something large moving through the trees, and heard the low grumble of a big bear. I felt the fur rise in a line along my back and neck, my lip curling to reveal fangs, but then I lifted my nose to the air and realized the grizzly lumbering into the clearing was Karl.

Even recognizing his smell, I still braced myself, adrenaline flying through my veins. He was huge. Bigger than a polar bear huge. Karl's grizzly form was at least ten feet long and six feet at the shoulder. Yeah. As a bear, he would be more than twice my height standing upright. He had to have weighed over a thousand pounds. Brown bears came in a variety of shades and markings, but Karl was distinct. He was blond, his gold fur deepening to brown on his lower legs and paws. And those paws were huge with claws as long as my human hand. He was enormous, powerful, his jaws big enough to crush my head. And in those jaws was a fish...a fish he deposited at my feet.

Uhhh, this was awkward. Was I supposed to eat this? I didn't know much about grizzlies, but I tended to cook my food first. Maybe I could pretend it was sashimi—sashimi that had been carried around in a bear's mouth for who-knows-how-long, and hadn't been gutted, cleaned, or filleted. I was a dominant wolf, but I wasn't a caveman...or cavewoman.

Karl made a huff noise and sat on his big furry rump, looking at me with brown bear-eyes that still had those familiar gold glints. I reached over and patted the empty beef jerky bag trying to communicate that I'd already eaten.

He still stared at me, waiting.

The things I do for sex. Closing my eyes, I took a tentative bite of the fish, trying not to gag. The skin was rough, the scales sharp, and the rubbery bones poked my gums as I chewed. The meat wasn't horrible, though. It was fresh, tangy, but very, very fishy.

One bite was it. I stared down at the fish, but try as I may I couldn't manage to choke down any more of this. I looked up to meet Karl's intense gaze and flattened my ears, trying for a cute puppy expression. His furry eyebrows shot up.

Seriously? I hadn't seen him eat any fish. For all I knew he was totally pranking me right now. Come next month's barbeque there would be all sorts of stories about how he got Sabrina to eat a raw fish.

Yes, he was serious. One courtesy bite should have been enough, but evidently I was required by some bear etiquette to continue, so I ate another bite, gagging and choking as I forced it down. I couldn't do this, I just couldn't. Maybe I was a wimp, but the next bite was going to either get me into guts or head, and I just wasn't going there.

Karl huffed then nudged me aside, nearly knocking me over. Then he snapped up the remains of the fish, crunched it with those massive jaws, and gulped it down.

I was so going to puke. Karl the human was smoking hot. Karl the grizzly was scary, and more animal in his bear form than I was in my wolf form. I dug into a second bag of jerky, just to get the taste of raw fish out of my mouth, and shared some with Karl. He was warm and I had every intention on snuggling up with him tonight. Better for the pair of us to have jerky breath than fish breath.

Then we curled up together underneath a tree, my muzzle against his shoulder, feeling the breath rise and fall in his chest, his scent filling my nose with clove, pine, and fur. There was something inside me that wouldn't settle being near him like this, a deep rooted instinct that was reluctant to trust him. Because he was a grizzly shifter? Because he was so darned huge? Because he'd crunched up a raw fish whole? Or because those glittery gold flecks in his eyes let me see a glimpse of a Karl I didn't understand—a shifter that seemed more beast than man. Outside of the incredible sex last summer, what did I really share in common with him?

Nothing, that's what. Absolutely nothing. But that still didn't tell me why his bear form made me wary, why the things I could overlook in Karl the human seemed right in front of my face when he was Karl the grizzly. Maybe I was imagining it all, blowing our difference out of proportion and giving him a darkness that in reality wasn't there. Maybe it was a day of scenting a rogue in the woods that had me on edge. Wild man didn't mean amoral psychopath serial killer. I'd had sex with this man—a whole lot of sex. Rough sex, but nothing shifters would find disturbing. If I trusted him enough to screw him all night long, then surely I trusted him enough to sleep next to him.

I pushed away the worry. I soothed the prickling along my back. I forced my eyes to close and my mind to drift into peaceful sleep. But as I floated into slumber, all I could see was gold flecks of light in hazel irises—gold flecks that hid something very dark.

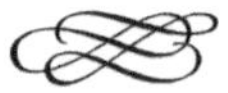

I awoke to find my muzzle resting on skin, long fingers curled tightly into the ruff around my neck. Flesh instead of fur, but Karl's scent was still the same wild spice-and-pine as it had been when he was a bear. When had he changed? How had I slept so soundly that I hadn't awoken to either a bear moving out from underneath me or shifting form?

"Ready for some breakfast?" His voice was deep and raspy, his fingers loosening to stroke along my fur.

Breakfast. I remembered the taste of the raw fish and shuddered.

He chuckled. "Such a princess. I can gather some berries, but I'm guessing you'd rather have that log of cooked meat in your duffle?"

The summer sausage. My mouth watered at the thought.

"Here. Since I've got hands at the moment and you don't." He took the meat from my bag and flicked open a knife, cutting hunks off and feeding them to me by hand. A girl could get used to this.

And I realized that in the light of day, with Karl in his human form, the unease I'd felt last night had receded. It hadn't completely vanished. It was still lurking deep inside me, dancing at the edges of my awareness, but at least I didn't feel the urge to bristle up my fur and snarl.

Karl handed me another piece and I took it gently, giving his fingers a quick appreciative lick. The taste of his skin sent a bolt of need through me and I closed my eyes, remembering last summer when I'd tasted every inch of him.

"You're making me hard, Brina," he complained. "I don't mind taking you like this, but if you couldn't manage to eat a raw fish, I doubt you'd be able to enjoy me fucking you in your wolf form."

Yeah, that crossed uncomfortably into bestiality in my mind. That it wouldn't bother him the way it bothered me was yet another reminder of how far apart we were.

I nudged his hand, and when he cut off another piece and handed it to me, I pushed it with my nose up toward his face.

"Thanks." He alternated feeding me and himself, then wrapped the remaining half of the sausage log back up and returned it to the bag. I trotted off into the woods a ways to take care of business, then returned, stretching and eyeing him with a questioning head tilt.

"Let's go." His voice was tight, his mouth a grim line as he looked out into the woods. Neither one of us wanted to be doing this, but we couldn't let a rogue run free. I dropped my nose to the ground and picked up the scent, leading the way. Within a few hours the smell of blood hit my nose and I broke into a fast jog, slowing as the scent grew overwhelmingly strong.

"Brina, slow down," Karl hissed behind me. I dropped to a trot, not wanting to burst in upon a rogue grizzly feeding.

We didn't find the rogue in the clearing up ahead with

smashed brush and gouged trees, but we did find a dead bear —a wild grizzly bear, not a shifter.

I skidded to a stop, staring open-mouthed at the slaughter. Wild bears fought over territory, but seldom to the death, and never with this level of carnage. The non-shifter bear would have conceded the fight and run for it long before he'd lost his life. Which mean the shifter hadn't allowed him to run. Instead of reacting defensively, then letting the wild bear retreat, he'd held him there, forced him to fight to the death, then mauled him.

Eaten him.

Bile rose in my throat. I was an omnivore. I didn't have anything against hunting. Actually I enjoyed a good hunt myself, and the entire pack benefited from the meat from our kills. This wasn't a hunt; this was a murder. And to eat the bear raw, in the field... I suddenly had an image of that fish from last night, of Karl crunching the whole thing down. Maybe this was a bear shifter thing? Maybe I shouldn't be such a bigot, quick to judge others by my ways. Maybe I shouldn't be such a princess.

Karl walked past me, his hand brushing the fur along my back. "This bear didn't have to die." He carefully turned the body, examining the bite wounds, gouges from claws, and the chunks of missing flesh. "I'd hoped we were wrong, but this is truly a rogue we're tracking."

I nodded, sniffing the body to get a better lock on the rogue shifter's scent. That's when I noticed it. On the wild bear's claws was blood, and that blood held a cloying scent that made my lip curl in revulsion. I'd never smelled anything like it—hot melted plastic and rotted bananas was the closest I could come to a comparison.

Karl did the same thing, frowning as he touched the blood on the claws and rubbed it between two fingers. "What the hell is that?"

I shrugged. Karl dropped my duffle onto a clean spot of ground and pulled out a plastic bag, carefully wiping the blood onto a napkin and sealing it up. Good idea. I had a pretty amazing scent memory, but it would be good to have a strong sample just in case this trail went cold and we needed to expand our search outward.

That done, Karl shouldered the bag and I once again put my nose to the ground, feeling bad about leaving the bear carcass behind, but knowing that the wildlife in the area would make short work of it and appreciate the easy dinner.

The shifter had picked up his pace after the kill, not bothering with stealth as he tore through brush and saplings off the existing animal track. It slowed me down to have to struggle through brambles and thick grasses, but I managed. Karl had a more difficult time on two legs, carrying the duffle, and he fell farther behind as I pressed on ahead. After the rogue's meandering, practically staggering-around-the-landscape trail, this was straight, direct. Had killing the wild bear given him a return to some sanity? Was his den somewhere ahead and he just wanted to get home? I didn't know why, but this rogue seemed to suddenly be moving with purpose and speed toward something.

The sun was dipping low on the horizon and my stomach was growling when I hit pay dirt. Fresh scent. The shifter was ahead, and by my nose he was only a half-mile away. I paused, waiting for Karl to catch up. He must have fallen farther behind than I'd realized because I could no longer hear him tearing through the woods like an elephant, cursing each time some bramble snagged the leg of his jeans. I held silent, waiting, because there was no way I was going to confront this crazy shifter on my own, especially after I'd seen what he'd done to that grizzly.

Then I heard a gunshot and a scream—a human scream. It was the type of scream that someone could have heard a half-mile away with or without shifter auditory senses. I yipped for Karl then ran, not caring about the noise I was making or that the airflow would bring my scent to the rogue. There was a human out here in the middle of nowhere, alone with a rogue shifter who had killed five humans and torn a wild grizzly to bits. If I didn't get there in time, this person would wind up dead as well. Actually even if I did get there in time, they might not survive. *Karl, hustle your furry ass up.*

I raced into the clearing, taking the situation in with a glance and throwing myself between the human and the rogue. The human was holding a pistol. The shifter had a bloom of red on his chest. I sent up a quick prayer that the human wouldn't shoot me, then squared off against the grizzly, and snarled.

He'd attack. And I'd lose without Karl to back me up. The only chance I had was to keep alive and keep this guy occupied until Karl had time to shift into his more lethal animal form. That could take twenty minutes. It's not like I had a choice, though. I couldn't stand by and watch this human get mauled while Karl changed form.

The shifter hesitated, recognition sweeping across his glazed eyes as he realized I wasn't a wild wolf. It made me hesitate too. A true rogue would have just killed anything in its way, but it seemed like this guy was fighting against it.

There was another gunshot. I winced at the deafening sound so close, expecting the pain of a bullet tearing through me, but the hiker had shot the bear again, another splotch of red spreading on his shoulder. The bear roared and charged, leaving me no time to consider strategy or do more than give a quick howl to warn Karl.

Ducking low, I danced to the side, sinking my teeth into the bear's lower leg then spinning out of reach. He whirled on me and swung with his right, claws barely missing my shoulder as I hopped back. Before he had time to swing with the other paw, I'd darted in for another solid bite, then danced away. Out of the corner of my eye I saw the human back out of the clearing and take off into a run. Good. It was never wise to show your back and run from a predator, but the rogue's focus was on me, and I'd fight with more concentration if I knew the hiker was safely away.

The shifter gave up the free use of his front paws and dropped from his upright position. Not that I would have tried to go for his exposed belly and risk being wrapped tight into a crushing grasp, but he'd been less stable on two legs than four. Now he'd have less reach, but he'd have those jaws in position to bite down on my back and snap my spine, and he'd be faster and quicker to maneuver like this.

I hopped back, ducking and darting as I evaded his attack. Seeing an opening I dove in to bite his muzzle then jumped back. I moved a hair too slow and a giant paw slammed into my ribs. Claws dug deep furrows and the force of the blow lifted me clear off my feet and flung me ten feet away where I crashed into the trunk of a tree. Down I went and stayed, winded, feeling the wetness of blood seeping from the gashes in my side. Five seconds. That's all it had taken for this rogue to take me out. Five seconds wasn't long enough for Karl to change form and get here, or for the human to be a safe distance away. I'd failed.

And I couldn't fail. Not when so much depended on me to keep going. Struggling upright, I ignored the pain and snarled. I was too hurt to do my dart-in-and-out routine. I was going to go for the jugular and hope I could pierce the bear's throat before he crushed me. The grizzly charged and felt a stab of shame for not being able to hold my own against this rogue for less than a minute.

I leapt on him, my jaws wide as I sank them through a thick ruff of fur. Powerful arms wrapped around me, pressing my ribs. I heard a crack, then something hit the grizzly with the force of a wrecking ball spinning him away from me. I dropped to the ground, my mouth full of fur, and I shook my head, struggling to stand and attack once more.

A roar shook the trees. My eyes widened to see two bears rolling across the clearing. When the tangle of fur separated I saw Karl. Or not-Karl. If I hadn't caught his familiar scent, I wouldn't have even recognized him. He'd been an oversized grizzly yesterday when he'd come back with the fish, but this time he was something else.

Fighting the rogue was an animal of legend, an animal I'd only seen in books and plaster bone-casts in museums. The bear facing off against the rogue was some prehistoric monster. He was double the size of the massive grizzly he'd been yesterday, weighing close to two thousand pounds, and at the shoulder he was about seven and a half feet. On two legs, the guy had to be close to fifteen feet tall. He was monstrous. He was terrifying. The same fur darkened on his lower legs and paws, but those legs were thick as tree trunks. Claws ripped chunks from the earth as he dug in. The rogue stared at him, eyes glittering red, then he roared.

Karl opened his mouth wide and returned the threat. As he bellowed, lips curled back to reveal savagely huge fangs. With no more than that quick warning he was on the grizzly, tearing, biting, and slashing.

As a smaller animal, my technique had been to bite-and-run. It was a pack method of bringing down larger animals and brutally effective in a group hunt. Solo, when the intent was to actually take down an animal, it wasn't as effective. Given time and enough maneuverability, I could possibly have worn the grizzly down enough to get in a killing bite, but the odds were stacked against a lone wolf in this fight.

Karl had better odds—far better odds. In his huge form he had the advantage of greater mass compared to his opponent, his only disadvantages were lesser speed and, strangely enough, not as long of a reach.

They came together with a crash, grappling as necks twisted and teeth snapped. Both bears sank their claws deep into the other's back, holding tight. The rogue bit down on Karl's shoulder, blood staining the dark blond fur a bright red.

They spun, giving me a chance to see Karl's face. There was a huge grin stretching his mouth—not a grimace of pain but a smile. His eyes had lost everything remotely bear-like, or even shifter-like, his irises an unworldly glowing gold.

He was enjoying himself. He was purposely holding back, letting the rogue bite deep into his shoulder because he *liked* it. We all got stoked from the adrenaline of the hunt, of a fight, but this was beyond that. Karl was lost in a strange kind of bloodlust where the joy of inflicting pain, of killing was all wrapped up with a very intense joy of his own pain.

I'd been crouched, watching and waiting for an opportunity to assist by hamstringing the rogue or attempting to distract him with small bites, but Karl's expression froze me in place.

His mouth opened wide, coming down on the top of the rogue's head, then he bit. I heard a crack of bone. The rogue yanked his claws from Karl, pulled his fangs from the other bear's shoulder, and shoved, trying to push the bigger bear away.

And Karl let him, opening his mouth and hopping backward with a few easy strides, not at all moving like a bear with jagged raw flesh at the shoulder and stripes of red along his back. The rogue shook his bloody, misshapen head, one eye unfocused, one side of his jaw slack, then with a twisted snarl, he charged.

They dropped, rolling and wrestling on the ground as I tried to stay clear, splintering the trunks of small trees and flattening saplings. Karl let the rogue bite and scratch him, holding himself back, all with that terrifying smile on his face. Then the giant prehistoric bear got serious.

The rogue's attack quickly turned to defense, then to panicked attempts to get away, but Karl held him in place, tearing with claws and teeth, bleeding him a little bit at a time, until the bear's struggles grew weak. Then he opened his mouth wide, and this time he sank his teeth deep into the rogue's neck. Blood gushed and I heard the crunch of pulverized bone. The rogue went limp, eyes unfocused, twitching paws slowing then hanging still.

Not content to just leave the dead bear, Karl stood up on his hind legs and shook the rogue like a rag, blood painting the nearby tree trunks. Then he dropped to all fours and ran over to one of those trees, bashing the shifter's body against the trunk. He was so powerful, and so deep in bloodlust that I should have been frightened, but instead I found the whole thing funny. So I laughed.

Yeah. Because I was in a lot of pain, and I'd just watched something out of Jurassic Park Caveman Edition toy with and take down a grizzly shifter with a disturbing amount of glee. None of this was amusing, but I was probably bordering on hysterics because laugh, I did.

Laughing as a wolf sounds kind of like a cross between a whine and a cough. Karl froze at the noise, his head swiveling. He loped over to me, letting go of the dead bear halfway. I dropped down, ready to roll over and play submissive, but the gold glint in his eyes receded and he sniffed me, licking my wounds with his nasty, bloody, gore-filled mouth.

Ewww. I didn't know much about bear shifters, but this wasn't cool. I tried to push him away with my front paws, letting out an involuntary whimper as the motion pulled on my injuries.

Karl's snuffling grew frantic, and he made a noise that

sounded an awful lot like Chewbacca. My remaining fear vanished. Silly guy. I was a shifter. I'd survived worse than this. Since I wasn't doing a good job of communicating to him in my wolf form, I closed my eyes to concentrate and began the process of shifting back.

It took longer than usual. It was more painful than usual. And when I was finally human again I realized that Karl was also human and was cradling me against his chest, my naked rear on his very naked lap.

My first thought was *how the heck does he change forms so quickly?* My second thought was *this dude has a serious boner going on right now.*

A boner. I had angry red gashes and a host of bruises around my ribs. They hurt. Even with Karl's gentle touch, they hurt. And they were sticky with blood and bear saliva. And human saliva. "Karl, cut it out. Stop licking me."

He paused, then nuzzled my ear. "Thought you liked me licking you, especially down—"

How could he be sexed up right now? I knew a lot of wolves who wanted to get it on after a fight, but this was a bit extreme. And was I just as twisted that his words were making me want to forget about my injuries, turn around, and straddle him?

"Yes, yes," I interrupted hastily. The boner against my butt was becoming insistent and now I was remembering how very talented Karl was with that tongue of his. "I do like you licking, but not when you're a bear, and not on my injuries. I'm a shifter. I'll heal just fine without the help of saliva."

"Wasn't healing. Was tasting." His breath was warm and soft against my skin. And thankfully it didn't still smell like blood and gore. "That bear was sick. Still can't get the taste out of my mouth. Wanted to make sure you didn't get infected."

Sick? Beyond the melted plastic/rotten banana smell that we'd smelled in the shifter's blood before, I hadn't considered him sick, just a rogue, a crazy bear. The rogue had tasted pretty horrible, but I'd never bitten a rogue before. And I'd never been a huge fan of blood in my mouth anyway. Medium rare. Not alive and kicking. Obviously Karl knew what rogue grizzly shifter blood was supposed to taste like. It made sense. They fought a whole lot more than we did, and their skirmishes were usually brutal. Grizzlies weren't as social as most bears, and they tended to fight over food, territory, someone parking in their favorite spot. We fought too, but not quite to their level, and once our hierarchy was established, everything was good. But come to think of it, if I bit a werewolf who was infected, I'd probably be able to detect it. I hadn't risen to second in the pack without my share of brawls.

"Real sick. It ain't normal. Shifters don't get sick." Karl shook his head, his hair brushing along my shoulder with the motion.

Sick. It made me think. "Do you think this sickness, the weird smell of his blood, the fact it didn't clot might be related to the shifter killings up in Kenai? Those hunters were using magically tainted bullets that forced a shift to beast and hindered the ability to heal the wound. If he was shot with one of those bullets and didn't get it out right away, he might wind up susceptible to illness."

Karl grunted. "Maybe. Didn't taste right. You think someone shot this guy with tainted bullets, and he went crazy?"

I thought, the pain beginning to subside to manageable levels as my body healed the wounds. "Could be. The bear killed up in Kenai was a grizzly shifter, and the hunters with tainted bullets nearly killed two werewolves. Maybe if that scientist was using something a little different, a version 2.0, it made the bear go crazy along the way to killing him."

The other alternative was that there was now some virus floating around that turned bear shifters into crazed killers. There wasn't anything I could do to battle a virus. Although I wasn't sure there was anything I could do to battle hunters with magical bullets. Or scientists with magical bullets. They still hadn't caught the guys responsible up in Kenai, and the police, although helpful, had given up, calling it a fluke.

It wasn't a fluke. A bear died. Two werewolves almost died. One of those hunters got away and I was pretty sure that behind the hunters was someone supplying them, organizing the trips and profiting from our deaths. But they'd seemed to vanish in the wind and we'd had no further incidents since this past spring.

"Do you think this guy going rogue is somehow connected to what happened in Kenai?" I asked.

"One way to find out." Karl slid me off his lap and stood, walking over to the body he'd discarded and carefully searching through the bear's thick fur. Throughout our entire sober conversation, he'd maintained that erection. He still had it. Crazy bear.

"Look at this, Brina."

I stood and went to him, careful not to pull at the healing claw wounds along my waist. When I knelt down I saw a spot on the grizzly's chest, a hairless patch with blackened crusty flesh and a raw wound. I was surprised Karl had found it among all the slashes and bites the rogue had suffered in their battle, but there it was—a gunshot wound. And not a new one either.

"He's got two more—another one in his chest and one in his shoulder from where the hiker shot him," I commented. "But this one looks to be a few days old and it didn't heal right."

Karl examined the other two wounds, digging in the rogue's flesh to pull the bullets out and place them in my hand. They looked like normal .357 bullets to me. Then one of Karl's nails elongated, sharpening into a short claw and he dug out the other, older bullet. As soon as he sliced the skin over the wound, a foul odor hit my nose.

Hot melted plastic and rotten bananas.

I held my breath, gagging and waited while Karl tore through putrid flesh to pull a smashed chunk of metal from the shifter. It was slimy, coated with a gray sticky rot. And the sight of it sent a wave of nausea through me.

I didn't want to touch it, but we needed to take it back with us, to compare it to the bullets that had been taken from Leon and Brent from the attack up in Kenai, to have someone who knew their way around a microscope test the coating on them.

We were naked. My bag was probably a half-mile away where Karl had, no doubt, dropped it when he'd shifted. Gritting my teeth, I held out my hand and took the other bullet, keeping it separated from the other two.

"That wound should have healed within a few hours, even with the bullet still lodged in his chest." I stood, looking around the clearing and finding the two casings from the bullets the hiker had fired. Scooping them up, I kept them in the normal-bullet hand.

Karl nodded. "Looks about right timing-wise, if you discount the shifter healing. Maybe he was trying to warn them out of his territory, and the scientists got scared and shot him. Grizzlies are aggressive, more than most bear shifters. If they shot him, he might have attacked."

"And if they shot him with some tainted bullets…" Brent said he'd had the urge to run, to get away when he'd been hit with one, but maybe bear shifters reacted differently than wolves. Maybe they got even more aggressive when the magic hit their blood.

Clearly there was something peculiar about this bullet for there to be an infected wound over twenty-four hours later, and the blackened flesh reminded me of what Brent had said about the smell of rot and necrotic tissue that came from the hunters' bullets up in Kenai.

The whole thing made me sick. We'd had to kill a shifter who had possibly been a victim himself. And if there were hunters in south coastal Alaska in addition to in Kenai, where else could they be? Was anywhere safe for us?

We'd need to figure out exactly what had happened between this shifter and those five humans studying fungus. And for that we'd need to talk to human law enforcement.

"Let's go find our clothes, get dressed and head back to the Jeep. We need to go back to Ketchikan and talk to the police. Then I need to get this bullet somewhere to be analyzed."

Karl sighed, wiping his hands on the rogue's fur as he stood. "Ain't our problem anymore, Brina. We caught the rogue and killed him. The job is done."

"No, the job isn't done. There's a group of hunters up north with tainted bullets who are killing shifters, and now I've got reason to suspect some of those tainted bullets can turn shifters into rogues."

"No law against selling bullets," Karl commented.

"There's a law against shooting people, and in Alaska shifters count as people," I argued.

"I doubt this rogue was human when he was shot. Maybe he was a grumpy bear who thought he'd frighten off some humans he considered trespassers and got more than he bargained for."

I couldn't believe I was hearing this. "Whose side are you on?"

"Mine. Don't mess with humans. Don't mess with other shifters. Mind your own business and keep to yourself and no one will bother you."

We were standing here, naked, arguing. I was injured, holding a bullet that made my skin crawl, and Karl wanted me to mind my own business? This *was* my business.

"The hunters up in Kenai shot two werewolves while the shifters were in human form. Based on that, I believe they also shot the grizzly shifter they killed when he was in human form. That's against the law. And it's murder."

Karl's eyes gleamed gold, that darkness pushing to the forefront. "Then track them and kill them. No need to involve human police. No need to investigate anything. Just drop your nose to the ground, find the human responsible, and make him disappear."

This Karl terrified me.

"That scent has long gone cold."

His lip curled into a snarl. "Then wait. He'll kill again, and you'll have him."

Oh, no big deal. We'll just sit around and wait while the hunters kill someone else, or cause more shifters to go rogue. It was obvious I wasn't going to change Karl's mind on this. He was a lone bear, an isolationist, where I was a pack animal with a sense of societal responsibility. Yet another glaringly obvious example of how we were miles apart.

"Okay. It's not *your* problem, then. I still need to let the police know that the rogue who killed five human scientists has been neutralized, so he and the others in Ketchikan can sleep at night."

I wasn't going to bury my head in the sand on this one. I'd find out where this bullet came from. Then we'd work with the police as we'd always done to handle the situation.

The gold dimmed in Karl's eyes and once more they were clear hazel. "We're going straight into Ketchikan? You're gonna make me walk around the town and talk to humans, aren't you?"

Oh the horror. Although I doubt he'd be much help in dealing with the police, plus there was the fact that he didn't have a shirt with him. "No. I'll drop you at your cabin and you can go back to chopping wood if you want. I'll go to talk to the humans."

He sniffed and stared into the forest, back along the path. "You'll come back?"

"Come back after I meet with the police? Or some other time? I'll see you at the barbeque, right?"

"After you're done with the humans in Ketchikan. I want you to spend the night at my cabin. I want your scent there."

If I spent the night at his cabin, my scent would be everywhere because we'd probably screw like rabbits all night long, in every square inch of the place. The guy scared me. His "not my problem" attitude pissed me off. But I wanted him so bad I could barely stand it. Besides, it would save the pack the price of a hotel room in Ketchikan. "Yes, I'll come spend the night, but I might need to leave early. I'll have to meet Dustin at the dock whenever he can bring in the plane for me."

He nodded and started off down the path while I fell in beside him. "You're just going to talk to the police and drop that bullet off somewhere, right? I'm not going home to chop wood while you're going after killers with bullets that kill shifters and make them crazy. I need you to be safe. I don't want you sticking your nose in something that gets you shot and killed."

I rolled my eyes and picked his pants up off a sticker bush, tossing them to him. "I'm just talking to the police, but I won't promise you anything else. I'm a wolf. I stick my nose in stuff. It's what I do."

He caught the jeans with one hand. "Then you need to let me know. This isn't my problem, but if you've got your nose in it, then it turns into my problem."

"So you'll come riding to the rescue like a knight on a white horse?" Yet another difference between us. I was a dominant wolf—strong, capable, a leader. While I appreciated back-up, I didn't need a rescuer.

He grunted. "I hate horses. And I'll always fight by your side, wolf."

Maybe I'd misunderstood him and that's what he'd meant all along. Not a rescuer, but an extra sword in battle. That I could accept. "You're handy to have around in a fight, Karl," I told him, because he was, and along with my pack, I'd appreciate a grizzly shifter with a giant prehistoric cave bear form to walk by my side.

"You're not so bad in a fight yourself, Brina."

The trek back to where Karl had dropped the duffle bag took a whole lot longer than our mad dash in, and gave me time to think. Twenty seconds it had taken me to reach the rogue and the hiker, and I doubt Karl would have traveled much faster. I'd been fighting the bear for all of five or ten seconds before my back-up had appeared. That meant it had taken him a maximum of fifteen seconds to change form, quite possibly less. That was unheard of in any shifter accept for Nephilim.

And that bear…that monstrous, extinct bear form of his.

"What are you, Karl?" I asked, breaking the silence as we walked. "Nephilim? Are you a Nephilim?"

Nephilim were the only ones among us that could assume more than two forms—human and one animal. But Karl didn't feel like a Nephilim, he felt like a grizzly shifter. Most of the time. Sometimes he felt…like I was looking into a fiery abyss.

"I'm not a Nephilim, I'm a grizzly," he countered. But even I could feel the edge of a lie in that.

"Karl, you changed form in seconds, and you weren't a grizzly back there, you were a giant bear-thing from the paleontology books and archeological digs."

"My mother was a grizzly," he insisted.

"And your dad?" I prompted. "A time-traveling extinct cave bear thing? What?"

Even if one parent was a Nephilim, the offspring still only had the two forms. What the heck was he?

"I'm not talking about my dad. Or my mom." There was this closed expression on his face. He was shutting down, but I wasn't about to let this one go.

"What other form can you assume, Karl? Hawk? Cougar? Saber-toothed tiger?"

"Bears. Any kinds of bears and that's it."

I got the feeling there was more. I got the feeling that the *more* was something really horrific. I remembered the glowing eyes, the glee with which he'd toyed with the rogue, like a sadistic monster playing with his prey. I remembered the twisted grin on his face as the other shifter had bitten down on his shoulder.

He'd told me once he liked it when I bit him. I'd thought it was just rough sex, but now… There was a dark power to Karl that drew me in, made me feel off-kilter, vulnerable. I'd likened it to a mountain, to an amoral force of nature, but I'd now seen something else in him. Under that mountain was a volcano, ready to break through the earth's crust at any moment and destroy everything in its path. And unlike the impersonal destruction of nature, I got the impression that Karl would enjoy every minute of it, that he'd have those glowing eyes and disturbing grin as the world burned around him.

"You're afraid of me, Brina?" His voice held disappointment and sorrow. "Strong dominant wolf like you is afraid of me?"

Of course I was afraid. A grizzly shifter would have made me feel wary, well aware that if I needed to defend myself I'd need to be alert, smart, use every bit of cunning and strategy to get out alive, but Karl with those glowing eyes and sadistic grin had made me scared—fear like I'd never felt before.

"Dominant doesn't mean you're not afraid," I told him, trying to deflect his statement into a different sort of conversation. "Dominant means you fight even when you're afraid, that you exhibit the type of leadership and skill that makes other wolves instinctively follow your lead. Over time their instinct is reinforced with your good decisions and your history of putting the good of the pack above your own welfare. That's dominance, not being foolishly aggressive or grinding every one of your packmates beneath your heel."

It was my philosophy. It was Brent's philosophy. It was the philosophy of the majority of wolf Alphas in our world.

"But you're afraid. Of me." The gold flecks sparked like beacons of light, and again I saw something dark and dangerous behind his eyes. "Why?"

Because he was supposed to be a grizzly shifter, but he'd just turned into some kind of prehistoric monster. Because he wouldn't give me a straight answer about his heritage. Because the power in him seemed off-leash and ready to kill with reckless, gleeful abandon.

"I'm less afraid of you like this than a giant cave bear," I told him, trying to avoid hurting his feelings. It didn't work.

"You'll fuck me like I'm the very air you need to survive, but you're afraid of me."

I caught my breath at the rawness in his words. If I was honest with myself, part of his appeal was that fear he inspired, that wild feeling of danger, that he could just as easily kill me as bring me pleasure. Sex with everyone else was enjoyable, fun. Sex with Karl was like mating with nature itself—full of beauty and brutality, life and death all rolled into one seductive, dangerous package.

"Dominance is fighting when you're afraid, taking the risk even though you're afraid," I told him, implying that it was also loving when you were afraid. I wasn't anywhere near ready to say the "L" word with him, but love didn't come without taking a chance, and in spite of our mountain of differences, in spite of my very real fear, I wanted to take that chance and see what a future for us might hold.

He stared at me, his scrutiny feeling like it tore through to my very soul. "I need you to trust me, Brina. Afraid or not. Sex or not. I *need* you to trust me."

And suddenly I had a glimpse of *his* soul, of a dark monster who would never submit, but might walk side-by-side with the right person, the right wolf. In his eyes I saw a glimpse of someone who longed for another to share his days and nights with. I could be that wolf. All I needed to do was trust.

Karl stuffed his jeans into my duffle bag while I dressed. And he watched me dress. I thought maybe he'd joke around or proposition me, but after our serious conversation, he'd fallen silent. Once again he was the brooding shifter of few words, naked, watching me as I struggled into a pair of jeans while favoring my still-healing wounds.

His had healed. Completely. He didn't even have a scar. It was another thing that made me think Nephilim, even though he'd denied it.

"You're going to hike naked?" I asked, easing into my T-shirt.

He shook his head. "I'll hike as a bear."

It was like he was waiting for me to say or do something. Or like he was trying to think something over and come to a decision.

"Should I wait here while you shift or will you catch up?"

He took a step back, then another. "I don't let anyone watch me shift. No one." He made eye contact with me, making sure I got the significance of what he was about to do, then he shifted. With Ahia, who as it turned out was a full angel and not a Nephilim, shifting was in an instant with a flash of light. With us, shifting was a painful contorting and re-forming of skin, muscle, and bone. For Karl, it was like a smooth, liquid transition. He slid into something bright and formless, like a molten metal taking shape midair, then expanded. It took seconds, and before me was a giant grizzly, his fur sparkling with gold lights before it dimmed to blond.

At least he hadn't turned into that cave bear thing, although his grizzly form still made my flesh rise, made me want to back away very slowly. I pushed down the instinctual fear. Trust. He was one scary mo-fo, but he'd done nothing that might make me think he would harm me.

"What's with the glitter?" I teased him. "Sparkly bear?"

He shot me an irritated glance, then shook his fur again, glancing down at his paws.

"Oh, it's gone now, but don't think I didn't see it. Is that why you don't want anyone to see you shift? Ahia would never let you live this one down. You'd wake up one morning covered in glitter glue."

He snarled, then made a huff noise and turned to head down the trail. I grabbed the duffle, wincing as it hit my healing scabs, then followed him. "Lead the way, oh Sparkly Bear."

It wasn't long before I realized that this hike was a bad idea. I was exhausted from the fight, from shifting, from healing my wounds. I'd been tracking the rogue for most of the day, and after all that had happened including a dump of adrenaline into my system, I was done for. Still I pressed on, not wanting to admit to Karl that I needed to rest, and wanting to make enough headway on our trip back that we'd arrive to the Jeep tomorrow with plenty of time to get into Ketchikan before the police sheriff had gone home for the day.

The urgency wasn't quite the same as it had been when we had a killer on the loose, but I still felt the need to hurry. If this was related to those hunters up north, then any delay might cost lives—shifter as well as human lives.

I stumbled, catching myself with a hand on a tree. Karl turned and I tried to brush it off as me being clumsy or lost in thought, but I could tell from the expression in his eyes that he knew. The next small clearing we came across, he began to circle, sniffing, shredding a few tree trunks, and checking the potential camp spot.

I plopped down the duffle, yanked out a light blanket, and curled up, using the bag as a pillow. The sun hadn't even set yet and I was ready to sleep. As I closed my eyes I felt the warmth of fur next to me, the thump of something huge settling down on the ground. Then I felt Karl's huge bear body press against my spine.

He was scary. I didn't quite know what he was, but he was scary. And right now, I was glad to have him at my back.

I wasn't sure how the heck Karl had done it, but his jeans were ripped in several important areas. Actually I was pretty sure he'd tried to shift before he managed to get all the way out of them, which again had me wondering what he was that he could change forms so quickly. Alphas could often do it in five minutes. Maybe Karl was dominant as all hell, or he had a higher than usual percentage of angel in his DNA, or both. Either way, his pant legs were separated at the side seams, the crotch had an indecent-sized hole and the zipper was hanging useless from a gaping fly.

We were at the car and close to the more populated areas, and even though Alaskans were fairly used to seeing bears wandering around, given the recent events with the rogue, we didn't want to risk the chance of Karl getting shot. Which had meant he'd needed to shift into a human form rather than jog alongside the Jeep, or ride as a grizzly. And human meant he should probably at least have some pants on.

The silly bear wanted to climb into the car and ride through the streets naked. As entertaining as the prospect was, I didn't want him arrested for indecent exposure. Plus, I'd probably wreck from the distraction of naked Karl riding shotgun. I was distracted enough by naked Karl trying to get his pants to stay together and remain up over his hips.

I'd begun to get used to his grizzly form. The shadowed darkness behind his eyes was quickly becoming part of the near constant attraction I felt for him. As we'd hiked to the car this morning, I'd found myself reaching out to brush a hand along his rough fur, watching the movement of his powerful muscles as he walked, warming at the very human expression in his eyes as he'd turned back to look at me.

And when he'd shifted in that smooth, liquid motion into his human form, I'd felt my mouth go dry. He was gorgeous, formidable...and dark. And he looked at me like he wanted nothing more than to drag me off into the woods and have his way with me.

I was kinda on board with that idea. But first I needed to get into town and talk to the police. Actually, first we needed to get his darned pants to stay closed.

I had a few safety pins in my duffle and some hair ties, so I tried to at least get the fly together with a weird combo of the two, figuring the ripped legs and hole-in-the-crotch weren't as critical.

I'd barely gotten the safety pins in place when I realized we had a problem.

"Dang it, Karl. Stop with the boner, okay? I can't get your jeans closed with your big dick trying to poke me in the eye."

He grinned. "Quick hand job would do the trick."

No, it wouldn't. "I've had sex with you. It doesn't go down. Even if I jerk you off, you'll be hard again in seconds and ready to go for another ten to twenty minutes. Just think unsexy thoughts or something, at least until I get your pants together."

I couldn't resist leaning forward and placing a lingering kiss on the tip trying its best to escape the jeans.

He groaned. "You're not helping. Actually, you *are* helping. Keep going with that."

Should I? How urgent was it for me to get back to Ketchikan? Ten minutes wouldn't matter in the scheme of things, and I was sooo tempted. I ran a finger over the exposed skin of his cock and he leaned forward trying to increase the contact.

"We need to get moving," I told him reluctantly, trying to stuff his hard cock back into the pants. It sprang free, teasing me, mocking me, tempting me.

There was a dead rogue in the forest. There was someone somewhere creating bullets that disabled, infected, and even killed shifters. There were quite possibly more hunters prowling around coastal Alaska. And I was about to give a bear a blow job.

Pushing the fly I'd just been trying to pin closed open, I pulled his cock free. Then I kissed the tip, licking underneath and tickling my fingers up his shaft. Karl's hips jerked forward, nearly punching me in the face with his dick.

"Brina, don't tease, girl."

I looked up at him from under my lashes. "I don't tease, Karl."

Then I took him in my mouth, encircling him at the base with my hand and bracing myself against his knees. His hands came up to tangle in my hair, urging me on as I sucked and licked along the skin of his shaft, running my tongue along the slit at the tip. Then I paused for a dramatic moment and took him in deep—so deep he bumped the back of my throat. His hands fisted in my hair as I built up a rhythm. I brought one of my hands up from his knee to fondle his balls, the other giving his shaft a firm stroke each time I pulled my mouth to the edge.

His breathing was harsh and ragged, his hands starting to be a bit demanding on the back of my head. A groan tore from deep in his throat and I laughed, the vibration sending him over the edge. He thickened and jerked his hips, shoving my head forward and holding me tight as he came down my throat. I felt his legs tremble, heard him let out a held breath, felt his grip on my hair suddenly loosen, as if he'd just realized he was holding me tightly in place, my nose pressed against the lower part of his stomach.

I pulled back, still sucking hard, and released him with a pop. Then I licked along his entire length before tucking him back inside his jeans.

"Sorry."

He was apologizing. And he had nothing to apologize for. It was actually quite flattering that I'd been skilled enough to make him come so quickly. Besides, it was a good thing he'd lost control when he had since I wasn't accustomed to marathon oral sex performances. If that was his expectation, I'd need to practice more and work up to it.

"It's been a year," he added. "Tough for me to hold back, ya know?"

Eek. "Surely you've taken care of things yourself since last August?"

His smile was slow, mirroring the sexy spark in his eyes. "*My* hand doesn't feel like your hand, or your pussy, and it especially doesn't feel like your mouth." His voice grew husky. "Been thinking about you all fall, winter and spring, Brina, hoping that you'd be wanting a repeat of last summer."

Yeah, me too. And that was just a shame when we could have been getting it on all fall, winter and spring. "Why didn't you reach out to me, Karl? I know you said you don't have a phone, and you thought sex was just a seasonal thing for us, but you could have let me know you were interested in something beyond a quickie by the stream."

"As I recall, that weren't exactly a quickie." He grinned, then ran his fingers through my hair. "Sows are seasonal about sex with male grizzly shifters, and they don't want contact with us outside of the rut season. Thought you might be the same and didn't want to ruin my chances with you by being pushy. I'm a patient man. I'm willing to wait eleven or twelve months for you to come into season, for you to want to take me to your bed."

Well I wasn't so patient. "I'm going to straighten this out right now. Werewolves are like humans. We don't have a season. We get turned on any time during the year, and it doesn't matter whether the object of our lust is a human or a shifter, we're always receptive. Having sex with someone and not contacting them for almost a year means you're either not interested or just want an occasional, no-strings-attached booty call, not that you're worried about being pushy."

He reached out and brushed the calloused pad of his thumb over my cheekbone, then down across my lower lip. "Then why didn't you contact *me*?"

Because in spite of being a dominant wolf, when it came to guys I was a bit of a traditional girl. And I'd been scared. Being a skinny girl with barely any boobs, bright red-colored hair and freckles meant I'd faced rejection more times than I'd like to admit. I'd learned to play it casual, to keep my heart safe, to act like a hook-up and no call wasn't any big deal. It was. And I'd been terrified to face rejection after the night we'd shared. I'd rather just not know and keep my pride intact.

"Could'a called *me*, Brina," he accused.

I snorted. "No cell phone. No consistent location. You bears are a pain to track down. And..." I needed to be somewhat honest here. "I thought you guys were solitary, that maybe you didn't want more from me than just one night. I didn't want to be pushy and look like that crazy wolf chasing after a bear."

His smile changed, becoming warm, affectionate. "Seems we both had the same misconceptions 'bout each other. How about I get a cell phone, and you be willing every now and then to go off the grid with me, and in the meantime we screw like monkeys."

"How bout we screw like monkeys even when we're off the grid or enduring the company of a whole pack of rowdy wolves."

"In front of them?" He was now smirking. "Didn't think you were into that sort of thing Brina."

I tugged the last hair tie around his pants and stood, placing a quick kiss on the corner of his mouth. "With you? I could be."

I drove back to Karl's cabin. He leaned over and kissed me before climbing out of the Jeep. It was the kind of kiss that made me want to change my mind and head into town tomorrow, but I'd have more fun with him tonight knowing I'd already let the police know that the rogue was no longer a danger.

"You coming back tonight?" he murmured, his lips brushing mine.

"Yes." I felt hypnotized by him, mesmerized. His was so darned distracting.

"I'll feed you," he announced, finally pulling away. "Don't eat any of that human food."

Smoked trout? He'd promised to bring some to the barbeque and my mouth watered just thinking about it. Having nothing but beef jerky and summer sausage for two days had left me craving fresh-cooked meat.

"I'll call you when I'm on my way," I promised. Oh, crap. No, I couldn't. The crazy guy didn't have a phone. "Actually hold off cooking anything until I get back. I'll try to make it before seven, but I don't want everything getting cold if I'm late."

He nodded, then spun around and without another word or glance headed over and began chopping wood once more. Strange, antisocial, weird-mannered bear. It didn't matter though, because I knew he was just as excited for tonight as I was. I hesitated a few minutes, just to see if my hair-elastic and safety pin job on his pants managed to survive the axe swinging motions, then drove off. I'd see plenty of naked Karl tonight. And I couldn't wait.

I was an hour out of Ketchikan when I got cell phone coverage and started to get the texts. It was Brent, wanting an update and telling me that there had been other reports of rogues in the Juneau area and northern Alaska. I pulled over to the side of the road to look at the YouTube videos he'd sent, staring with shock at my tiny phone screen.

They were horrifying. Three videos of campers and hunters, seemingly minding their own business when suddenly a shifter burst upon them in human form, shifted into their animal in a matter of seconds, then went on the attack. All three were werewolves, and all three seriously injured the humans before they were killed. The videos were jumpy, obviously edited, but the effect was still chilling.

But the videos didn't tell the whole story. Outside of Karl and Nephilim, I'd never seen a shifter who could change form that fast. Brent had said the magic on the hunters' bullets up in Kenai had forced a rapid shift—seconds instead of ten to twenty minutes. The parts that hit the cutting room floor must have included someone shooting a shifter. That and the campers and hunters who'd finally taken the rogue down clearly had magical weapons of their own. A few hunting rifles wouldn't kill a shifter, especially one gone rogue. Unless they had a stockpile of assault weapons at their campsite, they had "special" bullets.

My phone dinged again and I clicked the latest link that Brent had sent, feeling my heart sink further.

We'd always had a good relationship with the humans in Alaska, but word of these "rogues" had stretched beyond the state. News organizations and major outdoor/adventuring websites were warning people about shifter attacks.

It was bad enough that the humans we'd trusted in our own state would now eye us with uncertainty, but a world that hadn't even known we existed would now be terrified of us. The humans here who'd coexisted peacefully with us would be put in the middle, needing to either defend us against the scared folks in the lower forty-eight whose only knowledge of shifters was what these videos showed, or placate the scared tourists by placing restrictions on us.

I foresaw shifter registries, regulations on where we were to live, times and dates that we'd be allowed to assume our animal forms. We'd have curfews, have to wear something that would easily identify us as shifters to any human who saw us. And with these videos, any attack on us would be easily justified as self-defense. It wasn't just the pain of a bullet we'd need to fear, but death.

All the freedoms we'd had would be taken away in the name of human safety. Karl was wrong. We couldn't afford to mind our own business and let it blow over, or to just avoid humans. I didn't want to be forced out of my home and job, to have to choose between going off the grid and hiding in the wilderness or dealing with restrictions that were one step away from life in a cage.

We needed to find out who was responsible for this and stop them as well as repair our public image because Karl might be able to live like a wild man in isolation, but I couldn't, and neither could most of the shifters in Alaska. We needed to fight this, and we needed to win.

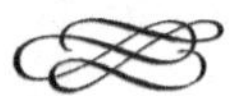

Sheriff Murray pulled me into his office and shut the door. "Please tell me you got that rogue bear."

I nodded. "Yes. He's dead. The official word was that this was a grizzly attack that killed the five scientists, right?"

Brent's texts and those YouTube videos worried me. If people thought shifters were behind this last string of killings, then it would just add fuel to the fire of hysteria.

"Sabrina, no one in their right mind is going to think a wild grizzly killed five people, one of them armed with a rifle. The locals know it was a rogue, and up until recently they've trusted you shifters to take care of the, frankly, very few problems. But there were three wolves up north that attacked people, and now this grizzly kills five. Word is out—and I mean out beyond Alaska. People know, and they're scared."

"Those videos were carefully edited. We don't shift that fast, ever."

Sheriff Murray lifted his hands up. "Then what's happening? Because people are scared, and it really looks like those werewolves were trying to kill those people."

"They're shot before they transform. Something on the bullets is causing a rapid shift. It kills us, and I think in some instances it's causing shifters to go rogue, to attack," I told him. "We're not like this. You've grown up around shifters. We don't attack people. We mind our own business and get along with the humans. We've lived peacefully among you for hundreds of years up here in Alaska, and I can count the number of rogue incidents on one hand."

"Before this week, yes. But there's been four reported incidents and five humans are dead, Sabrina." He pulled out a piece of paper and showed it to me. "This is a phone call we got from some hiker claiming a grizzly attacked him. He shot it twice and it didn't even flinch. Then he claims a wolf joined in the attack. He barely got away with his life."

Oh that ungrateful jerk. "It was the rogue that attacked him, and *I* was the wolf. But I was defending him, putting myself between the hiker and the rogue. Karl and I distracted the rogue then killed him. The hiker got away unscathed because we—two shifters—were there to help him."

"He wouldn't have needed your help if there hadn't been a rogue shifter attacking him," the sheriff countered.

"There wouldn't have been a rogue if he hadn't been shot with a tainted bullet. It drove him mad. He was probably a normal guy before someone shot him. The people making and selling those bullets are the ones you should be afraid of, the ones you should be going after, not us."

He scratched his beard and shook his head. "I like Brent. I've got a lot of respect for him, and the shifters I've met from his pack are good folk, but I can't ignore this. Five people are dead. People are panicking."

How could I convince him that the shifters weren't to blame for any of this? "In May there was a group of human hunters up in Kenai with some kind of magic coated bullets that forced us to shift, blocked our ability to heal, and killed us. They were hunting us. They'd already killed a bear shifter and nearly killed two werewolves. I think whoever made those bullets and sold them is behind this. We took a bullet from that rogue bear, and it was tainted. Someone shot him and made him go rogue—made him crazy. And if we hadn't killed him, he would have eventually died from what was on that bullet."

I handed him the bullets, separating the two that the hiker had shot from the tainted one. The sheriff picked up each one, examined it and shook his head. He couldn't tell the difference. I could feel the magic tainting the one bullet, but to the human, they were all the same.

"I don't know, Sabrina. It sounds pretty farfetched. I can't exactly defend you guys with a tale of magic bullets and some conspiracy theory of wizards or something out to kill shifters."

Great. "The world believes there are elves migrating to live among us, that angels walk the earth, that there is a dragon in a museum in London and mermaids in the Great Lakes. The locals believe that there are interdimensional rifts opening that spit out manticores and drop bears and hydras. They'll accept that shifters exist, but they won't believe that someone has the motive and ability to create magic bullets capable of killing us or driving us into insane killers?"

"They can see all those other things, but this bullet." He held it up to my face. "This bullet looks just like a regular bullet. If you can prove that someone is deliberately shooting shifters—and not in self-defense—then we can do something about it. Otherwise I need to do everything I can to protect human lives and keep everyone, tourists and locals alike, from panicking and taking the law into their own hands—for your safety as well as ours."

The police were already scratching their heads over the appearance of other supernatural beings in the world. We didn't have dragons or elves in Alaska, but I knew the humans were grappling with how to enforce the law when it came to beings that had magic, or breathed fire. We shifters had melded in with human society up here, but the police weren't equipped to prosecute someone for making magic-coated bullets, even if I could prove to them they existed. The only way we'd get human cooperation on this is if we found proof of hunters shooting shifters while they were in human form. If we could show premeditated murder, then we might have a chance of regaining human trust.

"It's not self-defense," I told the sheriff. "It's murder. I know there are some in Alaska who don't really like us shifters and would be happy to buy bullets that could take us down and kill us. Someone is capitalizing on that and providing bullets that can kill shifters."

He eyed me sympathetically. "There's nothing illegal about manufacturing and selling bullets. You can't prosecute someone for that. Most everyone is okay with you guys, but there's always those crazies that see you as animals, or some kind of demon that deserves putting down. If someone threatens you, or tries to take a shot at you, then you need to file a report and not try to take care of it yourself. You shifters are entitled to the same protections as humans, but you can't go taking law into your own hands."

We'd ignored those crazy people who saw us as animals that needed to be put down, because up until recently there hadn't been much they could do to hurt us. The laws prohibiting assault and murder covered us too, but the group of hunters in Kenai had been operating underground, taking the risk. And once we were in animal form, it would be hard to press murder charges. If a hunter had a license, saw a bear, shot and killed a bear and claimed to not know it was a shifter, he'd probably go free.

And now, with videos on the internet of shifters attacking

humans, with five dead from a rogue grizzly attack, I doubt any jury would believe our claims of magic bullets forcing us to shift. Self-defense, or a legal hunter claiming mistaken identity meant it would now be open season on killing shifters. And the real game changer was that evidently random people, including scientists, now had access to these magic-coated bullets that could kill us.

"I need to take the tainted bullet to someone who can analyze it," I told the sheriff.

He hesitated. "We really need to tag these into evidence."

I know he was still worried about us taking justice into our own hands. It was a valid concern. For the most part we played along with the rules of human society, but when it came to threats like this, we often colored outside the lines. I was pretty sure that neither Brent, nor Jake, the Swift River Pack Alpha, had reported those shifter hunters that they'd killed up in Kenai. Sometimes it was easier to just sweep it all into a crevasse than deal with the paperwork and questions of an investigation.

"I really need to compare this bullet with the ones used against shifters up in Kenai to see if there is a connection. And I'm also hoping that maybe we can find an antidote."

His eyes lit up and he slid the bullets back toward me. "If you could find an antidote so that all these rogue attacks ended, then we'd have a much easier time going after whoever is targeting you guys."

And if we could dig up enough on these guys that the police would know exactly who was targeting us, that would be even better. I hesitated a moment, wondering under what circumstances we'd feel that we needed to deliver our own justice. Brent had been raised with humans and it would take a lot for him to sanction taking the law into our own hands. If there was an immediate threat, if the police said their hands were tied and they could do nothing, then Brent might pull a discreet, select group of us to take care of these killers. Moira, the Denali Pack Alpha wouldn't get involved unless they were specifically targeted, but Jake, the Swift River Pack Alpha, would support taking action. One of his had been shot and nearly killed, and Jake wasn't the type of wolf to turn the other cheek.

I pocketed the bullets, shuddering at the feel of the tainted one. "I saw the videos with the attacking rogues, and like I said, I think they may have been shot off camera or that it was edited out. I believe that one of the five victims of this rogue shot the bear with this tainted bullet. Do you have their effects somewhere? Can I check and see if any of their bullets matches this one we dug out of the rogue?"

The sheriff scowled. "I'm not going to blame five scientists who lost their lives to this guy for shooting him. Like I said, selling bullets isn't illegal. And defending yourself against an attacking animal, whether they're a shifter or not, isn't illegal either."

I raised my hands. "I'm not blaming them. I'm just trying to find a connection. Maybe the rogue was shot with the tainted bullet before he even got to the campsite. Maybe one of the scientists is related to one of the shifter hunters and grabbed his bullets by mistake. I'm just trying to find a connection, if there is one."

Although why would the shifter hunters have bullets that made shifters go rogue? It was suicidal. Instead of a head on their wall, they'd most likely wind up dead right next to the corpse of the shifter. And by the videos, someone was setting up the attack.

Was that it? Was someone selling the rogue bullets as kill bullets, catching the carnage on tape and driving the public into a panic? Although they'd need to be stealthy. If hunters found out they were being sold bullets that would end up with them dead in addition to the shifter, public opinion would shift.

"All the effects are down at the morgue with the bodies." The sheriff gave me a narrow-eyed glare. "I'll call down and get you in, but you're to take nothing. Their families are making arrangements, and I don't want to hear that so much as a sock is missing. Got it?"

"Yes, sir." I reached out and shook his hand.

The M.E. pulled another slab out of the freezer, eyeing me as she spoke. "This is the last one. All five healthy males. All injuries consistent with a large animal attack—bear from my experience. Death from blood loss and trauma from said injuries."

I really didn't want to look at these mauled human bodies, but needed to be thorough. If there was anything in the rogue's attack that gave me a clue as to what happened, I'd take it. Unfortunately, I got an eye full of mutilated corpses and nothing else. The M.E. was right. They seemed to be nothing other than a large-animal attack. Bites. Claw marks. Defensive wounds. Hunting among shifters was quick and efficient with maximum consideration for preserving the meat. This was an attack fueled by rage. Overkill. An image flashed through my memory of Karl bashing the dead rogue's body around the clearing. Yeah. Like that.

One of these humans had been in possession of a rifle. And yes, it had been recently fired. Judging from what was left in the magazine and the damage to the stock, one of the scientists had fought back, shooting at the rogue at least four times before the gun had been swiped from his hands. But Karl had only dug one bullet out of the bear shifter besides the two the hiker had shot. Had three bullets missed? Or had all four missed and the one that had turned the grizzly shifter rogue had been from another shooter?

There was more to this than a simple bear shifter gone rogue. Who'd attacked first? I couldn't blame a shifter for defending himself, and there *were* the occasional idiots who panicked and unloaded on a bear who was just eating berries a little too close to their camp. I didn't expect that sort of behavior from most people, but the world was filled with noobs, and it wouldn't be the first time some poor shifter got an ass full of lead when she was just minding her own business.

Yeah. I still had the scars.

And then there was that bullet we'd dug out of the rogue. "Can I see their personal effects?" I asked the M.E. The .35 caliber .358 that I had in my pocket could have been fired by the Browning that one of the naturalists had fired, or whether it could have been fired by someone else.

The personal effects took up nearly an entire room. There was a neat pile of packed-up tents, coolers, foodstuff, and research equipment. Another pile held the bagged-and-tagged samples the naturalists had been studying along with several notebooks full of scribbled handwriting. In smaller piles were duffle bags.

"This was the guy that shot the rifle." The woman pointed to a small pile of bags. I got down to work under her watchful eyes and sorted through clothing, toiletries, more notebooks and pens, and a box of .35 caliber, .358 bullets.

They were all normal bullets, without the magic coating, but further down in the smaller dufflebag I came across something the shape of a crayon box with five bullets and an empty slot. Gritting my teeth, I pulled each one out and examined it, comparing the smell, the feel, to the one in my pocket. This was it. Out of the bullets in the rifle, one had been tainted.

He'd bought them separately and they'd come in this plain brown cardboard container. And clearly they were expensive or he would have loaded all of them in the rifle.

One, just in case any attacking animal was a shifter. Three, so he wouldn't waste all the expensive bullets on a wild bear. But where had they come from? This guy must have bought them specifically for this trip. And whoever was selling these bullets was complicit in the murders of not only the bear shifter in Kenai, but these five scientists. They had to be connected. Two different types of magical coating, but both affecting shifters, both in the same geographic area, and, I was willing to bet, both made by the same sorcerer and most likely sold by the same company.

"What was this guy's name?" I asked. "And did he have anything on him as far as receipts?"

The M.E. flipped through a chart on a nearby table. "Joseph Sebastian Floyd. Age thirty-five. Portland, Oregon."

"Any idea what he did for a living?"

She shrugged. "I take care of the bodies. I don't do the detective work. These guys were all scientists, but they were amateurs, not professionals. That's all I know."

"Did he have a wallet? Can I see what was in there?"

The M.E. looked like she was running out of patience with my questions, but nodded reluctantly. "Come on." She led me to a safe, then sorted through tagged cell phones and wallets. "Here."

It held about forty in cash, two credit cards, and a license. I quickly committed the address and birthdate to memory, then dug through the recesses of the leather billfold, pulling out a handful of receipts. One was from a stop-

and-go near Ketchikan for junk food and fuel. Others were dining receipts, more junk food, and an outfitter. I pulled my cellphone out and with a questioning glance at the M.E. for permission, I snapped a picture of the receipt. I didn't recognize the address, and the print out only showed the total, not the detail of what was bought, but at least it was a lead.

If I were lucky, this would be the place where Joseph Floyd had bought the tainted bullets. If I were lucky.

I left the morgue and glanced at the time. Then I typed in all I'd gleaned from the license and sent it plus the receipt picture to Brent along with a summary of what had happened. Did I have time to go hunt down this outfitter before they closed? And how late would that make me in getting to Karl's? As much as I was looking forward to getting naked and sweaty with the bear shifter, his promise of dinner was the greater draw right now. Two days of beef jerky and summer sausage weren't my idea of sustainable dining.

My phone beeped. *Where are you?* Brent asked.

Still in Ketchikan. Just left the morgue. Can you get Dustin to fly me back tomorrow?

We paid the Swift River Pack for the use of their plane and pilot, but it was getting to the point where it might be cost effective for us to buy our own plane and have a pack pilot, especially with Kennedy having to fly back and forth to the trauma center in Anchorage each week.

I got in my car and typed in the address for the outfitter, grimacing at the route and estimated arrival time. If I hurried, I could squeak in just before closing time. And be very very late for smoked trout tonight.

A half an hour later, I was pulling into the parking lot when Brent called.

"Dustin will be at the harbor to pick you up at six. I know

it's early, but he's got two other charters tomorrow and that's the only time he can squeeze a pick-up in."

Great. Get to Karl's around ten or eleven, and have to be out of there at four thirty at the latest. So much for any marathon sex sessions. And from experience, sleeping while flying in a tiny plane wasn't ideal, at least not for me.

"Thanks, boss." I meant it. A six o'clock pick up by plane was better than an eighteen-hour ferry and drive home. "How do you want to handle the bullets? And tracing Joseph Floyd's purchase?"

"I was thinking of sending the bullets up to Kennedy. She's a surgeon, not a lab technician, but she's bound to know someone. She's got resources, and can probably put a rush on it."

I wrinkled my nose, eyeing the store and wondering how quickly I could wrap up this conversation. "Does she have some kind of mage in the lab? I don't think it's a natural substance on there. Shifters have been around for ten thousand years. If this was some plant or mineral that had this sort of effect on us, I'm pretty sure we would have encountered it by now."

"I still want her to take a look at it. I've been up close and personal with the killing bullets, and while I'm thinking magic too, I don't want to rule out that there's a genetically modified foxglove that's lethal to us. But I'm thinking before we send it to her, we should have Ahia look at it."

Ahia was an angel, and might have a better take on magical spells or curses than I would. Even better, she was shacked up with an archangel—an archangel with billions of years of life experience and connections that spread far beyond Alaska, or even this realm of existence.

"Magic would be tricky, though. It would be a pain to have to spell every single bullet."

"I don't think it's mass produced, though. There were

only six bullets in this pack, and the naturalist had only loaded one tainted bullet in with regular ones. It's not like everyone is running around with these, and the hunters in Kenai that you encountered seemed to be an exclusive group. I'm thinking maybe they are individually spelled. If so, they'd cost a fortune and wouldn't be available to everyone or be the sort of thing you'd load a whole magazine with unless you were super rich."

"But then why release the bullets that cause a shifter to go rogue?" Brent asked, half to himself. "Mass hysteria is only profitable if you've got the volume of product to meet the need."

Well, I was the marketing expert. "Supply and demand. If people were scrambling, panicked, for the bullets, they could push prices way up. The market would bear a thousand percent increase if demand was there. And there's no saying they won't hire a bunch of mages to replicate the bullets on a faster scale if they had orders in queue."

"Hopefully we'll bring their business down before that happens," Brent said. "And I've given your information on Joseph Floyd to Marcus to see what he can dig up. Hopefully he can find enough to determine where he bought the tainted bullets. This is our only chance."

Well that and the store in front of me that was closing in…fifteen minutes. Crap. "Brent, I've got to run. I'll talk to you when I'm back home."

I hung up and ran for the store, feeling like an idiot when I burst through the doors to find myself in a silent room filled with life-vests, fishing nets, tents, rifles, and one very startled employee.

"Uh, can I help you?"

"Looking for some bullets," I told him, trying to slow my breathing and heart rate as I walked to the back counter.

He eyed me worriedly. I didn't blame him. I was a

disheveled red-head in dirty jeans and a crumpled T-shirt looking like I was desperate to shoot something before the sun went down.

"Caliber?"

".35. .358 diameter"

He pulled a few boxes out from under a cabinet. "How many do you need?"

"Uh, no. I need the special bullets." I tried to give him one of those knowing looks.

Instead he stared at me as though I were the "special" one. "Like hollow point, special? What are you trying to kill?"

"Bear." I clearly should never go into acting. "You know, *bear*. Like the kind that's not a bear, but then is a bear, and doesn't go down with regular bullets."

I felt like such an idiot, but someone sold these things. I doubted Joseph Floyd from Portland, Oregon cooked them up in his basement. And he did have a receipt from this store in his wallet. It was the only sound lead I had.

"Are you going into Canada? Did you get a special permit or something? You can't just go around shooting grizzlies in the woods." The guy started to put the bullets away, obviously thinking that I wasn't of mental soundness enough to be trusted to shoot even a BB gun.

"Self-defense." I now tried for the weak and helpless expression. I might be a skinny redhead, but I'd never appeared weak and helpless in my life. And I doubted that I was pulling this one off either.

"The best self-defense is to just make a lot of noise in the woods and ensure you've got your food locked into a bear-proof container. We sell those here. And bear spray too."

I reached out and grabbed his hand, trying not to hold on with excessive strength. "Five people were killed a few days ago—mauled by a rampaging grizzly. But he wasn't a grizzly, he was like a werewolf grizzly. And a guy out hiking said that yesterday a crazy grizzly attacked him. Bullets didn't stop this bear. If a wolf hadn't shown up and distracted the attacking grizzly, he wouldn't have gotten away."

His eyes searched mine. "Look, I've heard things. I don't know if I believe them or not. We've grown up knowing there are people in Alaska who have animal abilities. Some say they can even magically turn into an animal. None of these stories say anything about people getting attacked up until a few weeks ago." He shoved a box of .358 bullets toward me. "I can sell you these. I can sell you some heavy game ammo that should be enough to take down a polar bear if one comes at you, but that's all I have."

I got the feeling he was telling the truth. I also got the feeling he wasn't telling the whole truth.

"Five people are dead." I just let that statement hang there in the air between us.

He hesitated a second, then his expression hardened. "I can't help you. All I have is regular bullets. If you want something else, then you need to shop elsewhere.

"My friend bought some here." I pulled up the receipt on my phone and turned it to him. This was my Hail Mary effort. "He said you had them."

The clerk shook his head. "If he bought ammo here, they were regular bullets. A regular bear killed those five people. Maybe it was rabid, I don't know, but it wasn't some magical were-bear that attacks people. Even if it was, I don't sell those kind of bullets." He looked around the store then lowered his voice. "I went on a climbing expedition with a couple of guides that I'm pretty sure were wolf shifters. They were good people. I'm not about to go selling the equivalent of murder weapons in my shop. If you're afraid, then stay home, or get some spray. Otherwise, go elsewhere."

Now, I believed him. He knew where I could get the tainted bullets, but he wasn't about to tell me. And I honestly believed that he didn't carry them. But if he didn't, someone else had.

Someone. Out of the thousands of outfitters, of convenience stores, of bait shacks that sold bullets, someone supplied the tainted bullets to the hunters and to this Joseph Floyd. And it wouldn't have been good business to keep that sort of thing too quiet, or their customers wouldn't be able to find them. As Sheriff Murray had said, there was no law against selling bullets. These people advertised somewhere. I just needed to put on my marketing hat, think like a business owner, and figure out who, and where, they were.

I drove as quick as I could back to Karl's little cabin, breathless with excitement as I headed down the slashed-bark-lined path to the entrance. This felt big. Bears didn't let just anyone into their homes, and they were crazy possessive when it came to their food. Karl wanted me here, and he wanted to feed me.

He pushed open the heavy wooden door at my knock and motioned me into the tiny cabin.

I gaped in surprise. The dwelling was a single twenty-by-thirty room with a loft over the back third and a stout ladder leading upward. A woodstove doubled, no doubt, as a heat source as well as a method of cooking. There was a small refrigerator in the corner—an old-fashioned ice box with a section for a one-foot cube of ice and the food storage below it. The sink was a wash basin with a drain that led under the floor and outside past the rear of the house. There was no bathroom. There wasn't even an outhouse that I could see. The cabin was far more primitive than I'd expected, but that wasn't what had me catching flies with my mouth as I stood with my feet rooted to the hand-hewn oak floors—it was the books.

There had to have been hundreds of them. They were stacked in precarious towers on the floor, filling makeshift shelves that lined the walls, piled under the table and next to the sofa. I even spotted at least a dozen of them up in the loft next to the mattress.

"I thought you said you were a bear on the move, a sort of nomad shifter?" I commented as I walked into the house. "Do you pack the books up and ship them around every time you change dens? Or do you just leave them here?"

He wrinkled his nose and grinned sheepishly. "Leave them. I've got just as many in my other dens. Winters are long, and I'm alone a lot. Books make for good company."

They did indeed. And it blew my mind to think that Karl had just as many books in several other dens. I hated to admit that I'd been stereotyping, or that I was a snob, but I'd never thought of Karl as a reader. I'd just assumed he was one of those jacked-up, good old boys whose idea of reading was a copy of Field and Stream once or twice per year. The guy didn't have a cell phone, he didn't have internet or television, heck he didn't even have electricity or a bathroom. The idea of him sitting by the woodstove on a cold winter's night and reading…holy cow, the guy had a copy of Great Expectations.

"Sorry. The place is a mess. I tried to clean it up a bit today, but I didn't really build it to entertain a lady." He moved a pile of books and ushered me over to the sofa with a hand on my lower back. "There's nobody I'd rather have in my den, though. Glad you're here for the night."

Me too. He pushed me down on the sofa and wiped some spill off the maple-topped end table with his arm, then hustled into the kitchen, banging cabinets and firing up the woodstove.

Wait. How did he start that fire? He didn't have one of those long grill-starter thingies, nor did I see him pull any matches out of anywhere. I didn't have time to wonder though, because just as quickly as he'd begun dinner prep, he was pushing a glass of liquid into my hands.

"It's not fancy whisky, or wine, but it's not bad."

I took a sip and caught my breath. Holy cow, Karl had moonshine. And it wasn't half bad as moonshine went. Alcoholic as all get out, but with apple, cinnamon, and berry notes, and some herbal flavors that gave a refreshing finish to cut the corn-whisky bite.

"Dang, Karl. Are you trying to get me drunk and take advantage of me?"

"Hopin' I don't have to get you drunk for that. There's a still out back and I put down enough hootch to last me through the winter. Books and booze, know it? Now, what are you hungry for, my red-headed wolf? Fish? Fowl? Venison?"

"Romaine salad with goat cheese and croutons, and a light balsamic vinaigrette," I teased.

He shot me a mock scowl. "Then you best leave now and start driving to town, 'cause I ain't got no green shit in this den, let alone balsamic crap."

I laughed. "Seriously. If you've got meat, I'm gonna eat. You pick. Whatever sounds good to you is going to sound good to me."

"Fish then. I never had it until I came up here. Well, I did, but it was the frozen breaded fish sticks or the stuff in the can. Nothing beats fresh caught, but smoked is a close second."

I blinked in surprise, but didn't dig into why a bear shifter would have been raised on frozen and canned food. We were all picky when it came to our meals—well, all except for Ahia who seemed to exist on macaroni and cheese. I watched him pull spices and oils from the cabinet, then head out in the back of the den, down to the woods. He vanished into the trees and I got into my duffle, pulling out my laptop and cell phone, then wandering around the room to find a cell signal. Nothing. I felt itchy at the thought of being so disconnected. Yeah, I'd lived in Alaska my whole life. I was used to dead spots and having to wait until I got back into the city for decent internet, but somehow, sitting in this tiny cabin full of books with no electricity or running water, I was two seconds from having to breathe into a paper bag.

This would never work. Karl was totally hot. Sex with him was mind-blowing. I actually liked him, scary though he might be. But the thought of living like this, even for a few weeks or months of the year was terrifying. It would never work between us. Never.

Karl came back through the door with two huge fish in hand.

"I'm not eating that raw," I told him. "Especially with the guts still in it."

He laughed. "You could have knocked me over with one finger when you took a bite of that fish the other day. I was sure you'd turn up your nose at it."

"I didn't want to be rude." And I didn't want to seem like a girly-girl, squeamish wolf in front of him, even though I pretty much was.

He snorted. "Thought you were gonna puke."

"Thought I was gonna puke too. You crunching down the rest of that fish didn't help my stomach any, either."

His shoulders shook. I noticed he sliced through the abdomen of each fish, carefully peeling meat from the bones and insides. "Did it just to freak you out a bit. I gotta admit that I don't mind eating like that, in fact I kinda enjoy it." He turned to me, his eyes with those golden sparks that made him seem more "other" than human. "There's a lot of things I enjoy, Brina. I'm not the type of shifter that civilizes well. Don't like to be around people most of the time."

"You're more animal than human," I commented. It wasn't all that unusual. We had a few in our pack whose wolf-selves were more in control than their human half.

He stared at me a moment, the gold rolling over his hazel irises. The hair rose on the back of my neck. "More than animal, Brina. I've got bad blood, and it's better for me to live out here by myself. I like you. I more than like you. I want to make you mine and never let you go. And I realize that if I want that, I need to get control of my darkness enough to not kill your friends, to know which fork to eat my salad with. As well as actually eat salad."

Was I weird? That had to have been one of the sweetest, most romantic speeches ever. Karl would eat salad for me. He wouldn't kill my friends for me.

Wait. What?

"Well, I appreciate you cooking the fish this time." I watched as he turned his back on me and continued to work, my gaze sliding from his broad shoulders, down his trim waist, to his amazingly tight ass.

"What did you find out from the police?" he asked, reaching for an unlabeled jar of seasoning.

I told him about my conversation with the sheriff, as well as what I'd found out at the morgue. Then I walked over and showed him the video that Brent had texted me of the wolf shifter attack. The links didn't work since there wasn't a cell signal or internet probably within miles of this cabin, but thankfully one of the videos had actually saved into my phone's memory.

"The guy shifted too fast. It's not normal," he commented.

"No, it's not. That's what Brent said happened when the hunters shot him and Leon up in Kenai. Plus, the film's been edited, so parts are taken out. It's made to look like a shifter ran in, changed forms, then attacked. They would have had to shoot the wolf with the tainted bullet after he got there so that they could get the shift on film, otherwise everyone watching the video would just think a rabid wolf attacked them."

Karl frowned down at the screen. "Doesn't make sense. Why would the shifter run in on a group of humans like that? Gotta say, if some stranger came bursting into my campsite out of nowhere, I'd probably shoot him too."

Good grief. "Remind me not to surprise you while you're out camping then."

"I'd know your scent. You're not a stranger."

"Even upwind?"

"It's not just your scent, Brina. I'd know you. I can feel you near."

Okay, that was just weird. But I didn't have time to get into that. "You're right about the shifter in this video. What if there was an emergency and he was trying to warn them? What if the hunters or another rogue were after him and he was trying to tell the humans to get away?"

He squinted at the phone. "The humans don't look freaked out until the guy shifts from what I can see. If some guy came running into my camp hollering that a bear was after him, I'd be grabbing my gun. Actually, if some guy came running into my camp, I'd be grabbing my gun."

We'd already established that. "I need a bigger screen. If the video quality is good enough, I could see the shifter's expression and maybe get a better idea of what's going on behind the scenes. While you're cooking, I'll see what the video looks like on your..."

Oh yeah. The guy didn't have a cell phone, or indoor plumbing. I doubted he had a computer.

"Seriously? Ain't even got electricity, Brina," he huffed.

Yep. I should have known.

"I don't think there's going to be the panic you're imagining. Lots of humans are going to think those videos are fake," Karl added.

"And lots will think they are real." I thought about the guy in the outfitter shop. He'd been reluctant to believe the tales of attacking shifters. He'd refused to sell the tainted bullets or even point me to where I could get them, but that didn't mean others wouldn't. "Even Alaskan natives are going to start shooting first and asking questions later. They'll assume that every one of us they see is a potential killer. They know us, Karl. They're our friends and neighbors. They know who we are, but with five people dead and these attacks, they'll fear for their safety. And all the tourists… What's next, registration? If this keeps going on, we'll be considered a danger to all humans. If the angels don't intervene, human government will. We've always had more freedoms in Alaska than in the other states, partly because the angels haven't really bothered with us up here and the humans trust us. But now we'll be tagged and restricted. Us as well as all the packs in the lower forty-eight, and even in the rest of the world…we'll find ourselves declared dangerous."

He reached out and smoothed my hair, his other hand taking the phone from me and putting it on the counter facedown. "That's a long way off. Three or four rogues isn't going to turn the world against us."

I stared down at the phone. He was wrong. I, of all people, understood how things can catch fire in an internet age. "It won't take three or four rogues. All it will take is one rogue, and one clever marketing campaign."

* * *

KARL CONTINUED to cook dinner while I went outside and wandered his property, looking for a decent cell signal so I could do some research. There had to be noise on the internet, either on the comment section of these videos or in hunter and hiker forums about the attacks. And that was where I was sure I'd find some endorsement or referral to whoever was selling the bullets.

I glanced back at the flickering firelight shining through the cabin windows and felt guilty. Karl was making me dinner. He was happy to see me and was looking forward to some romantic time together, but here I was, type A, second to the Alpha, obsessing over all this. I couldn't help it. If I could just get a name and number, or at the very least an e-mail address or website, I could go back in and stick all this into a corner of my mind to deal with tomorrow.

I finally got a weak signal by standing on the hood of my Jeep and reaching my arms up as far as they could go, which made typing difficult. Still I managed, searching hunter and hiker forums and chat groups, looking for any reference to specialized bullets, or shifters, or werewolves. Nothing. Then I got an idea.

And I struck gold. Werewolf had yielded nothing, and neither had shifter, but grizzly attack had. Suddenly there was a whole list of threads with both hunters and hikers concerned over being mauled by giant, aggressive, rabid grizzlies in Alaska that didn't go down with even a round of .50 caliber bullets. There was an underground hysteria, and it seemed to have one source—a guy with the screen name of StraitShooter. And he was claiming to be with a hunting supply company outside of Juneau named Hit-The-Mark.

I did a quick search of the company, figuring I could always ask one of the Swift River Pack about it. Their main business interest was hosting tours and they knew all the outfitters and supply companies in the state. The website for Hit-The-Mark Outfitters was bare-bones. The internet marketing specialist in me itched to give them a redesign, but many of these smaller, mom-and-pop companies were content to merely have their contact information and location on the internet. This place didn't even have a physical address or a phone number, just an e-mail address and a vague mission statement about providing for every hunter and hiker's needs. It was so vague that it made me wonder what they were really selling.

I eyed the cabin and wondered if I had time to do more. As much as I wanted to e-mail Hit-The-Mark, I didn't want to tip my hand. Clearly their clientele already knew what they were selling, and they most likely wouldn't respond if they thought I was just some idiot who'd stumbled across their site in a blind search.

I was running out of time. And battery. While I still had enough juice to do it I sent Hit-The-Mark an e-mail, hoping I worded everything right, then I tracked down Straight-Shooter, grabbed his ISP and tagged a few of his posting trails as my phone was screaming low battery. Just before it died, I sent the lot to Brent with a quick e-mail, knowing he'd put a pack resource on it—someone with electricity and a decent internet connection, probably Elle or Allison, or maybe Zeph. That done, I hopped off the Jeep and headed to the cabin.

I was the worst date ever, I thought, watching Karl as he cooked, breathing in the intoxicating aroma of frying fish. "I'm so sorry. I know it was horribly rude of me to run off and do work-stuff with you in here making me dinner."

He shot me a smile. "You've got responsibilities. You're assertive and smart and driven. Don't think I'd like you as much if you just sat on my sofa for the last hour and stared at me."

"I promise, I'm done. And I really am because my phone is dead and even if I charge it off my car I have to stand on the roof and do some contorted pose just to get one bar of signal."

"Good." He flipped the fish. "Now you're all mine."

I shivered with anticipation. All his until some ungodly hour of the morning when I had to head back to Ketchikan and catch a plane. And then what? Get the bullet to Ahia. Track down this Hit-The-Mark place. Adjust my ad spend for the week and tweak some graphics for an upcoming sale. Then, in a few weeks, hopefully see Karl again at the barbeque.

I had a lot to do, but somehow the thought of seeing Karl was the highlight. Maybe I needed to take a vacation from work and the pack and see what his life was like out here. Could I do it? Could I hang in the woods for a week with no electricity, no internet, no plumbing? Just the two of us hiking, hunting, running on four legs? In the evening we'd take turns cooking, if I could figure out how to work the woodstove, read, then have sex. Actually we'd probably have sex several times during the course of the day if I had my way. It sounded ideal, but in reality would I be ready to crawl out of my skin within forty-eight hours?

I'd have to give it a try if we had any chance of making this work, just as he'd have to try the not-killing-my-friends and eating salad thing. Putting thoughts of Karl with his barely restrained violence aside, I turned my attention to the amazing spread he was putting on the table. "You do realize this is my personal fantasy to have a sexy guy fix me dinner while I finish up work."

"Ain't gonna be all that fancy, but think you'll like it." He shot me a quick glance then went back to the stove. "So what work do you do? Wolves work outside the pack, right?"

Oh my God. The fish looked amazing. And so did the veggies. Veggies! He'd actually dug up some veggies for me in spite of his obvious dislike of green things.

"Some of us. Swift River Pack keeps their businesses consolidated and their members work for them. We operate more like a club. We each have responsibilities, and every wolf knows that pack duties come first, but beyond that everyone except our Alpha has an outside career. I used to work for a corporation, but now I have my own company and do marketing for small businesses on a contract basis."

"Smart woman."

He sounded rather awed, even though I wasn't doing anything that a thousand other people weren't doing. "What about you?"

He put two plates on the table and pulled out a chair for me. I sat, salivating at the huge slab of fried halibut on the plate surrounded by honeyed carrots and roasted brussels sprouts.

"I sell the wood I chop, sell meat from my hunting. Don't need a lot of money. If I do, I'll do odd jobs for a bit of cash or trade."

I took a few bites, savoring the unexpected joy that was Karl's cooking before asking him to elaborate.

"How do you get the wood into town for deliveries without a truck? How do people know you're selling it if you don't have a phone or e-mail?" The whole thing boggled my mind. How in the world did people live like this?

"I go into town on occasion and put a note up on the board outside the grocery store. People drive out if they want wood or meat, or if they want me to pull up tree stumps for them. Some humans out here live the same way, Brina. It's not that odd."

It seemed odd to me. I envisioned some human showing up out of the blue with a pick-up truck to buy a cord of wood, or to ask Karl to hop in the cab and go off somewhere to pull stumps or clear trees. I guess it was no different than picking up one of the people who hung out in the home improvement store parking lot looking for day jobs.

"I only need enough for things like books, clothes, the occasional tool or hinge, or latch I can't make myself. And toilet paper." He grinned. "That's where I draw the line. Decent toilet paper is a necessity of life."

I'd never really thought of that. I shook my head to dislodge all the "bear crapping in the woods" jokes. "How long does it take you to walk into town?"

"Few hours if I walk. Less if I run. I make a day of it and enjoy the journey."

It hit me. That was pretty much Karl's philosophy on life. And I suddenly wanted it to be mine. I'd like to enjoy the journey too, instead of obsessing over crossing the next thing off my to-do list and living for what needed to be set up and accomplished to meet the next day's, the next week's, the next year's goals.

"Wait…" Something suddenly struck me. "How do you get to your other dens? It must take you weeks to get up to Juneau or Skagway if you're walking. Does someone give you a lift? Do you hitchhike? Use your savings to take a ferry?"

Every muscle in his body tensed. "I make my own way. Walk some."

What wasn't he telling me? "You better head out tomorrow if you want to make it in time for the barbeque, then. Juneau is a long walk, especially if you're going around the ice fields."

"I've got a den near Juneau. It's quicker traveling to my dens."

No. No, it wasn't. "What, the chimneys connect or something like in Harry Potter? How is it quicker for you to get to your den in Juneau versus some other place in Juneau?"

He sat his fork down. "My dens are beacons. They're home. If I want to move from home to home, I just do it."

Was he saying what I thought he was saying? "Like waypoints on a GPS? You close your eyes, click the heels of your ruby slippers together, then *poof*, you're there?"

"Don't know anything about GPS stuff, but my dens are home. Anything that's home to me, I can travel to. I just want to be there, and I go."

Teleporting. He was telling me that he could teleport. Ahia was a frickin' angel and she couldn't teleport. The gate guardian could. Ahia's main-squeeze, Raphael, could, but he was an archangel. Karl had sworn he wasn't Nephilim. Was he an angel? What in the heck *was* he?

"Can you do it right now? Can you show me? Go up to your home in Juneau, then back. I want to see you do this."

He shook his head. "I can't right now. I don't want to go there. I want to be here with you."

That was just plain weird. "There are days I don't want to get in the car and go to the grocery store, but I still can do it. Are you telling me there has to be a deep-seated desire to be at a different den for you to teleport there? You can't just say 'oh, I really want the copy of Sons and Lovers from the Juneau den' and pop back and forth?"

He grunted, then ate a few bites of fish. "I'd have to need that book. Not just think it would be nice to read it, but *need* it."

"And the barbeque?"

His eyes met mine. Heat pooled low in my body. "I *need* to be at that barbeque. It's more than want, Brina. Fact, I'm kinda worried I might be dreaming one night and wake up to find myself up at the den in Juneau."

I concentrated on my food, thinking about what he'd said. There was something visceral needed for him to teleport, and his feelings for me qualified. A wet dream might trigger a teleport. Wow…that was some sexual attraction. I'd never inspired that kind of lust before. Ever. It was a heady feeling to know he desired me that much.

I scooped the last bit of fish off my plate only to have Karl cut a section of his and slide it over to me. "Trying to fatten me up?"

I don't know why I said that. Probably because I was still a bit awestruck at Karl's attraction to me, his passion for me. And underneath all my confidence and assertive dominance was an insecurity about my skinny, non-feminine body. Carpenter's dream because I was flat as a board. Built like a boy. Skinny where women were supposed to be curvy. Hard where women were supposed to be soft. Good for a drunken one-night stand. Good to have as a buddy. Good to date until a better wolf came along.

"Like you the way you are. You're rangy and strong, lean and tough. You're smart. You're determined. You're powerful. You're the kind of woman a strong man needs by his side and in his bed. You're beautiful with hair like Indian Paintbrush in late summer, freckles like stars in the night sky, like spots on an orchid. I want to feed you because you like my cooking, and I don't have much else to offer you."

I caught my breath, feeling the sting of tears in my eyes. I guess we all had our own insecurities.

"I'm not a smart bear, Brina. I never went to school. I learned to read on my own. My folks taught me basic math because it was useful knowledge, but that was it. I don't know marketing or computer stuff. I don't know how things work in a pack. I can only manage to spend a day around big groups of shifters before I want to either kill someone or go into a cave and hide for a few weeks. I don't like humans much. I'm good at killing, at hunting, at chopping wood. And I'm good at cooking fish. That's all I got."

What a pair we were. All we seemed to have in common

was rocking sex. And the feeling that neither one of us had more to give than rocking sex.

I finished the fish, sat back and looked over at Karl, a heavy lump somewhere in my middle. "This isn't going to work, is it? This thing between us is going to flame out in a few weeks once we get all the screwing out of our system."

The gold rolled over his irises, lighting them up. "It will work. It's more than sex. You're more than just a good fuck, Brina. We're different, but we fit together like puzzle pieces. And there's no flaming out for us. There's no getting you out of my system."

There was an intensity in his deep voice that lit me up from inside. "I'll…I'll do the dishes," I announced, standing abruptly. Wait. No dishwasher. Did I have to lug water in from the well or something?

"Fuck the dishes," Karl growled. Then he stood and flipped the table over.

I yelped in surprise, then laughed as he grabbed me and threw me over his shoulder, climbing up the loft ladder and tossing me down on the mattress.

Karl shed his pants in one quick movement while I watched, grinning. Then he stood there, arms crossed, one eyebrow raised.

"Well?"

Oh. Guess I was supposed to get myself naked instead of waiting for him to tear the clothing off me. I stood, careful to position myself in the part of the loft where I wouldn't bang my head, which put me about six inches from Karl. I could feel the heat coming off his skin as I pulled my shirt over my head and shimmied out of my shorts. Then I gave him a naughty wink and slowly unsnapped my bra, letting it slide down my arms to his feet. He watched, silent, eyes shimmering with that eerie gold light.

Catching his gaze, I hooked my thumbs in the waistband

of my panties and waited for him to drop his stare downward, then slowly wiggled them down my legs.

"There. Naked and ready," I told him, my voice husky.

"Ready? Cause I haven't even touched you yet."

I smiled. "Ready. And I can clearly tell that you're
ready too."

He grinned, stepping forward and picking me up, nearly
banging my head on the rafters as he tossed me over his
shoulder. Then he dropped to his knees and slid my body
down along his until I was on my back with him straddling
me. We lay there, sharing a breath. I reached out a hand and
trailed my fingers along his face, feeling the scrape of his
scruffy whiskers, the hard planes of his cheekbones, the softness of his lips. Then he bent his head and kissed me—my
lips, my neck, my breasts, my stomach, until he was between
my legs and all I could do was close my eyes and arch my
back, moaning with each touch of his tongue.

My senses swirled together—the intimate cozy feel of his
den, the smell of wood smoke and pine, of Karl, of our lust
curling through the air, the sound of our movements against
the sheets, of my ragged breathing and Karl's murmured
endearments, of the sensation of him, so huge and powerful
looming over me, my legs tossed over his shoulders.

His fingers joined his tongue and before long I was
begging, pleading with him to make me come, but each time
I was close, he eased off and my climax danced just out of my
reach. Just when I thought I would go insane, he plunged two
fingers into me, sucking hard on my clit and my orgasm
roared through me. I threw back my head and cried out,
bucking against him, my hands gripping his hair. Then
slowly he shifted upward, my legs still on his shoulders as he
climbed over me.

"This okay?" he asked. I was bent double, his cock pressed
against my entrance, his mouth against mine.

"Hell yeah it is," I told him, my voice sounding breathless and light.

He chuckled and he pushed deep inside of me, swallowing my gasp with his mouth. Damn. He was big, and pretzeled-up like this he felt even bigger. But it felt inexplicably good being filled to the edge of discomfort, feeling him struggle to hold himself back as he drove himself in and out, kissing me like he was drinking water in the desert.

I gripped his arms, my nails digging into his skin. It seemed to send him over the edge, and his pace became fast and uneven. His mouth left mine and I heard him inhale sharply, I felt him thicken. He slammed himself deep, and I felt myself slip over the edge, felt myself shatter just as he shuddered and poured himself into me.

We soared. As he opened his eyes, that unearthly golden glow stared down at me. For a moment neither of us breathed. We just existed, two people, two beings who had come together and connected in an incredibly intimate fashion. There was something in his gaze, as if he wanted to tell me something, then he closed his eyes and exhaled, dropping his head so that his hair hid his face.

I reached up and smoothed it aside, pulling him down so that I could kiss his forehead, his eyelids, his cheeks and lips.

"Thank you for inviting me to share your den," I whispered. "There's nowhere I'd rather be tonight."

At my words his head lifted, his eyes searching mine. "It's your den now, Brina. It's all yours."

I woke up in a panic, not knowing what time it was and not wanting to keep Dustin waiting at the harbor. My phone was dead, and inexplicably, Karl had no clocks in his house. Although I guess it wasn't all that unusual for a guy with no electricity or running water to forgo a time-keeping device. Out here, so disconnected from anything resembling a nine-to-five, a clock wouldn't be necessary.

Unless you had a friend spending the night who needed to catch a plane at six in the morning.

I threw on my clothes, gave a groggy Karl a kiss and ran for the Jeep.

"Crap. Crap," I muttered, catching a glimpse of the dashboard clock. I'd need to hustle. And I couldn't leave a note or say a proper goodbye to Karl as I wanted to. Normally I'd just text him later. Normally I'd call him later.

This was so not going to work. How the heck could I tell him I'd had a wonderful time and wanted to see him soon? Did the guy even get postal service deliveries for me to send a quick post-booty-call postcard?

Except I didn't want this to be a booty call. We were so different. There was something deep down inside him that scared me. The sex was good, but a relationship needed more than sex to survive. Books? And I did like to hunt and fish. Maybe we could meet halfway. I hoped so because I really wanted things to work between me and this bear.

And if they didn't…well, we'd just screw each other until the attraction burned out, then go our separate ways. The thought made me sad, but it was what it was. At my age, I'd learned to take these things as they came and not try to force a long-term connection where there was none.

I made it. The clock hit six just as I pulled into the harbor parking area. I grabbed my duffle bag and locked the keys in the Jeep's console as instructed, and watched Dustin fly down Tongass Narrows in his landing approach. The guy could fly. Of course, he spent most of his time in this plane. Originally the Swift River Pack had used it, and Dustin, to shuttle their hiking/climbing/hunting tours to various Alaska destinations, but they quickly realized the other two wolf packs in the state needed frequent and reliable transportation. Jake, the Swift River Alpha, was shrewd like that, always on the lookout for a way to increase revenues for their pack. And Dustin was the perfect guy to take charge of this part of their business. He was smart, and had a chill-attitude. He wasn't what I'd call submissive, but he wasn't so dominant that there was a constant pissing match between him and his customers. Dustin had a friendliness that made everyone trust him and confide in him. He was like a bartender, only thousands of feet in the air.

The plane swooped down, a trail of mist in its wake as the pontoons touched down. Slowing, Dustin pivoted the aircraft around and made his way to the dock, expertly pulling alongside.

"Hey Sabrina!" The werewolf grinned at me, his blond

hair spilling over his eyes—which looked tired. If I'd been up early, Dustin had been up earlier. Although I doubted he'd been awake most of the night having sex with a grizzly shifter.

"Hey, Dustin. Busy day I hear."

He nodded, grabbing my duffle bag then helping me into the plane. "You. Then I've got to go up to Anchorage to grab a couple of the Denali pack and take them home. Then I've got a cold beer and a couple of steaks waiting for me back home."

Now that sounded divine. I took the headset Dustin offered and donned it, flicking the "on" switch so we could have a conversation over the loud noise of the propeller engines.

"You must have caught that rogue pretty fast," Dustin commented as he turned the plane around. "Although I'm not surprised. I heard you had help from one of the grizzly shifters. Those guys are downright terrifying in a fight."

I didn't ask when Dustin had ever seen grizzly shifters fight. "I did the tracking, and Karl did the rest," I admitted.

"Karl?" Dustin shot me a quick glance before turning the plane for our take-off. "That guy is more than terrifying. He's like hell on earth. I saw him get into it with a polar bear shifter once. The guy was a smear on the pavement when they were done. I swear, I don't even think Karl is a grizzly."

I leaned back in the seat as Dustin accelerated and we rose above the water, the plane tilting as it came around to head north. "I don't think he's a grizzly either," I admitted. "He said his mother was. He won't talk about his father."

Dustin nodded sagely. "Lots of people won't talk about their fathers. Not everyone had a great childhood, Sabrina. Although, I gotta say, I've always wondered if Karl wasn't secretly a Nephilim."

Me too. "He says he isn't. He says all he can do is bear and human forms. But there's something in his eyes…" I didn't know why I was discussing this with Dustin. Bartender. I swear the pilot was just like a bartender. Or hairdresser.

Dustin shrugged. "Maybe his father was a Nephilim. Most second generations don't have anything more than other shifters beyond enhanced fertility, but he could be the exception. All I know is I'm glad he's a pretty chill dude most of the time. Seems like it takes a lot to get him riled up, but when he gets riled up, I don't want to be anywhere near him."

I thought back on the last few days with the grizzly shifter. He'd said he'd never hurt me, that I could trust him. And I believed him. As frighteningly powerful as Karl was, as much as the darkness behind his eyes scared me, I got the feeling I was somehow precious to him.

The thought brought a smile to my face. "Do you mind if I sleep a bit? It was a long night." I told Dustin.

He shot me a perceptive look. Yeah. I'd not had time to shower even if Karl had indoor plumbing, and I probably smelled to high heaven of sex-with-grizzly-shifter. Dustin knew very well what I'd been doing all night.

"No problem. I'll wake you when we land."

* * *

Brent paced back and forth in his kitchen. I was sitting on a stool at the center island. Ahia and her angel, Raphael, were leaning against the counters, watching Brent.

"I don't like this. I don't like it at all," the Alpha declared.

Neither did I. "So what do we do? The police won't get involved unless we can prove people aren't acting in self-defense, which means we need to counteract the forced shifting and stop the rogue attacks."

"Basically negate what the bullets are doing," Raphael said.

"Yes. It's not just a matter of hunters targeting us anymore. We've got a public relations nightmare looming. And we need to get human law enforcement what evidence they need to be on our side. If we can prove that they're shooting us when we're in human form, then it's a matter of assault with a deadly weapon, or attempted murder. Until then, there's a whole gray area of self-defense for them to consider."

Brent growled and slammed his fist into the countertop, denting the surface. "Why is it *our* responsibility to come up with an antidote? We've coexisted peacefully with the humans for generations and they don't believe us on this one? Humans go crazy taking ice or LSD and they're victims. We're not even voluntarily taking this, and we're blamed."

I took a deep breath. "I'm with you, boss, but we're on our own with this. We need to play by the human rules and get out the warning so our pack members and other shifters don't get shot with these tainted bullets. Let's work this side of the situation, cooperate, communicate, and find an antidote as quickly as we can. Then behind the scenes we'll take it to them. I'm not saying sit on our hands and let the police do all the work. We can track them down, destroy their supplies, and possibly deliver our own justice toward those responsible."

I couldn't believe I was proposing this. But the alternative was bleak. There was no way I wanted to stand aside and bide our time while shifters went rogue, and others were killed and mounted on walls as trophies. No way.

Brent ran a hand through his short, dark hair. "So we have this SharpShooter guy posting on forums and riling people up. Then we have this Hit-The-Mark place that supposedly sells a solution to the rampaging werewolf problem."

"Now that I'm somewhere with decent internet, I'm going

to try to see if I can arrange a purchase from Hit-The-Mark and see if they're truly supplying the tainted bullets. That will get us one step closer to whoever is making these things. *That's* the guy we need to take out. We'll never get ahead of this tracking down hunters, or humans who bought these bullets out of fear."

Brent shot me a narrowed glance. "You're a werewolf, Sabrina. I don't like the idea of you going in this Hit-The-Mark place. If they're selling bullets coated in magic, they might have a way to detect what you are, and then you'll be trapped."

I hadn't thought of that. My whole life I'd walked among humans, and unless I confided in them, they'd never known I was any different than they were.

"You need a human to make the buy for you," Ahia chimed in. "Isn't Kennedy coming back from Anchorage today? Maybe she can help with the detective work."

Brent froze, tension in every muscle. I grimaced, knowing exactly what was going through his mind. Kennedy was completely capable. She was an ex-Army medic, a trauma surgeon, an amazing woman who was deadly with a rifle, who mountain climbed and hiked not in the least bit hindered by the fact that she was an above-the-knee amputee. But in spite of all that, she was human, and she was Brent's mate. His every impulse was to keep her safe. And that warred with his realization that she'd kick his ass and walk away if he tried to swaddle her and keep her safe. When Kennedy had mated with Brent she'd become a part of our pack, and she'd embraced every responsibility that entailed, even if she was human.

"She'll want to help," I told him. "And I'd be right outside, with my werewolf hearing, ready to intervene if necessary. Not that I think it will be necessary. I've seen her fight.

You've seen her fight. She's saved both you and Leon. She's just as capable as any wolf in this pack."

Ahia shrugged. "Besides, would these guys harm a human? It sounds like their whole business is built around the idea that shifters are monsters and humans need to be able to protect themselves."

I eyed Brent, knowing that I was about to add to his fears. "If it was just the hunters up in Kenai, I might think that, but from the videos, it looks like they're causing shifters to go rogue and siccing them on humans to prove their point. Five people died down in Ketchikan." Although I got the idea that those five weren't supposed to die. Maybe the bullets worked better with werewolves than grizzly shifters, and the manufacturers didn't know that.

"You're right," Ahia nodded. "Besides, if they knew she was part of a pack and was there doing reconnaissance, they might not care that she's human."

Brent scowled. "I'll ask her to help, but she just makes the buy, then she's out. Once it's confirmed where they're manufacturing these things, I'll want to work with the Swift River Pack to go in and take them out. We need a united front on this and I promised Jake I'd keep him in the loop. One of his wolves was shot too, and the hunting that happened up in Kenai was in his territory."

"Let's not jump the gun then. If we take out their supply, it might just drive them underground," I warned. "Maybe we should wait until we know who's spelling the bullets and go for them. Otherwise I worry that these guys will go stealth on us and we won't be able to dig out whoever is behind this whole thing."

Brent thought for a second. "I don't like the idea of leaving supply on the market for people to buy. If we take out their stock, we can slow them down."

"Or not," I countered. "Hit-The-Mark might just be a storefront. If we take out that store, they'll just set up shop somewhere else the next day, or do internet sales. Selling bullets isn't illegal. Let's take out their supply if we can do it without them tracing it back to us. Otherwise I think we need to wait."

Brent leaned forward, resting his hands on the kitchen island. "Okay. I'll defer to your judgement on this one, Sabrina. It's your project, and I'll trust you to make the call. As soon as we're done here, I'll phone Jake and let him know what's going on. Then I'll call Kennedy. In the meantime, we figure out what exactly the magic is on these bullets, and see if we can find an antidote."

Which was my cue to pull the bullets out of my pocket.

"You need us to look at these, Sabrina?" Ahia turned her wide smile to me, and I couldn't help but grin back.

"Why, yes I do. I could really use your angel mojo on this one. This," I shoved the one bullet in front of her, "is a bullet that that feels tainted."

Ahia caught her breath and exchanged a concerned look with Raphael.

"The wound didn't heal and the rogue didn't smell right," I added. "Karl said he smelled infected. Rotted tissue. And his blood was cloyingly sweet. Karl said that he'd fought enough bears in his life, killed enough rogues, that he knew this guy wasn't right."

Raphael reached out and took the bullet before Ahia could, shooting her a worried look. I wasn't sure if angels could be affected by whatever coated the bullets. Werewolves were descended from angels, but I'd assumed our relatively weak supernatural powers made us susceptible. I could understand Raphael's concern, though. Ahia was only five thousand years old—very young by angelic standards. He wouldn't want to take the chance.

"I can tell right now that this isn't exactly the same as

what was on the bullets Kennedy dug out of Leon and Brent. It's similar, but there's a slight difference." Raphael placed the bullet at the edge of the counter so only the front half protruded over the edge. A white light bloomed from his fingers, surrounding the bullet. After a few seconds, the light vanished and the angel slid the bullet back. "There's definitely a spell there, but there's also a natural, botanical component to it."

"So a mage, then?" I asked.

He shook his head. "An elf. This isn't just herbals used in a spell, the plant matter is actually a part of the spell. That's one of the differences between elven magic and what the human mages and sorcerers do."

An elf? I'd been assuming the person behind this was a human killer, perhaps a mage. I'd never considered an elf. I'd never seen an elf in my entire life, wasn't aware that there were any in Alaska. Was this guy, or gal, working elsewhere, shipping the bullets up here? The prospect of hunting all over the world, among seven billion humans, for one elf seemed an impossible task.

"What about the biologic?" I asked.

Ahia ignored Raphael's scowl and pulled the bullet over toward her, examining it. "Foxglove. Lilac. White pine. Thornapple. And larkspur, but that's only on the edges."

I didn't know if that was the sort of thing that combined together would affect shifters. We'd been around for thousands of years, and although there were some herbs and chemicals that made us sick, none of them had the same dramatic effects that they had on humans. We didn't get ill, we didn't need antibiotics. We didn't get cancer. And if we took cyanide, we'd be down for several days, but not dead.

"But those plant essences are the catalysts for the elven spell," Raphael added. "Slap them on a bullet by themselves and they do nothing. Add in elven magic and *that's* what makes it deadly."

"Who can we ask about countering the magic on the bullets? Do either of you know an elf?"

"Not any who would cooperate at this time. They're not all that pleased with the angels at the moment, and the few who are on our side don't have the skills to do this kind of magic," Raphael said. "There is a mage who is elven trained, and might recognize the spell, though. He's a friend of a friend of a friend, and he's in Hel, so it might take a while."

"Think this friend of a friend of a friend might also be able to come up with an antidote?" I asked.

"It depends. There might be a counter spell he could put together if what's on the bullets is within his area of expertise."

"Maybe ask him to work on a counter spell or antidote, or something like a protective amulet? Something that would block the magic, neutralize it before it took effect. That way we'd only need to deal with the bullet wound, and not the other effects."

A plain bullet we could cope with. It was the magic tainting them that was the problem.

"Or perhaps something that blocked the bullet entirely." Brent stopped pacing. "I feel like an idiot for not thinking of this before. We can't provide protective vests for every shifter, and it's not practical to wear them twenty-four-seven, but that might be a starting place."

I picked up the bullet and examined it once more. Outside of the magical coating, it *was* a regular bullet. I was touching it and not affected beyond the ick factor. If we could keep the bullet itself from physically penetrating our skin, then we wouldn't have to deal with the magic aspect of it.

"I agree," I told the Alpha.

"Good. Then let's get a dozen vests in different sizes for pack use and I'll authorize payment to this mage for any information he can provide as well as any magical item to counter the effect of the bullets." Brent turned to Raphael. "How much do you think he'll charge?"

"I've got no idea. From what I've been told, there is a currency they use in Hel, but they also operate on a barter system—mostly favors."

Brent frowned. "I don't know what favor a werewolf pack can provide to a group of humans in Hel, but I'm open to suggestion. Maybe we can trade them gems or plants or something."

In the meantime, there was one more open thread we needed to follow. "Did you manage to get anything on Joseph Floyd'?"

"Not much." Brent pulled out his phone and scrolled through his texts. "His e-mail address is linked to a username on a wilderness hiking forum. He'd expressed concern about the possibility of a bear attack on his upcoming trip to Alaska. Another forum member posted a link on his thread to the first video of the shifter attack, and told him '*this* is what you should be worried about.' There was a whole exchange of 'is that fake' and 'that can't be real' then the other guy sent him a link to Hit-The-Mark and told him he needed to be prepared."

I looked over Brent's shoulder at the screen shots. The conversation was a week before Joseph's trip. No doubt he'd bought the bullets and had them rush-shipped, probably thinking he was a fool buying snake oil the whole time.

And that snake oil got him killed.

"Can you forward that to Sheriff Murray down in Ketchikan?" I asked. Buying bullets wasn't illegal, but if we could push this from a different angle—that there was a company selling defective products that contributed to the killings—then maybe we could get the law to work on our side.

Brent pushed away from the counter. "Okay. Sabrina and Kennedy will check out Hit-The-Mark. Raphael is going to work with this mage in Hel to see about further identifying the spell, and possibly getting an antidote or something to shield against it. I'm ordering a bunch of protective vests and communicating with the other two packs on the situation. I'll put out that all shifters should be looking for an elf— which shouldn't be too hard to spot in Alaska—or someone who has access to an elf and has the know-how to run this kind of business operation. Our bad guy will understand how guided hunting tours work. He'll be savvy about guns and have connections or possibly work in the outfitter industry. Anything else?"

Ahia, Raphael, and I looked at each other, then shook our heads.

"Good." Brent thumped a fist on the counter. "Sabrina, be ready to head over to this outfitter with Kennedy in the morning. Let's go get these guys. And let's do it without anyone of us dying."

$\mathcal{A}$hia and I walked out together while Raphael stayed behind to nail a few things down with Brent.

"So," she elbowed me in the ribs. "You and Karl...?"

How had she known? I'd been careful to shower and clean up after our barbeque liaison. And had done the same when I got back from Ketchikan. I could see Brent picking up a trace of scent on me, but Ahia's nose wasn't all that good compared to us werewolves.

And yes, I was well aware that Dustin had known what I'd been up to the night before from more than ten feet away, but he'd politely not said a word, and wasn't the sort of wolf who'd gossip.

Ahia laughed. "Oh, the expression on your face! Girl, I saw the way he was eyeing you last summer, like he wanted to drag you off into the bushes and rip your panties off. Plus, there's a kind of mellow satisfaction about a girl who's been up all night fucking. Add to that the fact that he asked about you the few times I ran into him in the spring, and that Brent mentioned Karl was accompanying you on this rogue-hunting trip, and it wasn't hard to make the connection. Karl? Hunting a rogue? He's more likely to tell Brent to fuck off before going back to chopping wood. Sudden cooperation like this was only because he wanted to see you and get you into his bed. Or den. Or whatever bears call their sleeping spot."

"Den." My face felt like it was on fire.

"So? Is he as good in the sack as I've been imagining in all my lurid fantasies over the years?"

We came to a stop and I leaned against my car. "Let's just say I'm a bit obsessed. Sex with Karl is probably as close to a religious experience as I've ever had. But we're so different. I can't see this working out beyond the physical."

She shrugged. "Don't discount Karl. He's got his reasons for isolating himself like some hermit. I don't know what they are because the guy barely says more than two words, but I'm sure he's got them."

"Yeah, that. And his go-to response to any question is a grunt." I folded my arms across my chest. "How well do you know him? You said you run into him from time to time?"

Ahia had been a member of our pack for centuries, before that living with the indigenous humans in the area. She was quirky, warm, sweet, and funny, and had been alive for over five thousand years. She had wings, as in angel-wings, and when she put on the speed she was like a streak of light flying by overhead. It wasn't unusual for her to travel hundreds of miles away from Juneau for a quick afternoon jaunt.

"He's brooding, which is sexy as all hell. He's smart, but he doesn't talk a lot so some shifters just assume he's a dumb bear. He's observant. He notices shit that goes right over my head, stores it away in that mind of his, then remembers it later and puts a whole bunch of random puzzle pieces together. That's the kind of smart he is.

"And there's more," she continued. He replaced my truck

tires with bicycle ones, welded my fry pans together. He gave me a squeaky toy hamburger between two buns at last year's barbeque. Oh, and one time, he put a pissed off wolverine in my bathtub."

My eyes widened. Did he really do that? "And what did you do to deserve all those things?"

I might not know Karl that well, but I'd known Ahia all my life. Mischief was her middle name. The angel loved nothing better than a good prank, although she was usually on the giving end.

"Nothing," Ahia lied. "Absolutely nothing. But he's got a sense of humor, and in spite of the dark-brooding-Heathcliff aura, he can be pretty lighthearted and fun. It comes out of nowhere, totally surprises you, but it's there."

So they did prank each other. Something sour and ugly unfurled in my stomach. Were they...? Did they...? There seemed to be such an easy familiarity between the two, an affection that made me want to sprout claws and go nuts on the angel in front of me.

Ahia reached out and squeezed my shoulder. "We're just sort-of friends, Sabrina. He's never wanted even a quick fuck with me. I think he views me as an annoying younger sister. Which is kind of funny given that I'm five thousand years old and he's probably in his late thirties."

I knew Karl had that dry sense of humor, but I'd never thought him the type of guy who would put a squeaky toy in between a hamburger bun and give it to someone. Zeph, yes. Karl, no. Then I thought about all those books stacked up in his den. "He said he's self-educated, that his parents taught him basic math, but he never went to school and had to learn to read on his own."

Ahia grimaced. "Yeah. From what I've been able to glean, he didn't have the best childhood. I think it was probably one of those where his parents were neglectful, or crackheads, or serial killers or something."

I hoped Ahia was kidding. It was kind of hard to tell sometimes. "What was his father?"

The angel shrugged. "A douchebag?"

"No, I mean he said his mom was a grizzly shifter, but he didn't want to talk about his dad."

Ahia slowly shook her head. "Female grizzly shifters sometimes have kids with humans. Maybe his dad was human and never accepted that his kid, or the woman he'd had sex with, transformed into a bear?"

Maybe. But none of that explained Karl's odd abilities. "You said Karl was a grizzly in his animal form. Have you ever seen him shift into…something else?"

Ahia shot me a puzzled glance. "Like what? I've seen him dozens of times and he's always a human or a grizzly. Why?"

"The first time I saw his bear form, I thought he looked more like a Kodiak than a grizzly, then the second time he was a monster prehistoric looking bear. He said he could shift into any kind of bear form, but that he's not a Nephilim."

She grinned. "That's freaking cool. Any bear? Like, even a Koala bear? A polar bear? Maybe his dad was a Nephilim. Or maybe he's just some weird genetic throwback."

I couldn't imagine Karl as a Koala bear, not that Koala's were actually bears. "I like him. At least, I think I like him when I'm not terrified out of my skull because he's some extinct cave bear who looks like he's ready to devour every living thing in the state."

Ahia put an arm around my shoulder and squeezed. "Just let it all play out, Sabrina. Enjoy the ride—and I *do* mean enjoy the ride. If things work out, then all the little stuff won't be a problem. And if not, well have some awesome sex and stop fussing over the future."

She was right. I hugged her back, then turned to get into my car.

"Is he coming to the barbeque?" she asked.

"Yeah. He said he's bringing smoked trout."

Ahia gave me a thumbs-up. "Well, if you see him before-hand, give that fine ass of his a squeeze for me."

I laughed, then headed home. I was exhausted, and I needed to be at my best tomorrow, so I was planning on sleeping the rest of the day away. Half dragging my purse, I made my way to the porch of my house and stopped. There was a note on my door. And from the faint scent lingering in the air, I knew exactly who it was from.

Karl.

Sorry I wasn't more awake when you left this morning. Had a great time and hope to see you again before the barbeque. I'm at my Juneau den for the next few weeks. And I now have a cell phone, although I don't know how I'm going to keep it charged.

I looked down at the number he'd scrawled just above his name and grinned. The wild man got a cell phone. It was truly a miracle. I went inside, dropped my bag, and immediately called him.

"Hey," I said in response to his signature grunt. "I'm dead on my feet and am probably going to sleep for the next twelve hours, but if you want to lay next to a comatose woman and snuggle, then come on over."

There was a hesitation on the other end and I realized that the bear might have a cell phone, but he didn't have a vehicle. "Where is your den? I can come pick you up." Or just sleep there. I was so darned tired that the thought of driving to whatever remote wilderness Karl had stuck his den wasn't pleasant. I really wanted him to see my house, though. I wanted to see how he managed with a modern home that included indoor plumbing, plus I needed to be somewhere with a cellphone signal and internet in case

Brent needed to call or there was an e-mail response from Hit-the-Mark.

"No, I can teleport." There was another hesitation, as if he wasn't sure if he was welcome or not.

"Well then get over here, wild man. Come to *my* den and experience the joys of a microwave, a pulsating shower head, and a Sleep Number bed."

There was a knock on my door and I opened it to find Karl standing on my porch, a flip phone in his hand.

A flip phone.

"The twentieth century called and they want their phone back," I told him.

He grinned. "The guy at the quick-mart picked it out for me. I told him I only needed to call, and maybe text, and didn't need a lot of minutes. Plus, I only had twenty dollars."

Oh good, Lord. "Wait, where did you get twenty dollars?" Did Karl have a mason jar at home with loose change for emergencies? From what he'd said, it sounded like the majority of his jobs were cash under the table.

"Helped a guy pull his truck out of a ditch. He gave me twenty bucks."

I had a vision of Karl literally grabbing the frame of a truck and hauling it up to the pavement, shoulder and arm muscles bunching as he dragged the vehicle out of the ditch. Shirtless, Karl. Pulling a truck with one hand. It was a pretty hot vision.

"Come in." I stood aside and ushered him into my home.

"Nice place."

I was proud of my home. It was a little Cape Cod style with white paint and dusky blue trim. There were rockers on the front porch, a big two-car garage out back, and neighbors shouting-distance over a little wooden fence. Neighbors. I loved having people nearby. I loved sitting on my porch with a mug of coffee and my laptop, listening to the

Brecking kids playing with their new puppy, or Mr. Staley mowing his lawn. I'd wave when the couple that lived across the street headed off to work. I'd greet the mail lady when she brought a stack of flyers, bills, and the occasional package in the afternoon. I lived in a bustling neighborhood, and Karl lived in the middle of the woods down a barely accessible dirt road.

I remembered what Ahia said and pushed the *it's never going to work out* thoughts away.

"Kitchen is in through here. Help yourself to anything you want. TV remote is over there if my snoring keeps you awake, or you want to catch up on the news. Come on upstairs. Let's get naked and figure out what your sleep number is before I pass out."

As tired as I was I realized something was wrong. Karl stood awkwardly at the foot of the stairs, staring at me as if I were a creature from another planet. Surely he'd encountered a modern house and appliances before? Was there something about me that was different? Was he regretting this? Were the *it's never going to work out* thoughts running through his head, too?

I suddenly wanted to retreat to my usual casual attitude, my it-doesn't-matter-because-this-is-just-a-booty-call attitude. *Act like it doesn't matter and you won't get hurt.* Well, I'd get hurt, but at least he wouldn't know that and my pride would remain intact.

"Brina, when I teleported to Juneau, I didn't go to my den." There was something in his voice that made me think this announcement had earth-shattering significance.

"Where did you go?" I almost didn't want to know. Had he killed the guy whose truck he'd pulled out of the ditch? Had he gone to rob a bank first? Had he gone to see a wife and kids? Because somehow in my mind, that was even worse than killing someone or robbing a bank.

"I came here."

Thank God it wasn't the wife-and-kids scenario. Although I should probably double check that.

"Okay?"

He ran a hand through his hair. "Brina, I don't know where you live. I can only teleport between my dens. I had no idea where I was at first. I had to wander around the outside of your house before I caught your scent and realized what happened. I'm surprised your neighbors didn't call the police on me."

"Okay?" I still didn't understand where he was going with this.

"Your house is now one of my dens. I've never been here. I didn't even know this was where you lived, but somehow your house is now…mine. But not mine in that way. Mine as far as a location I can teleport to."

And now I understood. His hesitation made sense. If my house was now considered one of his "dens" then something inside Karl had labeled what we had together as important. This was far more significant than having a toothbrush in my bathroom, or a designated clothing drawer in my bedroom dresser. Or a programmed setting on my Sleep Number bed.

The idea made me happy, but did it make him happy? I eyed the bear, realizing that he was eyeing me back, the same expression on his face that was, no doubt, on mine.

"That's cool. It means I won't need to drive out to pick you up. Now if only you could teleport me to your house. Think of what I'd save in gas costs and wear and tear on my car."

Relief slid like a wave over his face and body, and I heard him suck in a deep breath.

"You're okay with this? I promise I won't come here unless I'm invited. I mean, I might accidently come here if I'm distracted and not concentrating enough on which den, or if I'm thinking about you, but if that happens I'll leave right away. I don't want you to think I'm some weird stalker guy who's going to be lurking outside your house at night."

I smiled and extended my hand. He took it, twisting his fingers around mine. Then I tugged him up the stairs behind me. "I don't want you to be that stalker guy lurking outside my house at night. I want you to be the hot bear shifter in my *bed* at night." I stopped at the landing so I could face him. "I like that you think of my house as your den."

His dark eyes searched mine. "I'd like it if you thought of my dens as yours as well."

I remembered the cozy cabin with the woodstove, the loft, the books stacked everywhere. It would be roughing-it for me to spend half my time in a rustic one-room house with no indoor plumbing, but he was committing to make similar adjustments for me. He'd bought a cell phone, for crying out loud. And he was about to be subjected to the electronic wonder that was my mattress.

"I'd be happy to call your dens home. Just warning you, though. I've got a lot of makeup. And I'll need more than one dresser drawer."

He grunted. "Brina, for you, I'd build an extra dresser and a whole damned closet for your makeup."

I led him the rest of the way to my bedroom. We got naked. We figured out his ideal setting on the mattress. Then I felt asleep with his arms around me, my head resting on his shoulder. And although our sleep numbers were miles apart, it was the most restful night I'd ever had.

I got an o'dark thirty text from Brent that Kennedy had been delayed in Anchorage. Since it had woken me up, and since I'm obsessive about my e-mail, I checked my messages. Karl grumbled next to me, putting a pillow over his head to block out the light of my phone.

There were three from new clients, another six discussing changes to some ads I was running, one from a graphic designer I was subbing work to, and one more from Hit-The-Mark.

It was a vague response from some guy named Dutch, stating that they did sell a variety of fishing supplies as well as ammo. They didn't yet have a catalogue or an online list of products, but if I knew exactly what I wanted, he could check availability.

Cautious. Careful. Just as I'd been when e-mailing my request. But Dutch hadn't been cautious enough because he'd attached pics of some items they carried sitting on top of a box. And in the corner of the box was an address for Hit-The-Mark.

I zoomed in on it and entered it into my map app. Karl

muttered something about "could I type a bit quieter," so I slid out of bed and headed downstairs. Ugh. This place was out in the middle of nowhere. Not ideal for a retail location, but their website was horrible for internet traffic and sales. How the heck did this guy make any money? I glanced out the windows at the tinge of pink and gray on the horizon. Four in the morning was too early to head to this place unless I planned on breaking and entering, and I wasn't quite there yet.

I set my phone down on the table and headed up the stairs, determined not to let anything else disturb our lazy morning sleep-in, and hopefully lazy morning sex, only to run back down and scoop it up, putting it on vibrate. Just in case. Because there might be an emergency with the Flying Fish Excursions campaign, or Brent might need me, or that graphic designer might be burning the midnight oil.

Then I hid it under my pillow to further muffle the sound, and wrapped myself around a very warm bear shifter, dozing off with my face against his back.

* * *

It was nice to wake up next to someone, to go through a morning routine with them, to have the kind of sex that rocked the bed against the wall and made the floorboards squawk.

Yeah, I'd slept almost sixteen hours. Yeah, it felt really, really good. But it hadn't felt nearly as good as sex in the morning. Oh, yeah.

"I like your shower," Karl told me as he walked into the kitchen, his hair wet, his clothing clinging to his damp skin. He'd popped back to his house while I'd started to make breakfast to grab some clothes and now had them in a drawer upstairs. He also had a toothbrush in my bathroom.

And I was well aware that this was moving too fast, but I was going to take Ahia's advice and just ride it out. What happened, happened. And I hoped it happened.

Karl walked over and kissed the top of my head, stealing a piece of bacon from the plate. "I wish your tub was big enough for my grizzly form."

"I don't." I swatted his hand as he reached for another bacon piece. "I have to dig enough hair out of the drain as it is. Cleaning bear fur out of my tub isn't my idea of a good time."

"Just as well. I don't think I could hold the shower massager with my paw. You'd have to get in with me and wash me," he teased.

I envisioned a dog-wash type scenario, only with me squashed into the tub with Karl's giant bear shape, rubbing shampoo into his fur. I'd need a whole lot of shampoo. "I'm more than happy to wash you as long as you're in your human form." Mmmm, now that was an image.

He wrapped his arms around me. "Let's eat. Then we can take another shower. This time together."

My phone beeped. It had been beeping all morning. Karl had announced repeatedly that he was going to throw it out the window or flush it down the toilet. This time he pulled away and glared at the device.

'I know I know." I turned and put a hand on his chest, grabbing my phone. "I swear when it's your turn and I'm at your den I'll leave it locked in the car."

He raised an eyebrow. "And be running out every five minutes to check on it?"

Maybe. If I could get a cell signal, that is. "Once an hour?"

"Once a day," he growled. "Otherwise I'm going to take my ax to it."

Crap. I was going to suffer some serious withdrawal in

this relationship. "Okay. Once per day I get to check my phone at your place."

I looked down at said phone and grimaced. Kennedy was assisting with injured from a building collapse and wouldn't be back for another three to four days at the earliest. I couldn't wait that long. None of us could wait that long. If Kennedy couldn't help me check out Hit-The-Mark, then I'd just need to do it myself and hope they didn't have some sort of magical doorway that identified me as a shifter.

"I take it from the look on your face we won't be taking that shower together?" Karl asked.

"No. I want to. I really want to, but I need to visit this outfitter and see if I can figure out who is manufacturing the tainted bullets. When I get back, we'll do some shower action, I promise." I handed him a plate of scrambled eggs and bacon, and shooed him over to the table.

Karl scowled. "I don't like the idea of you going after these guys. Let the humans handle it."

We'd been over this twice already this morning. "We need to find a way to negate the self-defense excuse and show the police that what's happening can be classified as a murder, and to do that we need to not be forced to shift when we're shot, and not go rogue. That's a magic thing and it's going to take a while to find something to counter the spell on the bullets. In the meantime, we need to make it so every human on the planet isn't packing these things. If that happens, we'll never be safe shifting. We need to cut off the supply and we need to do it fast."

Every time we were in our animal form and came across a human, we'd be vulnerable. There were penalties for hunting without a license, so very few humans could use the mistaken identity claim, but with the videos online and those five dead scientists in Ketchikan, there would be enough fear flying around that anyone could claim self-defense.

"I really don't want to be out eating berries and get shot," Karl admitted.

"Exactly. And it wouldn't just be 'crap, that hurts' shot either. It would be death—right away or eventually depending on how good of a shot the human was and if we could get to help in time."

Karl leaned back and fixed me with a hard gaze. "I went back to that rogue corpse after you left Ketchikan. I don't like this, Brina. I know you're strong and capable, but that bear was three times your mass and that bullet was killing him, driving him mad. I don't want that to happen to you. And I'm scared that if you take a bullet like that, you'll be dead before you hit the ground."

I didn't really know how to respond to that, so I tried to address his fear. "I'll be careful."

"I'd rather you wait for this Kennedy human," he grumbled.

Me too, but sitting around while other shifters could be dying wasn't going to happen. "She won't be back for days."

He scowled. "You said she saved Brent and Leon when they were shot."

"Saved them by operating and getting the bullet out of them. She's a trauma surgeon. And we wanted her to go in because she's human and she's new to the pack. It's not likely they'd recognize her, either as a local member of the pack, or a shifter."

Karl grunted. "She probably smells like Brent. There's just as good a chance she'd get shot too."

I didn't want to think about that. "Brent would skin me alive if I let anything happen to his mate."

"Well, I'm gonna skin *him* alive if something happens to you," he grumbled.

"I'll be careful." I repeated. "And all this is moot because Kennedy isn't here to go, and I'm not waiting for her to come back. I'm going to go check it out, then head to Brent's to brief him and do some research. Then I have my marketing work to do, which I *should* be doing right now. I'll be back later tonight." I eyed my phone. "I'll call you and let you know when I'm finished. Maybe I'll come over to your den tonight so I can see your place."

The bear muttered something under his breath and didn't speak again until he was done eating.

"I'm going with you."

It was a good thing I didn't have food in my mouth, because I would have choked from surprise at his words.

"Karl, you'll scare the crap out of them. You can't go with me."

He glowered. "If they can't tell you're a wolf, then they won't be able to tell I'm a bear."

How did I put this? "Your eyes glow sometimes, Karl. Actually, they glow a lot and that's not exactly human." It wasn't exactly shifter either, but it was clearly supernatural. "And besides that, you're this huge jacked-up guy who looks like he's two seconds from picking up a car and slamming it through the side of a building. One look at you and the clerk will be pushing that emergency button under the counter."

He considered my words. "I don't like being around humans very much. Never thought that they might be scared of me."

I'm sure the people who bought wood from him, or the guy who had Karl haul his truck out of the ditch were happy to wrap up the transaction and be about their way. "I love that you're a grumpy, scary bear, but this situation calls for a non-threatening, skinny, redheaded woman."

He laughed. I can't recall that I'd heard him laugh before and the sound thrilled me. Humor transformed him, turned a sexy, dark, brooding guy into someone gorgeous and lighthearted. Even the darkness that lurked behind the gold flecks in his eyes receded, nearly vanished, when he laughed.

"Brina, every inch of you screams confidence and determination. If I were looking for someone to rob, I'd pass you right by. You walk around like someone who would beat the ever-loving shit out of anyone who messed with her."

That had to have been the sweetest thing anyone had ever said to me. Forget his comparing my hair to Indian paintbrush, or my freckles to stars in the sky, *this* was romantic.

"Okay. Point taken. But my eyes don't glow gold. That's why you're not going. I'll be careful. And I'll see you tonight."

He scowled. "You'll call me when you leave the shop, is what you'll do. Or text me. I think my phone receives texts."

I picked it up off the table and flipped it open. "Yeah, you can get texts. And yes, I'll let you know when I leave."

"Promise?" He was still glaring at me.

"Promise."

"Good." He stood. "Because otherwise I'd worry. And if I was worried, I might be tempted to go to that store and gnaw on all those humans until they told me where you were. Might even kill them."

Shit. "That won't be necessary, wild man, because I will text you."

He gathered the dishes and went over to the sink, smiling as he turned on the tap. "I miss this running water thing. Wouldn't be too hard for me to do a gravity-fed tank to my sink at one of the dens."

No it wouldn't. And it would make me a lot happier than having to haul water around. But I didn't want him to change the way he wanted to live just for me. He was adapting to my place nicely. I could do the same at his place. I picked up the rest of the dishes and put them in the sink, grabbing a dishcloth to wipe the table.

"Ahia and Raphael were at Brent's yesterday," I said casually. "They examined the bullets and are going to pull some strings to get an antidote or counter spell or something. Seems Raphael knows someone in Hel that might be able to help."

Karl grunted. That was it. Just a grunt and no words. I swear the guy's communication skills made me want to whack him over the head sometimes. He was going to make me spell this out, ask all the embarrassing questions that I hated to ask, but really needed to know the answer to.

"So…how well do you know Ahia?"

"Well enough. She's okay for an angel."

That hardly sounded like he was harboring any unrequited feelings for her. I began to breathe easier, giving the table an extra wipe. "She said you put a wolverine in her bathtub."

Karl grunted. "She bear-tipped me when I was taking a nap. It was a good nap too."

"And the bicycle tires on her Jeep?"

"As I said, it was a really good nap. Can't let her get away with that shit, angel or not." He put his arm around my shoulder, shutting off the water with his other hand. "I've known Ahia since I came to Alaska. She's okay in small doses, but think I'd wind up killing her if I had to spend more than a few hours in her presence, know?"

And that put all my fears to rest. We finished the dishes together, then I left Karl at my house to head to Hit-The-Mark, promising once more to let him know when I left the store. It felt good driving away, knowing he was still in my house. We'd spent the last two nights together. We'd pretty much been in each other's company for four days straight. And I couldn't wait to see him again.

CHAPTER 13

I'd wondered why I'd never heard of Hit-The-Mark when it was practically in my own backyard. Now I knew.

There were two types of sporting goods stores around Juneau—the huge chain stores that carried everything from kayaks to golf clubs, and the specialty stores, which carried eighteen types of kayak oars and attachments in case you planned to fish in the middle of your paddling expedition. If you couldn't get it there, you'd need to go to the internet and wait for a week or two because overnight or two-day shipping to Juneau cost an arm and a leg.

Hit-The-Mark didn't even appear to be a store. It was a shack back off of a long dirt road. It looked like someone had turned a tiny, one-bedroom, pre-fab house into a ramshackle retail location. I sat in my car parked next to two others and wondered whether I dared go in or not. When I'd envisioned myself strolling into something like Cabela's, or at the very least Harry's Bait and Bullet, the idea of being shot in the middle of the store was ludicrous. This place was isolated to the point where I swear I could hear banjos. There were two

212

cars here, but they were probably employees, or belonged to someone who lived in the back room. Were they even supposed to *get* walk-in customers? Had I totally tipped my hand by driving out here?

Only one way to find out. I got out of my car and headed toward the front door. There was clearly a sign that said "open," so I went on in, trying to look like a confused tourist who wasn't sure she had the right place.

Inside the front door was one long room that spread two thirds of the length of the house. There was a doorway to the left of the room that might have led to a bedroom. Along the back wall was another door and a wide passageway next to a bar-style pass-through that was most likely a kitchen/dining area. There was a tiny electronic cash register in the room where I stood next to a scale and some ledgers on an old dining table. Most of the room was filled with stacks of unassembled boxes, fishing lures in plastic packaging, bins of duck calls, scent lures, netting and traps, and small boxes of bullets, the calibers clearly marked on the sides.

"Hello?" I called into the empty room.

A man peeked out from around the pass-through. He was chewing. There were ketchup stains on his blond beard. At least, I hoped they were ketchup stains.

He grinned sheepishly, then vanished only to reappear coming through the doorway, wiping his hands on a paper towel. "Hey. Sorry. Most time I get a customer they've called ahead. I'm surprised you found us out here."

"I did make a few wrong turns," I admitted. This guy seemed nice. Normal. Not the murdering sort. I'd expected a villainous dude twirling a mustache, or a group of squinty-eyed thugs, not cheerful Grizzly Adams with a potbelly.

"Need lures?" He glanced at my clothes, then out at my car in the driveway—the car that wasn't towing a boat and didn't have a kayak strapped to the roof. "Lots of times we come up on the GPS as the closest bait shop to Windfall Creek, even though I really don't have much in the way of bait here. Most of my sales are internet fulfillment as opposed to walk-in traffic."

Windfall Creek was a small, local secret. It was a great place to catch sockeye. Karl and I should come out to fish here sometime.

I shook my head to clear it of images of Karl and me relaxing on the bank of the stream, beers and fishing poles in hand. Or of Karl in his bear form, snatching salmon between two giant paws.

"No, actually I heard you had bullets. Are you Dutch? I e-mailed you a few days ago."

"Oh yeah." He scratched his head. "Yeah, I'm Dutch. I didn't realize you were a local gal or I would have just told you to come on out. Figured you were up around Skagway or something."

"My parents are in Sitka, but I've been in Juneau since I graduated college. You?"

He grinned, placing his fists on his hips. "Vancouver. I moved up here last year. Inherited a bit of money and have always loved fly fishing in this area. I'm calling it my early retirement."

I found myself really hoping this guy wasn't Sharp-Shooter, or that he wasn't knowingly selling the tainted bullets, but I sorta liked him.

"This is definitely a fisherman's paradise. Do you actually sell out of the store, or just online?"

"Both, although my website is a mess right now. I really need someone to whip it into shape, get a decent point-of-sale system, and figure out what websites are best for ads. Maybe run some on Facebook."

Okay, now I was itching to make this guy a customer. I

could seriously turn this spot into a hole-in-the-wall local best-kept-secret kind of thing.

Maybe later. After I'd determined that this Dutch wasn't murdering my people in cold blood, later.

"I'm hoping to pick up some bullets today," I said.

He nodded and walked over to a pile of boxes. "Absolutely. I don't have the biggest supply, but I've got a variety here. What 'cha shooting?"

It was a familiar question. He meant both what firearm was I using and what type of game I planned to hunt.

"I've got a Marlin 1895 and a Remington 870."

The clerk tapped a finger against his lip. "12 gauge on the shotgun? I've got a few boxes of those."

"Yeah, 12 gauge."

He rooted through the stacks. "Which model is the 1895?"

"The GBL."

He pulled out a box and set it aside. "Nice gun. Short range, though. Most women going for moose or bear don't want to be that close in. You hunting deer?"

"Maybe," I replied, trying to see if there were any special markings on the bullet boxes to indicate they might be "special" bullets. "I like to be prepared."

"You probably know this, being a local gal and all, but make sure you've got your licenses in order," he warned. "I swear the Fish and Wildlife wardens here outnumber the hunters. Don't take anything illegal because they *will* find out, and they *will* fine you and confiscate your kill. Some days I think they've got a bunch of crystal balls in their trucks or something."

I chuckled, thinking that I really liked this guy. I took the two heavy boxes he handed me and tucked them under my arm. "I also need some .44's."

He straightened, hands once again on his hips. ".44's?"

I nodded. "I've got a Smith and Wesson 629."

"You *do* like to be prepared," he commented, his words coming out slow and careful.

If you lived in a dicey urban area and wanted to be ready to defend yourself, you had a semi-automatic, a Glock usually. If you wanted to be ready to quickly defend yourself in the wilderness, a revolver was the weapon of choice. And the minimum bullet size you'd need to even think about stopping a bear was .44.

"How good of a shot are you?" he asked.

It was a good question. Tourists that went hunting or hiking and had visions of shooting down a marauding bear either came home with their bullets still in the box or they came home in a box. Wild bear generally stayed clear of humans. Make enough noise, secure your food and trash, keep an eye open for sows with cubs, and you'd be fine. If lightning struck and you did find yourself in a situation with an attacking bear, you'd need to draw and fire fast. And you'd need to be accurate enough to unload your magazine between the animal's eyes. Pumping a bunch of bullets into a bear's chest wasn't going to do much more than piss him off. That was with a normal bear. With a bear shifter, you had even less of a chance of taking him down.

Unless, you had *special* bullets.

"Good enough," I told him.

He eyed me. "Best leave that pistol at home, you know."

"Best be prepared, you know?" I gave him what I hoped was a meaningful glance. "I saw those YouTube videos. Now I don't know if they've been doctored up, or are some special effects, but why take chances? There's a guy in the hiking forums who said you were supplying the sort of thing that could protect a hiker, or hunter, against that happening. If it's all a hoax, well, then I'm a fool. If it's not and I go out there unprepared, then I'm a dead fool. I'd rather be a live fool than a dead one."

His face went blank, his expression suddenly unreadable. "You'll be fine. Those…that…you'll be fine."

"Fine? I'm out hunting with my friend, and some dude stumbles into our camp and turns into a bloodthirsty monster, and we'll be fine with shotguns and rifles? I don't think I could even get to my weapon in time. I'm taking the pistol. And I'd like it to have more than regular .44 bullets in it, if you catch my drift."

He hesitated.

"I'm a woman," I continued. "And not a big woman either. Now I know how to handle myself out in the woods. I grew up in Alaska, so I'm not some wide-eyed tourist. I'm not going to shoot some dude out fishing in his boat or a hiker who I think looks sketchy. I can keep my cool. I'll only shoot if a human comes into my camp and then suddenly becomes not-a-human."

"They're expensive," he finally admitted. "And the chances of you being attacked are probably less than winning the lottery. Why don't you just buy a box of plain old .44s, and forget about monsters in the woods."

I shook my head. "It's kind of hard to forget about monsters in the woods when five people got killed down in Ketchikan. Five."

His mouth opened. "That…that couldn't happen. It wasn't. In Ketchikan?"

He didn't know. I had a feeling the werewolf videos had been staged to create fear in the human public, but if this guy was as connected as I thought he was, then Ketchikan wasn't supposed to happen. What had gone wrong? What had happened?

"Yeah. Five scientists." I pulled out my phone and read the names. "Paper says there was a grizzly attack, but he wasn't really a grizzly, you know? He was one of those monsters. One of the guys shot him—some dude from Oregon. A

Joseph Floyd. But instead of going down, the bear shifter went crazy and killed all five of them. Then he went on a two-day tear through the woods, slaughtering animals, nearly killing some hiker he cornered. Took more than bullets to kill him."

Dutch was breathing hard, a bead of sweat rolling down his forehead. "No. Just…no. Joseph Floyd…" He turned around and grabbed the ledger from next to the cash register. "No…it can't… That didn't happen."

I nodded. "Yes. I've got friends down there and they're terrified. Heck, I'm terrified. Wolf-people. Bear-people. I just want to make sure if I shoot something, it goes down and stays down."

He was pale, his finger shaking as he traced a line down the ledger. "They're supposed stay down, or run away. Supposed to make it an even playing field."

"Well, then that's what I need."

He snapped the book shut. "No, you don't. I don't have those bullets. I can't sell you any."

Don't have them, or won't sell me any? Because those were two different things. "What do you suggest, then?"

"Regular bullets won't kill these monsters, but if you can get four or five well-placed shots into them, you'll take them down. And then you can run away."

"But the guys in Ketchikan shot this bear shifter. When they finally caught and killed him, they dug three bullets out of the guy. So it sounds to me like regular bullets aren't going to cut it. From what this SharpShooter guy says, I believe that. If the guys down in Ketchikan had been shooting these bullets, would they have been okay?"

Dutch clamped his jaw. "This SharpShooter guy isn't someone you should be listening to. Maybe. These bullets are supposed to work but…I'll admit that I sold the special bullets to Joseph Floyd. So maybe they only work on werewolves. Or maybe you need more than one to take down a bear shifter. Maybe he didn't have the special bullets loaded in his rifle. I mean, they're expensive. He might not have wanted to waste them."

"Why buy them if you're not going to be prepared," I argued. "Are you saying they don't work? That this Sharp-Shooter guy is lying? I mean, he referred people to you. You supposedly sell them, right?"

He wiped his face on his sleeve. "I do sell them, but I need… Let me contact the manufacturer. I want to make sure there isn't a quality control issue. I can't tell the bullets apart aside from a mark they put on the end. Maybe they got mixed up in the box before I got them. Maybe they don't work on bear shifters, or maybe there needs to be a special kind for the larger ones. Or maybe it's all fine and that Floyd guy shot the bear shifter with regular bullets. I don't know, but I've got a reputation I'm trying to build here. I'm not gonna sell any more of these until I'm sure they work as intended. The company that sells these to me markets them for werewolf protection. I'm thinking a bear-man is too big, and they don't have the same effect, but I want to check first."

It made sense. You didn't go bear hunting with a .22. Clearly whatever magical coating was on the bullets, it would take more, or different magic, to bring down a grizzly shifter.

Except…the hunters in Kenai had been shooting bear. I thought back on what Brent had said about the dying shifter he'd seen. The hunters were taking trophies. They were all about the hunt. They shot. The shifter transformed, and ran away in pain. Then they tracked it and took the killing shot. Or if the shifter didn't run away, they finished it on the spot.

The only difference was that now the shifters were fighting back after they got shot. It wasn't that surprising. Just like humans, we all had different reactions to situations.

The flight instinct kicked in for some of us, where in others it was the fight instinct. Maybe this wasn't a case of different bullets, but of different reactions from the shifter. And maybe a bullet that caused a grizzly shifter in human form to shift and run would have a lesser effect on an adrenaline-pumped, already shifted grizzly shifter who was pissed at five scientists for trespassing.

Maybe that bear down in Ketchikan was already on the edge of crazy, a hair's breadth from going rogue, and the bullet just pushed him over the edge. And maybe the were-wolves in the videos were dominant, aggressive wolves. There were three videos on the internet. How many videos were there of wolves that shifted and took off, that had to be hunted down? That wouldn't have made the sort of publicity these guys wanted.

Or maybe there were two different types of tainted bullets and, as Dutch suggested, something got switched at the factory. The "hunter and self-defense bullets" somehow got mixed up with the "make the shifter attack" bullets. Whoever was running this wouldn't want the world to know that their bullets hadn't saved Joseph Floyd and his buddies. In fact, their bullets got him killed. Maybe this would help counter some of the hysteria. But in the meantime, I needed to gather as much information as I could about the "supplier."

"I'm not leaving until tonight. Do you think you can call the manufacturer? Get it all cleared up? Perhaps at the latest by this afternoon? I'm local. I can swing back by and get the bullets."

Dutch hesitated and I could see the conflict in his face. These bullets were expensive. He probably made as much selling one or two of them as he did a case full of lures. But he clearly didn't want to be responsible for selling someone faulty goods—goods that might get them killed.

"Let me make a quick phone call."

Dutch walked back into the kitchen area. I could hear him, and because I was a werewolf, I could make out a word here and there from the other side of the phone.

"It's Dutch. I need to double check with you and make sure the supply you gave me is the right stuff."

"Of course. What do you mean?"

"I sold some to a guy, and he was just killed by a bear shifter down in Ketchikan, him and four others with him."

"Maybe he missed."

"They dug bullets out of the bear shifter body after they caught him and killed him. The guy shot him, and he didn't go down. I want to make sure something didn't get mixed up in the shipment."

"No…each one is custom crafted. There's no way…"

"You're not ripping me off, are you? Charging me for special bullets and just marking up regular ones and sending them to me?" Dutch suddenly sounded like a guy that shouldn't be messed with. "If I find out you're screwing me over, then I'm done. And I'll make sure everyone knows that you can't be trusted."

There was an ominous silence, then some words I couldn't make out.

"No, I'm not threatening you. I just want to make sure what I've got is legit. There's a woman here looking to buy some and I don't want to sell her anything that's fake. I don't want to be responsible for anyone's death."

"What woman?"

I tensed at those two words, half expecting to be surrounded at any minute.

"She e-mailed me, but she's a local so it was easier for her to swing by."

"The bullets are fine. Call me back when she leaves."

I didn't like the sound of that. Dutch walked back into the room, a smile plastered on his face. He was still sweating.

"I confirmed they're okay. I've only got two .44 ones. They're five hundred each. Do you want both?"

I caught my breath at the price. That was insane. Although if I really wanted to kill a shifter, I guess five hundred was the price I'd pay. "Uh, just one. I'll have to hope one will do it, right?"

He didn't answer me, instead turning to go through a box and pull an envelope out. I couldn't make out the address but the postmark was Anchorage, and the company name looked like it was Strike or something like that.

"Here." He hesitated handing the envelope to me. "If you grew up in Alaska, then you know that most people up here think these half-animal shifters are harmless. Heck, I've got a live-and-let-live attitude myself. There are bad humans around that kill others. I'm sure some of these shifter people are bad too. And there's nothing wrong with protecting yourself. Just don't cross the line into murder."

That was a very fine line to keep from crossing. I nodded. Then paid for the bullet, wincing at the fact that I needed to use my credit card since I wasn't exactly carrying around hundreds in cash.

Great. Between that and the e-mail, Dutch knew my name, and he knew I lived in Juneau with parents in Sitka. And the supplier wanted him to call back once I'd left.

Which meant there were some calls I needed to make as well. If these people didn't have a problem killing shifters or siccing rogue shifters on humans, then they wouldn't think twice about coming after me…or my family. I was such an idiot. I should have made some shit up about my parents or where I lived, although any idiot with my name and an internet connection could find me. I wasn't exactly off-the-grid. I'd never needed to be.

I'd be okay, but my parents might want to take a vacation in Montana for a few weeks. Or longer.

I got into the car, feeling edgy and aware the whole time. Then I drove a few miles to a more populated area, and pulled over in a parking lot with a restaurant that evidently catered to quite the huge lunch crowd. Later. Lunch later. First I needed to call Brent.

He answered on the first ring. "What's up?"

"Hey, I got a response from Hit-The-Mark so I went on over there this morning and checked it out."

I heard Brent swear softly. "You okay?"

"Yeah. For now. Dutch, the guy at Hit-The-Mark, is definitely selling the bullets. When I mentioned the scientists down in Ketchikan that got killed, he recognized one. He definitely sold Joseph Floyd the bullets, and was pretty freaked out when I told him they'd all been killed by a rampaging bear shifter, even after shooting the rogue."

"So what do you think?"

I sniffed. My stomach growled, and I eyed the fish-fry place across the street. "I think the guy is on the level. He seems like he's got a conscience and was worried that he'd gotten a bad shipment or that he was being screwed over. He called the distributor to check before selling me any of the tainted bullets."

I heard Brent typing something in the background. "Raphael's friend of a friend of a friend mage guy in Hel said the magic bullet from the bear and the two taken from Leon and me are definitely different. Which means they either changed their formula and there's a problem, or they have two different types of bullets, one for killing and another for staging these attacks with rogues, and the shipments got switched."

"I overheard the supplier say they were individually crafted, so any switch that occurred was intentional."

Brent was silent a moment. "Either someone inside their organization is harboring a grudge and wants to bring them down, or they want to drive the public panic into overdrive and are comfortable taking the risk that they may be discredited in the process."

As nice as it would be for there to be a saboteur within their organization, I cringed at the thought that shifters and humans would be collateral damage in their own personal vendetta. Not that the other theory was any more comforting.

"I've got an idea. Do you think Tony could spread a rumor that the family of Joseph Floyd is suing the manufacturer for defective bullets? That he was assured these expensive things would protect him. That the family has proof he shot the bear with one of these special bullets, and it didn't work. They're suing the manufacturer for wrongful death or something?"

Brent barked out a short laugh. "Brilliant. If they're looking to profit on public panic, we'll nip that in the bud."

"We also need to convince Sheriff Murray to go wide with this, to let the public know *not* to go shooting bears or shifters, because clearly these wonder bullets didn't work, and in fact, actually made the situation worse by making the bear go rogue."

"We counter their fear campaign with one of our own." I heard Brent typing in the background. "I'm on it."

"In the meantime, the bullets come from a place up in Anchorage. Strike something, or something Strike."

"I'll lob that one over to Jake. Anchorage is in Swift River Pack territory and I don't want to step on his toes."

Nobody wanted to step on Jakes toes. Tony, the king of social media, would handle the smear campaign. Raphael's friend of a friend of a friend was hopefully working on an antidote. Once the news got out, Dutch would be afraid to sell any more of his bullet supply. And Jake would put his wolves on tracking down the manufacturer. My job was done here, except for a few additional items of note.

"Umm, boss? A couple more things."

"Yeah?" Brent sounded distracted.

"The bullet I bought at Hit-The-Mark was five hundred dollars."

He sucked in a breath. "Okaaaay. We'll reimburse you out of pack funds for that."

Thank goodness. "And this Dutch knows who I am. I'm not sure if he'll bend under pressure and tell the supplier or not, but just in case I'm going to tell my parents to go on an impromptu vacation, and I'm going to stay at Karl's den for a few weeks."

Gah, it made me sound like I was such a coward, running and hiding behind a grizzly shifter just in case the big bad human came after me with a rifle.

"It's a good idea. I'll contact you there if I need you, or if I hear anything more. And be careful."

"Thanks."

I disconnected and dialed Karl. And because I was starving, I got out, locked my car, and headed over to the restaurant.

Karl picked up. And grunted.

"Done. And still alive," I teased.

"Good. I'm glad to hear it."

"We've done pretty much all we can do on this, so I'm going to come home and get my marketing stuff done, wrap up some things and maybe sub some work out. Then I was hoping I could hide out at your den for a while like a fugitive from justice. You can protect me in case the bad-guys come looking for me, right? Maybe I'll wear a frilly dress, and gasp and faint a lot and you can walk around shirtless and grunt. Oh wait, you do that all the time anyway."

Mmmm. This place had salmon. Or maybe I should get the fried halibut. And coleslaw. Yeah. I'd pick up extra in case Karl was still hanging around my house, although it would be cold by the time I got there.

"What happened?" he asked. "Not that I ain't thrilled to have you at my den for as long as you want. Can you be shirtless too? Hate those frilly dresses, although I plan to make you gasp and make all kinds of other noises."

Such a bear.

"The Dutch guy at Hit-The-Mark knows my e-mail, what I look like, and my name from my credit card. He seems like a pretty good guy, but things are about to get hot, and if he tells the manufacturer about me…well, I'm not all that hard to find. A Google search and they'd be on my doorstep."

I heard Karl growl.

"Down, wild man."

"Don't like this, Brina. Don't like it at all."

I rolled my eyes. "Fine. Meet me at my house if you're that worried. You can hover over me and glower at the doorways while I finish my work."

"You coming straight home?"

I'll admit it was kinda nice having someone fuss like this over me. "As soon as I score one of these fish sandwiches here. Want one?"

A familiar sound roared through my ears, and a millisecond later I felt the pain, felt heat scorch through my back. The phone fell from my hands to clatter along the porch decking. I crumpled, staring in amazement at the red pooling beneath me. I'd been shot. Right in front of a restaurant full of humans, I'd been shot.

And the bullet burning in the muscles of my back wasn't a normal bullet.

Pain ripped through me. My vision blurred to white. I felt myself writhe on the porch of the restaurant, bones twisting, muscles contorting. Shifting. I was shifting within seconds, and the agony of it was scrambling my thoughts. I felt another bullet rip into my flesh. Someone screamed and the sound was like a knife through my ears.

Thirsty. Hot. Cold. Pain. So much pain. Who was hurting me? I needed to bite them. I needed to kill them so they'd stop hurting me. All I saw was white and the heat signatures of living beings as they ran through the parking lot from the restaurant. All I heard was a buzzing sound and gibberish. All I could smell was a sickening sweet, foul odor—hot melted plastic and rotten bananas.

I stood on four feet and stumbled as I tried to run down the stairs. All I wanted was to bite, to rend flesh, to tear limbs and disembowel any living thing I encountered. Only then would the pain stop. Only then would this agony tearing through my body cease.

I could see people running in the parking lot. They'd

done this. If I killed them the pain would go away. This time I managed to stay on my feet and run, gaining on one of the humans, snarling as I coiled myself to launch at her.

A scream filtered through the static of my mind, then something large plowed into me, pinning me to the ground. I spun around, teeth snapping, claws digging deep into flesh. Something heavy was on top of me, holding me still, something that bled on me, that grunted as my teeth sank into his arm.

Pain. Pain. The monster on top of me flipped me over, slamming my face into the gravel of the parking lot and pinning me down. I felt him dig claws into my skin, but as much as I snarled and thrashed, I couldn't escape the iron grasp of whoever was holding me. Something slimy slipped out of my body. And another. My stomach twisted and I tasted bile on my tongue. Pain. Pain.

Then I threw up, gagging and choking as my vision started to clear. God, it hurt. It hurt so bad, worse than anything I'd ever felt before. I was shaking in agony, but the urge to kill anything and everything was gone. All I wanted now was to curl up in a ball and die.

I couldn't. Strong arms held me to the ground. I couldn't move. I could do nothing but dry heave and strain against the strong force pinning me in place. Then the brutally strong arms that held me gently rolled me over onto my back.

Holy shit. Turning over nearly made me pass out. My thoughts swirled, then surfaced and in the white of my vision a face appeared—a gorgeous guy with scruffy whiskers and wavy, dark blond hair. Hazel eyes stared into mine, gold flecks like lights sparking through his irises.

I bit him. I couldn't help it.

He grunted, then a strange grin creased his face, as if my assault only made him love me more. Then he bent his head to my side and I felt him licking one of the wounds where I'd been shot. What was with the licking? Every time I got injured he seemed to lick me. I growled, and heard him laugh, but that darkness still lurked behind the gold in his eyes.

"Come back to me Brina," I heard him say.

Something was hurting me. Someone was hurting me. I needed to kill them. I needed to kill everyone to take the pain away. But even as I thought that, I realized the pain was receding.

"Brina, my red-headed wolf-girl. I'll never let anything happen to you. I'll never let anyone hurt you. I want to lock you in my den and make love to you and feed you for the rest of our lives, but I know you've got a different idea of what you want for your life. And I'll work with that. I'll do anything for you. Anything."

There was a burning sensation working its way through my muscles and nerve endings. I blinked and stared into my grizzly shifter's gorgeous eyes.

"Can you shift back?"

I closed my eyes and tried, knowing that it would help me heal, and that the humans who'd been running and screaming in the parking lot would be a whole lot more sympathetic to a naked woman with gunshot wounds than a wolf with huge teeth and gunshot wounds.

It hurt, but with every twist of bone and muscle, I felt the horrible burning pain recede just a little. In what seemed like hours I was human once more, gasping and wincing as I looked up into my bear's eyes.

"There." He smiled at me. "That's better, darlin'. Now I get to wait on you hand and foot while you lay in my bed and recover."

Like hell I would. It had taken Brent a few weeks to be back to himself, and he still had the scars, but he'd been up and fighting pretty much as soon as Kennedy had dug the bullet out of him. If my Alpha could grin and bear it, then so could I. Gritting my teeth, I struggled to sit up, then thought better of it. Guess I wasn't quite the level of an Alpha yet. Maybe if I gave myself another half an hour.

But in the meantime, at least I could ask questions. "Karl. How…how did you get here? How did you find me?"

He bent down and pressed his forehead against mine. "Remember I said I could teleport between my dens?"

Man, this hurt. Hurt, hurt, hurt. "Yes. Waypoints. Is your den near here?"

He shook his head, and the smile on his face warmed me.

"Brina, it's not just your house. *You* are my den too. You're home to me. In fact, you're more home to me than any of my homes, my dens. Anywhere you are, I can be there. And I feel when you need me. I know when some asshole has shot you and you're in pain."

"Well, it didn't take psychic powers, dude. I was on the phone with you when I got shot." This time I managed to sit up, although I was holding onto Karl. Oooo, and I'd ripped him up good. And bit him. "Sorry about hurting you."

He grunted. "I'm fine. I'll be better once I've got you at my den, though."

Sirens sounded off in the distance. Humans were nearby, talking in hushed voices. I breathed deeply, trying to focus. "I need to get him. Shot me. The one who shot me. I need to get him."

Karl growled, and a bolt of fear shot through me at the sound. "*I* will get him."

I snarled back. "I'm not weak. Joking about the frilly dress stuff. Just give me an hour or two and I can trail his scent and track him down.

The bear shifter's eyes glowed gold. "You are not going anywhere in an hour or two. I'll track him down, but I'm not going to do shit until I'm sure you're okay."

I closed my eyes, not wanting to argue. The siren noise stopped. The police must be here. "Can you get me some clothes? There's some in my trunk." I didn't exactly want to make a police statement or walk around naked.

He hesitated. "You're not going to run off, are you?"

Umm, like I could run anywhere right now. Besides I was naked, and another shift would put me down for a twelve-hour nap with my injuries. "No. Promise."

He pulled away, helping me rise to my feet before walking across the street and popping the trunk of my car. There was blood everywhere—all over the gravel, the porch, the steps, covering Karl, soaking my clothing, coating the bullets that lay on the sidewalk. These weren't rifle bullets like the one we'd taken from the grizzly shifter, or the ones used to shoot Leon and Brent. These were from a pistol, a 9mm by the look of them.

A pistol. Shooting a shifter in the woods with a hunting rifle and claiming self-defense was a plausible excuse. Shooting me in outside a restaurant with a pistol, and with a human witness, didn't allow for anything except attempted murder. This attack wasn't to stir up fear of shifters, or to put my head on a wall. This attack was meant to kill me, to ensure I didn't continue investigating. Was this guy so stupid that he didn't realize he'd need to kill a whole lot more than just me to keep the wolves from his door?

A wound decorated my side, and I was sure there was an equally horrific one on my back. They'd scar. They'd take weeks, if not months, to fully heal. If Karl hadn't dug the bullets from me, I would have died, the magic in them hindering my ability to heal. Even with them out, my healing was slower than it should have been.

I winced, turning to face Karl as he trotted back across the road, clothes in hand.

"Someone shot her," a woman told the police. "She was

just standing by the door, looking at the menu and talking on the phone when someone shot her. My husband and I were walking across the parking lot and saw the man. We dove behind one of the cars, thinking he was one of those crazy mass-murder guys, then he shot her a second time."

I tried to wave off two paramedics who were intent on getting me on a stretcher. "I'm a shifter," I told them. "My boyfriend dug the bullets out of me. I'll be fine."

"Doesn't look fine," one of them grumbled. "At least let us bandage you up before you bleed all over your clean clothes."

I complied, since Karl was refusing to give me my clothing until they looked me over. It gave me time to hear the rest of the woman's story. I was completely the victim, an innocent woman shot by some crazy man in the parking lot. The fact that I'd turned into a wolf didn't seem to bother her at all. According to her story, I'd shifted, and was trying to attack the shooter and save the humans. The shooter fled, and I collapsed from my wounds, saved by my gorgeous boyfriend who'd arrived like the hero from a romance novel. Only romance novel heroes didn't sprout claws and dig bullets from their girlfriend's furry body. Or maybe they did.

Thank goodness for selective memory. I hadn't injured anyone. I'd been shot in front of witnesses, apparently a human minding my own business. Then as a werewolf, I'd acted to protect the terrified humans.

I wasn't sure how I felt about being sort of a victim, but this was a story we could spin to our advantage, and we could use it to counteract those horrible videos, maybe get people to start believing that we weren't monsters to be killed. And the best part of her story was that I heard her description of my assailant.

Six foot tall. Roughly one-eighty. Tan. Bald. Clean shaven. Broad nose and square face with a barbed-wire tattoo down his neck. Yes, she could describe him to a sketch artist. And you'd better believe we'd have a copy of that sketch before the sun was down.

By the time the paramedics were done with me I felt like I'd been swaddled in gauze and surgical tape. I gave my statement to the police, reiterating that we were being targeted by people who were trying to eradicate shifters. A hate crime. Attempted murder. And if I hadn't scared the guy off, he might have turned his gun on the witnesses just to cover it up.

Slowly everyone began to leave. The restaurant gave me a bag of fish sandwiches. I refused a ride from the ambulance and made my slow and painful way over to my car.

Karl took my keys.

"Um, what do you think you're doing?" At least I could talk in complete sentences now, and wasn't gasping for air with every step.

"Driving you to Brent's. I called him from your phone when you were talking to the police. He wants you at the Alpha house."

I totally understood why. We were a pack. He was my Alpha. There would be three dozen wolves there to sniff me over and fuss over me, reassuring themselves that I was okay. I'd go. And I'd probably accept Brent's offer to spend the night there, just to recover more of my strength. But that didn't mean I was going to let Karl drive.

"Do you even know how to drive? You don't have a vehicle. I got the impression you'd never had a vehicle."

"I drive," he huffed out. "How else was I supposed to steal all those cars and trucks when I was a kid?"

Huh? Karl helped me into the passenger seat of my car, and I let him because I got the feeling he was trying to tell me something big—something he didn't tell just anybody.

"Yeah, I stole cars. That's the least horrible thing I did when I was a kid. From when I was old enough to reach the pedals, probably six, until about ten. 'Cause when you're that age and the cops manage to catch you, they just take you home to your parents. Especially if you look at them with big eyes and tell them you're running away from home because Mom wouldn't let you have any ice cream."

I caught my breath, not sure how to respond. So instead of saying anything, I watched him close the car door, walk around, and get into the driver's side. He didn't speak again until he'd started the car and backed it out of the parking lot.

"When I was really little, I was the bait," he said softly. "Cute little kid in his mother's arms. People would stop to help her, then Dad would come out of nowhere and knock them out. Not that Mom needed Dad to help her. Lots of times she just dropped me on the ground and took the mark out herself. We'd steal all their stuff. Sometimes Dad got carried away and the human didn't live. We had to stop that ruse when I was about eight because people don't feel safe stopping for a woman with an older child."

I reached out a hand and placed it on top of his. He turned his palm-upward, and entwined his fingers around mine. "I'm sorry. I'm so sorry."

My heart ached, imagining Karl as a little cub with such horrible parents.

"Wasn't like I was unwilling, Brina," he said gruffly. "I had no problem jacking those cars. I stole. And when I was old enough, I didn't think twice about hurting someone to take their things. Humans were there for us to use. I have a hard time being around them even now, because I just don't see them as anything but prey."

"You were just a child," I countered. "You didn't know any better."

He shot me a wry glance. "Maybe at five. But when you get to be ten, that 'I didn't know no better' isn't an excuse. I did it 'cause I wanted to, 'cause it's what I'd done my whole life and I didn't see anything wrong in it."

"You're not like that now," I said softly.

"I am. That's the problem, Brina. I am like that now. And you've got your neighbors and human friends, and all those damned werewolves in your pack. I respect Brent. I respect Ahia and that angel she's shacked up with. I respect you. Hell, think I might actually love you. But the rest of them…"

"Karl, give it a chance. You spent the whole day with my pack at the barbeque last year. You had fun. And you didn't kill anyone."

A slow grin curled up his mouth. "I wanted to just get a burger and go, but I saw you and wanted to see if I could get you to bed. No, I was determined to get you to bed, even if I had to hang out with those damned wolves for a week."

Little did he know he could have gotten me to bed within the first five minutes of arriving at the party.

"See? Just think of all the great sex we're going to have and you'll be able to tolerate neighbors and random humans at the Walmart, and my pack family. And it's not like you'll need to do that all the time. I've promised to go out into the wild with you and stay at one of your dens, isolated from shifter and human. If I can manage to only check my cell phone once a day while I'm with you, then you can refrain from killing anyone and actually use silverware while making small talk with others for an hour or so each day. See? Compromise?"

He laughed, squeezing my hand. We rode in silence for a bit, and I noticed that he actually was a good driver, not at all what I'd expected. But then again, Karl had never been what I'd expected.

"Member how I told you my mom is a grizzly shifter?" he asked out of the blue.

"Yeah?" I waited, holding my breath.

He sighed. "Well, I don't really like others to know about it, but my dad is a demon."

That needed a moment to process. A *demon*? His father was a *demon*? It wasn't unheard of for demons to impregnate human women, either via rape or an uninhibited one-night stand, but a shifter woman? She would know exactly what she was sleeping with, and although rape was still a possibility, she could have been willing. No, she had to have been willing, unless that "Dad" Karl had referenced was someone else.

Karl turned to watch my face intently. "Mom was in love with him. Still is. They're like the Bonnie and Clyde of the supernatural world. When I was a cub we were all over North America stealing cars, robbing banks, pulling off scams. We stayed in places that rented by the week, or lived in stolen cars, or broke into houses of people that were on vacation and stayed there. Sometimes we broke into houses and tied people up in the basement and stayed there, but we always had to leave in a day or two before anyone found out. No school. Hell, I don't even think I have a birth certificate. The only reason they had me was because they thought a baby, a kid, would be useful in scamming people. I ran away at eighteen and haven't seen them since."

I caught my breath imagining what kind of childhood that must have been. "Did they track you down? Are you hiding out in the Alaska wilderness from them?"

His laugh was bitter. "Hardly. They never bothered to look for me. Weren't like they were mad or nothing, they were just too busy doing their thing to care. Once I was past the cute kid stage I wasn't of much use to them, beyond another mouth to feed. Yeah, I could help steal shit and whack any human who resisted over the head, but they could do that on their own. One night we were robbing a convenience store, and the clerk shot Dad. He beat the guy to death with his own shotgun, then stuffed him in the ice-cream freezer. Then he turned around and beat the shit out of me for not killing the clerk before he got a shot off. I left that night. Got no idea where they are. Honestly, they've probably killed each other by now. They used to get pretty violent when they fought and they fought a lot."

I think my heartache hurt worse than my bullet wounds. "You were eighteen and on your own with no one to help you? No money, no car, nothing?"

He nodded. "And I didn't really know how to be a bear. I grew up in cities, surrounded by tall buildings and thousands of humans, exhaust fumes in my nose. I rarely shifted form as a kid, didn't know how to hunt, to find shelter. Until I ran away, I hadn't had a meal that wasn't premade at a convenience store or out of a can. I made a lot of mistakes with the other shifter bears at first down in Montana and Idaho. Got in a lot of fights that I'm surprised I walked away from. I managed though, and got myself territory up here with some nice dens. Managed to not kill anyone yet. Managed to have civilized relations with a few other grizzly shifters and the local wolf pack Alpha." He grinned, a sudden bit of sunlight in the gloom of his revelation. "And you wolves *do* put on a mighty fine barbeque."

The grin wasn't enough. I leaned over to bury my face in his chest, hugging him tight, tears stinging behind my eyelids. "God, Karl. I'm so sorry you had to go through that. That was no way for a shifter, let alone a bear cub, to live."

His arm wrapped around my shoulders, nearly crushing me and I felt him kiss the top of my head. "I'm not good at this, Brina. Don't have any experience on how mates are supposed to be. And I'm not a smart man. Mom only taught me enough math to run a con. I never went to school or college. I like fishing, chopping wood, and my books. I like to move around every few weeks. I sleep outdoors more often than I sleep inside. And I'm in my bear form at least half the time."

But he *was* smart. He'd taught himself to read. Had a den stacked high with books, and no doubt had the same quantity of reading material in each of his other dens. He was wise, had good judgement, was thoughtful. I didn't need a guy who could do advanced calculus in his head, I needed someone with a good heart, and in spite of his childhood, in spite of what he said, I got the feeling that Karl definitely had a good heart. How a demon and an immoral bear shifter had raised this strong, sweet, rock of a man, I'll never know.

I smiled, inhaling the wild scent of his skin. "Well, I'm not having sex with you as a bear, so you may need to be human more often if you want to get laid. Otherwise I'm fine with the rest. If you need some alone time, just tell me when to expect you back, then go scoop salmon out of a stream for a few weeks. I'll be there when you come back."

The tightness left his body. "Think you might want to come scoop salmon out of a stream for a few weeks with me now and then?"

I had a flexible job, as long as I could log on now and then, and I was sure Brent would understand. It was going to be a challenge meshing my personality to Karl's roaming-bear lifestyle, but I'd make it work.

"Absolutely. Although I'll be on the bank catching the salmon you toss my way. We'd starve if it were up to me to catch fish. Now take me hunting, and it's another story."

By the time we got to the Alpha house, there were already a dozen cars in the driveway. I was assaulted by concerned werewolves before I'd even crossed the threshold, escorted to a sofa and fussed over. Everyone wanted to see my wounds. More people arrived, some of them carrying casseroles.

Through it all Karl hovered, his hand occasionally on my hair. I could feel his tension; practically hear the growl he was keeping locked tight in his throat. I knew he wanted nothing more than to carry me off to his den where he could stand guard over me. Even though he knew these wolves were my family, the bear in him was seeing all of them as a threat.

I pulled his hand over and squeezed it. "You need a break?"

"Yeah," he rumbled. "But I don't feel like I can leave you."

"I'm safe here. I know everyone rushing around, stuffing chicken tomato gratin under my nose is driving you crazy, but there are two dozen wolves here who would die for me.

Brent is here. My Alpha. A wolf is always safe with their Alpha."

Karl might have not had the typical shifter childhood, and grizzlies didn't structure their society like we do, but my words seemed to sink in. I felt some of the tension ebb away. He looked over at Brent, felt the strength and determination emanating from the werewolf, and knew viscerally that I was right. Karl might be a monster of a bear, but these wolves would protect me equally well.

"Go," I told him. "Turn furry and run through the woods. Shred some trees. Eat raw fish. Flip a few boulders. Get it out of your system, then come back."

He hesitated. "Don't want to leave you."

Okay, clearly another tactic was necessary. "I need you calm. You're ready to jump out of your skin and that's making me feel like I need to be at the ready, like I'm about to be attacked at any minute. Go do something to calm your-self down. Whatever it takes. I'll heal faster, I'll be more relaxed if you are."

He considered my words. "Okay. Need to borrow your car, though."

I'd hardly imagined Karl going for a quiet drive in the country to settle down, but if that's what it took, so be it. He was clearly a careful driver. "Sure. No problem."

He bent down and kissed the top of my head. "I'm gonna go do something, then I'll be back."

I watched him stride off, feeling a tad bit uneasy about what Karl's "something" was that he was about to do. Hope-fully it didn't involve anything that would get him arrested.

* * *

I WOKE up to a much quieter house. Once everyone had come through with their food offerings to check on me and reassure themselves that I wasn't dying, Brent had kicked everyone out to let me sleep. I was still on the sofa, because werewolf anxiety meant letting me sleep in peace in a bedroom was out of the question. I needed to be nearby, so they could see me as well as smell and hear me. Hovering over my bedside would have not only been creepy, but would have given the impression that I was at death's door. So instead I was napping on the couch with throw pillows and a blue crochet afghan while the few remaining pack members ate, drank coffee, and spoke in hushed voices that I could clearly hear.

"There better be a plate of chicken and dumplings over here, stat," I announced, easing myself upright. My wounds protested, but I felt that if I needed to, I could defend myself. Or at least quickly move to hide behind the couch.

"Here." Brent stuffed a handful of pills in my palm and handed me a glass of water. "Antibiotics. Per Kennedy, who also said we need to change your bandage and put some of this cream stuff on it."

I obediently swallowed the pills, but was far more enthusiastic about the plate piled high with food that Zeph was handing me. Shifters burned a lot of energy healing. I'd had sleep, and now I desperately needed food. Then I'd probably need more sleep.

I scarfed down the food, happy to see Zeph bringing a second plate to me. Kennedy must still be up in Anchorage, but I saw Brent, Zeph, Matt, Tina, and Ahia. My security detail watching over me as I healed. It was a bit overkill, but I was grateful that they cared enough to make sure the pack heavy-hitters were here.

But where was Karl? I went to check my phone for the time and couldn't find it. How long had I been asleep? More to the point, how long did it take an agitated bear shifter to drive around and calm down? I hoped I had enough gas in the car, otherwise Karl was in for a long walk back. Somehow I doubted he had money or a credit card on hand for a quick trip to the pumps.

I heard the door slam open. Everyone turned toward the noise, their eyes widening, their mouths dropping open. Karl appeared, dragging a whimpering man that he deposited on the floor in front of me like an offering.

It was Dutch from Hit-The-Mark. And beyond looking rumpled with a black eye and a few bruises, he was basically in one piece. Karl had clearly exercised great restraint. I was grateful. But I would have been more grateful if he hadn't basically assaulted and kidnapped someone that we really needed on our side.

"Karl? This isn't helping our public image," Brent commented drily. I could tell he was amused, that if he hadn't been guarding me, he might have done the same.

Dutch sniffed, wiping the crusted blood under his nose. "I didn't know. I tell you, I didn't know until you showed up and told me. I was completely surprised when I heard she'd been shot."

"You told them her name, her e-mail, what car she was driving and the license plate," Karl snarled. "What did you expect was going to happen?"

"They needed to keep track of who bought the bullets in case there was a complaint or a lawsuit. That way they could counter claims that the bullets were defective. I swear I didn't expect him to try to kill her." Dutch looked up at me. "Please believe me. I really didn't want anyone getting killed."

"Yet you sell bullets that kill shifters," Brent commented. There was a light in his eyes that I didn't really trust. Between him and Karl, I was pretty sure this guy wasn't going to live long. I exchanged a quick glance with Ahia, figuring that we'd need to intervene if necessary.

"Only for self-defense!" Dutch protested. "Every store

that sells pistols isn't advocating murder. I even told her to be careful and not go just shooting someone because they changed into a wolf. Didn't I?"

"Yes, he did." I put out a hand toward Karl. "Stop. Both you and Brent stop right now. This guy didn't do anything wrong, but he can tell us about the people who are. He can tell us about their operation, who they are, where they live. Right?"

Dutch nodded. "Mason Sharpe. He's my distributor. He lurks in all the hunting and hiking forums and posts as SharpShooter, referring people to buy from me, then he wholesales me the bullets to sell through my store. Although now that he's probably going to be arrested, I'll probably have to deal with one of the other owners."

I took a careful breath and got to my feet. "How many owners are there? And this is that Strikes company in Anchorage? They're the ones manufacturing the bullets?"

"Yeah." Dutch shot a wary glance at Karl, then also stood. "Three Strikes. The owners are Curtis Worth, Jesse Baker, and Mason Sharpe. I've never met Curtis or Jesse. They handle some other part of the business up in Anchorage. Mason runs the self-defense part of the company. He's spreading the word about the products and in charge of approving distributors. There aren't many of us, and it's hard to get supply. That's why they cost so much, and instead of selling a box of bullets, we usually only sell one or two at a time."

"And Mason is here, in Juneau?" He had to have been to get to where I was so quickly after the call with Dutch. He must have left right away, then seen me, and/or my car in the parking lot and decided to take me out of the equation.

"Yeah. If I don't have a certain bullet and he has it in stock, he runs it by. Otherwise he needs to call up to Anchorage and have them make it special for me."

"Which means the elf is in Anchorage," Brent commented.

"Elf?" Dutch blinked in surprise.

"So you don't know about an elf? They've never discussed how the bullets work?"

"No, that's proprietary information. They're hardly going to tell me that. And they've never mentioned an elf."

I believed him. The only thing for us to do, beyond giving this added information to Jake, was to wait for the police to do their job and arrest this guy. In the meantime, I was going to hang out at Karl's den, where no one would shoot me, and where he'd most likely eviscerate anyone who came within a mile of the cabin.

"Tell them the rest," Karl growled at Dutch. "Tell them about the meeting."

Dutch eyed him and took a few steps back. "Um, Mason called me right before this guy showed up. He said he was concerned about the supply and was recalling all the bullets. I'm to meet him tonight with all my stock and he'll pay me cash for them."

The guy was trying to cover his trail, get them off the market. And I got the impression that Dutch wasn't meant to walk out of that meeting alive.

"We'll be there," Brent said. "I'll put eight wolves on the perimeter, and two of us will close in once Mason shows up."

"No," Karl countered. "You have ten wolves on the perimeter, and I'll take this guy down."

"We need him alive, Karl," I reminded him. "For questioning, and to also show both the police and the public that we play by their rules." I wasn't thrilled that he'd roughed Dutch up, when the guy would probably have come in on his own once he knew I'd been shot.

"I'll try to not kill him."

"And I'm going," I added.

There was a chorus of "no you're not"s.

"I'll stay back, along the perimeter. If it helps, I'll stand near Ahia. And I'll wear a protective vest." I met each of their eyes in turn. "I'm second in this pack. I was the one who was shot. I'm going."

Karl reached out and touched my hair, his fingers gently smoothing downward to rest on my shoulder. "Okay. Be careful?"

I put my hand on top of his. "You're the one taking this guy down, *you* be careful. And don't kill him."

He grinned. "I'll try my best."

"Do I have to go?" Dutch asked.

I tried to smile reassuringly, but in all honesty we couldn't ensure Dutch, or any of us, would come out of this alive. "Yes. Yes, you have to go too. After all, you're the one with the bullets."

It turns out Karl had my phone. He'd used it to call Brent, then called up the address on the GPS that I'd used to find Hit-The-Mark. Sneaky bastard. The calming drive plus punching Dutch in the face didn't have the stress-reduction effects I'd hoped. The bear was on edge. Which worried me. He'd admitted to problems controlling murderous impulses, and I feared being face-to-face with my attacker would put him over the edge.

"Hate this fucking vest thing," he snapped, yanking at the thick Kevlar plates. Ahia was driving, because Brent hadn't ordered a vest big enough for Karl so he couldn't stretch his arms out straight in front of him to grip the steering wheel. And, evidently, nobody trusted a werewolf who'd been shot around noon to be driving eight hours later.

"You need to wear the vest," I repeated. "He'll probably shoot you on sight, and nobody wants a giant prehistoric bear going rogue just outside of the city limits."

"Ooo, I do!" Ahia exclaimed. "We could film it, dub in some audio, and voila! Paleolithic Grizzly versus old growth pine. I've got the perfect soundtrack."

Karl growled at her. I wanted to growl at her. Normally I found Ahia downright hysterical, but I was on edge too, and I was still in pain from being shot. Twice.

We pulled up roughly a mile from our meeting spot. Ahia drove the Jeep off-road to hide it and I nearly passed out from being bounced around the back seat. Maybe this wasn't such a good idea after all. I probably should have stayed at the Alpha house on the couch and slept.

"You okay to hike this?" Ahia sent a concerned look through the rearview mirror.

"Yep." Might as well act like this wasn't a big deal. I'd insisted on coming, and I wasn't about to wimp out now and stay in the Jeep. Especially because that would mean Ahia would have to stay with me on guard duty, and as our pack angel, it was important for her to be present in case everything went horribly wrong.

Please Lord, don't let everything go horribly wrong.

"I'm gonna run on ahead. If I can run in this motherfucking thing," Karl grumbled. "Brina, you good?"

No. "Yep, I'm good. Go. Be careful. Don't kill him."

"I'll try my best." Karl hopped out of the Jeep and vanished into the woods. Of course, since he was a bear shifter, he sounded like an elephant plowing through bushes. Hopefully he'd get there early enough to sit quietly out of the way because I was pretty sure even a human could hear him from a mile away.

Ahia purposely kept her pace slow to accommodate me, keeping me in her line of sight the whole agonizingly long mile. I was pretty sure she was poised to catch me in case I fell over. My babysitter. I should have stayed behind. Here I was, injured, pretty much useless, tying up one of our most powerful pack members to watch me. Next time I wouldn't let my pride get in the way of my common sense.

We got to our spot and I sat down, resting my back

against a tree. We'd hunted as a pack so many times that this felt familiar. I knew where Brent had stationed the others, could scent a few of them in the air. Ahia stripped, and with a flash of light shifted into her wolf form. Her eyes glinted silver in the moonlight, her black and tawny fur ruffling in the breeze.

We waited. Half an hour later, a truck pulled into the camping area and Dutch got out, carrying a box. He looked around then stood, highlighted by the truck's headlights. I wanted to hiss at him to get down. Idiot. I could collectively feel the wolves around me roll their eyes.

A branch snapped and a man emerged into the lit-up camping area. I snapped to attention, realizing that I hadn't even known he was there or heard him arrive. Had he been here before us? Did he know he was surrounded by shifters?

"Mason." There was relief in Dutch's voice. "I wasn't sure you were coming. Why couldn't you just meet me at the shop? This all seems ridiculously cloak-and-dagger."

I pursed my mouth in admiration, realizing that Dutch was a far better actor than I'd ever thought.

"Those the bullets?" Mason's voice was deep, echoing through the woods. He was an imposing guy, tall and muscled with a shaved head, just as the witness to the shooting had described. I couldn't see his neck tattoo from here, but I could clearly see the pistol at his hip and the rifle in his hand.

"Yeah, all the unsold ones. I also have a list of everyone that's bought them since I began distributing. I keep all that stuff for follow up. Repeat customers, you know." Dutch's acting skills were falling apart under pressure and he was now babbling. He shoved the box at Mason, and when the man didn't take it, he set it on a tree stump.

"Open it. Give me the .308s."

Dutch did as requested. I could see him trembling even from my distance.

Mason examined the bullets, then loaded them into the rifle. "Get the others, and put them in this bag."

He shrugged a small nylon sack off one shoulder and plopped it onto the ground. This was starting to feel like a bank heist. I wondered why Karl hadn't made his move yet. Did Mason have buddies in the tree line somewhere? He'd been invisible to me, so perhaps he had a dozen armed guys that none of us could see.

Dutch bent to pick up the sack, and the brush exploded with action. Karl rushed into the clearing along with four wolves. Zeph leapt on top of Dutch, pinning him to the ground and covering him with his tawny-furred body. Matt clamped his jaws around the box of bullets and took off into the woods. Just as Mason pointed and fired the rifle at Zeph, Karl plowed into him, knocking him to the ground.

Ahia shot me a quick "stay here" glance and took off.

I held my breath, praying that the bullet hadn't hit Zeph. If it had, then Dutch was dead. There was another gunshot. I saw the motion of wolves moving through the woods, closing in so that if Mason got away from the camping area, he wouldn't be able to flee far.

Karl was wrestling with the man, rolling on the ground. He'd managed to knock the rifle out of Mason's hand, but the man had grabbed his pistol and fired off several shots right into Karl's chest.

I heard him grunt. I smelled blood. And I snarled with fury to realize that he'd taken the vest off. Once this was over I was going to kill him. I was going to pin him to the ground and rip his limbs off.

And now I prayed that the pistol had only held regular bullets and not the spelled ones, because in spite of Ahia's comment in the car, a rogue prehistoric bear wasn't a good thing.

Mason kept shooting into Karl. And no one could help him because Brent, Ahia, and Tina were too busy keeping Zeph corralled away from Dutch, who was writhing on the ground.

Ahia transformed in a flash of light and wrapped her arms around Zeph, shocking him with a jolt of electricity, then hitting him on the head with a rock. Then Brent and Tina held him down, while Ahia frantically clawed the bullet from his shoulder.

Mason pushed Karl aside enough to get his arm free and hit him on the head with the pistol grip. Karl's head jerked to the side and Mason slid free, jumped to his feet and ran.

I did the same, not because I was worried that Mason would escape. He was surrounded. His deadly rifle had been knocked across the camping area and was somewhere under the truck. He had an empty pistol. No, it wasn't Mason I was worried about, it was Karl who had taken an entire magazine of bullets to the chest and been hit in the head.

Shifters can survive a lot of damage. Getting shot usually isn't a death sentence. But getting shot that many times could overwhelm our healing abilities. We weren't immortal. Even Ahia wasn't technically immortal.

So I ran, gasping with pain the whole way and not caring. I needed to get to him. And when I heard another gunshot, I put on a burst of speed, plowing into the clearing.

Karl was moving, but he was on the ground in a huge pool of red. I threw myself down beside him, scrabbling to pull the tattered, blood-soaked shirt away from his chest. He growled and I froze, hair rising along the back of my neck. Because that was the growl of something very pissed-off, something inhumanly strong, something that could take my head off with one swipe of a giant paw.

Karl's eyes were completely gold. I caught my breath, holding still like a rabbit caught in the briars. Were the bullets tainted? Was I about to be murdered by the man I might eventually someday soon love?

"Fucking told you to stay back," he snarled.

I let out a breath and collapsed, a sob ripping out of me as I smashed my face against his bloody shirt. "You're okay? You're okay. They were tainted? How many bullets did you take? Jeez Louise, Karl, you should be breathing your last right now."

"Half demon," he huffed out. "Guess this is one time I should be thanking the bastard who fathered me, huh?"

I sniffed and gave him a watery smile. I might be a dominant wolf. I might be second to the Alpha. But that had been the most terrifying moment of my life running down here and wondering if Karl was alive or not.

"You." His voice was stern, accusatory. "You were supposed to stay on the perimeter, not come hauling your cute ass down here. We had it handled. You didn't need to come down here to save the day."

Silly bear. "I didn't come down here to save the day, you fool. I came down here because I thought my boyfriend was mortally injured."

His eyebrows went up. "Boyfriend?"

Yeah. Sorta. "Bearfriend? Boybear? No, that doesn't sound right either. Bear-main-squeeze? How about that?"

He chuckled and ran a very bloody hand through my hair. Which was okay I guess since my hair was already red. "Did they catch him?"

Crap, I hadn't even bothered to look.

I got up, and Karl rose to his feet, pulling the bloody shirt over his head and wiping his body with the non-bloody parts of the fabric. Which was very distracting. Would we need to sedate him and dig the bullets out later? Had they gone through-and-through? Did his half-demon parentage mean he could somehow pulverize them inside his body and make them disappear?

"He's dead."

I turned at Karl's words and looked. Mason Sharpe was spread-eagle on the ground, eyes wide open, a hole neatly placed between his eyes. Around him stood half a dozen puzzled wolves.

"Who shot him?" I asked, glancing over toward the truck. The only gun with bullets was the rifle, and it was still on the ground with no one near it. The rest of us, except for Karl and me, had been on four legs.

Well, and Ahia, who was breathless and naked, looking like she wanted to punch something or someone. "It came from out in the woods. I think the bullets aren't the only magic they have access to. I didn't see or hear this guy before he walked into the clearing, and obviously there was someone else out there we didn't detect who had a rifle and a scope."

Great. All the positive PR we'd gained from me being the victim of this guy would now go down the drain. We'd be suspected of killing him, of taking the law into our own hands. I wasn't sure if even Dutch's witness statement would completely clear our name on this one.

And with Mason Sharpe dead, we'd lost the one person who might be convinced to serve up his two partners in return for a plea deal. Which was probably the reason he'd been killed tonight.

I felt Karl's arm around my shoulder. "It's gonna be okay, Brina. He's gone. We've got the bullets, and I doubt Dutch is gonna be selling them anymore."

Ahia nodded. "Without SharpShooter stirring up fear on the hunting and hiking forums, and the publicity of your being shot, I think we've put a dent in their business. Now it's up to Jake and his crew to do the rest."

She was right. But we'd still need to be vigilant. Because just like that hydra Ahia had killed this past spring, I had a feeling these guys were likely to sprout two heads for every one we took out.

We got Zeph back to the Alpha house. It was odd seeing him on the couch, going through the same casserole-and-visitor dance that I'd gone through not twelve hours before. He was milking it for everything he could, claiming that all the female wolves needed to "kiss his boo-boo," then kiss something else as well.

Brent, Ahia, Dutch, Matt, and Tina had stayed at the camping area to talk to the police. We knew them, the police that is, and they seemed to believe Dutch's statement that what was supposed to be a recall exchange had gone all wrong when his distributor had brought weapons and started shooting.

He'd not mentioned Zeph going rogue and nearly killing him, claiming that his injuries were sustained trying to get away from Mason. It was nice of Dutch, given that Karl had roughed him up and pretty much kidnapped him earlier, but I guess the guy knew that without us, he would have been dead. Without Zeph, he would be dead. And from the way he'd thanked us over and over again before we'd brought

Zeph back here, he knew the wolf had saved his live, nearly losing his own in the process.

It was nearly sunup by the time Brent and the others came back. Dutch was going to crash in one of the spare rooms for the night, then one of our wolves was going to accompany him back to his store/home, and basically provide security detail until this was all over. We couldn't very well lose one of our key witnesses.

I yawned, nursing a gigantic cup of coffee and thinking that I might want to take some aspirin and get some sleep, but Karl was prowling around like a grumpy bear. He was still pissed at me for not staying at the perimeter. And he'd told me in no uncertain terms that I was coming with him to his den and there I'd remain for the next few weeks.

I wasn't arguing. I'm sure I'd argue tomorrow once I'd gotten some sleep, healed further, and was itching to find WiFi somewhere, but for now I wasn't arguing. I was just waiting for Brent to print a few things out for me, then we'd be on our way, with Karl driving as he'd informed me not two minutes ago.

It worried me having these loose ends. There were still two guys with Three Strikes, and although the police said they'd question them, there was no proof that those two guys had done anything wrong. Yet. I didn't really need to worry though, because if there was anyone who operated his own system of justice, it was Jake with the Swift River Pack. With him on it, I was sure the other two members of Three Strikes would be out of business, and the whole hunting-magicked bullets issue would hopefully vanish.

But the elf…

Not my problem. Jake's problem, not mine. My problem was finding cell signal in Karl's little den in the woods, not going insane with only checking my e-mail once per day, and getting used to taking my potty breaks in a hole in the ground somewhere. Yikes.

"Ready to go, my wolf?"

I looked up into Karl's hazel eyes with their flecks of gold, then slugged down the rest of my coffee. "My place first so I can pick up my laptop, my clothes, my scented bath gel, my nail polish, my makeup, and my blow dryer."

He grunted. "Where the hell you gonna plug in the blow dryer, Brina? Ain't got no electricity, girl."

I wiggled my eyebrows at him. "My car has a battery, and I've got a thingie that converts the power. So you better believe I'm bringing my blow dryer with me, wild man."

He shook his head. "Fine. Long as you're in my den, I'll put up with blow dryers and nail polish and scented bath gel and your damned laptop. But the phone stays in your car except one time per day. Right?"

I slid off the stool and reached up to wrap my arms around his neck, pulling him down for a kiss. "Right."

I might wind up loving this bear. I was pretty sure I might wind up loving this bear in spite of our differences.

"Salmon for dinner tonight?" he asked.

Mmm. Yeah, I probably already loved this bear.

"Sounds like a plan, wild man." I kissed him once more. "Sounds like a plan."

WINTER FAE

NORTHERN WOLVES BOOK

CHAPTER 1

Dustin glided the plane onto the lake with practiced ease. It had been a long day: an early pickup in Ketchikan for Brent's second, then to Juneau to drop her off. Then off for another grab-and-go from Skagway to Anchorage, then this last flight. It would probably be close to sunset by the time he was back at the compound, grilling up that steak with a cold beer in hand, but so be it. These days he spent more time in the air than he did on solid ground, especially now that his Alpha, Jake, had arranged for contract charter service to both the Juneau and the Denali packs. Not that Dustin minded. He loved to fly, and it felt good that his services were bringing such money into the pack accounts. They all did their part, but feeling valued sent a warm glow to his chest.

He nudged the plane up to the dock, shutting down the propellers and jumping out to pull it close enough for his passengers to easily hop off.

"Thanks Dustin. Appreciate it." Mark climbed out of the plane. Dustin grabbed the werewolf's bag, then extended a hand to his companion. She took it with a smile, stepping carefully onto the dock.

"Thanks Dustin."

"Anytime." He touched his hand to his forehead and nodded, watching the pair of them holding hands as they headed off toward a cabin in the distance. This was the third time this week he'd shuttled members of the Denali pack to and from the coastal cities. Their members were spread out all over the interior and eastern section of Alaska, and his services meant these trips took them hours as opposed to an entire day or more had they traveled by car.

This was his last charter and he wouldn't have another until late tomorrow afternoon when he was supposed to pick up a pack member from north of Anchorage and shuttle her back to the compound. He could finally go back home, and after his steak and beer, socialize with his pack members, maybe shoot some pool with the guys. Although any plans he made needed to be flexible in case a call came in. He'd drop everything and go, because that was his job. That's what a good pack member did in support of the group. And it's not like he would have ever done otherwise when Jake sent him on a job. No one said no to Jake. Even if Dustin didn't have the utmost respect for his Alpha, he would never have done anything to cause that ice-blue glint in the shifter's eyes.

Once Brenda and Mark were safely to their house, Dustin turned back to the plane, untying the rope and hopping aboard. In seconds he had the engines fired up and was backing away from the dock, calculating the distance for his take-off. There was some bad weather moving inland, and as much as he wanted to take a scenic detour, he'd need to get back. Once in the air he radioed in, giving his course and ETA, then signing off and flying low by sight. This part of Alaska was very different than the Swift River Pack's territory near Anchorage, or even the Juneau Pack's down south.

The Denali Pack claimed the section of Alaska that was the most sparsely populated and dominated by the huge national park. The mountains and higher altitude through the territory meant there were still patches of snow on the ground even in early August. Today, fog shrouded the highest mountain peaks, the occasional black rock a stark contrast to the patches of grass and snow at the lower levels. Alpine forests dotted the harsh landscape, and thin ribbons of rivers twined through the steep canyons. Dustin swooped down, tracing the winding blue of the water before swinging west to cut across the lower corner of Denali. He'd flown this route weekly for the last two months and the beauty of the landscape never failed to awe him.

If he hadn't been flying so low, he'd never have seen the wreck.

Out here there were few roads, and most of them ended up covered with ice or snow for half of the year. In the winter people used snowmobiles, or heavy trucks equipped with chains and plows, but in the summertime, it was four-wheelers, and the chains came off the trucks. This narrow dirt road was barely more than a deer track, surrounded for nearly fifty miles on each side by snow and rock interspersed with the occasional pine. If the humans had a sat phone, they might be able to get someone out to rescue them in a few hours. If they didn't, then they were out of luck.

As Dustin closed in he realized it was a truck, on its side. There was a figure lying on the ground near the wreck and another person frantically waving. An injury, serious if the guy had been thrown from the truck as it appeared. He hesitated, knowing his next actions would mean the difference between life or death for that guy.

He could call it in, but it would take a few hours to mobilize and get a chopper here from Fairbanks. That person on the ground didn't seem to be moving. Dustin hesitated. Call it in and keep flying, hoping the guy made it in time, or land and fly the man in himself, saving an hour or two in getting him medical attention.

So much for that steak and beer.

There was no lake nearby to land on. His seaplane had floats since it was July and most of his charters involved a water landing. Dustin eyed the patchy snow, hoping it was deep enough, then banked around. Just before he began his approach, he radioed in, unsurprised to hear the static in response. Stupid weather. He'd try the satellite phone once he landed, thankful Jake had insisted each guide and pilot that went out carry one. After what had happened with Leon and the Juneau Alpha's mate two months ago, safety was of the utmost importance. Dustin shivered with the memory of how at least one grizzly shifter in Kenai had lost his life to hunters armed with special bullets. Leon still bore the scars and was lucky to have lived. And so was Brent, the Juneau Pack Alpha.

Nothing had happened for a few months and they'd begun to think themselves safe again, when there was another incident in Ketchikan where the magically tainted bullet had driven a grizzly rogue. According to Sabrina, the Juneau Pack second, the guy who'd shot him hadn't even been a hunter, but a scientist doing fungal studies. Anyone could be packing these bullets. The shifters in Alaska had always lived openly with the humans. It wasn't a secret what he was. Any human he met could have decided that as a werewolf, Dustin needed to die. And unlike a few years ago, they'd now be able to secure the means to easily accomplish that.

He eyed the two humans on the ground as he made his approach. Every shifter in the state had been warned about the presence of hunters targeting their kind. It was one of the reasons demands for their plane services had tripled. Until they were sure all the hunters had been eradicated, no one wanted to be caught out in the open unprepared. But he couldn't deny someone emergency medical attention out of fear that they might harbor ulterior motives. He couldn't ignore a human in need because there was a remote chance they might try to kill him.

Dustin set the plane down, plumes of snow and chunks of dirt and rock flying up on either side of the floats. He winced, knowing the take-off was going to be brutal, and that he'd damaged his pontoons. It would all come out of the pack funds as everything did, but Marcia, the pack accountant was going to chew him out for this one.

The propellers were still spinning down when he grabbed the first aid kit and the satellite phone and hopped from the plane. The man from the wreck was waving at him, and as Dustin grew near, he realized the man was holding a rifle.

It made him pause. How sad was it that he was suddenly suspicious of any human hunter he met out in the wilderness, that his worry for a person who might have suffered devastating injuries faded when he feared the guy on the ground might decide to point that rifle at him? It shouldn't matter that the guy was human or that he had a gun like ninety-nine percent of humans and shifters in Alaska. Until a month ago, it wouldn't have. He would have run to the aid of a human just as he would for another shifter regardless of whether they were armed.

Times had changed. And even though this man was hopping up and down with impatience as he waited for Dustin, he still felt the tension tightening his muscles, preparing for him to haul ass if needed.

"Do you need an emergency transport?" Dustin shouted.

The man pointed to the figure on the ground and shouted something else, turning and running to his injured buddy. Dustin ran as well, fearing the worst. He wasn't a doctor, and beyond basic first aid there might be nothing he could do for this man except watch him die.

He drew near and that's when Dustin realized that the truck rolled on its side looked like it had been gently laid over rather than flipped. And the person on the ground wasn't a person after all, it was a dummy.

He froze, dropping the medical kit and yanking the pistol he'd started carrying from his hip holster. Before he could flip the safety, the man lifted the rifle in his hand. Dustin heard the gunshot echo off the mountains, felt the bullet rip through his chest.

The pistol fell from hands that suddenly weren't hands, the satellite radio also dropping into the snow. His back curled then arched, bones snapping and reforming, joints twisting, muscles tearing and reshaping. The pain was incredible and Dustin felt himself fading, his vision narrowing to a field of white. Fur burst from his skin and a shift that should have taken him fifteen to twenty minutes was complete in seconds, leaving him panting and in pain on the ground.

Red splashed across the patchy bits of snow. His chest was burning from a bullet wound that should have already begun to clot and knit together. He wasn't healing. This guy was a hunter. And just like Leon and Brent, Dustin had been shot. Only in his case there was no gutsy female surgeon with a rifle to save him. There was no one here to save him.

He heard a triumphant whoop, heard the sound of another human. Had the other one been hiding in the truck? He hadn't smelled them. Actually, he hadn't smelled *any* of them. And they were both approaching with rifles, chatting between them as if they'd just brought down a ten-point buck.

Get up. Get up. Blood sprayed onto the snow with each breath, but something deep inside Dustin made him compartmentalize the pain and pull together the strength to rise. He nearly passed out from the effort. The men shouted, jumping back and scurrying to raise their rifles.

Run.

The wolf that had always seemed to be just another facet of Dustin's being suddenly ripped free of his psyche. The world spun around him, bile rising in his throat, his lungs burning with pain and bubbling with blood, but miraculously he ran. There was the sound of gunfire, bullets whistling by him, one slamming into his hip. The pain screamed through him, but there was someone else in charge, someone who didn't feel the pain, someone who wanted to live at all costs.

As if he were a disembodied spirit watching himself, he saw four paws tearing through the snow and patchy turf, skirting brush as he ran. Dustin felt himself climb the edge of a canyon, leap over rocks, and race toward a tree line.

He was heading toward a plateau, a thick forest of oaks and maples that had suddenly appeared in front of him like an illusion, like a fabled Shangri-La.

Every breath burned, every muscle screamed. The trees blurred before him, but still Dustin's wolf ran, swerving around trees in a desperate attempt to put as much distance between himself and the assailants as possible. But even as detached as he felt from the animal operating his physical form, Dustin knew his wolf was nearing the end of his sprint. Adrenaline was burning out, and the pain and blood loss was too much. The world narrowed to black for a few seconds and when Dustin finally floated once more to awareness, his wolf-self was again integrated with his mind and soul. He was bleeding. He was in agonizing pain. And he was staggering in a wide circle around an enormous hawthorn tree.

Why was a forest of hawthorns, oaks, and maples *here*? Why was this huge deciduous tree in the middle of an alpine environment? And it looked like it had been here for centuries, crashing up through the canopy with thick leaves and sturdy gray trunks. How had he never seen these trees when he'd flown over? How could he have missed this huge forest, and this weird, gigantic hawthorn?

Dustin staggered to the side, leaning against the rough, thorny bark, then slid down to his belly, nose in the trail of blood he'd made around the tree. So tired. So much pain. He was going to die. And oddly enough the only regret he felt was that he hadn't had that steak and beer he'd been thinking about all day. His pack would eventually find him. They'd find his body and give him a burial, mourn him. There was some solace in that.

At least the hunters wouldn't get him. At least he wouldn't be a pelt on someone's floor or a mounted head on their wall. And of all the places to die, this stately, powerful hawthorn, so out of place in the high altitudes of a mountain range, was better than most. Looking up at the chartreuse leaves, so brilliant that their green was nearly gold, he felt at peace. He felt like somehow he'd found home.

And just as he felt himself drift into darkness, he heard his wolf pull together enough strength to voice a mournful cry.

CHAPTER 2

Gwylla froze. Someone was at her heart-tree. Someone was circling it three times, marking it with the power of their blood.

And then out of the deep forest she'd created to hide herself from the world, from everyone, from *him*, she heard the cry. It was a knife to her heart, a sound that brought tears to her eyes. An animal was mortally wounded. An animal needed her. And unlike all the weird, stupid creatures this side of the gates, this animal had the sense to lay down its blood around her heart-tree, to phrase its need in a way that she could never refuse.

She darted from her domicile, not needing a coat or scarf, her breath frosting intricate patterns of ice into the air as she ran across the top of the snow. Her feet left no trace, her body was one with the wind, a part of the crisp purity that was her sanctuary.

A gasp burst from her when she saw him, sticky and still in the snow. His lips were curled back, his teeth bared in a grimace of pain. Thick crimson circled her beloved hawthorn, footsteps blurring the red to pink in some places.

She would have thought the animal dead had she not detected the faint thread of his heartbeat desperately pounding in a chest that was more blood than lung.

It was a wolf. Or maybe a coyote. Or maybe a dog. It was so hard to tell the difference here between the various breeds and species and whether one was domesticated or not. Out here in her little oasis, there would be few domestic animals. He was certainty large enough to be a wolf, from what little knowledge of this world she had, but some dogs here were large as well.

He was smoky gray and black with adorable white paws. And it was definitely a he from what was clearly visible between his sprawled legs.

She fell to her knees beside the animal, cradling his head in her hands. Humming, she rocked back and forth and sent healing energy into the wounds. What she saw of his injuries with her second sight shocked her. He'd been shot twice, and the bullets were coated with a foul magic that was rotting the flesh around it, tearing the spirit from his body. If he hadn't been so strong, his soul so determined to survive, he would have died before she'd arrived.

Her fingers probed the bullet holes, seizing each projectile and easing them from his flesh. The touch of the metal burned her fingers, the thick blood coating them the only thing that saved her from blistering and scarring. She gagged as she pulled them out, tempted to throw them away. But she didn't want to sully her beloved forest with their foul presence, and she needed to save them, to study them.

She needed to save them because she recognized this magic. And as horrible as it felt in her fingers, the guilt she felt was worse. This was her fault. This poor animal was near death because of her.

"Don't give up, beautiful boy. I have you. I heard your call, and I received your plea. I won't let you die. I accept responsibility for your life and spirit, and bind you to me in promise so that you may live."

Eyes flickered open. She caught her breath, expecting them to be dark brown or golden, but instead they were as verdant green as the leaves that formed the canopy above them. Then as quickly as they opened, the animal's eyes shut and he let out a low whine.

"Poor thing." She ran her fingers over his fur, healing him as best as she could. If only she could reverse this magic completely and heal him to full health with a brush of her fingers. At least he'd live. It would most likely take him weeks to heal, but she'd nurse him back to health. She belonged to him now, and he to her, and the vow she'd just made would ensure these two bullets wouldn't take life.

Her hands brushed through his coarse fur, feeling the powerful muscles beneath and something else—something very strange. There was something odd about this animal beyond the foul magic on the bullets. Of course, all the plants and creatures here seemed odd, but this dog was not the same as the other animals she'd met since she'd crossed the gateways from Hel. There was something about him that reminded her of the angels, a faint hint of a spirit being locked deep inside this flesh. Maybe he'd been given a gift by one of the heavenly beings. Or maybe canines were one of the animals that had caught notice of the angelic host and they were being assisted in their evolution. It's not like she or her kind had bothered much with the angels.

Angel-touched or not, Gwylla couldn't leave him here at the base of her heart-tree, not still injured like this. She'd vowed to nurse him to health. She'd responded to his plea and now his life was her responsibility. Gathering him onto a sled formed from ice and snow, she pulled the dog to her home in the hill, then gently slid him onto a blanket and dismissed the ice sled back outside before it had a chance to melt. Then she warmed water and washed his wounds, putting a bowl of water by his nose.

She needed to go out. The animal would heal on his own with rest, warmth, and care, but the men who did this must be near. She needed to safeguard her forest, to make sure the glamour and wards that surrounded her sanctuary were unbroken. It would be horrible if humans found her home—especially these humans. She knew where that foul magic had come from, and if the humans who were using it found her, *he* wouldn't be far behind.

The one she'd once trusted, that she'd once thought loved her. The one that *she'd* thought she loved. She wasn't ready to face him yet. She might never be ready to face him. It was best for her to stay here in sanctuary alone, hidden from him.

But she wasn't alone. Gwylla looked down at the dog on the blanket and smiled. The Goddess had seen fit to send her a friend, and with the bond between them that had saved his life, neither of them would ever be alone.

Dustin blinked one eye open, then the other, forcing the heavy lids to remain up long enough for the blurry gray of his vision to clear into sharp lines and bright colors. He wasn't dead. He couldn't be dead, because if he were, these sharp pains and throbbing aches in his chest and hip would be gone.

Besides, he doubted if the afterlife consisted of a snug domicile that looked like it had been dug into the ground. He was no longer in the woods, no longer outside in a pool of blood next to a freakishly huge hawthorn tree. He was on the floor in human form, laying on top of a soft dove-gray blanket and naked as the day he was born.

Of course he was naked. He'd been in wolf form, forced into a rapid shift by the magic of those horrible bullets. But why wasn't he dead? And beyond that, how had he managed to change *out* of his wolf form? From what Brent and Leon had said, the magic kept a shifter in their animal form, and even when the bullet was removed, the magic tended to linger.

Actually, the magic tended to kill, possibly turning the

shifter rogue along the short journey. It was only a human surgeon's quick wits and skill that had saved the Juneau Alpha and Dustin's pack mate from death. The grizzlies hadn't been so lucky.

Dustin tried to move, but none of his body seemed to want to respond beyond his eyelids. And mouth. He licked dry lips, wincing at the pain that shot through his head at the motion.

Where was he? There were no windows, no bits of glass, not even a doorway. And the dwelling was round, with a flattened, low roof, like one of those yurt tents he'd seen in a magazine once. There was a table with one chair, and a bedding arrangement that looked like a mattress on a platform piled high with colorful pillows and blankets.

Hey. How come he got one lousy blanket on the floor while the bed remained empty? It didn't seem very hospitable to rescue an injured werewolf and just leave him on the hard floor, although he probably shouldn't be looking this particular gift horse in the mouth, given that he'd most likely been near death and no one wanted a werewolf bleeding out onto their mattress and good linens.

Beyond the sparse furnishings, the room held little else. There were several glass washbasins, some bins that looked like the ones used to store potatoes and apples, an unlit fireplace with clay cooking pots and wooden utensils next to it. Lines of string were stretched like a spider's web near the low ceiling, bundles of herbs clipped and hanging along their white lengths.

Unlit fireplace? Dustin slowly turned his eyes and attention back to the cold hearth. Although cold wasn't an accurate description if he were to guess by the temperature of the one-room house. July in central Alaska wasn't like a summer day in Florida. There had been snow on the ground when he'd flown through here. At this altitude, outside it was most likely fifty degrees if it were daytime, slightly above freezing if it were night.

But inside this little round earthen dwelling, it was warmer. Even without a fire, with only those odd sparkly lights like fireflies in glass that illuminated the room, it was close to seventy degrees.

Which actually was a bit chilly given he was a naked man lying on top of his blankets.

A door formed in the brown earthen wall, silver-blue around the edges. It opened and someone entered, light streaming in momentarily until it was shut once more. It was daytime, then, although probably not the same day he'd been shot given the state of repair his wounds were in. Brent and Leon had both said the magic on the bullets had hindered their ability to heal. Even with Kennedy's skillful surgery, it had taken them weeks to fully heal. Had he been here weeks? Dustin's heart thumped wondering what had happened to his plane, if his pack was looking for him. They must think him dead.

His thoughts shifted, focusing on the person who had come through the door—a woman by her willowy form and soft voice that hummed an unfamiliar tune. She smelled odd, like no other human or shifter he'd ever known. Like no animal. Actually she smelled like sun on snowy leaves with faint hints of crocus, hyacinth, mint, and pine. And she smelled cool, not like the warm musky scent that humans and shifters naturally bore.

She had her back to him as she pressed the door closed, that silver-blue light darting around the edges before the opening merged seamlessly into the rest of the house. Her clothing was human—dark jeans, a modest black tank top. White-blonde hair hung straight past her shoulders, brushing against skin so pale it seemed almost translucent.

She tilted her head and he caught a glimpse of an ear, its pointed tip rising high through her hair.

An elf? He'd heard they were all sequestered on some island while the angels taught them how to live productively among the humans. The thought made Dustin want to chuckle. As if the angels knew anything about living among the humans. That one in Brent's pack was the only angel who seemed to know the human world in any detail and that was because she'd been raised by humans and shifters who'd thought she was a Nephilim.

The elf-woman said something in a lovely sing-song voice, and turned, a beautiful smile on her rosy lips, her light green eyes warm with compassion.

The smile froze. Her eyes widened. And her voice cracked as she screamed.

Even with the horrible pain in his chest and hip, Dustin couldn't help but clasp his hands to his ears. She had the type of scream that would shatter glass, or at the very least shatter a werewolf's ear drums.

The scream went on and on. Was she frightened? Of what? Him? Hadn't she brought him here? Maybe there was another resident of this bungalow who had neglected to tell his wife, or roommate, that he'd dragged home an injured werewolf.

"I'm sorry...I don't...please stop that noise." He scooted backward, trying to hike the blanket up over his hips in case it was his nudity she was so loudly frightened of. Not that he was *that* big. Sheesh, this was probably not the first dick she'd laid eyes on. It wasn't like he had a massive hard-on or had been in the middle of whacking off when she'd come through the door.

"Who...what...get out. Get out!" The last word of her heavily accented sentence ended on a pitch so high he was sure he wouldn't have heard it had he been human.

Get out. Dustin tried to scramble to his feet while bunching the blanket around his hips. He didn't even make it to his knees before crashing back to the ground. Wet trickled down his chest. The smell of copper filled his nose.

"Oh sweet Lady," she stared in horror at the blood oozing from his freshly opened wounds.

"I'm not a lady, Lady," Dustin slurred. Hadn't she seen he had a dick and balls? He'd always considered himself a fairly blessed werewolf in the genital size department, but maybe elven guys were huge, like pointy-eared John Holmeses.

"How can that be? You were a dog, I saved the life of a dog, not a human", she babbled.

"I'm not a dog," he told her, wincing in pain. As soon as the words were out, he realized she might have never seen a wolf before, or any canine. How long would it take elves to learn the various animals and plants here? And how long would it take them to come across werewolves and other shifters that they most likely didn't realize existed?

She waved an impatient hand. "Wolf? Or coyote? No, you're too big for a coyote, so you must be a wolf if you're not a dog. But you're not either. You're a human, and yet you were a wolf when I found you."

Wow, he hurt. It hurt to breathe. It hurt to think. It hurt to keep his eyes open. "Because I *am* a wolf." Did he say that out loud? Because it sounded like he'd just thought it. Or maybe he whispered it. "Wolf-man," he continued. "And I got shot. Cause bad guys."

There was this weird static sound, like a hundred bees swarming around his head. Her eyes were so green, her skin and hair like two shades of alabaster, those pink lips an 'O', a splash of color. They were the only things besides her eyes that relieved the whiteness of her skin and hair. Like jewels in snow. Like emeralds and drops of pale blood in snow. His blood was soaking her blanket. Guess it was a good thing she hadn't put him in her bed after all.

Although it would be nice to be in her bed. She was beautiful, like an elven princess from a fantasy role-playing game come to life. And those electric green eyes that were distorting and fading as he slipped into a sea of pain were breathtaking. They were the last thing Dustin saw before there was nothingness.

CHAPTER 4

How was he a man when he'd been a dog—or wolf —just an hour ago? Gwylla stared down at the human sprawled across her floor, bleeding dark blotches onto one of her favorite blankets. She'd barely known humans. In Hel, she'd seen them in the city or at various elven functions, but she had seldom been close-up with one. After coming through the gates to this strange new world, she'd seen far more humans than ever before. But never had she seen one that was sometimes a wolf.

He'd smelled like a dog. He'd looked like a dog. Yes, he'd smelled and looked a bit different than the other canines she'd seen in the last few months, but there had been nothing to indicate he was a human in wolf's clothing.

And he had broken open the thin scabs that covered his wounds—the wounds that didn't want to heal. The wounds that she was partially to blame for. With a tsk sound she filled a bowl with water and went to him, peeling the blanket from him and carefully washing each bullet hole, singing her spells of healing as she worked.

If he'd been found by anyone else, this wolf-man would

not have had a chance of survival, but she had pledged for his life. And she knew this magic that had infected him. It was the mirror to the magic that ran through her like a river. She could slowly redirect its flow, change its purpose so the wolf-man could heal. It wasn't easy, and these injuries required constant attention or they'd revert to the rot they were intended to cause. But it wasn't just her magic that was making this wolf-man better, it was something inside him.

He had remarkable healing abilities. She could feel it as she ran her fingers over his smooth golden flesh, caressing the hard muscle that curved like mountains and valleys across his chest and down his torso. His skin was so warm, so responsive to the stroke of her hand. It felt like heaven to touch him. It soothed her like the song of her heart-tree, like the sound of falling water. Was it the bit of angel she'd detected in him? Was that what allowed him to have two forms and heal?

"It was easier to care for you when you were furry," she muttered, pulling her hand away from his skin as his eyes blinked open.

Green eyes. Darker than hers with flecks of brown and gray. It had been a shock to come home and find a naked human on her floor where she'd left a wolf. If she hadn't noticed that he had the exact same injuries, she wouldn't have realized the wolf and the man were one and the same. Although if she'd gotten past her shock and actually considered the situation she would have remembered that there was no way a human could have seen, let alone entered her sanctuary without her permission.

Although the *wolf* had been able to. Animals could see her forest, could enter and exit without any special magic. That there were wolf-men who could enter her sanctuary was a surprise. It was a design flaw she'd have to address as she'd not accounted for wolf-men sneaking through in their animal forms.

But if that flaw hadn't been there, this man would have died, bleeding out at the edge of her sanctuary instead of using his blood to mark her heart-tree and call for help. Was it the wolf that had known to do that or the man?

"Please don't scream again," he told her, his voice raspy like he'd been swallowing broken bits of glass. "I don't think my ears can take it. My brain might explode."

He was funny. How long had it been since she'd heard humor? Since she'd laughed? Unable to stop herself, she ran her fingers lightly across the skin of his shoulder and down his arm. So warm. Warm, and smooth, and an appealing combination of hard and soft. "If you had rescued an injured wolf and returned home to find a naked woman in its place, you would have screamed, too."

He grinned, those green eyes dancing. "Absolutely not. I would have thanked God for answering my prayers. Every man alive hopes to find a naked woman sprawled across his floor when he comes home."

She felt her lips twitch upward at the thought. It had been a long time since she'd had someone flirt with her, felt this fluttering in her chest at the look in another's eyes. This wolf-man found her attractive, and unlike the stupid elves, she was not averse to taking pleasure where she found it. But he was recovering from his injuries, and the last time she'd shared passion with another, she'd ended up giving herself unwisely.

"There will be no more screaming, I promise," she told him. "I am not one of those who loses her mind at every unexpected event." She put the basin of water and cloth aside, touching a hand to her heart. "I am Gwylla. I accepted your plea for help and have saved you from death, so now your life is mine to protect."

Having a wild dog linked to her in spirit was what she'd imagined when she'd answered his call and accepted the bargain between them. But a wolf-man? This would be unusual. No, this would be unprecedented. A wolf would have continued to live as an animal, remaining in her forest and near her, but this wolf-man would no doubt be more comfortable here inside her home. She glanced at the bed. She'd need another, and another chair as well. Although there probably would be no need to construct another bed, not if she was reading the expression in this man's eyes correctly.

"I don't think I heard you right. Did you say that my life was *yours?*" The wolf-man seemed uncomfortable at that prospect. "Umm, I'm Dustin Schafer from the Swift River Pack. No offense, but as much as I appreciate your assistance, my life is most definitely not yours. I have an Alpha. And a pack."

He clearly was not understanding the situation. "I don't know this pack or the Alpha of which you speak. You laid your blood down around my heart-tree, cried your prayer into the wind. I answered the prayer, and the magic that holds death at bay now binds us together. You are now mine."

Yes, he was very uncomfortable, on the edge of anger even. How did he not understand?

"I'm kindly," she assured him. "I will not force you to do anything against your will or treat you unfairly."

"Oh, gee, thanks so much." Was that sarcasm in his voice? "I recognize that you saved my life, and for that I thank you, but no matter what you think, I'm *not* yours."

Silly wolf-man. Of course he was. Didn't he feel it? Couldn't he sense the threads that now bound them together, that would remain in place until one of them died?

She stood, taking a few steps to compose herself. "I am

merely stating the situation. Trust me, I am not pleased about this either. I thought I was pledging to a wild dog, an animal, not…you. Had I known you were a wolf-man, I would not have answered your call."

"So instead you would have left me bleeding out beside your tree? You would have just let me die rather than save a shifter?"

Yes, he was definitely angry. Which was okay, because she was starting to feel angry as well.

"You do not get one without the other. Either we are bound together as part of the magic that saves you from death, or you die. I would have rendered aid, but no, I would not have bound myself to a human. Or a wolf-man. Or anyone. I thought you were an animal."

"Well, I'm not an animal," he snapped, wincing as he tried to sit up. "And as much as I appreciate you doing whatever you did to keep me from dying, that doesn't mean I'm bound to you."

"Yes. You are. And I am as well. Even though I expected to be taking a wild canine to my side, I am bound by the agreement. As are you. You extended the offer. I simply accepted it. If anyone should be upset, it should be me for having been deceived into believing I was saving a dog. But it was my fault for not recognizing what you are or knowing the creatures here well enough to see that you were not a dog after all. I'm sure there was no deception intended on your part."

She'd said the words with a generous and forgiving spirit, but he seemed even more angry at her speech.

"That's not how things are done in here in America. I'm very grateful that you healed me, or whatever you did to keep me from dying, but that *doesn't* obligate me in any way. I'm not yours. I belong to no one beyond my pack and my Alpha. If you want to submit a claim for services rendered to my insurance company, feel free to do so." He stirred, obviously trying to rise to his feet.

She put her hands on his chest, pushing him gently downward. "No. No. You will bleed again. The magic needs time to seal your wounds. I don't want to upset you further. We will discuss this later, after you have healed completely. Just rest now. I will give you something to help you sleep if you need."

He glanced down at her hands, his breath hitching. His heart pounded against her hands.

"No, I don't need…" He shook his head, then pulled away from her touch. "Don't…I mean, how long have I been unconscious? My pack will think I'm dead. I need to get back to them, to warn the about the hunters. Do you have a satellite phone? Radio?"

Of course he would want to leave. She'd thought the Goddess had sent her an animal companion, then she'd briefly envisioned a human, or wolf-man, companion, but he had friends, family. He wouldn't want to stay here. And she wouldn't want to leave. That was going to be a problem, but she could hardly hold him against his will.

"You were wolf for five suns. If you rest, you will heal completely within four more suns, and then you can leave my home."

He blinked, a puzzled frown creasing his brow. "I can leave? I can go back to my home, my pack?"

"You are not my prisoner, not my slave. I must insist that you not leave until you are healed to the point that you can make the journey. It wouldn't be safe for you to travel in your condition. And I can better protect you here in my sanctuary. Here it is safe. There is no foul magic, no hunters with poisoned bullets. You can rest and heal and not fear being shot again."

"But my pack…"

"They will worry, but wouldn't they rather have you return to them healthy and whole after your absence? They would not want you to collapse in the mountains somewhere and die trying to struggle home."

His eyes met hers, pupils dilated, silver sparks lighting up the green with an inhuman glow. "Yes. You're right. I'll stay."

He sounded so reluctant that she felt a bit hurt. "Is it so terrible to remain here for a few additional days? I will make sure you heal completely, as quickly as possible. And when you are able to go outside we will walk among the trees, and you will see the beautiful home I've created."

Home? Or was this really her prison? No, home. Because to think otherwise would lead her to think about all the things she could no longer have—things like the family and friends that this wolf was eager to reclaim. She didn't blame him. If she could, she'd go home as well.

"Only a few days. I have a pack that depends on me. I have friends and family that are looking for me. I cannot... stay." He pulled his eyes away, lids heavy as he sank back down to the blanket.

They were bound. Distance would only hurt them both. She could enchant him and hold him here. He'd be happy— deliriously happy. She could weave her magic around him, guaranteeing he'd never leave, never betray her. But that would make her a monster. She'd made many mistakes in her life, but she'd never been a monster.

"Only a few days. As I said, you are not my prisoner, not my slave. I only ask that you wait until you are fully healed from your injuries before returning to your pack."

He'd attribute the discomfort to lingering issues from his injuries. She'd suffer worse, but part of that was because she could feel the threads between them. Maybe he'd be back someday, a friend to help keep the loneliness at bay.

"But I thought… You said I was yours and something about us being bound together."

"Not like a rope, bind. Not mine as in ownership." Gwylla pursed her lips, thinking of the best way to explain the magic in terms this wolf-man would understand. "We will long to be in each other's presence, to assist each other, to keep each other safe. I have committed to ensuring your survival for the rest of your natural life. I am bound to you and you to me. If there is trouble that threatens you, I must protect you. If there is someone who wishes you dead, I will…kill them."

"Whoa whoa whoa." The wolf-man went to put his hands up, then winced and lowered them. "Seriously. I completely appreciate you saving my life and all that, but you don't owe me anything further. And you certainly don't need to appear out of the ether and fireball anyone who gets pissed at me over…whatever."

"I cannot create fireballs. There are other ways I can protect you, though."

He shook his head. "I don't need protecting. Thank you, but I'll be fine. I appreciate your continued hospitality, but in a few days, once I'm able to, I'll leave and return to my pack."

He didn't understand. That was okay, the elves hadn't really understood either. Gwylla felt a wave of loneliness wash through her. This wasn't what she'd ever expected her life would be when she left Aerie for Hel.

But that wasn't his problem, it was hers. So instead of burdening him further, she smiled and placed a gentle hand against his shoulder. "Then rest. I will have food for you when you awaken, and with my continued care, you will soon be able to return to your pack."

His eyes drifted closed and she watched him a moment, admiring the way his brown hair curled across his forehead, the way his lips curved up as he slept. He wasn't what she would consider a handsome man, but his features were intriguing. And she liked him. She admired his determination, his commitment to his pack-family. She liked his humor, and the way his eyes darkened when he felt strong emotion.

She hoped that someday he would return to see her, because of all the beings she'd met in the last few decades, this wolf-man already seemed like a friend. And right now, Gwylla could truly use a friend.

By the time the wolf-man opened his eyes once more, the room smelled of fresh-baked bread, squash soup, and berry cobbler. It was also hotter than she would normally have liked her home, but even with an extra blanket, she'd noticed her patient shivering.

"Stay," she ordered when he began to move. "Food first, then we'll talk."

"Sounds good to me. My stomach feels like it's trying to eat itself. Is that bread you're baking? You *make* bread? Well, of course you do. It's not like you're going to pop down to Foodland for a loaf of Sunbeam or something."

Clearly the wolf-man was not understanding the "talk later" part of her command. "Yes, I made bread. You haven't eaten since I found you, so tonight will be soup, bread, and if you are feeling up to it, berry cobbler."

"Oh, I am definitely up for some cobbler. Do you have ice cream? Probably not, since I don't see a refrigerator."

She ladled the soup into a huge bowl and tore off a slab of warm bread, slathering it with butter. "Frozen cream? I was going to just pour the cream on top, but I can freeze it if you like."

"Ice cream is cream with sugar that's been churned as it freezes until it's the consistency of snow. But cream on top is just fine. Anything is just fine. I'm about ready to gnaw on your table leg here."

"Be patient. Do not eat my furniture. I promise I have made enough for a dozen wolf-men." She smiled and set the tray of food in front of him. "Here. I'll help you up."

She dropped down beside him and let him lean on her as he sat up, then she pulled the tray forward.

"Sorry. I'm not used to being too weak to sit up by myself," he told her, extending a shaky hand for the carved, wooden soup spoon.

She reached a hand forward to help, then drew it back, letting him manage by himself. He ended up with almost as much soup spilled on the tray as in his mouth, but that was no matter as long as he felt some measure of self-sufficiency.

"More?"

He nodded, tearing into the bread like a man who hadn't eaten…well, who hadn't eaten for five days. He ate nearly two loaves of bread, and she refilled his soup bowl three times before he leaned back against the pillows and sighed. The last bowl, his hand had been steady, and she could already see the strength returning to his limbs. His natural healing ability was amazing. She had no doubt he'd make a complete recovery within the next two to three days.

And then he'd be gone. And she'd be alone. But that was her life now, and she'd best grow accustomed to it.

"Let's start this again, without all the binding/ownership stuff," he said as she gathered up the dishes. "I'm Dustin. I'm a werewolf with the Swift River Pack."

"I am pleased to meet you, Dustin, who is a wolf-man.

Can you tell me how you ended up shot with magical bullets and dying next to my heart-tree in my sanctuary?"

He smiled, his dark green-brown eyes dancing. "Why, I would be happy to, Gwylla. I was heading back from a flight that returned two members of the Denali wolf pack home when I saw an overturned truck and someone signaling for help. I landed, and when I approached to render assistance, they shot me."

She turned, nearly dropping the bowl she was cleaning. "They just shot you? They lured you in, preyed upon your helpful nature, and then *shot* you?"

This was unforgivable. Attempted murder right outside her sanctuary. She refused to think that such a cancer was widespread among the humans. No, these were bad people who needed to be exterminated. But it wasn't her place to do so. This wasn't her world. These weren't her people.

But Dustin *was* hers. And if that didn't give her enough of an excuse to deliver some much needed justice, then there was the fact that she knew this magic. In a way, she was responsible. She couldn't hide here in her sanctuary forever, no matter what she'd intended when she came here to lick her wounds and heal herself. Instead of frightening, somehow the thought was liberating.

The hole inside her was still raw, but if it hadn't healed by now, it never would. It was past time for her to learn to just live with the ache and find some purpose. Righting this wrong was a noble purpose.

She turned to him, feeling as if she were about to make a vow. "After I assist you to heal to full health, you will return to your pack and I will track these hunters and kill them." She would also kill the one responsible, no matter how much she disliked the idea of coming face to face with him ever again.

"There's a whole lot of killing with you, isn't there?" The

wolf-man's voice held a note of amusement. Irony? He didn't exactly approve, but he didn't exactly disapprove either. She got the impression he found her statement humorous.

"Not always. We are generally a peaceful people, except when threatened. We are the light, the sun and the blossoming of life. We are the snow and the cold and the dreams of the dark. We are the seasons, the elements of the world, the dust of the cosmos."

He blinked. "Very poetic. I've never met an elf before. Are you all so…interesting?"

He thought her an *elf*? Although that was probably not surprising. Her kind didn't make a practice of revealing themselves to humans. If he'd never met an elf, he wouldn't have any basis for comparison. And they *did* both have pointy ears.

"I am not an elf. I'm a sidhe, people of the hill. We are a race of fae, the Tuatha de Danann."

"Aren't they the same? I mean, pointy ears, healing abilities, lived in Hel?"

She scooped the warm cobbler into two bowls, then pulled the jug of cream from a bowl of ice. "No, we are not the same. We are as different as the wolf and the coyote in your world. Similar, but different."

He stirred, interest and confusion in his face. "So you all live in Hel with the elves? Are the sidhe coming here to live as well?"

Frozen cream with sugar. Hmmm, honey would not work properly. Did she have any beet or cane sugar left?

"No, the sidhe live with all the other fae in Aerie. I am the only one who was in Hel and who came here with them. And I will most likely be the only sidhe ever to come here in your lifetime. We seldom venture out of Aerie."

He stared at her, fascinated. "Your English is very good.

Did you learn it from the human slaves in Hel? How long have you been here?"

Now this was a better, less dangerous, topic of conversation. Gwylla pulled a packet of sugar she'd been saving for something special and poured it into a bowl with the cream.

"I left Hel just over four of your months ago. Sidhe absorb languages. I can go anywhere in your world and be able to communicate. Given a few days of contact, I will know your slang, idioms, and regional dialects as well. I did absorb some of your languages from the humans in Hel, although I was not often in contact with them. Not enough to recognize all of your words."

"I'm completely jealous of that skill. And your clothing? I mean, I really expected you in gossamer jewel-toned silk robes or something, not jeans and a tank top."

She laughed, bringing the bowls over. "I was told they came from a place called Old Navy. I like the human clothes. They're different and unusual. Would you prefer me to dress like this?"

Sweeping a hand across her body, the human clothing vanished, replaced with something more in keeping with the elven or sidhe courts. It was transparent silk, the lightest green with gold threads, and it wrapped around her body, hugging her slim curves and leaving very little to the imagination.

Dustin stared, open-mouthed, his eyes darkening. "I…oh, wow. It's like Playboy, Dungeons and Dragons edition."

"Is that a good thing?" She sat down beside him, leaning over to pull the bowls closer. She noticed his eyes glued to her chest at the movement.

"Oh yeah. You should dress like this all the time. Screw Old Navy."

She hid a smile. "Now, pay attention. Well, pay attention to what I'm doing and not my body parts. I'm going to try to make this ice cream, but I need you to tell me when it's the right consistency."

"Ice cream. Yep. Paying attention." He dragged his gaze from her chest and stared at the cream and sugar mixture. Setting the bowl in her lap, she frosted the sides, keeping the temperature consistent as she stirred.

"Holy… You don't have a sister back at the castle with a white streak in her red hair, do you?"

"I have no siblings. Is there a reason you ask? Do you have a preference for women with red hair?" The thought bothered her that he might not think she was attractive. Well, clearly he thought she was attractive from the way he was ogling her body, but she'd not considered that he might prefer someone different, more curvy, more…human. Or a wolf-woman. Did he have a consort back in his pack? She didn't sense any consort bonds, but perhaps they did things differently here.

"No. It was a movie reference. A joke, because you're using magic to freeze the bowl. I actually like blonds." He added the last bit as if he couldn't help himself, his eyes wandering back to her chest.

"Good. Pay attention, Dustin," she scolded, secretly flattered. "I don't want to over freeze the cream."

"Sorry. It's done. Can I go back to looking at your boobs now?"

The laugh bubbled up inside her. She hadn't experienced such light-hearted fun in…well in a very long time. "Yes, you can go back to looking at my *boobs*. See? I have now learned a new word, thank you very much."

She scooped the ice cream on top of the cobbler and handed him a bowl and spoon, taking one for herself. The first taste was ecstasy—sweet and cold and creamy, countered with the warm, sharp tang of the berries and crumbly crust. "Mmmm. You wolf-people clearly know the very best sweets. I'm very fond of sweet things. I can see that I will need to visit this Foodland of yours and find out what other treats I can experience."

"Chocolate. And there are all sorts of flavors of ice cream that you need to try. Cookie dough is my favorite. You're going to love it." He was resting more of his weight against the pillows, his eyes somewhat unfocused. She took the empty bowl from his hand and stood, tucking the blanket around him. He was tired, too tired to continue this conversation. Which was a pity because she hadn't enjoyed herself this much in decades.

"I am excited to try it, especially as it is your favorite. Rest. Allow the magic to knit your flesh together and repair your wounds. When you awaken in the morning, we will talk of ice cream and chocolate some more."

His eyelids were drooping lower, partially shielding those green irises from her view. "Thank you. I don't think I said thank you for helping me. And I like it here. I mean, I need to go home to my pack, but it's weirdly comforting to think about staying here. Trust me, it's tempting. You're very beautiful, like an ice queen from a multiplayer fantasy game. And I like that dress thing."

She sat and watched him fall asleep, reaching out a hand to touch his brown hair and trace the roundness of his small ears. How peculiar this wolf-man was—peculiar and appealing.

And he thought her beautiful? An ice queen? A warmth stirred in her chest. Something about this wolf-man appealed to her, and it was more than just the bond that was established when she'd saved his life.

Dustin woke feeling less like he was on the edge of death and more as if he'd merely been driven over by an express train. The smell of spicy stew curled around his nose and made him struggle to his knees. Nothing broke open, no blood trickled down his hip or chest. Everything ached, but the pain was manageable, especially given the siren song of food and the effect the aroma was having on his hollowed-out stomach.

Stew. He'd slept through breakfast? Or maybe sidhe ate spicy stew for their first meal? Didn't matter. It was food, he was hungry, and he was going to make short work of whatever was steaming away in that pot.

He didn't dare stand, but he managed to crawl his way over to the fireplace, the blanket sliding off him after the first few feet. Screw it. She wasn't in the house, and she'd already gotten an eyeful earlier. Plus, food trumped modesty, not that he'd ever had much modesty.

On the floor in front of the fireplace was a piece of parchment that looked art-worthy. He picked it up and chuckled. Clearly Gwylla couldn't write English, even though she spoke it better than most of the non-native speakers he'd encountered in his life. On the parchment was a drawing of a wolf sitting with his head cocked to the side, one ear up and the other down, tongue lolling out of a smiling mouth. Then there was a plus sign followed by a bowl of steaming food. Then an equal sign and a wolf dancing on two legs, forelegs outstretched, mouth open in a happy grin.

The last few days had been weird, really really weird. First the trap the hunters had set for him in the middle of nowhere. Then an invisible world sanctuary that fortunately was near enough to the scene of his attack. Then the presence of some sort of fae powerful enough to heal him, this bonding and responsibility-for-his-life thing. Now this really humorous picture. What was a sidhe anyway? And why *was* she here in the middle of Alaska instead of back home in Aerie or with the other elves on that island?

Dustin struggled upright, using the packed-earth wall for leverage. With a shaking hand, he spooned the steaming soup into a bowl thoughtfully placed right next to the pot.

Gwylla had said the elves and sidhe were similar, but not the same. She had the pointy ears he'd always associated elves, but what would he know? He'd never seen an elf in his life. Actually she looked more like the ice queen he'd called her than what he imagined an elf would look like. Except for those Lord of the Rings elves. Suddenly he envisioned Gwylla in the draped see-through silk dress she'd had on last night, her white-blond hair braided around the crown of her head.

Yep. She was his total nerdy-guy fantasy woman. As a kid the dream girl had always been a toss-up between a Middle-earth elf or one of those hot blue alien women from Star Trek. All his human friends had been lusting after cheerleaders and Playboy pin-ups, his shifter friends had been lusting after female MMA fighters and Lara Croft, and he'd been into alien chicks and elves.

Easing himself carefully back to the floor, Dustin slurped the stew right from the bowl, feeling stronger as the warmth hit his stomach and spread throughout his body.

Hunters. In Denali. When he finally managed to get out of here, would he find that others had been killed? It wasn't just the Denali Pack that was in danger from these hunters. Dustin had been missing six days at this point. Jake would have sent a crew out to look for him, and if the hunters had lain in wait…

Would he leave here to find that several of his pack mates had been killed? Would he leave to find an out-an-out war? When would the hunters get tired of laying traps and take their sport to the pack compound itself? Shifters had always lived in harmony with the humans here in Alaska. Here their existence was public knowledge, out in the open. Their home addresses weren't exactly a secret. It would be easy for the hunters to find where members of the Denali and Juneau packs lived and taken them down one at a time, but the Swift River Pack lived in a compound.

That was both a blessing and a curse. A concentration of werewolves in one area would make it easier for them to defend themselves, but it would also make it easier for the hunters to mount a siege and take down the entire pack. The compound was set up as a social construct, for ease of pack life and management, not for defense. There hadn't been anything for them to defend themselves against in Dustin's memory. No one messed with the werewolves. And he had no idea if human law enforcement would arrive in time to help them—or even arrive at all. At this point Dustin suspected every human in Alaska.

He needed to get out of here and warn Jake. He needed to find out what was happening outside of this strange forest.

He needed to be there to defend his pack if they were attacked.

The door opened and Gwylla smiled over at him before she began sealing the edges closed. She was once more wearing human attire—a floral print dress, that wasn't see-through and was less formfitting then her fae outfit.

"You look much better."

"I'm feeling better, thanks. And thanks for the stew." He held up the drawing. "And the picture."

She laughed. "I didn't have time to learn to write your language. I was among the humans here only briefly before I left and created my sanctuary."

She walked over and grabbed some pillows from the bed, tossing them onto the floor beside him. Then she poured two glasses of what looked like wine, and swapped one of them out for the empty soup bowl in his hand. "Relax. Drink. And we can continue our talk from last night."

He sipped what was indeed a sweet wine and relaxed against the pillows while she sat next to him, her thigh brushing his as she folded her legs.

"Let's see. Where were we…? I fly tourists, pack members and other shifters around Alaska as my job for our pack. Do you know what a plane is?"

She nodded. "The big metal birds that humans use to travel long distances because they cannot teleport."

He eyed her in surprise. "You can teleport?"

"Yes, but I'm not powerful enough to do it repeatedly within a short period of time. It takes a great deal of magic that is often better used for another purpose. And besides, I do not often need to travel long distances."

Dustin took another sip of the wine. It was better than what Jake had at the compound. It was better than any wine he'd ever had before. "As I told you yesterday, I'd just flown two members of the Denali Pack from Anchorage to their home and was returning when I saw an overturned truck and someone, a human, signaling for help with another lying on the ground. I landed and grabbed my first aid pack but when I got near I realized something was wrong. The guy on the ground was a dummy, and the overturned truck wasn't an accident. Before I could run or do more than pull my gun, the man waving me down shot me. It was one of those magic-coated bullets like the ones that killed a grizzly shifter in Kenai and nearly killed two werewolves. I was forced into an immediate shift to my wolf form. I don't know how I managed to escape. My wolf took charge and somehow I ran. In the distance I saw a forest shimmer into view. Everything after that is blurry. I passed out, and then I woke up here."

"You know these men? You recognize the magic they've used on their weapons?"

She seemed distraught, her eyes dancing away from his to stare into her own glass of wine.

"I don't know them personally, but as I said, hunters have attacked us in the past few months. We're shifters, the descendants of Nephilim. We heal much faster than the humans do. Outside of a few strategic shots, we don't die from bullets. These hunters are targeting us, targeting shifters. Their bullets force a change of form that normally should take twenty minutes into seconds. And the magic on the bullets hinders our ability to heal. It kills us." He fixed her with an earnest stare. "They're hunting us in particular, taking our bodies as trophies. And they want us in our animal form. We managed to kill two of these hunters in Kenai almost three months ago, but one escaped, and obviously there are more."

Her breath hitched. "Dustin, I must confess something to you. I recognize the magic on these bullets. It's a mirror to my own, and I am positive that it is wielded by an elf I know."

He turned to her eagerly, catching his breath as the wound in his chest protested the movement. "You know him? Do you know where he is? If we can get to whoever is creating these magic bullets, we can put a stop to the hunters."

"You cannot stop him. He will be surrounded by humans with these weapons. You and your pack would be killed before you ever reached him."

"So we just sit back and let them kill us? We wouldn't storm in and get ourselves killed. We'd do surveillance, set up a trap of our own. We'd… I don't know, Jake will think of something. Or maybe we'll ask the angels to help."

"Perhaps the angels can stop him. He is powerful and brilliant. I would suspect he is already wary of attack by angels and has something in place to mask himself from them."

"Well, we still need to try." Something in the way she was fidgeting with her wine glass caught his attention. It was as if she didn't want to tell him something. "What is it about this elf? Is he a friend of yours? A family member?"

She bit her lip, still staring at the wine glass. "We were once lovers, and there was talk that we would be wed. I thought…I thought I loved him and that he loved me, but he betrayed me. He was only using me."

He felt as if she'd punched him in the stomach. "A lover? Your ex-boyfriend? And an elf? But *you're* not an elf?" Shaking his head, Dustin tried to get the image of Gwylla and some elf out of his head. "Okay. Backup a moment. What is the difference between sidhe and the elves? You said you're both fae?"

She took a quick drink of wine. "All of the fae are like cousins? Step siblings? We would be indistinguishable to many. With sidhe and elves, the line is often blurred. We are taller, and our powers are different. We were all once together—all of the races of fae. A very long time before the war in Aaru, the elves left, refusing to remain with the rest of us in Aerie. They made their kingdoms elsewhere, and when the angel wars began, they took advantage of the division and left with the Angels of Chaos to live in Hel."

"And why are you here in the middle of Alaska and not in Aerie?"

"I was sent to be an emissary to Hel. The queens want the elves to return to our fold, and I was sent to live among them, to show them the power and joy that would be theirs if they rejoined us. I found some receptive to the idea, but the high lords had different plans. When the elves migrated here, I followed, not wanting to abandon my assignment, but uncertain how to proceed."

He stared at her, fairly certain she was lying but feeling that he was not in any position right now to call her out on it.

"But here?" he asked instead. "In the middle of Alaska, where as far as I know there are no elves? Why are you living in an isolated, invisible parallel universe world in the Alaskan wilderness instead of on Elf Island, making your case for reunification?"

She looked down at the half-empty glass of wine, her white-blonde hair hiding her expression. "It's a place for me to recoup my power, to decide whether I should continue to act as an emissary, or return to Aerie and admit failure."

And that felt like a lie as well. Did her presence have more to do with the elf that betrayed her, the one who had the mirror image of her magic? Perhaps if he came back to this later, she'd be more willing to share the truth with him. So instead of continuing, he switched the topic.

"You said your powers are different than the elves'? What exactly can you do? Beyond creating invisible worlds with giant trees and healing mortally injured werewolves, that is."

She shot him a mischievous smile that made him acutely

aware of the fact he was sitting naked beside her. "Teleport. Control the environment. Elves have some limited skill with that, but we're better. We're also better at forming plants and allowing them to live in what would normally be adverse conditions, like my maples, oaks, and hawthorn in the high altitudes and cold conditions here. We can create an overlay world and hide it, ward it strongly against discovery or attack. As for me, I'm particularly skilled with snow and ice. This part of your world calls to me with its wintery beauty. We can affect time in a limited fashion, and enchant. If we choose, we can also serve as a conduit, in which I would share my energy and skills with another."

Her powers seemed to be more along the lines of defensive ones, like a magical chameleon combined with the abilities of a weather witch. Except for enchantment. Dustin eyed her, suddenly wary. She was beautiful in an otherworldly way—breathtakingly so. Was her appearance a form of illusion to draw him in, to make him want to stay? Because it seemed to be working. The thought of leaving her sanctuary, of leaving her, distressed him. Was this her magic? Or this weird bond thing she'd mentioned? Or was he just hurt and tired and wanting to curl up in a safe, snug earthen den with a beautiful, sexy woman?

Dustin shook his head, trying to focus on something besides the brush of her thigh against his. "Will you tell me more about this elf that betrayed you? I know it's personal, and probably none of my business, but if he's the one who is providing the magic bullets to the hunters, then I want to know all I can about him."

Her mouth twisted as she turned to look again into her wine glass. "I was with him when we crossed from Hel. The other elves went elsewhere, but I remained, and came here to Alaska with him. At that time, I was beginning to suspect…

but that is not important. He is a high elf, very talented, brilliant and powerful."

"And he's the one who is providing the magic for the bullets?"

She ran a finger around the edge of her glass. "I'm sure of it. The magic is too close to my own to be that of another elf. I shared my knowledge and power with him while we were in Hel. I held nothing back, because I…trusted him. But once here, I began to see a side of Talligie that I'd foolishly overlooked or ignored before. We had a disagreement. I refused to do something, told him that I was leaving him. He attempted to imprison me, tried to keep me there, but I managed to escape."

"And you came here?" Dustin felt the stew curdle in his stomach at her words. He'd imprisoned her. Had he hit her? Hurt her as well? All of this made him want to dig his fangs deep into the neck of this elf.

Her eyes were sad. "Yes. I had allowed myself to be a conduit to him, and I'm unable to sever the connection unless I face him to do so. Here in my sanctuary, I'm out of his reach. He can't use my energy while I'm here, and I've constructed this place so he cannot easily find it."

"And you intended to either return to Aerie or stay here forever? Hide out rather than face him?"

She winced. "Yes. At the time I just wanted to avoid the confrontation. Please understand, he is equal to me in power and strength. There is a chance he would best me, and I didn't want to be imprisoned and used by him. It seemed the better solution to hide here, out of his reach."

"But now?" he prodded. This elf was providing the means to kill shifters, and she was the one being who could find him, easily get within striking distance of him. Dustin understood her fear that she might not prevail in a battle between the two of them, but for her to stay here while shifters were murdered…that would wipe out any respect he had for her.

She sighed, finally looking directly at him. "I'd hoped with me hidden he'd abandon his plans, but it seems that isn't so. I have no choice but to leave my sanctuary and confront him. I only hope that I've been able to recover enough strength to break our conduit link, and take back everything I so foolishly gave him."

Reaching over to get the bottle, she refilled both of their glasses. He was tired and still in pain, and the food he'd just eaten plus the wine was making it hard to concentrate but he still had questions he needed answers to. "How long have you been here in your sanctuary?"

"Almost three months of your time. It took quite a lot of my power to escape and build this sanctuary. As I've regained power, I've enhanced the illusion, hiding it better and creating a barrier between here and your world. I'd never intended to leave here. But I will. I promise you that I will do everything in my power to stop him."

What if she wasn't ready? Having to heal him probably had depleted her even further. Was he being selfish in wanting her to face her ex-boyfriend when she wasn't ready? "How much longer until you're at full strength?"

Her laugh was short and bitter. "Ten, possibly twenty years. Maybe more. But I don't need to be at full strength to defeat Talligie. I just need to be smart, to be clever."

Dustin gulped down the wine, suddenly worried that this confrontation between Gwylla and her ex wasn't going to end well. "I wish…are you sure? Because we don't have ten years. He's killing us. And I'm assuming that he doesn't need a functioning link to you to make the magic for the bullets."

"No, obviously not." She downed her wine as well. "But if he finds me and he defeats me, then bullets will be the least of your worries. He'll take everything I have, leave me nothing but a shell. And the sum of our magic is greater than our individual parts. If he defeats me, then he will be a problem that possibly only a host of angels can stop."

He swallowed and tried to remain calm. "Okay, so maybe you *should* stay here for a few decades, or until you're strong enough to face him. I can't, though. I need to help my pack. If we have to, we'll fight this guy ourselves. We can't just hide and wait until you're strong enough to deal with him."

She winced. "I'm sorry. I won't wait ten years. I'll face him as soon as I'm able. And there are other things I might be able to do to help your people. If you have healers, or magic users, I can teach them how to counteract the magic. I can't reverse the magic, or heal it with a touch, but I can teach others to help your injured survive their wounds."

"Thank you. We don't have a healer in our pack, but the Juneau Pack has an angel. Two, actually." It would help. And as much as he wanted her to face down this elf that had betrayed her and take her revenge, the thought that her ex would kill her made him want to hide her away himself, to protect her.

Silly. He was a werewolf, and an injured one. What need did she have of his teeth and claws when she had powerful magic at her fingertips?

"You have an angel?" Her green eyes registered shock. "There are two angels here in Alaska? They are ideally suited to learn how to heal the magic. And they may be the only two here besides me who could fight Talligie and stand a chance of defeating him."

He had mixed feelings about that. It was a relief that there were two celestial beings in Alaska who could take this guy down, but troubling that it would take an angel to defeat an elf.

And what did that say about Gwylla when she was at full power? That she was the equivalent of an angel? He was so out of his league here. It was one thing to have fantasies about an elf-like being with white-blonde hair and a see-through silk dress, but those fantasies seemed even more farfetched- when he contemplated the scale of her power.

Dustin looked down at the wine glass, thinking it had been a bad idea to indulge in alcohol. It was dissolving the few inhibitions he'd had. There was a bed over there. He was still injured, but maybe he could just lay there and she could be very gentle…

Now *that* was a fantasy. He'd need to think more about that when he had some private time.

What were they discussing again? Oh yeah, the ex-boyfriend elf that was trying to kill him and the other shifters. None of this had answered the question of why an elf was targeting them, though. "Why would this elf want to kill us?"

Gwylla took a deep breath. "He doesn't, other than you are a stepping-stone to what he wants to achieve. If he can create a weapon to kill shifters, he is on the right path to create one that will kill angels. And if he stirs the humans to act against shifters, he can also convince them to overthrow the angel 'masters' who are attempting to control them. He'd have the humans do the killing for him. The angels are reluctant to hurt humans, and even with their power, they are few and the humans here are many."

The alcohol was clearly messing with his head, because he couldn't have heard her right. "Kill the angels. You're serious. The elves want to kill the angels?"

She nodded. "Elves do not have warm feelings about the angels. Neither do the sidhe, but the elves originally placed themselves under angelic tutoring thinking that they would become more powerful and be able to overthrow the queens and rule Aerie. It might have happened but for the war in Aaru.

When it was clear that the heavenly host would be forever divided, the elves had two choices—remain allied with the Angels of Order and move here where they would be under strict scrutiny and be forced to shepherd a bunch of lower life-forms into positive evolution, or join the Angels of Chaos in Hel. They chose the latter, but neither was the option they wanted, and after nearly three million years, they are no more powerful than they were before the war. In fact, they are less powerful."

Great. So now in addition to interdimensional rifts opening up across the world and spitting out monsters, there was a crazy, souped-up powerful elf with a plot to arm humans with weapons to kill the shifters and eventually angels. Then what? Enslave the humans and take over the world?

"So he'll cause human hysteria about the shifters and Nephilim, give humans the tools to eradicate these spawn of angels, and the angels won't care because we're their dirty little secret anyway. Then they'll turn on the angels."

She nodded. "But I don't think Talligie can summon the power to enchant enough weaponry to kill angels without my help—willing or not. One item he could possibly manage, but one item won't be enough to kill a host of angels. He'll need an arsenal of enchanted weaponry, and for that he will need me."

Well, that was a small consolation. But in the meantime, how many shifters would die before those two angels with the Juneau Pack caught up with this Talligie and stopped him? And if they did stop him, would it be too late? How many bullets were out there already? How many humans were armed and prepared to kill?

"I'm so sorry," she whispered, putting her hand on his leg. "I recognized the magic on the bullets I took from you, and I knew what it was. I knew that Talligie had continued with his plans just as I knew that you were meant to die from that magic."

"Die and be someone's trophy on a wall," Dustin muttered trying hard to ignore her fingers on his naked thigh. "If these magic coated bullets are being distributed widely, we've got a bigger problem. We can't just go killing every human we see. We need a way to get rid of the bullets so humans are no longer a threat to us."

"Getting rid of the bullets might be a problem. The magic is out there and could possibly be replicated by any elf, or maybe even humans with magical ability." She turned to him, her eyes full of sorrow. "I'm am very much afraid, Dustin, that going forward, you and the other wolf-people will forever be vulnerable to these sorts of attacks."

CHAPTER 7

*D*ustin felt a sense of panic. They couldn't put the genie back in the bottle. Even if they could hunt down this Talligie and the human hunters, even if they could destroy the businesses that were running these shifter-hunting expeditions as well as their inventory, they would still be at risk. Any human who wanted them dead might be able to get these bullets.

"I need to go. I can't stay here any longer. I need to go and help my pack." Dustin struggled to his feet, leaning heavily on the wall and trying to catch his breath. This was ridiculous. He wouldn't make it five feet out the door in this state—even if he knew how to open the door.

"You are a very stubborn wolf-man." Gwylla frowned up at him, but didn't try to stop him or urge him back to the floor. "You will do your pack no good if you bleed out naked in the woods trying to get home. Stay and heal. And then I will help you and your people."

She'd helped him already. He owed her his life. That didn't bother him as much as her alarming insistence that she was somehow now glued to his side for life, that he belonged to her. Which would be kind of hot if it wasn't stemming from a sense of responsibility and duty rather than any sort of attraction on her part. He never did get the hot girls. Who was he thinking this ice-blonde fae would go for a somewhat skinny werewolf pilot? Not in the way he wanted, anyway.

"Dustin?"

He'd been daydreaming. And trying to keep from passing out.

"Yeah. What? What did you ask?" He swayed and gripped the edge of the fireplace, his knuckles white.

Her hands were soft and cool as they smoothed the skin of his back. "You're very pale. Do you need to lay down? In the bed?"

He needed to be uninjured so he could warn his pack, pass along what Gwylla had told him about the elf. *Do* something rather than lying on the floor sleeping.

Dustin cleared his throat, trying to take a step toward where he'd seen the doorway and almost falling onto his face. "I *need* to get to my plane, to my satellite phone. I know I'm not strong enough to hike out of here, but if I can call and warn my pack, tell them what you've told me…"

She put an arm around his shoulders, easing his weight against her side, which shifted his focus from pain to the soft feel of her body against his. "You're in no condition to travel. Tell me where the plane is. What does this phone look like? I'll need to wrap my hands so the metal doesn't burn me. Is there a way I can get into the plane with mittens on? I will go get it for you. Just please don't injure yourself further."

Dustin frowned. He couldn't describe where the plane was because he didn't know where the heck *he* was right now. After he'd been shot everything had gone blurry. His wolf instinct had taken over and he wasn't even fully conscious for most of that mad dash through the snow. All he could remember was pain, blood bubbling out of his mouth as he gasped for air, a forest of trees shimmering like an oasis in the distance, then waking up naked in this cabin.

And was his phone still in the plane, or had he taken it with him and dropped it when he shifted? Had the hunters ransacked his plane? Had they stolen it? And even if she did manage to find it and bring it back, would a satellite phone even work in this weird, alternate-universe thingie that was her sanctuary?

"I'll have to go myself," he told her, well aware that he was barely holding himself upright at the moment. "How long do you think before I'm mobile?"

Her hand caressed his shoulder, fingers tracing circles over and over in a soothing rhythm. "I will try to hurry your healing. I know it's important for you to warn your wolf-people, but collapsing from injuries and exhaustion, leaving yourself vulnerable in the open, is not a wise choice. Plus…"

He heard the worry in her voice. "Plus what?"

"Healing you is not easy. The nature of your injury, the magic used to harm you, makes it far more difficult than it would be had you suffered a normal wound."

In other words, there was no rushing this. He'd just have to hope and pray his pack mates were safe. "How long before I'm fully healed?"

She hesitated, her hand brushing low on his hip as she helped steady him. "You should rest. In my bed, too, now that I know you are not a dog. Or wolf."

She was teasing, but all he could think about was her bed. The one bed in the room. Where would *she* sleep? On the floor herself? In the bed with him? Naked? Oh, Lord. And just when he was starting to get his mind away from the land of erotic fantasy. What had he asked her again? Some question she was trying to avoid answering. Oh, yeah.

"Gwylla, please answer my question. How long before I'm

healed?" He'd meant that to be a firm, commanding state-ment, but instead it had come out breathy and lacking in any sort of compulsion. Sheesh. Even injured, probably even on his death bed, Jake would have been snapping out commands that no one could refuse. It's not that he was submissive, or weak. He was just a middle-of-the-pack, somewhat skinny wolf who would rather read comics and play Xbox than order people around. Totally not the sort of guy gorgeous fae women went for.

"Three days, possibly four."

Two. He couldn't risk depleting her energy any further, but two days should be enough for him to be able to get out to his plane and get the satellite phone. Then he could crawl back to her sanctuary, collapse in an exhausted heap, and finish healing.

"Let me help you to the bed before you fall on your face and I have to heal your concussion and skull lacerations."

She was right. He could hardly stand upright. If he made it two feet outside her door, he'd be lucky. If he could even find the door, that is.

"Okay. You win. I'll head out to my plane in two days. If they're still out there looking for me, they'll be armed, so I'll go myself. Then after I make my phone call, I'll come back and bleed some more on your blankets."

She made a huff noise. "If they're out there still, they will shoot you and you will die before you make it back to bleed on my blankets. I will *not* allow you to face them by yourself. I will attempt to heal you further, to speed the process, and I will go with you to the plane when you are ready."

Bossy. Honestly, she sounded more like his Alpha than he did. Figures. Dustin tried to straighten his shoulders, but a short stab of pain through his chest made him give up any idea of a show of strength. "It won't do me any good if you get shot and killed," he told her. "Unless bullets don't harm you?"

Her fingers stilled. "They will harm me, not because of the magic, but because of the metal. But that is of no importance. We will discuss this later and come up with a solution together, because I tell you right now, wolf-man, I will not let you face this danger alone."

He should be arguing with her, asserting his dominance and telling her he wouldn't allow that at all. But, in all honesty, it felt good to have her quiet strength beside him, to know that a powerful sidhe would have his back.

"Now, come to bed."

There was something in the way she said those words that made his mind take a sharp right back into erotic fantasyland.

"Just a minute. I need to catch my breath for just a minute. If you could go stand over there...away from the bed."

"Now. Before I have to drag your unconscious body across the floor." There was a firm tone in that her words that gave him strength. He pushed away from the fireplace, his back straighter than he'd been able to manage before. Holding his head high he walked as near to a straight line as he could to the bed, trying to ignore the fact that Gwylla followed behind close enough to catch him if he fell.

The mattress was amazingly soft, as were the pillows, and the blanket. Dustin sighed, feeling the pain ease to a dull ache now that he was no longer trying to stand or walk.

"And now I will heal you. Since you are awake, I need to warn you that it may hurt somewhat." She placed her hands on his chest and hip, right over where the bullets had penetrated his flesh. Ice and heat shot through him, stinging, burning, an intense combination of both relief and pain. He felt flesh knitting, infection searing away, damaged muscles and nerves forming and connecting. It was agonizing, but there was something liberating about the feeling. When she took her hands from his skin, he still felt the dull throbbing ache of his injuries, yet he knew that in the morning, he would feel ten times better.

She smiled, her eyes betraying how much the effort to heal him had cost her. "There. Sweet dreams, wolf-man."

"I don't get a goodnight kiss?" He hurt. He was exhausted. But hey, nothing good came to those who didn't try, right? Worst case scenario, she'd laugh and call him a silly wolf and walk away. It wasn't like she'd slap him or anything. Not after just healing him.

"Is that a custom among your people?" Her lips curled up. Was she flirting, too? That had to be a good sign.

"Yes?" he put as much hope as he could into the word, trying for an innocent puppy-dog expression.

"Well then, far be it from me to not honor the customs of my hosts." She leaned over him, light green eyes staring into his darker ones with a teasing glint. He smelled cedar and magnolia, green and crisp cold snow. Her hair fell around them, creating a private spot of white silk. Her breath had a hint of frost, like she'd been eating those sharp peppermints. Then her lids fluttered, hiding those beautiful eyes. Lips touched his, soft and surprisingly warm. Her mouth clung to his for an instant, then hovered a breath away, as if she was waiting.

Even as injured as he was, he knew an invitation when he saw one. With a groan he lifted his arms, ignoring the pain in his chest to pull her to him and bring her lips once more to his.

She cupped his face with her hand, using the other to keep her weight from falling onto him, and he deepened their kiss, brushing her bottom lip with his tongue. All too soon she pulled away, looking once more into his eyes. Then her gaze roamed down the length of his body to where his erection was tenting the blanket. There was no hiding *that*. So instead he smiled sheepishly, determined to just brazen it out.

She chuckled. "You have lost a considerable amount of blood, wolf-man. I suggest you try to keep the remaining amount in the upper part of your body. It does you no good all concentrated down between your legs."

He glanced downward and grinned. Oh, it did a whole lot of good down there, just not right now when he would be liable to pass out doing anything about it. What was it the erectile dysfunction ads always said? "Check with your doctor to see if you're healthy enough for sexual activity"? Well, right now, he got the feeling his doctor would say no even to masturbation.

So he adjusted the blanket and closed his eyes, smiling at the thought of what his dreams might hold. Which wasn't helping circulate the blood through the rest of his body.

"Gwylla?" he whispered, suddenly feeling as if he could barely stay awake. "Thank you. For everything."

As he drifted off, he could have sworn he heard her respond. "And thank *you*, my wolf-man. Thank you for being the sunlight in my darkness."

Gwylla stared down at the sleeping wolf-man. Dustin was sprawled in a tangle of sheets and blankets, taking up nearly every inch of the bed and leaving no room for her. Not that she would have risked accidentally hurting him while he slept by climbing in beside him.

She had two more days before he left. She was going to do everything in her power to make sure he was healed enough to defend himself and survive any possible attack. And she was going to use the next two days to ensure that when he returned to his pack, he remembered her, because she certainly would remember him. Even if she never saw him again, she was grateful. He'd shown her that she didn't have to be alone, hidden away in her sanctuary for the rest of her life. He'd given her hope that this world might welcome her, might be a home for her. He'd given her the confidence that she might be ready to face Talligie, and that she'd have the support of the wolf-people when she did.

She was no longer alone. And that brought her more strength than anything had in centuries.

Sidhe weren't meant to be alone. Her solitude the last few

months had been cathartic, allowing her to heal both her emotional wounds and her pride, but she longed for company. And she found herself becoming very attached to this wolf-man in the last two days. He didn't try to woo her with false flattery and honeyed words. He was funny and honest. He didn't hide his vulnerability, or pretend to be anything more than the wolf-man he was.

And the wolf side of him was just as appealing as his human side. Her affection for creatures had led her to readily accept his wolf's cry for help and keep him from death. Dustin as a human had that same earnest, unadorned, authentic nature. She already considered him a friend. And right now, she really needed a friend.

Dustin awoke to singing. Under any other circumstances, that would have annoyed the crap out of him. Any sound, pre-coffee, was an irritant that needed to immediately halt and wait until at least two cups had been consumed. But Gwylla's voice was soft and lilting, almost hypnotic as she sang. He stirred in bed and she turned, a bright smile on her face.

"Good morning!"

Okay, that was too much. The fairy lights in the hut had been turned up to daylight brightness. She was unreasonably happy and energetic for…whatever hour it was. She most likely didn't even have coffee.

"Humph." He'd make an exception for singing, but not actual communication.

Dustin rolled over to smash his face into a pillow that smelled like lavender and mint. That's when he realized that he felt better—he felt *way* better. The aches were still there, a sharp twinge every time he moved a certain way, and he did feel tired, but that was it. What had been barely-able-to-stand pain less than twenty-four hours ago was now move-carefully/don't-overexert-yourself twinges. He peeked from the pillow to eye Gwylla, wondering how much energy she'd used for this level of improvement. She didn't seem tired. In fact, she seemed to be glowing slightly, exuding something that tugged and pulled him to look at her, to be near her. Enchantment? Good grief, the woman hardly needed to enchant him. He'd been more than willing to molest her last night, kissing her like he was a teenager dropping off his prom date for the night. And that boner…

The boner was back. Which was pretty normal in the mornings, but this was a bit excessive, and had more to do with his acute awareness of a beautiful woman not twenty feet from him as he lay naked in bed. Good thing he'd rolled onto his stomach.

"Breakfast?" She approached and knelt beside the bed, face-to-face with him. Her flowery herbal smell washed over him, her hair like silk on his arm. Her light-green eyes, framed with dark lashes, tilted upward at the outside edges like a kitten's. God, she was beautiful. All she needed was an ornate silver crown and a bejeweled necklace, and she would look just like every wet dream he'd ever had.

Boner drilling through her mattress to China right now.

"I have berries with cream, and warm bread with butter and honey."

Breakfast. That's right, she'd been asking him about breakfast. But that would require him turning over.

"Can I sleep a little longer? And I'd like to clean up a bit before eating, if you don't mind." She shouldn't mind. He probably smelled like a yak at this point. And his breath… good lord his breath must smell like gym socks left in a bag in the sun for a week. And she'd kissed him last night. With not-brushed-my-teeth-because-I-was-unconscious-for-nearly-a-week breath. That was probably the last time she'd kiss him. So much for ever seeing second base, let alone crossing to home.

And now the boner was going down.

She smiled warmly. "You must feel better if you're wanting to groom yourself. I'll prepare a bath and enchant it so it stays hot, then go out so you can sleep some more. Rest and heal, my wolf. I will return later." She kissed the top of his head, which put her breasts right into his face. Annnnd the boner was back.

The next time he awoke, the house was quiet. True to her word, Gwylla had left a big tub over to the side of the bed. The water steamed, smelling of sandalwood and pine. There were soaps, a washcloth and towel, and a stick-like thing that he assumed was supposed to be a toothbrush.

The water felt amazing, the heat seeping into his stiff muscles as he sank into the deep tub. How had she managed to move this heavy thing? Or fill it? Or keep it hot? And where did she store it, because the tub hadn't been in the house earlier. Dustin imagined some interdimensional pocket, like a ten-by-ten at the storage rental place. Of course none of that explained how strong she must be to have moved it. Or how strong her magic must be.

He suddenly felt very small and weak. In a world of humans, he'd been the one with superior strength and speed, as well as his ability to heal just about any wound in a matter of hours, or days at the most. He didn't get sick like the humans did. He was a big fish in a very tiny pond. But now...

Angels walking among them. Elves—elves that made werewolves seem like stupid magically inept creatures on steroids. Even this thin, delicate-looking sidhe could probably beat him at arm wrestling in the first three seconds without even trying. Dustin wasn't an Alpha. He wasn't even close to being in line for that position behind Jake. His pack mates liked him. They said he was easy to talk to, that he was the sort of guy you could confide in. He wasn't a leader of wolves, or of men. But being low-middle of the pack of werewolves seemed even lower when surrounded by other supernatural creatures who could not only kick his butt, but could most likely kick his Alpha's butt as well.

And that was a scary thought. That any being less than an angel could best Jake was a difficult pill to swallow. Their world had been turned upside down by these hunters. It was on the edge of being flipped once more.

Submerging his head in the hot water, Dustin scrubbed himself clean and climbed out of the tub feeling better than he had since he'd been shot. Not recovered enough to run for his life or fight back against anything much stronger than a Chihuahua, but better.

There was a note over in the kitchen area—a picture of a wolf walking through a doorway, then another of a wolf sitting at a picnic spread of food by a stream, small woodland animals by his side.

He was hungry enough to eat those animals, but how the heck did he get out of a hut when didn't have the magic to open the door? Or even see the door? And then there was his glaring lack of clothing. Looking around, Dustin found a ball of twine that Gwylla must use to hang the herbs from her ceiling. He used his teeth to cut off a piece and tie it around his waist. Then he grabbed one of the towels, draping it over the twine in the front, passing it between his thighs, then draping it over the twine in back. An instant loincloth, although it felt more like a horribly bulky diaper between his legs. It wasn't like he was going to be running through the forest in his condition, so it would have to do. Taking a few experimental steps around the hut, Dustin cut a second piece of twine to reinforce the first. He didn't really trust this stuff not to break, but it wasn't like Gwylla hadn't seen his goods already.

Clean, and somewhat dressed, he set about trying to find the door, patting the earthen walls around where he'd seen the sidhe come and go the previous two days. He yelped as his hand sank into one spot as if it were a hologram. The door lit silvery-blue around the edges and he found himself facing an opening.

Weird. He hadn't left this hut in seven days. He barely remembered running into the odd forest that was Gwylla's sanctuary as a wolf. All he could recall of that panicked, pain-filled flight was the oddity of oaks, maples, and other lower-altitude deciduous trees in what should have been an alpine forest of pines and aspens. Taking a breath, he stepped through the doorway, a bit disconcerted to see it close up behind him, leaving nothing but a hill of soft grass where the dwelling had been seconds ago.

Well, there was nowhere to go but forward. The picture had shown him picnicking by a stream, but he had no idea where that might be. There were several paths branching out in front of him, and when Dustin lifted his head to scent the air, water seemed to be in every direction. He ended up picking the path where water smelled the closest, figuring that she wouldn't have selected a location requiring a long walk when this was the first he'd been able to truly stand for long, let alone take even a short hike.

Three steps in the world morphed around him, shifting and turning as if he were suddenly hit with vertigo. Dustin grabbed a tree, wondering if he were going to faint. But as quickly as it came on, the dizziness passed and he found himself deep in the forest, the patches of snow giving way to a small mossy clearing with tree-trunk seats, and a spread of food on a white tablecloth. A stream rushed by, dancing over rocks that sparkled with mica and fool's gold. Sunlight streamed through the leafy canopy, spotlighting the clearing. And sure enough, squirrels and birds, chipmunks and butterflies as well as a doe with a fawn stood around the perimeter, ignoring the food on the white cloth, and instead staring at him.

Of course they were staring at him. He was a wolf, a predator. He was surprised they weren't running away. He was even more surprised when he walked into the clearing, and their eyes tracked his movement without fear. The fawn flicked a white tail and turned from his mother to drink from the stream.

He sat, lowering himself gingerly onto the mossy ground, careful to not lose his loincloth or break the string holding it on. There was a shimmer of light on the other bank of the stream, and all the animals turned their heads as Gwylla appeared. She walked across the top of the water, bits of frost and ice forming then melting with each footstep. The animals approached, the birds and butterflies hovering around her hair and lighting on her outstretched hand. It was like a live-action Disney movie. She was an ethereal combination of Snow White and Elsa from Frozen.

"Hi." Idiot. Although, in his defense, it was difficult to know what to say to this fairy princess who walked across water and magicked big tubs of heated water from who-knows-where.

"Greetings. You seem to be feeling much better after your sleep and nap." Then she tilted her head, looking quizzically at his makeshift loincloth. "What are you...you're wearing a towel?"

He adjusted said towel, which was becoming even more uncomfortable under her scrutiny. "I can't keep walking around naked."

Her green eyes were big and innocent. "Why not?

Certainly naked would be more comfortable than having a thick towel bunched up between your legs."

It would be. And right now, if he was back among his pack, he wouldn't have thought twice about walking around in the buff. Shapeshifters didn't have much in the way of body modesty around each other, but it still felt weird to be naked before this woman.

"Well, you're wearing clothing. It seems rude not to at least make an attempt to do the same."

She gave him an odd look, as if she didn't quite believe the excuse. "Would it help if I was naked too? I apologize. I never realized that it might be awkward for you to be unclothed while I wasn't. Fae use clothing as adornment and don't have any taboos about nudity, even in formal social situations. It's always acceptable to be naked, although high-status fae do like to embellish their appearance with cloth, jewels, or precious metals as well as flowers and leaves. I would be happy to take my clothes off if that is the socially proper thing to do among wolf-people."

"As much as I would love to see you naked, I think it would probably be best if you kept your clothes on. For now. I'm reserving the right to change my mind later," Dustin choked out. "And I'll keep the towel on. For now. Although I might take it off later."

He wanted to take it off now. It was bulky and uncomfortable, but not as uncomfortable as having an obvious erection constantly popping up in her presence.

She smiled, walking over to him and plopping down on the moss, her hip brushing against his. Then she gestured toward the food. "Eat. And then, if you are up to conversation, we will talk some more."

Oh he wanted to do a lot more than talk. But the mention of food reminded him about the gnawing empty hole in his stomach. She'd put down a beautiful spread—the berries in cream as well as the bread and honey butter that she'd mentioned earlier. There were little leaf-bowls of candied nuts, and something that looked like oatmeal with blueberries scattered across the top. It looked amazing, but Dustin couldn't help but eye the doe over by the stream with longing. What he wouldn't give for a plate of eggs and a huge steak right now. Mmmmm, venison. He was pretty sure that he could consume a big ten-pound roast in two bites.

Gwylla followed his gaze. "Oh, there is no need for concern. The animals in my sanctuary have plenty to eat. They won't disturb or try to eat the food I've prepared for us."

That was so not what he was thinking as he eyed the doe, but it would probably be horribly impolite to chase down one of her woodland friends and sink his teeth into its hide. So instead, Dustin sighed and turned his attention to the fruit, and nuts, and oatmeal. It was all surprisingly filling, each bite far more flavorful and enjoyable than any food he'd eaten before. Was even the cuisine here enchanted? How much of this was real, and how much a contrived illusion? He looked over at Gwylla, unable to keep his eyes from wandering down her body. Didn't some legends say that fae were actually hideous creatures who used glamour to appear beautiful? Like magical cosmetics, or something?

"Are you tired?" She shifted, stretching her legs out as she leaned back on her elbows. The white tablecloth with the remains of the food blurred and vanished, soft grass and moss in its place.

"No, not really." Tired wasn't the right word. Full. Content. At peace. There was something about this place, something about sitting next to her that made him feel complete, as if all were as it should be, as if the whole world outside could disappear and he wouldn't even care. Which was wrong. So wrong. What was happening to him?

"How are your wounds?"

He lay back as well and spread out on his side, facing her, his head propped on his arm. "So much better. I can't believe that I could barely stand last night and I was actually able to bathe and walk here today. I don't think I'm ready for any long hikes, or to run, but I feel almost like myself again. Thank you."

Maybe just a little nap. The mossy ground here was so soft, and his stomach was full. Content. And happy. With a beautiful woman laying inches from him. One of the birds began to sing and he felt his eyelids grow heavy.

"You are welcome."

She snuggled up against him, draping an arm around his waist and positioning her head just under his chin. He could smell the cool floral scent of her hair, feel the softness of her body against his. His arm went around her, and he marveled at how perfectly she fit against him.

Enchantment? Maybe, but he was just going to go with it. He'd leave soon, but for now he'd relish this idyllic moment and let himself have something to dream about, something to hold on to whenever life got hard. Because illusion or not, this moment, this feeling he was experiencing here in Gwylla's sanctuary with her pressed against him was pure magic.

Dustin awoke, still feeling that incredible sense of contentment. He'd shifted onto his back, and Gwylla was draped across him, her head resting on the unin-jured side of his chest, her fingers gently tracing the lines of his ribs.

"Do you love my sanctuary, Dustin?" she asked with a small smile. "Do you feel the bonds now? Do you long to stay here by my side? I would be happy if you did."

Something in the soft words gave him pause. In another day or two he'd surely be able to leave this place to find the satellite phone and contact his pack, and maybe he'd be healed enough to head somewhere that they could land a chopper and pick him up. Or at the very least hike to a road and catch a ride to the nearest town. The thought chipped away at that sense of contentment.

"Your home is beautiful, Gwylla. But I don't belong here. These bonds you talk about aren't enough to make me ignore the obligations I have to my pack, or throw away the life I have back home. I'm sorry, but this is like a beautiful vacation. Well, aside from getting shot, anyway. Yes, I love it here, but I also love my home, and that's where I need to be."

She sighed, her fingers drifting down to his hip, tracing the edge of the towel across his stomach. Oh my. Maybe he could stay here a bit longer. Make a phone call and tell Jake everything he knew, then inform his Alpha that he was taking a two-week vacation to hopefully get laid—a lot. And he'd need a few extra weeks because as much as he wanted to make love to this beautiful woman in the next twenty-four to forty-eight hours, he wasn't sure he'd be able to do so without reinjuring himself.

Wait. Had that been her plan? Was this a plot to ensnare him, make sure he never left, or if he did that he'd return? He'd be a fairy princess's sex slave, or something like that. And as much as certain parts of his body were on board with that, his brain wasn't.

Actually, his brain kinda was. There were worse ways to live out the remainder of his life. Hadn't this always been a fantasy of his? And if it hadn't been for her finding and healing him, he would have been dead. So staying here and eating berries and hopefully having sex four or five times per day shouldn't be a problem.

Except he *hadn't* died. He had a life, a pack, an Alpha, and those last two needed him. But he could come back…and if they got rid of this elf guy, she could even come stay with him at the compound for a while. Would she? Because if she was willing to do that, then she could weave her spells around him all she wanted. Dustin imagined her at the compound, in his home, and just couldn't see it. Dark jeans and tank top from Old Navy aside, she belonged here in her sanctuary, surrounded by animals and flowers and berries. The idea of Snow White/Elsa living in his house with his pack… His home and life seemed a world removed from this idyllic paradise.

But he wanted her. And that seemed to be overcoming any warnings from his rational side that she might be enchanting him somehow. He shifted on the moss and winced as his chest gave a warning twinge. Clearly sex wasn't going to happen anytime soon. Although maybe she'd give him a blow job. He could lay here, his hands tracing her skin while her mouth brought him the release he was desperately craving. It would probably be rude to suggest it, though. And it would probably be just as rude to reach down and jerk himself off, so Dustin gritted his teeth, thought unsexy thoughts, and once more contemplated a possible death by blue balls.

"Are you still in pain?"

He opened his eyes to find her face close to his, her breasts smashed against his chest. This wasn't helping.

"Um, not much. I'm okay. I think I'd be better if we both sat up. We could sit here and talk." Talking was good. That would hopefully get his mind away from the idea of her giving him a blow job.

A mischievous smile curved her lips and she rose, folding her legs as she settled her back against a tree trunk.

"What is your life like, wolf-man?" she asked, scooting close to him as he sat beside her. "You said that you fly the plane around to transport people. What else do you do?"

Eat steak. Drink beer. Play pool or darts with the guys. Go on hunts with the pack. Occasionally go on a date if he found a werewolf who he was fairly certain would say yes. But he got the feeling she was asking for more than those facts.

"You mean my childhood? I grew up in Pennsylvania, the only offspring of a werewolf couple who were right at the end of their fertility. We generally live to be a hundred to a hundred twenty years, and can have kids until we're about eighty, although it varies by wolf. We're not very fertile, and many couples can't get pregnant, so I was a happy surprise."

"You were spoiled," she teased. "Fae adore children. Any young are a blessing, whether it is a fae, human, or an animal baby. We would have spoiled you, too."

He laughed. "Yes, I was spoiled. Our pack was in a big city as part of the existence contract that the angels put in place. We needed permission to move, permission to hold our hunts, permission to pretty much do anything. We were forbidden from marrying or having children with humans, so we tended to keep to ourselves."

A frown creased her forehead. "The angels did this? Because you are descended from Nephilim, and they hoped eventually you'd die out?"

Dustin winced. "I'm sure some thought that. Mostly the angels were undecided whether we were of Nephilim or not, and until they made a determination, we were held under these strict rules."

"But you obviously have angel in you. I can see it clear as the stars in the nighttime sky. How could the angels have been so blind?"

"Back then most angels never left Aaru. And now I think the ones who were here were covering for us. Because if we were found to be descendants of Nephilim, we would have been slaughtered. Wiped out. Genocide. Living under draconian rules was better than that."

Her eyes were huge. "What happened? You said this was the past?"

He nodded. "The very recent past. The secret got out among the general population of Aaru, and there was a push to exterminate us, but the Iblis, the Angel of Chaos who rules Hel and the Fallen, claimed us as hers. I'm told she stood naked on top of a conference table with her sword in hand at a Ruling Council meeting and proclaimed that the offspring of sinful angels were under her purview, and that the other angels couldn't touch us without going through her first."

Gwylla put her hands together, her face a study of rapt attention. "I would like to meet this Iblis angel. Go on, though."

"There was a vote, and some fighting, but the Iblis has powerful friends, and she prevailed. There are still some angels who want us dead, who watch us carefully and report on any wrongdoings, but I've been told they have other priorities. And now we are free to move from pack to pack, congregate and hold hunts, and marry who we choose. The Alpha down in Juneau just mated with a human woman. As long as we don't go around slaughtering humans, the angels seem pretty much content to leave us alone."

"So you are newly arrived to this part of the world from Pennsylvania? Since these strict rules were lifted?"

He shot her a sly smile. "No, I've been here for the last seven years. My mother passed away ten years ago, and my father didn't live long after her death. The Alaska packs have always enjoyed freedom from the rules and angelic interference that the others haven't. We're sort of under-the-radar. So I snuck up here, and I joined the Swift River Pack. I like the way Jake runs things. There's a lot of structure, and a sense of community. We all live together in a compound, work for the good of the pack. I was an only child in a small Pittsburgh pack. This is like finally getting the big huge family I'd always wished I'd had."

She rested her chin in her hand. "And you fly a plane for your pack. Are your customers primarily wolf-people?"

"Up until recently I mainly flew tourists. The pack owns three outdoor adventure companies. I pick the customers up wherever they're staying, then fly them to wherever they're beginning their hike, or climb, or fishing expedition, or paddling trip. They meet the guides there, or sometimes I'll fly the guides, too. Then I go pick them up in a week or so when they're done. I'll have pontoons on the plane during the summer for lake landings, and in the winter I'll equip it to land on the snow and ice."

"But lately?"

He sighed, remembering the day his workload had doubled. "It's not safe for shifters now, not with these hunters. I get them where they need to go quickly, and I can be trusted. A human charter…"

"Might be a trap," she finished softly.

Dustin waved a hand. "But hopefully someday that won't be a worry. How about you? What was your life like in Aerie?"

"One endless party." She smiled at his laugh. "I'm not joking. Small feasts, large feasts. Dances. Celebrations. There's a lot of inebriation, a lot of sex, and a whole lot of intrigue. The non-stop merrymaking actually covers up all the attempts to garner favor from the queens, their consorts, or other powerful fae and the ugly politics in our society. Then once a year we have The Hunt."

Dustin's blood quickened and he glanced once more at the doe. "We hunt as well. It's a time when we get to really be wolves, to truly bond as a pack. Hunting together is one of my favorite activities."

She shivered, a tremor running down her body. "We don't discuss The Hunt with those who are not fae, but I'm sure your event is not the same as ours."

Ah, a topic that was off limits. He had an idea of what their hunt might entail from her comment about political intrigue. And if he was right, then she was justified in not wanting an outsider to know the sordid details.

"And what about when you went to Hel? Was that an endless party as well?"

She scooted down in the moss, resting her head back to

look up at the sky. "The elves certainly enjoy entertaining, but on a lesser scale. And with their high lords and fractured kingdoms, they have their political interplay as well. It was somewhat relaxing to be there. As an outsider, I wasn't thrown into the middle of all the intrigue as I'd been in Aerie, although I *was* expected to attend every function that I was invited to."

"I'll bet you were invited to a lot of things."

"I was. These elves are the descendants of those who first made the decision to cross into Hel, and they have never had a chance to experience what it's like in Aerie, or know the power that the fae wield when together except through legend. I understand why they chose to live in Hel. It's bad enough in Hel to live next to powerful demons, but to be in Aerie with the sidhe ruling over them, being equals with fairies, pixies, and brownies would have been a blow to their egos."

It was the big-fish, little-pond thing again. Only where he was used to having bigger fish living under the thumb of the angels until recently, the elves weren't. He'd been told they lived an autonomous existence in Hel, side-by-side with their powerful demon neighbors, but not subject to their rules and laws.

But there was one bit of information about Gwylla that she hadn't mentioned—one that he really wanted to know.

"How did you meet Talligie?"

Her lips turned down and she shifted her head, deliberately not looking at him. "He is the son of a high lord in a Kingdom called Wythyn. He was next in line to rule. After his father died unexpectedly, he was briefly high lord. When the kingdoms were combined and then a united elven alliance was created, he was still highly placed and powerful."

"Okay. Elven prince. Brilliant. Powerful. Quite the catch. How did you two end up…together?" The word stuck in his throat, and he wanted nothing more than to punch this elf in the face.

"We met at a spring equinox celebration while his father was still alive. He was very obvious in his admiration. After that he was at every function I attended, sending gifts to me and expressing great interest in my becoming his consort."

Dustin frowned. "How would that have worked? I mean, I assume with your diplomatic assignment that you'd be called back to Aerie eventually. From what you've told me, he doesn't seem the sort of guy who would abdicate the throne to go live with you in Aerie."

She shifted on the grass. "I would have remained in Hel as his consort, the Lady of the kingdom of Wythyn. The queens would have allowed me to stay and not return to Aerie."

There was something off about what she'd said. It wasn't quite a lie, but he got the feeling it wasn't the complete truth either. Did she love this elf so much she would have forsaken her homeland, all of her friends and family, possibly angering these queens and never being able to return to Aerie again? Dustin thought of his connections to the pack and couldn't imagine loving to the degree that he would turn his back on them forever. Although his pack would never have issued an ultimatum. No matter who he eventually chose as his mate, he was certain they would find some way to welcome her into the pack.

"So you were to be wed, but he betrayed you?"

She nodded. "There seemed nothing untoward about his affections. He seemed sincere. Our relationship was very public and open. There was a clear alliance between us, one that the other elves recognized and accepted."

"Marriage?" He choked the word out, wondering if he'd need to kill this Talligie himself.

"Fae do not marry in the same way as humans do. We have consorts, which is generally a romantic and political alliance that lasts more than a few centuries. There are casual, short-lived entanglements. There are consort relationships that are public, extend beyond the bedroom, are longer lasting, and also result in social and political alliances. We also have…pets. I'm not sure that's the right word. We sometimes have romantic relationships where there is an imbalance of power. These are loving and respectful relationships, but they can be a bit one-sided because of the inequality between the pair, like between a high lord and someone of the elven worker class. I know it sounds odd, but those are generally relationships that last until one partner dies."

Pets. It was a horrible word for what seemed similar to what European royalty had done hundreds of years ago. A spouse of equal social level for political alliance and children, and a low-born lover that held your heart.

She might say she had loved this elf, but surely that love was enhanced by the advantages such an alignment would give the both of them. She was a diplomat from Aerie, which probably was fairly high in their social ranks. Through her ex-boyfriend, she would have been the equivalent of a queen, with a husband who ruled over an elven kingdom. In some people's eyes, that might be worth giving up your homeland, and for all he knew she had no family or few friends there to miss.

Of course, this all meant the only position open to Dustin would be the second one. A pet. Or a casual fling, a one-night stand. Although that was definitely putting the cart before the horse given they'd kissed once. *Slow it down, Dustin. Don't let those fantasies get in the way of reality.*

Still, a powerful sidhe and a werewolf of far lesser power. If there ever was more than a goodnight kiss between them, he knew where it *wouldn't* be going. There would be no "consort" for him. There would only be casual sex, or a future as a "pet".

Well, screw that. He'd just keep his dick in his pants. Or in his towel as the case may be.

"So, this ex-boyfriend of yours, I'm assuming he's over near Anchorage or thereabouts? Do you think he could sense you if you left the sanctuary for a short period of time?"

She sighed and turned toward him, her expression sad. "He knows I have hidden myself to recover my strength, and he probably spent the first month searching for me, but from what you've said, I believe he's turned his attention to these hunters and ways to bring death to you and the angels. He will be patient and wait for me to come out of hiding, but I doubt he will find me quickly. I feel fairly certain I could walk among you for a few weeks outside my sanctuary before he noticed my presence here once more."

"Good." Dustin nodded. "I want to leave tomorrow to try to get the satellite phone. I'd appreciate it if you escort me to the border of your sanctuary at the very least. If you feel comfortable, I'd welcome the back-up until I get the phone and can call my pack."

"I will protect you and ensure you are not harmed while retrieving your phone," she vowed.

He couldn't help but flinch at her words. She'd protect him. Because as a werewolf, he needed protecting. A pet. He'd be no more than just a pet.

"The next thing I need to ask is about weaponry. Obviously you don't have any guns. Bow and arrows? An axe? Knives?"

She held up her hands. "These are my weapons. If attacked, I use my magic."

"I mean for *me*," he told her.

"I don't have metal. Perhaps you can sharpen a stick on a rock?"

Right. Because caveman weaponry would be sooo effective against men with rifles and bullets that killed werewolves. He was going to have to rely on the things he did have, which were claws and teeth, speed and strength. And for that, he'd need to shift into his wolf form. He wouldn't be able to communicate with her like that, or have opposable thumbs to pick anything up, but at least he'd be able to defend himself, and possibly her, from attack. At least in his wolf form, he would be more than just a pet.

The next day Dustin knew he was ready to leave. Outside of a few aches, he was fully recovered, although the lack of meat in his diet was driving him crazy, as was the caffeine withdrawal. He'd give anything for a big mug of coffee right now. Anything.

And it was becoming difficult to resist the urge to stay. This place was seductive. It wasn't just Gwylla's beauty and companionship, it was the sanctuary itself. The world pulled him in, swaddled him in soft blankets, promised the kind of peace and joy that was found by drinking of the river Lethe. As tempting as it was, the whole thing grated something in the back of his mind, made his wolf restless. He feared if he didn't get out of here soon, he'd never be able to leave.

And then he would be a pet. Or solidly in the friend-zone. Neither option appealed to him in the least.

Of course, there were two problems with his plans to leave. One, he suspected that without Gwylla's help, he'd spend the rest of his life wandering around in circles in a magical forest. And two, he had no clothes.

He wasn't a tall wolf, but Gwylla was a good four inches

shorter than he was. Worse, he couldn't even force a pair of her pants over his hips, let alone manage to button them. And the one T-shirt he struggled into was so uncomfortably tight he felt he could hardly take a breath.

The sidhe found the whole thing hysterically funny. He would have found it funny too had he not been stir-crazy from an eight-day confinement and eager to let his pack know he was still alive.

"Can't you make clothes?" He was being rather snappish, but she'd not seemed to notice. "Ahia can make clothes, although I've never seen her make them for someone else. Can't you?"

"You mean magic clothing into existence?" She snapped her fingers. "Like that? No, I cannot do that. I cannot even manage to shape clothing with needle and thread, let alone through my magic. That is why all my human clothing came from that delightful place called Old Navy."

"You could have just said no," he grumbled. "I'm going to have to shift and go as a wolf."

"You said you were going to do that anyway," she pointed out. "Because you are faster on four legs and can evade the hunters if they try to shoot you."

"Yes, but I'll need to grab the satellite phone with my mouth and hope I don't accidently crush it while dodging bullets." And if he needed to get into his plane, he was hosed. Plus, there was the fact that eventually he'd need to shift back into his human form. He'd at least need to do so to operate and speak over the satellite phone. Which meant he'd be standing vulnerable and naked out where he'd been shot last time. There weren't many other alternatives, though.

If he returned here, which he was hoping wasn't necessary, he didn't want to have to choose between nudity and a towel loincloth. If Jake sent a chopper to pick him up, he'd either need to shift back and wait in wolf form, or stand naked, flagging down a helicopter. And if Jake couldn't send transport, he'd need to hike naked to the nearest town, then ask some human, who hopefully wouldn't shoot him, to give a nude man without money a ride to the pack compound.

Yeah. No.

"I'm going with you. I'll have hands to carry things, although if the phone is metal, I'll need to wrap my hands to pick it up. And I'll need a bag to carry it in."

She was *that* sensitive to metal? For some reason he'd thought anything but pure iron would be okay. He looked over at her, realizing she was going to be potentially dodging bullets herself, and risking burns from what he'd always considered everyday objects.

"Actually, I've changed my mind. You stay inside your sanctuary. The plane can't be far. I'll be out and back in a few hours at the most. And if I need to, I'll shift into my human form to get into the plane."

No he wouldn't. It took him twenty minutes to shift, and three shifts in as many hours would have him facedown in the snow with exhaustion, even if he wasn't still recovering from the gunshot wounds. Dustin fingered the blanket wrapped around his hips and wondered if he could carry it and throw it on as a loincloth/toga thing that wouldn't excessively hinder his mobility.

Gwylla folded her arms across her chest. "I'm going with you. Two of us will be more aware and alert to any possible attack by these hunters. And if you need to, I will help you open the airplane doors and carry anything." She turned around and grabbed a strip of cloth, making a show of wrapping it around her fingers and palm, as if she were prepping to dress as a mummy for Halloween.

If there was one thing Dustin had learned in the last few days, it was how pointless it was to argue with her when she had that stubborn look on her face. "Okay," he sighed. "I'm going to begin to shift into my wolf form. It's not pretty. You might not want to watch this."

She tilted her head, shooting him a quizzical glance before turning her back. "I do not have a queasy nature about such things, but if you are shy, or do not want me to watch, I will honor your wishes."

Dustin began the painful process of changing into his wolf form. And as the muscle and bone twisted and contorted, he could have sworn he heard her grumble: "It's not like I haven't seen all your naked body parts already. There is no longer any need for modesty between us."

Yes, there was. It was one thing for her to see him bleeding and close to death, for her to see him with an erection. This was something he'd always kept from anyone outside his pack. When he shifted, he was vulnerable, he was in pain, he was weak. He felt weak enough in her presence without having her witness him at his weakest.

When he was wolf, he got to his feet and shook himself to settle his fur.

"Are you done?" she called, her back still turned.

Dustin couldn't help himself. He snuck up behind her with soundless footsteps, then goosed her in the rear with his nose.

She shrieked that high pitched sound that made his ears want to bleed and launched herself forward. He laughed, knowing the sound didn't translate well in this form, and was surprised when she laughed in return.

"Bad wolf-man," she teased, shaking a finger at him. Then she went to where he'd learned the doorway to the house was, tracing a seam with her finger. As the edges glowed a blue-silver, she pushed and the door opened wide.

Dustin blinked at the sudden bright light, then followed her outside, turning to watch as she closed the door to her house, turning it once more into simply a barrow, built into the side of a rolling green hill that had no place in Alaska. By the time she'd sealed the door, the entrance was undetectable. Even with his heightened senses, he could walk up and stick his nose right against it and not know that this was anything except a grass-covered hill of dirt and rock.

She patted the grass then turned, leading the way through the forest. He'd grown to know a bit about her over the last few days, her sense of humor, her warmth, her caring, her odd way of speaking. But he'd never realized the power she held until he walked with her through this forest of her own creation. It was like she'd sliced open reality and brought forth a world of her own making. The size and types of trees weren't typical, and certainly not typical for this part of the planet. As she walked, the world seemed to bend and skew around her. He could have sworn they'd passed the same tree at least a dozen times, that they'd been traveling far longer than they should have. He'd been shot, and ran for his life while bleeding profusely from what should have been fatal wounds. There was no way he'd ran for hours through the normal Alaskan wilderness, then another few hours inside her acid trip of a sanctuary. There had to be something wrong. Were they going around in circles? They should have been outside the sanctuary by now.

"No, we're not at the exit, and I wanted us to leave at the same spot you came in as that's probably the closest to your plane."

He jerked to a stop, staring at her as she continued forward. She heard him? She'd heard his thoughts? A powerful fae that claimed he now belonged to her, that was most likely enchanting him with her magic and her beauty to stay, and now even his thoughts weren't his own?

She must have sensed he was no longer following, because she stopped and turned back to look at Dustin quizzically. "Is there something wrong?"

If she could read his thoughts, then she would be very aware that there *was* something wrong.

The sidhe sighed. "Dustin, I would never intrude on your thoughts normally, but you're unable to speak when you are a wolf, and I felt it important that we be able to communicate. I promise not to go beyond the surface, or intrude into things you want to keep private." She took a step forward. "But I *do* want you to know that I'm not enchanting you. Humans are drawn to us, and since you are part human, that is normal. I can't turn that off any more than you can stop breathing. As for the bond…I can't turn that off either, and I am just as affected by it as you are. This was the pact we made when you called to me and I saved your life. Yes, you did not realize what your wolf had done, and I did not know you were any more than a mortally injured animal, but we have entered this contract, and neither of us can break it."

He didn't like any of this. If she'd been a human, or a shifter, who had found him in the woods, taken him in and nursed him back to health, he would have been fine. But she was some otherworldly creature with powers he didn't understand. He didn't trust whether the attraction he felt was real or some glamor, or this weird bond. And wrong as it might be, he blamed her for the bond that tugged at him to stay in the sanctuary. Moments like these he wasn't sure if death wouldn't have been the better option.

Gwylla watched him, and from the patient expression in her eyes, he knew she wasn't reading these thoughts.

He patted the ground and looked at her intently. *This forest couldn't be as big as you say. I had lost a lot of blood and was running flat out. I couldn't have gone far before collapsing.*

"You were an injured animal in need of help," she replied. "My forest shaped itself so you came directly to the center, to my heart-tree. My sanctuary is huge, and although I can, and am, folding it so that we do not take all day to leave, it still takes time to reach the border. Folding space takes energy, as does teleportation. And that is energy I need to have available in case we are attacked."

So he owed his life to her forest as much as to her. Was it fate that led him in this direction, that brought him to these trees? Was it fate that the forest, instead of rejecting him, or letting him wander lost until he died of blood loss, pulled him directly to the spot he needed to be to call to Gwylla for help? It seemed far too much to chalk it all up to coincidence.

Dustin figured it had to have been a two-hour walk before they reached the edge of the sanctuary. There was no line delineating the border, no gate or stream to cross. One moment he was in a thick forest of green leaves and icy white frost, and the next he was in an Alaskan alpine meadow. He turned around to catch sight of the forest behind him and saw nothing but a continuance of the meadow with craggy pines, rock, and patches of snow. It was gone, like an illusion from a fantasy movie. And if he needed to find it again, he was pretty sure he'd not be able to. At least he wouldn't be able to find it unless Gwylla, and the forest itself, wanted him to.

It bothered him. He wanted to be able to see it. He wanted her sanctuary to be his secret place, too, something they shared between them. He wanted it to always be open and welcoming to him. But the reality was, even with her talk of bonds and responsibility for his life, there was nothing permanent in this thing between them. Maybe she'd always check on him or have some awareness of his health and well-being, but after the hunters were stopped, after this Talligie was stopped, he'd go back to his pack and she'd go back to her forest. And unless there was some unusual circumstance, like if he crashed his plane or got into a fight with a polar bear, he'd probably not ever see her again.

The thought twisted his chest like it was caught in a vise.

"Look." Her voice was hushed as she crouched down, pointing to something at the edge of a patch of snow. It was a footprint.

Bending his nose to the ground he inhaled, trying to find a scent. Whoever had left this print, they'd done it at least a week ago. But that didn't mean he hadn't come back more recently.

Dustin was tired, and starting to feel those nagging twinges in his chest and hip from the long walk through the sanctuary, but he couldn't lead Gwylla into a trap. Dropping his nose again to the ground, he swept back and forth, cataloging all the varying scents and ignoring everything that wasn't human.

There had been two. He was pretty sure these were the two that had shot him, given how remote this section of Alaska was and that this was the very spot where Gwylla said he'd entered her sanctuary. They had followed the blood trail —which he was sure a blind man could have followed. There were no recent scents, so they must have given up at least five days ago and left. But…he eyed Gwylla who was frowning down at the patch of snow where she'd seen the footprint. What would the hunters have thought about a significant blood trail that just vanished. No tracks. No blood. No dead werewolf body. Just a spot in the snow where everything stopped. Experienced hunters would know there was something odd about that, and hunters who knew about the existence of shifters probably knew about the existence of magic as well. Had they gone back to whoever their boss was and told him about the strange anomaly? And had that person known enough to let the elf working with them know someone had snatched a mortally injured wolf out of thin air?

It was a stretch. And he was being paranoid. No doubt they figured he'd managed to overcome the bullets—that they were either defective somehow, or that he had abilities beyond most werewolves. Why would they bother to relay something so trivial to the elf?

He walked over and nudged Gwylla's hand, looking up into her face. *I'd really prefer you stay here, close to the borders of your sanctuary.*

"No. They came after you, but they left. These tracks are old—even I can tell that. And you're getting tired. I won't leave you."

He was getting tired, and it would be best to get going and stop arguing or else Gwylla might have to carry him back to the sanctuary.

Taking the lead, Dustin trotted ahead, sniffing the ground occasionally to pick up the old, faint notes of his own scent as well as the hunters to make sure he was on the right path. Once he found the dirt road, he traced it back to the ditch where the truck had been overturned. There was nothing except churned up dirt and black snow. He'd run for roughly two miles after being shot—an amazing feat given how much blood he'd lost along the way.

And about fifty yards from where the truck had been was his plane. The doors were open, the pilot's side one hanging from one broken hinge. He ran to the plane, knowing before he got there what he'd find. Putting his paws on the seat he peered in and saw a mess of hacked up wires. It had been stripped. All the instruments, all the controls were gone. Hopping down and circling it, he saw the propeller was bent, mechanical components completely missing. The fuselage had several huge holes poked in it, and from the lack of spilled fuel, he knew they'd siphoned it and taken it somewhere else.

The fuselage wasn't the only thing with holes in it. The plane looked like the hunters had used it for target practice as well as hit it with a sledge hammer a few times. The sight made him want to curl up and cry.

Destroyed. He'd loved that plane. He'd been flying it for seven years now, and this plane was like a second home to him. Yes, Jake would authorize the purchase of a new one, and the next one would have more passenger and cargo space, have additional bells and whistles, but nothing would replace *his* plane.

Gwylla put a hand on his head, smoothing his fur back. "I'm so sorry, Dustin. I can tell you are aching inside because they have damaged your plane. You are just as upset about its loss as them shooting and trying to kill you."

She was right. Was that weird that he'd nearly lost his life, and yet he was ready to go on a rampage because they'd destroyed his plane? Well, the aircraft might be a loss, but there still might be the satellite phone somewhere nearby. He remembered he'd had it in one hand, the first aid kit in the other, when they'd shot him and forced his shift. He'd dropped it, the kit, and his pistol. And with any luck, the phone would be lying in the dirt nearby.

Dustin put his nose to the ground, picking up the faint degraded scents of the hunters and cataloging them to memory as he retraced their steps. The fallen first aid kit was gone except for a stray bandage that must have fallen out of the box when he'd dropped it. There was no sign of the pistol or the satellite phone beyond a few broken pieces of plastic partially embedded into the ground. They must have taken the gun and smashed the phone.

And there went his hope of contacting Jake and the pack. He'd need to pull together enough strength to hike out to the main road, then hope some passerby didn't mind picking up either a naked man with a towel or a wolf, and giving him a ride to the nearest town.

"What's this?"

Gwylla had left his side and was walking over to a dark shape on the ground next to two trees. Dustin trotted after her, wondering what the very thorough hunters could have left behind. Then he smelled them—five humans had been there, and within the last few hours.

"Is this your phone? It looks like it might–"

He'd yipped a warning, but it was too late. A net shot up from the ground, gathering Gwylla up and hauling her into the trees. She gasped in surprise, then began to laugh. "Oh how clever! They must have known you'd return, or possibly that your pack would send someone searching for you and the plane."

She might think it was funny, but he didn't. The net held her high above the ground. It would have been easy enough for a werewolf to bite through the ropes and escape—if the net hadn't glowed with a magic that made the hair stand up on the back of his neck.

Dustin knew without a doubt if it had been him caught in that net, or any other shifter, they could have chewed and clawed to their heart's content and not escaped. It was meant to hold them until the hunters returned. He'd set enough snares in the last seven years that he knew the importance of checking them regularly. They'd be here before nightfall. Heck, for all he knew, they had some type of spell that let them know when the trap had been triggered.

Can you get yourself out of there? We need to go?. He tried to put as much urgency into the thought as possible.

She swung the net from side to side, poking her fingers through the holes and testing the rope. "Yes. This is not a complex spell. It's similar to the nets the elves make to hold demons they find trespassing in their lands. See? I just counter the magical current at the junction here, then reroute it—"

The magic vanished, the net fell apart and Gwylla

shrieked, frantically grabbing at the rope as she fell to the ground. Dustin began to rush forward, to try to break her fall, then stopped, realizing that it wouldn't do Gwylla any good to land on top of a wolf. And it most certainly wouldn't do him any good to have a woman landing on top of him either. Feeling rather unchivalrous, he watched her crashed onto the snow and grass, the net a tangle of ropes on top of her.

And now he rushed over, pulling the deactivated net from her and poking her with his nose. She looked up at him. "Ouch. Don't let anyone tell you that sidhe always land on their feet, because you have now witnessed what an untruth that is."

He laughed, relieved she wasn't hurt. Then he gripped the net in his teeth, yanking it over to the side. *We need to go, and fast. If they've set this trap, they check it regularly. They might be on their way right now.*

Gwylla got to her feet and straightened her clothes. "Back to the sanctuary? Or is there somewhere you'd like to hide and lay in wait for these hunters to arrive?"

He hadn't thought of that. His first impulse at this situation was to get Gwylla back to the sanctuary where they both could be safe, and where he could make plans for getting to the nearest town. Could they ambush the hunters? The idea appealed to him, but he was injured, he had no idea what use Gwylla's magic capabilities might be in this situation, and the hunters were packing bullets that could easily kill either of them—Gwylla by the metal in the bullets, and him by the magic coating them. No, it would be best to run back to the sanctuary and hide.

The hunters would follow them. And this time they'd know something was up when two tracks vanished in the same place where the blood had stopped before. And then, instead of having the element of surprise on their side, he and Gwylla would be trapped in the sanctuary under siege by humans with magic bullets and a powerful elven ex-boyfriend.

Let's stay, he told her. *Although it might be uncomfortable. We'd need to find a spot to shelter and hide for hours.*

"I can make the ground soft and dry, and assist with an illusion to hide us better," she said.

He shook his head. *They might have something that would sense the illusion. I don't want them to know we're here until we are on top of them. No sense in taking the chance that an illusion would give us away.*

"How far away should we be? How fast can you run?"

He looked around. They'd want to be on top of the hunters before the humans had a chance to take stock of the situation and begin shooting.

I'm fast, but we should probably be no farther than a hundred feet from the net. They'll be ready to aim and shoot, and hyper-aware once they see the net is disabled and on the ground.

"There?" Gwylla pointed to a patch of briars. Dustin winced at the thought of spending hours where every movement would send sharp thorns jabbing into his side. It was the best cover available at a reasonable distance, though, so he headed toward it, only to stop when a light appeared over by the plane. It was a long sliver of light that reminded him of the transporter beams on Star Trek.

"Elves," Gwylla hissed.

His skin prickled. Elves? As in plural? Was this the ex-boyfriend come to retrieve Gwylla? If so, he'd have a fight on his hands. Dustin might not be an Alpha, but he wasn't going to die being shot in the back as he ran away—not when Gwylla's life also was on the line.

The light expanded, and as if they were stepping through a doorway, three hunters appeared, their guns at the ready. They took one look at Dustin and pulled the trigger.

Time seemed to slow. The flash of gunshots, Gwylla's outstretched hands. He leapt forward, determined to at least take down one of these hunters before their bullets killed him. Two steps in he hit something solid, something cold.

Ice. A wall of ice. Somehow Gwylla had managed to erect a wall of clear ice between them and the hunters. It wasn't thick, and the hunters seemed to realize that, as their bullets chipped away at the barrier faster than Gwylla could repair it. The humans moved closer, the force of their gunshots nearly penetrating the wall. She couldn't keep this up for long. He'd need to run around the wall to attack, and they'd see him coming, they'd shoot him dead before he could round the corner. And in the time it took him to do that, they'd be through the barrier and have killed Gwylla.

On my word, drop the barrier, he told her. *I want them close enough that the rifles are ineffective and we can grapple.*

The idea of Gwylla grappling with the hunters was ludicrous, but it was the only thing he could think of. Hopefully she'd be able to at least hold her own while he killed them one-by-one. Then he thought of the wall of ice before him. She wouldn't need to punch and wrestle, she could probably deep-freeze them with a touch.

Wait. Wait. He cautioned, as the hunters drew close. The bullets were nearly through the ice and Gwylla was breathing heavily, her hands shaking as she tried to increase the thickness of their wall.

With a shower of ice chips, one of the shots broke through. Gwylla cried out, clapping a hand to her shoulder, and the wall fell like a waterfall to the ground. Dustin saw one of the hunters take aim, and sprang, knocking the gun from his hands as he dove for the man's throat. In his peripheral vision he saw the other hunters turn from Gwylla to train their rifles on him. He tried to ignore them, sinking his teeth deep into the man's neck and feeling the rush of blood.

One down. And that was probably all he had time for. But instead of the agony of magicked bullets ripping through his flesh, he heard shouts and curses, and turned to see the two men dropping rifles that were suddenly freezing cold. Actually, more than freezing cold. The guns smoked as if they'd been stored in dry ice.

Not wanting to take the time to contemplate that, Dustin sprang on the nearest human, feeling the guy's frostbitten hands fumble clumsily with his fur. There was still one hunter, and Dustin wasn't sure how much magic Gwylla had left to use.

When he lifted his head, blood dripping from his muzzle, he saw the man running to the plane, clutching something in his hand. With a burst of speed, Dustin raced after the human, closing the distance with each stride. The white elongated light appeared once more, and Dustin tried to pump his legs harder, feeling the twinges in his chest and hip rip into agony. He was five feet away when the man began to step through the light—easy jumping distance, but if he leapt, they'd both be propelled through the passage, and Dustin was pretty sure there would be a whole host of humans on the other side ready to fill him full of lead. Instead of jumping, he skidded to a stop, watching the light fade. Then he turned and jogged back to Gwylla.

She was sitting next to the two dead hunters, breathing heavily, her hand still on her shoulder.

Let me look at your wound.

There was a lot of blood, but from what he could see the bullet had just grazed the top of her shoulder. A werewolf wouldn't even have blinked at such an injury. A human would have gone in for stitches and been fine in no time. But Gwylla was neither human nor werewolf.

How bad is it? Was she going to die? Was this like a sort of blood poisoning, that being grazed by a bullet could kill her?

And what metal was she sensitive to? All? Only iron, like in the fairy tales?

She bunched up a piece of cloth that she must have torn from her shirt and pressed it against the wound. "It hurts, and it will scar, but I'll live." She sniffed, shaking her head. "I've been injured many times, and nothing has hurt like this little flesh wound. And I've never had a scar. Such a thing on a sidhe is unheard of."

A scar. She was worried about a scar when he was fretting that she would wither and die right before his eyes. Then Dustin remembered the pain he himself had felt when he'd been shot. It didn't look like much, but he knew that injury had to hurt like heck. Even hurt she'd managed to freeze two guns. And that wall of ice…once more she'd saved his life. If it hadn't been for her quick thinking, they would both have been dead.

"You saved my life," she echoed his thoughts. "Thank you."

He tilted his head. *And back at cha'. We make quite the team, you know. We work well together.*

She smiled at him. "We do. Our powers are complementary. We are like…twins when we are fighting."

Twins? Why did his mind immediately go to Sunday morning cartoons? *We're Wonder Twins! Power of ice. Form of a wolf.*

She tilted her head. "Wonder Twins. I like that. Where should we go now?"

We should probably head to your sanctuary. I don't think either of us is in any condition to fight a dozen armed humans right now.

She fixed her gaze toward the horizon, a sad expression on her face. "We can't return. That man who got away will tell the others of a woman with long white hair who creates ice from nothing and freezes their weaponry. They used an elven transportation method to arrive and leave. Talligie must be in close contact with them. As soon as he hears that man's tale, he will know where I am. The sanctuary is no longer safe. I have no desire to hide there like a rabbit, waiting for him to eventually hammer through my defenses. I would rather we find your people to warn them. Then, hopefully, I will be strong enough to face Talligie and end this thing between us."

He watched her, knowing the need to abandon her beautiful sanctuary was just as painful as the wound on her shoulder. And he could read between the lines of her speech. She'd take him somewhere safe, where he could be with his own kind, then she'd set out to what might be her death—and she hoped that before he killed her, she managed to take Talligie down.

Gwylla followed Dustin's lead. She wasn't sure where they were going, but trusted that in his wolf form, he would have the senses to lead them in the right direction. Against his silent protests, she'd robbed one of the dead men of his clothing, knowing that if they reached a human town, Dustin would need to revert to his bipedal form—and that being naked would only hurt his cause if not get him arrested and put in jail. There had been a carrying case of sorts on the man's belt, and she'd taken it too, as well as the long gun, which she'd wrapped carefully with the clothing. The awkward bundle made it difficult to hike across the rocky, uneven terrain, but she didn't want to use the energy to create an ice sled to haul it on.

Actually she barely had enough energy to put one foot in front of the other. The ice wall had taken a lot out of her, as had freezing the human weapons. It had been a bit overkill to ice them down to that point. She was pretty sure those guns would no longer be functional, even if they thawed out, but the one she carried should be usable since it belonged to the first one Dustin had killed. Well, usable by the wolf-man, as she was trying hard not to touch the thing.

How in the world had the hunters planned this? She doubted Dustin flew this route every day. She'd picked the spot for her sanctuary because it wasn't a high-traffic area. If the hunters had camped out in a randomly selected location, waiting for a chance occurrence to kill a shifter, they would have probably been waiting for weeks if not months. Even she knew that was a complete waste of time.

Hunters knew their prey. The foxes knew where the rabbits played and fed, knew where their dens were. She doubted a human hunter would just walk out his front door and wander around until he happened to come across a wolf-man. No, just like the fox they'd know where their prey frequented by studying the landscape and their habits. And if a hunter wasn't familiar with the area, he'd hire someone to show him the right spots, to increase his chances of seeing, and shooting, his intended prey.

Which meant the hunters knew the shifters on sight. In his human form, Dustin blended right in. She wouldn't have been able to tell him apart from the other humans visually. And even in wolf form, she'd thought him only a bit off from the non-shifter canines she'd seen. Gwylla might not have been around humans for long, but she was reasonably sure they didn't have heightened senses that she didn't possess. Either they were working from a list of shifters, including where they lived, what they did, and their habits, or they had a magical means to identify them—like an amulet or stone that would detect the miniscule bit of angel in them and alert the hunter that the human he was facing was not, in fact, a human.

She wasn't sure which theory was more disturbing.

Is it possible for the hunters to have a magical means to identify shifters? Like an orb that glows blue if we're a werewolf, and stays white if we're human?

Gwylla turned to Dustin in surprise. Had he been reading *her* thoughts? There was so much she didn't know about these children of angels. She'd made so many assumptions in the last few days—so many false assumptions. She'd seen Dustin as no more than a wolf, and no more than a human, completely forgetting that the wolf part of him came not from an animal, but from an angel. There had been something when he'd fought the hunters, some hint of his angelic ancestors. It was locked tight, but it was there. And it made her curious to know more about him.

"It's possible that the humans are using a magical device," she replied. "I thought you were a dog when I first saw you, and when you're in your human form, I couldn't tell you apart from other humans. But I've not been around a lot of humans, canines, or even shifters, and there is something that feels unusual about you. I'm sure the elves or possibly a human sorcerer could narrow that down and enchant an object to indicate whether someone was a shifter or not."

Or they have a database of who we are. It wouldn't be hard. We haven't been secretive about our existence here in Alaska. It would take time and work, but eventually someone could have detailed information on enough shifters that they could set up these hunts and give reasonable guarantees that the hunter would bring home a shifter pelt.

The thought wasn't exactly reassuring.

"Where are we heading? I'm not familiar with the cities and towns here."

As far as she knew, they'd need to cross mountains to reach any nearby city and neither one of them were in any condition at this moment for a long, grueling hike.

Right now I'm just trying to get us out of this valley and somewhere with a good vantage point so I can get my bearings. Then...

maybe Cantwell. It's is the closest city as the crow flies. Except we aren't crows and flying isn't an option. Pretty much everything would involve crossing several mountain ranges unless we want to hike southeast. It's farther distance-wise, but we could cover it at a faster speed, so we'd probably make about the same time in arriving in a populated area or near a road.

"Days? A week or two? How far is it to walk to this Cantwell village?"

If we go through this range, then northeast, it should be around 40 miles to Route 3 just outside of the preserve. We're bound to encounter someone eventually along the road. If not, we'll walk south and toward Cantwell.

"I'm a bit worried about encountering someone along the road," Gwylla replied. "Who can we trust if any human you encounter might be intending to kill you?"

Sitting on the roadside waiting for a shifter to drive by wouldn't be a good use of time. I'm hoping that once I'm in my human form and dressed, I won't be recognized as a shifter. Unless there are thousands of magical devices that can identify us and they're in wide distribution, the odds are in our favor.

She still didn't like it. "Can't we just go to the home of one of your wolf-people? Didn't you say you were coming back from transporting two of them when you were deceived into landing?"

That's actually a good idea. They're in McKinley Park, just north of the town. It's a bit farther north and west, but probably a better plan than hitchhiking into Cantwell.

"How far?"

The wolf evaded her eyes. *Fifty miles, give or take. It's not easy terrain, so it will probably take us a couple of days. I can hunt for food, and we can put together a makeshift shelter for us.*

This was a terrible situation. Gwylla had left the sanctuary with no thought that they'd be gone for more than the day, and here they were hiking through the wilderness with nothing but clothes, and a gun. They could find water, and she could provide a shelter, but the thought of plodding along, injured and tired, for two days wasn't thrilling.

There was no other alternative. Well, there was an alternative. Fifty miles. The two of them. She'd be pushing it, but once safe with Dustin's wolf-people friends, she could rest and recharge. "Do you have knowledge of where these shifters live? I mean, a picture in your mind, and a way to pinpoint their home in the geography of this land?"

He looked up at her in surprise. *Of course. I was just there, and I'm a pilot. I can visualize the flight path, the approach, and the lake where I need to land. Why?*

She took a deep breath, knowing what this would cost her. But time was running out, and getting them safely to Dustin's people was more important.

"Because I need you to show me where this place is in order for me to teleport us there."

* * *

Dustin stopped in his tracks in surprise. He knew she was right. Neither of them were fit for this journey on foot, and they'd reach their destination probably weaker than if she used the energy to teleport them. But how much energy could she expend and still be able to fight and beat this ex-boyfriend of hers? How much could she expend and be able to fight him and live?

At Brenda and Mark's he could accomplish multiple tasks at once—alert the Denali Pack of his attack, call Jake and let him know what happened, and maybe buy Gwylla some time. This ex-boyfriend of hers would be searching for her near her sanctuary, perhaps wasting time battering down the defenses so he could enter. The more distance he could put between the pair of them, the quicker he got her out of the area, the harder it would be for that elf to track her. And it would give her time to recover and be prepared to fight him.

How do we do this?

"You should probably shift into your human form and wear these clothes. Then I'll read your thoughts as you picture the place where we're to go. I do the rest."

He envisioned a sort-of Vulcan mind-meld and then the transporter glowy-light thingie. *How much will this tire you?*

She smiled. "Fifty miles isn't too bad."

He noticed that she hadn't answered his question. Which meant it would tire her more than was safe given that there might be a homicidal elf on their tail right now.

Okay. Put down the bundle of clothes and turn around. I'll shift into my human form and let you know when I'm finished.

She did as he asked, grumbling about his silly wolf-man modesty. As soon as her back was turned, Dustin began his shift.

When he was done, he picked the clothing, grimacing as he examined the heavy, army surplus camo cargo pants and shirt. Putting them on over naked skin just felt gross, and once he got them on, he started to laugh.

Gwylla turned around and began to laugh as well. "That shirt is big enough for you and me both," she giggled.

"You think that's bad, watch this." He let go of the waistband and the pants immediately fell to his ankles. The only thing keeping his nether regions from view was the knee-length shirt.

There had to be something somewhere to help him hold these pants up. Dustin picked up the pack that had been on the man and began to rummage through it. If there wasn't any twine, maybe he could rip down a vine from a tree and use that. Although the only vines around here were most likely poison oak. He might be a werewolf, but poison oak was still no fun.

"That shirt is like a dress." Gwylla grinned. "I didn't realize our attackers were giants. You should be proud that you so quickly bested a man so much larger than you."

Multi-tool. Skinning knife—he didn't want to think too deeply about that item. Lighter. Carabiners. That might work. He could gather the waistband and hook them through the belt loops. Figures the one guy they strip wasn't wearing a belt.

"Well, to be fair, I am a werewolf, and he was a human." Which meant size didn't really factor into the equation as it would with two humans fighting. He still had the unfair advantage.

"Yes, but he had a weapon as well. Do not be humble. You chewed his buttocks."

"Kicked his ass," Dustin corrected. "Actually I chewed his jugular, if you want to be precise." He looked around the ground at the rifle and the pouch. "Crap. We didn't think to grab his shoes."

Gwylla clapped a hand over her mouth. "Oh, I am so sorry! I took them off his feet to pull the pants off, then was so concerned about wrapping the gun that I didn't take them. Perhaps your werewolf friend has a pair you can borrow?"

Hopefully Mark's shoes would be a better fit than this dead guy's clothes. Actually, he hoped Mark had clothes he could borrow as well. Anything would be better than these nasty camos stripped off of a man who'd been trying to kill him.

That done, he gathered up the pouch and the rifle and spread his arms wide. "I'm ready when you are. What do we need to do to make this happen? Click our heels together three times? Hold hands and sing? Get naked and have sex like monkeys?"

"You just got dressed," she pointed out. "All I need is to

touch you, and for you to envision where we are going, and I will do the rest."

"I like a woman who takes charge," Dustin wiggled his eyebrows. "Touch me where? Do I get to pick the spot, because I have preferences, you know."

She tried to hide a smile. "I'm sure you do, but as you are holding a gun in one hand with *metal* on it, I would prefer to stand on your other side as far away as possible and touch your shoulder."

He sighed. "Maybe next time."

Gwylla put her hand on his shoulder and he closed his eyes, picturing the lake and Mark and Brenda's house. Suddenly he couldn't breathe, as if the air had been sucked right out of his lungs. He felt as if he were tumbling, as if the world was closing down on him tight, like a vise squeezing his entire body. The only thing that kept him from panicking was the feel of Gwylla's hand on his shoulder.

Then it was over. He sucked in a breath, then staggered a few feet to the side. The world was still spinning when he opened his eyes and it was all he could do keep the contents of his stomach in place.

"Where is the house? Is it hidden from view by some magic?"

"No. It should be...give me a moment until I can see straight again." He closed his eyes, waiting for everything to stop spinning, then opened them again.

There was the lake. And he was pretty sure that brown dot was the house. Crap. When he'd pictured it all in his head, he'd envisioned it as he saw it from the plane. Luckily Gwylla hadn't transported them five thousand feet in the air, but they were three miles off where they should be, and quite a bit higher in elevation.

"Uh, I hate to admit it, but I screwed up. See that dot down there by the lake? That's where we're going."

Gwylla stared where he was pointing. "This is humor, right? You are joking with me?"

"No." He let that sink in a moment. "The good news is we can get there before nightfall."

"The bad news is you have no shoes, and from what I remember of your naked feet, they are not conditioned for long treks across rocky ground without some sort of protection on them."

She was right. "More good news, I'm a werewolf and I'll heal any cuts or blisters or bruises."

"More bad news. You'll still feel the pain, and we'll need to go incredibly slow while you carefully pick your way through this rocky ground."

He glared at her. Shifting again would push him to exhaustion. He was just going to have to suck it up and deal. "I'll be fine. You lead the way, and I'll worry about my feet."

By the time they made it to the lake, it was getting close to dark. Gwylla had been right. His feet were killing him. The non-stop cuts and bruises had healed almost instantly, but still hurt. He vowed that when he got out of all this, he was going to spend more time barefoot and try to build up some calluses. Gritting his teeth, Dustin put on a burst of speed, pain bringing tears to his eyes as he pushed himself hard. The cabin was off around the other side of the lake, and he nearly wept as he saw it.

There were no lights on, but it wasn't dark yet. And even if Brenda and Mark were out, he knew they wouldn't mind him going in and using their phone, and borrowing some clothes, under the circumstances. Gwylla was right behind him, urging him to be careful, but Dustin ignored her, pushed himself forward as fast as he could, energized now that his goal was in sight. He'd let Mark and Brenda know what happened. They'd sound the alarm within the Denali Pack. He'd call Jake. And soon, he'd be home.

Dustin jumped the porch steps two at a time and came to an abrupt stop. He smelled blood. It took a second to register, then he closed his eyes, inhaling deeply and trying to catalogue all the scents assailing him.

Brenda and Mark. Humans. Blood. Gunpowder. The sickening smell of entrails that had been decomposing for days. Knowing what he was going to find, Dustin waited for Gwylla on the porch and choked back his tears.

CHAPTER 12

$\mathcal{H}$is wounds hurt. His feet hurt. His muscles ached. He wanted nothing more than to go lay down and sleep, but a nightmare awaited him. And looking up at Gwylla, he could tell that she too knew what was inside the cabin.

"I'm sorry. Even I can smell…" she whispered. "I don't want to go in there first. I don't know these people, and feel you should be the one to enter their home first. I did do a spell to see if anyone was inside."

He waited, raising his eyebrows.

"There is no one alive inside. They've left."

Was it too much to hope that Brenda and Mark had been injured and, like him, had run to safety? Although without a surgeon or a sidhe nearby, running away would have ended in the same death as staying to fight. He only hoped that the entrails he smelled belonged to a human.

Standing, he swayed and leaned against the side of the house to get his balance. Then he went inside. The door was unlocked, but that wasn't unusual for people who lived far away from any town or road. Inside, the house looked like there had been a robbery. Tables and lamps were knocked over. The phone had been ripped out of the wall and smashed. Sofas were pushed to the side. The dining room table had been flipped, and had several bullet holes in it. Dustin wondered if one of the werewolves had tried to use it as a shield.

There was blood splatter on the floor, spray on the wall. Then in the kitchen were huge pools of blood all over the floor and piles of intestines and organs. The hunters had shot them, bled them, and field dressed the werewolf couple in their own kitchen. Dustin remembered dropping them off at the dock, watching them walk toward their cabin hand-in-hand. And now this. Now they were dead and most likely in some taxidermist shop. Just eight days ago they were alive. Just eight days ago he'd seen them.

Dustin turned to the kitchen sink and retched, but he hadn't eaten since breakfast and there was nothing in his stomach for him to throw up. He felt cool hands on his back, soothing his neck and shoulders.

"Monsters have done this," Gwylla told him. "It is murder, and they will pay for their crimes."

He nodded. They would. Eventually. But how many would die before they managed to catch them? It wasn't just a matter of stopping Talligie and cutting off the supply of spelled bullets any longer. There were humans among them they could not trust, humans who wanted them dead, who were eager to track them down and hunt them in their own homes. These people weren't just murderers. This wasn't a crime of passion or a robbery gone bad, or even hunting for food. These humans were psychopaths. They justified murder, no doubt, by claiming that the shifters weren't human. But in all honesty, they were one very small step away from killing humans as well. And psychopaths like this *would* kill humans eventually. The shifters just needed to convince the police that this was murder, and that if these people weren't stopped, humans in Alaska were next on the kill list.

But that was something to face tomorrow. Right now he was facing a pile of rotting entrails in a blood-splattered house, and wanting nothing more than to mourn these two wolves. He couldn't bury Brenda and Mark, but at least he could bury what was left of them.

"I'm going to go dig some graves," he told Gwylla, pushing away from the sink and heading out the back door. She didn't protest.

There was a shed out back. Although the ground was warm, it was rocky as all get out, and it was full-on dark by the time Dustin had found a shovel and managed to dig holes big enough for what remained in the kitchen.

"This isn't very respectful, but it was all I could find," Gwylla commented, handing him a cardboard box with a plastic bag inside. "I put what remained in there. And I cleaned up the blood. I know it's not ideal given what happened to your friends, but we should probably stay here for the night."

He was sweaty and beyond exhausted digging out in the dark. Gwylla was right. They would need to spend the night here. Maybe more.

He took the box from her hands and lowered it in the ground, thinking once more about Brenda and Mark walking off together from his plane. He hoped they were at peace. He hoped there was some sort of afterlife where they were together. He hoped they knew that he'd avenge their deaths.

Scooping a shovelful of dirt and rock, Dustin tossed it on top of the box, wincing at the sound of it hitting. Gwylla began to sing and he continued to fill in the grave. It wasn't a sad song. He could tell even though he didn't understand the words. This was a song of springtime, and new beginnings, of blossoms that burst from trees that had appeared dead all winter. She was a winter fae, her magic of death and rebirth. How fitting that she should sing for Brenda and Mark, and that what might have been a dirge was instead a song of hope.

Patting the last of the dirt on top, Dustin gathered up the larger rocks he'd set aside when he was digging the hole, and placed them across the surface. There. A cairn. And that too was fitting.

He stared down at the grave for a moment, everything crashing down on him. What the heck was he supposed to do about any of this? He wasn't a warrior. He wasn't a fighter. He was a pilot who liked to play video games in his spare time. Yet here he was. He'd managed to survive an attack by the hunters. He'd just buried two of his own. And no matter how ill prepared he was, it was time to be a fighter.

But first, sleep. Actually first would come a shower, and maybe some food, and then sleep.

Gwylla followed him into the house, unusually silent. To be careful, he went around and shut all of the shades and curtains before turning on any interior lights. If the hunters were waiting for more shifters to come by the house, if they were periodically checking, then he didn't want them to know anyone was inside.

Gwylla had done an amazing job of cleaning the house. The broken lamps were gone. The tables and sofa were righted, and the floor was clean. The only way he knew anything had happened was the gunshot holes in the dining room table.

Deciding that food was probably more of a priority than a shower, Dustin went into the kitchen and looked through the refrigerator. Gwylla's stew was good, but it was nice to see a fridge stocked full of meat. He pulled out two pounds of ground beef, a pair of steaks, and a container of pre-cooked meatballs. Popping a few in his mouth, he grabbed two fry pans. Steaks went in one, burgers in the other. Throwing two more meatballs in his mouth he began going through the cupboards for spices.

"Are you a burger or a steak woman?" he asked Gwylla. "Better let me know now because I'm probably going to eat mine half raw and I want to make sure I save one for you."

She'd been quiet, following him around the house and sitting on a stool at the edge of the kitchen island. She hadn't spoken since her song outside.

"I don't eat meat."

What? *What*? "You're joking."

She shook her head. "No meat. Only plants."

He stared at her. "You're a vegan?"

She wrinkled her brow. "I do consume honey and dairy products, so I guess your word for it would be vegetarian."

A vegetarian. "Are you telling me that for four days I've been eating only vegetables? No wonder I'm exhausted. No wonder I haven't healed yet."

She flushed. "You're exhausted and haven't healed yet because you were shot with magical bullets, not because you ate wholesome and nutritious food. I'm not criticizing you for frying up a bunch of dead animals in those pans. Don't you dare criticize me for refusing to eat them."

Crap. "I'm sorry. I didn't mean to insult you. It's just werewolves…well, we're omnivorous, but we tend to have a high percentage of meat and fish in our diet. I'm not sure I could survive as a vegetarian."

She scowled and tossed her white-blonde hair. "You could. In this form you're not any different from a human as far as digestion and anatomy. There are humans who don't eat meat, right?"

He squirmed. "Yes. But I'm not a human. I'm a werewolf and I *need* meat."

"You don't *need* meat. You're used to eating a meat-heavy diet because it's what you've eaten your whole life. No doubt your parents told you that you needed to eat meat, and that notion has been reinforced by your werewolf peers. That doesn't make it true, just habit."

He shoved two more meatballs in his mouth and flipped the burgers and steaks. Actually it was a good thing she didn't eat meat because he was hungry enough to eat all this food himself and probably want more.

"I'm a werewolf. Our metabolism is different. Wild wolves eat meat. I don't see you out there in the forest, insisting the carnivores eat broccoli and carrots. I don't see you telling predators that they shouldn't hunt." Wait, hadn't she said something a few days ago about the sidhe hunting? "And you do too, right? If you guys hunt once per year, what do you do with the meat? Waste it? How is that any better than eating it?"

Her light green eyes sparked with anger. "It's not that kind of hunt. We don't eat meat. Elves do on occasion, but we don't. And I see no need for you to hunt when you can satisfy all of your nutritional needs with non-meat foods."

He was so not going to get laid tonight, or possibly ever. "What part of werewolf are you not understanding? My pack and I shift into our wolf forms and hunt together. Yes, that means we kill animals, and we eat them, although unlike wild wolves we take the kill home to cook first. And guess what? Like a lot of people in Alaska, I occasionally go fishing. I'm not that crazy about hunting with a rifle, but I've got nothing against it. I just don't do it because I'm a lousy shot and I don't feel like sitting up in a deer stand before dawn, freezing my butt off for hours just to waste a bunch of bullets and go home empty handed."

She got up. "I'm going outside. The smell of your food sickens me."

And now he felt like a total jerk. Could he blame it on hunger? On exhaustion? On his injuries that were screaming at him to lay down? On the fact that he was cooking burgers and steaks in a house where two werewolves had been murdered, where he'd just finished burying what was left of them?

No. There were no excuses. He was just a jerk. He didn't have a whole lot of experience with women. Yeah, he'd dated on occasion. And he wasn't a virgin, although his hand saw more action that it probably should. He was normally more diplomatic, less argumentative. He'd always prided himself on being a good listener, not sticking his nose in where it didn't belong, on being that easy-going guy that anyone could talk to. And yet here he was, snapping at the very woman who'd saved his life.

Dustin turned off the stove and ate the food straight out of the pan, finishing off the meatballs afterward. Then he cleaned the pans, found a bottle of air freshener, and sprayed it liberally all over the kitchen. The lemony pine scent made him want to sneeze, but hopefully it covered up the smell of cooking meat. Then he went and took a quick shower, finding a pair of Mark's pajama bottoms to wear, and once more looked in the fridge.

Cheese. And the yogurt? Baked beans? No, they had pork in them. Dustin dug through the shelves and cabinets, cursing the fact that this werewolf couple probably didn't even have a piece of celery in the house.

Grabbing what he felt were safe options, Dustin arranged them on a plate. Raisins. Sunflower seeds. There was a tomato and the cheese. He took them out, grabbed a knife and hesitated. Wait. She had some sort of metal allergy. If he sliced food with a steel knife, would that hurt her? What else was he supposed to use? It wasn't like Brenda would have had gold-plated knives lying around. Eventually he found a plastic one and hacked his way through the tomato, hoping that it didn't look too mangled. He added a lemon that he'd sawed in half with the plastic knife, then he sliced up the cheese and stacked it on the side.

He found Gwylla on the front porch, sitting in a rocker and staring out toward the lake.

"I set wards a hundred feet out around the house," she said, not looking at him. "It won't give us much time to prepare in case of attack, but at least we'll have a warning, and not be caught in bed asleep."

"Thank you." He sat beside her and extended the plate. "And I'm sorry about earlier. I was a total jerk and that's not normally me. Here. Peace offering?"

She took the plate, her lips trembling slightly before curling up into a smile. "A lemon? Is there some significance to you giving me a lemon? Am I a sourpuss?"

He laughed. "Two werewolves live here. True or not, they, just like other werewolves, have a fridge stocked full of meat with very little in the way of fruit or vegetables. This was all I could find that I was sure was vegetarian friendly."

She picked up a lemon half. "I'm sorry, too. I was wrong to criticize you for your food. And for your hunting. I don't know your world. I don't know shifters. I'm making assumptions that have no basis in fact or experience. As difficult as it is for me to believe, you probably do require the types of protein in animal flesh. Just because I felt you all over and healed you doesn't meant I know everything about your metabolism or digestion."

"Apology accepted." He grinned. "Did you really feel me all over?"

She put down the lemon and scooped some raisins into

her mouth. "Of course. I needed to ascertain the extent of your injuries, and that required a thorough examination."

"While I was unconscious? Doesn't that violate some kind of sidhe doctor ethical rule?"

"While I would rather you had been awake, at least for part of the examination, it was probably just as well. As injured as you were, I wouldn't have wanted to risk exciting you too much."

He was getting pretty excited now, and Mark's pajama pants weren't doing much to hide it.

"As it was, you had a surprising physiological response to my touch that I hadn't expected in one so injured. Clearly you are very sensitive."

Even unconscious he could get it up. He'd figured as much from wet dreams and morning wood over the years, but that he could be shot twice, lose a huge amount of blood, be at death's door, and still get an erection was gratifying. The thought made him rather proud.

"I'll bet you're sensitive, too. Can I examine you? I mean, it was a long difficult journey today, and we were moving fast."

"Not that fast," she countered. "I'm sidhe. I can move quickly and for long distances, even though I'm not accustomed to it."

"Still, if you're not accustomed to it, you may have...pulled a muscle? In fact, I'm sure teleporting may have resulted in some sort of injury. I should check you over, just to be sure. And if I find any tight muscles, I can massage them. I'm good at that, I'll have you know."

"Are you?" She shot him a wicked grin before turning her attention back to the almonds on her plate. "I'll admit that I *am* tired. Perhaps this examination should take place in the bed where I can lay down."

Holy moley. Was this going in the direction he thought it

was? Did sexual innuendo carry across their cultural barriers? Because it would be horribly embarrassing if he were to make a move on her only to have her slap him down. He didn't want to mess this up. And he wasn't exactly Casanova when it came to women.

"Finish your dinner, then you lay down and I'll massage your back. We can save the full examination for later. Some other time when we know each other better."

He was botching this big-time, but the fear that she'd say no loomed over him. Better to delay, to hopefully convince her that he was charming and sexy and someone she'd want to sleep with. Well, charming if not sexy.

"Oh." She cast him a bewildered look. "That's fine. In fact, I'm sure you're very tired yourself, and you're still injured. We should probably just sleep, and save the rubbing and examinations for some other time."

Yep. Shot down. At least it was now and not after he'd groped her or tried to kiss her or something. This way he could always claim misunderstanding.

And he *was* tired. And in pain. Although he was pretty sure he'd rally if she wanted to get naked under the covers with him.

Gwylla finished her food, leaving the lemon untouched and he followed her back inside.

"You look like you're ready to fall over. Go to sleep. I'm going to get a shower after I wash this plate," she told him.

And there went his last chance at getting in her pants tonight. With a sigh, he bid her goodnight and headed to one of the bedrooms that did not have Mark and Brenda's scent all over it. It was clearly a guest room, with a patchwork comforter and a little desk in the corner of the room. He pulled the sheets aside, and was asleep the moment his head hit the pillow.

CHAPTER 13

*D*ustin woke up with a naked woman in his arms.

In his defense, the bed wasn't very large. It was what would have been called a full-size, which should have been adequate for two people who were accustomed to some intimacy. The bed size didn't excuse the fact that he was spooning Gwylla, her ass pressed against one of the hardest erections he'd ever woken up to.

Her blonde hair was across his face, tickling his chest and arm. It smelled like vanilla and brown sugar and was still slightly damp from her shower. Her skin was like silk against his, her small body contouring perfectly to his shape. She was slight, thin, but soft in all the right places.

Soft. Oh sweet mother of pearl, his hand was cupping her breast. Wow. This was…awkward. And kind of awesome. Both. At the same time.

What was she doing in his bed? Oh, yeah. There were two bedrooms in this cabin, and it wasn't like she'd want to sleep on the couch or in Mark and Brenda's bed. He could completely understand that, but naked? Why was she naked? He'd coopted a pair of Mark's pajama pants.

Why hadn't she borrowed something of Brenda's? Unless Brenda didn't have any pajamas. Maybe the werewolf was the kind who slept naked. Still, she probably had some oversized T-shirts that Gwylla could have borrowed to sleep in. Every woman had oversized T-shirts, didn't they?

But no. The sidhe woman had climbed into bed with him, stark naked, then proceeded to cuddle up against him. Although to be fair, she might have cuddled up in her sleep. He'd certainly been asleep when he'd grabbed hold of her breast.

Should he move? All the scenarios ran through his head. Gwylla could hardly be angry at him for their compromising position, not when she was naked in bed with him. But still… It would be mortifying if he was found groping her and trying to poke into her ass with his dick. He didn't want to be that pervy guy who felt up a sleeping woman when he wasn't sure she wanted to be felt up.

But she'd teased him last night, saying she'd done the same to him. Maybe she wouldn't be upset. Maybe she was expecting him to make a move. While he was thinking this through, he absentmindedly brushed his fingers against her taut nipple. She sighed, squirming her butt against him.

And now he could pound nails with his cock. Great. He was torn, uncertain whether he wanted her to wake up or not. Not. It was all too embarrassing. Carefully he pulled his hand away and scooted backward until he could safely ease off the bed. Then he ran for the shower.

* * *

GWYLLA HAD SLEPT like an oak in winter from the moment her head hit the pillow until the sunlight came through the window and touched her face. This bed was comfortable, and she had the vague memory of how warm Dustin had been curled up against her.

It was nice having someone to sleep next to her. His arm around her made her feel safe, which was ridiculous given her abilities.

She liked him. Really liked him. He was goofy and sometimes shy. He'd never asked anything of her. He'd been alarmed when she'd told him she'd bonded to him to save his life. If that had ever happened with Talligie, the elf would have immediately thought of some way to use that connection to his advantage.

Dustin was so different than Talligie. He was different than any of the sidhe or elves she'd met. She never tired of being with him. She could converse with him all day and still long for his presence. He made her laugh. And he made her feel things she probably shouldn't feel for a wolf-man.

Crawling out of bed, she stretched, then put on her clothes. She'd cleaned them in her own way since she had no idea how to work the machines, even if they hadn't been made of metal. She'd barely managed to figure out their plumbing system last night to take a bath, using the wash cloths to guard her hands against the metal. But oh, how that bath had felt good. And the female werewolf who lived here had some very nice smelling hair and skin products.

That poor woman. After her shower, she'd been undecided about what to do. There was no way she could wear a dead woman's clothes, even just to sleep in. It was one thing for Dustin to borrow their clothing. He'd known them. She hadn't. It would be disrespectful. She'd stood over the dresser full of pretty clothing and felt ill at the thought of putting any of it on. The same with the other bed which clearly had been used by the two werewolves. It had been their bed, used for sleep and lovemaking. She couldn't desecrate that space.

Which left the couch, which did actually look rather

comfortable, or the other bed where Dustin lay half-naked, his warm body sprawled across the mattress, the sheets tangled around his legs.

It hadn't been a difficult decision, although she did feel that sleeping naked next to the werewolf was probably pushing things a bit. She wouldn't have been surprised to wake up to him sniffing her hair or awkwardly trying to hide an erection. But she'd woken up alone, and from the sounds in the other room, Dustin was taking a shower.

Hadn't he cleaned himself last night before bed? Were werewolves so fastidious that they preferred to shower twice each day? Whatever his cleanliness needs, he seemed to be taking an inordinately long time about it.

The shower shut off and a few minutes later Dustin appeared, a towel wrapped around his waist. Another was in his hands as he rubbed his hair dry.

"Oh. Hi." He stopped in the doorway, flushing as he saw her. His hair was standing up all spiked on the top of his head. It made Gwylla want to smooth it down.

"Hi, did you sleep well?"

"Uh. Yeah. Okay, I guess."

Why was he so flustered? After her earlier thoughts of their easy way of conversing this was the most awkward few sentences they'd ever exchanged.

She got up to leave, and he put out a hand. "Wait. Um, I have a question." He shuffled his feet while she waited. "Why…why were you naked in bed with me this morning?"

Was that wrong? She'd thought maybe she was pushing it a bit, but why was he so disturbed by it all? "Because I slept there. Should I have slept on the couch instead? Or in your murdered friends' bed?"

He winced. "No. No, I meant…why were you naked? You could have borrowed something of Brenda's to wear."

He didn't like her naked? That hurt, but she made a note

of it for future reference. Teasing was okay as was sexual innuendo, but naked was not.

"Because her sleeping clothes looked very uncomfortable." And she hadn't wanted to wear a dead woman's clothes, but as Dustin was wearing the other wolf-man's clothes, he probably wouldn't think that an adequate reason.

He frowned at her. "What do you mean, uncomfortable?"

"I'll show you." She pushed past him and went into the other bedroom, returning with a few of the items which she held up and showed to him. "I don't understand how anyone could sleep in these. I'm not even sure I know how to put it on properly."

He stared at the narrow pieces of scratchy lace in horror. "Oh, God. That's more than I ever wanted to know about Brenda and Mark."

"I mean, do they go like this?" She held a piece up over her breasts and stretched the other down to between her legs. "Or like this?"

"I don't…I'm not sure even I know. Can you just put those away and go in the other room or something?"

She gathered the lace back into her hand. "Sure. Are you coming?"

"Yes. No. I'm going to get dressed." He darted out of the room, leaving her to stare after him. Strange wolf-man. Rather than wait for him, she went into the kitchen and looked around for something suitable for breakfast.

Dustin hadn't been kidding about the contents of the refrigerator. Bacon. Sausage. Steak. Eggs. A block of cheese that was so large it could double as a weapon. There was a little container of diced peppers, tomatoes and onions that she pulled out, along with a bag of sweet potatoes. And luckily the werewolves' dislike for vegetables didn't extend to grain products. Two loaves of bread and a package of tortillas. She could work with this. She could definitely work with this.

By the time Dustin walked in breakfast was almost done. He was wearing a pair of jeans that were a bit loose on him, and a blue T-shirt that was not loose on him. He'd shaved the fuzz from his cheeks and chin, and smelled like sandalwood and pine. Mmmm.

The werewolf sniffed then went to look in the pan. His face fell.

"Oh. That looks…good."

She bit back a smile. "I believe you would call it a hash. We can roll it up in the tortillas."

"Can I add some sausage to that tortilla? And bacon?"

He sounded so hopeful. Her stomach turned at the thought but she took a deep breath and tried not to think about it. "Can you wait until I have mine so I can go out on the porch? I don't like the smell of cooking meat."

He pulled the sausage from the fridge. "Sure. It's already cooked, so I can just microwave it. Is it okay if I join you on the porch when I'm done cooking it? We can eat together."

Yuck. Just yuck. But if she had any hope of spending time with this werewolf, she'd need to get used to his eating habits. "Yes, I'd like that. If you joined me, I mean."

He set the sausage on the counter and filled up a glass container with water from the sink, pouring it into a plastic device. Then he scooped some fragrant ground-up brown stuff into a paper cup and stuck it in another part of the plastic device. Before she'd removed the hash from the stove, there was brown liquid pouring in a steady stream into the glass container.

"How do you like your coffee? There's some non-dairy creamer in here. And sugar. I don't trust that the milk hasn't gone bad from the date on the carton, so it's fake or we drink it black."

Was she expected to drink that brown stuff? She'd turned up her nose at the meat last night, it seemed rude to refuse to try this. "I don't know," she confessed. "I've never had coffee before."

He stared at her in astonishment. "We'll try a few things and see what you like then. Here. Read the ingredients on this and let me know if it's okay for you to eat it. Or drink it."

She took the container and read the back. "I don't know what these things are. I will drink milk, but what is Dipotassium Phosphate? Or Silicon Dioxide?"

He took it from her. "I don't know what they are either. Let's nix this and try something else."

He didn't know? Werewolves ate things when they had no idea what was in them? It seemed rather risky, but perhaps they had an innate sense of what was healthy for their bodies and what wasn't.

"Yes!" Dustin turned from the freezer and showed her a container. "This! Brenda is probably the only werewolf in the state that has coconut milk ice cream in her freezer, and there are no things-I-can't-pronounce on the ingredient list. You're going to have iced coffee. And you're going to love it."

She hoped so because it would be terribly embarrassing to spit the drink out all over the porch.

"I'm looking forward to it." She handed him a plate with his hash on a tortilla. "I'll be on the front porch when you're ready."

It was a bit chilly still outside, but the view was lovely with the mountains, the lake, the wildflowers swaying in the breeze. She could see the outlines of her wards, and was relieved they were intact and undisturbed. A human, or anyone else, would have set off the alarm by crossing them, but she'd worried if it were Talligie who'd come, he'd be able to disarm them without triggering the alarms.

But he wouldn't come. Not yet, anyway. Hopefully all

they had to fear right now was humans who were hunting werewolves, or looking for Dustin in particular. But once Talligie realized she was here, once he knew she was out in the open, not hidden in a sanctuary, then he'd come. And when he did, she needed to make sure Dustin was safe, and that she was far enough away he'd not be hurt.

Talligie would hurt him. Talligie would kill him. Not just because of jealousy. The elf *would* be jealous of her wasting her power on another, but that was all, and there wasn't much power she could grant a werewolf. No, Talligie would kill Dustin because it would hurt her. It would give the elf more power over her. And more importantly, it would give him revenge. It would be his punishment for her leaving him.

She needed Dustin to be safe. She'd vowed it when she saved his life, but there was more to it than just the vow.

The werewolf walked out on the porch. His wonderful breakfast tainted with the smell of meat. She ignored it, smiling at him instead. And ignoring it got a whole lot easier when he shoved a mug into her hand.

The drink was…pungent. It certainly overpowered the meat smell, and for that she was grateful. It was the color of a muddy river that had stirred up a chalky limestone bed. It smelled sweet and bitter and nutty.

And Dustin was staring at her. Expectantly. She lifted the mug to her lips and took a sip, careful to control her expression.

It wasn't terrible. She gave Dustin a smile that was probably more of a grimace and took another sip.

"Too sweet? Not sweet enough?" he asked, sitting down in the rocker next to her.

"It's sweeter than I'm used to, but there's something really bitter that the sweetness isn't quite managing to cover up. I'm not sure I'd find it tolerable without the sugar."

His face fell. And Gwylla felt horrible.

"Maybe it's an acquired taste." She took another sip, just to prove that she was attempting to acquire this taste. "How is your breakfast?"

He took a bite. "Love it. I've never had this with sweet potatoes before, and with the spices and everything, it's really good."

"Would you like it just as well without the sausage?"

He took another bite, considering the idea. "I don't think I'd like it as well, but I'd like it. It would be good plain, but for me, the sausage makes it perfect."

Well, at least it wasn't horrible and the sausage wasn't the only thing bearable about it. Gwylla drank more of the coffee, and thought. He'd seemed to like the stews she'd made at her sanctuary, but that had been when he was injured and most likely so hungry he would have eaten a table leg. But at her home, he'd need to eat what she cooked, because there was no way she would ever allow meat into her home. And she hoped he'd come back to visit her, maybe stay for a while. Gwylla was under no illusions that she'd be happy living long-term among the werewolves in Dustin's home. Not that he'd asked her. Although if he did, she would try it for short stretches of time to see if she could manage it. Hopefully he'd find her effort proof that she did like his company.

Of course if she wanted to even visit him wherever the werewolf lived, she'd need to take care of Talligie. She couldn't have the elf track her to Dustin's home. She couldn't have him know she cared about others, put them in his path, risk their lives. No, she'd need to make sure Talligie couldn't track her, couldn't hurt those who were her friends. And to do that she'd need to kill him.

Could she do that? She'd once thought she loved the elf. Could she kill him? Glancing over at Dustin she remembered his wounds, remembered finding him near death in his wolf form at her heart-tree. Yes, she could. She could kill Talligie. She just needed to do it in a place where others wouldn't be killed in the process.

"There's something I want to do before we head out today." Dustin eyed her uncertainly. She got the feeling this wasn't something she was going to enjoy.

"Does it involve the meat in the refrigerator?"

"No, it involves metal. We need to find out what metal you have a problem with and what is okay for you to touch. I can't believe you're sensitive to *all* metals."

This was a bad idea. She instinctively reached up and touched the still-healing wound on her shoulder.

"Legend says fae can't touch iron, but from my D&D days, I remember having some lively arguments about whether that included steel or alloys. I used a plastic knife to cut your food last night just to be safe, but it would help you to navigate this world better if you knew exactly what was going to be a problem and what wasn't."

"When we crossed the gates, an elf with us touched one of your transportation devices, and his hand blistered. It took him days to heal. I decided it was best to avoid all metal."

"Okay, so that was a car, and it was probably steel, although a lot of cars have aluminum, plastic, and carbon fiber components. We also need to find out how close you can get to them. Can you stand inside an elevator, or a building with steel beams as a structural component, or will it bother you being near them?"

She thought for a moment. "I'm fine in this house, and I'm certain there is iron and steel here. When I used the bath, I covered my hand to touch the shiny faucets, just to be safe."

"It *could* be that you're fine with steel and it's just an elf thing and not a sidhe thing," Dustin mused.

"But the bullets? They are steel, are they not? And that

gunshot wound still hurts and has not healed properly. That makes me believe I cannot touch steel."

He frowned in thought. "Touch it or have it touch an open wound? Because that would be the difference between you being able to ride in a car and not."

This was ridiculous. "I'm not going to be riding in your cars. I can teleport. And as soon as you are safe back with your pack and I take care of Talligie, I'm returning to my sanctuary where there are no metal objects to burn and scar me."

Why did he look so sad at that idea?

"Please? Just try a few of them, okay?"

She sighed, unable to resist when he looked so earnest and enthusiastic. "I will try."

He took both of their plates into the house and returned with a tray. On it were an assortment of metal objects.

"This one first, because I think you'll be okay with it."

He held it out to her and she reached a tentative finger to it, tapping the surface of the disk briefly. When she felt no burn from the contact, she touched it again, this time for a few seconds.

"It's bronze. Now let's try brass, which is an alloy of copper and zinc. Bronze is copper and tin."

She touched the brass with more confidence. "So I'm fine to touch bronze, brass, and therefore copper, zinc, and tin?"

He nodded. "Now gold. And this one is silver. Werewolves can sometimes have problems with silver. A lot of us get hives with repeated contact, a few blister and scar like you do with iron."

She handled both with no problem. "Can you touch the silver?"

He laughed. "I'd rather not because it makes my hands itch. Sometimes I'll grab something silver by accident and need to go take a Benadryl. Brenda obviously didn't have any problems with the metal since these are her necklaces."

She nodded, then inhaled sharply as she saw the other items on the tray. "Those are iron?"

"Nothing pure iron. Some steel and alloys. We'll start you out with this. It's a chrome plated brass fitting. If you can touch this, then most bathroom fixtures are okay."

She exhaled in relief when her fingers brushed the metal with no pain.

"And now stainless steel silverware. It's iron, but has ten percent chromium to keep it from corroding."

She touched the fork and yelped, yanking her hand back. There was a round blister on her thumb that ached like she'd been bitten by something poisonous. "Ninety percent iron is too much."

He grimaced. "Sorry. The chromium coats the surface, so I'd hoped that would protect you from the iron. Let's try this one."

"No," she shook her head. "I can tell you right now that I can't touch that."

He picked up the hammer. "But you're okay sitting a few feet from it, right? If you put a towel over your hand, could you touch it? Gloves?"

"I don't know. Maybe? It bothers me being this close to it. It's like standing next to a very hot fire. You know that one wrong move and you will be burned."

"As bad as I feel that you are so affected by a metal that's pervasive in our everyday lives, I have to admit this kinda makes me glad. Your ex-boyfriend is hardly likely to take over the world when Billy Bob can kill him with a screwdriver."

She laughed. "I'm sure he hasn't realized the incredible disadvantage of this sensitivity. He probably sees it as an inconvenience, and I'm sure the humans he's working with are scurrying to keep everything iron and steel away from him. Talligie is like that. He's a high lord and people just fall to do his bidding by nature."

"And did you fall to do his bidding?" He dark green eyes were intense, as if the answer to this question was of the utmost importance.

"I thought I loved him. When you love someone, you do things to please them. He never had to command me to do anything. In fact, that would have sent me packing. Instead he just smiled and said it would make him happy, and I did it." She snorted. *Weak fool. How could you have been so blind?*

Dustin turned a dazzling smile on her. "It would make me so happy if you did the dishes this morning."

She laughed again. She'd had more laughter in the last week then she'd had in decades. "I believe the human saying is 'go stuff it'."

He grinned. "That's my girl!"

Was she? Was she his girl? Because sitting here on the porch, chatting, she definitely felt like she was his girl.

"And now that I've made my feelings clear, I'm going to help you do the dishes, and then we can leave to go into town." She stood and something caught her eye again over by the woods, something shiny that reflected the light. Something that most definitely hadn't been there yesterday."

"—if so, I'm game. Hello? What are you looking at?"

She'd completely missed what Dustin had said. "Over there. Do you see that in the woods? A prism or something."

He stood as well, she felt the tension radiating off of him. "I'll go check it out."

"No, *we'll* go check it out. Remember, we have complementary powers, like the Amazing Twins people."

"Wonder Twins. Okay, but stay here a minute while I get the rifle. If that's your ex-boyfriend, then I'll apologize in advance for being a little trigger happy."

"Stop calling him my ex-boyfriend." But Dustin had left and she wasn't sure he'd heard her.

Dustin insisted on leading the way, the gun at his shoulder. Halfway there he lowered it. "I don't smell anything fresh, but someone was here and it wasn't an elf, it was a human."

A neighbor checking on the werewolves who had owned this cabin? Or one of the hunters, dropping by to see if there were additional werewolves here to kill. Her wards had been undisturbed, so whoever he'd been, he hadn't ventured beyond the woods.

Gwylla edged past Dustin to the mirror hanging from a tree branch that swayed in the light breeze and caught the sunlight. Hanging from the bottom of it, like a wind chime, was a glass tube etched with runes.

"Should you touch that?" Dustin asked, putting out a hand to stay her as she reached for the tube.

"I can see the magic. It's a simple spell that keeps anyone but fae from opening the glass tube." There would be a scroll inside. And there was only one being in Alaska who would be leaving messages that were clearly meant for her.

"That doesn't reassure me one bit. If your ex-boyfriend sent that, it's liable to explode when you open it."

Except Talligie didn't want her dead. Not yet, anyway. "It won't explode. And stop calling him my ex-boyfriend. Call him Talligie."

"I don't want to say his name," Dustin growled. "Can I call him Jerk Face instead?"

She snapped the tube off the branch and twisted the top. "Jerk Face is acceptable. See? No explosion."

"Well, that's a relief since I'm standing all of six inches from you. What's it say?"

She unrolled the scroll. "That he wants me to come back

to him. That he's sorry. That he'll alter his plans for world domination if I'll just come back to him. Etc. Etc."

That wasn't what the scroll said, but she wasn't about to tell Dustin that Talligie had threatened to kill "her wolf-man toy" and exterminate all of the werewolves unless she returned. Stupid elf. In all the years they'd been together, hadn't he realized that threats never worked with her?

"Why am I thinking that you're lying and that what's on that scroll is more stick than carrot?"

She rolled the scroll up, then set it on fire, watching it burn to ash in her fingers. "Because you are a very perceptive wolf-man. He does want me back. And neither stick nor vegetables of any kind will convince me to rejoin him."

They watched the scroll burn until the embers were gone, the smoke had drifted away, and she brushed the ash off on her pants leg. Then Dustin put his arm around her shoulder, keeping pace with her as they walked back to the house. "Good. Because I'm not going to let you go back to Jerk Face in some noble attempt to sacrifice yourself for the good of others. You're mine, remember? Bond and all that stuff?"

It was the first time he'd acknowledged it. The first time he hadn't seemed angry or upset about it. The thought brought a smile to her lips and made her snuggle into his side. "Yes. Bond and all that stuff."

Gwylla cleaned the dishes and tidied the house while Dustin went outside to pay his respects at the little grave he'd made for his friends. She watched him outside the window, a horrible feeling in the pit of her stomach when she remembered what they'd found when they came into the house. Dustin had been so distraught.

These people had killed his friends. They'd tried to kill him. And for that they'd pay with their lives. But first Dustin needed to contact his other werewolf friends and make sure they were safe. First she had to deliver him to this Alpha who would take care of him and protect him while Gwylla went to find the elf responsible for this whole mess. Then after she found him, she'd do what she should have done months ago and take Talligie's life.

But she couldn't think of that right now. Now she needed to be sharp and ready to protect Dustin as they walked to the nearby town and tried to find a human communication device. And maybe a conveyance that would allow them to travel faster than a walk or jog.

She still wasn't at full strength. And putting up the wards

last night hadn't helped. She could only pray to the Lady that she didn't encounter these hunters until she was strong enough to deal with them, to protect not only Dustin, but herself.

It was late morning by the time they set out, and not quite noon by the time they walked into town—if the place could even be called a town. The houses were spread far apart, with a few hotels and tourist shops clustered near the park information center. Dustin headed toward the information center, then spoke for a while with one of the humans wearing a brown shirt and pants with an official looking patch on the collar while she went over to look at the informational items stacked on a shelf beside the door.

* * *

Dustin had no money. And of course Gwylla had no money either. If he'd have thought about it, he would have checked to see if there was even a jar with change in it at Brenda and Mark's place.

"Someone shot you?" The ranger gave him an odd look. "And you hiked fifty miles through the park to get out?"

A year ago he wouldn't have hesitated to tell the guy that he was a werewolf, but right now Dustin was wary and suspicious of every human he met. But beggars couldn't be choosers. It was time to be up front with the guy and hope he didn't pull a rifle out from behind the counter and shoot him dead.

"I'm a werewolf with the Swift River Pack. I flew Brenda and Mark Edmonds from Anchorage to their home and was returning when I saw an overturned truck, and two guys on one of those little service roads. The one guy looked injured, so I did an emergency landing and went to help them. They shot me."

"They shot you?" The guy repeated, still with the odd look. "Why?"

Here went nothing. "Because there are humans who are hunting shifters. They killed at least one grizzly and shot two werewolves in Kenai. Evidently these guys were using a trap to draw me in, and they shot me."

Still with the odd look. "But don't you guys just shrug off gunshot wounds? I'm sure Mark told me one time that it hurt like heck and took a day or so to heal all the way up, but bullets weren't a big deal like they are to us."

The guy knew Mark. Oh no, he was going to have to tell him that Mark and Brenda were dead.

"These aren't normal bullets. They have a special coating on them that makes us shift to our animal form, and hinders our ability to heal. Unless we have someone nearby who can quickly get the bullet out and provide medical attention, we'll die."

And now the guy didn't have that odd expression, he seemed interested? Curious? Either way, Dustin didn't like it one bit.

"So these bullets make it so you're just as vulnerable as us humans. Huh."

"Except they also cause us to shift into our animal form. Then the hunter can take our pelt or drag our bodies off to a taxidermist and hang a shifter head in his living room. Somebody who shoots you while jacking your car doesn't hang your head on the wall afterward."

That was probably a bit harsh, but at least the ranger no longer looked curious. Horrified was a much better expression, one that mirrored how Dustin felt about the situation.

"That's...that's freaky psychotic serial killer stuff right there. How did you get away from them? It's not like there's a hospital in the middle of the park or something."

Dustin pointed to Gwylla who was looking at a stack of

brochures. "Her. She's got...medical training, and happened to be nearby."

He looked at the sidhe. "Is she one of those elves? I've only seen them on television, although I heard they're on some island getting trained to work with us or something. As long as they don't take my job, I'm okay with it. Although the guy that I saw seemed to be a bit of a pompous jerk."

Dustin was sure that the ranger hadn't meant to insult her. Either way, he needed to talk less about elves and more about borrowing the guy's phone.

"When I was well enough to travel, we left the park and went to Mark and Brenda's. But the hunters got there first." He paused to let the words sink in. "They field dressed them in their own kitchen and took their bodies."

And now horrified wasn't a strong enough word to describe the expression on the ranger's face. "Mark and Brenda are dead? Murdered? By these psychos?"

"Yes. That's why I need to borrow your phone. I need to call the Alpha at the Denali Pack to let her know what happened. And I need to call my Alpha, too. He most likely thinks I'm dead. I was supposed to be back nine days ago."

The ranger slid the phone over to Dustin, his hand shaking.

The first thing he did was call Moira, the Denali Pack Alpha. As desperate as he was to let Jake know his status, and that his plane was destroyed, it was more important for Moira to be aware that two of her wolves had been murdered.

He got her voicemail and hesitated, uncertain if he should leave this kind of news on a message or not. It might be a while before he had access to a phone again, and Dustin had an uneasy feeling that more wolves might be targets, so he left the message, noticing that the ranger looked rather ill as he detailed exactly the scene at Brenda and Mark's house as well as where he'd buried their remains.

Then with an apologetic glance at the ranger, he dialed Jake.

The phone rang and rang. Dustin started to panic, wondering where everyone was, if he was the only werewolf left alive in a horrible Mad Max post-apocalyptic scenario. He nearly passed out with relief when he heard his Alpha's gruff voice on the phone.

"It's Dustin. I'm alive." That seemed the most important thing to get out there. Jake wasn't the sort of Alpha who liked long monologues.

There was a shout from the other end of the phone that nearly took Dustin's eardrum out. "I sent a team northeast looking for you," Jake told him. "I've got three guys on the ground in Denali with Moira's approval combing the mountains. You nearly gave me a heart attack, Dustin."

He couldn't help the shiver that ran through him. Jake was so…intense. Sometimes having him as an Alpha was like holding onto the bare end of a live wire. But in spite of the tension crackling across the phone line, Dustin knew his Alpha well enough to understand the subtext. He was valued —highly valued. And Jake had been unsettled, no he'd been scared, by Dustin's disappearance.

"I saw an emergency on the ground and landed to help," Dustin told him. "But it was a trap. They shot me. I ran for it, but by the time I was healed enough to go back, my plane was trashed and everything was gone. I had to sort of hike out and borrow a phone. And Brenda and Mark were killed, their bodies taken as trophies."

It was a lot, and Dustin hoped he'd conveyed it in a succinct manner. Short and to the point was how Jake always wanted his reports.

There was a silence that seemed to stretch on for hours.

Dustin shifted his weight, feeling like all the blood had rushed out of his body. He noticed the hand holding the phone to his ear was shaking. He should have been dead, like Brenda and Mark. It was only sheer luck that he was here alive, talking to his Alpha on the phone.

"Why aren't you dead?"

Dustin knew his Alpha well enough to know that Jake was shocked he'd been shot with one of the magic-tainted bullets and survived, and this was Jake's rather brutal way of expressing that disbelief. And relief.

"I...., um..." Dustin looked over at Gwylla who was still looking at brochures, although he was pretty certain she'd heard every word of the conversation. "My wolf took over and I ran, and through some miracle I managed to wind up being found by a healer before I died."

Yet another long silence stretched across the phone line. "A healer. On the edges of Denali Park, which is six million acres big and filled with the highest mountains in Alaska. No one lives there. You can hike for days and not come across a human or shifter, but you managed to find...a healer? What was he, a trauma surgeon like Brent's mate Kennedy? And he was hiking or mountain climbing nearby?"

Dustin shot another glance at Gwylla. He was reluctant to tell Jake about her. Why? He'd always been open and honest with his Alpha about everything, but he didn't want anyone to know what Gwylla was. Was he trying to protect her? Or was he trying to protect Jake?

"It was a one-in-a-million thing," he confessed. "She's... she's a fae. Otherwise I think I'd be dead because I was shot twice and I'd lost a lot of blood when she found me."

"An *elf* saved you?" Jake sounded incredulous. "The magic on the bullets is from an elf. Those angels of Brent's ID'd it, and he had it confirmed by some mage in Hel who is supposed to be working on an antidote. Do you think she's the one who made the magic on the bullets? Or knows who does?"

A lot had happened since he'd been shot. And he really, really didn't want to discuss all this with Jake over the phone. Or at all.

"I wanted to let you know I'm alive and I'm in McKinley Park at the visitor center. I've got no money and no phone, and I'm wearing borrowed clothes. Can you send someone up to get me? And one other person. Then I'll tell you everything that happened and what I know in detail."

"I need you to tell me right now about the elf that saved you. And you're not intending on bringing her to the compound, are you?" Jake sounded suspicious. And a suspicious Alpha wasn't likely to be a welcoming one.

"She's not an elf. She's...some other kind of fae. A sidhe. They're like cousins to elves. It's a long story."

"I'm ready to hear this long story of yours. And I've got a problem with strangers in the compound right now," Jake told him. "We have humans who are trying to murder us, and evidently they're being assisted by an elf. Then you tell me you stumbled across an elf in the Denali Pack territory. An elf. No one has seen any elves in Alaska, but now there are two wandering around? They must know each other."

"She's a sidhe, not an elf. She saved my life, Jake. And yes, she knows who the elf is that created the magic on the bullets."

Jake inhaled sharply. "Okay. I need you to stay put for a few days until I can charter a plane or chopper to pick you up. Is there somewhere safe for you? And for her? I want you to protect her with your life, Dustin. If she knows this elf, then she's valuable to us."

As if he'd do any less. Dustin frowned at the implication. "Yeah. We'll... I guess we'll hole up at Mark and Brenda's. There's a clearing for a chopper, or a plane with pontoons can land on the lake. The coordinates are in the log book in the office."

He had no money. He was wearing borrowed clothes. As uncomfortable as it was to go back to stay at Brenda and Mark's, it was the best option available to them. Dustin looked over at Gwylla and thought about the message hanging from the mirror on the tree. Jerk Face knew they had been there. He'd sent a message last night, but he'd most likely appear in person next time. Dustin would just have to hope that Gwylla's wards held. And that Mark had a whole lot of steel and iron in that shed of his.

"Good. I'll try to get someone there as fast as I can. And I'll call Moira about Brenda and Mark. She's already got her hands full, but she'll want to know."

"I couldn't reach her just now, but I left a message." Obviously it was good manners for Jake to call and give his condolences and express support in hunting down the killers, but Dustin wanted his Alpha to know that Moira might already be aware that two of her wolves had been murdered.

"She didn't pick up?" Jake seemed bothered by that, and there was very little that bothered Jake. "When I called her a few days back, she told me that she'd had a wolf go missing. It seems the hunters might have shifted focus from Kenai to the Denali Pack territory."

"We'll get them," Dustin vowed. "We'll get this elf, and we'll get these murderers as well."

Jake made an approving noise. "I hope so, because all I care about at this point is killing every single one of them."

As in most things, Dustin agreed with his Alpha on this.

CHAPTER 15

$\mathcal{A}$fter a silent walk back to the cabin, Gwylla went to reinforce the alarm system she'd put around the property while Dustin headed to the shed to see what Mark had in there that might serve as a weapon against an elf.

He was worried. That scroll… Gwylla might have at one time had a romantic entanglement with this guy, but Dustin had a feeling he wouldn't hesitate to use force to drag her back. And once she left and he imprisoned her, Dustin feared they'd never rescue her. They'd either never find her, or they'd find her body in some basement somewhere.

Gwylla was too smart to be persuaded by threats or promises of his safety to voluntarily leave with the elf, but Dustin feared she'd die fighting him. Which was why he was knocking the heads of hammers to use with a slingshot and loading shotgun shells with nails.

The hunters had ransacked the house for weapons, but they'd overlooked this old shotgun in the shed, and Dustin still had the rifle from the dead guy. Plus, the hunters had obviously been looking for human weapons—things that could be used against humans. They never would have considered that half the stuff in this cabin would be lethal to an elf. If he could only get close enough, he could stab the guy with a butter knife and most likely kill him. Or throw a toaster at him from across the yard.

Thinking of all the ways to kill Jerk Face with random household appliances made him feel better, and by the time he went back into the house with his deadly stash of tools and supplies, he was whistling.

Gwylla definitely wasn't feeling his optimism. As he deposited his armful of metal, he saw her at the bullet-riddled dining room table, her head in her hands.

"Hey. It's going to be okay. You've set up a perimeter. I've got plans to kill your ex-boyfriend with a toaster. Trust me, we've got this."

She lifted her head, a smile trembling at the corner of her lips. "Toaster?"

"Yeah. I'm a werewolf, so I can throw things really hard. I shotput the toaster into his face, and boom! Dead elf."

"And if you miss?"

"Well, then, there's always the mixer. Or the microwave."

She laughed, then her face grew serious. "Dustin, I barely escaped him before. He won't be fooled like that again. If he thinks he can't force me to come with him, he'll kill me."

"Not if we kill him first. Remember? Toasters and microwaves. He's arrogant, and he knows very little about this world, the humans, or us. One stupid mistake and he's mine. And trust me, he'll make a stupid mistake. They always do, usually about the time they deliver their long, boring villain monologue."

She shook her head. "I can't believe this, but you're actually convincing me that we can win this. I'd hoped your Alpha could get you, that you'd be safe with your pack, and that I could face Talligie alone. I didn't intend to drag you into this fight."

"Well, it's a good thing you did, because there is no one better at slinging small appliances than me." He walked over to the table and sat beside her, wrapping an arm around her shoulder and pulling her against him. She relaxed, putting her head on his shoulder, and he kissed her hair. "Together we'll do this. Wonder Twins, right?"

He felt her smile against his shoulder. "Right."

"Then let's celebrate. We'll feast, which for me will mean lots of meat, and for you probably more raisins and possibly that tub of yogurt if it's not expired. Brenda's got a few bottles of wine, too. We'll toast to our victory. But no getting drunk."

She snorted. "I doubt these werewolves have enough wine in their house to get me drunk. We sidhe know how to party, and we are better than anyone about holding our liquor."

"Well, you've never seen a werewolf drink before. Once this is over, you can come over to my house for vegetarian pizza and beer and if you're lucky, I'll break out the tequila and drink you under the table."

She lifted her head to look at him. "To your house? You'd invite me to your house?"

"Well, yeah. I mean, it's not as nice as your little place in the hill, but it's pretty sweet. Usually only mated couples get houses and the rest of us live in dorms, but I got a house since I fly the pack plane and I get called out for jobs at weird hours sometimes. It's not big, but I've got a dart board, and a nice TV. We can watch a movie after pizza, before I get you drunk."

She watched him, fascinated. "And what happens after I get drunk?"

He was going to go with this. Yes, he was going to make a giant fool of himself, but oh well. "We make out, then I take you into the bedroom and we have the best sex of our lives. Although, maybe we should do that before I get you drunk, that way you don't pass out on me, or puke in the middle of it."

Smooth. Yeah, real smooth.

She blinked, then nodded. "Okay."

Okay? Was that *okay*, okay? Or just okay?

"Then we have a plan. Kill your evil ex-boyfriend. Fly out of here on whatever Jake sends to pick us up, then enjoy our amazing pizza-tequila-and-sex night." Was she really agreeing to this? Was he dreaming, or was she joking? Or was she really going to at the very least eat pizza and drink tequila with him? And sex?

"Will you visit me at my sanctuary, too?" she asked. "I'll make some fresh bread, and a mushroom pate and I have wine. And we can have sex before you get drunk at my house, too."

He could barely breathe. "Yes. Absolutely. That sounds lovely. Especially the sex part."

"Good." She stood. "Then this is settled. We will spend lots of time at each other's houses, eating and drinking and having sex. Three things that we sidhe enjoy the most. And I will be especially happy to do them with you, because I like you Dustin."

He pinched his thigh hard. Definitely not dreaming. "Yes. Good. Let's scavenge for whatever is edible and drinkable in the kitchen, then get on with killing this psycho ex-boyfriend of yours, because I'm eager to start doing these three favorite things of yours."

She laughed, then leaned forward and kissed him. It was different than that soft kiss when he'd been injured and in her bed. This kiss was passionate and full of promise. Before he knew it, Dustin's arms were around her, pulling her down onto his lap, his hands tangling in her hair. Her hands scooted up the bottom of his shirt, cool against his stomach.

He pulled away, reaching down to still her hands. "No. I

want to wait. I can't believe I'm saying this, but I don't want this to be an oh-my-god-we're-gonna-die thing."

Her fingers caressed the skin along the top of his waistband. "Are you sure?"

No. "Yes, I am." He leaned forward and kissed her once more, just because he couldn't help himself. "Oh, this is the most difficult thing I've ever done in my life, but I want to wait. I don't want heat-of-the-moment sex. Well, I *do*, but I want the first time to be because we're really feeling it for each other."

"I am feeling it for you." She rested her forehead against his. "But to prove it to you, I'll wait."

He scooted her off his lap. "Good. Because we're not going to die."

She grinned. "No, we are not, because you are the toaster-man, or toaster-wolf, or whatever. And now let's go drink human wine and eat raisins and celebrate, for tonight we kill the evil ex-boyfriend known as Jerk Face."

The sun was a ball of tangerine, lighting the sky above the lake in shades of peach and turning the lingering clouds into a violet contrast. They'd cleaned out most of the contents of the fridge, and Dustin had managed to find a glass jar full of change, vowing that if they were still here tomorrow evening, they'd go into town for dinner of burgers—veggie or meat—and milk shakes. Gwylla's earlier confidence had faded with the light, but instead of fear, a feeling of resigned calm settled over her. What would be, would be. She would need to trust in the Lady to guide her hand—and guide Dustin's aim with the toaster. And the uncomfortable sense that she needed to reveal her secrets to someone—to Dustin in particular. She didn't want to die with all this deception between them. And if she lived—well, deception between friends was a terrible thing, and it seemed that they might become even more than friends.

"What would you do if you were ever ousted from your pack?" she asked, rocking as she watched the last bit of sun seemingly vanish beneath the surface of the lake.

"Oh, sheesh, that's a horrible thought. I guess I'd petition to join another. If I were ousted, I'd figure that it hadn't been a good fit between us, and I'd research carefully before I requested to join another pack."

"But what if you were blacklisted? That's the correct term, right? What if no wolf pack would allow you to join? Where they all shunned you?"

He shot her a perplexed look. "I'm not really suited to be a solitary. Male bear shifters do that all the time because they don't have a pack structure, but they seem to have the personality for living completely alone and isolated. I'd probably go live among the humans. My wolf wouldn't be happy, but at least I'd have companionship."

"But you already live among the humans, so that wouldn't be terribly difficult, would it?"

He shrugged lifting his hands. "In some ways, no. We look human, so that's not a problem. We've embraced their technology, mirror their social structure to a great extent. I could get a job, go to happy hour with the guys after work, eventually move out of an apartment into a house in the suburbs. But deep down inside, a part of me would feel empty and alone. No more hunting in wolf form, my pack by my side. No more sharing experiences and feelings that only shifters can relate to. There would be a huge portion of myself that would forever remain unsatisfied."

"And you'd always feel like a stranger in a foreign land," she mused.

"Yeah, but the humans would never know, they'd never understand. They'd probably just think I was prone to occasional fits of depression or something. It would be hard, but I'd survive. And I'm sure in time, I'd come to love and cherish many things about life as a human. After all, it wouldn't be completely different than my life as a werewolf. Maybe thirty percent different."

She let his words sink in while she rocked, watching the sky slowly darken as Dustin observed her.

"Is that how you felt among the elves, Gwylla?" He broke the silence. "Is that how you feel here? Why didn't you return to Aerie and tell your queens that the elves aren't ready and that you'll try again in a few hundred years or so? Why didn't you return when you escaped Talligie? He would have never been able to reach you in Aerie, and I'm sure your link would have been broken, not just muted."

He sounded hurt, and she knew he didn't want her to leave.

"I can't. I lied, Dustin. I'm not an ambassador sent to convince the elves to come back to Aerie, I'm an exile. I can never return. Never. I fabricated that story because I knew the elves would never take me up on that offer, and the ruse allowed me to have a status in elven society that I otherwise would not have had."

He watched her for a minute, his expression unreadable. "Okay."

Okay? Just okay? "I lied, Dustin."

"Yeah. And what would have happened if you hadn't lied? What would the elves have done had you told them you were exiled and banished to Hel?"

She shuddered. "I would not have had the implied protection of the queens to keep me safe. I would have needed to trade my magic abilities for food and shelter. I would have most likely been preyed upon by someone who promised to be my patron in return for exclusive use of my magic, then fallen into a sort of slavery to him."

Which was ironically what had ended up happening with Talligie, anyway. How the fates always found a way to deliver the outcome they desired, no matter her efforts to lead events to an alternate conclusion.

"Then you were right to lie." He turned in his chair to face her. "History is full of people who did what you did. There are thousands of stories of false foreign princes in various courts, mingling with the nobles and pretending to be on vacation or on diplomatic missions when they had a death sentence over their heads back home. In the last few centuries, that hasn't happened as much because there's faster and more thorough global communication, but it happened."

"Don't you want to know what I did to deserve my exile?" she asked, dreading that his friendship might vanish just as quickly as the setting sun once he heard.

"If you want to tell me."

She took a few breaths to steady her nerves. "Treason."

He chuckled. "It's treason when you lose. It's overthrowing a despot for the good of society when you win. Gwylla, this country was founded by a bunch of traitors who took a huge risk on the very slim chance that they could wrest this land from the control of the British monarchy and form a nation of their own. If we had lost, the very heroes whose faces are on our currency right now would be called traitors. And they would have faced the hangman's noose, not exile had they lost."

How very strange these humans and wolf-men were. "I didn't want to take over Aerie. The queens are very powerful, and such a thing would have been far beyond my abilities. And I do not want to rule. I merely orchestrated events so that something the queens were putting in place failed. And I was discovered. Remember how I said fae society is very political? Well, those who wished to see me discredited seized upon my wrongdoings and amplified them. I was accused of many things that I did *not* do in an effort to make sure I did not manage to wiggle out of punishment."

"So you were framed? You weren't really guilty of treason, just…I don't know what to call it. Minor betrayal? Dissent?"

"Oh no, it was treason," she assured him. "Any action that goes against the queens' mandates is treason. Piling on additional accusations didn't lessen the fact that I was guilty of the worst crime. Not that I was alone in my actions. Many fae each year have committed the same type of crime. Some are able to escape the charges, but most face The Hunt."

He nodded. "I wondered if that's what you meant when you told me about your hunt. There must be a lot of dissent if you have enough criminals to hold this event annually."

"Many commit suicide before the annual Hunt, but others try to keep up their strength so they can have one last moment to defy the queens. They always are killed in The Hunt, but sometimes a few hunters are injured or even killed before the convicted are."

"Doesn't sound like even such a punishment is an effective deterrent. Your queens must be horrible."

She shrugged. "Not horrible. The truly powerful sometimes become misguided, their judgement clouded by a false sense of divine purpose. It happens."

Dustin grimaced. "Yeah, it does. So how did you avoid this Hunt and get banishment instead? Or did you manage to escape the queens as you did the evil ex-boyfriend?"

"A few supporters convinced the queens that for me in particular, banishment would be a worse fate. I arrived in Hel thinking that they might be right, but then everyone believed my lie, and I began to think that perhaps I could make a life for myself with the elves, that in time the whole ambassador story would fade and I'd just a sidhe consort to a high lord. I went from one crime to another."

"I don't see your lie to the elves as a crime, Gwylla. Who was hurt by your deception? Didn't those hosting you for dinners and other functions enjoy your presence? Your conversation? You cost them little, and gave as much as you got, I'll bet. Forgive yourself."

"You don't understand, Dustin." She fixed an earnest gaze on him. "I lied. Talligie would have wed an exiled traitor, not an envoy important to the queens. I thought I loved him, but in all honesty I used him just as he used me. I loved the idea that I would be his consort, that I would be secure in a high position in elven society. He used me for my power and what I could give him, and I did the same. I used him for what he could give me. The words of love we spoke to each other were lies on both of our parts. And I may have continued with this horrible arrangement, even after I realized this truth, had the elves remained in Hel. If the elves had not decided to cross the gates, I would be consort to a dictator, to a high lord who would have worked to bring all of Hel under his control."

"You're not being fair to yourself, Gwylla." Dustin reached out and grabbed one of her hands, holding it tight. "You were scared, an exile among people that would have practically enslaved you had you not lied. And I know if the elves had stayed in Hel and you and Jerk Face had wed, you would have worked your butt off to make sure he didn't turn into a dictator. You risked death to do so in Aerie, defying the queens for what you thought was right. And you did the same here, leaving Talligie when you realized what he planned. Don't ever think that you'd just sit back and watch him trample others just so you'd get to wear a crown. I don't believe that, and you shouldn't either."

The sun had set and the moon broke free of the clouds, illuminating the landscape in shades of gray, sending streaks of white across the surface of the lake. Gwylla felt the same light, same clearing of clouds in her heart. He was right.

"You could have sent me out to get the satellite phone on my own and continued to hide in your sanctuary," Dustin continued. "You could have left me after the fight at the plane and teleported thousands of miles away to create another sanctuary, safe from your evil ex. Instead you helped me. You continued to help me. You're sitting here beside me tonight, ready to battle this jerk. And don't tell me it's because of this weird bond, because I know better. Those aren't the actions of someone forced into them by a magical tie. Those aren't the actions of a traitor. Those are the actions of a hero."

She lifted his hand and placed the back of it against her cheek. "I love that I'm a hero in your eyes, Dustin."

He turned his hand to cup her chin, rubbing a thumb across her lower lip. "You're more than a hero in my eyes, Gwylla. Now let's get ready to kick some evil ex-boyfriend butt."

There wasn't much sense in trying to get any sleep, so Gwylla and Dustin sat on the porch in companionable silence, watching the stars and listening to the insect song as they rocked. It would have been romantic if they hadn't been waiting for the inevitable confrontation.

Close to midnight, an elf walked out of the woods by the lake. Gwylla felt every muscle tighten as she watched him make his way toward the cabin. He practically glided across the ground, every step smooth and unhurried. A wind blew the long golden hair that hung loose, showing the tips of his pointed ears.

"I take it that's the ex-boyfriend? I mean Jerk Face?" Dustin's slumped posture in the chair looked relaxed and casual, but Gwylla knew better. She could tell he was struggling to keep from going on the attack.

"Yes."

What else was there to say? She watched the elf slowly approach, and something twisted inside her. Regret? He was beautiful, and brilliant. They'd been a powerful couple. And in the beginning when he'd promised her the sun and the moon, everything seemed as if it would be perfect by his side. She thought she'd found that perfect match for her, a partner that brought status and power, safety and security to her life as well as affection. But he'd been lying about his intentions, not that she'd been much better. She glanced over at Dustin. He looked so much like a human. He didn't have a presence that commanded attention. He didn't have the ability to perform magic. But he was honest and true, and was *here*, ready to fight by her side. And she was fairly certain that if he ever professed a love for her, it wouldn't be flowery but it wouldn't be a lie.

"Should we kill him?" Dustin's voice was just as casual as his posture, but again she heard the tension as well as the hopefulness in his words. It made her smile.

"Eventually. I think it would be beneficial to parley with him first. He will want to assess my strength and size you up as a potential threat, and we can gain information on his plans so your pack can better strategize their plan of action."

He made a sharp, brief nod. "The villain soliloquy. They can't help it. It's like it's in their DNA or something. That and the overly complicated method of murder, like dangling us over a shark tank with a candle slowly burning the rope."

She had no idea what he was talking about. "Yes. That."

Neither of them budged as the elf neared, then came up against the line of wards that Gwylla had placed around the cabin.

Dustin snickered. "Is he going to huff and puff?"

Most likely. Talligie stood for a few moments, his gaze locked with hers. "Trying to keep insects away, Gwylla? Or possibly humans? I'm hurt if you think this ward could possibly stop *me*."

She stood, deciding now was a good a time as any to have

this conversation. "It is merely to give me warning of those too rude not to announce their arrival in a proper fashion. The owners of this cabin weren't afforded that courtesy, and I doubted I would be either."

"Must we shout across the lawn? Come here, or dismiss your wards."

He could break them, but that would be a blatant declaration of war, and clearly Talligie had something else in mind. At least for now. Brute force would most likely follow her rejection of whatever proposal he was about to make.

She walked down the steps, noting that Dustin followed about five feet behind, carrying the toaster under his arm. "Why are you here, Talligie? I thought I had made myself clear the last time we spoke that I wasn't about to be a part of your plans."

He spread his hands wide. "Why not? You sidhe have no love for angels."

"No, but we do not seek to eradicate them."

His jaw clenched. "Because the sidhe will not budge themselves for anything. All the queens do is feast and frolic, plot and intrigue and have orgies. Your talents were wasted in Aerie. They won't be wasted here. Once the angels are gone, this world will be ours. You and I will rule. You'll be the queen you should have been in Aerie."

She caught her breath. Did he know? Had the stories of her treason somehow made it to Hel and his ears? Or was that a random observation, more of the false flattery that she used to believe was sincere admiration?

"But I won't be your queen, will I Talligie? You'll use me, use my power, and when I'm no longer useful, I'll meet an unfortunate end. You'll never share power with anyone, not even me."

His eyes widened with hurt, and there was a sincerity in

them that was so real she almost believed it. "I loved you, Gwylla. I still love you. You are the only being fit to be my queen, the only one I've met that has ever been my equal. Come back to me and I'll listen to your counsel. These shifters are not my true target. If you care about them so, then we will spare them. Now that I know the effect of this magic, I can tailor it to create a weapon that kills angels, and leave the shifters in peace."

Would he? She thought back on all their times together. Talligie was a high lord, used to getting his way. He might compromise in the short-term to achieve a long-term goal, but in the end, he wouldn't compromise on that goal. He'd end up killing the shifters because they couldn't be controlled or enslaved, and anyone that couldn't be controlled or enslaved, including her, would end up dead. Besides, this world didn't belong to the elves *or* the angels, and trading one overbearing master for another would do the humans no good.

She curled her lip and lifted her head, channeling every haughty queen she'd ever been in the presence of. "You don't have the power to create a weapon that would kill the angels. I've seen your bullets, and they are a child's trick. All they do is force a shifter to change into animal form and prohibit them from healing their wounds. How could you possibly alter that in any way to create a weapon that would destroy a being of spirit?"

His eyes sparked. "You doubt me? You, of anyone, should know the skill and power I hold. At first I thought to use a blade, but getting close enough to an angel to strike brings with it too great a risk. These weapons of the humans are perfect for enchantment. They could kill from a safe distance. Even a human could kill an angel with these."

And that's what he intended, no doubt. Make the humans

do the killing, so if the tides turn and the angels win, the elves would look innocent in all of this.

"With bullets that hardly are strong enough to affect a shifter? That take days to kill even them with their miniscule amount of angel essence?" she scoffed. "You are a fool."

"I am no fool!" he declared hotly. "The bullets were my test, to make sure that was the correct path the magic should take. The stupid humans who believe they are my partners pay enormous amounts of money for them. They pay for the privilege of killing shifters. And they will pay for the privilege of killing angels. It's possible. I've created a blade—several of them that have enough power to kill an angel. It is a simple thing to transfer that enchantment to a bullet. All I need is to be able to produce enough enchanted bullets to supply all of the humans, then I will stand back and watch and wait."

Her heart sank. He'd produced a weapon, the issue was scale and mass reproduction of it.

"These weapons of the humans can also be turned against us," she cautioned. "Who is to say that once they drive the angels from their home, they won't do the same to the fae?"

He shrugged. "The difference is the angels don't want to hurt the humans. They think of them as some special little project to pamper and coddle. Elves have held humans in slavery for thousands of years. We know them. We know how to make them obey."

Dustin growled. Even in his human form, it was an intimidating sound. And it got Talligie's attention. The elf eyed the shifter in surprise.

"Gwylla, your pet has teeth? Of course you took him in and healed him, a dying wolf at your door. You always did have a soft heart for injured animals. Come back to me and I will let them all live. You can have as many pets as you wish —a whole harem of them."

"No." She pulled back her shoulders and called forth a bit of ice, just enough to hang like talons at the ends of her fingertips. "The elves have no right to this world. You are welcome to go to Aerie and kneel at the feet of the queens, or you may stay in Hel with the demons, but you cannot seize this world and enslave the residents."

Talligie didn't appear at all daunted by her statement. "But I will. And if you won't join me, then *you* have a choice. You can return to Aerie, or you can stay here and die by my hand." He took a step forward. "Which leaves you *one* choice, does it not? Because if you return to Aerie, you'll be imprisoned and this autumn you will face your death at the teeth of the hounds."

She felt cold. He knew. He'd probably known all along. He'd take her and use her as a battery. She'd be nothing more to him than a source of energy to fuel his power. He never wanted her as a queen, as an equal. He only wanted her as a tool.

Before she could reply a toaster shot through the air. Talligie lifted a hand, arrogantly catching it midair, then shrieking and dropping the appliance, his hand blistered red.

"Next time it's the microwave, dickhead," Dustin told him.

Was it too soon in their friendship for her to tell this wolf-man she loved him? That would probably have to wait until after pizza, tequila, and sex.

"I will stay here," she told the elf. "And *we* will make sure that you don't take this world."

Talligie snarled, shaking his injured hand. Then he extended a finger to touch her wards. They rippled, distorting him and the landscape behind him. Pain shot through her head, and she gritted her teeth, fighting to keep the barrier in place.

It fell, the sound of shattered glass filled her ears,

pounding into her head. Everything went white. She wasn't sure how she remained standing, but when her vision cleared, she was still upright, her hands clenched by her side.

Talligie smiled. "I will return tomorrow at dawn, Gwylla. And if you run, I will find you. Best say your prayers, because tomorrow, I will kill both you and your pet."

CHAPTER 18

"Nice job with the toaster," she told Dustin as they walked back to the house.

"Thanks," he climbed the stairs and turned around, staring out at the spot where the elf had been. "Think he'll keep his word and wait until morning? I wouldn't mind getting some sleep, setting an alarm, and being fresh and alert for the Great Appliance Throwing Battle."

"It's unlikely. Talligie is the type to make a big show of honor and keeping his word, then pay someone to poison the rival high lord the night before the battle. He likes to win. And he can justify all sorts of actions to get whatever it is he desires."

"Then we might want to get ready for a long night on the porch. Can you keep watch while I go gather supplies?"

She nodded and sat back down in her rocking chair, sipping the now-cold tea as Dustin came and went from the house, stacking up appliances, eating utensils, knives, tools, and the two guns, as well as a slingshot with a small pile of what appeared to be the tops of hammers. All the metal in such close proximity to her was making Gwylla nervous, but

Dustin was careful to keep it on the side of the porch away from her.

"Are you able to set any alarm wards, or even a barrier like you did before?" he asked, finally returning to his seat.

"I'm better off saving all my energy for the battle," she replied. "It's not like a barrier is going to stop him. You saw what he did to the last one."

"Yeah, but it might stop human hunters. I was thinking about what you said—that he'd send someone to poison the high lord the night before the battle? Made me wonder if he wouldn't prevail upon his human buddies to be his cannon fodder and attack us in the night. If they kill us, well then there's no need for a big battle at dawn. If we kill them, we'll be exhausted and probably injured and at a disadvantage going into that battle at dawn."

Gwylla sighed, rubbing a hand over her face. This wasn't the life she wanted to live. She wasn't a warrior. She wasn't a hero. All she wanted to do was live at peace in her sanctuary.

No, That was a lie. She wanted friends, a community to care about, who cared about her. She wanted to rock on porches in silence with Dustin by her side, drinking tea. She wanted to have picnics by the stream in her sanctuary with Dustin. She wanted to stay at his house and eat pizza, drink tequila, and have sex. And to do all those things, she needed to be a hero first. Sometimes running away and hiding does nothing but get everyone you love killed. Dustin would never run away. And she couldn't either.

"I'd better set wards then, and possibly a trap for the back door and other entrances of the house. If a group of hunters attack, they will most likely distract us with fighting here in the front while others sneak through the house to shoot us in the back."

Dustin nodded. "My thoughts as well."

She set a simple alarm fifty yards out surrounding the

house, Dustin walking by her side with the rifle in his hands, just in case. Then she put a freeze spell on the door and the downstairs windows all the way around.

"Now sleep," Dustin told her when they had returned to the porch. "Either the alarms or I will waken you if anything happens. I want to make sure you're well rested."

He was right, once again. She grabbed some blankets and pillows from the bedroom and came out to find Dustin had set up a little space for them in front of the door. He sat beside her, and she closed her eyes, her head in his lap, dozing off to the feel of him stroking her hair.

* * *

THE ATTACK CAME a few hours before dawn. Dustin was grateful that Gwylla had been able to get some sleep before the alarm woke her, but a fight this close to when they expected Talligie to arrive would mean they'd be pretty battered facing him.

Even before the wards had chimed their warning, Dustin had sensed the humans. Six. They had been in the woods for the last hour, observing, strategizing, taking position around the house. The hunters had been sold their trips as a tourist shoot-a-shifter expedition, but he could tell from the way these guys moved and set up that this group was on what they thought was a paramilitary exercise.

Thank you, "Call of Duty."

Which brought the question to Dustin's mind of whether these were actual trained mercenaries or, like him, a bunch of guys whose only military experience was with a game controller in hand? Dustin hoped the latter, because he'd always been good at team warfare games, and the ace in his pocket was that Team Werewolf/Sidhe had abilities these guys had probably never encountered outside of an Xbox.

He shook Gwylla gently. "Hey. We've got company. Six humans. I haven't been able to catch sight of them yet, but from the way they're setting up, I'm expecting they'll set the wards off in front of the house, and try to draw us out front while they approach from the sides and rear."

She stirred, rubbing the sleep from her eyes. "Would we be better inside the house, not out in the open like this?"

Dustin shook his head. "I want to be free to move about and not risk being trapped in the house, especially if they've got some kind of explosives. I wouldn't put it past them. It would take McKinley Park a while to respond to an explosion. By the time they got here, all they'd find is a burning house with our bodies inside."

She wrinkled her nose. "I don't plan on being blown up or set on fire."

"Me either." The chime sounded, from the front as Dustin expected. "Showtime, babe."

A shot sounded from the woods, showering them with wood splinters as the bullet slammed into the door jamb right next to Dustin's head. Gwylla yelped and scurried behind the row of potted plants as Dustin yanked the front door off its hinges to use as a shield. Inside was looking better and better.

A hail of bullets exploded the planters, sending dirt and terra cotta fragments all over the porch. More punched through the solid wooden door, two of them tearing through Dustin's arm and shoulder. He waited for the shift, for the agonizing burn of magic and felt nothing.

"Regular bullets," he shouted to Gwylla. They were still deadly to her, but at least she didn't have to waste time worrying about him. Clearly the strategy was to wear him down, or injure him to the point where someone could move in with the magical bullets and finish him off.

There was a faint thump on the roof, and Gwylla looked upward, her eyes blazing. "Oh, no you don't."

Her fingers spread outward, and Dustin felt the air around him drop fifty degrees. There was a shout, a crash, and a man dressed all in black slid off the roof to land heavily in front of the steps, his clothes covered in frost.

She'd iced the roof. Good girl. "Cover me."

Gwylla formed a wall of ice and he ran, quickly snapping the neck of the fallen human and dragging him onto the porch amid a barrage of gunshots and flying ice chips. Then he quickly set the door against the porch railing and grabbed the dead guy's gun. He couldn't shoot worth shit, but these guys didn't know that. Maybe he'd actually get lucky and hit one of them.

"On the right," Gwylla announced, diving to the ground as another round of bullets riddled the front of the house. Dustin turned, emptying the magazine on the guy. He went down, but the werewolf took two more to the chest. This was starting to really hurt, and he was getting shot faster than he could heal. Two hunters were down, but there were four more, and if he took another dozen bullets, he'd most likely be down for the count.

But it was more important to protect Gwylla. She wouldn't recover from these bullets, and she was the one who needed to be strong enough to fight Jerk Face at dawn. So he pulled the magazine from the rifle and dug through the dead guy's pouch for another.

"Do you want to get that gun?" Gwylla asked.

"Let me see if I can kill another one of them first." He really didn't want her to exhaust herself, and two were still in the woods, the other two circling to the back entrance. Dustin heard a scream and felt another wave of cold. He lifted an eyebrow at Gwylla.

"He touched the doorknob." She smiled with satisfaction.

"And now he is stuck to it and going into cardiac arrest with hypothermia."

"You're amazing," he told her, propping the gun back on the door-shield and eyeing the woods.

There was the sound of breaking glass from the rear of the house and Gwylla winced. "He used the stock of his rifle to break the window. Good news is the rifle is now useless. Bad news is there is a bad guy in the house."

If he was just closer, he could get these two in the woods, while Gwylla dealt with the one in the house. "Can you teleport me to the woods? Or do you have to come with me?"

"I have to be with you." She reached up and put a hand on his shoulder. "The guy in the house is less a worry than the two out there with guns."

She was right. He nodded. And again he felt the pressure and vertigo as she teleported the pair of them. He staggered a bit when they materialized, but even with his poor aim, it was pretty easy to kill two men by unloading an entire magazine of bullets into their backs.

One left. "Stay here." Dustin tossed the rifle aside and picked the two up from the fallen humans, then ran full speed across the field toward the house. A figure appeared in the front doorway, knife in hand. Then he saw Dustin and dropped the knife, grabbing the nearest firearm. It was the shotgun—the one with shells loaded with iron nail fragments.

This is going to seriously hurt. He was already injured. The four gunshot wounds were no longer bleeding, but the torn muscles hadn't quite healed yet, and two still had bullets lodged in them. Gritting his teeth, Dustin forced his body faster, cringing when he heard the shotgun blast and felt himself peppered with tiny iron fragments. The hunter shot the second shell, then the third.

He'd been hit with buckshot a few times in his life. It

always sucked, but other than having to pick hundreds of tiny pieces of metal out of his body, there were worse things in life.

The human racked the weapon, but Dustin was on him before he could fire again, slamming the man against the wall of the house. The guy lifted the gun, trying to use it as a wedge to push Dustin away, but the werewolf head-butted him, then grabbed his head and twisted.

Then he slid to the porch floor along with the dead human. It was an hour until dawn, by the look of the sky. Hopefully they wouldn't have to deal with any more human hunters tonight. And hopefully Gwylla was strong enough to face Jerk Face, because he wasn't sure he would be much help.

"Dustin!"

He heard her voice close by, smelled her cool, floral, minty scent, felt her soft hands on his skin. Then heard her shriek as she pulled her hands away.

"I can't get the metal out. It burns."

Yeah, because it was hundreds of chopped up iron nails. "I'll get it. Eventually. Sorry, until I manage to get it all out, I'm not going to look all that pretty. And my priority right now is trying to get the two bullets out of my shoulder so I can heal properly."

She picked up the dead man's knife, handling it gingerly. "Where? If I cut you deep enough, can you remove the bullets yourself? And will you be able to heal before dawn?"

That was the big question. "Let's just leave them for now."

"You'll heal all the way around them, won't you? It will hurt ten times as much having to dig them out of your body after you heal."

"Yeah, but they're wedged in the bone. I'm not sure I can get them out by myself without tearing the crap out of my shoulder muscles. If I wait, I'll just have someone at the pack do it for me. Honestly, it will cause less damage that way."

She eyed him sadly. "I wish I could do this. I wish I didn't have this problem with your metals. I could touch metal just fine in Hel, or even in Aerie. This is…this really puts me at a disadvantage."

"Yeah, but luckily it puts Jerk Face at a disadvantage as well."

"Who will be here in an hour," she commented, looking at the sky.

Which meant there was no time for them to rest. Dustin struggled to his feet. Grabbing the dead humans, he pushed them off the porch into a pile in front of the steps, then he tried to put the door back on its hinges, giving up when he saw how bent they were.

Reloading the shotgun, and inventorying his pile of weaponry, Dustin sat on the porch steps beside Gwylla and waited.

They didn't have to wait long. Just as the sky began to lighten, an elf walked out of the woods and toward the house. Dustin took aim with the shotgun and pulled the trigger. Unlike with the toaster, this time Talligie was prepared. He waved a hand and the metal fragments halted a few feet from him, dropping to the ground. Dustin kept at it, figuring that if he got lucky, one or two might get through, if not, at least he was keeping the elf busy and hopefully tiring him.

Before he could reload, the elf launched a fireball at the house. Gwylla countered with a wall of ice, and the two began an exchange of magical attacks that left the grass in front of the house as well as sections of the front porch both wet and singed. All the while, the elf continued to counter Dustin's bullets and even the slingshot hammers. Slowly the elf advanced on the house, his fire weapons starting to overpower Gwylla's ice. She reached out a hand, and vines sprung from the ground, tangling around the elf's legs, only to blacken and crumble within seconds. One of the fireballs hit the house, exploding and sending flames onto the porch. Gwylla cried out, frantically extinguishing the little fires while Dustin began throwing everything he could find at the elf. This wasn't going to work. Talligie was far more powerful than he'd thought. He had nothing to counter fire, or magic. He was only a werewolf. The only abilities he had were strength and speed. And souped-up healing.

Healing. Out of the three of them, he was the one who could take the most physical damage and survive. That was pretty much his superpower, and it would have to do.

Looking down at the pile of metal by his side, Dustin grabbed a hammer and nails and looked down at his hand. This was going to hurt like a mo-fo.

"Distract him," he told Gwylla and got to work, gritting his teeth as he drove the nails through his left hand.

After a quick horrified glance at what he was doing, Gwylla turned back to the elf. "Io shilla thettah tenslgna missilltah ossa wikath anath."

Even through the pain of driving nails into his hand, Dustin felt the impact of her words. Suddenly he saw the thread of their bond, the silvery light that stretched between him and the sidhe. He also saw a line of red light that connected her to the elf.

"Ossa wikath anath," she repeated. And the red light began to crumble.

Talligie fell to his knees and screamed. Fire streamed from his hands, hitting the porch and the front of the house with a wave of heat. This time the flames took hold. Dustin felt his skin blister, smelled the burning of his clothes. Wincing he hammered one more nail into his hand.

"Ossa wikath anath," Gwylla screamed, and the red line connecting her and Talligie snapped.

It was now or never. Dustin jumped up and launched himself off the porch and onto the fallen elf. Talligie grinned in triumph, reaching his hands around Dustin's neck as he slammed into him and setting him on fire. It hurt like nothing had ever hurt in his entire life. Even the magic bullets rotting through his flesh hadn't compared to the agony of being burned alive. Dustin heard Gwylla scream his name, and focused, raising his left hand and smashing it with all of his strength into the elf's face.

Talligie shrieked, his hands leaving Dustin's neck to claw frantically at his face. The werewolf pushed the elf backward on the ground, using his weight to hold him down as he continued to press his hand into Talligie's face. The iron nails sank into the elf's flesh, smoldering with a sickening sweet smell. Dustin felt flesh melting into goo around his hand and pushed harder. Talligie stopped struggling, his hands falling limply to the side. Still, Dustin kept pushing until his hand hit the dirt, and all that was left of the elf's head was a sticky puddle of goo.

Then he stood and looked down at the headless elf for a few seconds before turning around. Gwylla was on the porch steps, the entire house soaking wet, but no longer on fire. She was staring at him with a mixture of horror and admiration on her face.

"You, wolf-man…do not let anyone ever tell you that you are not my equal. You are a match for me in every way."

He nodded and grinned, feeling the blistered skin of his face crack and ooze. A wave of agony swept over him, and Gwylla blurred. "Complementary powers," he slurred. "Wonder Twins, right?" Then he felt his knees buckle. Everything went white and then black as his face hit the dirt.

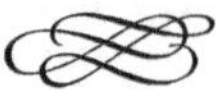

CHAPTER 19

Gwylla was pretty sure she was going to die.

First, there was the fact that the metal hollowed-out bird-like contraption she was flying in was *metal.* She could feel it buzzing around her, too close to her skin to ignore. If this conveyance lurched and she fell a few inches to the side, she'd be burned. Badly. Painfully. And she would scar. Would Dustin still find her attractive if she had ugly scars all down one side of her body? Although, it hardly seemed fair to worry about her scars when Dustin was still healing some truly horrific injuries.

She'd barely had the strength to get him inside the house. Then she'd put on a pair of leather gloves that she found in a closet and used one of the tools Dustin had on the porch to pull every one of those horrible metal nails from his hand. Not that yanking those nails helped with the burns all over his body, or the metal embedded in his skin, or those two bullets still lodged in his shoulder. Concerned that if she expended the energy to help heal him, she wouldn't be strong enough to fight off any other attacks, Gwylla had cut the clothes from his body with some plastic-handled scissors, and covered him with a burn salve that she'd found under the bathroom cabinet.

Then she'd sat on the floor of the kitchen, amid broken glass and bits of burned wood and curtains, cradled Dustin's head in her lap and cried. A few hours later he'd woken, and she'd given him water, even cooking the horrible meat in the microwave so he could eat. He looked horrible. His burns had faded to bright red skin and blisters, and his hair was singed to the point where she thought he might need to shave his head and just let it grow in.

She hadn't left him until the helicopter landed out front, and then it was to stand on the front porch, her jaw set, ready to freeze anyone who came to hurt them. But there were two werewolves in the big metal insect-shaped thing, not humans with weapons. They'd taken Dustin into one of the bedrooms and dug the bullets and metal fragments out of him, and when he'd come out, he looked even worse, with bloody bandages on his shoulder, and small scabs all over his skin.

Those were probably healed, although she couldn't tell since he now had clothes on. His skin still looked like he had a horrible sunburn, and his hair was still singed, but he'd never looked more beautiful to her. This wolf-man had driven nails into his hand and thrown himself at Talligie, risking death to kill him. She'd thought no one but her or perhaps an angel could kill the high elf, but a werewolf had done it. And not just any werewolf, but *her* werewolf. Her wolf-man. Never again would she ever underestimate him.

Dustin reached out and took her hand. His still had little hard bits of skin from where the nails had been, but she was sure they would be gone by tomorrow. Then he tried to say something, but it got lost in the noise of the machine and the wind outside of the machine. She had something covering the lower part of her ears, but it did little to muffle the deafening sound, and she couldn't get the talking- part of it to work properly. So she just smiled like an idiot at Dustin and prayed to the Lady that they'd land soon. Safely. And that she'd never again have to put herself in a metal box of death in the sky.

The helicopter dove downward and Gwylla squeezed her eyes shut, gripping Dustin's hand so hard that she was sure her fingernails had broken the skin. There was a lurch, then the conveyance held still. Dustin tugged on her hand and she opened her eyes to see the wing-blades slowing. They were on the ground and all around them were large wood and brick buildings, a line of metal transportation devices in front of several.

All this metal. How could she ever be comfortable here? She should have walked right back into the mountains where there was no metal to burn her. If she never saw another rifle or hammer or steak knife again, it would be too soon. She should have gone back to her sanctuary.

But she couldn't. Dustin was hers now, and she was his. It wasn't just the bond that would make her ache with longing if she was apart from him, it was her heart.

Dustin slid the ear-protectors off her head.

"We can get out now," he told her.

"But the wing-blades are still rotating." It wasn't safe. It clearly wasn't safe. She was torn between fear of the metal box she sat in and the metal spinning overhead.

"This is as slow as they are going to get," he replied. "Cam needs to take off after we get out, and it's a waste of time and fuel to completely power down. Just duck once we get out so you aren't decapitated."

He was teasing. She knew he was teasing, but he'd just voiced her very real fear. The metal all around her was hindering her abilities, blocking the flow of magic through her. Under normal circumstances she could bend the reality just a bit and either halt the propellers, move herself at supersonic speeds, or teleport the short distance it would take to clear the deadly objects. But in a box of metal, even metal she was not touching, she'd not be able to do any of those things. In reality, she'd be lucky if she didn't throw up before clearing those wing-blades.

"Now." Dustin opened the door and tugged at her, his head bent low. And she went, not because she was suddenly brave when it came to these guillotine blades spinning above her head, but because the longer Dustin stood there, holding her hand and bending himself over, the more he risked being decapitated himself.

And she could never put Dustin at risk, especially over fear for her personal safety. This was his world. If he said duck and run, then she'd duck and run.

But she was never so grateful as when that stupid bird-insect conveyance left in a tornado of wind and flew into the distance.

Dustin held her hand, then he slowly tugged her forward. "Come on. I can't wait for you to see my house. I promise I will throw away anything metal. I'll make it completely safe for you. I'll even decorate it how you want, in any colors you want." He pulled her close. "Anything to make you want to stay with me."

"I want to stay with you. Although…how long until you will be able to stay with me at my sanctuary?"

He looked over to a huge log building. "I'll need to talk to Jake, my Alpha, about a schedule. It's going to be tough, Gwylla. I have a job here. They need me, and this is my pack. I can't just take off every other week to go with you."

What did he mean? Did that mean she would only see him now and then? Whenever his Alpha said he could visit?"

Dustin wrapped his arms around her and hugged her tight. "I want my home to be your sanctuary, Gwylla," he whispered into her hair. "I want my pack to be your pack. I want you to have friends here, to think of my pack as your family. I know you love your sanctuary and I would never keep you from it, but I truly hope you come to love it here just as much."

She blinked away sudden tears. "But I'm not a werewolf. Will your Alpha allow me to stay? Will your pack-friends even like me? What if they don't want a sidhe in their family?"

He pulled back and cupped her face in his hands, leaning forward to kiss her. "We're bonded. Jake will definitely allow you to stay, especially when he hears all you've done to help us, and me in particular. And if I love you, then my pack mates will, too."

Gwylla slid her hands under the hem of his shirt and up his back, marveling that the smooth, warm flesh didn't have the slightest hint that he'd been shot and burned less than twelve hours earlier.

"Do you love me?"

He smoothed his hands through her hair. "Absolutely."

When she'd left Aerie, she'd never thought life would be this wonderful, she'd never imagined what joy the Goddess had in store for her. How ridiculous she'd been to ever think she'd loved Talligie. Her feelings for that elf were nothing compared to what she felt for her wolf-man.

"Well good, because I love you, too. Now I seem to remember a certain werewolf promising to introduce me to the wonders of pizza and tequila."

He kissed her again. "Will you be happy here, Gwylla?"

She looked into his dark green eyes with their flecks of brown and gray. "My beloved wolf-man, I will be happy anywhere you are. Anywhere."

BAD SEED

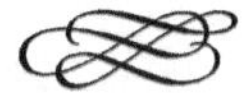

NORTHERN WOLVES BOOK 4

PROLOGUE

*I*t was surprisingly peaceful in Jake's meeting room despite the fact that three Alphas, three seconds, one human mate, a bear shifter, and two angels were squeezed into the space along with a werewolf pilot and a sidhe. But then, a threat that endangered every shifter in the state served as a catalyst to bring them all together.

"We have these, courtesy of a mage in Hel." Brent, the Juneau Pack Alpha deposited a multi-sectioned box on the conference table. He pulled a glass vial from one section and held it up, the red liquid inside shining like rubies in the room's fluorescent lighting. "Potions. They won't heal the damage, but they'll halt the progress of the rot and allow our bodies to heal the wounds. It will still take us about as long as a human to recover from being shot, but at least we won't be dead. And we won't go rogue."

Jake didn't want to think about how much that must have cost the pack. When it came to the lives of his people, no price was too high. "I'd like to purchase enough for each member of my pack to have one, plus as many spare vials as we can get."

"I only have fifty right now, and I want to have some available for any bear shifters that need them. Ten for the bear shifters and ten for both mine and Moira's pack, and I'll let you have twenty since you have the biggest pack in Alaska."

Twenty. For sixty werewolves. Jake winced. "How soon can we get more? If I make sure Dustin and those working for the outfitter companies have them, that only leaves five for the rest of the pack."

"Ten isn't enough for us either," Moira, the Denali Pack Alpha said. "My wolves are practically on lockdown. They're ready to shoot first and ask questions later when it comes to humans."

"We're trying to get more as fast as we can," Brent told them. "There's only one mage in Hel who is producing these. Now that he knows the formula, the process should be faster. It still might be a few weeks until I get more, and probably a couple of months until we have enough for every shifter in Alaska."

"Then we need to think about the shifters outside of the state," Sabrina, the Juneau Pack second said. "If supplies of these magically enhanced bullets reaches the lower forty-eight, they're at risk as well."

Brent nodded. "I'll coordinate with the other pack Alphas, but my priority is Alaska right now."

Jake tapped his pen on the table. "Until then, I'll hold back as many as I can, and make carrying one mandatory each time one of us is in a situation where we'll be interacting with humans—or where the possibility of being shot is at all a risk. Just like the flak jackets."

"I'm getting push back on those," Moira, the Denali Pack Alpha spoke up. "We don't live in a compound, and my wolves don't want to put on a bulky protective vest every time they take out the garbage or run to the grocery store."

"Mine either," Brent added.

"The potion might stop the spread of magical infection, but it does nothing to repair the wound itself," Brent's mate, Kennedy chimed in. She was human, but a trauma surgeon and had proven herself more than once to be the equal to any shifter at this table. "A werewolf that can't run because he's full of gunshot wounds that will take weeks to heal is going to be slaughtered, potion or no. And if those bullets destroy a shifter's vital organs, they won't have the luxury of weeks to heal. A shot to the heart that can't be immediately healed is going to be fatal even with a potion on hand. Those protective vests are just as important, if not more so, in saving shifter lives."

Moira sighed. "Mandatory flak jackets. I'll just have to get snarly about it. The potions *will* save lives, though. Our thanks to the Juneau Pack for taking the lead on this and making it happen."

Brent nodded in acknowledgement.

"Other good news is that our media campaign is taking hold," Sabrina added. "My shooting, painful as it was, did a lot to put shifters in a good light and bring public attention to the situation with the hunters. That, along with some key human testimony has brought law enforcement to our side. They're discrediting the videos showing shifter attacks saying that they're unsubstantiated and possibly fabricated, and warning the public that any attacks upon us will be treated the same as at attack on humans—assault and attempted murder charges will be brought against any human who shoots a shifter. The onus will be on the human to prove self-defense."

That was a huge positive turn of events. With law enforcement on their side, it would be difficult for the hunters to just hold up a wolf carcass and claim they had been attacked. There were now witnesses to the effect of these bullets, and proof that, at the very least, Sabrina's shooting had been completely unjustified.

"Talligie may be dead, but there're still many bullets that he managed to spell, plus the risk that another elf or a human mage may be motivated enough to continue the project," the sidhe, Gwylla, added. "And of course, the blades and bullets that were enhanced to use against the angels are going to be an issue." The last was said with an apologetic grimace toward the two angels in the room.

"I've brought it to the attention of the Ruling Council," the archangel, Raphael, assured her.

"And taking out the current supply of ammunition along with either the arrest or timely death of the humans organizing and profiting from all this will go a long way toward making us all feel safer, even if there's a possibility that someone else might attempt to create more," the other angel, Ahia, commented.

"Which leaves me." Jake stood. "We'll need to find out where in the Anchorage area they're keeping their supply, and destroy it as well as bring those humans to justice. I'll take charge of the project, since it seems to be in my own back yard."

Nobody disagreed, and nobody questioned what sort of justice Jake was proposing. Like Ahia, most of those in the room wouldn't be terribly disturbed if the humans who had been hunting and killing their own were found dead. And he'd prefer it. Jake knew there was quite a lot a human criminal could continue to accomplish from behind bars, and he was determined that the businesses these three humans had begun would never operate again.

"I'm okay with that," Brent said.

"Whatever you need us to do, Jake, we'll do it," Moira vowed.

They'd taken care of the hunters who'd been murdering

in her territory, or rather Dustin and Gwylla had taken care of them, but there had been two bears that vanished up near Fairbanks and another one of her pack was missing and presumed dead. That was more than enough to light a fire under the normally standoffish Alpha and her widely dispersed pack.

"Gwylla has offered to do a divination." Jake nodded at the sidhe. "She has to wait for the right astrological alignment, but that should give us a bead on where the spelled items are being held, and possibly where we'll find the other two partners."

It had been huge for the reclusive fae to remain here away from her sanctuary, but Dustin had convinced her of the importance of finding the humans selling the magic that the hunters were using to coat their bullets. And it had become quite clear that what was important to Dustin was going to be important to Gwylla. Jake glanced over at their entwined hands and felt a stab of envy. His pack pilot had found his mate. He should be happy for him, and not wishing that he had the same.

He was ninety years old. He'd most likely live for four or five centuries, if not more. Someday there would be a werewolf for him. Someday. He just needed to be patient. And to keep lying to himself that he'd ever meet a werewolf, or any shifter, who'd be his match, his mate.

"Conditions should be right in the next two to three days," the sidhe spoke up. "I'm confident that I can trace the supply of bullets through the magic used to coat them."

Jake smiled at her in thanks. "In the meantime, Moira will continue to police hunters in her territory, with the cooperation of human law enforcement. Brent, let me know if things heat up your way, and if you need any assistance." Not that the Alpha would be likely to call upon Jake for help with two angels in his pack.

Brent nodded. "Will do. And I'll send three of my best wolves up to Anchorage and Kenai to assist in policing hunters here. Sabrina is in charge of coordinating with you on that, as well as assisting you in scouting out the location of the ammunition storage once you've determined where it is."

They would just need to wait for Gwylla to do her thing and to make sure the hunters felt the squeeze...and to make sure that no more shifters died in the meantime.

Everyone made to stand, but Jake halted them with an upraised hand. "Hang on. Before you guys leave I need you to know about something. A courtesy FYI, so to speak."

There was one more reason Jake had asked the two other Alphas to meet him here. And even though he wasn't thrilled about a half a dozen others overhearing this, it was best that they knew as well.

He pulled a folder from a desk drawer, opened it, and slid it over toward Brent and Moira. Both Alphas sucked in a breath.

"Jake, you're not seriously thinking of taking her in, are you?" Moira asked, her voice sharp as she passed the folder down the table toward the others.

"I already have. She arrives tomorrow. I'm just giving you a courtesy heads-up in case the worst happens and she gets out of hand."

Jake waited until the folder made the rounds, noting the looks of confusion and alarm on the other faces before handing the folder back to Moira and Brent. They looked at it once more, shaking their head as they read the details in the contents.

"You're insane." Brent spun the folder around and pushed it back toward Jake. "Tell L.A. to put her down. It should have been done decades ago."

"*Can* they even put her down?" Moira asked. "I mean, isn't she immortal? We'd need to call in an angel or something."

Everyone turned to look at the two angels in the room.

"I'm not killing her," Ahia said firmly. "You guys need to deal with her, or bump it up the ladder if you need her dead."

Raphael raised his hands. "Werewolves and Nephilim aren't under my sphere of influence, honorary pack member or not. If she needs killing, and you guys can't manage to make her stay dead, then you'll have to ask the Iblis to do it."

Everyone sucked in a collective breath. Nobody wanted the Queen of Hel, the most chaotic being in the universe, to turn her attention to their little corner of the world.

Jake shook his head and looked down at the picture paper-clipped to the folder. It looked like a mug shot. A woman with purple spikey hair, tattoos, and piercings stared out at him. Her eyes were cold, dead. Others saw a shifter that had been a ticking time bomb in every pack she'd belonged to. Others saw a notorious wolf who had been shuffled from pack to pack because eventually she challenged her Alpha—and won. But she couldn't lead. No one would follow her. She had an aggressive dominance, but no leadership skills whatsoever, no ability to hold a pack together, encourage them, make the sum greater than the parts. Others saw a genetic experiment gone wrong, a shifter who was more demon than angel.

Jake saw desperation. He saw a woman who had preemptively sabotaged everything she wanted in life. He saw someone who was at the end of the line and had given up on herself. He saw someone who needed a chance—a real chance, not some half-hearted pack membership with an Alpha who didn't have a clue what was boiling inside this woman.

"She arrives tomorrow. I'm it. I'm the only Alpha alive

who is willing to take her on. If I fail, I'll put her down myself. And yes, if I kill her, she'll stay dead."

None of them liked involving angels in their business, present company excluded. For hundreds of years, the Alaska packs had been off the angelic radar. There might be two of them in the Juneau Pack territory right now, not including the gate guardian, but that didn't mean any of them wanted more. And there was no way Jake would ever have asked Ahia to do something like this. No, if this bad seed was beyond his ability to save, then he'd do the job himself. He owed it to her. And he owed it to himself.

"The timing is terrible, what with everything else going on," Moira warned.

He nodded. "I agree, but she can't stay in L.A. until this is resolved. She needs a pack now, and I'm it."

Brent shook his head. "Jake, you've got a tightly run pack here. I might not agree with your management style, but you get results, and your wolves are satisfied with their lives; they're happy. She's going to ruin everything. She'll upset the harmony you've achieved here."

She would, but he needed to do this, both for her and for him. And if he was such a lousy Alpha that his pack couldn't withstand a tsunami in their midst, then so be it.

"What are you going to do with her?" Moira asked. "I mean, does she have skills that your pack will find useful, or are you just going to chain her to a pole twenty-four-seven?"

The Juneau Pack members had pack duties, as well as jobs in the civilian world. They tithed to a central account for pack benefit. Brent was the only full-time pack member as their Alpha. The Denali pack took Brent's loose structure one step further. They were more a gathering of solitaries than a real pack. They also tithed, but Moira had a job and duties outside of her Alpha ones.

There had been those who had accused the Swift River

Pack of being a cult, or a para-military group. They all lived on a compound—every single one of them with no exception. Everything was pack-owned except for the clothing on each wolf's back and their personal items. Mated couples, and a few select others whose jobs were more of an on-call nature, were granted a small family house. Everyone else lived in a dormitory-style arrangement. All the businesses were pack businesses. Jake decided who did what. The cooks submitted the weekly meal plans to his second for approval. The tour, flight, and other businesses submitted their weekly financials and status reports to his second. But Jake reviewed everything. No one sneezed in his pack without his permission. This tight level of control eased his mind, and it seemed to suit those who called Swift River their pack. Wolves were free to transfer elsewhere. He'd never hold a wolf here against his or her will. But it was gratifying that so few left. Of the three Alaska packs his was the most profitable, the largest in terms of members, the most stable.

And he was about to dump a grenade right in the middle of all that. Brent was right. He *was* crazy. But it was too late to back out now, even if he'd wanted to.

Jake leafed through the file, thinking of Moira's question. What was he going to do with this rabid wolf? In the last fifty years she'd been a mechanic, an equipment operator, a lumberjack. She'd plowed fields, dug ditches, hammered nails. Outside of the operator job in the seventies, she'd always been assigned manual labor, no doubt in an attempt to physically exhaust her and blunt her aggression. Obviously that tactic had been unsuccessful. Maybe she needed to be forced to be around humans and other shifters. Maybe isolating her in physically demanding jobs had only been gasoline on the fire of her isolation and disrespect, reinforced her lack of empathy. Maybe she needed to mentor, to be forced to lead, to bond. Although woe to those who she was mentoring.

He'd throw her off balance. He'd keep her so unstable that she didn't have a chance to set her feet and attack. He'd throw so much at her so fast that all those layers of anger and defiance were stripped away, exposing the raw, terrified, insanely powerful being that lay within.

"I have no idea," he replied with honesty. "I've got no idea, but I'll find something."

CHAPTER 1

Dustin set my duffle bag onto the dock then turned to give me a hand out of the plane. Good thing, too. Otherwise I would have ended up taking a dip in what I was sure was near-freezing water. It wasn't just my unsteady legs on the rocking pontoons, it was my eyes looking everywhere except where my feet were going as I took in the breathtaking landscape of my new home—my *last* home. Because I either made it stick here with this pack, or I'd wind up six feet underground, with my head, no doubt, buried a few miles away from my body.

The pilot steadied me as I planted both feet on the dock, then bent to retrieve my bag.

"That's the Alpha House?" I couldn't keep the awe from my voice. We'd flown over what seemed like an entire town of buildings clustered within a quarter mile of the lake, and here at the edge of it all was a huge, sprawling, two-story log house with a wraparound porch and nearly as many windows as logs.

"Yep, that's the Alpha House." There was a note of pride in Dustin's voice. "This is the pack compound. We all live here."

Here? In the middle of nowhere? All together? The packs I'd been a member of in the lower forty-eight tended to operate on more of a human-society structure with shifters living wherever they chose, only meeting monthly for pack business at a local VFW or rented fire hall. I felt claustrophobic just thinking about a "compound", but it's not like I had any choice in the matter. They could stick me in a windowless basement room and it would be better than dead. Maybe.

"How far do you guys have to commute to work?" In Dallas, Richmond, L.A. and Philadelphia, work hadn't been too far of a daily drive, where many of the Minneapolis pack had needed to drive an hour each way from home to their jobs. Once again I wondered what I'd do to support myself here in the wilderness.

Easy answer—whatever I could find. And whatever the new Alpha told me to do. No fighting. No disrespectful behavior. No disobedience. This was it. Shape up, or get off the bus. I gritted my teeth, determined to make this one work. Although I'd been determined to make all the other ones work, too.

"We're all employed at one of the pack businesses, so it depends. Robin has the worst commute with two hours each way. Books on tape are her friends."

Books on tape? Didn't they have internet out here? And who the hell still had a tape player in their car? My worry over whether Dustin meant cassettes or eight-track vanished as I saw a four-wheeler heading our way. Eyeing my pilot's stance, I quickly determined that this wasn't my new Alpha approaching. I relaxed, still bowing my head slightly and staring at the dock planks six feet in front of me. This was a new pack and I didn't know where in the hierarchy I stood. No sense in starting off my first five minutes with a fight for dominance, especially with *my* reputation. I'd sit happily at the bottom rung until I'd earned their acceptance and respect.

No you won't, that voice inside me snarled. *Bottom rung, my ass. You're more powerful than this pilot, more powerful than this woman on the four-wheeler, probably more powerful than the Alpha himself. They bow before you, or you make them bow.*

Or they kill me. There were over sixty wolves in this pack. That was more than enough to take me down, even if my beast went on a rampage. This was my last chance. *Don't fuck it up*, I told the voice.

The four-wheeler came to a halt. I peered up enough to see a blonde who looked like she might double as a Sports Illustrated Swimsuit Edition model in jeans and hiking boots. Her glossy golden locks were pulled up into a pony tail. She didn't look particularly welcoming, but she didn't look like she was ready to sprout fur and rip into my jugular either.

"Good luck," Dustin muttered. I shot him a quick smile of thanks and walked over to the blonde, waiting until she addressed me before I spoke. The beast inside me bumped against the edges of my skin, desperately wanting to pin this bitch and possibly pee on her. The sensible part of me hoped that none of that aggression was apparent.

"Tupper Mills."

It wasn't a question, but I nodded. "Yes, ma'am."

"Get on."

I had no idea who this woman was, what her position in the pack was, and that bothered me far more than it did my beast. I wanted to fit in, and fitting in meant knowing my place and acting in the correct manner toward my new brothers and sisters. My beast didn't give a shit. Keeping my gaze lowered, I shouldered my bag, climbed onto the back of the four-wheeler, hooking my feet around the pedals and bracing my hands on my thighs. As expected, the blonde stomped on the accelerator, taking off toward the Alpha House. It would have been improper for me to hold onto her waist, so instead I gripped with my thighs and tried my damnedest to keep from flying off the back of the moving vehicle. Thankfully it was a short ride. Without any further communication from my chauffeur, I hopped off the four-wheeler and followed her into the house and through several doors.

It was glaringly obvious when I was in the presence of my new Alpha, and not just from his position behind an enormous solid chunk of desk furniture. There were six people in the room besides the blonde and me, every one of them a werewolf, and every one of them looking like they could give me a run for my money in a fair fight. Not that I ever fought fair.

The guy behind the desk was different. Alphas always exerted some sort of pressure on me, as if they had their hands firmly planted on top of my head. This dude felt more like he had his claws embedded deep inside my chest. He made me nervous. And when my beast got nervous, she got hostile. I wasn't an Alpha, but I couldn't help but want to dominate every single shifter I met. It was a character flaw that would kill me before my ninetieth birthday if I couldn't find a way to overcome it.

The Alpha ignored me. They all ignored me. The blonde stood patiently just inside the door, her hands clasped in front of her. I was two feet behind, with my hands clasped behind my back as if I were a prisoner waiting my turn on the gallows. Glancing up, he nodded at the blonde. She turned and left, knocking me with her shoulder as she passed. My beast snarled, but I was too thrown off kilter to act. Should I enter? Should I sit? No, I shouldn't do anything until instructed. There was a reason this was my last chance. The Swift River Pack was known for the military way they ran their organization, and their Alpha, Jake Linton, was uncompromising. Others might rule their werewolf group with a kinder, gentler touch, but this guy didn't mind bashing heads and cuffing ears. You did what he said, the exact way he said it, or you paid in blood. If my beast wouldn't submit to him, it was over for me.

Half an hour I stood there like a statue, listening to the others discuss flooding, the season's excursion schedule, something about dead bears, and a recipe for fish stew from a guy named Yeti. My beast grew bored and settled, their voices fading into a soothing monotone of sound. I was nearly asleep on my feet when the four who were standing around the desk filed by me and out the door.

A few more minutes passed before the Alpha finally looked up, catching me as I observed him and meeting my disrespectful, lifted gaze. I should have immediately dropped my head, but I couldn't help but stare. He was obviously of African descent with his dark, coffee-brown skin and short, black, curly hair, but his eyes were an eerie light blue. They reminded me of the surreal shade I'd seen in the glacier ice on the trip up here. And the expression in them was just as cold and hard as those jagged chunks of ice.

Then the ice shattered. I felt something like electricity sizzle through me. His expression registered surprise, as if he'd felt it too. Warmth. Recognition. I didn't know him. I'd never met him, but there was a familiarity about him that made my beast sit up and take notice. I was all the way across the room, but I felt myself touch him—not his skin, but *him.*

He jerked backward, and the contact broke, his expression once more icing over.

"Sit," he commanded.

My ass was in a chair before the last consonant left his

lips. I still couldn't look down, though. He had a sharp, angular face, the severity not at all relieved by his full lips. I had no idea how tall the guy was, but his shoulders were wide enough that I'll bet he had to turn sideways to get through narrow doorways. And judging by the size of his arms, he took upper body day at the gym pretty seriously. The guy looked like he should have been a linebacker on a football team, if he'd been wearing anything but a suit, that is.

I wanted to touch him again, but I was afraid if I repeated that weird experience, he'd punch me across the room.

"Should I behead you now and save us all a lot of trouble?" my Alpha asked, his voice low and smooth as the silk of his jacket.

I grinned, trying to fake a composure I didn't have. "I'd rather you give me a chance to screw up first."

The corner of his mouth twitched. "And what makes you think this time is going to be any different than the last five —" he checked the paper in front of him, "—no, ten packs. Ten."

"Eleventh time's a charm, sir?"

Again with the infinitesimal twitch of his lip. "I doubt it, but I can't just kill you outright. That would mean paperwork, and I'm a busy man. Although, I'm not averse to filling out a few hundred pages of forms if you piss me off, Mills. Understand?"

He stood and I jumped to my feet, knocking my chair backward and wincing at the sound of the crash of it against the floor. "Understood, sir."

"Jamie!"

The door opened and the blonde stood there, ample chest heaving as she panted. "Sir?"

"Take Mills to her quarters." He turned to me. "You'll be

staying in the bottom-bitch house until you earn your way into the higher-level dormitories."

Or until he executed me. The bottom-bitch house. Dormitory-style living. I swallowed hard, thinking this was going to be the shortest pack membership of my life.

Jamie handed me off to a young brunette named Mir and informed me the dorm super would be by later to give me my work assignments for the week. Then she left and Mir eyed me nervously.

"Which bed is mine?" I slid my bag off my shoulder and looked around. There were no bunk beds, just singles with a trunk at the foot of each one. Across from the row of beds was a line of metal lockers, each with a number. I was guessing I'd be taking one of the plain beds that wasn't personalized with a colorful comforter and pillows, and I was right.

"That one there. Your locker is number fifteen. The higher level dorms have four to a room, some only two to a room. I like rooming with five others, though. I like having lots of people around me."

Well, not me. I set my bag on the trunk at the end of the bed. Hopefully they had a blanket I could use. It might be August, but the weather here was colder than I was used to, and my other belongings were being shipped up. At least I thought they were. My former pack might have kept them thinking I'd be dead before the boxes arrived. Or they may have burned them.

I wasn't sure what I'd be able to keep anyway. It didn't look like there was much room here for personal belongings. And there was one other issue.

"There are no locks on the trunks or lockers?" My beast wasn't too happy about that, and neither was I. I liked my privacy. And although I didn't own anything worthy of theft, I didn't want to be the subject of such practical jokes like a locker full of shaving cream or flaming dog crap.

"No. We're shifters. It's pretty easy to tell who has been messing with someone's stuff. And there's zero tolerance for theft." Mir shuddered. "Rule one, don't break the rules. Jake doesn't give second chances and you don't want to know how creative he gets with punishments."

"What about kids? Are they also subject to these rules and draconian punishments?" That's where these authoritarian types always fell apart. It was hard to hold a young wolf to adult standards.

"Depends on their age. Older ones are held accountable for their actions. Younger ones are considered their parents' responsibility and it's one of the parents that takes the punishment."

I didn't like it, but I didn't have to like it. It's not like I was ever going to have kids. Like, ever.

"We're up at five for breakfast and pack drills, then you can go back to sleep or head in to work depending on your assignment and shift. There's a wing for the third shift wolves so they can get undisturbed sleep. It's got black-out blinds and everything. On the weekends we run hunts or hunt simulations." Mir grinned, her dark eyes sparkling with excitement. "Last week we divided into four teams and had a paint-gun war. The week before we battled on the lake in inflatable rafts. The team with the most dry at the end won a fishing excursion this fall. This weekend it's steal the steaks in wolf form."

It was like corporate team-building on steroids. And the daily pack drills before breakfast? My wolf was none too happy about that.

"We're a big pack, so we only hunt all together maybe twice a year, but we all get several chances to go out in small groups to hunt. And, of course, you can always request permission to do a solo or partner hunt, if you like."

We'd only had annual hunts in my other packs, and I'd always been forbidden from joining in. Seriously injure a few pack mates one time and no one would ever let you forget it.

Mir sat on the bed next to mine and I began to unpack, taking out the small piles of underwear, shorts, pants, and T-shirts. I had a small bag of toiletries and a larger makeup bag that I put in the trunk next to my clothes.

"All of your food is provided, three meals a day," she continued in a cheerful tone. "There are usually two to three choices, and if you're picky, you can just eat cereal or beef jerky. There's a kitchen in each dorm, and once you start earning money, you can always buy food and cook it yourself for a special meal. Most of us don't, because why buy food when what's in the cafeteria is free for all pack members? And it's good. And that way you can eat with your friends and family and everyone else and not all alone in the dorm common area."

I had no friends or family, and the thought of eating every meal in a cafeteria made my stomach knot up. It's not like I had any money to be cooking my own food, though. So it would be cafeteria, or a pretty severe weight loss program.

"I'll take you over to the compound shop this weekend and you can pick out any clothes you need," she continued. "That's all provided, too. You'll get a wage from your assignment, and with that you can buy special clothing or treats."

"You guys order things online?" I wasn't sure what was permissible in terms of shopping here. Although I was hardly likely to be doing much shopping. I had very little money of my own, and hadn't really ever been interested in knick-knacks or fancy clothes.

"Sure. If you save up enough, you can buy anything you want. There are computers in the resource center that are for public use, and if you save enough, you can buy your own laptop."

Okay, that wasn't so different than the other packs. The main difference seemed to be that the tithe here was hefty, but that wouldn't matter since it seemed the pack provided for every basic need.

"Are there are lot of mated pairs in the pack? I'm surprised to see such big dormitories."

She nodded. "All the little houses out front are for mated pairs or people who have on-call kinds of jobs. There are larger ones for those who manage to have pups. Those are clustered together so the kids can play without having to run across the compound. The kids are all eager to move into the dormitories as soon as they're old enough, though. It's nice to be independent and not have parents breathing down your neck at every step."

Which made me wonder… "How old are you, Mir?"

She flushed. "Sixteen. How old are you?"

Here we go. "Eighty-four."

She gasped. "You look maybe twenty-three at most."

And I'd most likely continue to look that age for a century or so. If I lived that long.

"You've been in eight packs?" she asked, her eyes wide.

"Ten. I've been kicked out of ten packs, not including the ones where I was a temporary guest until some Alpha stepped forward to take me in."

She shook her head. "Why didn't you just go solitary if you can't handle being in a pack?"

Because I needed to be in a pack. It terrified me to think what might happen if I were out on my own with no structure, no one to hold me accountable—at least no one to try to hold me accountable. But I wasn't about to tell Mir that.

"Solitary in the lower forty-eight can be a death sentence, unless you never shift and want to live as a human. The angels still keep an eye on things there." I looked around the dormitory. "Things are different in Alaska." And things were very different here. Hopefully different would be a good thing for me.

"I'll admit I was a little scared when I heard you were coming here." Mir eyed the tattoos on my arms. "And I was really scared when they said I needed to show you around and get you used to the pack rules."

She didn't need to be scared. She was young and although she wasn't what I'd term submissive, she wasn't dominant. As far as my beast was concerned, she didn't exist. And that was a good thing for both her and me.

"I won't hurt you," I told her, just in case she was still scared.

She shot me a mischievous smile. "Not intentionally, but if you get into trouble, I've got a feeling you'll be dragging me into it as well."

Probably. Poor kid. It wasn't like I could help it, though.

Mir gave me the grand tour of the dorm, then we walked all over the compound as she showed me how to sign out a car if I needed to go out anywhere, the enormous supply of fishing supplies, kayaks, and climbing gear that I could use, and where the library, media rooms, and cafeteria were, where I was supposed to sign out a bottle of antidote for something or another if I had to leave the compound, and a dozen other places that I probably wouldn't remember or ever be able to find again. It was like a university, an entire self-sufficient community by a lake and mountains. Not that I'd ever attended a university.

"So do you guys grow all your own crops? Cows and pigs and chickens out on the back forty somewhere?" I asked.

Mir giggled. "We're not a hippy commune. Some of the cafeteria employees do food runs. Produce and perishables are bought weekly, where meats and other groceries are bought in bulk monthly. We do have fresh meat and fish from hunts, but it's hard to feed the pack off hunts alone. You should see the freezers and the storage rooms. I think we could survive a zombie apocalypse with all the food they have in there."

"Are you always this cheerful?" I teased. She'd been at it for hours now, her happy enthusiasm never fading. It should have irritated the crap out of me. By this point I normally would have been either clawing my eyes out, or clawing *her* eyes out. But for some inexplicable reason, I liked Mir. And instead of grating on me like nails on a chalkboard, her chipper commentary was infectious. No, I wasn't about to start skipping and singing pop tunes, but I did feel less hostile than usual. Even my beast had begun to take notice of my companion and now seemed somewhat charmed by this young wolf.

"Yes. Well, most of the time. I'm excited to meet you. I mean, I was kind of scared, but you're so cool. You've got purple hair, and piercings and tattoos, and you're like older than my Mom, but look like you could be my big sister. And you haven't hit me or anything, so maybe we can be friends."

I blinked, not sure what to address first. "Is that your criteria for friends? That they don't hit you?"

She laughed. "No, silly. It's just that your reputation... well, I heard that you fight a lot. I've never been in a fight. If you hit me, I'd probably cry. But I get the idea you're not going to hit me."

It was getting hard to keep from smiling. And my beast was practically purring, filled with some weird maternal, or possibly fraternal, instinct that she'd never exhibited before. "No, I'm not going to hit you. Do you want purple hair, piercings, and tattoos?"

Her brown eyes grew huge. "Yes! But I think my parents would kill me. They're not happy about me living in the dorm, but I'm safe here in the compound, and it's not like they live far away. I think if I showed up for dinner with purple hair, I'd be living back at home before lights-out."

Lights-out? Werewolves could see really well in the dark, so it seemed kind of silly to have a lights-out rule, but I wasn't in any position to be complaining about the rules. I just needed to shut up and follow them.

"I wish I could at least get a tattoo, though." Mir looked at my arms with envy.

"You do know that you can get piercings in places where your parents aren't likely to see them?"

I didn't think her eyes could get any bigger. "We're werewolves. We see each other naked all the time. The only place I could get a piercing where no one would see was—oh. Oh! Wouldn't that hurt? I mean, really, really hurt?"

I winked. "Hell, yeah. But, once it's all healed up, then it's game on, girl."

She grinned. "I want one. Like, I want one now. Could you do it? Maybe I could steal some whisky and do a few shots first so it won't hurt as bad."

"That's something that really calls for a professional," I told her. "I'm sure there are tattoo and piercing places in town. Or we could go to Anchorage and make it a weekend trip, assuming I ever get a day off whatever work I'm given."

Wait, she was sixteen. Was that too young to get a piercing? I'd seen human children with pierced ears and noses, so I was assuming it was okay. I'd probably need to lie and say I was her parent or something and sign a consent form, none of which would be a problem for me.

"Let's do it! And once I get brave enough, I'll get a belly button ring like yours, and a tiny tattoo on my ankle. Something cool, like a dragon, or a rose with flames, or Mickey Mouse."

My head whirled trying to figure out what was cool about those three things. Maybe a dragon, but a cartoon mouse? And a rose with *flames*?

"Let's start with the piercing, then when you think you parents will be open to it, a little tattoo."

"I've got an idea." Mir grinned. "I'll tell my parents I want to get a tramp stamp, then when they're done screaming and yelling, we'll compromise on a pretty little ankle tattoo."

Huh. There was a little more devil in Mir than I'd ever imagined. It made me wonder what other surprises were in store for me here at the Swift River Pack.

CHAPTER 3

Mir gave me some time to myself, promising to return in time to escort me to dinner. I wasn't sure what I was supposed to do with this time. Nap? Contemplate my precarious position in life? Deciding to combine the latter two, I lay on my bed and thought about my new Alpha.

Hot. Scary. Suffocatingly dominant. And what the hell had been that thing between us? I'd experienced insta-lust before, and although I had no doubt that Jake could rock my world in bed, what had happened in his office had been more than lust. If I were one of those sappy chicks who read romance novels, I would have thought we were destined to be together, or some shit like that. I didn't read romance novels, and I wasn't a sappy chick, so I was going to explain it away as a weird reaction to a guy who was the most powerful Alpha I'd ever met in my life.

And yeah, I did want to fuck him. But then again, I wanted to fuck just about every good looking guy I came across—werewolf or human. No biggie. Nothing special. Time to forget about the weird electricity thing and move on to think about more important things, like how I was going to be able to survive in a pack with this many rules and this much order.

Swift River Pack wasn't so much a commune or university than a military camp without all the marching. I wondered what job I'd be assigned to do. I wondered how long I'd manage to toe the line here until I fucked up and got myself killed. It would probably happen sooner than at the other packs. In the past I'd usually managed to avoid other werewolves and humans and throw myself into an isolating work-rest routine. But although I'd physically wear myself out, I never could stand being alone for long. Funny that everyone was afraid of me and hated me, and although that was usually due to my own actions, I longed to be around them. Well, I longed to be around them and sometimes to pick a fight.

In the other packs, the werewolves had been skilled at de-escalating the conflict and getting me the heck out of there before I got to brawling. On the occasions when I did fight, I'd always win, and usually had to be hauled off my opponent by my pack mates before I killed him or her. Then they'd cover it up out of pride, until they could cover it up no more. Which usually happened when the Alpha got tired of my defiance and disrespect and finally decided to try to teach me a lesson.

Try. That was always the end of my membership in that pack. We were werewolves, and both dominance and a mixture of strength and smarts were necessary to be a leader. But that wasn't all. The pack needed to *want* to follow you. They had to see their Alpha as someone who would look out for their best interests, who would put the good of the group above his or her own personal gain. No one would have followed me as an Alpha. And neither my beast nor I wanted to lead a pack anyway. We just wanted to fight. And win.

The idea of leading a pack and being responsible for others scared the fucking crap out of me. And it scared the crap out of my beast too. I think for all her ferocity and bravado, she was just as lonely and scared as I was. And the more lonely and scared she got, the more difficult it was to control her. I gave myself two days before I tried to rip someone's throat out. I got the impression Jake wouldn't brush that sort of thing under the rug. I could tell things were strict here. The incident would be brought to him, no doubt along with me, and he'd take me out in the woods and do it.

The thought was oddly comforting. I'd been a mistake, a monster that never should have been born. And I had gotten to the point in my life where living was harder than dying. I'd try my best to make this work, but I didn't have a lot of faith that after all these years I'd be able to fit in with this pack. After all these years, I didn't have a lot of faith in anything at all.

Two women who I was sure I was safe to assume were some of my new roomies came in. I'd heard them enter the building, taken their scent, caught snippets of their conversation as they came down the hall. One looked to be in her late twenties with a bit of muffin-top visible between the waistband of her jeans and her too-short tank top. She had brown hair scraped back into an unflatteringly severe knot at the back of her head and had been a bit heavy-handed with the mascara. The other looked about five or so years older and was slightly shorter with the kind of build that looked like she could bench a couple of elephants. She also had on an excess amount of mascara. Don't get me wrong, I'm a huge fan of ultra-black lashes and a thick line of kohl around my eyes, but these girls had the clumpy, overly curled, long lashes that made them look like kewpie dolls.

They both ignored me. Because, of course, they'd

scented me and knew I was here long before they entered the room. And, as everyone else in the compound, they knew who and what I was. I was positive Jake wouldn't have brought a viper into his pack's midst without warning them first.

I ignored them as well, gathering from their conversation that Muffin Top had a job that had something to do with scheduling, and Muscles was in security. Or accounting. Accounting security? I had an easier time envisioning her patrolling the compound for wrong-doers than running accounts receivable reports, but maybe not. I'm sure there were accountants out there in the world who liked to spend their off-hours lifting at the gym.

I gave my beast the side-eye, trying to gauge how she felt about these new roommates. She wouldn't care about Muffin Top, but Muscles had enough dominance and swagger that my beast might suddenly awaken and decide she needed to teach this poor woman a lesson.

"Nice tats," Muffin Top said, finally glancing my way.

"Thanks." It was safer not to engage in lengthy conversation until I knew I had my beast under control.

Muscles glanced my way and frowned. *Oh no, here we go.*

"How often do you have to touch-up the purple in your hair?"

Okay. That was a safe question. "It fades pretty quickly. Usually I do it every two weeks, when I bleach my roots."

She nodded. "I tried to put a streak of red in my hair last year, but it didn't show up at all."

Because her hair was nearly black, that's why. "Pre-bleach the strand just ten minutes or so, and the red should take. If you want it really bright red, you'll need to bleach the streak a lot. As in probably two steps and some toner a lot."

Wasn't there a stylist on the compound she could go to? At the very least a barber or someone? Was I going to bond with these women over hair color techniques? Maybe I should suggest a different mascara.

"Cool. I'll have a professional do it next time I go to town. I'm half afraid that if I do it myself, I'll burn a chunk of my hair off."

Muffin Top snickered. "You'd look like Sandra that time she caught her hair on fire."

What? *What?* I had no idea who this Sandra was, but I *had* to know this story.

Muscles laughed. "She was at dinner trying to flirt with Jake and did this hair flip thing. Her hair hit the candle flame, and with all the product she had going on, it went up like a torch. Jake grabbed her head and dunked her face-first in a pot of spaghetti sauce to put her out."

Holy shit, that was funny as hell. "So I take it she bombed out on any attempt to score with our Alpha?"

Both women shouted with laughter. "She bombed out even before the hair-on-fire incident. Jake doesn't date inside the pack. I doubt he dates at all. I mean, I'm sure he probably gets some action whenever he feels like going into the city because he's smoking hot, but nobody in the pack knows about it."

Or nobody wanted to risk their lives telling anyone that they knew about it. Still, it made me curious. Everyone had needs, and I couldn't believe a guy like that, an Alpha, wasn't getting stroked regularly by someone besides himself.

CHAPTER 4

uffin Top and Muscles had left, and no one else came to the room by the time Mir arrived to get me for dinner. I was bored. And I was a bit anxious about meeting the other two women who shared this room with me. I'd always lived alone in an apartment. The idea that I was going to be in a dormitory with two dozen women, and in a bedroom with five others worried me.

The moment that plane had landed and I'd entered this pack, I'd felt off kilter, anxious and uncertain of what to expect next. You'd think that would cause someone like me to go on the attack in some sort of fear-based aggression, but if anything the weird situation seemed to defuse my normal hostility. I was scared. And instead of stepping up to give me the sort of confidence that would get me killed, my beast took the confusion as a cue to retreat. Bitch had gotten me kicked out of every pack I'd ever joined, and now that I felt afraid and on-edge, she'd abandoned me.

But at least I had Mir. And the irony didn't escape me that

I was clinging to a sixteen-year-old girl as my anchor in an unfamiliar environment.

"Do I need to dress for dinner or something?" I asked her, jumping from my bed in relief when she came through the doorway. Lying in bed alone wasn't helping my anxiety any. In fact, all the silence and solitude was making me question what the hell my life was going to be like going forward.

Mir added to that anxiety by handing me a large envelope. "No, silly. It's not Buckingham Palace or anything. Even if you get invited to dine at Jake's table, or at the Alpha House, you don't need to get all swanky. Most people are there in their work clothes. We're not a fancy-dress kind of pack."

Good, because I didn't even own a dress, let alone anything remotely formal. I opened the envelope, reading the note inside while Mir peered over my shoulder.

"Garbage collection." Mir pronounced my job assignment like it was a death sentence. "Yuck. But I guess someone's got to do it. I wonder what the 'special assignment' thing is?"

I wondered as well. I was to report to a building at the edge of the compound at seven in the morning tomorrow where I would given a four-wheeler with a trailer attached to go around and collect garbage that pack members had put out in the approved receptacles. Then I was to take it to the incinerator and burn the lot. This was a twice weekly activity. Another twice weekly activity was to go around and collect the recyclables, sort them and box them by type, then take them via truck into the nearest recycling center which was most likely a hundred miles away.

"You'll get to sign out a truck for recycle days," Mir pointed out. I assumed from her tone of voice that signing out a truck was a perk. "And that's only four mornings per week of work. I wonder if you'll get a secondary assignment for the afternoons?"

I hoped so. Sitting around and doing nothing while everyone else in the compound worked would drive me crazy, and it would foster resentment among my pack mates. "Maybe this special assignment thing is the full time gig?" I asked.

"You're meeting with Jamie at the Alpha House after dinner to find out."

"Jamie?" My stomach twisted at the thought that I'd be taking orders from someone. The garbage job was ideal. I'd be working solo, and outside of some initial instruction, I'd be completely on my own. Those types of jobs tended to be what I preferred, and tended to last longer than the ones where I had to play nice with others, or follow orders.

"Jamie. She's Jake's second. Have you met her yet?"

I immediately thought of the Baywatch Babe who'd driven me in on the four wheeler. "Blonde? Pretty? Looks like she could be a pin-up model?"

Mir giggled. "That's her."

My mind cycled back to the conversation with Muffin Top and Muscles. "Are she and Jake an item?" It wasn't unheard of for an Alpha and their second to be involved. They usually worked together closely, and sometimes that closeness led to bedroom activities and occasionally a mated pair.

Mir shrugged. "Maybe. She's really beautiful, and Jake relies on her a lot. I know there are nights where she stays overnight in the Alpha House, so I guess they could be doing it."

"And that doesn't bother you?" It bothered me. If I hadn't wanted to kill the woman before, I certainly did now.

"No. It's not like I'd ever have a chance with him. If he ever even looked at me like he was interested, I'd probably pee myself in fear. Jake is scary."

Yeah, scary hot. Wait, *Jake* was scary? "So he's scary, but I'm not?" I was kind of insulted by that.

Mir laughed. "You're not scary. I don't understand what all the fuss was about. I mean, don't get me wrong, if bad things were happening, I'd really, really want you on my side. I'm pretty sure you could take down a grizzly single-handed and not smear your make-up. But being kick-ass and being scary are two different things. You're kick-ass. Jake is kick-ass and scary."

Yep, I was definitely insulted.

"Now hurry up," she continued. "It's prime rib night, and if you get there late, all the good cuts are gone."

Now *that* was motivating. I freshened up in our bathroom, noting the amount of makeup and products lining the shelves, then headed out with Mir. We walked across the compound, past the Alpha House and through a tidy garden to a long low building that smelled of meat and potatoes. Inside, the cafeteria was one giant room with long buffet tables and two sets of doors that I assumed led to the kitchen. There were rectangular tables that seated ten, and smaller round tables. Along the edge of the room, next to the windows overlooking the garden were a series of two-person tables. I would have called it romantic, except that I couldn't imagine having a romantic dinner in a cafeteria with my entire pack staring on.

Mir pointed out that each buffet held different food choices. There was one with vegetables, another with a sort of pasta bar, and another with salad. Off to the side was a round table with cakes and pies, and a soft serve ice cream machine. The longest line was for the table where a man was carving slabs of meat off a huge rib roast. I eyed the meat, then the line, and was convinced that I'd be eating pasta for dinner tonight. By the time we got up there, we wouldn't even have the end scraps.

"Don't worry, they'll be bringing out another one. Or two. No one goes hungry here. Jake makes sure we all get as much meat as we want, and have other choices, as well. I was joking about us getting the scrap cuts. Usually there's plenty left over, which ends up as sandwich meat or in soups."

We stood in line, and I noticed that although everyone smiled and greeted Mir, they quickly averted their gaze and turned their back on me. Once again, my reputation was making it hard for me to feel welcome. I'd need to earn their trust. I only hoped I could.

The guy carving the meat did smile at me and didn't hold back on the portion size when it came time to slap a piece on my plate. I noticed it was really good quality, not the cheap stuff like I'd seen at some of the inexpensive all-you-can-eat buffets. This was tender and juicy with lots of fat around the edges.

Even though there was no room left on my plate for anything besides the enormous slab of prime rib, Mir still led me over to the vegetable table where she piled roasted potatoes, fresh green beans, and an ear of corn on top of the meat, creating a precarious mountain of food. I did the same, my stomach growling in anticipation. I'd been too nervous to eat much for breakfast, and had completely skipped lunch. I was starving.

We paused at one of the long tables. Mir motioned me to a chair and slid her plate carefully onto the table, plopping herself down and unrolling her silverware. My stomach twisted as the other occupants turned to stare at me. I wished I could just eat alone. I wish that Mir had chosen one of the two-person tables along the edge. Maybe if I just put my head down and didn't make eye contact, and shoveled my food in as fast as I could, I could get out of here in ten minutes or less.

And then what? Go back to the room that I was sharing

with five other people and eventually have to deal with them? I suddenly regretted this whole thing, wishing that my last Alpha had the guts to just put me down, or that the people in this pack would quickly realize that I'd be much better off on my own, alone.

"Mom, Dad, this is Tupper," Mir announced cheerfully. I hid my horror at the fact that she'd brought me to eat dinner with her parents.

"Hi," I squeaked. The pair returned the greeting with a quick nod.

"How did you...why are you with her?" Mir's mother asked, her voice strained. "She's not living in your room, is she?"

Yep. Just talk about me as if I weren't here, or deaf. My beast glared at the woman, sizing her up and flexing her claws.

"I'm in charge of showing Tupper around and making sure she knows where everything is, that she meets people and feels welcome in our pack," Mir proudly replied. "Jake asked me himself. And yes, she's staying in our room with us. Isn't that cool?"

Her father stared down at his steak, a resigned expression on his face at the mention of the Alpha. The mother, on the other hand, clamped her lips together and narrowed her eyes.

"Jake asked you to show her around and...mentor her? He does realize you're sixteen, right? Maybe he should have asked our permission first?"

"Kathleen," the father hissed. "Don't."

She ignored him. "Sixteen. You shouldn't even be living away from home in the dorms yet, let alone living with....a dangerous shifter."

I'll admit a part of me admired the woman. She wasn't sugar coating it. She was honestly expressing her feelings and clear disapproval of me. At least she wasn't a hypocrite, smiling at me and telling me how welcome I was then stabbing me in the back as soon as I turned around.

"Mom! Tupper is not a dangerous shifter. And you agreed to let me live in the dorms for six months to see how it went. Stop treating me like a child."

"You *are* a child." I could feel the anger coming off Mir's mother. "And I intend to speak with Jake about this. He should have asked our permission."

"Kathleen, please," the father pleaded.

"The prime rib is really good," I told them, determined to shift the conversation before my beast got pissed off enough to start swinging at this woman. I liked Mir. My beast liked Mir. And my beast was particularly upset that Mir's mother thought me to be a bad influence on her.

I tried to calm my inner monster down, reminding her that if she didn't chill, we wouldn't be alive for very long. Then I ducked my head, ate as fast as I could, and attempted to get through dinner without making eye contact or speaking with anyone. Survive dinner. Somehow manage to survive a meeting with my Baywatch Babe Second, who I was pretty sure hated me. Survive an evening in my room with five other people. I just needed to make it through tonight, then I'd make sure I ate alone, worked alone, remained as far from any of my pack mates as possible. Maybe then I'd stay out of trouble and live long enough to see another year or two.

CHAPTER 5

After dinner, Mir took me by the Alpha House and pretty much left me at the door. I got the feeling she was abandoning me for my meeting with Jake's second, and it bothered me. Sad that a scary monster like me was clinging to a sixteen-year-old girl for comfort.

I forced myself to climb the stairs and not watch Mir skip off to the dorms. This morning when I'd been in the Alpha House, I'd gone straight from the heavy carved doors to Jake's office on the first floor. This time I let my nose guide me and found Jamie in a side room full of cushiony chairs and couches, and walls lined with bookshelves. A few newspapers sat on a coffee table next to a carving of a salmon leaping from a stream. Jamie stood next to an unlit fireplace, her blonde hair still in the ponytail. A twinge of envy shot through me. She was tall with that perfect swimsuit model body, her face the sort that could easily launch a thousand ships. She waited a second after I entered the room, just to reinforce my lower status, then turned, her eyes narrowed.

"Sit."

I sat in the closest chair, like an obedient dog, and waited.

Jamie slowly made her way to me and gracefully lowered herself onto the couch across from me.

"Is your dorm acceptable?"

"Yes, thank you."

She nodded. "And you received your work assignment?"

"Garbage duty starting tomorrow morning. Recycling twice a week."

"I'd advise that you collect at all the houses and dorms first, then make a second trip for the cafeteria trash. They usually have more than enough to fill the trailer."

Was this a check-in meeting? I'd thought it would have something to do with this mysterious assignment, but maybe Jamie was merely ensuring that I was settling in nicely and hadn't killed anyone yet.

"Thank you. I'll do that."

She nodded again. Was that a habit of hers? Bobble head-itis? "Did Mir tell you about the special assignments? That's the reason you only have what amounts to a part-time job. These assignments might take you away from the compound for a day or more, and would take priority over your garbage collection duties. You may go months without an assign-ment, then need to be away for two weeks on one."

It was all very mysterious, as if they were asking me to conduct some sort of espionage for them, or superhero work. Would I have a secret identity? I hoped I got to wear a cape.

"What is the nature of these jobs?" I asked. It might not be respectful to grill my second about this, but I felt like I had a right to know. And I suspected that the assignments might involve killing large groups of people. Why else would they single me out? Killing was clearly something I was good at, something my genetics had unfortunately supported.

"Jake will discuss that with you tomorrow. After lunch, you're to come here to the conference room for a meeting, and he'll outline everything at that time." She stood. "I'll check in with you throughout the week to ensure that you have everything you need, and that you've been provided appropriate instruction and training on working the incinerator. Mir is acting to onboard you and acclimate you to our pack, but I realize she is young, so if you have any questions, or there is something that would be inappropriate to ask or discuss with Mir, please feel free to contact me."

I stood as well. "Why are you being so nice to me?" I could tell she hated me. I could tell she was afraid of me. But in spite of all that, her behavior just now had been unusually welcoming.

"Because Jake told us all that we are to judge you as you stand before us, not based on your past actions. Don't get me wrong, I don't want you in this pack. I don't want you in the state. I don't trust you. But if Jake says that I'm supposed to give you a chance, then I'll do it."

I was stunned, reeling. She'd give me a chance? She'd overlook a lifetime of violence and judge me based on my actions from today forward? No one had ever said such a thing to me. And it was on Jake's orders—orders that clearly no one would ever think of disobeying.

"Can I see him?" I asked Jamie's retreating figure. "Jake, I mean. My Alpha."

She stopped and turned, her eyes suspicious. "Jake never requires an appointment. He's in his office right now. If you ever want to speak with him, just go on in."

Jamie left and I stared at the empty doorway, filled with uncertainty. Her statement had almost been a challenge. Even with her announcement that she'd give me a chance, I could tell she wasn't ever going to be my friend. Was this a trap to get me in trouble? Would I go to Jake's office, only to find that I'd just broken some huge etiquette rule?

Fuck it. What was the worst that would happen, me

getting yelled at by my Alpha? Wouldn't be the first time, although I got the feeling that getting yelled at by Jake would be a singularly unpleasant experience.

Heading out into the hall, I retraced my steps from earlier today and found myself just outside of the closed door of Jake's office. The entire Alpha House was a mixture of pack scents—Jake's primarily, but also all the other werewolves who had been in and out of here throughout the day. But just as I'd been able to trace Jamie to the little side room, I was able to tell right away who was behind closed doors with the Alpha. It was Mir's mom. And even if I hadn't picked up her scent, I would have known because she was yelling loud enough for a half-deaf human to hear.

Yelling. At Jake. That woman had some serious balls. I wasn't sure *I* had balls that big. She was not only reaming the Alpha a new one, but the objects of her tirade was her daughter and me.

"Sixteen! She's sixteen! I didn't want her to move into the dorms this young, but I deferred to your judgement and agreed to a trial period for her to stretch her legs a bit. I did *not* agree for her to be endangered like this. That woman is a monster. She's bunking right next to my young daughter. I won't be able to sleep at night worrying that she'll snap and rip Mir's throat out in the middle of the night. It's not like the others can even protect my daughter if she goes crazy. Did you hear what she did in L.A.? And in Atlanta? It's not if, it's when, and I'm not about to sit here while my daughter is in danger."

Jakes voice was so low that I couldn't hear his reply, but I could tell by his tone that he was trying to calm the woman.

"That doesn't reassure me one bit. I'm not happy about that...thing being in our pack, but I know my place. It's your right to admit whoever you want, and if I don't like it, I'm free to leave, but this is my *daughter*." Mir's mother voice cracked on the last word and I heard her choke back a sob.

I heard the creak of a chair, the rustle of someone moving and backed up a few steps. But instead of the door opening, I heard crying, and Jake's soft reassuring voice.

This was clearly not the time to be here. I tried to be as quiet as possible as I backed away from the door and into the hallway. Once there I turned and headed out of the Alpha House.

The sun was still high off the horizon, although I figured it had to be going on toward eight at night. It would take me a while to get used to reading the sun this far north. It would take me a while to get used to everything here, and not just the unfamiliar way this pack was run. Eyeing my dorm in the distance, I turned the opposite way and headed toward the lake where the plane that had brought me in had touched down.

The compound wasn't walled or gated in any way, but it was surrounded by what I estimated to be over ten miles of wilderness. Past the last row of houses was a quarter mile of meadow filled with wildflowers and tall grasses. That led to the lake, or off to a thick forest if I'd turned left or right. And all around me were mountains—huge, rocky, snow-capped mountains that pierced the clouds above. The compound was in a sort of valley, although clearly not at sea level from the headache I'd been sporting all day. I made my way down to the lake, awed at the beauty that surrounded me. I'd lived in some amazing cities, and there had been truly gorgeous scenery, but this was unlike anything I'd ever seen before. Glancing up I eyed the angle of the sun, I saw the pinks and lavenders of the sky reflected in the glass-like waters of the lake and felt a sense of awe.

The plane that had brought me in this morning was there, tied to the dock. I'd been a bit surprised when the pilot,

Dustin, had picked me up from Juneau since the plane appeared brand new and was fancier than I'd expected. Clearly this pack had money. With nothing else to do for the evening, and reluctant to return back to the dorm and face my new roommates, I sat on the dock. The air was cool with a breeze that rustled the aspens that bordered the far edge of the lake. Frogs croaked and splashed into the water, and fish surfaced, rippling the calm surface. It was idyllic, and unable to resist, I took off my shoes and socks, and dipped my feet into the water.

Holy crap it was cold. Did people ever go swimming around here? And if so, how did they keep from turning into icebergs? Clearly too much of a wimp to endure this frigid water, I pulled my feet out, and let them dry, laying back on the dock to watch the sun slowly make its way toward the smaller set of mountains to the west of us. There I stayed until the sky grew dusky gray, with only a faint band of pink where the sun had gone behind the ridgeline. The lights would be on in the compound right now, and I finally felt ready to go back, to try to fit in with my new pack. I put my socks and shoes on, then got to my feet and turned around, nearly colliding with a tall, broad-shouldered, dark-skinned man who had been standing right behind me.

My heart nearly ripped out of my ribcage. I hadn't heard him; I hadn't scented him. I'd just turned around and there he was, five feet from me, staring at me with his ice-blue eyes.

And again, there was that sharp electricity that arced between us, making me want to touch him.

"Damn it." I slapped a hand onto my chest and tried to slow my heart rate. "Next time cough or something. You scared the piss out of me.

"You were by my office earlier." It wasn't a question. I'm sure he caught my scent right outside his doorway, or maybe he'd heard me out there when Mir's mom was chewing him out. Or perhaps Jamie had told him that I had been going to see him. Either way, it would be clear that I'd overheard that conversation. I wasn't sure if I was more embarrassed about eavesdropping, or that I'd heard a woman yell at my Alpha.

"Yeah. I just wanted to pop in and ask you something, but you were busy. It wasn't important."

He tilted his head, and I felt uncomfortable under his intense gaze. "I'm here now. What did you want to ask?"

I'd wondered about the mandate he'd told Jamie, that I was to be judged on what I did since arrive at the pack, not my disturbing past, but here in the chill of the evening, after a gorgeous sunset, it really didn't seem important. I'd do my best. Then I'd fuck up. And the entire pack would know why my past wasn't something that could be overlooked or swept under the rug. I wished it could be different. I wished some magic would happen and I could actually have a pack and a family, have friends. It bothered me that I'd never have that. It bothered me that Jake had stuck his neck out for me, and I was bound to disappoint him.

For some reason, I really didn't want to disappoint him.

"It really wasn't important," I finally replied.

He nodded and turned, walking beside me as we headed back to the compound. "You overheard Kathleen."

Mir's mom. "Yes. Don't worry. I don't blame her at all for what she said. Although if she gets in my face, I might end up punching her."

I wouldn't want to, but it might happen. My beast didn't like her. I think it had less to do with Kathleen's dislike of me than with my beast's fear that she would try to separate Mir from me.

"She'll calm down in a few days once she realizes you're not going to turn her daughter into a purple-haired, violent rebel with tattoos."

I remained silent, figuring anything I might say would incriminate me further.

Jake sighed, rubbing a hand over his short hair. "Oh no. Please tell me you haven't already gotten out the hair dye and given Mir a prison-style tattoo."

"Uh, no. But I'm pretty sure the piercing thing is going to happen."

"One of those giant earlobe holes? The hoop thing under her nose? In her eyebrow? Belly button?"

Probably all of the above. "Sorry. My bad. She's probably going to get her hood pierced to start with."

He stared at me. "What do you mean? I'm assuming you're not referring to a car hood."

I pointed between my legs. "It's not a huge piece of jewelry, and it's not a spot where everyone would see it. I mean, maybe when she's shifting to hunt if she waxes pretty aggressively and flashes you guys a spread-leg crotch-view before she goes furry, you'll see it, but otherwise the only one who will know it's there besides her is whoever she's fucking. Even then…well, I hope whoever she's fucking is going down on her, because that's awesome. And when that happens, the guy, or the girl because I don't know how Mir swings, is going to get an eyeful. Well, more of an eyeful than usual."

I'd done it. I'd completely shocked my cool, calm, and collected Alpha. Jake looked horrified. I was pretty sure no one had elicited that expression on him in…probably in forever.

"People don't…women don't…why would someone *do* that? Why would anyone jab a piece of metal through such a sensitive part of their body?"

I was so going to hell. "Because it totally enhances the sexual experience. Dude, every thrust makes that little ball rub up against—"

"Okay. I get it. Do you…I mean, I'm assuming that you…" His eyes dropped to the portion of my anatomy under discussion, then jerked back up to meet mine. I'd flustered my Alpha. I'd completely rattled the guy. Score one for me.

"Of course. I'd hardly be in a position to recommend such a piercing if I hadn't experienced it myself."

Jake sucked in a breath and shook his head. "She's sixteen. Her mother is going to kill me."

I snorted. "Hardly. You'd kick her ass."

"I just sat for half an hour while Kathleen chewed me out. I no longer have any confidence that I could 'kick her ass'. If she finds out her daughter got this hood piercing, we're all dead, starting with me. I don't even think the archangels will be safe from her wrath."

"Then why? Mir said you'd assigned her this job. Why do that to a sixteen-year-old girl?"

"There are good reasons I asked Mir specifically to take you under her wing and help you acclimate to the pack," Jake said.

I waited a few seconds, then decided that I needed to ask if I wanted him to elaborate. "And those reasons are?"

"She's young and eager to be of use in the pack. She's of an age where the idea of a rebel, someone who seems independent and unconcerned with others' opinions is appealing to her. She wants to go against her parents, to be an adult living on her own and making her own choices, but that's scary. I knew that she'd admire you."

"I'm not exactly someone that young werewolf girls should admire," I told him. "I'm starting to agree with her mother that you screwed up on this decision."

"Mir has a clear head. She may admire you, but she will only gain confidence in her ability to live independent from her parents from you. She won't emulate you."

"That's what *you* think. She's already talking tattoos and piercings."

Jake winced. "Please try to dissuade her from that, or at least convince her to wait until she's eighteen. I'd take it as a personal favor if you did."

It would be awesome to have the Alpha in debt to me, although I was kind of to blame for putting the idea into Mir's head anyway. "Sure. I'll do my best." Which meant Mir would probably have a tramp stamp before the week was out in addition to her genital piercing.

"The reason I wanted Mir in particular to help you fit into the pack was because I think *you* need *her*. I get the idea that you haven't had much of anyone in your life who admired you, or who seemed to enjoy your company without being nervous or suspecting every single move you make. Mir is fascinated by the whitewashed versions of your past that her parents have told her, but she judges you as you stand before her today, she judges you for how you act toward her and treat her. And she likes you, so she's not afraid."

In other words, Jake picked someone that he felt would actually be a friend to me. My first friend in…well, in ever. And she was a sixteen-year-old girl. If I was as young as I looked, then Mir could have been my little sister. Instead, she might have been my granddaughter. Was it weird and kind of creepy that my only friend was a minor?

Oh well. It's not like I had the luxury of being picky about my friends. Mir was it. And I liked her. My beast liked her. My beast really liked her, and seemed to be treating her as if she *was* my granddaughter or something.

We walked through the compound, the few people still out and about trying hard not to stare at us as we passed. I turned to head to my dorm, and was surprised to feel Jake's hand on my arm.

"Come with me. I want to talk to you a minute now that you've gotten unpacked and a bit settled in."

I hesitated, wondering what it was he wanted to say that couldn't wait until tomorrow afternoon when I was supposed to meet with him after lunch. But curiosity got the better of me, and I let him steer me toward the Alpha House, noting that he kept his hand on my arm the whole way up the stairs and in the door. What, was he afraid I'd run off or something? My initial impulse was to pull away once we started walking, but I let it go. It wasn't just that I didn't want to piss Jake off by yanking my arm free of his grasp. I kind of liked him touching me. The only touching I'd had or done in decades had either been in fights, or fast, hard, usually drunken sexual encounters. None of them had the same steadying, comforting, guiding feel as his hand on my arm.

He let go once we were inside and I followed him to the office, taking a seat when he gestured.

"How are you feeling? Any issue with your new pack mates? Have you met your roommates yet?"

"Other than Mir's mom, everyone has pretty much not spoken to me." Or made eye contact, or even come within five feet of me. "I did meet two of my roommates besides Mir, though. They were friendly."

They were, and it shocked me to realize that. Muffin Top and Muscles might have been wary, but they'd still initiated conversation with me, and even shared that hysterical story about hair-on-fire woman. I didn't want to believe it. I kept thinking that I must be mistaken, but something inside me wondered if I'd make friends in this pack.

Nah. Within a few days, we'd fight over something, and my beast would decide she needed to kill them. Hopefully someone would drag me off before that happened, and then they'd drag me to Jake and he'd do what should have been done decades ago.

Which brought me to something I really wanted to ask. "Why *didn't* you just kill me? I get that the Alpha down in L.A. didn't feel comfortable doing it. Actually, I beat her to a pulp, so I'm thinking she couldn't kill me even if she tried. I half expected that joining Swift River was a pretense for being led out into the woods and put down. No sane Alpha would take me into his pack. I didn't really expect that you would either."

Jake sat on the corner of his desk. His stance was relaxed and casual, but I knew that one wrong move and I'd be pinned to the floor. I got the feeling he was fast and strong, and that as crazy as my beast was, she wouldn't be able to get the jump on him.

"Well, I can't kill you without provocation. Not now. Mir would never forgive me, and I'd be going against the rules I set up about pack behavior. I asked you to join us. If it doesn't work, I won't shy away from doing what I need to do to protect my wolves, but that wasn't my intention in bringing you up here. And I truly hope it doesn't come to that."

Me too. "But why? I've failed at every pack I've been a member of. Why do you think I'll succeed here?"

"Because I think you can get control of this thing. I think you can manage to integrate your beast and be a valuable member of our pack. I don't put wolves down for small infractions. If you kill someone, I'll put you down. Until then...well, I won't promise you won't have a broken bone here or there."

That was reassuring, but it wasn't really the answer I was looking for. "Why bring me up here at all? There is no other pack in the world that would have me. I was on a fast track to execution by angel when you volunteered to take me on. Why bother? And don't give me some crap about thinking I can be rehabilitated. I might not know you, but I can tell you're not some goody-two-shoes Pollyanna type who thinks there's sunshine and roses in a garbage pit."

There was a forced sternness in his eyes that made me think he was fighting not to smile. "When I heard you needed a pack, I had to offer to take you in. I know the circumstances of your birth, Tupper."

It wasn't a national secret, although the werewolves that had been alive at the time preferred to let that ugliness become buried, a forgotten sordid part of our history. "Yeah, I was one of many test-tube werewolves, an attempt to combine two Nephilim and come up with an angel. Hundreds of attempts and I was the only embryo that survived to birth. And once they got a load of me, they halted the experiment and forbade anyone from ever trying again. That's one of the reasons why Nephilim are placed in packs away from each other, just so they don't get another one of me."

He was quiet for a long while, the gaze of his ice-blue eyes disconcertingly intense. "All of those experiments? They were trying to produce another me."

I couldn't have heard that right. "You? You're saying you're the product of two Nephilim? I mean, no offense, you're damned powerful, but you're no angel. Where are your wings?"

"I haven't been able to manifest them since I was an infant."

He was serious. Fuck me to the moon and back, he was serious. "You're an angel."

"I doubt I'm a full angel. Most likely three quarters, but possibly more. I learned to mute my powers and hide my energy signature since before I could walk. My life depended on it. My parents already had a death sentence on them just for being Nephilim, imagine what the angels would have done to me if they'd found out. Imagine what they'd still do."

An angel light. No fucking way. "But Dustin told me that there is an angel down in the Juneau Pack. The angelic host hasn't dusted her, and she's flying around the state like some damned winged Mary Poppins."

"She is the product of an angel and a demon, not two Nephilim. And believe me, if the angels had discovered her even five years ago, they most likely would have thrown her through the gates to Hel or killed her. I have no faith that the angels would welcome me with open arms. I'd rather live as a werewolf and lead my pack, than try to live my life as a wingless, almost-angel."

I still wasn't sure I believed him. "So your parents were in love? Or they just screwed and your mom got knocked up? How did two Nephilim even meet when they're rare as hens' teeth?"

He actually looked embarrassed. "They were pen pals. And my father snuck away to meet my mother because he'd fallen in love with her. He snuck away repeatedly. Eventually they came clean to her Alpha when my mother became pregnant, and that put an end to the sneaking away."

That…that was a sad story. Like Romeo and Juliet, forced to be forever apart, only no one died. At least, I didn't think so. "Did your Mom commit suicide after you were born?"

I don't think I could have shocked him more if I'd spit in his face. "No! Why would you ask that? Of course she didn't. She raised me. She's still with her pack. I visit her on holidays and call her weekly. As I do my father."

Okay. Not so Romeo and Juliet then. Even with the sad story, I felt the stab of jealousy. I was a test tube embryo, born to a surrogate mother and passed around from family to family each year. Or month. Or week. However long it took me to alienate everyone who'd taken me into their home. Even as an infant. I would have given anything to have someone to visit on holidays, who would worry if I didn't call weekly. Someone. Anyone. It didn't have to be a parent figure. Even a friend would be nice.

Cut the pity party. I looked up at Jake warily. If he had so much as one ounce of sympathy in his face, I was going to punch him regardless the consequences. But instead of pity, I only found calm disinterest. Strangely it helped. The beast settled, satisfied that I hadn't appeared vulnerable in any way.

"So, what? You feel somehow responsible for my birth, because they were trying to replicate you, or create a better-than-you? I'm your pet project to assuage your guilt?"

He laughed. "Guilt? I carry no guilt for deeds that are not my own. Just as I'm no Pollyanna, I'm no martyr. I am almost-an-angel. You're almost-a-demon. If I was given a chance to live and make my home here, you should be as well. That's why I took you in, not through any sense of guilt or obligation."

I shook my head, confused. "But my beast…I can't control her most of the time. She'll challenge you."

"And she'll lose. Do you think it was easy for me to control the beast inside of me? He clamors for me to punish even the slightest infraction, to set rules and procedures so strict that no one would ever stay in my pack. I give him enough leeway to put him at ease, bring him satisfaction, but I don't allow him to control me, to make me a wolf that would be unable to live among others."

I'd tried. Didn't he think I'd tried? Over the decades, I'd begged, badgered, bribed my beast to submit, to compromise, to just calm the fuck down long enough for me to have a home, to have one friend, one lover, someone, anyone. "And how do you propose I do this?"

"Your beast wants to fight, wants to be top of the pack, but doesn't want to lead, or to rule, correct?"

I nodded.

"Then let her fight."

I snorted. "Holy shit, why did I not think of that myself? Oh, that's right, because I've spent my entire life beating the crap out of my pack mates and Alphas and it hasn't got me anything but shuffled off to the next pack, homeless, friendless, reviled and hated."

"Don't fight your pack mates. You know you're more dominant than they are, and they do, too. Fight me. I'm the one who sets your beast the most on edge."

Strangely enough, he was the one that *calmed* my beast, but at his proposal, she perked up her head in interest. Adrenaline shivered through me. Something other than adrenaline shivered through me. Lust. That weird electricity. That desire to reach across the few feet that separated us and touch him. Strange how those things all seemed to go together when it came to this Alpha.

"In the gym, in private. You can fight me anytime you choose, with whatever weapon, in whatever form you want. We can fight until first blood, or until one of us yields, or until one of us is unconscious. It won't be a fight for control of the pack, it will be a fight to give your beast what she wants. And then, when you walk out, and the doors of the gym close behind you, she will be satisfied. She will be at ease."

"I...I..." I didn't know what to say, how to reply. I'd never had someone offer to fight me before. Usually I, or rather my beast, challenged, and my opponent accepted with barely hidden fear, to save face. No one willingly fought me. Because everyone who did, lost. And everyone who did barely escaped with their lives.

"Say yes, Tupper." There was something seductive in his voice, as if he were asking me to his bed, and not to his private battleground. "Say yes, and know the first peace you've known in your life. Or say no, and continue to fight with your beast until you both kill each other."

I inhaled, filling my lungs. I hoped….no, I didn't hope. For the first time in my life, I trusted.

"When do we start?" I asked.

"We start now." He grinned, and it transformed him from a stern, unflinching Alpha into a man of unearthly beauty, it transformed him into an angel.

CHAPTER 6

The gymnasium was down in the basement of the Alpha House, far from the meeting and dining rooms. It was huge, with padded walls and mats on the floors. Across the back was a row of heavy bags. In one corner, a metal rack pulled down and locked into place with speed bags. Jake swung open one of the padded walls and turned on a light switch, illuminating yet another room with boxing gloves and sparring weapons.

"Some of our pack members use the weight room or other workout equipment in the common usage exercise area, but for those who want to practice boxing or martial arts, this room is always available."

"So the Alpha House isn't just yours?" I asked. In most packs, the Alpha House wasn't truly a private residence. It was more of a pack-owned resource where the Alpha may, or may not live. The packs in large cities tended to not have an Alpha House, instead using rented facilities for their gatherings. It was nice having a common space where anyone could congregate, but given the level of order and structure in the

Swift River Pack, I'd assumed the Alpha House was Jake's sole domain, only to be entered with permission.

He gave me an odd look. "I'm not a monarch. I have private rooms here, but this building belongs to the pack. Everything belongs to the pack. I don't get special exceptions from the rules because I'm the Alpha."

That wasn't what I'd expected at all. "So this isn't all in your name? Just like the others in the pack, all you own is the clothes on your back and a handful of personal belongings?"

I waited, expecting there to be all sorts of reasons why the slick Range Rover, the yacht, the private plane, were all his. But nothing else. Oh no, it was all very communal, aside from a few paltry luxuries that he deserved as the Alpha.

"Yes. The Swift River Pack is incorporated and everything is owned by the corporation. We have a board of directors, a governing body, and a charter. There are rules, regular financial statements and corporate reports. I own no more of the corporation than any other pack member. Once you've established yourself and are past your probationary period, you'll begin to receive shares of the corporation as well. We hold corporate stock aside for new members, and children."

Was this guy a fucking saint? I would have at least gotten myself a private jet out of the deal. I mean, he *was* the Alpha, after all. "And if members leave?"

"We buy their shares. Once they leave the pack, they're unable to continue to hold stock in the corporation."

Once again I was speechless. I could only gawk at Jake as he walked into the room and surveyed the weapons.

"Bare-fists? Gloves? Do you want to use staffs? Or perhaps fencing?" He turned to face me, his blue eyes eerie in the bright light.

"I...I...I don't know." I *didn't* know. And my beast was no help. She was reeling, completely knocked off kilter by everything that had happened in the last few hours.

"Maybe you'd like to fight in animal form, instead?"

I wasn't sure that was a good idea. Wait, was he a wolf in animal form? Or something else?

"You mean fight as wolves?" I asked, careful not to betray my anxiety over what his answer might be. I was never certain what form my beast would take—something that was frequently the nail in the coffin with my other packs. He was some sort of souped-up Nephilim, so he most likely had more than one form. Although he probably had control over his, where mine might end up a wyvern, or a gryphon, or a cat-dog for all I knew.

"Wolves, big cats, hawks." He shrugged. "You choose."

I couldn't. That was part of the problem. "Let's fight as humans." That way at least I'd have a modicum of control over my beast. If I let her off the leash, there's no telling what would happen. I was pretty sure I wouldn't be able to kill Jake—and that was a first—but I could piss him off enough that he decided to take *my* head off.

"Human. Bare fist, then." Jake ushered me out of the weapons room, turned off the light and closed the door. We stood in the middle of the room, neither one of us saying anything, neither one of us dancing around or shadow boxing, or anything that might indicate we were preparing to spar.

"Whenever you're ready," Jake told me.

He was still just standing there, as if we were in the middle of having a casual conversation about the weather or the local sports team. I felt this strange sense of indecision. I knew he was waiting for me to make the first move, to go on the attack, but right now the human part of me was in charge—the rational part of me that screamed it was suicide to hit my Alpha. So instead I reached inside to the beast, the monster that rode me, that frequently ruled me. She was always ready to fight. She wouldn't hesitate to attack Jake, no matter how dominant and scary he was.

And for the first time in my life, the beast was unwilling. She was confused, and curious. Instead of an angry, brawling, kill-or-be-killed monster, I had this. *Great.*

I opened my mouth to tell Jake to forget it, and he hit me. The blow came out of nowhere. I swear I hardly saw him move at all, although in my defense I hadn't really been paying attention. One minute we were both standing in front of each other, relaxed and casual, the next his fist was connecting with my jaw, knocking my head aside and sending me staggering.

It was cliché, but I saw stars. It hurt like a motherfucker. Several teeth were loose, my neck ached, and the lower left half of my face felt like it had been bashed clear into Canada. Within the second it took my vision to clear, everything was healed. Which was a good thing, since the next punch took me right in the stomach. I doubled over, then I flew back as his knee slammed up into my face.

And now I was on my back, wheezing blood and snot on the mats. Stupid beast. She'd gotten me kicked out of every pack I'd ever been in. She'd nearly gotten me killed more times than I could count. And when I needed her, she was sitting back on her haunches blinking at the events as though she were fucking Bambi or something.

Jake waited for me to get up, resuming his we're-just-conversing-casually-about-the-weather stance. I stood and tried to rush him, not because I really wanted to but because my pride was begging me to do something. He side-stepped, pushing me down and under his arm, and using my momentum to flip me over. I slammed on my back hard enough to knock the air from my lungs and blinked up at him.

My eyes met his, and that's when I saw his beast. I saw

whatever it was inside of him, that cold, emotionless, unbending dictator who refused to allow any transgression to go unpunished. I *saw* him. And so did my beast.

And he saw me. There was that odd moment of electricity again, that strange sensation of touching, although this time it felt as though he were the one reaching out to me. It felt like every nerve ending in my body came alive. And that's when my beast finally decided to get with the program and wake the fuck up.

She leapt to the surface, and there was an instant of awareness between us, an acknowledgement of who we really were. Then I swung my legs to the side, hooked an ankle around his, and pulled. He didn't fall, but I yanked him enough off balance to give me time to leap to my feet and land a hard kick to his left knee.

I heard bone snap, but instead of dropping to the floor, he spun and was ready for my second kick, grabbing my leg and pushing into me. I went down, Jake on top of me, and felt my knee dislocate as he twisted my leg to the side.

"Fucker! Not fair," I shouted as he got to his feet. The bastard's leg had already healed, while I had the joy of trying to get mine back into the socket.

"Absolutely fair," he replied coolly. "Here, let me help."

He knelt down and grabbed my leg at the ankle and knee, pulling it out and twisting it into place while I clenched my teeth to keep from screaming. As soon as he was done, I rewarded him by kicking him in the face. I put everything into it and was gratified to see his head rock backward, the force of the blow knocking him to the floor.

Jake might have waited for me to rise before attacking, but I wasn't shy about hitting a man while he was down. I jumped on top of him, straddling his legs and trying for a choke hold—trying and failing. He did a move straight out of MMA 101, and freed his arms, slamming mine downward and twisting a leg to hook around my neck, flipping me over. And instead of lying on top of me, he was basically sitting on me, his body weight concentrated on my upper body while my legs flailed helplessly trying to get purchase. I snarled and he leaned into his position, the arm across my neck mirroring the choke hold I'd just been trying to achieve.

I should have tapped out. He had me, and both my beast and I knew it, but there was some perverse part of me that wondered whether he'd push me to unconsciousness, or do the chivalrous thing and let me up even without my signaling a yield.

The pressure increased. There was a buzzing in my ears that should have given me my answer, but I kept fighting, digging my nails into his skin hard enough to draw blood. The buzzing got louder, and my vision was starting to swim, but I refused to yield. I wasn't scared. I knew deep down that he wouldn't kill me, otherwise my beast would have taken on a more lethal form and been digging claws into him rather than human finger nails. Finally, as everything began to grow dim, I felt my beast do something she'd never done—yield.

I wasn't able to say the word, but I pulled my nails from Jake's arm and placed it palm on the floor. He loosened his grip a fraction, enough to allow me to gulp some much needed air into my lungs.

Alpha, my beast whispered. She wasn't cowed, she was awed. She was filled with respect for this man two millimeters from choking me into unconsciousness. She was also filled with desire and a strange feeling of connection.

The obvious desire was kind of embarrassing. Yeah, I'd had my share of crazy sexual encounters that both my beast and I had enjoyed, but she'd never wanted anyone like this. The human me wasn't sure how I felt about that. Jake was damned hot, but he kind of scared the human me, which was probably why my beast was ready to bump uglies. Well, the beast would just have to take "no" for an answer on that one, because screwing my new Alpha was so not a good idea. Even if he were remotely interested.

I saw a moment of surprise cross Jake's face, before his usual impassive calm expression returned. He carefully eased off me, giving me a second to heal and catch my breath before extending a hand to help me up. Any other time I would have taken that hand and thrown him to the floor, but the beast was surprisingly meek and I wasn't about to push it, so I let him help me up.

"Thanks," I said, because I wasn't sure what else *to* say. What *did* one say to one's Alpha who had just beaten the snot out of you?

"Welcome." He nodded abruptly. "We'll do the same tomorrow evening at eight. Meet me down here in the gymnasium."

Okaaaay. There was a clear, curt dismissal in his tone. Was he angry with me? He'd been the one who'd suggested this. Why was he pissed all of a sudden?

"Yes, sir." I turned my nod into a short bow, my eyes downcast as I headed for the stairs.

"Mills?"

I turned at my name, noticing he'd stopped calling me Tupper. "Yes, sir?"

"You're covered in blood. Make sure you clean up before heading to your dorm room, unless you're prepared to answer questions."

No, I most certainly didn't want to explain why I was covered with blood to my young roommate. "Will do, sir."

Tired, bemused, and oddly content, I climbed the stairs, and headed out of the Alpha House to cross the compound to my home. My home. Yes. For the first time ever, I finally felt like I'd come home.

I woke up before dawn, disoriented and confused by the noise around me as well as the scents of others. It took me a few seconds to realize that I was in Alaska, in a dorm room, and that the sounds and smells were of my five roommates, all up and about while I was still sprawled across my mattress drooling on my pillow.

"Time to wake up. Pack drills start in ten." Even Mir's whisper sounded cheerful.

"Fuck this," I muttered into my pillow. Then I dragged myself out of the bed and eyed the meager selection of clothing in my trunk. I was assuming I'd need to do calisthenics, so those skinny jeans and my favorite tank top were a no. The others were in yoga pants and T-shirts and I made a mental note to stop by the pack store later and pick some up. I didn't think I'd ever worn yoga pants in my life, but if this was a regular occurrence, I might as well dress appropriately. No sense in trying to do burpees in skinny jeans.

I was yanking on a pair of cargo pants and wondering if my bra was up to the task of daily exercises when I smelled it —coffee.

The two roommates that I hadn't met yet were holding cups and pouring the elixir from a small French press they'd set up on one of the trunks. They'd both been in bed asleep by the time I'd gotten back last night. I wondered how rude it would be to ask for coffee before we were even introduced?

"Hey, do you guys have any extra?" I asked. Screw courtesy, it was some ungodly hour of the morning. I was about to do jumping jacks and push-ups without a sports bra. I *needed* coffee.

The one holding the French press gave me a once over. She had reddish-blond hair and a long, narrow face with an equally long narrow nose. Even her eyes were narrow, but I think that was more from disapproval than any natural shape.

"No." Fox Face turned to pour the coffee into her friend's mug. I noticed she wasn't sharing with Muffin Top, Muscles, or Mir, so I shouldn't have felt that her rudeness was directed specifically at me. Still, my beast bristled, urging me to punch her in the face and steal her cup. Or her friend's cup. The other woman was someone I'd describe as more fluffy than curvy. It was kind of hard to tell if she was overweight or if her enormous boobs just made her seem that way.

"We'll grab some at breakfast after the drills," Mir told me, shooting a worried glance at Fox Face. "I never eat or drink anything before exercising, not after that time I puked while sprinting the mile."

I barely heard her. My beast had been busy taking everything in yesterday and more interested in getting a feel for our new surroundings than asserting her dominance. It seemed the acclimation period was over because she was itching for a fight, scratching at my skin to get out. Jake was wrong. Sparring with him last night hadn't helped at all. My beast wasn't satisfied. She wanted me to put this woman in her place and do it with claws and teeth.

The pot was empty, and both women were chatting as they sipped their coffee with exaggerated motions. It was like they were asking me to beat the crap out of them, inviting me to swing the first blow.

"If you guys are done, maybe I can just re-use your grounds?" I asked, trying to find a compromise. It would be weak coffee and lukewarm since I didn't have time to heat the tap water.

"No," Fox Face repeated.

"Don't be a jerk, Stace. You're just going to toss it anyway," Muscles told her.

"It's our coffee pot and grounds," Boobs sniffed. "She wants coffee, she can get her own."

"She just got here yesterday. It's not like she's had time to buy a coffee maker." Mir was antagonistic, standing up for me. I thought it was a bit embarrassing, but my beast was oddly proud.

It's not like I had the money to buy one right now. I was sure the pack would provide me with yoga pants no charge, but I doubted membership came with a French press and a bag of dark roast.

"No," Fox Face said once more. Before I could make fun of her for her monosyllable responses to everything, she picked up the French press and dumped the grounds into the garbage.

My fists curled. My beast snarled. Everyone in the room looked over at me—Mir and Muffin Top with alarm, Muscles with a resigned sigh, and both Fox Face and Boobs with defiance. I struggled to keep my beast inside, only succeeding because a sharp whistle from downstairs broke my attention.

"We gotta go." Mir grabbed my arm and tugged. "You don't want to be late to drills."

I followed her out, wondering if being late to drills had been what had resulted in Mir vomiting while doing sprints?

There weren't sixty wolves in attendance this morning, but most of the pack was out in the grassy section in front of the Alpha House, lined up in neat rows and columns. I fell in between Mir and Muscles, squinting to see the lake in the dim morning light. Why wasn't everyone here? I thought this thing was mandatory. We were werewolves, so it wasn't like people could call out sick or something. Were the missing pack members ones who needed to work away from the compound for days on end? The ones who cooked in the cafeteria? Or did they just get special waivers. I needed one of these special waivers. I needed a lot of these special waivers, because it was far too early in the morning to be doing a workout.

Jake clearly missed out on the special waivers because he was up front, barking out orders for us to do an insane amount of sit-ups, push-ups, and burpees. Then we all sprinted around the compound, stopping at designated areas to throw logs and cement blocks back and forth at each other, do dips from benches, and kick holes in a brick wall that looked like it had recently been repaired. At the end of it all, the sun had come up and the sweet smell of eggs and bacon was permeating the air. I was sweaty, ready to go back to bed, and wishing that some other pack had volunteered to take me in.

On my way to the dining hall it hit me—no one had taken attendance at this thing. There had to have been forty wolves all clustered together doing exercises and running around. I knew there was supposed to be a dorm leader, or super, or something, but there hadn't been anyone checking up to see if we were all present and accounted for. If I ditched morning drills, would anyone notice? Maybe not every day, but every other day? I could probably count on Mir, and possibly Muscles to cover for me, but I'd need to watch out for Fox Face and Boobs. They'd tattle if they thought I slept in.

Dead wolves don't tattle, my beast reminded me.

I grabbed a plate of scrambled eggs, a few pounds of bacon and French toast that had been coated with cornflakes, then tried to decide whether I should head back to the dorm and shower or go straight to my job. Given that I was going to be handling garbage all day, it was probably wise to save the clean-up for later. If I hustled, I might have time for a shower in between lunch and my meeting with Jake. Eating as quickly as I could, I wished Mir a good day, then headed out to my new job.

A werewolf who introduced himself as Stanley met me by the incinerator. Operating instructions were straightforward, and just in case I forgot, there was a laminated safety sheet next to the huge metal chute where the trash went.

"Trash collection is twice a week," Stanley repeated. "Recycle twice a week. The dumpsters here are for emergencies, like if there's something wrong with the incinerator, or you're out of town on vacation and no one is covering for you. We burn the trash as soon as we collect it, but if we can't for some reason or another, it needs to go in these dumpsters with the lids, otherwise bears will get into it and make a mess. Jake doesn't like a mess. One thing you'll learn fast is that he's an Alpha that's strict about rules, policy, procedures, safety protocols, and he likes the compound neat and clean. Everything in its place."

I wasn't particularly clean or neat, and "in its place" tended to be wherever I dropped something last. I could completely see the need for such rules when there was a group of werewolves living in close contact like this, but I had a tendency to wing it on most things. One more item on my "I'll eventually screw this up" list.

Stanley showed me the four wheeler with the trailer, and told me the best way to go about collecting the garbage. Then he wished me luck and gave me his cell phone number on a sticky note in case of questions. I pocketed it, not bothering to tell him that I didn't have a phone. If I had questions, I'd just figure it out myself. It was trash collection. How difficult could it be?

Within the first hour, I realized that I loved my new job. I swear some people had put bricks in their trash bags, because a few of them were heavy as fuck. And a few of them broke when I went to pull them out of the containers, which meant I had to scoop trash off the pavement and somehow manage to keep it from blowing out of the little trailer. I'd made four trips, stuffing my bags into the incinerator chute before I remembered that I still needed to collect from the dining hall before I fired this thing up.

Jamie had advised me the cafeteria would take several trips and I saw why once I got there. Instead of the metal cans with latch lids, or the bear-proof locked trash areas, the cafeteria had big metal dumpsters. I didn't have any big equipment to dump them or haul them off, so I had to flip the lids open and climb inside, tossing trash bags into my trailer. It took me four trips, and when I was done, I was sweaty and stinky with pleasantly sore muscles. Anyone else would have hated the thought of digging through dumpsters and hauling smelly refuse around, but the dirt and stink made me strangely happy. Maybe I had been Oscar from Sesame Street in a former life, because this seemed a pretty weird thing for me to enjoy. One more oddity to chalk up to my freaky genetics.

The lunch whistle blew, and I still had the men's dormitories and one street of houses to collect. Mir had told me that lunch ran for two hours to accommodate everyone's work schedules, that the whistle was mainly to let those working in the compound know that everything was out and ready. Those who worked outside the compound, like the pilot and the folks with the outfitters and adventuring companies, had the option of picking up a box lunch in the mornings before they left or utilizing an expense account. Mir said many of those people preferred to grab the box lunch because the expense account was more like a per-diem and they got to keep what they didn't use at the end of the month. She said the only restriction was that people couldn't skimp on their food. Jake evidently had some weird obsession that his people be fed, and if a wolf was found to be hoarding his expense account and not eating the pack lunches, he'd lose the per-diem privileges.

Well, Jake was going to have to deal today, because I wasn't done with work, and the post-lunch meeting at the Alpha House wouldn't leave me any time to run by the cafeteria for a sandwich.

It took me another hour to finish the trash collection and fire up the incinerator. I waited to make sure everything was set and the sickening sweet smell of burning trash was spiraling in white smoke into the air before I headed out. I didn't have time for lunch. I didn't even have time to shower or do more than wash my hands before jogging over to the Alpha House for the meeting.

I'd expected a large group, but Jake and Jamie were the only two in the conference room when I entered. They looked so right together, her blonde hair brushing against his dark skin as they bent over what looked like a map. She'd worn it loose today, and in the sort of stylish golden waves that women spent hours at the salon to achieve. In contrast, I was sweaty and smelled of old garbage and ash from the incinerator, my spiked purple hair partially flattened from where I'd slept on it, not a stitch of makeup on my face. I could deal with the sweat and stink, but the lack of makeup bothered me. With sufficient eyeliner, I would have felt badass and tough, like I'd just come out of a Mad Max movie. Without it, I felt like a street urchin.

Jamie was certainly looking at me as if I were a street urchin. She opened her mouth as if she were about to command me to sit, or chew me out for my appearance. Then she shut it with a snap, gaze sliding to Jake.

Yeah. Because it wasn't her place to either order me around or chastise me with the Alpha right next to her.

"Take a seat, Mills," Jake told me, still not glancing up from the map. He didn't comment on my pungent aroma, but Jamie looked at the seat cushion in alarm at his directive.

I sat, squirming a bit to make sure any dirt along with the smell of garbage was firmly embedded into the upholstery. Not that I wanted Jake's conference room chair to stink, I just wanted to annoy Jamie.

He looked up at me, not even the slightest bit of surprise or dismay at my appearance. "What do you know about our situation up here with the hunters and the magically tainted bullets?"

Not much. I'd seen the YouTube videos of wolf shifters attacking humans, and been perplexed at their rapid change of form as well as alarmed at the bullets that killed them. Bullets that could force us to shift and that caused an agonizing death were almost as terrifying as the thought that there were humans tracking us down and killing us to mount our heads on a wall. I told Jake what I knew, feeling a bit uneasy about what this special assignment was supposed to be. My beast wouldn't bat an eye at the thought of killing a group of humans, but I really didn't want to have a bullet strip me of what little control over her I had, let alone rot my insides while my body struggled in vain to heal my wounds.

Jake slid the map over to me. "The elf that was creating the magic on these bullets is dead, but there's a warehouse full of them somewhere in the circled area. We're hoping to find out where through a divination spell, then take out their supplies."

That sounded just as dangerous as killing human hunters, but far more intriguing. I'd expected to be used as a sort of killing machine. That Jake might want me for reconnaissance or a search and destroy, thrilled me. Did he actually see me as more than a monster? More than a thug to do the brutal violent work? If so, he was the first.

"So what do you want me to do?" I asked, mentally hoping that this would be my chance to prove myself a valuable member of the pack—valuable enough that they'd overlook me smashing in the face of one or more of my roommates and encouraging a young wolf to get a piercing.

"First we have to hold the divination. It needs to be tonight at midnight and the sidhe who is doing this will be vulnerable. I've got a team who is going to be doing security, and I'd like you on it. It's the team's responsibility to make sure Gwylla isn't disturbed, or shot, or harmed in any way while she works her magic, or that the compound isn't attacked while this is going on."

I winced, thinking that I would be better doing this sort of thing solo. Team work wasn't my strength, and I wasn't sure if this group would even want me along, or trust me not to kill them as well as any intruder.

"Spend the rest of your day getting familiar with the land around the compound," Jamie told me. "Take Mir if you need. The kids here know every den and tree within a ten-mile radius so she can save you some time."

"If this works out, then we might use you in the raid on this warehouse," Jake said.

I knew that was supposed to be incentive, but the thought of another team mission chilled me. I wanted to be useful. I wanted to fit in with this group of wolves, to finally feel like I was a part of a pack. But I wasn't sure this was the right way to go about it. Throwing me into a group that didn't trust me, making me responsible for a critical task, was just setting me up for failure.

Is that what Jake wanted? But if he wanted me dead, he could just do it. No one besides Mir would give a damn if he took my head off. There had to be some other reason he'd do something so risky, so crazy.

Jake stood to leave and Jamie jumped to her feet. I did the same, since that seemed the appropriate protocol, but when I made to leave the room, the Alpha halted me.

"You didn't eat lunch."

It sounded accusatory, as if I were on some sort of hunger strike as a rebellion. "No. I didn't shower either. I'll grab something on my way back," I told him.

"A granola bar and some jerky isn't going to cut it," he argued. "I can hear your stomach growling from across the room. Go shower and change, then come back. I'll throw together something."

I nearly fell over in shock. "You cook?"

It wasn't that I doubted he could broil a steak, it was more that he'd just offered to cook for me. Dinner was in four hours. It wasn't like I was going to starve or something. I got the weird feeling there was more to his offer to cook for me than I knew. And I was pretty sure that if anyone in the compound found out, the gossip would spread like crazy. I'd been in the pack just over twenty-four hours, and the Alpha was cooking a late lunch for me. How weird was that?

Late lunch. Was that a dinner-lunch? A lunch-dinner? Dunch? Linner?

"Okay," I said rather breathlessly, my thoughts a jumble. Then I took off, running out of the Alpha House and to my dorm, practically plowing over a few of my pack mates along the way. The dorm was thankfully empty, and I was able to shower and dress undisturbed. This time I did throw on my skinny jeans—the ones with slashes ripped across the thighs—and a dark red tank top. There was a mini laundry room on our floor but I had no time to wash my clothing, so I tossed it on the floor by my bed and put on my makeup. I was done in record time, making my way back to the Alpha House at a more sedate pace, feeling a whole lot more attractive as I let myself in and headed toward the kitchen.

Jake was making omelets, flipping them out of the pans and onto plates as I walked in.

"You're just in time." He slid a plate onto the table next to a neat place setting that included an actual cloth napkin. I'd never used one of those outside of a restaurant before. In fact, I usually didn't even have the paper napkins at home. Paper towels worked just fine.

"Sit. Eat," he commanded. "Do you want coffee? Tea? Juice or soda?"

"Coffee, please." I eyed his fancy-schmancy coffee maker with envy, and my beast urged me to steal it for my room. Then I jabbed my omelet with my fork and took a bite. It had a whole pig worth of bacon and ham inside along with a spicy cheese. Add amazing cook to the list of my Alpha's talents.

"How was the first day on the job?" Jake asked.

This was so weird, him cooking for me and asking questions about my day as if we were dating or something. At least, this is what I assumed people who dated did. In books and television shows they did this, so there must be some basis in reality to those tales.

"I love my job. Can I just do garbage twenty-four-seven?"

He shot me a questioning look, as if he thought I was kidding.

"Seriously," I told him. "There's something cathartic about

gathering up everyone's trash and burning it. I think I like burning it the best. That incinerator is wicked cool."

"That scares me. Please don't burn down the compound, or stick any of your roommates in there."

I chuckled in between bites of omelet. "My own personal body disposal tool. What a great idea."

"No, it's not, although I was envisioning you using it as an execution device."

Wow, this guy had been watching too many horror movies. "Nah. I like using claws and teeth. It's far more satisfying to watch someone bleed out than burning them alive."

"I hope you're not speaking from personal experience," he commented dryly. "So, are there bodies for disposal? Do I need to account for everyone at dinner tonight?"

I hid a wince. He was joking, but with my past, it wouldn't be a stretch for him to truly fear that I'd killed one or more of my pack mates.

"Not yet. I came close to knocking one of my roomies out this morning, though. I don't think I would have killed her, but she might have not been able to participate in this morning's drills if I'd let loose."

"What happened?" He put a mug of coffee in front of me and sat down to his own omelet.

I shrugged. It took so little to set my beast off, that it seemed pointless to discuss what happened and why. "I was tired, disoriented from waking up in a new place, and without caffeine. She was a snotty bitch and I wanted to teach her a lesson."

"No, I mean, why didn't you hit her? What held you back?"

I immediately thought of Mir, her face pinched with worry when she'd realized that I was ready to sprout fur and go on the attack. Yes, I'd been interrupted before I could act by the whistle to go to drills, but it had been Mir that brought my beast back under control, not the need to do jumping jacks in the compound. I'd been worried that she would be hurt in the brawl. And I'd not wanted to see the disappointment in her eyes, the realization that I was just a monster after all.

"I don't know," I lied, not ready to bare my soul to this guy. Not yet, anyway.

"Did sparring help?" he pressed.

"Maybe?" It had made my beast feel less ready to go start a fight, but she was still reactive with a hair-trigger temper. I didn't want to admit to Jake that the sparring wouldn't be the cure-all he'd hoped, because I wanted our sessions to continue. My beast enjoyed them, and so did I.

"Well we won't have time for them tonight, not with the prep for the divination. Do you want to reschedule for tomorrow after lunch instead?"

"And a second one in the evening?" Because getting the crap beat out of me by my smoking hot Alpha once per day wasn't enough?

"Let's do afternoon, then if you feel like you need a second bout in the evening, come on by around ten."

Oh, I'd be by even if I was so exhausted I could hardly stand, because there was something that sparked in me last night when we'd fought down in the gym—something that I was desperate to feel again. It wasn't just the fight. It wasn't just the fact that Jake had bested me and I wanted another chance at him. It was *him*. There was something about this Alpha, this wolf, this almost-angel that drew me in like steel to a magnet.

CHAPTER 8

It was late afternoon by the time I left the Alpha House and headed back to my dorm. I didn't know where Mir worked—or even *if* sixteen-year-olds worked—so I wrote a note and put it on her pillow. If I didn't see her before, I'd certainly catch up with her at dinner. With the divination thing at midnight, we should at least have a few hours for her to give me the outside-the-compound tour before I needed to join this team. That done, I decided to make a list of things I needed from the compound store, as well as what I'd need to purchase once I got paid. Workout stuff for these morning drills. Sturdy clothing for my garbage job. A cell phone. A coffee maker. I flipped the lid on my trunk, mentally inventorying my clothing and froze.

Someone had been going through my things. The scent wasn't overwhelming, but I could tell that Fox Face had opened the trunk and actually handled the contents. I carefully picked up each piece, inhaling the scents it held and checking it for damage. Nothing was stolen. Nothing had been slashed or peed on or even spit on. But Fox Face had rubbed her scent over every single article of clothing.

If she'd stolen or damaged something, I could have gone to the dorm super. I wasn't a fan of ratting someone out, preferring to take care of things like this one-on-one, but I knew that theft or destruction of personal property was pretty high up on the list of things-that-would-make-Jake-go-ballistic. Fox Face had been careful to do neither. Which meant I had a choice. I could go to the super and complain that she'd been touching my stuff, which would make me look like a weak, whiny tattle-tale, or I could do nothing. Doing nothing would also make me look weak and reinforce her claim that she was the dominant wolf and had the right to rub her scent all over my stuff without complaint or repercussion on my part.

Let's just say that Fox Face was messing with the wrong bitch. My beast wanted me to track her down and beat the ever-loving crap out of her, or at the very least take a huge dump on her pillow. But for once, my less reactive human brain prevailed. I would absolutely not let such an insult pass, but I needed to retaliate in a way that wouldn't put me in Jake's crosshairs, and wouldn't jeopardize the almost-friendship I was on the edge of developing with Muffin Top and Muscles.

And Mir. I couldn't let her down. I couldn't do anything that might cause her mother to put down her foot and yank her out of the dorm and out of my life.

I'm a monster with many talents. Most people only see the killing one, but I do have others. Folding my clothes and neatly returning them to the trunk I went over to Fox Face's bed, knelt down beside the blankets, and inhaled deeply.

Scents are intricate things. Millions of complex chemicals combined in varying proportions to make up an aroma that identifies a substance, a plant, an animal, a human, or a shifter. I let the beast in me process through these chemicals, analyzing and recreating them until I'd successfully duplicated Fox Face's scent over top of my own. Then I went to both Muffin Top and Muscles' trunks and carefully went through their things, laying the artificial scent trail down. I should have done Mir's as well, but I couldn't bring myself to disrespect her belongings, so I hoped no one would catch that hers had remained untouched. Then I dismissed the artificial scent, returning to my own natural one. It wasn't perfect. If a shifter had a really, really good nose, they would catch subtle differences between the one I'd created and Fox Face's. But even shifters with good noses usually attributed those differences to the effect that emotions, food consumed, and even environment have on personal scents.

Basically, my charade had always been good enough. Yeah, I'd done this sort of thing before. No, I'd never been caught. Shifters didn't have the ability to change their scent signature. Neither did humans. As far as I knew, only demons could do so, and most of them didn't bother. But no matter what people said about me behind my back, and sometimes to my face, I wasn't a demon—not really. I was a shifter, and shifters were all about scent. So if I wanted to cover my tracks, then scent was how I did it.

Okay, maybe I *was* a demon. If Jake was an angel-light, then perhaps I was a demon-light. It would explain a lot about me and the beast inside me.

I left the dorm, thinking it would be too much of a coincidence to ignore if I were found there when the others discovered Fox Face's scent all over their belongings. With only a few hours until dinner, I took it upon myself to head out past the lake and look around the wooded area. The lake was beautiful as usual, the plane that Dustin flew was not at the dock, no doubt flying wolves and tourists around to make money for the pack. I skirted around the marshy areas and past a huge cluster of pines, then through a meadow filled with grasshoppers and brilliant red and yellow flowers before dipping down a rocky trail into the woods.

Everything was a vivid green. Ferns. Bushes. Groves of mountain laurel that arched over the trail creating a light-speckled tunnel. Small trees trying to push their way up through the space in the canopy created by the larger ones. I caught the scent of water and followed a narrow deer track to what was either a large creek or a small river. Judging by the sediment and gullies spreading out from the banks, this creek flooded often. Right now it was fairly shallow, the rocky bottom clearly visible through greenish-tinted water. I followed it downstream to a small set of rapids, then a section of deeper water, complete with a half-finished beaver dam. The flooding had caused a shallow-rooted tree to topple, the dirt-covered root ball stretching to the sky. The trunk made a natural bridge across the creek, the top branches partially submerged about two feet from the oppo-site shore. A bridge, if you didn't mind getting hip-deep in icy water for the last couple of feet.

I wasn't willing to get wet, so I passed it by, taking a side path that led down to a larger river—this one bordered on my side by a huge, slick, flat, rock face that a hundred feet later became a sheer wall of gray. I scrambled up and over it, regretting that I was wearing my cute skinny jeans and shoes that weren't exactly hiking friendly. The cliff was roughly twelve feet high, and once up, the path continued on, winding around shorter rocky outcrops that would make perfect dens for large as well as small animals. It was at one of these "dens" that I paused, a weird smell capturing my attention.

Correction, it wasn't a weird smell, it was a weird lack of smell. I'm one of those shifters with a really, really good nose. And since I tend to mask my scent with a manufactured one at times, I'm particularly sensitive to those subtle anomalies that occur when a smell is not natural.

But this wasn't truly fake. It was just…oddly perfect. It was as if someone had magically Febrezed a section of this rock, covering up a scent they didn't want known with one they felt blended better with the surroundings. Camouflage. Except it was too perfect, too organized in pattern. Nature is chaos. If there's a pattern, it's so complex that it never appeared perfect. I moved in closer to the den, but couldn't see anything that would indicate someone or something had been here recently. And try as I might, I couldn't break through the magical Febreze to figure out what it was covering up.

It was dinnertime, so I headed back, not sure what to do about the experience. I was confident that I was the only one who could tell there was something off about the den's scent, and I wasn't established enough in the pack for anyone to take my word for it that something was off. Plus, I wasn't familiar with this area at all. There were shifter types I'd never met before, angels down in a pack in the south part of the state, something called a sidhe, whatever the fuck that was. For all I knew there were magical groundhogs that had a way of covering up their scent so the wolves—shifters as well as wild ones—wouldn't eat them. It would be horribly embarrassing to go to Jamie or Jake with this, only to find out I'd dragged them out of the compound to check out a magical groundhog den.

I met Mir in the dining hall, and try as I might, I couldn't wiggle out of sitting with her and her parents again. I was torn between wanting to make new friends so I'd have an excuse to eat elsewhere and the desire to hang out with the girl that my beast seemed to have adopted. Even if I were to try to sit elsewhere or eat alone, she would have scratched at my skin, pacing and fretting until I moved to a table with Mir.

Mir's mom stared at me the whole meal, as if she expected me to stick my fork into her daughter or something. Mir's dad cast me a sympathetic smile, then focused his entire attention on his food. It was awkward. And I'd had enough of this shit. I was a member of this pack. I was their daughter's roommate and friend. I still wasn't sure I wouldn't be dead in a few weeks, but until then, I was going to do my damnedest to make peace with these people and show them that I might be a monster, but I would never hurt their daughter.

"Jamie suggested I go out with you today so you could show me all the places outside the compound I might need to know about," I told Mir, noting that her mother stiffened at my words. "I explored a bit this afternoon past the lake. There was a spot where the creek branches off and feeds into a bigger river with some rocky spots."

"Oh yeah," Mir replied. "Those are cool spots to hide when we're doing capture the flag and weekend mock battles. Upstream from the creek are a bunch of downed trees that are overgrown with brush and weeds creating a huge deadfall. If you're little and don't mind getting scratched a bit, you can squeeze in through them. There's an open spot underneath that's really cool. Matt and Aaron tried to track me by scent one time, and never found me. I think they knew I was in there somewhere, but couldn't figure out how to get in without the whole thing crashing down on their heads."

Mir's mother sucked in a breath. "I've told you I don't like you going in there. Those trees are rotting, and there's a good chance they will crash down on *your* head."

The girl rolled her eyes, but did it in a direction so her mother couldn't see. "I'm careful, Mom. If I can't lift a bunch of rotted trees off my head, then I'm a pretty poor excuse for a werewolf."

"How about that fallen tree bridge? How stable is that?" I asked.

"The one that came down this summer is solid, but there's another one upstream a ways that you don't want to cross over. The beetles have tunneled all through it and half the bark is off. If you don't slip off the side from the moss and slime, then it will probably crumble under your feet."

I could tell this was driving her mother crazy, but I liked that Mir was reinforcing the idea that she did all kinds of risky things completely on her own, before I had even arrived at the compound. The worst I'd do is help her get a piercing in a very private area. With me here, I'd be the one trying the log bridges and deadfalls before I ever let her enter. If anything, her parents should be thanking me for ensuring all the crazy stuff Mir did came down on my head before hers.

I peeked out the window of the dining hall. "We should get going if we're going to do our tour before it gets dark," I told her.

She stuffed a last bite of chicken into her mouth and nodded. "I need to run back to the room and change my shoes and then we'll head out."

"Be careful," her mother pleaded. Then she did something completely unexpected, she looked me right in the eyes and what I saw in them was far from hate. "Please watch over her. She likes to think she's a big bad wolf, but she's only sixteen."

"Mom!" Mir squealed.

"Nothing will happen to her," I swore. "I'll guard her with my life."

Mir huffed following me out of the dining hall and across the compound. "You didn't have to say that. Ugh, how melodramatic. 'I'll guard her with my life'. You're my friend, not my nanny."

"Hey, if it makes your mom think I'm a decent werewolf, then I'll say anything," I lied. "I gotta impress your parents, so they'll think I'm a suitable friend for you."

She laughed. "I think Dad actually likes you. He'd never admit it in front of Mom, but I get the impression he thinks you're one of those tough chicks with a soft heart."

I wasn't, except when it came to Mir. Funny how I'd lived for this long not giving a crap about anyone, even the guys I slept with, and a sixteen-year-old werewolf had wormed her way into my heart in one day. Less, if I were to be completely honest.

We climbed up the stairs to our room. I heard the loud argument before I'd even entered the building, and acted surprised and clueless. It was hard to keep from smirking, especially when Mir opened the door and I saw Muscles and Muffin Top waving shirts and underwear at Fox Face, whose mouth was open in a confused "O".

"Why were you in my stuff?" Muscles demanded. A muscle twitched in her jaw. My eyes drifted down to her arms with their very admirable biceps and again I had to force back a smirk. Fox Face was so going to get a beating.

"I wasn't. I didn't go in your stuff. I didn't touch anything," Fox Face shouted back.

Boobs was backing away from the argument, looking like she wanted to be anywhere but in the room at the moment. Mir ran to her trunk and sniffed the contents, sighing in relief as she shut the lid. "No one was in my things," she said.

"Well she was in mine," Muffin Top replied, shoving the shirt toward Fox Face once more. "And Brianne's as well. Mills, check your trunk. I'll bet she went through your things, too."

I was biting my lip hard enough to draw blood. Opening

the lid of my trunk I made a show of sniffing loudly as I went through the clothes. "Yep. I can smell her on my stuff."

Fox Face shot me a look that should have burned me to a pile of ash, then she turned back to Muscles and Muffin Top. "I swear I didn't go through your things. Why would I do that? I've got no reason to bother with your stuff."

All the shouting brought the dorm super upstairs. She was a dark-haired woman who looked like she might have had some Alaskan native in her background. "What's going on?"

The room erupted in a shouting match, Muscles and Muffin Top accusing Fox Face while Boobs cowered in the background.

"Wish I had some popcorn," I told Mir, sitting on the end of my bed to watch the show. I didn't have to watch long. The super tried to shout louder than the others to get them to calm down and talk one at a time, but no one paid any attention to her. Muscles was practically brushing her nose against Fox Face's forehead, still screaming and waving her underwear in the woman's face. Then it happened. I felt the adrenaline, felt the shift in emotion, sensed the subtle changes in scent that came when bodies are readied for action. Fox Face didn't have much room to maneuver, but she made the best of what she had and hit Muscles in the jaw with an uppercut. Her right fist impacted with enough force to snap the other woman's jaw shut with a crack, jerking her head backward sharply. I was positive that there were chipped teeth and whiplash involved at the very minimum. But Muscles was a werewolf, and it would take more than a solid blow to the jaw to knock her down.

Muffin Top seized the moment and got in the action, rushing forward and slamming into Fox Face, pushing her backward into the wall. The super tried to pull her away and got an elbow in the face for her trouble. After that, it was a melee of action. Muscles clearly had the physical strength, but Fox Face was one hell of a fighter. She managed to hold both Muscles and Muffin Top off by herself, punching, kicking, biting, head-butting, and even pulling hair. The woman fought dirty. If she hadn't been such a bitch to me, I might have liked her.

By the time Jake arrived, the furniture was scattered around the room, and blood decorated the floor. Mir and I were over near the bathroom where we could duck in if the fighting came our way, not because I was worried about getting hurt, but because I was determined that Mir not suffer even a papercut in this melee. Jake didn't say a word. He strode across the room and grabbed Muscles by the neck, slamming her into the wall hard enough to leave an outline of her body dented into the drywall. Then he reached out and grabbed Fox Face's shoulder, throwing her to the ground and grinding his foot into her back. Muffin Top danced out of the way, her hands raised and her eyes huge as she dropped to the ground and lowered her head.

"What in all of creation is going on here?" he demanded. There was an edge to his voice that was like taking a whip across the face. I felt Mir shiver beside me, and smelled urine. Glancing around, I realized that it was from Boobs who was cowering between two of the overturned beds, whimpering.

"She went through our stuff," Muscles choked out, wheezing from a bruised windpipe that hadn't fully healed yet.

"Did she steal anything? Damage anything?" Jake demanded.

Muscles lowered her eyes. "No. But she has no right to go through our things. I don't need anyone pawing at my underwear and bras, and seeing personal stuff that I've got in my trunk."

I suddenly wondered what personal stuff Muscles had in her trunk. I'd only spread the manufactured scent through the top few layers of clothing. Maybe she had dildos or something in the bottom underneath everything. I was tempted to check later and satisfy my curiosity, but now wouldn't be a good time. Maybe in a few months, once all this had settled down and I could figure out a good excuse for going through her things, or to blame someone else for going through her things.

"You could have complained to the super," Jake commented. "Brawling, damaging furniture and getting blood all over the floor wasn't necessary."

He'd damaged the room far more than the women had with the Muscles-shaped drywall dent he'd created, but I figured it would be best if I kept my mouth shut and stayed out of it all.

"I didn't do it," Fox Face mumbled, barely audible with her face pressed against the linoleum floor.

Jake tilted his head and looked down at her, a puzzled expression on his face. Then he lifted his foot and nudged Fox Face in the side. She rose, her eyes still lowered.

"I didn't do it," she repeated.

It hit me. Jake was an angel-light. Just as I had talents no other werewolf had, he also had talents of his own. And I was getting the feeling that one of his talents was in detecting falsehoods. Fox Face wasn't lying. She hadn't messed with Muscle's trunk. It had been me. And if Jake could sense a lie, then he could also sense that she was telling the truth.

I was so fucked. It was just a matter of time before he came around to asking me some very difficult questions. Could I get away with lying to him? Would demon-light skills counteract angel-light skills? Or should I come up with some pitiful excuse as to why I'd framed Fox Face?

"You are telling me that you did not go in either Brianne or Miranda's trunks at any time in the last three days?"

I winced. Three days was the freshness limit of scent. After that point, the aromas degraded and faded, shifting and altering in strength and tone. With my nose, the changes began within a matter of hours, but most shifters, it was days before they could sense the degradation.

"I have not been in Brianne or Miranda's personal belongings, or in their storage trunks *ever*," Fox Face vowed. "I swear it. It was her," she pointed at me.

I forced my muscles to remain relaxed and rolled my eyes. "Girl, if I was going to get into anyone's trunk, it would be yours to steal that French press of yours as well as the bag of dark roast coffee that I can smell from across the room." I turned to Muffin Top, since Muscles was still pinned to the wall. "Did I go in your things? Did you catch my scent at all in your stuff?"

"No," she declared. "The only scent in my trunk was my own and Stacy's."

Jake looked completely perplexed by this. I held my breath, hoping he didn't figure it out. And in those few seconds I wavered, wondering whether I should speak out that Fox Face had been through my stuff as well. It would ring true, but it would also bring attention to the cause of all this. Jake struck me as a very smart guy—smart enough to figure out if Fox Face admitted to going through my things, I probably was somehow responsible for the rest of this in retaliation. So instead of speaking out, I kept my mouth firmly shut.

Rather than grill me further, Jake dropped Muscles, who collapsed on the floor gasping and holding her throat. Then he went over to her trunk, flipping the lid open and bending down to rifle through her clothing as he inhaled deeply. I leaned in closer, hoping to catch a glimpse of the gigantic dildos that I was sure were at the bottom of the trunk, but sadly Jake did not dig that deeply among her clothing.

He lifted his head, brows knitted together. Then he pinched his nose, and bent down for another deep inhale. I held my breath, trying to look as if I were only mildly interested in what was going on. I don't think I was very successful, because Mir shot me a suspicious glance.

Jake stood and moved to Muffin Top's trunk and did the same, with the same intent expression on his face. Then he moved to Boobs's trunk, then Mir's, then mine.

If he had my super nose skills, he'd clearly be able to tell the difference between the scent among my clothing and the one in Muffin Top and Muscles' trunks. He took longer among my things, tilting his head and shaking it slightly as he analyzed the scents. Then he stood and walked over to me. I couldn't help but tense.

"She was in your trunk as well."

It wasn't a question, but I still nodded in reply.

"Why weren't you ripping her throat out?" he asked.

"Because Muscles was already tearing her a new asshole by the time I arrived. I was waiting my turn." Cocky, but hopefully it would convince him that I was innocent in all this.

"So you just *now* noticed that Stacy had been in your things? You didn't notice, say, when you came back after our meeting to shower and change your clothing? Or after late lunch?"

Fuck. He had a good enough nose to know Fox Face had been in my stuff right around our lunch together. Time to put on my best poker face and bluff like crazy.

"Yeah, but what the hell was I supposed to do? She wasn't here to beat the crap out of. Nothing was stolen or damaged. I'd look like a total pansy if I went to the super or you and bawled that she'd been pawing through my undies. I figured

I'd confront her later, when we were alone and I could take the time to break her fingers one at a time without being interrupted."

There. That was damned good, if I did say so myself. I totally deserved an Oscar for that one.

I could see Jake putting two and two and two together, though. I'd mentioned a near run-in with one of my room-mates when we'd had lunch together. She'd gone through my shit, and if he had as good a nose as I thought he did, then he could tell Fox Face had been through my stuff hours before the other two. There was a time difference in the snooping. I'd indicated I'd had a problem with a roomie earlier. And I was worried that Jake could tell the difference between the scent on my stuff and the scent on the others'. Damn it all, I wished I had gone over my things with the fake scent as well, but then there would have been a weird overlap and I would have had to figure out a way to explain that as well.

"Swear to me," he commanded. I felt it deep in my bones, as if he were trying to wrench the truth from me. For one hot second, I almost confessed it all, but my beast slapped that idea down, and instead I pulled myself up to my full five-foot-four height and looked my Alpha straight in the eyes.

"I swear to you that I had nothing to do with that were-wolf's scent on my clothes. I came in this afternoon and noticed it. And I swear to you I had every intention of making sure she paid for that trespass at some point."

There. Truth. Evasion. And I'd found that being honest about my violent intentions often masked the sneakier shit that I'd already done.

Jake's eyes narrowed. He stared at me for long enough that my own were starting to water. I could feel the tension in the room, feel the nervous anticipation of my roommates. Then he nodded.

"Stacy, report to Jamie at four tomorrow morning for punishment."

Fox Face bit short a wail, and nodded, tears welling up in her eyes. I clamped my teeth together hard and continued to meet Jake's eyes, waiting for my punishment. Surely I'd be punished as well. He knew. I knew he knew. But would he act on his instinct, or hold back unless he had substantial proof that I'd done wrong?

Without another word he turned and left the room. I felt myself sag, swaying slightly in relief. I still wasn't in the clear. I was darned sure that Jake knew I'd been the instigator of all this, but he was too tied up in his rules and procedures to punish me unless he could prove I'd been involved. I'd gotten away with it. The toughest, smartest, strongest, most dominant Alpha I'd ever known, and I'd managed to get away with this. I should be relieved, but instead I was worried.

Because I was positive I hadn't gotten away with anything at all, only temporarily evaded an inevitable punishment.

I met my team at ten o'clock outside the dining hall. For all the pack's quasi-military environment, the group looked more like a bunch of coeds getting ready to study for a test than a security team. The leader was a blond dude with a man bun and a soul patch. He read a bunch of stuff from a clipboard about sub teams, assigned areas, and communication protocols, then he sent one team of six to the east of the compound. One he designated to guard the actual compound area. I was in the team that was to head to the west, opposite the lake. Aside from the group remaining in the compound, we were all supposed to guard on four legs.

Hence the communication protocols, because it was darned hard to operate a walkie-talkie or a cell phone with paws, and growls and barks could only communicate a limited number of things. Soul Patch was leading my team, so we all followed him out past the lake to the trail I'd explored earlier in the day. Then everyone began to shed their clothing and shift into their wolf form.

I hesitated, wishing I'd been assigned the compound duty

instead so I didn't have to shift. Normally I would have requested a transfer, citing that my beast wasn't always cooperative about what animal form I took, and they might not want a lion roaming around an Alaskan forest, but after my close call with the roommates, I was reluctant to rock the boat. I was already on Jake's radar. Plus, being labeled uncooperative and defiant wouldn't help me establish myself in the pack.

Waiting a few minutes until everyone was focused on their shift, I stripped my clothes off, pleaded with my beast to cooperate for once in her life, then changed form.

Werewolves take about twenty minutes to shift. It's gross and painful, and they can't do it too often in one day or they're too exhausted to stand. I'm all sorts of special, so shifting form takes me about three seconds and I can do it all day long without fatiguing myself. The only hitch was that I didn't always end up a wolf. Lion wasn't all that bad. Lion-ass with a giant eagle front and a snake head was a problem. Previous packs had been freaked out enough about the non-wolf forms I occasionally wound up in, but the mix-match ones usually sent everyone running and screaming.

My beast must have been in a good mood because I wound up a sort-of wolf. I was bigger than the others, my fur a matte black that blended in with the shadows. I had the lowered hips of a show-quality German Shepherd with joints that would allow me to easily stand and walk on two legs if I so chose. The toes on my feet were more like fingers in terms of length and dexterity, and my jaw was broad—built for crushing rather than slicing and dicing.

The others finished their shift and shook out their fur— fur that immediately stood on end as they saw me. I grinned, going for that friendly monster look, but the sight of my gleaming fangs didn't help relieve them of their unease over my appearance.

Soul Patch narrowed his eyes at me, but there wasn't much he could do in wolf form to ask me questions or demand I turn into something more traditional, so he swung his head and pawed the ground. That was our signal to take our respective guard spots. Every one of them gave me one last nervous glance, then headed out. I loped silently through the woods, traveling just above the ground to keep my scent trail and sound to a minimum. I made my way to the designated area, close to where the creek dumped into the river. We were only six and there was a lot of area to patrol, so thankfully this wasn't a job where I had to sit on my butt for hours and stare at the trees.

Deciding that patrolling along the established pathways wouldn't be the best way to perform guard duty, I went off track, through bushes and weeds that were tall enough to brush against my hips. The occasional breeze brought the scent of my pack mates, orienting me to their positions and locations. Two hours I prowled around the woods, enjoying the sensation of being in an animal form, but not noting anything that would give me cause for concern. I glanced up at the moon and stars, so incredibly bright in the Alaska sky. Midnight. This was when that sidhe was supposed to be doing the divination. We were supposed to guard for another hour, then head back in.

I was looping by the area where Mir had told me the deadfall was when I felt something. Freezing in place, I lifted my nose to the sky and swiveled my ears. All I could smell were the normal scents of my surroundings and the occasional whiff of my pack mates in the distance. All I could hear were insects, frogs, the careful footsteps of a herd of deer about half a mile away. But there was something off, something that felt as if someone was rubbing sandpaper across my fur. A moment later I felt a burst, like someone had pulled apart a juicy orange and sprayed it right in my face. My skin prickled, and then it was gone.

What. The. Fuck. I'd never been around magic before. Well, I'd never been around real magic anyway. There'd been a few tarot card readings I'd indulged in from local psychics with a sign in their window, but I'd never felt anything unusual during those sessions. And I'd definitely never felt anything like this.

I shook myself to try to rid the feeling from my skin and fur, then continued my patrol, hoping that I'd be able to go back to the compound soon and go to bed. I'd been up early, had a physically demanding day, and was tired. Although I wasn't sure how well I'd sleep in a room with all the drama earlier this evening—drama caused by me.

Making my way through the rocky area with the little dens, I felt it again. The too-perfect scent areas were stronger, recently reinforced, and there was that sensation of sandpaper on my fur. I hesitated, but my beast urged me forward, to make my moves as casual as possible. I did, and that's when I saw them.

Something so indistinct I could barely tell it from the surroundings. It was dark over by the dens, and all I could see was the occasional distortion, so tiny, so brief that I almost missed it. Watching out of my peripheral vision as I continued to move by, I put all the distortions together and came up with six figures.

I couldn't smell them, hear them, or even see them, but they were there. My beast grinned, delighted that we now had prey to hunt. Walking on, I waited until I was far enough away that they couldn't see me, but close enough that I could still feel the weird magic they were using, then I begged my beast to shift once more.

A human form wouldn't do me any good, but a huge

monster wolf-like creature wouldn't either, especially with humans that were most likely carrying bullets that would rot me from the inside out. For once, my beast listened and I felt myself shrinking down, taking the shape of a mink. I hoped they had minks in Alaska, otherwise I'd be screwed. I wasn't sure six guys who were most likely packing rifles and who were using some magic to cloak themselves would give a damn about a mink prowling around in the brush. They were hiding from werewolves—either in human or in wolf form—not a mink.

Luckily I could be a really fast mink, because after twenty minutes, the hunters moved, and they moved fast. I followed the silent, odorless, faintly blurred forms as they traveled down the path along the creek. I watched from underneath a briar as they crossed the log bridge, their feet not even splashing or breaking the surface of the water as they jumped off the log to wade the last few feet to the opposite creek. I waited for them to be out of sight because I knew I'd be exposed crossing the log myself, and that my swimming through the water for those last few feet wouldn't be silent.

The water was really cold, even as a mink, and when I climbed up to the other side of the bank, I realized I had lost my prey. It pissed my beast off, but I was determined, confident that I could catch that weird sensation of magic again as well as that artificially perfect pattern of scent. I searched in a grid pattern, finally managing to trace the hunters through the woods for three miles to a road.

There had been a vehicle, and whatever magic they'd used, they hadn't bothered to coat their car with it. I morphed back into my sort of wolf form, and ran, easily following the car's scent for another twelve miles until it turned onto another road.

I needed to make a decision. Judging from my sense of time, it had to be close to four in the morning. Should I continue on for possibly hours, or days, tracking this truck? I had no way of contacting Jake and the pack, and I could only imagine how alarmed they'd be when I didn't return. They were probably already alarmed, and I wasn't sure they'd be able to track me down since I'd been very careful to alter my scent to that of a mink. I could keep tracking, but the odds were that a car moving at speed would eventually evade me. And then I'd need to drag my ass back to the compound without six hunter heads on a stick, and need to tell my rule-crazy Alpha that there was a good reason for me to take off for a day or so without letting anyone know.

I needed to get a cell phone. Although where the heck I was supposed to put a cell phone while I was a mink or a sort of wolf was beyond me.

Giving up, I headed back, speeding up as I saw we were getting close to sunrise.

I expected some degree of chewing out when I returned, but I wasn't prepared for the absolute chaos in the compound. They'd clearly scented me coming because I could see them waiting for me as I came around the edge of the lake and headed for the Alpha House. There must have been ten of my pack mates gathered there, half of them in wolf form. Soul Patch got on a walkie-talkie as I approached, clearly calling in some sort of search party. I hadn't encountered anyone on my way back, so they must have been a pretty lousy search party and heading in the absolute wrong direction.

"You okay, Mills?" Soul Patch's face was pinched with worry. I'd just met the guy. It was flattering that he'd been worried about me, although one look at Jake's face made me wonder if my team leader's worry wasn't for my well-being, but for the trouble he was in for losing one of his group.

"Yeah. Sorry, I went to check something out and it led me pretty far away from the compound."

"And you didn't think to check in?" he shot back, worry dissolving into irritation.

"I don't have a cell phone. Besides, where would I have put it in my wolf form, up my ass?"

"You were supposed to find a team member and let them know if you saw anything. You were supposed to go check out that something in teams of no less than two, not head out on your own."

Jake wasn't speaking up, so I got the impression that they were tag-teaming this verbal abuse. Soul Patch first, then my Alpha would no doubt finish me off.

If I'd gone and gotten someone, the hunters would have most likely been gone when we'd returned, and they would have thought I was a liar. Even if the hunters were there, they probably couldn't have sensed them and thought I was a liar anyway. Plus, I wouldn't have been able to track them with a werewolf trotting beside me, potentially setting off all sorts of magical alarm shit and getting the both of us killed. It seemed pointless to tell Soul Patch all this, though. He wouldn't believe me, would think it was just a bunch of excuses. So instead I tried to look cowed and submissive—and was well aware that I was failing at that.

"Sorry. I won't do it again. I promise next time I'll shove a cell phone up my ass and dig it out to text if I see anything."

Snark probably didn't help the situation. Soul Patch growled and stepped forward, his teeth bared. Jake grabbed the man by the shoulder and pulled him back, clearly saving a member of his pack from death or serious injury at my hands.

No, I'd mistaken my Alpha's motives, because no sooner had he shoved Soul Patch aside, than he grabbed me by the arm, twisting it around behind my back and marching me up the stairs of the Alpha House. I was too shocked to struggle or protest, until we were inside. Even then, trying to twist myself free did nothing but wrench my shoulder nearly out of its socket.

He shoved me into his office, slamming the door behind me. Then he grabbed me once more, pushing me against the wall. I tried to get a knee up between his legs, but he was too close and too strong for me to move more than a few inches. Instead of hitting him in the balls, I just ended up pushing my thigh against his crotch, which was far more seductive than I'd intended it to be. Not that my beast minded. She liked screwing just as much as she liked fighting, and she really wanted to do some of the former with Jake.

The Alpha blinked at me in surprise for an instant, then his expression returned to one of fury.

"We couldn't find you. The patrols came in, and you didn't, and no one had heard from you. Hours we searched. Hours."

It was my turn to blink in surprise. They were worried about me. Well, maybe not Soul Patch and the others, but Jake clearly was. He was so pissed that steam was nearly coming out of his ears, and that was less because I'd broken the rules, and more because he had been worried that I was injured or dead somewhere.

"I saw something," I told him. "Well, not saw exactly, more like I sensed something. I didn't have time to tell anyone, and I needed to be stealthy, so I tracked it. I'm sorry, but I thought that following the hunters was more important than checking in."

He growled. "Hunters. You were following hunters."

"Yeah, that's what I said. Hunters." Duh. That was the purpose of having us patrol wasn't it? To make sure the divination went off without a hitch, and to keep intruders from attacking?

Jake scoffed. "Right. I was out there with three of my best trackers, and we smelled nothing."

"That's exactly it. The scent pattern is like their surroundings, only more symmetrical. It's too perfect and organized, and it lingered in the spots where they'd been. I could feel their magic when I was up close, and if I watched carefully, I could see a faint distortion in the background where they were."

He stared at me for a moment. "You expect me to believe that you can smell odors to the point where you're reading the patterns at the level of chemical molecules? And that you somehow can sense magic that none of us can, see things that none of us can?"

I squirmed. "Maybe if you'd been there you would have seen the distortion and felt the magic as well. But as for scent, yes."

He stared at me in disbelief. I knew what he was thinking, that if he, an angel-light, couldn't do these things, then I shouldn't be able to either.

"I followed them through the woods to a road, then followed the scent of their vehicle, but it was getting close to morning and I needed to come back. Besides, the farther ahead of me they got, the greater the likelihood that I'd mistaken the trail or lose it entirely. I didn't want to be gone until midafternoon or longer and come back empty-handed."

"You followed them. You mean to tell me that you, in that giant weird wolf form Stevens said you'd taken on, followed a group of six magically shielded humans for miles and they didn't notice you? They somehow have the magic to be invisible and leave no scent trace, but they don't have the magic to detect a shifter in their midst?" Jake scoffed. "Admit it, Mills. You saw a herd of deer and couldn't resist going hunting. You left the area you were supposed to patrol and went off to do something more interesting."

Oh, I so wanted to punch him in the face. "Fuck you. I didn't go chasing off after deer. I patrolled my area, and clearly I did a better job than those other morons you had out there because I was the only one who sensed those hunters. Fuck. You."

"Then why couldn't we track you? Me. And three of my best trackers. We had your scent until just after midnight, then it vanished over near the rock face by the river. You didn't check in. You didn't call. And you didn't leave any kind of trail for us. Where were you?"

"I was following the hunters," I yelled at him, punching the wall with my fist. It made a nice dent in the drywall. "I fucking told you that. I saw them, sensed them, and *knew* that they saw me. I knew they'd shoot me if a big-ass werewolf started following them, so I acted like I didn't see them, went off a ways, then changed form into something they wouldn't expect. That's why my scent vanished."

Actually my scent should have remained the same no matter what form I was in. Subtle differences due to form, but clearly still me. I didn't want to go down that path, because a discussion of how I could alter my scent would lead Jake to realize I'd been behind the drama in my dorm room this evening.

"You have another form." Jake said it as if he didn't quite believe me. Again. It was clearly the morning for disbelief.

"I have many forms. And a lot of the time they get all jumbled up together. I knew they wouldn't expect something small, so I followed them as a mink."

"But your scent trail vanished. I'm your Alpha. I, at the very least, should have been able to find you no matter what form you took."

Shit. I was busted either way, but I'd rather take my lumps for the dorm incident than have him not believe me about tonight. For some reason, it was very important that Jake not think I was slacking off and chasing deer, very important that he knew these hunters had been close to our compound, no doubt doing reconnaissance.

"I figured that the hunters might have some kind of magic that lit up in the presence of a shifter, so I actually became a mink, not a shifter-turned-mink, a mink. That means I looked like a mink, smelled like a mink, and, I hoped, looked to a magical device like I was a plain old mink."

He shook his head. "I've met demons before, and they all smell the same no matter what form they take. They smell like the form they are in with faint touches of the souls they own and a weird burnt chocolate smell. I've never met one that completely masked their scent before."

"First off, I'm not truly a demon just as you're not truly an angel. Secondly, demons weren't raised around shifters with their heightened sense of smell. It's not that they can't mask their scent, it's that they don't think to do it. And even if they tried, I don't think they'd be all that great at it because they're not used to experiencing the world through their noses. I was brought up as a shifter. My entire life I've honed my olfactory skills. That's the sense I've practiced to the point that it's far more sensitive and skilled than any of my other senses. And because I'm all about my nose, I've learned to adjust my own scent signature."

"Do it." He narrowed his eyes. "Smell like something else —something not Tupper Mills."

It was tricky to do it without changing physical form, but I concentrated and shifted my scent to that of the mink. Jake leaned close, sniffing. Then he leaned even closer. I could feel his breath as he scented my neck and hair, felt the heat of him so near that he was almost touching me. My beast preened, urging me to present myself, to offer sex. The timing was terrible, but I couldn't help but catch my breath, the scent of arousal trickling out into the mink. His breathing changed in response, and he hesitated, almost touching me. It was one of the most erotic moments of my life, millimeters away from him, his breath tickling my neck as I held myself absolutely still, willing him to do something, do anything. Kiss me. Stroke me. Bend me over the desk and fuck me like the animal I was.

Instead he stepped away. "You do smell like a mink."

Yeah, a horny mink in heat, but a mink. I took a deep breath and tried to dampen down the sexual excitement. No boinking for me. Not now. Probably not ever.

"And I clearly picked up the aroma of a mink where your regular scent trail vanished." Jake sat at the edge of his desk. "Tell me everything about these humans you tracked."

That was it? No apology? No "gee Tupper, you're amazing and I should never have doubted you"? Asshole.

I was irked, but my beast wanted to show off and I really did want him to be aware of this threat, so I told him everything, from sensing the odd lingering spots of magical camouflage this afternoon to following the hunters' car.

"Were they armed?"

I shrugged. "The distortion wasn't enough that I could see whether they were carrying weapons or not. I'm assuming so, given that they were spying on a compound with sixty werewolves. They'd be idiots to come here unarmed, invisibility magic or not."

He nodded. "How close did they come to the compound?"

"I don't know. They were at the rock face when I saw them, and from my exploring this afternoon, that's the only place with the lingering spot of magic. There's a whole lot of ground I didn't cover though. It would take me a while to do a thorough sweep of the area to see where else they may have been and how close they came."

"That's your work then, after our post lunch sparring. I want you to take Robin with you just to see if she can pick up anything that you're sensing. It would be good to have another wolf with the ability to spot these guys. If you need more time, you can do it the next day as well."

Ugh. Work. Then sparring. Then this assignment, all on zero sleep. I was going to crash hard after dinner and not wake up until the whistle for morning drills the next day.

"Will do, boss."

He stood. "Then get going."

No rest for the wicked. It all felt so satisfying, though. I had a place here. I had value here. I was an asset to my pack, had skills my Alpha admired. Hopefully I had other things he admired as well. And best of all? I'd totally gotten away with the dorm room incident. Guess Jake wasn't as smart as I'd thought, because he hadn't put two and two together on my abilities to change my scent and what happened with Muscles and Muffin Top's trunks last evening.

I headed for the door only to turn around with my hand on the handle as I thought of something else. "I gotta ask, do I really smell like burnt chocolate?"

"Yes, you do. And Mills?"

I hesitated. "Yes?"

"Report in an hour to Jamie in the center of the compound for punishment. And try not to kill Stacy."

Busted. Guess I wasn't getting away with that after all. I wondered what this punishment would be, then thought of how Fox Face wasn't going to get a last minute pardon, and grinned. "I'll try not to kill her." Try being the operative word here.

One hour was just enough time for the exhaustion to set in. I dug out the sweaty garbage-scented clothing that I'd worn yesterday and put it back on, vowing that I needed to at least run it through the laundry tonight if I didn't make it to the compound store to buy extra workout, and work, clothing. Then I brushed my teeth and left behind my sleeping roommates to go meet Jamie.

Well, sleeping roommates minus one. Fox Face hadn't been there, although from the hastily-made bed, I could tell she got more sleep than I had last night.

Jamie and Fox Face were both waiting for me, the latter with a slightly puzzled look on her face.

"What did you do?" she asked, not masking the hostility in her voice.

"Killed seven in one blow," I told her. Judging from the wary expression on her face, she didn't get the fairy tale reference.

Jamie glared, ending the conversation, then she looked at the stopwatch in her hand. "Ten-mile circuit. If you're not back in an hour, you need to do it again. Two-legged, human form only. Go."

Fucking hell. I'd just spent the whole night walking all over the woods, not including my run back to the compound. Shifters were fast, but holding a six-minute pace for ten miles was brutal. But I didn't have time to contemplate that, or much else because Jamie had clicked the stop watch and Fox Face had already taken off.

Having only been here a few days, I wasn't as familiar with the area as other pack members, and although I knew the ten-mile circuit was the trail with the red blazes, I'd waste too much time slowing down to check for the markings on the trees to finish in the required time, so I did something that had my beast ready to rip out of my skin—I followed Fox Face.

My beast was pissed off beyond belief that I hadn't passed her, or attacked her, but even she didn't want to run a second ten miles in one morning, so I held position, keeping close enough to Fox Face that I didn't lose her. I had no idea if we were on the right path or not since I was jumping rocks, winding around trees, and splashing through shallow streams at top speed, having no time to check the trees for the red blazes. I only hoped that Fox Face was equally reluctant to do a second ten-mile run, and wasn't leading me off course on purpose.

My lungs were burning, but when I snuck a peek at my watch I saw we were only four miles into the run, and not going to make it if we kept up this pace. I edged closer to Fox Face, and she yanked a branch forward as she rounded a corner, letting it fly back to smack me in the face.

Bitch. I could feel the blood on my face before the wound sealed, and ducked to avoid another branch. I needed to pass her. Not only was the idea of running another six miles dodging branches completely unacceptable, but Fox Face was going too slow to make the run in our required time. Either she planned on pulling some Usain Bolt sprint the last few miles, or she wasn't able to hold the pace. And if I stayed behind her, not only would my face be covered with whip marks from the branches, but I'd find myself needing to scream past her and run the last mile at the speed of a jet airplane. I needed to get around her now, or reconcile myself to doing a second ten-mile run.

Of course, getting around Fox Face proved to be problematic. The trail was narrow, and the few times I tried to pass her, she swerved and cut me off. There's no way I could head through the brush and keep up the speed I needed to get around her, so I held back and waited.

Three miles left. There was another stream crossing and I took it wide, speeding up to get around her. She did the same and we reached the bank at the same time. I flung out my arm to knock her back, and she did the same with her foot. I tripped, landing face-first in the mud, looking up to see Fox Face vanishing around a corner.

Fuck. Fuck! Not only was she still ahead, but I'd need to waste time looking at the blazes or risk getting lost. My beast and I both snarled in frustration, and I jumped to my feet, fury fueling my adrenaline.

I caught up to her with two miles left to go, and when we came out of the woods and into a meadow, I put on the speed, each breath like fire as I pushed past her to take the lead. But even ahead, I still couldn't slow down, not if I wanted to make it in time, so I kept running, gasping for air as my muscles quivered and screamed. My watch beeped just as I rounded the corner of the lake, and I tried to sprint, giving everything I had to make it up that hill and to where Jamie stood waiting with her stopwatch. I tore past her, heard her click the watch, then fell to the ground, tears in my eyes as I struggled to steady my breathing. Fuck, that was tough. If I didn't make it in the hour and needed to run it again, I was going to just walk the damned thing.

Fox Face ran past Jamie. She was obviously beat, but still had enough energy to place a weak "accidental" kick in my thigh as she went past. Jamie looked at her stop watch and strolled over to us as we lay panting on the ground. I heard Fox Face retch and grinned. I was in pain. I was exhausted. But at least I wasn't dry heaving in the grass.

"Mills, fifty-nine minutes and twenty seconds. Hammond…"

Please let it be over an hour. Please let it be over an hour.

"Fifty-nine minutes, fifty-eight seconds."

Damn it all, she'd made it with two seconds to spare. I shot Jamie a narrow-eyed look, wondering if she'd fudged the time for Fox Face. It certainly had seemed like I'd come in more than forty seconds ahead of her, but I'd been too winded to check my watch.

"Nice job, ladies," Jamie commented, stuffing the stop-watch in her pocket before turning to leave. "Let's hope I don't see either of you here tomorrow."

* * *

I'D BEEN a bit peeved to find out that my punishment run didn't take the place of morning drills. No sooner had Fox Face and I returned to the dorm, but we needed to head back out again for more sprints, this time carrying logs. After that, I managed to grab a quick shower, then drag my aching body into work. It was recycle day, which wasn't quite as dirty and smelly as regular garbage day, I discovered. After collecting everything from the bins, I sorted it, then loaded it into the bed of a pickup and headed into town.

This was my first time off the compound since I'd arrived, not counting my tracking the hunters last night, and

I was a bit concerned about getting lost. The truck had a GPS on the dash, and I'd been left a map and a set of directions for the recycle center, but I still took it slow, pausing at each turn. Once I was out onto the paved road, the drive went quicker, and the town was only fifteen miles away, not the hours I'd been dreading.

I had no idea what this town was called. No one had told me, and there wasn't a sign as I pulled into town. Following the directions, I headed toward the rear of a gas station, where there was a line of dumpsters, each labeled with the appropriate recycle type. I tossed the contents of my bins in accordingly, then raided the truck's cup holder for enough change to buy a soda.

It was pretty sad that I didn't have enough money to buy a vending machine drink. The last two days I'd gotten kind of used to having the pack provide everything, but this brought home to me how very little I had in life to call my own. Not that I'd ever needed much, but it would be nice when payday came and I could at least have enough cash on hand to get a soda or order a new pair of jeans.

By the time I pulled back into the compound, it was lunchtime, and I was starved. I'd skipped breakfast in favor of a lengthy shower, and my stomach was reminding me very loudly of that fact. Work done, I grabbed a quick bite to eat, changed my clothes, and headed to the Alpha House for the afternoon sparring session with Jake.

I was nervous, and not just because I was stupid enough to have eaten right before I was going to get the crap beaten out of me.

Jake was in his office, and far from taking me to task about my part in the dorm room incident, he barely even spoke to me as we walked down to the gym.

"Are we sparring on four legs today?" Jake asked, eyeing my jeans.

"No, I'd rather fight in human form." It had been hard enough to control my beast on patrol last night. I feared sparring would quickly turn into more purposeful fighting if I let her out of my skin, and I didn't want to put Jake in a position where he'd have to rip my head off to save his own.

"Fencing? I'd suggest boxing, but I think those jeans are a bit tight for the footwork."

I reached down and unsnapped them, scooting them down over my hips. "I'll spar sans pants, then. I don't have any workout clothes besides the pair I wore this morning, and they could probably stand up on their own after that ten-mile sprint I had to do."

His lips twitched. "You've only got one pair of leggings? No sweat pants? Jogging shorts?"

"One pair." I folded my jeans and set them to the side, bending over at the waist so he could get a good look at my ass. Too bad I didn't have any fancy underwear. Hopefully Jake found six-for-three-dollar nylon panties sexy. "So are we going to do this or not? You gonna take off your pants too? I mean, we should really make this fair."

I turned around to see him watching me with an odd expression on his face. "Think I'll keep my pants on. Feel free to take your shirt off, though."

I ignored the sarcasm in his voice and pulled my shirt over my head, tossing it on top of my jeans. My sports bra covered more than a bikini top would, and it wasn't like shifters weren't used to seeing each other naked all the time anyway.

He shook his head, and I felt a bit let down that he wasn't overcome with lust at the sight of me clad in only discount-store underwear. His loss.

An instructor, heck, a gentleman would have waited for me to make the first move, but I'd hardly taken a breath to ask which style we were using today when I was on my back from a solid kick in my stomach. I hooked a leg around his ankle and pulled, but didn't have the best angle for leverage and barely budged him. Another kick came toward my side and I rolled toward it, grabbing his leg. I yanked, twisting the one leg while pulling the other and managed to at least get him on his ass for a hot second before he sprang to his feet.

Guess that was my cue to get up as well.

"Did you check up on my story today?" I asked, trying to distract him with conversation.

He threw a quick series of jabs and I danced backward out of reach. "I followed your mink scent to the road, and picked up the smell of the car you were following, but lost it ten miles out. I never did smell any humans, though."

He didn't believe me. He figured I just turned into a mink and went on a merry jaunt through the forest instead of patrolling like I was supposed to. Now I was the one distracted, and I found myself on the receiving end of an uppercut to the jaw that rocked my head and spun me around. I spat blood and a tooth to the ground and wiped my mouth on my arm. Damn, that one hurt.

"Kind of odd, you know, smelling a moving car without the scent of humans in it. As far as I know, we don't have any self-driving vehicles here, so whoever was in the car must have had a magical means of hiding their scent."

He did believe me.

"Maybe they just had a really big-ass bottle of Febreze."

I smiled and swung a few wild punches, leaving a stupidly big opening on my left. Jake swung for it and I spun, nailing him hard in the shin with the heel of my foot. I heard bone crack and he staggered back, bending down to position the leg so it healed properly. I took that opportunity to bring my knee up hard into his face and he fell back, nose gushing blood.

"Dirty trick, Mills," he commented, wiping the blood on the bottom of his shirt.

"All's fair," I quipped, snapping another kick at him as he rose. This time he was ready and grabbed my leg, tucking it under his arm and turning. I felt the strain on my hip and tried to turn with it, but wasn't fast enough. With an agonizing pop, my leg came out of joint.

It's really fucking hard to dislocate someone's hip, even for a shifter. They are big-ass joints, with a deep ball-and-socket fit. So even though I was squirming on the ground in pain, I was filled with admiration at the strength and ability of my Alpha to do it in one quick move.

Luckily my hip had snapped back into joint once he'd let go and it took me seconds for it to heal enough for me to stand. It still hurt, as did my jaw and my ribs where he'd kicked me. Shifters heal fast, and we're fairly impervious to pain, but that didn't mean those recently injured nerve endings didn't keep sending lovely reminders to our brain that what just happened wasn't something we wanted to repeat.

Unlike I'd done, Jake hadn't hit me when I was down. He waited until I'd gotten to my feet before sending me backward with a lightning-fast series of kicks and punches. I redirected as many of them as I could, but still found myself with my back to the padded wall. Jake had me hemmed in and try as I might to duck or scoot to either side, he blocked me at every turn. Suddenly he was too close for me to hit or kick at all, too close even to head-butt. I tried to raise my knee and nail him in the balls, but his thigh blocked my action.

"Yield?" He asked, his arms caging mine in, his breath against my face. Fucker was so close I couldn't do much more than bite him. Or kiss him.

I did the latter, gripping his shirt at the waist with my

hands to make sure he didn't squirm away. I could feel a very satisfying sense of shock and surprise, but instead of pulling backward or even breaking our kiss, he deepened it, his tongue tasting and exploring. He pressed himself against me and I felt breathless—both from his kiss and the weight of him. I was far from a virgin, but the force of this man, the raw power that poured from his skin like a fire against my own was intoxicating. I felt myself mold to him, unable to do more. Every inch of him was pressed to me, immobilizing me against the wall. I couldn't even get in a hip grind if I tried.

Finally, he broke our kiss, his lips so close they were still almost touching mine.

"Yield?" I asked him, my voice husky and low. Right. I was absolutely helpless, unable to move. Clearly he had the upper hand. For now.

He chuckled, leaning in for another kiss—this one soft and lingering. "Mills, I'm pretty sure I yielded the first day you walked into my office."

Then he pulled away, striding across the room to pick up my clothing and toss it toward me. "Get dressed. Get some sleep. I need you to come to a meeting after lunch tomorrow —a continuation of this special project. Make sure you're well rested."

That was it? No screwing on the floor? Or sex against the wall? Hopefully this was going somewhere or I'd be spending my first paycheck on a good vibrator. Or heading into town to pick up some human for a quick fling.

I was frustrated, but I was also humming with a very unfamiliar excitement. I didn't want a vibrator or hard-and-fast sex with a human, I wanted Jake. And as I slid on my pants, I realized something else.

I was fitting in. I might still be a square peg in a round hole, but I was starting to find a place in this pack. I had a friend, even if she was a sixteen-year-old girl. I had an Alpha that could kick my ass, and seemed happy to do so on a daily basis. I had an Alpha who believed me, who valued the weird psychotic skills I brought to the table. And I got the feeling that if Jake valued me, it would only be a matter of time until the rest of the pack did as well.

They might not completely trust me. They might still be a bit afraid of me. But at least they'd value me. Finally, after all these decades, had I found a pack to belong to? Had I found an Alpha that my beast respected?

Had I found a man that I could possibly come to love?

CHAPTER 12

I woke up in the morning staring at the pile at the end of my bed. I wasn't the only one. Presents. Just like Christmas morning, except without the bows and wrapping paper. Mir stirred in her bed, her eyes foggy with sleep until she saw the stash. Then she bolted upright and stared just like the rest of us.

Well, it wasn't like I expected these things to explode so I eased out of bed and went over to the pile to sort through it. Three pairs of workout pants and tops. Two pairs heavy-duty tan work pants. A cell phone, activated and loaded with numbers that I assumed were for my pack members. And best of all, a coffee maker and two bags of dark-roast coffee grounds.

I had no doubt who they'd come from, because the whole lot smelled like Jake. I did wonder how the heck he'd managed to sneak in the dorm room like a werewolf Santa Claus, deliver these gifts, and leave without anyone noticing.

"Something you wanna tell us, Mills?" Muffin Top asked with a grin.

"Nope," I replied.

"Jake never gives presents," Boobs announced. "Well, except for the year-end gifts that everyone gets."

"Did you have sex with him?" Fox Face asked. "How many blow jobs did you have to give him?"

Muscles snorted. "Like any of us would need to be bribed to give Jake blow jobs. Heck, I'd probably pay *him* for the privilege."

"And for a bunch of stuff I could get free at the compound store, if I ever had five minutes to go there and get them?" I scoffed. "I don't think any of this warrants even one blow job."

"Cell phones, coffee makers, and coffee aren't free at the compound store," Mir pointed out, scooting to the end of her bed to pick up the cell phone. "And Jake put his phone number in your favorites. That's so romantic."

I snatched the phone out of her hands. "I've got some special assignment things I'm doing. There was an issue the other day where I didn't have a phone to report in on something. I'm sure this will all come out of my paycheck."

No one looked convinced at my words.

"Seriously," I told them. "It's not like he gave me a flowers and edible underwear or anything. This is all work stuff. Totally non-romantic."

"Seems pretty romantic for Jake," Muscles chimed in.

"Think you're still gonna owe him at least one blow job," Fox Face added.

I couldn't help but smile with uncharacteristic happiness as I put on my new workout clothing and brewed up my coffee. It was early, and I was still tired even though I'd skipped dinner and gone straight to bed. All the physical activity had worn me out, and I'd nearly fallen asleep doing sweeps around the compound with Robin trying to pick up the scent, or rather the lack of scent, from the hunters.

They'd come disturbingly close to the houses and dorms.

It made my beast bristle to realize that right under the sensitive noses of my pack-mates, these guys had snuck near enough that they could have shot and killed quite a few of us before we were able to take cover and defend ourselves. She was on high alert, demanding that I walk the perimeter several times a day just to make sure they weren't coming back.

Physical exhaustion was one thing, but being in a constant state of awareness, tense and ready for any attack drained me even more. I was the only one who could sense these guys. I was the only one who could sound the early warning if we were about to be attacked. Me. The safety of this pack depended on me. And *that* was the most terrifying thing of all.

CHAPTER 13

$\mathcal{I}$ hadn't been told where in the vast house the meeting was being held, so once more I used my nose, working through a whole host of unfamiliar scents to isolate both Jake and his second and follow them to the rear of the building. I thought I was on time, but when I entered, I realized I was probably the last to arrive. Jake was seated at the head of a huge table, Jamie to his right. To his left was a skinny redheaded woman that I'd not met yet. Next to her was a bear shifter—a really hot grizzly guy. My beast perked up because he was sexy as all get out, a grizzly, which was pretty rare in the lower forty-eight, and there was something weird about him. He smelled one hundred percent like a grizzly shifter, but there was something my beast sensed that made her drool a little.

Well, she was out of luck because it was completely obvious the bear was screwing Skinny Redhead.

Next to Jamie was my pilot from the other day, Dustin. And next to him was a woman who I assumed was an elf from her pointy ears and white gossamer-fine hair. As much as my beast wanted to rub herself all over the bear, she was scared of the elf-woman. Scared. My beast wasn't scared of anyone, not even Jake who she had a sort of wary respect for, but she was close to terrified of this elf.

I sat next to the bear, which put me across from the elf. I wasn't happy about being that close to her, but at least she was in front of me where I could keep an eye on her. My beast would have ripped out of my skin if I'd had this pointy-eared woman at my back, so this was the best compromise I could come up with.

"Tupper Mills," Jake announced. Then he introduced the others. Skinny redhead was the second from the Juneau Pack, and the bear was her mate. The terrifying elf-woman was that sidhe who'd done the divination the other night, and from the careful language Jake used I gathered she was an advisor to the pack, as well as a guest member, and a few formalities away from being Dustin's mate.

That made my eyes bug out. Dustin, the cool, chill, friendly, gets-along-with-everyone pilot was the almost-mate of this ethereal creature that I was pretty sure could kill me with a snap of her elegant fingers. I'd thankfully never met an angel before in my life, but I honestly thought she was probably just as intimidating as one of them would be.

They all stared at me awkwardly. The grizzly's eyes swept over me, then narrowed, but he didn't say anything.

The sidhe did. "She's not a shifter."

Even more awkward.

"She's the newest member of our pack," Dustin told her gently.

Gwylla, the sidhe, looked over at Jake for a moment, a strange look of comprehension descending on her face. "Oh. Because, Jake…I completely understand."

Well then, she was the only one. Jake smelled like a shifter, no matter what his parentage. No one else in my entire life had ever told me there was anything amiss with my scent aside from Jake the other night. Unless I purposely changed it, that was. Right now I smelled like a werewolf. At least I thought I smelled like a werewolf.

"Sabrina, can you begin by briefing us?" Jake said to the skinny redhead, not acknowledging what Gwylla understood or inquiring into what she thought I was.

The Juneau Pack second slid a tablet into the center of the table with a map on it. "Karl and I confirmed that the spot Gwylla identified is where the hunting company has their weapons stockpile."

"All we need now is the go-ahead to take them out," the bear said.

Jake's blue eyes met mine. "That's why Tupper is here."

Here, at this meeting, or here in the pack. I felt cold at the thought. Had Jake taken me in because he thought I might be worth saving, or had me taken me in because I could be of use to him and the pack? My mind detoured into cynic territory. I was a killer. Murdering humans in a spectacularly bloody fashion while destroying an arsenal of weapons wouldn't be a moral problem for my beast. And when all was said and done, the Alpha could act shocked and dismayed that such brutal justice had been delivered. I'd be put down, as I was no doubt going to be anyway, and my killings along with my death would serve a purpose. I'd deliver the justice they wanted, and they could make me the scapegoat, claim I was rogue and excuse my behavior with apologies to the local law enforcement, stating that I'd been put down. How useful my death would be.

Something flickered in Jake's light eyes. "You're here because you're smart, Tupper. You're new to the pack and to Alaska and you'll provide fresh eyes and insight into things that the rest of us might overlook. Plus you have a talent— one that you've proven to me. We need you."

I wasn't sure that I believed him. I was a tool. Just when

I'd thought maybe I'd found a pack I might be able to fit into, friends, a way to keep my beast on her leash, a job I kinda enjoyed, I walk into this meeting and realize that was all a fantasy. I'd never fit in. At least this way my death would have some sort of purpose. A martyr was better than just some crazy experiment gone wrong that needed to be killed and wiped from the history books.

"Anyway," Sabrina said, her gaze darting back and forth between me and my Alpha. "The bullets are being warehoused here." She pointed to a spot on the map, then spread her fingers to zoom in to a concrete building that looked like it had been a gas station at one time, out in the middle of the woods on a rural paved road. "There is security around the building, as well as a guard. There are also magical wards and traps which made it impossible for us to determine the exact nature and quantity of what's inside."

Maybe we could just nuke the whole thing. Fly over it in Dustin's plane and drop one big-ass bomb on it all.

"We need to get in, destroy the ammunition or steal it so we can destroy it elsewhere. And to do that, we need a plan," Sabrina added.

I immediately thought of my nuke-it-from-above idea. I hoped they weren't relying on me for a feasible plan, because I hadn't had a feasible plan in my life—not even concerning what was for dinner or what to do on the weekend.

"Gwylla can't do this for us," Dustin said. "All it takes is one bullet, one knife, or a toaster to the head, and she's seriously injured or dead. I don't want her to take that risk unless it's absolutely a last resort."

"I'll go," the bear volunteered. "I'm pretty sure bullets won't affect me the same way they do other shifters. I'll just need an idea of what I might be up against magic-wise and some suggestions on how to counter those spells."

"I'll go as well," the skinny redhead chimed in.

"No, you will not," the bear replied.

There was a staring contest between them, a struggle for dominance that had me sweating. The rest of the table remained silent, so I did, letting this bear and his mate battle it out.

Finally, he brushed the hair back from her face with his hand, and tucked it behind her ear. "Can't lose you, Brina. You got shot once already. I can't go through that again. Please let me handle this one without you."

Her eyes softened and she turned her face into his palm. I resisted the urge to gag, secretly wanting to kill the pair of them. I'd never inspired that sort of worry, ever—not even the wolves who'd been tasked with raising me. Never had there been someone who told me something was too dangerous, that they couldn't risk losing me. Between Dustin expressing that for the sidhe, and this bear with his mate, I was having a serious case of envy.

"I don't want you to go by yourself," the skinny redhead told the bear, her voice soft.

Gag. Ick. Yuck. Puke.

"Then I'll take her." The bear jutting a thumb over in my direction. I looked behind me, just to make sure he wasn't pointing at someone else.

"Me?"

"Yeah, you," he grumbled.

Jake nodded. "Good. This needs to happen soon. Mills, you're relieved of your other job for the next twenty-four to forty-eight hours with the possibility for extension. I'll set up an expense account for you to use while you're off the compound. Let Miranda in accounting know if you need anything specific. Karl, make a list of weapons, equipment, or other things and we'll provide them."

I clamped my jaw tight and schooled my expression into one of bland indifference. I was expendable. Gwylla couldn't go because a valuable pack resource couldn't be at risk. Sabrina couldn't go because her mate loved her and didn't want her to be hurt again. But no one loved me. I was expendable. No one cared if I lived or died. I had been about to propose dropping a nuke on the place, and now I realized that that's exactly what they were going to do. I was the nuke. Why they were bothering to send Karl was beyond me. Probably to keep me in line and make sure I didn't kill half the state in the process of taking this facility out.

And if I died, oh well. One less thing for Jake to have to take care of. It wasn't like anyone would miss me. Mir's mother would most likely have a party and dance on my grave.

Sabrina pulled up a satellite view of the building on her tablet and began making little red X's on it with a stylus. "There's a guard, most likely armed with a fully automatic weapon positioned here. He circles the building every half hour, but he's got to be bored sitting out there in the middle of nowhere."

"Don't underestimate his ability to be alert and ready," Jake added. "And there will most likely be alarms that will go off before you even get near the building."

"Physical alarms are here and here," Sabrina said. "And my nose tells me there are explosives in these spots. They tried to cover up the smell with bear urine, but they used too much."

Karl grunted. "As if a brown bear would walk that close to the building and empty a gallon of piss on the ground. Dumb asses."

"The magic wards and defenses will be subtler," Gwylla said, pulling the tablet over toward her. "There are most likely alarm wards surrounding the building, one probably a barrier keyed to keep shifters out. I think it would also keep angels out, since the magic Talligie used plays off the angel within your systems."

The bear nodded. "I can probably break through those, but there's nothing I can do about not setting off those alarms."

"You'll just need to hurry, and maybe one of you can act as a decoy for the other," Gwylla said. "Then here, here, and here are where there are likely to be additional defenses."

Dustin pulled the tablet his way and frowned down at it. "Who put these in place? Did Talligie do this before you killed him?"

Gwylla shrugged, the human gesture looking odd on her. "Possibly. I don't want to rule out the chance that these men could have a mage or another elf working with them. You'll need to be extra careful."

That wasn't a word in my vocabulary, and I got the feeling it wasn't in Karl's either.

I reached across the table and slid the tablet over my direction, figuring if I was going to be the sacrificial lamb, or rather sacrificial monster, I had a right to see what I was up against.

"One guard. Explosives and magical shit. The ammo is probably locked up." I turned to the bear. "You know how to pick a lock?"

"No, I was just going to bust a hole through the safe or haul it out with me."

"It's probably too big to haul out with us, and punching a hole through several inches of steel takes muscle we probably don't have. And if we do, it will take time we don't have."

"I'll get you a set of lock picks by tonight," Jake told me. "I'm assuming you know how to pick a lock?"

Because I was the bad seed, the monster who killed and vandalized and stole shit. But he was right, I did know how to pick a lock. "Yeah. Get me some C-4 while you're at it, because there are some locks I can't pick."

The Alpha didn't even bat an eyelid. "Will do."

"So I can assume I'm going to be shot full of bullets, most of them coated with magic that will force me to shift, rot my insides, and probably turn me more rogue than I already am. I'm going to most likely be blown up once if not twice. Then there's some magical shit that will fireball my ass, and turn me into a frog or something."

"Hope it turns you into a huge, badass frog," Karl commented. I was beginning to like this bear.

"With fangs and claws, and poison spit," I told him. "I'd be okay with the frog thing if I could spit poison at people."

"Of course you would," Jake interrupted. I could tell he was holding back from a major eye roll. "And if you do this smart, you won't be a frog, get shot, or get blown up."

Smart like how? Because I was a force of destruction, the muscle. I wasn't the sneak in and get shit done kind of person.

"What's the plan?" I asked Karl.

The bear raised an eyebrow and I could tell he was not the sneak in kind of person either. "Can you shoot? Maybe we can sniper the guard and at least we can cross getting shot off the list."

Dustin winced. "What if he's just a guy hired to do security duty? It's not going to look good if we sniper-shoot a mall cop picking up some extra money on the side."

"He's not a mall cop," Sabrina assured him. "He's got an automatic weapon to guard what looks like an abandoned gas station. And he wouldn't hesitate to shoot and kill you."

"Doesn't matter because I can't hit the broad side of an industrial complex," I told them. "How about Dustin flies overhead and I jump out of the plane?"

Everyone stared at me in amazement. "You have a form

with wings?" Sabrina asked, exchanging a quick glance with Karl. "Or you just have wings?"

"Like an angel?" I snorted. "Uh, no. And I don't have an avian form either. I was just thinking of jumping out of the plane. It would hurt, and I'd probably smash right through the roof, but I'd be in without being exploded or turned into a frog, and it would provide a huge distraction for Karl here to jump the guard and be the one getting blown up."

"Unfortunately the magical protections most likely extend to the roof, so you'd still wind up a frog," Gwylla said.

"Guess we're both getting blown up after all," Karl told me.

That, or we thought of something else once we were there and had an opportunity to check the place out first hand rather than staring at it on a tablet. "When do we leave?" I asked Jake.

"After dinner." He slid a set of keys across the table to Karl. "Take the black truck. I'll have weaponry, the C4, the lock-picks, and other supplies loaded and ready."

Hey, how come I didn't get to drive? I might have only been a member of this pack for a few days, but I was still a member, where Karl wasn't even a werewolf.

"Shotgun," I told the bear, even though I was the only other one going on this trip.

He nodded. "Only if you behave. One wrong move from you and you're riding in the truck bed."

I grinned, knowing that he wouldn't hesitate to follow through on that threat. Although truck bed would be a whole lot better than tied like a dead deer to the roof. Which, from what I could make of this bear, wouldn't be completely out of the question either.

$\mathcal{M}$ir once more led me over to her parents' table for dinner. I was perversely delighted and plopped my ass down next to her mother with a huge smile. I would have hugged the woman had I not been convinced that would start a brawl that might end up with someone dead. Not me. Although if I killed a pack mate, I had no doubt Jake would be lopping my head off come sundown.

"How did your day go?" Mir asked, bubbly with excitement and enthusiasm. "I can't imagine taking care of the garbage would be much fun. After your three-month probationary period, you should ask for a reassignment."

"I like it," I confessed. "It's physical, which is something I need. And it's solitary, which is also something I need." There was something else I liked about the job that I couldn't quite put my finger on. I got the idea it had to do with cleaning up the compound, disposing of the unwanted and undesired remnants of living here. It might be a cliché metaphor, but I was finding that I liked being the one who took out the trash.

"And what about the special assignment? You had another meeting today?" Mir's eyes were huge, and although she whispered, it was loud enough that I'm sure every shifter in the compound could hear it. Her parents certainly could because they looked over to me in surprise.

"I'm not sure that I'm at liberty to discuss the details, but I'm heading out after dinner and probably won't be back until late tomorrow or maybe the next day. So don't worry if you don't see me around for a few."

It was important to me that Mir not worry, that she knew my absence didn't have anything to do with her or our friendship. I'd miss her. I'd been excited as all get out to see her after work and have dinner with her.

"Oh." Mir's face fell. "I'll miss you. Be careful. I mean, I'm sure nothing bad will happen, and you're probably better able to take care of yourself than any werewolf in the compound, but be careful."

My tiny little heart grew ten times the size at her words. "I will. I'll bring you back a present."

I don't know what made me say that. It wasn't like I was going to some exotic location where they sold tourist baubles. I would bring her back something, though. Maybe a broken part of the safe, or a piece of the building.

Mir clapped her hands together at the idea. "Oh, cool! I like red, by the way. And I wear a size four."

I was pretty sure the guard wasn't wearing red and that he wasn't a size four, so that ruled out bringing her his shirt. Hopefully she'd accept something besides a T-shirt as an appropriate gift, or I'd be trying to convince Karl to detour to a Walmart on our way back.

Did they even have Walmarts in Alaska? I guess that was something I'd need to check into.

"You're leaving? On a special assignment?" There was disbelief in Kathleen's voice. And relief. I knew she was hoping I wasn't going to be coming back.

"Who are you going with?" Mir's father asked. It was the

first I'd heard him say anything besides his panicked pleas with his wife to not rock the boat with our Alpha the other night.

I shrugged. "Some Karl dude. He's a bear. Evidently he's the mate of the second in the Juneau Pack."

They both stared at me in shock.

"He's…" Mir's father grimaced. "Well, at least we don't need to worry about you killing him."

Probably not. I got the impression Karl could hold his own in a fight. Funny that I'd spent most of my life trying to keep my beast from wanting to kill just about every shifter or human I met, and in the space of less than two days, I'd met several beings who my beast was uncertain if she could best. And that didn't include that sidhe, Gwylla, who she just wanted to avoid like the plague.

"We've been working with the other two Alaska packs to deal with the hunters." Mir shot me a concerned look. "Did you hear about that down in the lower forty-eight? There are humans up here with special magic on their bullets that kill us. And they're hunting us like we're animals. We're not supposed to leave the compound alone, and we're supposed to carry a satellite phone and wear a protective vest as well as carry a bottle of that antidote if we go out."

"Jake briefed me," I told her. Hopefully Jake would put the satellite phone, vest, and antidote in the bag with the C4 and lock picks, because I didn't have time after dinner to go grab all this stuff.

"Make sure you take a bottle," Mir reminded me, her voice full of worry. "Just in case you get shot. That way you won't die."

"Don't worry," I assured her. "I'll be careful, and we'll take care of the bad guys. Soon it will be safe for you to go into town and shop and hang with your human friends again."

"I hope so," she whispered. "I used to go to the human

school, but my parents pulled me out in May when Leon got shot."

"They didn't seem to be targeting our young, or shifters in populated areas, but we can't be too careful when it comes to our children," Mir's father explained.

"Well, they shot Sabrina in front of a restaurant full of humans, so I think we made the right choice," Kathleen countered. "At first we thought it was just psychos trying to take our pelts as trophies, as if we were some exotic game, but it seems to be more widespread than we'd thought."

Mir nodded. "It was those YouTube videos of shifters attacking people. It got everyone scared of us, even the Alaskan humans who know we exist and have lived side-by-side with us for generations. It gave people that hate us an excuse to claim they were killing us in self-defense, and scared the piss out of the humans in the lower states who didn't even know we existed."

"Mir. Language," her father warned. "As horrific it was that Sabrina was shot out in public like that, it did a lot for our PR. Lots of human witnesses defended her, saying she was shot in cold blood while just standing there reading the menu, and that the shooter endangered everyone with his actions. Then another guy came forward and exposed a bunch of them as murderers, saying that the self-defense thing was a sham. If we could just take out the rest of these murderers, I think we could go back to living in peace with the humans."

"I don't know," Kathleen countered. "I'm all for taking out these murderers, but I'm not sure I can ever trust humans again. Where were they after Leon was shot? Why did none of them come forward to defend us when those videos came out? There were humans who I'd known my whole life, who I had lunch with, bowled with, carpooled with, and none of them stood up for us."

I'd never thought of any of this when I'd been down in L.A. Here were hundreds of shifters who might never again trust their human neighbors, who might separate and grow even more isolated in the world. And when groups held themselves apart and didn't mingle in society, suspicions and fears went into overdrive. Things had been easier down south where we worked next to humans, not ever letting them know that we were werewolves. There we could fly under the radar, at least for a while. Here, the wolves were known. And especially in the Swift River Pack where we all lived together on a compound. Here such a division between humans and shifters would only hurt us both.

"Well, I want to go back to school," Mir announced. "I miss my friends, and I know they don't believe we're dangerous or weird. They'll stand up for me. They'll protect me if someone tries anything."

I wanted her to believe that. I wanted Mir to keep her Pollyanna innocence and faith in the good in people. I'd fight to keep her innocence, even though I was just as jaded as her parents. More so, because in addition to not trusting humans, I didn't trust shifters either.

Oddly enough, the conversation had served to shift Mir's parents' animosity from me to the human hunters, and for a brief moment, I felt as if I were truly an accepted part of the pack. It didn't last and by the time we'd finished the pulled pork and cornbread, they were back to frosty silence and wary side-eye glances.

After dinner Mir and I headed back to our room and she helped me pack for my assignment. We both agreed that I should take eyeliner and that kick-ass red lipstick, as well as my mascara. Just in case the assignment went overnight, we decided an extra pair of jeans and a black tank top along with a change of underwear would be appropriate. I stuffed my bug-out-bag of toiletries in the duffle, and turned around to see Mir holding up a leather corset with metal studs and grommets that I'd bought on a whim.

"Since I don't know what kind of special assignment this is, I'm going to recommend you bring this," she announced.

I snatched it out of her hands. "Uh, no. First of all, I don't want to get this bloody because it cost a fucking—I mean, fricken—fortune. Secondly, that bear Karl is screwing the skinny redhead and I get the impression he won't be looking twice at me. He loooooooves her."

"Wow," Mir sighed. "I hope some bear shifter feels that way about me someday."

I did a double take. "Don't you mean wolf shifter?"

Mir giggled. "Bears are really hot. Don't tell Mom, she'll freak, but I'd totally do a bear."

I'd been having sex since I was twelve, but I wasn't sure if Mir had at sixteen. "Have you…I mean, are you still…?"

"A virgin?" she scoffed. "No way. I've done it with two different human guys. One was at a party last year, then the other was this spring right before my parents pulled me from school. And I've gotten to second base with Dallas Strider in the woods next to the lake. I might have done more, but he's a really sloppy kisser. Ick. I hope other werewolves are better than Dallas, because otherwise I'm going back to screwing humans."

I had to force my jaw to close. "I really think you should wait until you date someone a few times, Mir. I mean, you're better than hooking up with random humans and some bad-kisser werewolf."

She frowned. "I know, but it's fun and I like sex. Don't you? I thought you would be all about screwing just because it felt good."

I was. And my beast was ready to slap a chastity belt on Mir for being the same as me.

"I do like sex, and yes, I screw every chance I get. But

hookups are like eating junk food. It's yummy and gives you a sugar rush, but it's not satisfying in the long run. Don't think the sugar rush is all that, because really caring about someone you have sex with is a million times better."

There. That sounded like something a normal person would say, something from a movie on the Hallmark Channel. *Do as I say, not as I do.*

She tilted her head and pursed her lips. "Did you care about someone? I just assumed…which is probably my bad. Was there someone you loved in your other pack? Do you miss them?"

My mind went to Jake, to that kiss in the gym. But that had been just an in-the-moment thing. I was a tool, a monster to launch at their enemies. I was expendable. All I'd had in my life was quick fucks—hard and fast and over the moment we'd both orgasmed. I ached from the lack of connection, just as I ached from the lack of friendship or any kind of loving parental figure. I didn't want Mir to go through that. This might be my life, but it didn't have to be hers.

"I've had more one night stands than you could count. And if I ever found a guy—shifter or not—that was more than just scratching an itch, I'd hold on with all my might. I'm broken, Mir. I'll never find that. I'll never find someone that loves me. But you will. Have fun and be safe, but don't have so much fun that you let that really awesome guy pass by. Because that's going to change your life. And I want you to have that."

She observed me as if I were an animal in a zoo—a really pathetic animal in a zoo, then launched herself at me and wrapped her arms around my waist in a tight hug. "I want you to have that too, Tupper. You're awesome. I love you already and I know there will be a great guy who will love you too. That bear shifter might be in love with Sabrina, but there will be a better guy for you. Maybe Jake. He needs someone to love him. And he bought you a coffee maker and a cell phone. I think you should fall in love with Jake."

I nearly choked at the thought. Sex with Jake might be on the table, but love? I was pretty sure that I could easily fall in love with Jake, but I doubted he'd ever be falling in love with me.

$\mathcal{I}$ was a bit later than expected heading out of my dorm room, but it had been hard to leave Mir behind. With my duffle over my shoulder, I jogged over to where all the pack vehicles were parked and found Karl standing beside the black truck, looking like he was on the verge of dozing off.

"Let's go, motherfucker!" I shouted, delighted to see him jump. Then I threw my bag in the bed and dashed around the back of the truck only to run head-first into a solid wall of man.

Jake.

I recovered quickly, bouncing away from him. "Seriously? Are you here to see us off? Are you going to break a champagne bottle on the side of the truck and throw streamers at us or something?"

"No, I'm going with you."

That caused my brain to do a screechy thing. "Why? Don't you trust me? Why bother to send me if you don't trust me? Why bother to even put me on this special assignment team if you don't trust me? And what exactly do you expect me to do? Kill the bear? Because I doubt I could even if I really, really tried. Screw up? Cause' that's a given, and you should have known that before you assigned me this shit."

Jake reached out and clamped a hand across my mouth. "Stop, before you say something that pisses me off and I have to kick your butt into Russia. I trust you to be you. No, I wouldn't have put you on this team, or agreed to let you go, if I didn't trust you to get the job done. And I'm going because this is serious. What happens here affects every shifter on a global scale, and I want to make sure it gets done the way I want it done. And I've got a bad feeling about this—call it a premonition. I don't want either you or Karl to wind up dead because I didn't listen to my intuition."

I blinked up at him in surprise, because that was a far more emotional statement than I'd ever expected cool, calculating Jake to be making. Whatever that premonition was, it had to be disturbing as fuck for him to be as unsettled as this.

"I'm going because…well, because I worry about you. I want to make sure you don't get shot or blown up or turned into a poison-spitting frog or something."

Someone worried about me. *Jake* worried about me.

He still had his hand over my mouth, so I bit it gently. He narrowed his eyes, and removed his hand. Then he leaned forward and kissed me, and all the fears, the worries I'd had melted away in a swirl of desire and emotion.

"You ready to do this, Mills?" he asked.

I was so ready to do this, but I got the feeling he wasn't referring to having hot sweaty sex up against the side of the truck with Karl standing on the other side.

"I'm ready," I told him. "And I still get shotgun."

His eyebrows lowered. "You most certainly do not get shotgun. I'm the Alpha here."

"Then you drive and Karl can ride in the back," I said, trying to edge around him.

He shoved me and I flew backward to skid across the gravel on my ass while he ran for the passenger door, laughing. Asshole. I jumped up and ran after him. Of course he was already in the passenger seat before I got there, smiling smugly and indicating with his thumb that I was to either climb into the tiny back seat or in the bed of the truck. I climbed in and plopped my ass down on his lap.

For a hot second he let me sit there, then he grabbed me and hoisted me over top of the seat into the back, slapping my rear firmly on the way. I heard Karl chuckle as I landed face-first in the cramped space.

"If you two are gonna start that shit, then you're going on your own. Don't care if you're Alpha of this pack or not, Jake, I'm not gonna ride along with you two acting out a low-budget porno in the truck."

I snickered, liking this bear more by the moment. But I felt the change in Jake, felt him suddenly realize how out of character he'd been acting. I don't know if that whole strict-as-shit Alpha was an act or not, but clearly he was a bit embarrassed by our shenanigans.

"All business, Karl," he promised. "Sorry about that."

Karl turned to face him, eyebrows practically in his hairline. "You're not one bit sorry. And don't be a stiff prick-face on my behalf, cause' I don't give a shit. You wanna grab ass with that demon-wolf, ain't no business of mine. Just don't wanna get all worked up myself without my Brina here to relieve the frustration. Know what I mean?"

Sadly, there was no more grab-ass. We drove through the night and well into the morning, stopping at a gas station where Jake ran in and bought a plastic bag full of beef jerky, granola bars, and Gatorade for our breakfast. The guys switched places with Jake driving exactly the speed limit with mind-numbing precision. Karl drove like an old lady. Jake drove like the car was set on auto pilot. I dozed, not really able to get more than ten minutes of sleep at a time.

"Last food until morning unless you catch it and skin it yourself." Karl's low voice woke me from a fitful nap and I blinked my eyes open to see the sun setting as Jake eased the truck into the parking lot of a burger joint.

We got out to stretch and Karl ran in with our food order, emerging with enough to feed a small army. I hadn't expected it to take us nearly a day to drive to wherever this stockpile of ammo was. The long roadtrip had blunted my excitement a bit and I found I'd settled into a kind of Zen peace, where I listened to Karl and Jake talk about the coming winter weather predictions, where we argued over the radio, where I occasionally caught Jake glancing at me through the rearview mirror as if he couldn't keep his eyes off me.

"Five bacon triple cheeseburgers and a bottle of water," Karl announced, handing a bag to Jake. "And the same with an extra-large chocolate shake for demon-wolf," he told me.

I opened the bag and inhaled, thinking nothing smelled so heavenly as bacon cheeseburgers. Then I scooted into the driver's seat and grabbed the keys out of the console.

"No. No you don't." Jake scowled. "Karl's driving the last stretch."

"Which will take three hours more than if I drive," I told him. "It's my turn. Karl can ride in the bed like a dog and you get the passenger seat. I'll even let you grope me while I drive."

"I'm not riding in the bed," Karl announced.

"And you're not driving." Jake reached in and hauled me out of the driver's seat, dumping me facedown over his shoulder.

That electricity arched between us. I lifted his shirt and put my hands on his warm skin, sliding them as far under the waistband of his pants as I could. Damn, this guy had an ass that could crack walnuts.

Jake didn't protest, letting me molest his backside as he carried me around the truck to the other side. Karl climbed into the driver's seat, and Jake hesitated a moment, allowing me to get a few seconds more of feeling him up before he slid me off his shoulder and down along the front of his body. Pulling my hips tight against him, he dug one hand into my short, purple hair and kissed me.

I ground against him, breathless, wanting him desperately.

"Any day now, guys," Karl growled.

"Five minutes in the burger joint bathroom," I whispered to Jake.

"I'm not making love to you in the bathroom of a roadside fast-food joint," Jake informed me, still making no move to pull away from me.

"Who said anything about making love? Let's fuck. Hard. Fast. Just bend me over the sink and shove yourself in as deep as you can go."

He inhaled sharply. "It's dirty in there. It's nasty."

I rubbed myself along him. "I'm dirty. I'm nasty. Three minutes, Jake. Or less. I'm so fucking wet right now that I'll probably come in two strokes."

"Guys." Karl growled.

Jake kissed me and I realized it would most likely take less than two strokes for me to come. Damn, I wanted this guy.

But he stepped back, his hands on my shoulders to keep me from closing the sudden distance between us. "No. Not here. Not like this. After we're done and can go somewhere with an actual bed and clean sheets. Not in a dirty bathroom."

"I'm starting the truck," Karl announced.

"But after we're done, I'll most likely be a poison-spitting frog," I complained. "Are you going to want to fuck a frog?"

"I'm driving away, now," Karl told us.

Jake chuckled. "I promise I'll have sex with you even if you're a frog. There. Are you happy? Because I've never said or envisioned saying anything as disgusting as that in my whole life."

"Leaving. Leaving now."

I smiled. "Stick with me baby. Fucking poison-spitting frogs is only the beginning. Be prepared for all sorts of perverted nastiness."

Karl edged the truck a few inches forward, and Jake hopped into the passenger seat. Then he grabbed me and yanked me in, setting me on his lap as he closed the door. Instead of shoving me into the back, he wrapped an arm around me holding me in place. Then he grabbed my bag of burgers and plopped them on my lap.

I ate, drank my milkshake, then dozed off for the best nap I'd had since we began this road trip, happily snuggled in Jake's arms.

It was full-on dark by the time Karl finally pulled off the road and edged the truck down a narrow dirt path. I could hear the branches slapping against the sides of the truck and scraping along the windows. He turned the headlights off, and even with my night vision, it was still creepy. I hoped the bear knew where we were going because I really didn't want to experience going over a cliff in a truck to smash onto a bunch of rocks and trees a few hundred feet down.

The truck slowed and stopped. Karl turned it off and slipped the keys above the visor. Jake opened the door and I scooted out. We were in fight mode. I knew things were serious because Jake didn't pinch my butt as I slid off his lap or even say anything to me. I stretched beside the truck while both Karl and Jake climbed out.

I'd never realized how truly dark it was out in the middle of fucking nowhere when there wasn't the slightest bit of light pollution. I'd been in the woods before at night, but this was completely different. The sky was like a blackout curtain that a moth had gnawed, the tiniest star clearly visible, the swoosh of constellations a blur of lighter gray amid the dancing white lights. I'd always felt comfortable making my way around the forest even on a moonless night, but the woods we were in were so thick with trees and leaves that outside of the spots where the sky was visible overhead, my surroundings were a solid black.

"You get used to it," Karl told me as he came around the front of the truck to join us. "I member' when I first came up here, I felt like maybe I'd gone blind. Worried that something had happened to my eyes at first cause' I couldn't see shit at night anymore."

"I'm less worried about seeing shit than walking off the edge of a cliff," I teased him. Although I wasn't sure if there were any cliffs nearby. The trees were different. The smells were different. Even the insect song seemed different. The whole thing had an odd rainforest feel that made me wonder how close to the coast we were.

Karl pulled a paper from his back pocket and unfolded it, spreading it out on the still-hot hood of the truck. "We're here. The old gas station is here."

I squinted at the map. Obviously, the old gas station that was our target was off of an old road. Whatever wards and traps the hunters had in place, they must have made allowances for the fact that a car or truck might occasionally go by every so often. It would have been stupidly obvious for us to just drive down the road, park and try to walk into the old gas station, but the hunters must have planned for the chance that a human might do that very thing. Someone stretching their legs in the middle of a long drive might use the old gas station to pull off the road and walk around, or even pull off to take a nap. That made me assume that either the protections would be set off by actual breaking and entering, or that they were somehow magically set up to only go off if a shifter crossed the lines.

And I was pretty sure if a human pulled in to take a nap, the armed guard would tell him to move along.

"You want to take the back and I'll take the front?" Karl asked Jake. "I'll shift and draw their fire, while you deal with the wards on the building?"

Jake frowned at the map. "Let's do a one-hour observation first, just to get an idea of the guard's routine and possibly get a feel for the other security, then we can pull back and decide on our actual attack strategy."

It was a smart idea. There was no knowing whether the security had changed since Karl and Sabrina had been out here a few days ago. Plus there might be things that Jake and I could pick up that the other two couldn't. Me especially. I clearly had the advantage nose-wise, and I seemed to be the only shifter so far that could sense the magic.

Jake and Karl looked at their watches, synchronizing them. I didn't have a watch. I did have a nifty cell phone I could use, though, if I really needed to be precise about time.

"We gotta be careful about sunrise," Karl added. "Ain't gonna be night for long."

"One-hour reconnaissance shouldn't push us too tight time-wise," Jake told him. "And if we're at all uncomfortable with proceeding, we can always push the actual attack to tomorrow night and spend the day observing and planning."

That would drive me fucking nuts. I just wanted to go in there, blow shit up, and take the ammo. I got the feeling if it had been just me and the bear, that's what we would have done. Jake was the cautious, planning one, and although Karl seemed okay going along with that plan, I was feeling like I wanted to knock my Alpha upside the head and do it my way.

"How quiet are you in your bear form?" Jake asked.

Karl chuckled. "Brina says I sound like a stampede of elephants. 'Course I'm not much quieter on two legs either."

"I'm thinking we send Tupper in, then." Jake turned to me. "Can you do something small? And sense any magical alarms enough to evade them? Ideally I'd like you to get inside and give us a better idea what we're up against once we take out the guard and make our way through whatever minefield they've got out front."

I nodded. "I can do a rat, and depending on how they have their magical wards set up, I might be able to get through them without them going off." I'd been thinking about this one. Those magical alarms had to be shifter specific, or else every fucking mosquito would be setting them off as well as the human guard. I was pretty damned good about masking my scent, but whether I could get through undetected or not would depend on what would trigger the alarm—and I just didn't know enough about magic to be sure on that.

"Gwylla feels most of the shifter-specific magic is triggered by the angel in us," Jake warned. "Don't be cocky and get blown up."

Angel. I was pretty far from an angel. I got the impression that although angels and demons were opposite sides of the same coin, things didn't always work the same between the two. And I was far more demon that I was angel.

"We'll have to go in slow," Karl said. "When Brina and I did our reconnaissance, we didn't want to get too close in human forms and tip them off."

Jake nodded. "This isn't the sort of location where hikers and pedestrians would be commonplace. They might suspect a wolf coming in close, but wild bears are more bold around humans."

Karl grunted. "I'll shift when we're near, so if the guards hear us and turn on a spotlight or use night vision goggles, they'll just think I'm some grizzly looking for berries in the woods."

"Then let's do this," Jake announced.

Karl folded up the map and stuck it back in his pocket.

"Do you want me upright, or on all fours right now?" I asked. I wasn't as noisy as Karl claimed to be, but I certainly wasn't as silent as Jake was. It would truly suck if I stepped on a twig and revealed our presence to the guards.

Something sparked in Jake's blue eyes at the sexual innuendo, and I heard Karl snort.

"What's your primary animal?" Jake asked.

I'd never had anyone ask before. They always assumed I was a werewolf since I'd been shuffled around wolf packs since the moment I was born. The truth was my animal was whatever my beast wanted to be at the time. Usually I could assume a fairly convincing wolf form, but there were times when she did something weird and I ended up looking like some horrifying animal mash-up. I blamed it on weird genetics.

"Wolf," I told him, figuring that was most likely what I'd be if I shifted. Then I added a "sometimes" in the spirit of honesty.

Jake's eyes narrowed. "And when you're not a wolf?"

I shrugged. "Lion, with a bird ass and no wings, and scales. Fuck if I know. It's a roll of the dice whether I'm a wolf or some horror-movie nightmare."

"Thinking you better stay on two legs then," Karl said. "Hoping when you do your rat thing, you look like a normal rat, though."

Yeah, me too. I followed the guys through the woods, glad they were leading the way and not me. Karl, true to his word, managed to step on every stick in our path. After about a half hour of walking, he stripped, stuffed his clothes into one of the backpacks then walked into the woods to shift. I can't tell you how thrilled I was that the moon was out and we were in a bit of a clearing so I could see Karl in all his naked glory.

Skinny Redhead was a lucky gal because, damn, that man had a sweet bod.

Seconds after Karl had walked into the woods, I felt something like static brush across my skin, sending every hair on my body upward. One of the biggest grizzlies I'd ever seen strolled out of the woods, shaking his fur into place.

"Kinda big, Karl," Jake commented. "Can't you do something a bit smaller, otherwise they're going to shoot you anyway."

Karl stared at him and curled his lip, revealing some truly lethal teeth.

"Okay," Jake sighed. "Let's go. Quiet from here on out. And Karl, stay about fifty yards off to the left of us in case they hear you. I don't want Tupper or me to get spotlighted or picked up in night vision glasses."

"I can drop my body temperature if that would help," I told him.

"It's forty-five degrees out here," Jake replied. "A few degrees difference in your body temperature is still going to show up."

I opened my mouth to tell him I could drop my temperature to forty-five degrees, but then decided to keep my trap shut. Some secrets were best kept to myself, and I didn't really want Jake to know that I could shamble around like a zombie without any ill effects.

Karl was even noisier as a bear, and Jake waved to him, increasing the distance between us. After another hour I saw the thin gray ribbon of road through the trees, as well as our target.

We halted, then Jake motioned to me to do my thing. I stripped then shifted in one fluid movement into a rat.

Well, sort of a rat. I got the feeling that I was more like a diminutive wolverine, and from Jake's exasperated sigh, I probably didn't look like a creature that would be found in this world, let alone in Alaska.

I concentrated, glaring at my beast and trying to impress on her how serious this was. There were some minor adjustments that made me less of a freak, but still a nightmare-sewer-rat. I looked up at Jake for confirmation. He nodded, and with a squeak, I took off to the old gas station.

The place was a total dump. If Gwylla hadn't been so sure this was the spot, I would have walked right on by. It looked exactly like an abandoned gas station, complete with a collapsed awning over two ancient, rusted pumps, and plywood over the windows. As we got closer I realized that the plywood was strategically hinged, and the boards over the door would swivel out of the way to let someone in. I also noticed that the locks on the solid metal door were new, even though someone had smeared them with some greasy dirty substance to try to dull the shine. Weeds grew up through cracked pavement, and thick poison ivy covered the east side of the building. There were no lights, and I couldn't scent either the human guards, their weapons, the explosives, or any magical defenses.

I did smell bear pee. And like Karl said, it was insanely concentrated, as if an entire Russian circus had pulled off the road for a quick potty break. It made my nose itch and I struggled against the urge to sneeze.

Jake had pointed to the east corner of the building with all the Devil's Club and I made my way in that direction. I hesitated a few times, wiggling my nose and trying to see if I could manage to pick up anything untoward. Nothing seemed out of place, although to be fair, with the heady aroma of bear piss, I really couldn't smell much of anything else.

The guard rounded the corner and sat down on a concrete step leading up to the boarded-up door, setting the rifle by his side. He took out a phone and began typing. I doubted anything significant had happened for him to be alerting his boss because the dude hardly seemed on high alert. He was probably surfing Facebook or playing Super Mario or something. I kinda felt for the guy. This had to be the most excruciatingly boring job in the world, walking around an abandoned gas station with an assault rifle just in case a wolf decided to attack. He probably would have been better off with a mall cop job.

I ran to the second set of pumps, and a movement caught my eye at the edge of the building. It was tiny, as if a fly had disturbed one of the leaves on the wall, but as I looked, I saw another slight movement. And put together I realized that there was a second guard, this one employing the same magical cloaking means as the hunters had outside the compound. He was standing in front of the wall, completely unnoticeable except for little movements. There was no heat signature, no scent, nothing to indicate that a human with a big fucking weapon stood there, ready to blow my head off if I so much as sneezed. Which I really wanted to do. Fucking bear pee.

The guard moved, and if I hadn't been staring at him hard enough to make my eyes water, I would have missed it. He completely blended in with his surroundings and even his movements were no more than a faint ripple in the air. Illusion or an invisibility spell. Either way it was kick-ass and I wanted to know how I could get one of these myself. Mir said I'd get paid a wage for my sanitation job and that the money was mine to do with what I wanted. I'd been thinking I probably needed to get a cell phone, but since Jake had already bought me one of those, an invisibility spell just moved up on my most-wanted list.

"Is it midnight yet?"

I nearly jumped out of my fur, thinking for a split second that the guard was talking to me.

"No," the shimmer by the corner of the building replied. "Another twenty minutes. I hate this."

"Me too," the guy on the steps said, still typing on his phone. "When I took this job, I thought I was going to get to shoot some werewolves, not stand around an old building in the middle of nowhere."

"If I'd had five grand, I would have paid for a hunt. At least then I would have maybe had a chance at bringing home a trophy." The blur moved over and sat down on the steps next to the other guard.

"Grab a couple of those bullets in there before you leave tomorrow, and just go shoot your own werewolf. Or that bear woman on your block you keep talking about, the one with the BMW." The guy paused his typing and looked over his shoulder toward the building. "Not like those guys aren't pocketing a few right now."

"Five hundred a pop." Blurry guy snorted. "Even if I don't shoot that bear woman, I can sell them on the internet and make more than I am here."

These guys clearly weren't going to budge, and that shift-change or whatever was going to happen in twenty minutes wasn't something I had time to wait for, so I made my way forward. I could feel the magical wards, setting my fur to twitching from their weird static feel. I could smell the copious amounts of bear urine covering the physical explosives. With a careful, twisting path, I managed to make it to the porch, only to freeze in place as the guard suddenly turned around and saw me.

He yelped. "Jesus Christ, that's the biggest rat I've ever seen in my life."

Was I about to get shot? I really didn't want to get shot. The good thing about being a rat, no matter how huge, was that I was a smaller target than I would have been as a human. If I ran really fast, there was a good chance that this guy would only end up shooting a bunch of holes in the concrete wall of this building.

Blurry guy chuckled. "There's some as big as a small dog in New York City."

Really? Damn, I needed to step up my game. The guard kept a wary eye on me, and I did the same as I headed toward a hole in the concrete by the door. It would be a tight squeeze, but I was betting that I could make it through.

"Think I should warn Darren and Scott?" the guard asked.

Blurry guy laughed. "Let the giant rat scare the piss out of them. That'll teach them to leave food and chips lying around in there."

Two guys inside. I wondered what other surprises awaited me on the other side of this concrete wall. Hopefully they didn't involve me turning into a poison-spitting frog, because as cool as that sounded in theory, I was pretty sure in reality it would suck.

I managed to get through the opening with most of my fur intact. A wash of static brushed over me and I held my breath, expecting an alarm to sound at any minute or for me to explode.

Neither happened. Either my rat-form was spot-on, or these guys had some pretty sub-par magic now that their main elf was dead. Past the static-barrier, I darted across the room and surveyed the inside, which seemed much bigger as a one-pound rodent than a human. There were indeed two guards inside the building, as well as half of a bologna sandwich that someone had dropped on the floor. I shoved the sandwich in my mouth, partially as a convincing prop, and partially because I was hungry. That bag of burgers had been over four hours ago, and I had just hiked through miles of woods. I needed a snack, and I actually liked bologna.

The two guards were playing cards, smoking, drinking, and eating. There was food everywhere and a box full of empty beer cans on the floor. I was positive their "guard-this-shit" assignment hadn't included drinking beer and playing cards. Clearly boredom made for inattentive mercenaries.

One guy did a double take and yelped, shoving his chair backward to stand and dropping his cards. I noticed he had a pair of twos. Loser.

The other guy followed his gaze and cursed, also jumping to his feet and backing away a few steps. Full house, fives high. Winner, winner, chicken dinner.

Or in my case, bologna sandwich. I sat on my haunches and ate, watching the two.

"Shoot it," Pair of Twos commanded.

"Are you joking? Unload in a room filled with a bunch of magical crap just to kill a rat? One stray bullet would blow us all up, or turn us into mice or something."

Two guards outside, one invisible. Two guards inside. A magical ward around the building walls. And more inside. I finished my sandwich and decided it was time to take a tour of the small room. Up by the front door was a glass-fronted case that had once held lottery tickets and cigarettes by the faded stickers. The table with the food and cards and two chairs was in the center, and along the back wall, lined up along unlit refrigerator cases, were stacks of boxes. I scampered over to sniff them, amused to note that the two guys kept me in sight, shuffling around so they continued to face me.

Gunpowder. And I could feel the magic, although instead of static, this magic felt rotted and slimy. The boxes themselves didn't appear to have any physical locks, or magical protection, but there was a ring of something that surrounded them. Powdery and white, and loaded with tingly magic. It would be kinda stupid to have an explosive ward around boxes of live ammunition, so I assumed this magic was of the turn-me-into-a-frog kind.

I'd learned enough, and knew if I lingered too long I was going to have a giant bear and an angel-light bursting through the door. Still, I wanted to mess with these guys a bit, so I loped toward them, amused to see them jump out of my way with high-pitched squeals. Hopping on the table, I grabbed one of the small bags of chips, then hopped back down, racing toward the hole in the wall.

"Hey, he stole those chips!"

Yes, yes I did.

"Let him have them," the other guy replied. "Not like I'm gonna risk getting rabies to take those chips back."

It was an even tighter fit through the hole with my contraband, but I managed. I also managed to run right past the other two guards as they shouted and danced out of my way. Safely into the woods, and far enough away that I was sure I wouldn't set off any of the detection wards, I shifted back into my human form, opened the bag of chips, and went to find Jake and Karl.

"*B*et you fifty dollars I can." I'd finished telling the guys everything I'd discovered on my rat-patrol. And I'd finished the bag of chips. I hadn't shared.

Jake rolled his eyes. "I can't collect fifty dollars from you if you're dead. Besides, I don't think you even *have* fifty dollars."

I didn't. But I'd eventually get paid, although I had no problem with conveniently forgetting to pay Jake if I lost.

"I can do this. I got past the barrier without setting it off before, and all the guards did was hop around and scream like little girls when they saw me. I get in. I whack the two guards inside. You guys take care of the two outside, and I'll open the door for you and start handing you boxes. Easy peasy."

"Can't see one of the guards outside," Karl complained. "How the hell am I gonna kill a guy I can't see?"

"He'll be the one shooting at you," I told him.

"Oh, excellent plan," Jake scoffed. "You're inside as a rat trying to gnaw a hole in two armed guards while we're getting blown full of holes and trying to kill a man we can't see."

"Yep. It's an excellent plan," I replied.

Karl grunted. "I ain't got no problem killing these four humans, but Brina is always telling me it's not good public relations or some shit like that. Maybe we should try to knock them unconscious instead, like they do in the movies."

"Trust me, that's harder than they make it out to be in the movies," I said. "And it would be a bummer if one came to in five seconds and shot us after calling for reinforcements. They've got cell phones, you know."

Karl nodded. "Maybe I just won't tell Brina about the killing part, then. Okay. Jake and I take the two guards outside after demon-wolf sneaks in and slaughters the two on the inside."

"I've grown rather fond of this demon-wolf and I'd be pretty bummed if she got killed sneaking in and slaughtering two guys with magic bullets on her own." Jake gave me a side-eye.

That warmed my tiny little heart. "Tell you what. I'll sneak in, and the moment you guys hear gunfire, you roll in like the cavalry and save me."

From the expression on Jake's face, I could tell he liked the idea of saving me. I didn't, so the idea of me being some damsel in distress made me even more determined not to get caught.

Jake sighed. "Okay. Deal. But you take one of these before you go in, just in case." He dug in the backpack and handed me a vial with some sparkling liquid in it. "Drink this."

I felt just like Alice in Wonderland. "Will it make me freakishly tall? Or super tiny?"

"No, it will make sure you aren't forced to shift form when they shoot you. And it will negate the magic that rots your flesh."

I was all about not having my flesh rotted, but how would the magic bullets force me to shift if I was already in animal form? Would they work in reverse, turning me from a rat into a giant, naked human? Because that might actually work to my advantage somewhat.

"They're not going to shoot me," I told Jake. "They're afraid if they hit that line of magic around the boxes, they'll be turned into mice. Besides, I'm going to be a rat. No one shoots a rat that's attacking their friend. They'll try to whack me with a shovel or a chair or something."

Jake glared at me. I got the feeling that this was a non-negotiable mandate, so I drank the contents of the vial, grateful he wasn't making me wear a tiny rat-sized flakjacket as well.

"Go. You've got ten minutes, then we're coming in."

Shifting back into my rat form, I darted off toward the building. Ten minutes would be right around the time the guards were doing their switcheroo. I really didn't want to have to take on four of them all at once, so I'd need to get in and take out the two inside with as minimal noise as possible, and get it done before the other two came in and discovered a giant rat standing over two dead bodies.

The outside guards didn't jump this time when I hopped up on the porch, but they did give me a wary side-eye.

"That rat's back," the visible one commented. "Or maybe it's one of his buddies. We need to get some poison in here fast. I don't like the look of this one."

The invisible guy laughed. "It's a rat, not a bear. Pussy."

Little did they know I was probably worse than the bear in the woods behind me. Probably. I got the feeling Karl was damned lethal in a fight, so maybe not.

I scampered in through the hole and saw the two inside guys playing cards once more. Full house guy had a shitty hand this time, so I went after him first, running up and sinking my teeth deep into the exposed skin under his pants hem.

He screamed and flipped the table in his haste to get up, so much for minimal noise.

I held on as the guy frantically shook his leg, trying to dislodge me. The two outside were laughing, yelling slurs about the inside guy's manhood. Pair of Twos, meanwhile, was standing like he was frozen in place, staring wide-eyed at his co-worker.

"Do something! Get it off me!" Full House screamed.

"Do what? I don't want it to bite me," the other guy replied. Then I guess he decided if he didn't do something, he was liable to be next, because he picked up his rifle and pointed it at Full House's leg.

"Don't shoot me, you idiot." Full House hopped over to the wall and tried to slam me into it. I jumped off just in time, then leapt upward and sank my teeth into whatever I managed to grab hold of. It was his upper inner thigh. Two more inches of vertical leap and I would have been biting his dick.

One of the joys of being a genetic freak was that I could alter individual parts of my body as I so chose—well, as my beast so chose. Sometimes that meant I was a lion-chicken-snake. Sometimes it meant I was a big-ass rat with teeth the size of steak knives. Which meant I had the perfect tools to sink those pearly whites into both the guy's femoral artery and femoral vein.

Blood gushed, blinding me as well as choking me. I let go, gagging and sputtering, and was nearly crushed by the guy who immediately collapsed from the sudden blood loss. I gave him a minute tops.

Pair of Twos screamed. "Help! Giant, crazy, rabid rat! Help!" Then this time he actually shot at me.

Luckily, a terrified person is a very poor shot, because the rain of bullets did nothing more than blow chunks of concrete off the walls and shower white dust into the thick blood that was rapidly spreading across the floor. I hid under the body until I realized the guy was turning his aim on his dead co-worker, then I ran across the floor, trying to avoid the ring of magic around the boxes as well as the bullets being wildly shot around the room.

Even big magazine clips run out. As soon as the shooting stopped, I ran for Pair of Twos and jumped. He screamed, trying to hit me with the stock of the rifle as I bit and clawed my way up his body. Then as I latched onto his neck, he grabbed me with both hands, squeezing tight.

I didn't get as lucky with this bite as I had with the other one. Without an arterial strike, I was left to chew up the man's throat and hope he bled out before I needed to actually breathe. He did. And this time I did get somewhat crushed when he fell to the floor on top of me.

My ribs hurt. I was sticky with blood and cement dust. There was a two-hundred-pound guy crushing me. Still, I hesitated, waiting for the other two guards to come rushing inside now that Pair of Twos wasn't liable to kill them with his wild aim. I heard nothing but silence. Finally I couldn't stand to wait any longer. Shifting into my human form, I pushed the dead guy off of me and stood. Surely the guards outside would have at least called out to see if their buddies inside were okay by now.

There was a knock on the door that sounded like someone was hitting it with the butt end of a rifle. Then someone did call out—Jake.

"Tupper? You okay in there?"

I brushed my hands against my thighs, which did nothing to clean off the blood and dust. Then I grabbed the less bloody of the two dead guys and hauled him over to the door, using his hand to turn the latch, then using his body to prop open the hinged plywood.

The static feel of magic vanished. I didn't know if it was the human body interrupting the flow, or the guy's blood, or what, but I gave Jake and Karl the all-clear thumbs-up, and stood back.

They had to hunch over to get through without scraping against the hinged plywood. Inside they straightened up, then stared.

"The fuck? Looks like five humans got run through a chipper shredder in here," Karl commented.

"Not the neatest job by a long stretch, but she got it done," Jake defended me.

Karl grunted. "She looks like she rolled in it, too."

"*You* try to avoid arterial spray," I countered. "And concrete dust really sticks to blood."

The place did look like a war zone with blood everywhere and chunks blown of out of walls. Sad when the two dead guys on the floor were the least alarming thing in the room.

"Am I right in assuming there's some magic protection around the boxes?" Jake asked.

I nodded. Then I went over and grabbed the second dead guy, dragging him over toward the boxes. When I shoved the top half of his torso through the ring of dust, it sizzled, then caught fire with a bang.

The fire was blue. It didn't feel hot, but the guy's skin was melting.

"How much C4 did you bring?" Karl asked Jake. "I'm thinking we just blow it all up and call it a day."

"I've been warned that blowing up areas with magical wards might result in a catastrophic incident," Jake told him.

"Well, the owners of this shit had to have some way of getting the bullets out in case they needed them," I said. "The two guards out front were talking about pocketing a few of them as a little side bonus to their paycheck. They knew there was a magical barrier, so they must have had something on them to make stealing a few a possibility."

Karl grunted and went outside, returning moment later carrying an arm.

"We stack up the dead guards then use them as a bridge to get to the cases?" I asked. "Or we keep shoving dead human body parts into it until the magic runs out of juice or overloads or something."

"Guy had an amulet that made him invisible," Karl told me. "I yanked it off when I killed him, and noticed this ring. Looks kinda elf-like to me, you think?"

Jake and I stared at the delicate filigree gold ring on the thick, stumpy man-fingers of the severed arm.

"Let's give it a shot," I said. "Worst thing that happens is the arm catches on fire, and you lose out on a few hundred dollars in scrap gold."

Karl shoved it into the magical barrier, and I felt it fall. The blue flame extinguished, although the dead guy that lay across the barrier still was blistered and burned. Jake motioned me back and carefully extended a hand across the barrier. We all exhaled when nothing happened.

"I'm going in," Jake told us. "Karl, you keep holding the hand there. Tupper, I'm going to hand you boxes."

I didn't like this plan. "I should go in. I'm the one who can sense the magic. For all we know there's an additional ward on those boxes."

"You're not going in. I am." Jake's voice was commanding, and I knew there was no arguing him out of this. The Alpha had spoken.

He slowly made his way through the barrier, stepping over the dead guy. "Here goes nothing," he commented wryly. "If I turn into a frog, will you still have sex with me?"

I laughed.

"I'm not gonna fuck you, Jake," Karl growled. "Now hurry up. I'm getting tired of holding this dead arm here."

Jake handed the boxes through to me and I stacked them over by the door. There were twenty of them, each one weighing over fifty pounds. How the heck we were going to get all of these to the truck was a mystery. When all the boxes were moved, Jake stepped back through the barrier, and Karl removed the arm. I felt the static of the magic springing to life once more and saw the blue flame leap across the dead guy.

Jake hadn't been turned into a frog, and I couldn't feel any magic on the boxes themselves, so I ripped one open, pulling out a box of shotgun shells. "Huh. They feel normal to me," I commented.

Jake and Karl exchanged worried looks. The bear took the box from my hand, running his fingers over the tops of the shells.

"Cause they *are* normal," he announced.

His words set off a flurry of activity and we all tore into the boxes, running our hands over all of the bullets and separating the ones that fell all gross and slimy with magic from those that didn't. By the time we were done, there were empty boxes and stacks of bullets all over the blood-soaked floor. Only a few hundred of the thousands of bullets were coated with the magic.

"Do you think they sold the rest, or they have another warehouse somewhere with more?" Karl asked.

"Or they knew we were coming and moved most of the magicked bullets out of here," I added darkly.

Jake shook his head. "Gwylla would have picked up on another warehouse. They either moved them, or sold them, and as much as I dread the thought, I'm leaning toward sold them. One of their partners is dead as is the elf that was creating these bullets. Their videos are being debunked and with law enforcement on our side, their organized hunting tour business is going to eventually be impossible to maintain on any sort of decent scale."

"Best to sell the stock, make a ton of money, and move on," Karl added.

"From what Gwylla said, the elf was the one driving the whole 'kill the shifters and angels, drive the humans to rebellion, and take over the world' plot. These guys were using fear of us to make money, and with their supply cut off, and the increased risk of facing murder charges…"

"So there are a ton of these bullets dispersed all over the country?" I asked, looking down at the boxes.

Jake sighed. "Probably. I'll see if someone can verify it, but in the meantime, at least we have these bullets off the market and out of reach of hunters."

Karl scooped them up in his arms, stuffing boxes into pockets and his waistband. "I'll walk you guys back to the truck, just to make sure you don't meet with any unexpected surprises. Then I'll take off back south and deliver these to the angels. Let them deal with disposing of them."

Jake eyed the bullets. "Sounds good to me. I sure as heck don't want those things in my compound."

"Thinking that was a smidgen too easy," Karl commented, echoing my thoughts. We were back at the truck, the sky a dark gray in preparation for the coming sunrise. I was tired, dirty, bloody, hungry, and my clothes were rather fragrant. Yes, Mir had helped me pack and I had another pair of jeans and a shirt, but I was reluctant to put them on over my very filthy body.

"I'd expected more ammunition," Jake said, eyeing the boxes that Karl carried. I figured total there was about two thousand rounds in there. I was no expert, but if someone had to magic each and every bullet, two thousand was a damned lot. According to the briefing the elf had been at it for three to four months, that worked out to a hundred and twenty days, which meant that elf was cranking out around sixteen bullets a day. That was if he never took a day off, and there weren't any duds.

Assuming the bad guys had sold a thousand rounds already to hunters and paranoid humans, that would up the production to twenty-five bullets a day. Was that even possible? I had no idea the effort it would take to magic a bullet, or if twenty-five a day, every day, for four months straight was feasible.

"And we're still missing the bullets that kill angels as well as the blades the elf told Gwylla he created," Jake added.

"And what's already been sold," Karl said. "We'll never be able to find all those bullets. A hundred years from now, some human's' grandkid could still have a few of them. We'll never be safe, never be absolutely sure that some crazy isn't gonna try to pop one of us."

I could understand why shifters were scared. Heck, we'd been practically indestructible all our lives and gotten used to the idea that humans weren't a threat to us. In all honestly, even that had been a lie. I'd seen wolves killed in serious auto accidents. I'd seen them drowned, decapitated, and even killed with a really well-placed gunshot to the head. We could be blown up to the point where we couldn't heal. And let's face it, remove our heart and we wouldn't be able to regrow one fast enough to keep from going brain dead. Yeah, we didn't get sick, and we weren't so fragile that we died from things that killed most humans. We weren't immortal by any stretch of the imagination, though. And five bullets in some dude's attic weren't going to wipe out our entire population.

"Say a thousand rounds have been sold," I spoke up. "And of those, maybe half ever end up getting used. Face it, if you've spent five hundred bucks on one fucking bullet, you're not going to waste it. You wouldn't want to have it in a magazine and inadvertently use it while taking down a buck during hunting season because you grabbed the wrong magazine. Most of these bullets are going to be locked away in a safe somewhere and never used. The werewolf panic—it's like the zombie apocalypse. Everyone wants to be prepared, but no one wants to waste their magic weapons until they are absolutely sure they need them.

"And eighty percent of the time humans don't even fucking hit what they're shooting at. Yeah, some are probably skilled hunters, but how many psychos are going to be convinced to tromp out into the woods and shoot someone who looks like a human with a five-hundred-dollar bullet?"

"That's why we need to concentrate on getting as much of the ammo off the market as possible," Jake told me. "That way it won't fall into the hands of the psychos who will actually use it. If we can do that, and take down the people who are stirring this all up and organizing the hunting expeditions, then I think we'll be able to start trusting again."

"Maybe," Karl grunted. "Ain't never trusted or liked humans. Who's to say some idiot decides the werewolf living next to him needs to go and organizes an accident? We're stronger, faster, and don't get ill. That's enough to piss some people off, make them think we've got an unfair advantage over them. You think the psychos are only the ones hunting us for pelts, but in my opinion, they're all one good excuse away from trying to kill us."

"We have to trust that the government and law enforcement will support us," Jake countered. "We pay taxes the same as the humans do. We volunteer, and purchase their goods and services. Take out as much ammo as we can and the ones instigating this, and we'll go back to trusting each other."

Karl shook his head. "I don't see it. It's not just us, Jake, it's how everything is changing. This world is sliding into chaos, and the humans are going to feel powerless. People that feel powerless end up trying to take that power back in a violent way. They'll want things to return to the way it used to be when humans were the top of the food chain. Now there's elves, and angels, and dragons and other shit coming through those rifts faster than anyone can do anything about. Human are gonna start feeling puny and weak, and they're gonna lash out. We may have been living side-by-side with them for thousands of years, but they won't see that. They'll lump us all in with the elves and mermaids and other shit. They'll want us all gone—us and them. They'll want this place to be human-only as far as sentient life goes."

Jake scowled. "The angels won't go for that."

"Won't they? They've got their own problems from what the guy down in Juneau says. Angels wouldn't cry if we were wiped out. And a good number of them are probably ready to wash their hands of the humans and go back to Aaru and lock the doors behind them. And as for the elves…well, you've seen how Gwylla is with metal. She says the elves are the same way. I give them a few years and they'll be running back to Hel where at least they don't get third-degree burns from leaning against a parking meter."

Or taking a toaster to the head. But there was something Karl had left out of his scenario. "So the angels go home. We all get killed. The elves say 'fuck this' and leave. That means the humans are stuck here with a bunch of interdimensional rifts opening up and all sorts of freaky shit coming through. They've got no way to close them, and no way to stuff the monsters back through to the other side."

"Yep. But humans don't think far enough ahead to see that. They'll just deal with the problems they can, then cry big tears when they're here alone with dragons and manticores and mermaids."

I'd met a wolf from Chicago that told me about the mermaids in Lake Michigan. Talk about freaky shit.

"You know those mermaids eat people, right? I mean, everyone thinks they drag sailors down under the sea where they suddenly breathe underwater just fine and get to fuck a bunch of hot, naked mermaids. Idiots. Mermaids drown them, then eat them. There's no fucking involved."

Both Jake and Karl stared at me as if I were insane.

"Well, that really sucks," Karl grumbled. "If they're gonna drown me and eat me, they should at least give me a hummer first. Wouldn't mind dying if I could get in a decent fuck beforehand."

I rolled my eyes. "Dude. From what I can tell you're getting tons of decent fucking, and that skinny redhead doesn't seem to want you dead. Yet. That might change. And you should watch out for the skinny girls, too. She gets hungry enough, you might wind up on the table with an apple in your mouth."

"Annnd we do not need to go into the sexual innuendo of Karl naked on a table with an apple as a gag in his mouth and how kinky that might be," Jake interjected.

And now Karl and I were staring at him.

"Will you eat me if I lay naked on a table with an apple in my mouth?" I asked him.

Karl snorted. "Girl, he's gonna eat you without the table and apple. And I'm getting out of here before all that starts going down." He shook hands with Jake and wished him luck, then turned to me and grabbed me in a tight, rib-crushing hug. "Don't kill him, kay'? Thinking we're gonna need him for a while."

I grinned, hugging Karl back and grabbing a handful of his tight ass while I had the opportunity. "No promises."

And then he was gone, leaving Jake and me with a pickup truck and a twenty-four-hour drive ahead of us.

"Thinking of stopping halfway and getting a hotel room," the Alpha commented casually.

I wasn't fooled. He didn't look tired. I'd bet he could

easily go another day or two without sleep, possibly more. "A hotel room with a table and an apple?" I asked.

"No on the apple. I want your mouth available for other things."

Oh yeah. I was so gonna get laid. "Shotgun!" I shouted and ran for the passenger door.

We drove halfway back to the compound, detouring a bit off the road at sunset to an area with something nicer than a no-tell motel. I would have been happy with a rent-by-the hour place, heck I would have been happy with Jake taking me up on the hood of the truck, but clearly the guy had standards.

Standards that meant the moment we'd checked in, he was on the phone, discussing business. Even with a hands-free speaker, Jake wouldn't call while driving. Or go over the speed limit. Or park outside the lines in our designated spot. I swear I could be here naked on the bed, my ass in the air, and an apple in my mouth, and he'd have to complete his phone call first.

But then I thought of our kiss in the sparring room, his lighthearted playfulness as we were setting out on this trip, his insistence that what we were going to do would be "making love", his wicked smile when he'd implied there was something other than an apple that he wanted in my mouth.

Maybe, in time, I could get this guy to break a few rules.

And maybe, in time, he'd get me to actually follow a few of them.

"It looks like two cases…Yeah, I thought there would be more, too. Can you have someone look around the net' and see if any of the company names they're using have been selling a lot of these bullets? Or anyone is selling a lot of these bullets?" Jake paced as he spoke on his phone. I wasn't sure if he was talking to his second, Jamie, or to the Alpha down in Juneau, but from the set of his shoulders, he was tense as all get out.

I was hoping to relieve him of some of that tension. I mean, we were in a hotel room for the night. I had every intention of taking advantage of this sweet king-sized mattress and getting as little sleep as possible.

But first, room service.

"Rare on the steak?" I asked Jake.

He nodded and kept talking.

"I'm assuming no on the salad?"

He nodded, then shook his head, then lifted his head from the phone. "No salad."

"Baked potato with sour cream and butter? And what do you want for dessert? I'm eyeing this caramel apple pie thing here. Hope you're paying for this because I've got no money."

"Tupper, I'm trying to talk," he growled in frustration. "And I'm taking this out of that fifty I owe you."

Jerk. "Fuck that, the steak is almost fifty bucks. I'm just charging it to the room." Which was on his credit card.

"I'm not buying you dinner. It's coming out of your paycheck."

I wondered what Jamie, or that other Alpha guy was thinking about our sidebar conversation.

"Hey, I thought I got a per diem or something? And what kind of cheap date is this anyway where you don't even buy me dinner?"

Jake's eyes bugged out. "This isn't a date," he sputtered. "We're not on a date. This is business."

Yeah, whoever was on the other side of the phone line was getting an earful. And they were about to get even more of an earful.

"I'm not fucking you unless you pay for dinner," I said loud enough that a half-deaf human on the other end of the phone line could have heard. "You rent us this sex-pad hotel room with oils and lotions and vibrators and crap, and expect me to fuck your brains out, but you won't spring for a damned steak?"

I thought Jake might be on the verge of having a heart attack from the expression on his face.

"I'm not…she's joking," he said into the phone. Then he held it to his side and told me to order whatever I wanted. As if that would keep any shifter on the other end from hearing.

"Thanks, babe," I told him loudly. "You're totally getting a blow job tonight. I'll even swallow. And if the apple pie is as good as I think it is, we can do anal. You being the one getting stuffed, that is. I'm pretty sure I saw a strap-on some-where in this drawer."

The door slammed as Jake went outside to continue his phone call. I laughed and placed the food order, getting four steak dinners and a side of spiced shrimp. We were shifters—kind of—and we hadn't had a decent meal in over twenty-four hours. I don't know about Jake, but my stomach was on the verge of devouring itself.

The food had arrived before Jake returned to the room. In spite of his threats, he signed for the check and tipped the guy, then turned a stern expression on me.

"Tupper, I do not need Brent thinking that I'm having inappropriate relations with a member of my pack."

What was this, the thirteenth century? A nunnery? Were-wolf packs tended to be rather far apart in distance and, until recently, we'd been under strict rules that made having a relationship with a member of another pack difficult if not impossible. Add to that the fact that we'd previously been forbidden from mating with humans and all the rules had created an environment where relations between pack members—even with the Alpha—were commonplace and accepted.

Unless by "inappropriate" Jake had meant my joking of oral and anal sex. Maybe he was one of those missionary-only wolves. I certainly hoped not.

"Like Brent thinks we're actually holed up here fucking each other in the ass with sex toys," I scoffed. "I know you've got a sense of humor somewhere in that thick skull of yours, Jake. Calm down and eat your steak."

The air crackled with tension. Jake's eyes glowed, their light blue intense. Clearly telling my Alpha to "calm down" wasn't the wisest thing I'd ever done, although the lure of a juicy steak must have been too much to resist, because he did sit down and yank the silver lid off his food, carefully spreading the napkin on his lap before cutting into his steak.

"I need you to treat me as your Alpha around the others, Tupper. This isn't going to work if you insist on behaving like this in front of other Alphas and our pack."

The only reason I wasn't reaching across the table to punch him in the face was the slip he'd made in calling Swift River "our pack". It wasn't just that he was acknowledging that I was a member, it was him saying he thought of me as a potential mate. Because as mate to the Alpha, Swift River *would* be my pack. A mate ranked above the second in the pack, and although there were occasional scuffles about whose authority was higher, the mate tended to win those arguments.

Besides, I could totally take Jamie in a fight. I wouldn't come out of it unscathed, but I'd win.

"I thought we were heading in the direction of an intimate relationship," I told him, my voice admirably calm and reasonable, especially for me. "You've implied that with actions and words, and I've made it quite clear I'm receptive. Are you saying that you've reconsidered?"

Because if he had, I was going furry and this hotel room was going to be trashed beyond the limit on Jake's platinum MasterCard.

His fork halted on the way to his mouth, and he set it down to rub his face. "No. Tupper, don't think that. I love being with you. You're different, so very different. It shakes me up, which is a good thing, but it means I'm struggling to figure out how to be with you and not go crazy."

Reassuring, if not somewhat insulting. But since I'd never really had a relationship before I could understand where he was coming from.

"I'm never going to be like Jamie, you know. I'm going to get in fights, break the rules, pinch your ass in public. There's a good chance instead of calling you 'sir' in a meeting with all the other Alphas, I might call you Honey Buns."

He grimaced. "I know. And in the spirit of fair disclosure, I'm still going to make you do sprints for stuff like that stunt you pulled in the dorm room with Stacy's scent on your roommate's things. I'll still beat the crap out of you sparring, yell at you in front of the pack when you are disrespectful or break the rules."

It might sound weird, but his speech made me want to rip my clothes off and screw him right here on the floor. "Babe, I wouldn't love you if you *didn't* do those things."

"I worry that 'those things' are going to be the very things that make you decide you can't deal with my overbearing self anymore," he confessed.

I had the same fears, but hearing Jake voice them—confident, uber-Alpha, always-in-control Jake—made me feel better about this thing we were heading toward together. We were both lonely, longing for that special someone to connect with. He hid his fears by throwing himself into the governance of his pack. I hid mine by fighting and pushing away everyone that even tried to come close to me. Except for Mir, and now Jake.

What a pair we were.

"So what do we do?" I eyed the steak. "Besides screw like monkeys and get no sleep at all, that is. What do we do to make sure this thing we have between us doesn't fracture the pack and kill us both?"

"We face it the same way we go swimming in October."

What the everliving- fuck was he talking about? "Hypothermia and the possible need for limb amputation?"

"Just jump. If you stick your toes in the water, you'll never get in. Just jump and get it over with."

That didn't sound like a good relationship metaphor to me. *Get it over with.* "And die of a heart attack from the shock."

He grinned. "What a way to go." Then he grabbed me and yanked me across the table onto his lap, plates of steak, potatoes, and apple pie crashing to the ground.

I gasped and laughed. "I'm not eating a cold steak off the floor once we're done screwing. Just letting you in on that little fact."

His hands roamed up under my shirt and unsnapped my bra. "We'll order more. I'll take it out of your paycheck."

I traced the line of his jaw and leaned toward him, my eyes on his lips. "Like hell you will. You're paying or I'm not fucking you."

I was totally going to fuck him, whether or not he paid for dinner.

"Okay, I'll buy," he breathed. "And if I get that blow job, then I might spring for an extra slice of apple pie."

Then his mouth was on mine, hot and demanding and just as intoxicating as a shot of hundred-proof whisky. I brushed my tongue against his and wound my arms around his neck, feeling my way down the nape to edge my fingers along the collar of his shirt and trace the ridges of his shoulders.

He pulled his mouth from mine, startled blue gaze meeting my eyes. Then he laughed. "Tupper Mills, you're a handful. You know that, don't you?"

My hands skated along his shoulder blades, feeling the powerful muscles under the soft cotton of his shirt. "Yes, I do. Now hurry up and fuck me."

He bent his head to trace a line down the column of my neck. "Make love. I refuse to fuck you."

By all that was unholy, the sensation of his lips on my skin was the best thing I'd ever experienced in my life. I felt hot and alive, that weird zing of electricity arcing through my body. He was hovering over me, his lips the only part of his body touching me, but I *felt* him. It was as if the eternity of him, the very essence that was Jake had surrounded me, enveloping me, teasing me with the promise of something that would transcend every sexual experience I'd ever had.

It turned me on. It scared the ever-loving piss out of me. It made me retreat into a defensive crudeness that felt totally inappropriate for the moment.

"Love. Fuck. I don't care, I just want your cock in me right now," I snarled, feeling strangely vulnerable and balking at the unfamiliar experience.

He hesitated. For a second my heart stuttered, thinking that he was going to get up and walk right out the door.

Then he turned me so I was straddling him, grabbing my ass and rubbing me forward against his erection. "Making love. I'm not fucking you, Tupper. I'm never fucking you. Don't you ever forget that."

Then he kissed me again, slow and languorous when I was desperate for him to be fast. I rocked against him, trying in vain with my hands to reach between us and undo his pants. Finally I gave up and tried to take another approach, running my hands across his chest and making desperate moans into his mouth. His one hand stayed on my ass, holding me firm against him, while the other came up to grip my wrists and still my roving hands. All the while, his mouth slowly explored mine, tasting every inch before easing back to nip my lower lip firmly.

That's when I realized that nothing hurried Jake. He'd do things his way, in his own sweet time. The thought was strangely liberating.

"What are we doing?" he murmured, nibbling along the edge of my jaw to my ear.

My heart raced as he traced my ear with his tongue, pulling the lobe into his mouth and sucking gently. "What are we doing?" he repeated.

"Making love," I panted, held so firmly in place with his hands and arms that I could only quiver. "Can you make love faster, though?"

He chuckled and it sent a bolt of need through me. I was wet before. Now I felt like I was soaking right through my jeans. If I could just angle my hips a bit and rock, I was sure I could get off right here on his lap.

"No. I want to take my time and enjoy you." He bit down on my ear lobe and tugged, then continued to move lower, kissing, nipping, and licking his way down the column of my neck. I just closed my eyes and breathed, letting myself sink into the feeling of his body against mine, the sensation of his mouth on the sensitive skin of my neck.

I popped my eyes open as he scooted the chair backward and stood. I slid my legs down from his waist to stand still pressed against him, his one hand still firmly on my ass, the other still gripping my wrists tight against his chest. Then he freed my hands and brushed his fingers around my waist, edging me backward, his breath against my hair.

My knees hit the edge of the bed. I expected him to shove me backward, but he stopped, his hand inching up my ribs to grab the collar of my shirt. With a sharp pull, the fabric ripped down the front.

Not to be undone, I did the same to his, running my hands across his warm skin, feeling the curve of his ribs, the sensitive skin of his waist, and the jut of his hip bones right at the waistband of his jeans. He eased my shirt and bra down off my shoulders, stilling the motions of my hands as the fabric bunched around my wrists and pushed my arms backward. I shook off the torn fabric, and he did the same, then traced his own fingers across my breasts and taut nipples, his eyes devouring every inch of me.

"Take off your pants. Slowly," he commanded. Before my hands had unsnapped my jeans, he'd bent his head to pull one of my nipples into his mouth, laving and sucking as I shimmied my pants downward where they caught at my ankles.

His fingers were feather light as they traced my ribs, and I carefully eased my shoes off and stepped out of my pants, trying to keep my movements slow and easy, not wanting to disrupt the heat building up inside me at each flick of his tongue. I shivered when he pulled his mouth away and blew gently on my wet, swollen nipple, turning his attention to the other one.

Hesitating, I reached for his pants. When he didn't grab my hands or protest, I worked the button loose, easing the zipper down, then sliding them off his hips.

It seemed we both shared a love of going commando,

because there was nothing to keep his cock from springing free to knock against my stomach. And there was nothing hindering my hands from gripping his incredible, rock-hard ass. This guy had the best butt ever. Someone should create a monument to Jake's ass. A Mount Ass-Rushmore or something, with only his glorious back-end on display for people everywhere to admire.

That was the moment when mouth returned to my lips, and his fingers strayed south, to brush through my wet folds, one finger slipping inside to curl and press confidently in that perfect spot just as his thumb smoothed along my clit rubbing against my strategically placed piercing. I hovered on the edge, sucking in a deep breath, my mind emptying of every thought. *Right there. Just once more, right there.*

Instead Jake pulled his hand away. Before I had a chance to do more than whine in protest, he'd pushed me back onto the bed and knelt down between my legs.

"Thought I was supposed to be the one going down on you," I gasped.

"Raincheck," he whispered. Then he teased my piercing with his tongue. "I want this more."

So. Did. I. He worked magic with fingers and tongue while I fisted the sheets and tried to keep from thrashing around. Jake must have noticed because he slid his shoulders under my legs, using his weight against my hips to press me down into the mattress and hold me in place. I let myself go, shaking and twitching against him, all sorts of incoherent noises and fragmented curses pouring out of my mouth as he continually brought me right to the edge of orgasm only to pull back just before I peaked. When I thought I'd surely go insane, he took my piercing in his mouth and tugged, curling two fingers inside me as he pressed and slid his thumb upward against my clit. I shattered, crying out as I came apart in what had been the most earth-shattering orgasm of my life. My first thought as I floated through the aftershocks was that I was never going to let this guy out of the bedroom. Never.

He kissed his way up my body to my mouth, then rose up on his arms, looming over me a brief second before easing himself into me. I felt myself stretch around him, felt the ball of my piercing tip forward against my swollen, still-sensitive clit. We held there, him deep inside me, our eyes locked together.

My gaze drifted past his shoulder, to the weird gold tracings that came from his shoulders, shifting and expanding as if they were the remains of fireworks, dropping their sparks from the sky. Wings. Was this what they'd looked like when he was a baby? Would they never be fully physical, feathered and capable of supporting him in flight like I'd been told the real angels had. Suddenly I wanted him to have wings. Angel-light was hardly inadequate in my view, especially when that angel-light was Jake, but the thought of him taking to the skies was intoxicating.

Then he leaned forward, rocking his hips against mine and all thoughts of wings vanished. as he slowly moved in and out, shifting and exploring different angles and rhythms until he found the one that brought us both together with a gasp. I matched him thrust for thrust, tensing again with another approaching orgasm as I felt him swell inside me. With a sharp inhalation, Jake threw back his head and slammed into me, breathing out as he came. I followed, not as intense as the first, but wonderfully satisfying—and just as fulfilling as I watched the expressions sweep across his face.

Then something odd happened. I felt my beast yield—not to him, but to me. She rolled and vanished, sliding into every cell, integrating for the first time in my whole life. The electricity between us increased to near painful intensity, and I felt something beyond his physical self slide into me, expanding and enveloping every part of who I was until we were no longer separate beings. It wasn't me looking into Jake's eyes, it was us—fully together with only the tiniest fractions of ourselves anchored within our physical forms. The closest I could come to describing it was the feeling of freefalling-, or flying.

Jake grew hazy and indistinct, a blur of white around him like an aura. Then the gold tracings exploded in light, manifesting into wings of white and a shocking tangerine color—like a noonday sun bursting from the whitest clouds. They were huge feathery things, extending outward the entire width of the room. With a jolt of surprise, we snapped back fully into our physical forms, and Jake flexed the wings, sending lamps and furniture flying as well as punching a long dent into the drywall.

"Ow." He grimaced. "That hurt. These things feel every molecule of air, every brush of fiber."

"They're way cool," I breathed, reaching out to touch one. It was silky, and hummed with the same hot electricity that I felt deep inside Jake's physical self.

He caught his breath as I touched the feathers and I felt his cock jump and harden against my leg. "Wow…that's… I hope I can manage to hide them."

"Why would you want to hide them? They're gorgeous." If I had big-ass feathery wings, I'd walk around flapping them all the time.

"Well first, I don't think I can fit in the truck cab with these things."

"Cool. I'll drive, and you can ride in the truck bed with your wings."

He shot me a narrowed glance. "Secondly, I'm not sure I can get out the doorway with them."

"Dude, you just punched a hole in the drywall. Just smash through the wall like that Kool-Aid pitcher guy."

"Did I mention how sensitive they are? I'm positive that punching through a wall with them would be like getting kicked in the balls. Which brings me to number three. They're sensitive. If I can't hide them, it's gonna be like me walking around with my genitals exposed. I bend one, it's gonna hurt. I whack one on a building because I misjudge the distance going around a corner, it's gonna hurt. I get a wing caught in a sticker bush when we're doing weekend games, it's gonna hurt."

I leaned forward and licked one, my tongue teasing the feathery filaments.

Jake shuddered. "Oh, God. Do that again."

I did, deciding this was going to be just as much fun as a blow job. "Too much?"

"No," he breathed.

I pushed him back and stood up, reversing our positions and shoving him down on his back this time, careful not to bend those gorgeous wings. Then I had my way with him, thrilled to see him lose control to me the way I'd lost to him.

The wings eventually faded back to the gold tracings, but not until we'd completely worn ourselves out fucking—no, *making love*—in every conceivable position. When we finally hovered at the edge of sleep, arms and legs tangled together, I couldn't help but smile and place a kiss on Jake's shoulder. I'd come home, and oh how sweet it was.

* * *

THE SUN HAD RISEN by the time we crawled out of bed and began to gather our things together. I wanted to stay here for at least another week, but we had responsibilities back at the pack compound that couldn't be put off any longer.

Responsibilities. Me with responsibilities. Go figure.

I felt mildly guilty about housekeeping having to deal

with the plates and cold food all over the floor as well as the porn-flick mess we'd made of the bed. Oh well. I wasn't cleaning it up. I wasn't going to take a shower either. I loved having Jake's scent all over me, imbedded into my skin and hair, each inhalation reminding me of him inside me. Let every pack member within twenty feet realize what we'd done. I was happy to carry such an announcement on my skin.

Jake seemed to feel the same because he made no move to take a shower of his own, nor suggest that I do so. I did brush my teeth after he did, though, and made sure to steal something from the bathroom on my way out.

"What are you doing?" Jake demanded as I shoved the logo-embroidered bathrobe into my duffle bag.

Should I take the towels? Maybe I should take some towels as well.

"It's a present. I promised Mir that I'd bring her back a present, and I forgot to get one at the gas station. Not that I think she'd want anything from there since it was all covered in blood and concrete dust. Although she did say that red was her favorite color." I eyed the bathrobe, which was white, but did have a lovely red on the embroidered logo.

Jake chuckled. "Fine. But just the bathrobe. And Tupper?"

I looked up at him as I struggled to close the zipper on the over-stuffed duffle. "Yeah?"

"I love you, you crazy freak-of-nature demon-wolf. I love you."

Jake. I got the feeling he'd never been one to hold back anything, that all his insistence on rules and procedures meant that he also needed to be brutally honest about his emotions. Cool, calm, and collected, except when it came to me.

"Yeah? Well, I might sorta kinda maybe care about you a little bit too, Almost-angel."

His smile was warm and intimate. Again I felt that zing of electricity, that sense of us touching even though we were across the bed from each other. And I knew then that no matter how much I tried to hide, tried to deny my feelings, Jake knew as well as I did that I loved him too.

CHAPTER 20

It was dusk when we pulled into the compound. Jake had texted our ETA before we'd left the hotel, and was unsurprisingly spot-on. That plus the fact that the werewolves could hear the truck a mile away meant we had a few dozen pack mates clustered by the road in. They smiled, and I felt the pack relax as a collective, relieved to have their Alpha back among them. Jamie probably had done a great job managing things, but wolves always felt more secure in the presence of their Alpha.

Jamie was the only one who followed us to the parking area, although the others milled around to ensure they had a good vantage point. Jake was at my door, his hands on my waist to help me out of the truck before I could even step foot on the running board. I wanted to protest this kid-glove treatment, but just as I opened my mouth, he kissed me, his one hand twisting my short hair into his fist.

Holy shit, what a kiss. And right smack in front of everyone, too. Even those who were too far upwind to get a whiff of our scent would know. As we broke apart, I heard Jamie make a strange gurgling noise.

"Go. Shower. Get some sleep. I'll see you in the morning," he told me.

There was an odd emphasis on the word "shower" that made me grin.

"You reek of sex," he said, loud enough for everyone to hear. Then he spun me around and sent me off with a slap on my ass. He reeked of sex as well, and I noticed there was no haste on his part to go wash my scent from him. Instead he turned to Jamie and started talking to her about the business at hand, ignoring her wide eyes and the nostrils that flared as her gaze whipped back and forth between the Alpha and me.

Oh well. Whatever lingering fears I'd had that Jake might be ashamed of what we'd done, that he might want to hide it and sneak me in and out of his bed, vanished.

I did not shower, at least not right away. Instead I strolled into the dorm and up to my room, smirking at the astonished expressions on my roommates' faces as I plopped my duffle bag at the end of the bed.

"Got you a present, Mir," I announced proudly.

"You sure did," she squealed. "Are you moving into the Alpha House? I'll miss having you as a roommate, but I'm so glad that you and Jake are getting it on."

"Screwing doesn't mean moving in." Fox Face wrinkled her nose. "Take a shower, Mills. Sheesh, how many times did you guys do it? You smell like a walking bordello."

Yes. Yes, I did.

"Glad somebody's getting some," Muscles groused. "I think I'm a virgin again it's been so long since I got laid."

Muffin Top rolled her eyes. "Please. Thirty days doesn't make you a virgin again. I *have* a boyfriend and I haven't gotten any in a week."

"I get some every night," Boobs announced.

"Liar." Muscles threw a pillow at the woman, and

suddenly everyone's pillows were sailing across the room with great precision.

I pulled out the bathrobe and handed it to Mir with a bow.

"Ooo, you stole me a bathrobe!" She lifted it to her nose. "And you didn't wear it either."

"Yeah, Jake and I weren't really bothering with bathrobes," I told her.

"You clearly weren't bothering with personal hygiene either," Fox Face retorted, holding her nose.

"I brushed my teeth," I told her. Then I dug in my trunk for my bag of toiletries and some underwear, because I'd made my point and I really *was* dying for a shower.

By the time I was done, Mir, Fox Face, Boobs and Muscles were asleep. I assumed Muffin Top, not wanting to be outdone in the most-recently-had-sex category, had gone out to find her boyfriend. I was hungry, and not very tired even though I'd not gotten more than an hour of sleep the night before, so I headed to the dining room, remembering that Mir said there was always some food out and available for those who were in late from work or who were stricken with late-night munchies.

I filled two bowls with Rice Krispies, dumped about a pound of sugar on top of each one, then floated the whole mess in whole milk before sitting at a table in the darkened room to eat. It was weird. I'd spent most of my life eating alone, and in just a few days I found it strange. I missed the buzz of conversation, the clank of the trays in the buffet, even the glares Mir's mother always sent my way. What used to be relaxing, companionable silence felt...lonely.

The door opened, spilling moonlight across the floor in a column of silvery white. I felt him before he'd even stepped across the threshold, before I even smelled his distinctive scent.

"Got news," he said in that deep voice that sent everything below my waistband to quivering. He'd showered, but it had done nothing to wash me from his skin. Now he just smelled crisp and clean with a sandalwood-pine fragrance accenting the I've-been-screwing-with-Tupper scent.

"Yeah?" I pointed my spoon at a chair and kept shoveling in the Rice Krispies as he sat.

"Sabrina called." Brent put her in charge of tracking down the bullet sales and monitoring the websites that these hunter guys have been using. "They've disbanded all the sites. They've shut down their operations."

"That's a good thing," I said with my mouth full. "We killed one of their partners, killed their elf, stole their shit. They gave up."

"Yeah, but before they threw in the towel, they sold over fifty thousand rounds of bullets by Sabrina's reckoning. The bulk of them went to an organization out of Montana, but the rest are individual sales spread all over the world. We'll never be able to feel completely safe again."

I knew this upset Jake, but it didn't particularly bother me. Werewolves had been pretty darned close to invulnerable since that first Nephilim had children. Now we faced the same fears of mortality that humans did every day. Actually we faced far less, because it took one heck of a car crash, or boating disaster, or fall off a ten-thousand-foot cliff to kill us. We still didn't get diseases. We still didn't lose our lives from a stab wound, or gunshot with a normal bullet.

But I didn't want to seem unsympathetic so I paused from chewing my cereal and made what I hoped were supportive platitudes.

"She's tracking down the place in Montana." Jake sighed and rubbed a hand through his short dark hair. "There's no way we can get tens of thousands of individual bullets off the streets, but if we can manage to find the spot where this particular group is warehousing them and seize those, it will help."

I swallowed the cereal. "So when do we leave?"

He shrugged. "Sabrina's gotta find the place first. I might see if Gwylla can help again, although the last divination took quite a toll on her. She's resting in her sanctuary, and I've given Dustin an open-ended leave to attend to her."

Attend to her. Fancy word for sex, I'd bet.

"Let me know when you need me," I told him. "Until then I'll be taking care of the garbage and recycling, stirring up trouble with my pack mates. Oh, and taking Mir to get that piercing I promised her."

He ignored the last statement and reached out a hand to touch my cheek. "We'll resume sparring tomorrow night. Will you join me for dinner first?"

I leaned my face into his hand. "I'd love to. Should I meet you at the Alpha House? What time do you want me there?"

"No, have dinner here with me. I want to share a private meal with you here, in the dining room."

Suddenly I realized the purpose of those little private tables along the edges. It wasn't just someone's clueless idea of what a romantic date should be, it was for couples to declare their partnerships in front of the entire pack. I was starting to realize that there was something sacred about sharing a meal together. No doubt that's why so many of this pack came to the dining hall to eat instead of using their dorm or house kitchens. It wasn't just that the food was included, it was a time of bonding, even if some of these werewolves didn't say a word to each other. Eating together, living together mattered for these wolves. And demonstrating a united partnership, a mate-relationship, in front of all your community was one step toward a mating ceremony.

I felt tears sting my eyes, and I didn't even have a plate of onions to blame it on. Damn him for making me feel all these things. Damn him for turning my still-lethal beast into a loyal, fiercely loving side of my personality.

"Yes. I'd be happy to join you here for dinner," I told him. Then I watched as he rose with a smile and headed out of the dining room. I had a mate. I had a pack, and I had a mate.

CHAPTER 21

I was on my way to the four-wheeler, the sky a pre-dawn light gray when I felt a prickle of warning down my spine. I stopped, turning towards the woods over by the lake and lifting my face to scent the air. Pine. Aspens. The crisp smell of water, and the murky odor of frogs and fish. Hundreds of varieties of grasses, brush, flowers, and berries. My fellow werewolves, the scent of breakfast bacon. Deer, bear, the muskrats down by the river. Nothing that should be making the hair rise at the back of my neck and my lip curl upward in a snarl.

They're here. I feel them. Many of them.

I trusted my beast's intuition, but I couldn't detect the smell of gunpowder, or the peculiar metallic smell I'd come over the decades to associate with firearms. I wanted to sound the alarm, but how? The compound wasn't gated. We didn't have guards—werewolf hearing and other senses were such that we weren't easy to sneak up on. Who would believe me when I told them that my beast was excited, wary, and ready to attack? As far as my pack was concerned, my beast was always excited, wary, and ready to attack.

Jake. Jake would believe me.

I forced myself to turn my back on what I was positive was a threat and tried to look casual as I walked to the Alpha House. It was never locked, so I pushed open the heavy door and walked in. Jake met me just outside his office.

"What?" His voice was tense, and I knew he was feeling the same sense of pending danger as I was.

"Do you feel it? Lots of them, in the woods by the lake." We had pack mates who were still asleep, pack mates who were showering and getting ready for their workday, pack mates who were right now in the dining hall preparing breakfast or grabbing a quick bowl of cereal before heading out.

"They'll disable the plane." Jake grimaced. "Dustin is going to explode if they damage it. He's lost one plane already this year. If he loses another he's going to go on a rampage."

I wasn't particularly concerned about the pilot going on a rampage, but I knew if he was upset, his sidhe mate would also go on a rampage. And I really wanted to make sure I was out of the blast radius when that happened.

"So is there some early warning system? A group text to all the pack that you can send out in a kind of alert?" It would take these werewolves twenty minutes to shift into animal form—the form that would best serve them in a fight. If these hunters were loaded with the magicked bullets, we'd still suffer losses, but already in wolf form, the pack wouldn't be reeling from a forced shift as they tried to defend themselves.

Jake was dialing his phone. "That's a good idea and I'm going to implement it as soon as this is over. We have an emergency flare, but it will also alert the attackers that we're onto them."

And with twenty minutes to shift, they'd attack when we were at our most vulnerable. "They're probably waiting until dawn to get as many of us in one place as possible. It will be easier for them to attack if most of us are in the dining hall or out in the open, as opposed to having to go house-to-house."

"Go make your garbage rounds like nothing is wrong," Jake told me. "Go to the dorms then the houses on the outskirts first and tell everyone to shift as quickly as possible. Children are to be secured in the basements and lower rooms with weapons if they're old enough to handle them. I'm alerting the inner houses as well as the businesses and the dining hall. Tell everyone to shift and wait for my signal. Stay close to the houses with the kids. You're responsible for making sure none of the hunters gets in and hurts the children. Got it?"

I nodded and spun on my heel, ready to go. Protect the pups. That I could do without any worry about losing control and killing my pack mates.

"Tupper? If everything goes south and we look like we're losing, I want you to let your beast loose. I want you to shift into whatever she wants and kill every one of those hunters."

I swallowed hard. "I can't guarantee she won't kill my pack mates," I confessed. "And if I let her loose, I can't always stop her. She could end up slaughtering the hunters as well as everyone else in the compound. I can't control her Jake. Here...since I've come here she has seemed calmer, more content, but if I tell her to kill, I'm worried that I won't be able to rein her in."

His ice-blue eyes met mine. "If she's out of your control, I'll step in. She'll listen to me."

No she wouldn't.

"Jake, I'll admit she's pretty attached to you, but that doesn't mean she'll stop killing because you ask nicely, or even command her to do so. Killing and violence are more fun to her than sex. They're more important than my pack, my Alpha, even my own continued existence."

His fingers paused on the phone and he looked up at me in surprise. "Your beast is you. And she's more than attached to me. Trust me, and go. We don't have much time."

He was right—about my beast being more than attached to him as well as us not having the time to get into this. Jake was powerful, brilliant, and I loved how instead of being afraid or repulsed by my beast, he seemed to like and respect her. She liked and respected him back.

Who was I kidding? My beast loved this guy just as much as I did.

And I did trust him, so I headed out, that feeling of anxiety and excitement ratcheting up as I made my way to the dorms and houses. I had to wake a few of the werewolves up, and many were reluctant to believe me when their noses and ears weren't telling them that anything was amiss. But I'd been chosen to go out with Jake and Karl on that special assignment, and he'd made it quite clear in full view of the pack that we had something important going on between us, so in spite of their misgivings, every one of the werewolves I spoke to began to shift.

I noted which houses had young, and planned to keep close to them and protect the pups when the attack occurred. I didn't trust these hunters to spare children, and as unhinged as my beast was, she was a softie when it came to pups.

I'd managed to go to all the dorms and most of the houses when the first shot rang out right at sunrise. Instinctively, I hit the ground, looking around to see who'd been hit. The noise echoed, making it difficult for me to figure out exactly where the shooter was, but my gut told me over by the lake.

The woods moved, and armed men swarmed out of the tree line, laying down a cover of bullets as they advanced. Instead of hitting us like hunters taking down prey, these guys moved like they were on a paramilitary exercise, dividing up as they reached the compound and using the buildings for cover. A flare shot up from the Alpha House, lighting up the sky like a second sun. Wolves ran from the buildings, darting across the open spaces and ducking under vehicles. The air was filled with their barks and yips, and above it all I heard a howl that shook the ground.

Jake. He stood at the top of the steps of the Alpha House, a huge silvery gray wolf with ice-blue eyes in a dark mask. He scanned the compound, and I realized that he was communicating silently with the pack, directing them in groups to take up positions around the edge. He planned to pull the attackers in, surround them, then move in for the kill. It would have been a great plan had these guys just been shooting regular bullets, but with the magic ammunition and the rapid-fire action of their assault rifles, we wouldn't come out of this unscathed. We might win the day, but we'd win it having lost most of our pack to those bullets.

Seconds after Jake's call to action, gunfire filled the air. He stood exposed on top of the steps, taking their fire as bullets ripped into him and blood splattered across the front of the building. I bit back a cry, certain that even Jake couldn't take that many hits, and my beast slammed against my skin, desperate to break free and protect our Alpha.

He was drawing their fire, keeping their attention away from the wolves that were now moving in on the humans. Jake fell to his knees, bits of flesh and fur flying from him in chunks. I wanted to run to him, but I needed to guard the homes with the children, and I knew in my heart that he'd be fine, that an almost-angel could take whatever these hunters were dishing out and repay them with death—just as soon as the pack was in position and ready.

Screams of humans suddenly rang out—now as loud as the gunshots. I saw the hunters dashing across the compound, using buildings and vehicles as cover. A brownish-gray wolf plowed full-tilt into one, closing his jaws on the man's arm as another wolf bit down on his leg. The man swung his weapon in the other hand, trying to push the one wolf away while shooting at the one on his leg. The wolf nearly exploded in a spray of red, bringing a fierce growl from the other. I heard bone crunch, saw the man trying to bash the wolf in the head with his weapon as another of my pack mates swooped in for the kill. We were winning, working together as a wolf pack should, but at what cost? Would we lose half of our pack to these guys? Would we mourn, only to have another group come back in a week or so to attack us again? How long could we hold out until they eventually killed us all?

I saw a shadow over by one of the houses, a man quickly looked around, then kicked the door in, vanishing inside.

Oh no you fucking don't. I snarled, scooting out from under the car and running full-tilt to the house. Bullets churned up the dirt and asphalt around me but through some miracle, I reached the doorway without being hit.

There was a muffled scream. I heard the thump of heavy steps on the stairs and grabbed the closest thing at hand, which happened to be a brass statue of a whale. The man appeared on the landing and I ran, but before I could get to him, he shoved the child aside and brought up his gun.

I threw the statue, but what truly saved me from being shot full of holes was the pup who had been pushed backward and onto the stairs. He'd landed hard, then with the speed and strength of an adult werewolf, he kicked the human in the ass, sending the man tumbling down the steps.

The statue clattered behind him, thankfully missing the child. The gunfire blew drywall chunks in a line across the foyer. Before he could bring the gun around, I was on him, stomping his wrist, then grabbing his head and twisting.

It wasn't as satisfying as sinking my fangs into his neck,

but dead was dead, and I was sure if one of them had snuck in to grab this child, others would be doing the same.

"Can you shoot?" I asked the kid. He nodded, so I reached down and grabbed the rifle, shoving it into his hands. "Get in the bathroom, lock the door, and hunker down in the tub. If anyone human tries to open the door, shoot him. Got it?"

He nodded again and I ran, wincing as I realized I'd just given a ten-year-old child an assault rifle with bullets magically coated to kill werewolves. It was too late for me to regret what was probably a very bad decision, though.

The next house had a broken-in door, and the two children were gone. I noted signs of a struggle—dented drywall, scratches, a door half off the hinges. Running to the next house I saw a man leaving, carrying a struggling child in his arms, a dish cloth jammed in the kid's mouth. Putting on a burst of speed I tackled the guy. The kid went flying, rolling across the pavement and pawing at his face to dislodge the dishcloth.

"Run," I told him, using my knee to hold the guy's gun arm pinned down as I grabbed his head and smashed it onto the pavement. He had a helmet on, so it took considerable force for me to crack the thing and then crack his skull. We'd need to patch the asphalt in that section of the driveway. Oh well.

A flash of light caught my eye and I launched myself off the dead guy, running through the compound and behind the dormitory. A bullet grazed my ear, and I felt blood trickle down my neck and shoulder. My beast roared to get out, to kill them all, but I needed control—control it was becoming harder to maintain. The bullet wound burned and refused to instantly heal, but the blood clotted, and the cloying scent of dead flesh and infection slowly reversed.

Karl had been wrong. The bullets did affect me, but not to

the degree that they affected the other shifters. For once my fucked-up DNA worked in my favor.

I rounded the corner and saw them—three men, one holding a gun, one with a baby in his arms, the other holding Mir.

She looked pissed. There was blood on her head from a wound that had already healed. Her hands were twisted behind her back and upward. Mir was strong, and I knew she would risk getting shot, even getting killed, to free herself and rip these assholes to shreds. What was stopping her was that the gun in the one man's hands was pointing at the baby.

It stopped me too. It didn't stop my beast. My fragile control shredded, and I felt my skin tear, bones and muscles pop as I shifted. It would have taken other werewolves twenty minutes. It took me seconds. And from the expression on the humans', as well as Mir's, face, the form I was assuming wasn't a wolf.

Whatever it was, my beast was pretty damned confident that whoever held that gun on the baby would be turning it to shoot me instead. That would free up Mir to attack. And my beast was so furious, so lost in rage at this moment, that the guy could have had an endless supply of bullets in that magazine and he wouldn't have stopped me. I was going to kill the both of them.

But the guy with the gun didn't point it at me, he kept it on the baby, shouting at someone to hurry. My beast sprang forward in spite of my panicked protests, ready to sacrifice the baby if needed. The man holding Mir pulled something out of his pocket—something that looked like a stone with carvings in gold on the surface. Then he shouted words in an unfamiliar language. There was a flash of light that blinded me, the smell of burning hair. I felt myself fly through the air where there had once been three humans and crash, skidding nose-first across the ground.

Gone. They were gone. They'd taken Mir and a baby and vanished. My beast went insane with grief and fury, and pushed the rest of me down, taking control of my body. Everything healed—the remaining injury to my ear, the road rash, the broken tooth. It all healed in a blink and I rose to four legs, feeling my size stretch and expand, horns bursting from my head, curls of smoke puffing from my nostrils. Huge claws dug deep into the ground, I lifted my head to the sky, and I roared.

CHAPTER 22

The rest was a blur. I ran through the courtyard, across the compound, circling around buildings and attacking every human I saw. They were in pairs or small groups, and each time I took one down, his friends turned their weapons on me. I felt the burn of the magic, and stamped it down, healing slower than I would normally have, but still healing. As many times as they shot me, I kept going, bullets hitting the ground with a metallic clink as my body rejected them and healed. I was fast and efficient, quickly snapping spines, opening arteries, and crushing skulls, then turning to the next attacker. With each group, they'd quickly realize that their bullets weren't taking me down, then they'd try to run. I was too fast for them. One guy managed to shout something into a walkie-talkie before I killed him. After that, the hunters began to disappear with the same strange words and gold-etched stones as the guys who'd taken Mir. I quickly realized that not every one of them had such a device, and that quite a few humans were running, frantically trying to find those who did so they could escape with them. When I saw one pull a stone from his pocket, I tried to take him down first, hoping that if I killed the ones with the teleportation devices, the others would be trapped here—trapped with me.

My pack was as terrified of me as the humans were, and rightfully so. If one of them had accidently been in my way, I would have killed him or her without a second thought. What had started as "kill the humans, they've taken Mir" was now just a gleeful celebration of blood and slaughter, of death by my claws and teeth.

My pack mates must have realized this because they stayed out of my way, circling with their fur standing straight up on their necks as they herded the humans inward toward me, killing those they could and leaving the rest for me to deal with.

I rounded the dining hall and saw a group of hunters converging in a central area. One took out a stone, and I launched myself at him, a blur of speed. The stone clattered to the ground as I landed on top of him and sank my teeth into the Kevlar plates and into his chest.

The other humans screamed, a few trying to grab the stone, while the others shot me. There must have been six of them, and six attackers unloading fully automatic weapons on me was having an effect. It wouldn't kill me, but it was hard to bite through this fucking protective vest while projectiles were filling me full of holes.

The bullets ripped my flesh. There was a burning pain, a nearly uncontrollable urge to revert to a wolf form instead of whatever the hell it was my beast had decided to become. It was as if I had a horrible itch and was desperate to scratch it. These bullets hurt. The hunters were running and screaming, the few of them that were left. And I was determined to make sure none of them made it out of here alive.

I was too late. One of the men had grabbed the stone before I'd finished killing the guy with the protective vest and ran toward the others. As soon as he reached them, he shouted the words to the spell and four of the six vanished, leaving two behind.

One of the abandoned humans froze, his head tilting upward as I rose to my feet. He shot me a few times, backing up as quickly as he could. Then he dropped the rifle, spun about and ran.

My claws tore chunks from the pavement as I pursued him, careful not to get so close that he'd lose any hope of getting away. Chasing was such an adrenaline rush, especially when flavored with the hunter's fear and his optimism that he might actually have a chance of getting out of this alive. I have very little patience, so before he'd reached the edge of the compound, I was on him, pressing him to the ground as he screamed and cried. It was too much—too much excitement, so I indulged in my desires, sinking my claws deep into his shoulders and clamping my jaws on his neck.

His head came off, because I'd forgotten how fragile these silly humans were. Blood geysered everywhere and I lapped at it as if I were drinking from a fountain. Then another human caught my eye. He was standing over a small cream-colored wolf, aiming his rifle for the kill shot. In seconds I was on him, crushing his rifle in my jaws before knocking him down. He scrambled to his feet, looking at the destroyed rifle before trying to run.

I snarled and snapped my teeth. Then with a leap and a swipe of my paw, the hunter was down with me straddling him. His soft flesh called to me as he pounded and kicked me. I batted him with soft paws, just to play a bit before I killed him.

Mills.

I let just enough claws out to scratch the man's skin and tear his clothing. His hands gripped my neck, fingers sinking into my thick fur as he tried to hold me away from the soft skin of his face and neck. I let him think just for a second that his strength would be enough, then eased my head down, fangs bared.

Tupper. Tupper don't kill this one. Stop.

The words were like an annoying fly buzzing around my head. I let my hot breath wash over the man's face.

Tupper.

There was a collective gasp as I felt a hand on my back. I tensed, expecting to be pulled backward, expecting the assertive dominance of an Alpha. But instead the hand stroked me, fingers tickling through my fur and lightly scratching my back.

I'd never known the soothing touch of a parent, but even through my bloodlust, I could tell this wasn't the same. This touching was intimate, reassuring, as if the person behind the hand didn't condemn me for what I was, as if they understood. It was the hand of a lover. Not just a sexual partner where physical gratification was a primary goal, but someone for whom touch was both sensual and emotional.

Tupper, we need him alive. Let him live.

I looked down at my human hands, fingers white as they gripped the man's torn shirt. Blood covered my skin, dripping down my face. I tasted the copper on my tongue and along my teeth. The man beneath me was still struggling, trying in vain to push me off of him. I grinned down at him, licking the blood from my lips.

And all the while, that hand kept stroking my back, my very naked back.

"Nice job, Tupper. Now get off him, please. We need to have a few words with this man."

I looked up into the startling blue eyes of my Alpha. There was no fear in his face, no uneasiness, no shock over what he'd just witnessed. I'd completely let my beast off-leash. She'd killed with the sort of reckless and joyful abandon that I'd always been terrified of anyone witnessing. But in spite of that, Jake's expression was warm and loving. His hand left my back and I felt my world tilt to the side. I needed his hand. I needed him touching me. I needed him like I'd never needed anyone in my life before.

"They took them," I told him, my voice rough. "I guarded the kids, but they took Mir and a baby and I lost it. I just went crazy."

I felt sick at the thought. I'd gone crazy, gone on a killing spree and left the children unguarded. If more had been taken, if any had been killed, it would be all my fault.

"You did a good job, Tupper," he insisted. "Can you help interrogate this guy with me? Do you need to take a moment?"

A moment and do what? I guess clean up, put on some new clothes, maybe become less of a psycho. I stood and staggered a few steps away from the man on the ground, not really trusting myself to say anything at the moment.

They took Mir. They took Mir. I need to get Mir back. I need to save Mir.

I did, but I needed Jake to help me because I sucked at strategy. Case in point, I'd been ready to kill this guy, the only survivor of my rampage, and if I had we would never be able to find out where the hunters had taken Mir and the baby.

Jaimie stood to his side ten feet back, and her expression was not impassive. She stared at me, shock and horror in her face. From her I felt the slight tendril of fear, although she quickly hid it. I looked around at the rest of the pack. Many were tending to the injured who were still in their wolf forms, but the others stood in a ring around us, their expressions mirroring Jamie's.

I stood back while Jake pulled the man to his feet, then followed as he and Jamie hauled him along.

As we walked, my pack edged away from me any time I came too near one of them. I'd never had my beast loose like this before. Never. They were terrified of me. They'd seen exactly what I could do and how little control I had over my baser instincts. They knew I was dangerous before, but now I was a threat to them all. I knew every last one of them wondered what might set me off, what minor incident might cause me to snap and tear through the pack like a rabid monster. I knew they'd want me dead.

I'd started out this morning thinking I finally had a pack to call my own, an Alpha strong enough to manage me, a lover that was my equal. Now I wasn't sure I had any of those.

CHAPTER 23

Jake had dragged our prisoner across the compound and back behind the incinerator where the bear-proof dumpsters lived. It was a good spot for an interrogation, and just to make it clear what I thought we should do with this guy, I fired up the incinerator.

Jamie didn't protest my tagging along. Other than Jake and I, Jamie was the only one present. Everyone else was off taking care of any wounded that needed assistance, or checking to make a count of who had been taken and who we'd lost to the hunters.

I had no idea how many of our pack were dead. And injured...was there enough of that antidote stuff to heal those who weren't already dead? Was there a limit to what that stuff could counteract? I remembered the bullets that had hit me, still feeling the wounds that were taking what felt like forever to heal. Then I thought of Mir, praying that she was still alive. She had to be alive. They wouldn't have taken her just to shoot her in the head, would they?

Mir is gone! My beast was nearly insane with panic and

rage. My friend. My only friend and they'd taken her. The only consolation was that if they wanted her dead, they would have shot her and left her body with the others in the compound. There was a reason they wanted Mir and that baby alive, a reason they'd been trying to take the children rather than just killing them. Whether it was for ransom and negotiation or to sell on the black market, or for other nefarious purposes, I couldn't think of that right now. The only thing keeping me sane was the conviction that Mir was alive. I'd rescue her. Gwylla would heal any of her wounds if she'd been shot and we ran out of antidote. Fuck, I'd haul her off to an angel if I had to. Anything for Mir to be okay.

Jake propped our prisoner against a dumpster. He wasn't tied, since we could easily catch him if he tried to run for it, and without his weapons, there was little he could do to hurt us. He was fucked, and he knew it. His chin might be up, but there was a slight tremble to his jaw that I didn't miss.

"Why did you attack us?" Jake asked.

The guy sneered. "Because you're monsters that never should have been born. Because the world will be a better place once you and the rest of these scum are gone."

Well, that was no surprise.

"You failed," Jake told him. "Even with the special bullets and a small army, we still managed to kill almost all of you."

His eyes slid to me and I knew what he was thinking. Things could have gone differently if I hadn't gone on a berserk killing rampage, if there hadn't been an almost-demon in a pack of werewolves. I was beating myself up over having lost Mir and a baby and potentially more children, but my spree had probably saved werewolf lives.

"We'll eventually kill all of you, and the ones we shot will eventually die," the man vowed. "There's nothing you can do to save them."

"That's where someone's been lying to you." Jake leaned

over the man. "Two shifters that were shot in Kenai survived. One shot in Juneau survived. We've got an antidote. And we've also got a healer with more magic than you planned for, and between the magic potions and our healer, those who you wounded will survive."

I hoped Jake was right, but in my heart I worried that many had died before they'd ever had the chance to drink that jewel-like liquid.

"Still killed a lot of you," the man countered. "And we would have killed a lot more if…" He looked over my way. "What is she? She's not a shifter."

"I'm a monster," I told him, walking close. "Where did you take the girl and the others? Where are they?"

He smiled. "They're as good as dead. And next time we'll be ready for you. We've got ammunition that can take out an angel. You won't bounce back from that one, wolf-monster."

I looked up at Jake, wondering if the guy was bluffing. From the expression on my Alpha's face, the man wasn't. Bullets that could kill an angel? I should be flattered that they'd think to waste such a thing on me, but instead I was calculating how many of these fuckers I could take down before they managed to shoot me with something that actually ended my life.

"Where. Are. They?"

I shivered at the look in Jake's eyes. The man held his gaze for a few seconds then looked down. "Dead. You're all dead. It's just a matter of time."

Jake stood back and stared at the man. "Jamie, would you go check on the others? See if any children besides Mir and that baby were taken?"

Jamie paled, shooting the man a sympathetic glance. "Will do."

She left and I remained, determined to stay until Jake told me to go. Actually I'd probably argue with him to stay even if he tried to send me off. I was barely in control of my beast now. If he tried to make me leave, she'd rip through and start killing again.

The Alpha stepped forward and put his palms on either side of the man's face. The guy's eyes widened, and his hands came up to grip Jake's wrists, but even though the muscles in his arms bulged, there was no way he could pull the Alpha's hands away.

"Where are they?"

I felt it, some sort of compulsion that seriously made me want to kneel and confess all to Jake. The hunter shook, sweat beading on his forehead, but he didn't reply.

"Let me try," I told Jake.

It was my beast that wanted at this guy. Although I wasn't sure I could do anything beyond what Jake was trying to do. If physical pain, if Jake's weird compulsion trick didn't get the man telling us all he knew, then I probably couldn't either.

Jake shot me a surprised look, then hesitated as though he saw something in my eyes that convinced him I could do this. He stepped away from the man. As I moved in close, I saw a fear in the human's eyes that hadn't been there when Jake had questioned him. My hand shot out, closing around his throat and pinning him in place.

Then something weird happened. My beast took control, but instead of ripping the guy to bits in a fit of rage, she pulled on him—not on his physical self, but on something deep within him. The hunter gasped, absolute terror in his eyes. He trembled, and I felt something tear, as if I were pulling the insides out of his cells. Tiny bits of blood surfaced in red dots on his skin and he screamed.

"Where are they?" I purred. "Where?"

There was a garbled sound as blood dripped from the man's mouth. His screams choked into wet bubbles of red saliva, as I began to ease the man slowly free from his body. Suddenly his mind was mine, all his experiences and memories. Everything he knew was mine.

And he was mine as well, to keep forever, to play with, to torture and torment for all eternity.

I smiled into the hunter's eyes, saw the knowledge there of what was happening, then his gaze shot to Jake.

"Kill me. Kill me. Please kill me," he begged the Alpha. "Don't let her have me. Don't let her take me."

"No," I whispered. "I don't want you to die. I want to play. Don't you want to play? You'll never die. You'll live forever in eternal torment. The only respite you'll have is so you can contemplate the return of the pain, knowing that it will never end. Never."

"Kill me!" he screamed to Jake. "I'll tell you anything. Don't let her take me."

"But I already know everything," I told the man. "He has no reason to save you. None at all."

"Tupper," Jake said, his voice sympathetic. "If you have what you need, let him go."

No! He would not deny me my prey.

"Tupper. Let him go." There was a heaviness in the air as Jake forced every bit of his Alpha dominance into the command.

I stayed my hand, turned my attention to my Alpha, and snarled. He would not deny me this. I would fight him for this.

"Tupper." Suddenly I felt him. It was as if Jake reached through the distance between us, past my skin to touch a hand to the head of my beast. "Don't do this. I'm asking you to please not do this. I'll let you kill him, but please don't Own him."

I saw the choice before me. My beast wanted this man to Own, but she also wanted Jake. We both wanted Jake. And for once in my life, the non-beast part of me cast the deciding vote. I wouldn't keep this man. I'd grant his plea for death. I'd do what Jake asked because I loved him and that's what people who loved each other did. I'd let this man keep his soul, and instead take his life.

But that didn't mean I had to be merciful about it. I let go, and he snapped all the way back into his body. Then as he screamed, I dug my fingers into his neck and let him slowly bleed out, not letting go until he stopped thrashing and I felt him leave his body.

It was a horrific death. And what I'd wanted to do to him had been even more horrific. I felt the rush I got from killing him, felt at one with my murderous beast. I lost myself to her and she stopped fighting me in return. I understood what Jake had been telling me during our sparring sessions. I'd been so afraid of trusting my beast, doubting that if I let her even a moment of freedom she'd go on a killing rampage. If I found a way to satisfy her nature, could we possibly coexist without tearing each other apart? If I let her have an outlet like sparring with Jake, like interrogating and killing this murderer, would she finally give me peace?

All I knew was that two seconds ago, she had been in charge and I'd enjoyed it. And when it was over, she'd been happy to let me take the wheel without any kind of fight.

I felt a hand on my shoulder and looked up into Jake's ice-blue eyes. They were warm with approval and affection. As much as I wanted to take that man's soul, this look in his eyes was more than an adequate trade.

"You know where they took Mir and the others?"

I nodded.

He took my face in his hands and it struck me how very different this was than when he'd done the same to this hunter. "You were amazing. Watching you was…well, it was the closest thing to a religious experience I've ever had.

You're fierce and beautiful, like a Valkyrie, like an avenging angel."

I caught my breath, shocked that he'd felt that way watching me go on a killing rampage, then almost rip the soul from a human and torture it for all eternity.

"You're amazing," he repeated. Then he kissed me. I swayed, then stepped forward to press myself against him, my hands reaching around to grip his waist. He deepened the kiss, one hand sliding around to hold the back of my head and the other skimming down my back to grip my ass.

When he finally let me up for air, I was barely able to stand.

"Later," he said, leaning down for another quick kiss. "After we find Mir and the others, I am going to haul you off to my bed and never let you leave."

Later. Because I'd seen not only where those men had taken Mir, but what they had planned for any shifter children they'd managed to capture.

Mir first. Sex—no, making love—later.

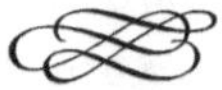

CHAPTER 24

"I know where they are. I know where they are." It was like a mantra as I paced the floor, struggling to keep my beast inside. We couldn't leave until we'd taken inventory and found out how many the hunters had taken with them. It wouldn't do to mount a rescue attempt, only to find that we'd inadvertently left some of our pack mates behind. So while Jake and the others did a count, I cleaned as much blood off of me as I could and put on some clothing before returning outside to wait impatiently for our go-ahead to leave.

"Soon," Jake said coming up to me. "Almost everyone is accounted for."

"Only two are missing," Jamie said, panting in between words as she suddenly appeared before us. "Mir and Emma."

Mir, I knew. Emma must be the baby. I closed my eyes and envisioned her in my mind. Any child younger than six was a baby in my mind, but from what I saw of Emma, I was judging her to be less than two. Truly a baby.

I'd absorbed that hunter's mind. I knew what they had planned for Mir and Emma. I knew that they'd planned to take more—as many male and female young children as they could find as well as any teen girls. Sexual slavery for the teen girls. The others would be sold as pets, and that most likely included sex for some perverts with enough money to buy one as well. Emma was so tiny, but it was the remembrance of what that man had wanted to do with Mir that made my beast ready to kill every living being I could find.

I needed to get out of here. There wasn't enough time, and I was terrified that without magical transportation of our own, they'd be gone by the time we arrived. If they moved Mir and the baby somewhere that the human I'd read hadn't had knowledge of, we'd never find them.

Correction. I'd eventually find them. Because I'd spend the rest of my insanely long life tracking Mir down and punishing those who had anything to do with kidnapping her or hurting her. And as far as my beast was concerned, vengeance for Mir's suffering extended to friends and family of those hunters. No one was innocent in her mind—not even my own pack who she felt should have done more to protect the only friend I had.

Jake turned to me. "Where are they?"

I opened my mouth only to shut it with a snap. Visions of land stretched before me. Mountains—not as tall as these, but still tall. South, in the lower forty-eight. I knew exactly where they were, but couldn't articulate it.

Wait. A sign. In the vision I saw a sign. Grabbing my phone out of my pocket, I typed the name into the search engine, then pulled up the images. Yes, that was it.

"Philipsburg, Montana."

Jamie and Jake both peered at my phone.

Jake growled. "I can fly us in to whatever airport has the next flight out of Alaska, then we'll rent a private jet if we need one to get to Billings, then rent a car. We'll get there. I'll get us there."

My vision blurred with tears. I honestly think this was one of the only times in my life I was ever on the edge of crying. "There's no time for that. We need to be there now before they move them, or we'll never find them again. They'll be sold. And there's not any doubt in my mind that those guys who vanished with them will recommend stuffing Mir and that baby into a big box and onto a truck to take to Minnesota, or Phoenix, or even Mexico until they can get the highest price for them. We don't have time to fly to Montana and rent a car. We don't have time."

I was on the edge of hysterics at this point. Jake grabbed me and folded his arms around me, crushing me against his chest. "I'll go find Gwylla and see if she can teleport us. I don't know where her sanctuary is, or even if I can find it, but I'll try…"

He knew as well as I did that traipsing around the Alaskan wilderness for days looking for a sidhe's hidden Shangri-La wasn't any better than flying commercial.

"Sir." Jamie cleared her throat. "That archangel down in Juneau…"

Jake pulled away from me and yanked out his phone. "Brent," he barked into it. "I need Raphael. The hunters attacked our compound and a few of them teleported away with a sixteen-year-old girl and a twelve-month-old baby. They're in Montana, and I need a teleport down there for Tupper and me."

I heard Brent's response and winced. Evidently angels were all about trading favors. This Raphael guy might want to help out of the goodness of his heart, but angels were weird creatures.

Who was I kidding? I was a weird creature. If it hadn't been Mir who'd been kidnapped, I would have been shrugging my shoulders and saying "so what" myself. For all I knew, this Raphael was the same.

"I will owe him a favor, whatever he asks of me as long as it doesn't go against any other vow or promise I've already made." Jake's tone sounded oddly formal, as if he knew how important this was. Then he stuffed his phone back in his pocket and turned to me.

"He may refuse, but I think not. His mate, Ahia, has a soft spot for children and he in turn has a soft spot for her. He'll be here."

I clenched my jaw, wondering how much of a delay there might be until this angel showed up, wondering if he'd agree to transport me once he saw what I was, wondering if Mir would still be alive when we got there.

Stuffing down the panic, I tried to think of something else, like peeling the skin off every hunter who had touched Mir, who had even *thought* about touching Mir.

I didn't need to wait long. We'd barely made it out into the center of the compound, when the angels appeared—both of them. My pack mates were dealing with the injured and starting to clean up the bodies—both of our own and of the hunters we'd killed. Our clean and neat home was a mess of blood and destruction. The angels looked around in astonishment, the female's brows lowering when she saw our dead.

"Take us there," I demanded, hardly able to stand a second more of waiting.

"Wait." Jake put his arm in front of me. "This rental car place in Philipsburg, Montana." He showed his phone to the male angel. "I don't think it would be wise of us to just pop in without knowing what we're facing."

I closed my eyes and envisioned the route the dead hunter had taken from Philipsburg to the cabin in the mountains where they'd intended on holding the kids. Half an hour. I wasn't happy about that, but Jake was right—it wouldn't be wise to just teleport in and find ourselves blown up, or shot full of magic bullets, or turned into frogs.

"We can't stay and help you." The female angel seemed quite pissed at that. "There's some fucking meeting we have to be at. You're lucky you caught us before we left."

I snarled, letting my beast right to the surface of my skin. "Just get us there and I'll do the rest."

The female angel blinked in surprise and I heard the male angel laugh softly. "I almost feel sorry for the hunters. Okay, folks. Next stop: Philipsburg, Montana."

CHAPTER 25

The angels dropped us off at a car rental place in a town that didn't look like it had many more residents than the Swift River Pack compound. Jake and I dry heaved for a while dealing with horrible vertigo from the teleport, then we rented a car.

He drove. I navigated. The road was a series of winding switchbacks, and then a dirt road that ended up so completely washed out into gullies that we could go no further in our little rental truck. Which was okay with me. I'd rather hike the next mile to the cabin than drive up to their front door while getting shot at.

I was too panicked, worried that they might have relocated Mir in the hour and a half between when they'd vanished from our compound to our attack at their cabin. What if they'd teleported here, immediately stuffed Mir and the baby into a magic cage, and driven away? I kept telling myself we would have passed them on the road, but my beast was still terrified that they'd slip through her claws and we'd never see Mir again.

There were two Jeeps parked in front of the cabin along

with a huge, jacked-up pickup truck with a cap over the bed. I smelled six humans. I smelled the baby, Ellen, or Elaine, or whatever her name was. I smelled Mir. My beast raged against my skin and I was fighting a losing battle to keep her inside.

"Let her go," Jake murmured. "Do what you do best, Tupper."

I yanked off my clothes and exploded into fur and talons and a broad mouth with a double row of sharp, serrated teeth that had more in common with a shark than any mammal. With a furious roar, I charged, smashing the door clear off its hinges.

The humans were unprepared, but there were six of them and they were too spread around the cabin for me to take all of them at once. I grabbed the closest one, unhinging my jaws to wrap them around his thick waist. Then I closed them, shaking my head to shred through tissue, muscle, and cartilage, then biting down hard to hear the satisfying crunch of pulverized vertebrae.

It took seconds, and seconds was all the others needed to grab guns and begin shooting. I'd been shot before, but these bullets burned their way through my body, rotting everything they touched and demanding that I become a wolf.

I almost laughed. If my beast wouldn't list to my demands regarding what sort of animal form she took, I doubted she would obey a bunch of magicked bullets. Still I felt fur sprout from my weird leathery skin, felt my body heat to an abnormally high temperature as it tried to fight the magic. All the while my body was recreating flesh just as fast as the magic on the bullets destroyed it. Karl had been right. I wasn't immune, but I was oddly resistant, and I had no doubt that I'd overcome this magic in a matter of minutes, no matter how many bullets they pumped into me.

I lunged for another human and heard a voice off to my right scream.

"Angel!"

For a second I thought they meant me, then I saw Jake. He'd come in through the back door, and was holding one of the hunters by the neck, the man's toes dangling two feet off the floor. He was glowing as if he had a weird silvery-white aura, his eyes nearly neon blue. But it was the wings that had the hunters scrambling for some magazines on the table.

Damn, I loved those wings. Someone was so gonna get laid tonight.

Later. After we rescued Mir.

I got an idea what was in those magazines the hunters were slamming into their rifles, so I finished off my prey with haste, dropping his broken body onto the floor.

Jake had done the same to the man he'd strangled, and grabbed another, spinning him around as a human shield and bringing his rifle up across the man's neck. I didn't trust that those angel-specific bullets weren't going to go clear through the human and into Jake, so I did something totally weird—I shot out a giant ten-foot long sticky tongue and wrapped it around the other guy's rifle, yanking it toward me just as he pulled the trigger.

Bullets sprayed into the cabin walls, inches away from Jake. I reeled my tongue in like I was deep sea fishing, then dug my talons into the man's waist and yanked them upward. Guts spilled onto the floor and the man screamed, dropping the rifle.

I didn't have time to finish him off, because the last guy had bolted and was heading for the vehicles. I hadn't a doubt in the world that I could run him down, even if he floored it going down that insanely rocky gulley of a road, but I didn't want him to get that far.

He saw me coming and quickly realized that he'd never

get the Jeep started and in gear before I was on him, so he ran for it, dashing around the house and into the kitchen where he grabbed something that looked like a cross between a sword and a giant fucking fillet knife.

I had a bad feeling about that knife. He swung it at me wildly, like the guy was far more used to shooting his victims than trying to stab or slash them. For the first time in my life, I was cautious jumping back and biding my time, ducking under one wild thrust to slam him against the wall, digging my talons into his wrist with enough force to make him drop the knife without severing his hand.

I had no doubt the guy Jake had been strangling along with the one I'd abandoned disemboweled on the floor were dead, which meant this guy was the only one left alive. I'd been absolutely aware the whole time I'd been fighting that Mir hadn't been in the room. I hadn't heard her. And although I could smell her, that scent could have been from before we'd arrived. My stomach twisted at the thought that we were too late, and I suddenly regretted my impulsive killing of the other humans. What if this guy knew nothing? What if they'd snuck my only friend out of here and the dead guys were the only ones who knew where she was?

Aware that I could hardly interrogate this man as a gorilla/lizard/wolf/shark, I sent my beast back into my skin and assumed a human form, keeping the talons and some of the shark-teeth. I also kept the lizard eyes because I knew they were probably fucking terrifying.

"Where are my wolves?" My voice was like gravel. "Where is my girl and the baby?"

"Screw you," the man panted.

I extended a serpent tongue to lick his cheek and hissed, showing him those lovely shark teeth, knowing he'd seen me bite through his friend.

He blanched, swallowing hard. "Screw. You."

There was an easy way to do this, and I no longer cared whether Jake scolded me not. Mir wasn't here, that much I knew, and the longer I stood here bantering with this guy, the more time whoever took her had to get away.

I tore into the man's mind, hacking my way through the stupid inane memories of his sad childhood and whiny-ass emotions concerning some woman he couldn't get to go out with him. Within seconds, I was where I wanted to be, absorbing his experiences with the hunters, witnessing his thrill at the attack on the compound, seeing him arrive back at the cabin with Mir and the baby and his friends. Then I saw the rest. I saw what had happened in the hour and a half it had taken for us to arrive. I felt sick at all the perverted thoughts and images that filled my head. Nausea turned to anger as I came to an image that had caused this man much joy. Mir, naked, crying as the humans laughed and did unspeakable things to her, one off to the side with a knife to the baby's throat.

It was my fault. Why had it taken us so long to arrive? Why couldn't I teleport? Why couldn't I have gotten to Mir before they'd activated their transportation device? Why couldn't it have been me, instead of my young, innocent friend?

I snarled, guilt shifting to fury. Death was too good for this man. Death was too easy for him. My only regret was that the others were already corpses on the floor.

"You all are monsters. None of you deserve to live," He gasped his last bit of defiance and tried to spit in my face, the liquid dribbling down his chin instead.

"They're not the monsters, I am." I smiled at him and stroked the side of his face. I knew Jake would be unhappy with me, but my beast needed some quality time with this man. Perhaps a few decades and I'd let him go. Maybe.

"I'm the real monster in this room," I told him. "And that

girl you hurt? The pain you caused her is nothing compared to what I'm going to do to you."

He screamed, his voice growing hoarse as I ripped him slowly from his body, tucking him safely away in that spot within me that I'd created just for him. Then I tossed his empty body onto the floor and went outside.

CHAPTER 26

"They escaped," I told Jake as I snatched my clothes from the Jeep and yanked them on, stuffing my phone in my back pocket. "Mir took the baby and ran for it."

The news didn't seem to cheer him any. "There's blood here—Mir's blood."

I thought of the memories of the man I'd just killed and Owned. Of course she'd bled after what they'd done to her—all seven of them.

"I'll track her. I can find her." Even without the blood, I'd find her.

"It's a lot of blood," Jake warned.

She was a shifter. The physical wounds were no doubt healed within minutes. It was the emotional ones I was worried about.

I picked up her scent, wincing at the volume of blood at the edge of the forest. Every quarter mile or so there was more blood, making me realize how quickly Mir must have been moving.

Then suddenly, after five miles of twisting, off-trail path, Mir and the baby's scent just vanished. I sneezed a few times and pinched my nose, then inhaled again. "Do you pick it up anywhere?" I asked Jake.

He knelt down and inhaled. "She's good at this. I don't like to bring too much attention to it, but her skills in the weekly games are some of the best in the pack. She doubles back, takes to the trees, covers her tracks, even heads down the middle of the darned river swimming under water to hide her scent."

Smart girl, especially when she didn't know what sort of tracking skills or magic these hunters might have. I let Jake crawl around on the ground and jumped, scaling the nearest tree. Then I closed my eyes and inhaled, sorting through all the complex scents. There. So faint that I could barely pick it up. I wasn't sure how Mir had done it, but she'd managed to climb a tree with a baby in her arms, and jump from limb to limb. Following her path and admiring her freakish monkey abilities, I climbed down near a stream.

Jake had followed me from the ground and was now frowning at a spot by the stream. He stirred the leaves with his foot and the smell of blood wafted up to me—Mir's blood.

How was she still bleeding? How badly had those men hurt her?

"She got in the water," Jake told me. "But I don't know which way she went. We'll need to split up, then call each other when we pick up the scent again."

We did the same, one of us heading upstream while the other headed down. Two miles I waded, crossing back and forth between the different banks just to make sure I didn't miss her exit point.

I did almost miss it. If it hadn't been for the watered-down puddle of blood on a rock, I would have kept going. Instead, I texted Jake, frustrated that there didn't seem to be cell service where I was, then followed her trail, only to have it vanish again in another mile. I climbed trees and scoured the area, starting to panic when I couldn't find a trace of her anywhere.

Then I saw it—a giant deadfall where a rockslide had taken out an entire grove of trees and piled them all up in a jumble of decaying wood and leaves. I approached it slowly, then called out for her.

"Tupper? Oh, Tupper." I heard her sob, then the soft cry of a baby. "I'm in here, but I don't think I can get out without bringing the whole thing down on Emma's and my heads."

She crawled out, naked, the baby securely tied around her with a pair of jeans. Tears streaked through the dirt on her face, her eyes puffy and her nose red.

And she was covered in dried blood and bruises. Not just dried either. I smelled fresh blood on her and the baby, and choked back a sob of my own.

Mir fell into me, the baby sandwiched carefully between us as we hugged.

"They were going to sell us, Tupper," she said in between tears. "They yanked my clothes off, then held a knife at Emma's throat and told me to do what they said. Then they took turns with me and made me do…things. And they put things in me and laughed and it hurt and I wanted to kill them all, but I was afraid they'd hurt Emma. They could do that stuff to me, as long as they didn't hurt Emma."

"They died too quickly," I told her, smoothing a hand over her hair. Well, except for that one I'd kept. He was going to pay for every moment of Mir's pain. He would pay for the sins of every last one of those hunters.

"When they were done and thought I was broken, they put Emma down. That's when I made my move. I hit one of them as hard as I could, then grabbed Emma and ran. I took my pants, but didn't have time to put them on. I ran so fast, Tupper. I tried. I tried."

"You did great," I told her soothingly. "You saved both yourself and the baby. You did great."

"They shot me before I got to the forest," she choked out. "A few inches to the right and they would have blown Emma's head off. I turned into a wolf in seconds, but I grabbed Emma and my pants with my teeth and ran so fast. It hurt. It wouldn't stop bleeding. I knew what it was, but I didn't want to stop because then they'd get Emma."

My heart stopped. "They shot you?"

Slowly my hands roamed her naked body, finding the open wound in her shoulder. The bullet had gone all the way through, but it wasn't healing.

It wasn't healing. But she wasn't still a wolf, and she wasn't dead. I didn't smell rotted tissue. Was Mir a Nephilim? Did she have something about her that made her immune? She still needed immediate medical attention, but I didn't get the feeling she was on the verge of death.

"I had a vial of antidote in my pants pocket." She laughed and it choked on a sob. "I'd put it there when the alarm for the attack when up. Mom is such a worrywart that it was second nature for me to run to the supply cabinet and grab one. But I gave Emma some of it just in case some of that bullet had nicked her. You should have seen me trying to get it out of the pocket and get the stopper off with my paws and teeth. I did it, though."

Now it was my turn to cry. I hugged her so close that Emma let out a squawk, then pulled back, planting a kiss on Mir's forehead. "Jake should be here soon," I told her.

She looked down at her breasts and flushed. It made me laugh that after all she'd been through, she was worried about her Alpha seeing her like this. Sheesh, it wasn't like the pack hadn't seen everyone naked on pretty much a daily basis.

I stepped back and yanked my shirt off, them shimmied out of my pants. "Here. I'll take Emma. You put these on."

"But then you'll be..." her eyes widened as she realized I wasn't wearing either a bra or underwear, and that given my propensity for waxing, my numerous piercings were in plain view—including the one in my hood. "Is that...?"

"Yeah. And I'm not worried about being naked." I winked. "Jake's seen it all before anyway. Trust me, he's had an up-close-and-personal with all my body parts. Put my stuff on."

She eyed the top. "I'll get blood all over this."

"Bloodstains are cool." They were, although I wasn't too pleased about them being from Mir's blood. We needed to get her to a hospital. I could carry her the eight miles back to where the hunters had been holed up, then take one of their trucks. I'd let Jake carry the baby, because I wasn't much of a baby kinda gal. I'd never liked children. I'd never wanted children.

But for some reason, I glanced down at Emma, at her little fists waving in the air, her pissed-off expression as she glared up at me. Would my kid look like this? Mine and Jake's, if we ever decided that was something we wanted?

I envisioned a mocha-skinned baby with fierce blue eyes and wings. Yeah maybe.

Then I looked up at Mir and smiled. She was okay. The baby was okay. Lots of bad guys were dead, and I had my own personal one to torture and play with for as long as I wanted.

Better yet, I had a pack. I had a friend. And I had something I'd never thought I'd ever have—a mate.

CHAPTER 27

*N*ormally there would have been no bribe or threat in the world that would have made me go to a giant wolf-pack barbeque down in Juneau, Alaska. Normally there would have been no bribe or threat in the world that would have made me go to a wedding/mating ceremony. But here I was.

Jake and I had flown down the day before where I'd actually sat in a church for an excruciatingly long religious service without combusting into flames. Kennedy wore an elegant cream-colored gown, her dark hair in coils on the top of her head, her sexy, sleepy eyes expertly made up. The woman knew how to pick her cosmetics as well as apply them. She was stunning. And Brent was a grinning, love-struck fool holding her hands and stumbling through his lines, all the time shifting from foot to foot trying to hide the fact that he was sporting a woody in the middle of church.

Afterward we'd all gone to their Alpha House, which was big enough to rival Jake's, and witnessed a repeat ceremony where instead of exchanging rings, they bit each other on the back of the neck with a vow to be as one flesh, one mind, and one soul for as long as they lived. Kennedy's blunt human teeth barely made a mark on Brent's skin—a mark that healed within seconds—and Brent was oh-so-careful to leave more of a hickey than a bite on the back of his bride's neck. Still, the two glowed as they received everyone's congratulations, the fact that one was human and the other wolf not mattering one damned bit to them or anyone else—even Kennedy's parents, who looked on both ceremonies with teary-eyed fondness.

The next day was the barbeque with a food-laden drunken debauchery that was more in line with my tastes. Many from both the Swift River Pack as well as the Denali Pack flew down to join in, goofing off in the pool, playing volleyball and drinking games. Brent and Kennedy vanished early on into the upper reaches of the Alpha House, leaving Sabrina in charge. The skinny redhead looked like she was two seconds from abandoning her post to the young, good-looking werewolf who was the third in the pack and dragging her hot bear shifter off into the woods.

It made me want to drag Jake off as well, but he was in business mode, making the social rounds and discussing what sorts of security and procedures should be put in place to ensure something like the attack on our compound never happened again.

Our compound. I glanced over at Jamie, who was doing shots with that Juneau Pack third—Zac, I think his name was. She'd been unexpectedly gracious about my elevation to almost-mate. I was pretty sure we would argue about a lot of things, and that some of those arguments might end up with blood on the floor, but I knew that she respected me.

And I respected her, which was something totally new for me. My pack. They didn't all trust me, and most of them were still scared of me, but they knew I'd fight for them. They knew that when they had a need, I'd be there, standing at Jake's side, to keep them safe and defend their way of life. That was another first. I'd never had it in me to lead. I'd never be an Alpha. But I was perfectly happy to be the muscle, the weapon that Jake launched toward our enemies. And with him as a moral compass, and my beast well in hand, I no longer feared that my violent tendencies would harm my own.

That was the trick. I'd needed to consider them mine. Just as I would never have wantonly destroyed a beloved pair of jeans or a favorite piece of jewelry, I wouldn't harm those my beast saw as her possessions. Yeah, she thought my pack mates were her possessions. And that was a little secret that was best kept to myself. The means didn't matter as long as the end was what it should be.

And Mir… My heart softened then ached as I looked over at her by the pool. She spent more time alone lately. And sometimes when I looked at her, I could see the darkness of a shadow that seemed to seep deep down into her soul. She tried to be her old self, but both of us knew that was impossible now. We'd gone to get that piercing, even though I'd pleaded with her to wait. It hadn't helped. Nor had the tattoo she'd insisted on that covered the scar from her gunshot wound.

Covering scars, ornamenting a part of her body that held the most horrifying memories of her life wasn't going to help her heal, but I didn't know what would. I wanted so badly to make things right for her. She was planning to return to the human school this fall, but all the joy she'd once had about finishing high school with her friends was gone. Most of her joys about anything were gone. I hoped that tiny spark of innocence inside her hadn't completely died out, because I don't think either my beast or I could take it if that happened.

I grabbed a couple of beers from the cooler and walked

over to her, biting the caps off with my teeth and spitting them into the pool. Sitting down, I extended one toward Mir.

"I'm sixteen," she told me, her voice wooden under a forced cheerfulness.

"Do I look like I give a shit? Drink the damned beer."

There was a ghost of a smile as she raised the bottle to her mouth. "I like Brent's mate," she confessed. "I think werewolves should give human men and women more of a chance when thinking about a possible mate, because Kennedy is pretty cool for a non-shifter."

"You thinking of a boy from school?" I asked, remembering her saying she'd had a few human sexual partners.

Mir shuddered. "No. I don't think I can ever be with a human again. Not that way. Not after…"

Okay. No humans. I didn't blame her one bit for that.

"Maybe you should give bears a chance," I told her, looking over at the very-hot Karl, then at a cluster of male grizzly and Kodiak bears that were clawing a big oak tree. Jake had told me that bears, especially brown bears, tended to be reclusive, but Karl had convinced a group of his buddies to join him.

Yeah. I couldn't imagine Karl having buddies. They were all guys, because female brown bear shifters didn't like to hang with the males, or even other shifters, preferring to live a human-like existence except for a few times a year when they felt the mating call of their own kind too strong to resist. There were five of Karl's friends at the party, their insanely oppressive dominance like a weight on everyone's chest. Three looked to be in their twenties, one old enough to probably be even my grandfather, one of them about Mir's age.

She looked over and flushed bright red, jerking her eyes back to the pool. I felt her stiffen and pull deep inside herself. "No. I don't want a bear anymore. Or a wolf or a human. It's my junior year in school. I need to really study if I'm going to get into a good college, so I don't think I'm going to date much for a while."

"And that's what you want?" I asked her gently. "To go to college?"

She nodded, her hair shielding her expression from me. "I take my SATs next spring and I'll start touring and applying to colleges next summer. With early admission, I'm hoping to get accepted by next fall."

I watched her carefully. This was the first that Mir had mentioned college. "Where are you thinking of going?"

She sucked in a ragged breath. "Florida. Georgia. Maybe Louisiana."

Those were all states, not colleges. Mir was set on a location as far from Alaska as possible within the U.S., not on a particular course of study or a college known for excellence in that area.

Instead of asking her what she wanted to major in, I cut right to the heart of the matter. "That's really far away. I don't know, Mir. Think I'm going to either be doing a lot of crying next year or buying a lot of plane tickets."

She laughed, and it sounded more like a sob. "I hate that I can't get past this, Tupper. I'm afraid to leave the compound. I'm terrified about going to school in a few weeks. The only reason I'm here at this party is because you and Jake are here. Well, because you are here. I'm over the edge of a panic attack whenever you even leave the compound to drive the recycling in to town. What kind of life is that for me? I need to be able to stand on my own two feet. Maybe if I force myself to go to a college a gazillion miles away, where the climate is different, where there aren't any mountains or anything to remind me... Maybe then I'll finally be okay."

I swallowed hard, gulping beer to keep the tears from coming. "Be patient with yourself, Mir. And remember that any time you need me, I'll be there. I'm your own guardian-almost-a-demon." Wait, this wasn't the right tactic to take with her. "And you don't fucking need me anyway. Mir, you endured and survived something most shifters and humans couldn't to save a baby. And you had the fucking guts to grab that baby and save the pair of you the moment you had the chance. You got shot with bullets that have killed shifters, and still hauled ass through the forest, disguising your trail to the point that Jake and I almost couldn't find you. You rescued yourself. Not me. Not Jake. You. And that baby—Elaine, or Eustace, or whatever the fuck her name is. You are the one who saved that damned baby, not us."

She looked up at me, her eyes sparkling with unshed tears. A smile twitched at the corner of her mouth. "Emma. Shit, Tupper, you need to start being better about people's names. This is your pack, after all."

I cuffed her shoulder. "Language. Cursing is fine for an almost-demon, not for a young werewolf who is illegally drinking beer right now."

She stood, taking another swig from the bottle. "I'm not human. Human laws don't apply to me. Well, their stupid laws concerning alcohol anyway." Then she straightened her shoulders and walked over to the group of bear shifters like a girl heading toward her execution.

She'd be okay. I knew it in my heart, even though it hurt every time I thought of what she'd been through at her young age. Mir was a tough girl. She was an amazing girl. I only hoped that Jake's and my children turned out half as badass as Mir. Well, if Jake and I ever decided to grace the world with our scary offspring, that is.

I smiled and looked over to my mate. Because ceremony aside, we were most definitely mates. An almost-angel and an almost-demon. How could we be anything *but* mates? And the rest? Well, whatever happened happened. Between the pair of us, we'd protect our pack. The world might fall apart, but nothing was going to happen to the Swift River Pack as long as Jake and I were there. We'd face whatever came our way together, and woe to whatever tried to hurt us and ours.

My pack. My mate. It felt good to know that. It felt damned good.

***

Want Ahia and Raphael's story? Pick up Northern Lights and fall in love with heaven's bad boy angel.

ACKNOWLEDGMENTS

A huge thanks to my copyeditors Kimberly Cannon and Jennifer Cosham whose eagle eyes catch all my typos and keep my comma problem in line, and to Damonza, for cover design.

Most of all, thanks to my children, who have suffered many nights of microwaved chicken nuggets and take-out pizza so that Mommy can follow her dream.

Debra lives in a little house in the woods of Maryland with her sons and two slobbery bloodhounds. On a good day, she jogs and horseback rides, hopefully managing to keep the horse between herself and the ground. Her only known super power is 'Identify Roadkill'.

www.debradunbar.com

The Templar Series

Dead Rising

Last Breath

Bare Bones

Famine's Feast

Dark Crossroads (2018)

* * *

The Imp Series

A Demon Bound

Satan's Sword

Elven Blood

Devil's Paw

Imp Forsaken

Angel of Chaos

Kingdom of Lies

Exodus

Queen of the Damned

Half-breed Series

Demons of Desire

Sins of the Flesh

Cornucopia

Unholy Pleasures
City of Lust

* * *

<u>Imp World Novels</u>
No Man's Land
Stolen Souls
Three Wishes
Northern Lights
Far From Center

* * *

<u>Northern Wolves</u>
Juneau to Kenai
Rogue
Winter Fae
Bad Seed